ANNO DRACULA 1918

THE BLOODY RED BARON

ALSO AVAILABLE:

ANNO DRACULA
PROFESSOR MORIARTY: THE HOUND OF THE D'URBERVILLES

COMING SOON:

ANNO DRACULA: DRACULA CHA CHA CHA
ANNO DRACULA: JOHNNY ALUCARD

ANNO DRACULA

1918

THE BLOODY RED BARON

KIM NEWMAN

TITAN BOOKS

ANNO DRACULA: THE BLOODY RED BARON

Print edition ISBN: 9780857680846
E-book edition ISBN: 9780857685346

Published by Titan Books
A division of Titan Publishing Group Ltd
144 Southwark St,
London
SE1 0UP

First edition: April 2012
10 9 8 7 6 5 4 3 2 1

Visit our website: **www.titanbook.com**

Did you enjoy this book? We love to hear from our readers. Please email us at readerfeedback@titanemail.com or write to us at Reader Feedback at the above address.

To receive advance information, news, competitions, and exclusive offers online, please sign up for the Titan newsletter on our website www.titanbooks.com

A CIP catalogue record for this title is available from the British Library.

Printed and bound in Great Britain by CPI Group UK Ltd.

To Paul McAuley

'It'll be over by Christmas.'

'Mechanical contrivances have been greatly exaggerated in comparison with the value of infantry. There must also be artillery and cavalry as well! …Each war has certain special conditions so some modification of organisation will be necessary but if our principles are sound, these will be few and unimportant. The longer the War has gone on, the more satisfactory do the principles of our training manuals appear.'
Field Marshal Sir Douglas Haig, 1918

'This little book gives one a useful insight into the enemy's methods, and more than a little respect for at any rate some of those whom we are at present endeavouring to kill.'
C.G. Grey, Preface to the first British edition of Manfred von Richthofen's *The Red Air Fighter*, 1918

CONTENTS

PART THREE: MEMOIRS OF A FOX-HUNTING MAN

PART FOUR: JOURNEY'S END

ANNO DRACULA 1923: VAMPIRE ROMANCE

PART ONE

ALL QUIET ON THE WESTERN FRONT

1

CONDOR SQUADRON

Four miles from the lines, heavy guns sounded as a constant rumble. Cakes of frozen snow gleamed vaguely in the pitted black road. The fall was days old. Bundled in his trench-coat and a useless tartan blanket, Lieutenant Edwin Winthrop was stung in the face by insect hailspits. He wondered if his frozen moustache would snap off. The open-top Daimler was unsuitable for this cruelly cold French winter night. Sergeant Dravot had a dead man's indifference to climate. The driver's night eyes were sharp.

At Maranique, there was a delay. Winthrop froze further while a corporal cast a sceptical eye over his papers.

'We were expecting Captain Spenser, sir,' explained the guard. He was twice Winthrop's age.

'Captain Spenser has been relieved,' Winthrop said. He did not have to explain himself. The corporal had made the mistake of getting used to Spenser. In this business, a bad habit. 'There's a bit of a war on. Maybe you hadn't noticed.'

Blood-coloured fire-flashes stained low clouds over the near horizon. If a shell caught the wind a certain way, its whistle was distinguishable from the babel of bombardment. In the trenches, they said you only heard that particular shrilling if the shell was the one that would kill you.

The corporal plainly recognised Dravot. The staff car was finally passed through. The aerodrome was a converted farm. Deep cart-ruts marked the track to the house.

Condor Squadron had been Spenser's show until this afternoon. After an hour's cramming, Winthrop was not really *au courant* with the mysteries. He had been briefed on tonight's work but given only the barest sketch of the big picture.

'Do well, young man,' Beauregard said, 'and there's a pip in it.'

He did not see how a civilian, even one attached so firmly and mysteriously to Wing, could promise promotion, but Charles Beauregard inspired confidence. It was an open question, though, whether he had inspired confidence in the lamented Captain Elliott Spenser.

Winthrop had been in France long enough to know how to avoid the shivers by tensing every muscle. The memory of Spenser, smiling through blood trickles, undid the trick. Aching cheek muscles gave way and he chattered like a puppet.

The farmhouse was blacked out, but faint light-ghosts outlined the windows. Dravot held the car door open. Winthrop stepped down, frosted grass crackling under his boots, scarf dampened with huffing steam. Dravot stood to attention, eyes frozen unblinking, tusk-like teeth sticking out of his moustache. The lack of white puffs from mouth and nostrils proved the sergeant did not breathe. He could be trusted to hold the bridge against barbarian hordes. If Dravot had personal feelings and opinions, they were unreachable.

A door opened. Smoky light and brittle hubbub spilled out.

'Hullo, Spenser,' someone shouted, 'come in and have a tot.'

Winthrop stepped into the billet and talk ended. A gramophone wound down, drawing out the agony of 'Poor Butterfly'. The low-ceilinged room was a makeshift mess. Pilots sat about playing cards, writing letters, reading.

He was uncomfortable. Red eyes fixed on him. All these men were vampires.

'I'm Lieutenant Winthrop. I've replaced Captain Spenser.'

'Have you now,' a gloomy-looking soul said from a far nook, 'have you indeed?'

This man held the rank. Major Tom Cundall. At first, Winthrop could not tell whether the flight commander was warm or not. After nightfall, almost everyone in the war had the predatory, haunted cast of expression associated with the undead.

'A warm fellow,' Cundall commented, vampire mouth curving. You could always see it in their smiles. 'Diogenes sticks to its old ways.'

Spenser was a living man. At least, he had been the last Winthrop saw him. So was Beauregard. It was not consistent policy, just the way things worked out. There was no preference for the warm. Quite the reverse.

'Has some sneak bombed Diogenes?' asked a pilot, smiling savagely.

'Steady on, Courtney,' said another man.

Huns who attacked rear positions were almost heroes to front-line men. A staff officer's red pips were a mark of Cain. The scarlet blots on his insignia invited scorn. Winthrop had not asked for a safe posting, any more than he had asked to be roped into the Diogenes Club. Again, it was just the way things worked out.

'Captain Spenser has had a nervous collapse,' Winthrop said, affecting cool. 'He has suffered self-inflicted wounds.'

'Good Lord,' said a man with red hair.

'Careless with a jolly revolver,' sneered Courtney. He had burning daredevil eyes, an Antipodean twang and a razored double dash of moustache. 'For shame.'

'Captain Spenser drove four three-inch nails into his skull,' Winthrop said. 'He is on indefinite leave.'

'I knew something was not right with the man,' said a hollow-voiced American, looking up from a Paris paper.

'If a chap's caught trying to give himself a Blighty one, it's usually the firing squad,' said Courtney.

'Captain Spenser was under a great deal of strain.'

'Lot of that about,' commented the American. A black hat shaded his gaunt face, but his eyes burned in the dark.

'Leave Winthrop be, Allard,' Cundall insisted. 'Don't kill the messenger.'

Allard pointed his prominent nose back at the newspaper. He was following the exploits of Judex, the vigilante. According to the press, Judex was a vampire too.

The vampire with red hair wanted more news of Spenser but Winthrop had nothing further to report. He had only glimpsed the officer as he was taken to the ambulance. He was being despatched to Craiglockhart War Hospital near Edinburgh, commonly known as 'Dottyville'.

There was discussion about the singular method Spenser had chosen to make an invalid of himself. Allard said that in the old days it was the practice in parts of the Russias for vampire killers to favour iron spikes in the skull over wooden stakes through the heart.

'Where do you get all this grue?' Courtney asked.

'I make it my business to know evil things,' said Allard, eyes like coals. Suddenly, for no reason, the American laughed. His throat-deep black chuckle grew into a resonant, mirthless explosion. Winthrop was not the only one to cringe.

'I wish you wouldn't do that, Allard,' Cundall said. 'It sets the dogs to howling.'

Even for vampires, the pilots were unnerving. Like the French *Groupe des Cigognes*, Condor was a squadron of survivors, almost a squadron of sole survivors. To win a place, a man had to outlive his fellows many times over. Some were famous, among the highest-scoring Allied aces. Winthrop wondered if any resented assignment to duties which offered fewer opportunities for individual victories. At Wing, some disparaged Cundall's Condors as glory-hounds and medalled murderers. Beauregard warned him not to let the pilots rag him too much.

With a deal of clumping, a young vampire dragged himself down a twisted staircase. His limbs were bent out of true but he got around capably. He wiped his red mouth with a white scarf. From his flush, Winthrop knew he had just fed. Away from the lines, there were usually grateful, if pricey, French girls. If not, there was livestock.

'Spenser's tried a Moldavian headache remedy, Ball,' Courtney told the crooked man. 'Nails in the brain.'

Ball pulled himself across the room, making monkey-use of hand-holds on the beams. He settled comfortably into a chair by the gramophone, eyes swimming in blood. Some vampires lulled in repletion, like snakes. In the old days, when *nosferatu* were hunted like plague rats, they were at their weakest after feeding and hid in coffins or graves. Ball slumped, mouth slightly open, a smudge of red on his chin.

'I need a pilot,' Winthrop said, more quietly than he had intended.

'You've come to the right shop,' Cundall commented.

Nobody stepped forwards to volunteer.

'Take Bigglesworth,' Courtney said. 'The *Daily Mail* calls him "a knight of the air".'

A young flight lieutenant coloured slightly, cherry spots appearing on his bone-white cheeks. Courtney clearly understudied Cundall for the role of resident cynic.

'Give it a rest, old son.'

The flight lieutenant was backed up by cronies who rumbled disapproval. Courtney did not seem bothered by the schoolboy clique.

Major Cundall considered and said, 'Bit thick up there to make a trip worthwhile, surely?'

Remembering Beauregard's briefing, Winthrop explained, 'Diogenes wants to snatch a look at something special. A lone spotter can get over the lines above cloud, then dip down to take photographs.'

'Sounds a doddle,' Cundall said. 'Probably win the war, this show.'

Winthrop was a little put out by the flight commander. Ragging was all well and good, but formalities should be observed. Diogenes was not in the habit of wasting its time on fools' errands.

He commandeered a card table and unrolled the map on the green baize.

'Here's the site Diogenes wants to know about,' he said, pointing. 'We've heard strange whispers.'

Some pilots were intrigued enough to crowd around. Ball crab-walked out of his chair and hobbled over. He put a cold hand on Winthrop's shoulder to balance himself. A complete cripple on the ground, Albert Ball was magically agile in the air, reckoned the Allies' ace of aces.

'The Chateau de Malinbois,' said the blushing lieutenant. 'That's a Hun field.'

Jagdgeschwader Eins,' put in one of his pals, whose hair was almost as red as Albright's.

'Quite right, Ginger. Dear old JG1. We're fast friends.'

'That's the Richthofen Circus,' Allard intoned, ominously.

At the mention of the famous name, Ball spat. A thinly blooded streak missed the map and soaked into the baize.

'Don't mind Ball,' Ginger told Winthrop. 'He was shot down by the Bloody Red Baron's fiendish brother, Lethal Lothar, and has a feud on. Family honour and all that.'

'Our intelligence is that the chateau is more than a billet for Boche fliers,' Winthrop said. 'There's odd nocturnal activity. Comings and goings of, um, *unusual* personages.'

'And Diogenes want photos? We did a batch on this site last week.'

'By day, sir.'

Winthrop took his hands off the map, which curled into a tube. He laid out photographs of the Chateau de Malinbois. Black bursts of anti-aircraft fire, known to one and all as Archie, were frozen between castle and camera.

Winthrop tapped areas of the picture. 'These towers have netting draped around them. As if the Boche doesn't want us to know what he's up to. *Camouflage,* as our French allies would say.'

'The sort of thing that makes a fellow inquisitive,' Ginger commented.

Cundall was doubtful. 'Be a bit bloody dark for photography tonight. I doubt if any of 'em would come out well.'

'You'd be surprised what we can read from a dark picture, sir.'

'I'm sure I would.'

Cundall looked closely at the photographs. He laid his hand on the table and drummed thick, pointed nails.

'The pilot will have a Verey gun. He can pop off a flare to throw some light on the subject.'

'"Pop off a flare?" Very likely,' Cundall said. 'Verey likely. That's almost a joke, isn't it?'

'I'll wager JG1 will be delighted at our company,' Courtney said. 'Probably lay out a red carpet.'

In the pictures, the Archie was uncomfortably close to the visible struts of the photographer's aeroplane.

'The Circus will be busy toasting each other in Rhine wine and virgin blood,' said Cundall, 'lying about the number of Britishers they've downed. Only we are dolts enough to send people aloft in this mucky weather.'

'Very unsporting of the Hun,' Ginger commented. 'Not coming out to play.'

'The flare'll prod him,' Albright said. 'There'll be Archie. Maybe an Albatros will make it into the air.'

'Inferior bird, the Albatros,' Courtney said.

Cundall seemed hypnotised by the photographs. The castle was bashed a bit about the battlements but still far more imposing (and, presumably, comfortable) than the farmhouse. Like every other breed of fighting man, the Royal Flying Corps were convinced the enemy had it cushier.

'Very well, Winthrop,' Cundall said. 'Pick your man.'

This was not what he expected. He looked at the pilots. One or two turned away. Cundall smiled nastily, showing sharp tips of teeth.

Winthrop felt like a live mouse in a cattery. He remembered the bloody nailheads in Spenser's scalp.

'The best qualified would be the man who took these.'

Cundall examined a serial number scrawled on the edge of a photograph.

'Rhys-Davids. Not a good choice. Went west two nights gone.'

'He isn't confirmed,' Bigglesworth said. 'He may be a prisoner.'

'He's lost to us.'

Winthrop looked around again. No one stepped forwards. Though well aware of the crucial differences between war as waged in the jingo press and war waged in France, he somehow expected a dignified competition of volunteers.

'Here's a list. Pick a name.'

Cundall handed over a clipboard. Winthrop looked at Condor Squadron's roster. He couldn't help but notice names with lines drawn through them, including 'Rhys-Davids, A.'.

'Albright, J.,' he said, taking the first name.

'Fair enough,' said the red-headed captain. Though in RFC uniform, he was another American. Cundall's catch-all squadron had more than its share of foreigners.

'How's your crate, Red?' Cundall asked.

Albright shrugged. 'Better than she was. The camera's still slung.'

'Highly convenient.'

Albright seemed a steady man. Though a vampire, he was sturdily built, square-faced, firm-jawed. He seemed made entirely of solid blocks. The wind would not blow him away.

'Ball, you'll have to make a fourth,' Courtney said. 'Red promised to partner Brown in bridge against me and Williamson.'

Albright shrugged a can't-be-helped as Ball shifted himself to the cards group.

'I'll be back by midnight,' Albright said.

Everyone groaned, in on a private joke.

Winthrop felt obliged to shine a lantern under the lower wings of the Royal Aircraft Factory SE5a to inspect the cameras rigged up in place of Cooper bomb racks. They were operated like bombs, by pulling a lanyard in the cockpit. The plates were fitted properly. One of Dravot's responsibilities.

Uneasily aware he was the only man on the field who could not see in the dark, Winthrop shut off the light.

Albright hauled himself into the cockpit and checked his guns, a fixed Vickers which fired through the propellor and a swivel-mounted Lewis attached to the upper wing. On a jaunt like this, he should get back without firing a shot. The idea was to creep in and get photographs before the enemy could muster. That was why this was a one-man job: too many aeroplanes would alert Malinbois that they were coming. As a rule, the Boche didn't take to the air unless they had to. Allied policy was to mount offensive patrols constantly, to remind the Central Powers who owned the skies.

Cundall and his cronies had ventured out to watch Albright depart. The pilots took a professional look at the SE5a, examining the fuselage where bullet-holes had been darned. They agreed the aeroplane, a relative newcomer, was acceptable. Through Diogenes, Condor could get whatever machines it wanted, but each pilot had preferences.

Stamping to get feeling into dead toes, Winthrop was completely in the dark. The aeroplane was a large shadow skeleton. Vampires were as comfortable in the night as he was on Brighton pier at midday. With their adapted eyes, the undead were suited to night-flying, to night-fighting. Thanks to them, this was the first round-the-clock war in history.

Ginger spun the SE5a's propellor. The Hispano-Suiza engine did not catch first time.

'A bit more elbow-grease,' said one of the cronies, Bertie.

Of course, without vampires (specifically without the brute now calling himself the Graf von Dracula) the war would not have been fought at all. The Graf's latest attempt at European power had led to a conflict that seemed to involve every nation on the globe. Even the Americans were in now. The Kaiser said modern Germans must embody the spirit of the ancient Hun, but it was Dracula, proud of blood kinship with Attila, who most epitomised twentieth-century barbarism.

Ginger spun the prop again. The engine growled, prompting a ragged cheer. Albright gave a salute and said, 'See you at midnight.' The machine taxied along bumpy sod, plunged into the shadow of the trees and soared upwards, wobbling a little as wind caught under its wings.

'What's the business about midnight?' Winthrop asked.

'Red always gets back by then,' Bertie said. 'Does the job quickly and comes home. That's why we call him Captain Midnight.'

'Captain Midnight?'

'Silly, isn't it?' the pilot grinned. 'So far, it's brought him luck. Red's a good man. Flew with the *Escadrille Lafayette* until they disbanded. We got him because the Yanks rejected him for their show as medically unfit. The American Air Corps is exclusive to warm men.'

Albright's crate rushed up into the underside of a low-lying cloudbank and passed quickly from sight. The engine drone faded into the wind and drifting music from the farmhouse gramophone. 'Poor Butterfly' was waiting again. Sergeant Dravot's eyes were fixed on the night sky.

Major Cundall consulted his watch (one of the new wrist affairs they wore in the trenches) and noted time of departure in a log book. Winthrop checked his own pocket watch. Half-past ten on the evening of February the 14th, 1918. St Valentine's Day. At home, Catriona would be thinking of him, intelligently worried.

'Nothing for it now but to wait,' Cundall said. 'Come in and stay warm.'

Winthrop had not realised how chilled he was. Slipping his watch into its pocket, he followed the pilots back to the farmhouse.

2

THE OLD MAN

Throughout the crossing, Beauregard was uncomfortably aware of the wounded man lying in a corner of the cabin. Given his condition, Captain Spenser was unnaturally quiet.

When an orderly had found him, Spenser was on the point of driving in a fifth nail. It seemed he intended to porcupine his entire skull. The inevitable diagnosis was a failure of nerve, but Beauregard thought it must take a steady hand to perform such an operation upon oneself.

Beauregard reproached himself for his failure to appreciate the strain put on Spenser by the demands of Diogenes. A man may know too many things. Sometimes, Beauregard wished his own skull would open and let his secrets escape. It would be pleasant to be innocent and ignorant.

After years of service to the Diogenes Club, Charles Beauregard sat with the venerable Mycroft and the eccentric Smith-Cumming on the Ruling Cabal, highest echelon of the Secret Service. His whole life had been lived in the dark.

The Channel was gentle. He chatted with the Quaker stretcher-bearer, Godfrey. He had chosen ambulance duty over prison and been decorated for bravery under fire at Vimy Ridge. Beauregard recognised as a better man one who would die for his country but not kill. He regretted each time he had killed; but he also regretted, in a single instance, not killing. At the sacrifice of his own life, he might have put an end to Count Dracula. Often, as he got older, he thought of those seconds.

At Newhaven quay, nurses awaited a small group of maddened officers. As a group, the men were quiet and pliable. They were shepherded with kindly firmness by the nurses. Four years ago, the army had considered shell-shock deplorable cowardice. After seasons of gruelling war, breakdowns were almost *de rigueur* for the better sort of officer. The second son of the Duke of Denver was among the current crop of Dottyville cases.

No light showed on the dock. German submarines were rumoured to be in the Channel. Beauregard wished the uninterested Spenser good luck and gave Godfrey his card, then crossed the shadowed platform to board the fast train for London.

He was met at Victoria by Ashenden, a youth who had proved himself a cool hand in Switzerland, and driven through the dark city. Despite rain and unlit streets, purposeful night crowds were everywhere. Even in the heart of the Empire, touched only by an odd air raid, it was impossible to forget the war. Theatres, restaurants and pubs (and, doubtless, vice dens and brothels) teemed with soldiers desperate for forgetfulness. Around every group of men in uniform swarmed crowds of hearty fellows eager to stand 'our boys' rounds of drinks and hero-worshipping young women intent on bestowing hot favours. Posters blazoned severe penalties for evading the call-up. Fire-eyed vampire girls scoured Piccadilly and Shaftesbury Avenue with white feathers for presentation to any of their undead brothers not in the King's service. A model trench in Hyde Park impressed an idea of conditions in France upon non-combatants; its cleanliness and home comforts provoked bitter mirth among those on leave from the real thing. At the Queen's Hall, Thomas Beecham conducted a No German Concert: the selection of pieces from English, French and Belgian composers excluded any note of the diabolical *kultur* of Beethoven, Bach and Wagner. The Scala Cinema offered reels taken at the front (mostly staged in the shire counties) and Mary Pickford in *The Little Bat Girl*.

If motion pictures were taken in the streets, a million details would confirm this as a city at war, from women traffic police officers to armed guards in butcher shops. To a man of his advanced years, many specifics reminded him of the Terror, the period thirty years gone when Britain had struggled under the yoke of the then Prince Consort. Commentators like H.G. Wells and Edmund Gosse argued the world war was the consequence of a job left undone. The Revolutionists of the '90s merely drove Dracula from the country when they should have hoisted the demon prince on one of his own stakes. By the second coronation of King Victor in 1897, there had been enough blood. Another civil war was narrowly averted when Lord Ruthven, the Prime Minister, persuaded Parliament to confirm the succession, cutting off his former patron, Dracula, from any right to rule.

Young Ashenden was patient with the crowds obstructing the car's way. As they idled, waiting for a Salvation Army band to pass, a rap came at the window. The driver looked out, quietly tense in what Beauregard recognised as a habit of their profession. A white feather puffed through the open crack of window and fluttered down.

'A penalty of serving in secret,' Beauregard said.

Ashenden put the feather in a tin box by the gears. Inside were a revolver and three or four more tokens of shame.

'You're accumulating plumage.'

'Not many chaps my age in mufti this year. Sometimes ladies converge on me like a pincer movement, competing to pass on the feathers.'

'We'll see what we can do about getting you a medal ribbon.'

'No need, sir.'

The Terror was the most vivid period of Beauregard's life. Nights of danger stayed fresh in the memory. His long-healed neck-bites troubled him. He remembered his companion of those nights, the elder Geneviève. These days, he thought more often of his wife

Pamela, who had died before Dracula stirred from his Transylvanian fastness. Pamela was of the world of his youth, which now seemed sunlit and charmed. The world without vampires. Geneviève was the fall of twilight, exciting but dangerous. She had left her mark on him. He would have sudden intuitions and *know* what she was doing, what she was feeling.

Soldiers lifted the barrier to allow the car into Downing Street. The Prime Minister's guards were elders, Carpathians who had turned against the Impaler during Ruthven's revolt. They wore quasi-mediaeval cuirasses and helmets but carried carbines as well as swords. If Dracula came for Ruthven, these vampires would stand up to their former commander. They had no choice, for Dracula would try to kill them on sight. He was not a forgiving soul, as this war bore out.

Dracula had left England as he came, as flotsam. When the country turned on him, the Prince Consort surrendered and was put in the Tower of London. It was a ruse: the Tower's spidery master, the Graf von Orlok, loyal to his fellow elder, assisted a daring escape. Floating through Traitors' Gate in a coffin, Dracula gained the Thames, then the open sea.

When Dracula escaped, Geneviève insisted on guarding Beauregard's bed. She feared the Count would take the opportunity to avenge himself on them. They had struck the blow which began the end of the Terror. Evidently, Dracula had had more pressing business; he never bothered to strike them down. Geneviève was slightly peeved by this neglect. They had altered the course of history, after all. Or so they liked to think. Perhaps individuals could do little to change the tides.

The car halted outside Number Ten. A liveried vampire footman darted out of the doorway, an unfolded *Daily Mail* held over his periwig as a shield against the drizzle. Beauregard was ushered up the steps to the Prime Minister's official residence.

In Europe, Dracula drifted Lear-like from court to court, embarrassing and threatening, playing on his hosts' dislike of parliaments that sacked monarchs. His bloodline spread through houses to which he was connected by his marriage to the late Queen Victoria and by his long-diffused mortal get. After centuries, the crowned heads of Europe all counted Vlad Tepes among their noteworthy ancestors.

When giving up his overcoat, Beauregard noticed his boots were still liberally coated with the mud of France. That foreign wars were so close to home was a miracle of the modern era. Though his old bones resisted, he had men like Ashenden and Edwin Winthrop whisked back and forth by air.

In Russia, Dracula turned thin-blooded Romanovs, whose shapes shifted catastrophically. Rasputin rose to power, claiming sorcery could assuage the raging lycanthropy afflicting the Tsarevich. Now, the holy charlatan was dead, dismembered by a *upyr* prince. The Tsar was imprisoned by the bolsheviks. The Diogenes Club understood Dracula had personally arranged the smuggling of Lenin back into Russia in his egregious sealed train.

Number Ten had been redecorated again. The reception hall was a gallery of portraits by distinguished hands of the last three decades: Whistler, Hallward, Sickert, Jimson. To the despair of Cabinet colleagues, who viewed as suspect anything other than a nice Constable landscape, Ruthven now declared himself a passionate Vorticist. Beauregard looked in vain for paintings on subjects other than the current Prime Minister. The grey, sardonic face cast cold eyes from a dozen canvases. Ruthven's craze for himself even embraced works which depicted him in a less than idealised manner, like Wyndham Lewis's representation of his visit to the front.

In July of 1905, the Romanov yacht *Stella Polaris* had conveyed Dracula to the Bay of Bjorkoe, off the coast of Finland. He was transferred by rowing boat to the *Hohenzollern*, the elegant white and gold yacht of another of his great-nephews by marriage, Kaiser Wilhelm II. At the time, the Diogenes Club had intercepted communiqués between Prince von Bülow, then the Kaiser's Chancellor, and Konstantin Pobedonostsev, the Tsar's close adviser, couched in the usual royal

European language of mutual distrust coated with cousinly diplomatic smarm. The Kaiser fervently wanted to believe the Dark Kiss would heal his withered arm. The Russians boosted the Dracula bloodline, concealing the state of the barking Tsarevich, to dupe Willi into taking on the burden of the former Prince Consort.

Beauregard signed the visitors' book and hurried through a corridor to the Cabinet Room. Carpathians armed with silver-tipped pikestaffs lined the passage. Kostaki, a rehabilitated elder whose fall in the Terror was now rewarded with a trusted position, touched his helm to Beauregard.

Assuming the title of Graf, Dracula became an ornament to the Imperial Court in Berlin. With all due ceremony, he turned Wilhelm. The Kaiser could at last straighten his hated arm and make a proper fist. The first thing Willi wished to do with his new fingers was sink them into the throats of fellow monarchs, to wrestle away their mastery of the seas, and sundry African, Eastern, Asian and Pacific dominions. Germany, he said, must turn vampire, and find its place in the moonlight.

British and French authors wrote novels in imitation of *The Battle of Dorking*, prophesying a coming war between Dracula's Germany and the Civilised World. Viscount Northcliffe serialised such yarns in the *Daily Mail*, achieving great success with William Le Queux's *The Invasion of 1910*. Paid-for strategists suggested the New Huns would favour lightning attacks on isolated outposts. Since there was little likelihood of increased circulation of the *Mail* in such hamlets, Northcliffe insisted the story feature invasions of every major town in the land. The citizens of Norwich and Manchester relished lurid descriptions of their fates when besieged by undead Uhlans. Beauregard remembered the *Mail*'s sandwich men strutting about town in German uniforms, a foretaste of the imagined occupation.

The Diogenes Club noted the Kaiser's programme of industrialisation and naval expansion, though the intelligence little affected Ruthven's programme of gallery openings and society balls. German rails snaked across the continent, an aid to rapid mobilisation. Britannia's dreadnoughts ruled the waves, but Willi's submarines took command of the deeps. When Heath Robinson, England's engineering genius, took the lead in the development of aircraft, Dracula employed the Dutchman Anthony Fokker to sketch design after design for fighter and bomber aeroplanes.

Vampirism spread through the Central Powers. Elders who had cowered through nomadic centuries returned to live openly on estates in Germany and Austria–Hungary. The condition had run unchecked in Britain, but Dracula now insisted on regulating the turning of new-borns. Edicts forbade specified classes and races of men and women to turn. Wilhelm sneered that Britain and France elevated poets and ballerinas to immortality; in his domains, the privilege was reserved to those willing to fight for their country and hunt their own human prey.

In 1914, having occupied a succession of military and political posts, Dracula assumed the twin positions of Chancellor and commander-in-chief of the armies of the Fatherland. Beauregard wondered how the former Vlad Tepes countenanced alliances which ranged him against Romania, the land for which he had fought, and alongside Turkey, the empire he had devoted his warmth to resisting.

Outside the Cabinet Room, Beauregard was greeted by Mansfield Smith-Cumming, the monocled spymaster who served with him on the Ruling Cabal. It was rumoured the vampire had amputated his own leg with a penknife to free himself from the wreckage of a car accident so he could drape his coat over his dying son, who complained of the cold. His leg was regrown past the knee joint; under a bundle of bandages, a new foot was forming.

'Beauregard,' Smith-Cumming said, smiling broadly, 'what do you think of the disguise?'

Smith-Cumming took boyish delight in the element of deception in his profession. He sported a large, patently fake beard. He leered, twitching his horsehair moustache like one of Fred Karno's comedy troupe.

'I look a proper Hun, what? Can't you just see me biting out the throat of a Belgian nun?'

He showed huge false fangs, then spat them out to reveal delicate real ones.

'Where is Mycroft?' Beauregard asked.

Smith-Cumming looked as serious as was possible for a man in disguise. 'Grave news, I'm afraid. Another stroke.'

Mycroft Holmes had been on the Ruling Cabal of the Diogenes Club as long as Beauregard had been a member. His plans had held the nation together throughout the Terror. Subsequently, he had done much to moderate the odd enthusiasms of the new King and his eternal first minister, Ruthven.

'We're all under a strain. You've heard about Spenser.'

Smith-Cumming nodded, appalled.

'I've had Winthrop step in. He's coming along fast. I trust he'll catch up.'

'Frightening nights, Beauregard,' Smith-Cumming said.

It had started on Sunday, the 28th of June, 1914, in Sarajevo, far from the borders where European powers snarled like dogs separated by fences.

Archduke Franz Ferdinand, nephew of King-Emperor Franz Joseph, was touring Bosnia with his morganatic wife Sophie, Duchess of Hohenberg. Left to its own devices in 1877 by the collapse of the Ottoman Empire, Bosnia was hardly the most desirable patch of Europe, but Austria–Hungary saw it as a natural addition to already swollen and ungovernable holdings. Franz Joseph had almost surreptitiously annexed the province in 1908. Serbia, not unfairly deemed a catspaw of Russia, also had designs on Bosnia and its sister province, Hercegovina.

The Archduke was *nosferatu*, a provocation. The Slavs and Muslims of Bosnia–Hercegovina did not accept vampires, especially as rulers. Serbian irredentists trumpeted the prevalence of the undead at the King-Emperor's court to stir up those in Bosnia–Hercegovina who wished to be free from bloodsucking Habsburgs. With fine hypocrisy, the Tsar's undead advisers (notably excluding the fanatically warm Rasputin) sent agents to Sarajevo to agitate torch-bearing mobs of vampire-hating Orthodox Christians, Serbian nationalists and café trouble-makers. Pamphlets appeared giving obscene accounts of the Archduke's marital relations with the plumply warm Sophie, a Czech caricatured as a bloodmilk cow.

It was the unshakable belief of the Central Powers that Tsar Nicky personally ordered a student Van Helsing named Gavrilo Prinćip to empty a revolver at Franz Ferdinand, putting silver in the Habsburg's vampire heart and incidentally murdering the scabby-necked Sophie. Equally, any adherent of the Allied cause was required to believe Prinćip a lunatic acting independently of any of the Great Powers, or even a paid agent of a warmongering Kaiser.

Beauregard once asked Mycroft if Russia was involved. The great man conceded no one truly knew. On one hand, the Okhrana certainly dispensed cash (and, probably, silver bullets) to many of Prinćip's stripe; on the other, even Artamanov, the attaché responsible for handing over funds, was unsure whether the obscure assassin was one of his contacts.

The Kaiser, seeing an opportunity to redraw the map of Europe, egged the ascetic bureaucrat Franz Joseph into issuing a communiqué to Serbia which must be construed as a preparation for war. Russia was pledged to defend Serbia from Austria–Hungary, Germany was required to stand with the King-Emperor in war with Russia, France was bound by treaty to attack any nation that warred with the Romanovs, Germany could strike at France only by invading through Belgium, Great Britain was obliged to preserve Belgian neutrality. Once Prinćip's silver bullet transfixed the Archduke, the cards fell one by one.

That summer, Beauregard, contemplating his sixtieth year, was considering retirement. As each alliance was invoked, each nation mobilised, he realised he could not leave his post. Reluctantly, he conceded there would be war.

In 1918, the question of who ruled Bosnia was remote. The Romanovs faced death by a hammered stake and beheading sickle. Franz Joseph's mind was gone, his empire governed by a feuding rabble of Austrian and Magyar elders. The Kaiser had long since ceased to supervise the conduct of the war, which was entirely in the hands of the Graf von Dracula and his new-born clique, von Hindenburg and Lundendorff.

The doors of the reception room opened and the two active members of the Ruling Cabal were ushered in to see the elder who ruled Great Britain under the standard of King Victor.

'Gentlemen,' said Lord Ruthven, 'come in and sit down.'

The Prime Minister was clad entirely in dove grey, from spats and morning coat to ruffled stock and curly-brimmed topper. He was at his bare desk, posed archly beneath another of his own portraits, a martial study by Elizabeth Asquith. The indifferent canvas might have earned a place because the artist's father was Home Secretary in Ruthven's Government of National Unity.

Others sat in deep armchairs around the room. Lord Asquith sourly contemplated despatches. Field Marshal Sir Douglas Haig was in France, but General Sir William Robertson and General Sir Henry Wilson of His Majesty's General Staff were present, kitted out in dress uniform. Churchill, the baby-faced Minister for Munitions, wore a smock-like robe which tented over his considerable bulk and an American belt with holstered pistols at his hips. Lloyd George, Minister of War, stood by the window chewing on an unlit pipe. Sitting meekly by the Prime Minister was the little-publicised Caleb Croft of the Home Office, his bloody hands in woolly gloves. Croft's duties were too frightening to consider.

Beauregard and Smith-Cumming took chairs in the centre of the circle.

'Tell me,' Ruthven purred, 'how goes the secret war?'

3

PAST MIDNIGHT

Courtney kept winding the gramophone and setting the needle back to the beginning. 'Poor Butterfly' was the only record in the billet. Winthrop wondered if the choice struck anyone else as unhealthy. Butterfly kept waiting but Pinkerton never came back, the swine. Every three minutes, the unfortunate Cio-Cio-San wasted away, drained cold and abandoned by her vampire lover. The story always upset Winthrop, and this version, distilled to a few verses, was the most concentratedly upsetting.

'We used to have a rare selection,' Williamson claimed, when Winthrop voiced a complaint at the limited repertoire. '*The Bohemian Girl*, *Chu Chin Chow*, "Take a Pair of Crimson Eyes"…'

'But there was a binge and they all got smashed,' said Bertie.

'I miss *The Vampyres of Venice*,' said Ginger.

'Heroic binge, though,' Courtney said. 'A veritable binge of binges. The *demoiselles* can still feel the bites.'

The record finished and the gramophone stuttered, hissing. Courtney lifted the needle. 'Poor Butterfly' started again.

The bridge game had evaporated. The pilots lounged in the mess, not talking of Red Albright, regarding Winthrop with a mixture of curiosity and suspicion. He fancied some of the vampires looked at him hungrily.

'Will you be permanent?' Bigglesworth asked.

'Nothing's permanent,' Courtney got in. 'Not even immortality.'

'I'm given to understand that I'm to be your liaison with Diogenes in place of Captain Spenser.'

'Oh joy,' said Brown, a sour Canadian.

'Mind your head then,' said Williamson.

'I intend to.'

'Deuced mysterious, Diogenes,' Courtney commented. 'It's hard to see a pattern in what they ask of us. Photograph a road here, bomb a bridge there, bring down a balloon, convey a silent passenger over the lines…'

'"Ours not to reason why",' Bertie said.

Courtney snarled humorously.

'I don't know any more than you do,' Winthrop felt obliged to say. 'It's intelligence. It's supposed to be mysterious.'

'Sometimes I think we're split-arsing around just to confuse the Hun,' said Courtney. 'Playing some complicated practical joke.'

'Then why isn't it funny?' asked Williamson.

Winthrop looked at his watch three or four times a minute. Midnight did not seem to get nearer. He overcame an instinct to hold the timepiece to his ear to make sure it still ticked.

The record started again. Lacey returned from a trip upstairs to visit 'mademoiselle'. The Englishman, one of the Bigglesworth clique, was quickened after feeding, eyes darting, sharp fingers fidgeting.

Allard laughed again, like glass scraping bone.

'First name on the list,' he mused. 'Last week, that would have been me. I'd be flying out to the chateau.'

'You were right to complain,' said Cundall.

Allard was silent. He leaned into a nook, disappearing in shadow.

'They used to misspell Allard's name,' Cundall explained. 'They'd miss an L and he'd be A-L-A-R-D. Put him ahead of Albright on the roster. He threw a squawk and Lieutenant-Colonel Raymond issued a stern notice to the fool typists at Wing. They've started spelling it properly.'

'Perhaps you'll make it to the top again,' said Courtney. Nobody laughed.

'You ought to be a pilot,' Cundall said to Winthrop. 'Begins with a W. You'd never have to go up. Williamson would be in the air before you.'

Picking the first name on the list was a fatuous idea. But any other choice would have been as arbitrary. Cundall's ragging irked Winthrop. It was the flight commander's responsibility, no matter that he had manipulated someone else into making the decision.

Even the vampires were restless, jittery. Conversation took silly turns. Bertie and Lacey compared eccentric, fearsome aunts.

Winthrop thought of Spenser, wondering what made a man drive nails into his own brain. As he was taken away, Spenser was smiling. He seemed not to be in pain.

There was a long-case clock in the room, face cracked across, stopped at ten to seven. Winthrop alternated looking at the broken clock and his watch. It was twenty to midnight.

The Chateau de Malinbois was forty miles off. An SE5a could make a hundred-and-twenty miles an hour but flying above the cloud, navigating by the stars, Albright would go slower. It might take several dips to look at the land before he found the objective. Captain Midnight was only human, even if a vampire.

If Albright wasn't back by twelve, it didn't mean he wasn't coming home.

'Poor Butterfly' slowed and Courtney wound her up again. After a comically sped-up squeak, she settled into her usual rut.

Waiting, waiting. Wasting, wasting.

Winthrop thought of Catriona. He must write and tell her his duties had changed. He could not mention Diogenes, of course. Also, the censors would blank anything about Spenser. No wonder the army provided form postcards; fill in the gaps, strike out anything that didn't apply and sign your name. He missed being able to talk things through with Cat. She had a keen intellect and usually found a different way of looking at a thing.

'Two minutes to,' Williamson said.

Winthrop checked his watch. Time had lurched forwards. After a moment lasting a quarter of an hour, a quarter of an hour had gone in a moment.

'I think I hear him,' Bertie said.

Courtney, swift as a snake, lifted the needle from the record, cutting off 'Poor Butterfly' in mid-waste. Winthrop heard noises in his head and the everlasting shelling, but nothing more. Then, perhaps, something.

With exaggeratedly casual gait, Cundall ambled over and opened the door. There was definitely a distant sound, a whine or a rumble.

'He'll be on the dot,' Courtney said. 'Captain Midnight returns.'

Cundall stepped outside and everyone followed, elated. Light strayed across the field from the open door. A tall figure stared into the sky. Dravot had stayed at his post all the time. Winthrop would not have been surprised if an icicle were hanging from the sergeant's nose.

Nobody had said they thought Albright would not make it home, so they couldn't now be relieved when he did.

'It's an SE5a all right,' Williamson said. 'No mistaking that cough.'

Winthrop saw the black bubble outlines of the clouds. He strained to see more.

'There, look,' Ball said, extending an arm that kinked at the elbow and wrist.

Something dipped out of cloud. Winthrop heard the engine clearly. He realised he was holding his breath and exhaled a plume of condensation.

'Can he see the field?' he asked.

'Of course,' Cundall snapped. 'Eyes like an owl. But there's no harm in giving him a flare. Allard, pop one off, would you, there's a dear.'

The American, wrapped in a cape, produced a Verey pistol and fired upwards. A purple shell burst high, colouring cloud from within, bathing the field in violet.

The SE5a rounded to approach the field. Winthrop had seen pilots stunt to impress fellows on the ground (some who survived dogfights broke their silly necks trying to look heroes to pretty nurses) but Albright was better than that. Cundall's Condors probably couldn't be much impressed by stunting.

Winthrop saw what excited the press about aviators. They were lone eagles, not anonymous masses. The only knightly heroes in the gash of bloody mud that stretched across Europe from Belgium to northern Italy.

Violet light failed as the flare came down. Allard sent up another.

'What's that?' Winthrop asked.

Above the SE5a was a winged shape, indistinct in the purple cloud. He heard only Albright's engine. The shape swooped down, more like a huge bird than an aircraft. Albright put a burst up into its belly. From the ground, the gunfire was a tiny sparkling. The shape fastened on to the SE5a and hauled it upwards. Entwined, they climbed into cloud. Allard sent up two more flares, one after the other.

Major Cundall's face, outlined by the violet glow, was hard.

Engine drone continued for seconds, then choked into silence. The cloud seemed to part. Something fell, whining. Albright's aeroplane spiralled tightly towards the ground, wind screaming in its wires. One set of wings tore loose. The SE5a ploughed nose-down and crumpled like a box-kite. Winthrop waited for an explosion.

People ran towards the wreck. The fizzling purple bonfires of fallen flares lit the mess. The tail was snapped off, the remaining wings shredded. Parallel slashes in the canvas looked like clawmarks.

Winthrop reached the SE5a just after Cundall. They skidded to a halt a few yards away, cautious. The fuel tank might explode. Burning petrol killed vampires as nastily as it did a warm man.

A crowd ringed the crumpled aircraft. The Lewis gun, barrel still smoking, poked out of twisted metal and fabric. Dravot pressed forwards and rooted through the wreck, ripping apart the remains. He found one of the cameras and checked the plate. It was smashed.

'Where is he?' Bigglesworth asked.

The cockpit was empty. No one had seen the pilot fall.

Had Albright taken a parachute? If so, it was against regulations. It was thought parachutes encouraged cowardice. They were issued only to balloon observers.

'Look,' Allard said.

Winthrop followed the American's gaze upwards. The last purple faded in the clouds. The flying shape was still faintly visible, weaving this way and that on the currents. It could be some strange sort of batwing kite. Then it was gone.

'Something's falling,' Ginger said.

There was a whistling and everyone scattered. It was just his luck to be under a bomb when he had a promotion in the offing. He flung himself on cold grass, covering his head with his arms, thinking briefly of Catriona.

An object thumped into the field, a dozen yards from the wreck, and did not explode. Winthrop gathered himself and stood up, brushing grass and ice-chips from his coat.

'Good God,' Cundall said. 'It's Red.'

The vampires stood in a circle around the fallen man. Winthrop was allowed through to look.

The twisted thing wore a midnight black Sidcot, ripped open from neck to crotch. A human face was shrivelled on to the skull, lids shrunk from staring eyes. It was a caricature of Albright's solid, features, bled white. In the throat was a sucked-dry wound the size of an orange, exposing vertebrae, pale sinew and the underside of the jawbone. The body was insubstantial, a scarecrow of sticks wrapped in thin linen. Albright had been emptied, leeched of all substance.

Cundall and the others looked up at impenetrable skies. Winthrop fumbled his watch out of his pocket. It must have cracked when he threw himself down, for it had stopped at midnight precisely.

4

GREY EMINENCES

'I would appreciate it if Diogenes could enlighten us about the Chateau de Malinbois,' said Lord Ruthven, admiring his diamond-shaped fingernails. His expressionless monotone always set Beauregard's teeth grinding.

Smith-Cumming, who had doffed his disguise, deferred to Beauregard.

He cleared his throat and began, 'There's a definite air of mystery, Prime Minister. We have Condor Squadron on the problem just now. You're familiar with *Jagdgeschwader 1*, the Richthofen Circus. At first, we assumed the fuss around the castle was what you'd expect of such a valued unit. The Germans are fond of their fliers.'

'As are we of ours, sir,' declared Lloyd George. 'They are the knighthood of this war, without fear and without reproach. They recall the legendary days of chivalry, not merely by the daring of their exploits, but by the nobility of their spirit.'

'Quite so,' Beauregard agreed, assuming the Minister was quoting one of his own speeches. 'But our heroes are, on the whole, modest men. We do not require the battery of press agents and portrait photographers the German Imperial Air Service employs to puff a Max Immelmann, an Oswald Boelcke or a Manfred von Richthofen.'

The name of the Bloody Red Baron hung in the air.

'It would be a good thing if this Richthofen were shot down,' said

Sir William Robertson. The warm general disapproved of new-fangled contraptions like aeroplanes and tanks. 'It would show there are no short cuts in war. No substitute for a good horse and a better man.'

'There is indubitably something to be said for the position,' admitted Beauregard, not stating what precisely could be said for it. 'But what concerns Diogenes is that the Circus have been unnaturally quiet since they put up tents at Malinbois. They log victories with monotonous regularity but the thrilling details so beloved of the German press and public have grown scarce. And JG1 has seconded unusual personnel.'

'Unusual?' Ruthven prompted.

'The commandant of the chateau is General Karnstein, an Austrian elder known to be close to the councils of Graf von Dracula.'

Ruthven's cold eyes evinced interest. The Prime Minister kept abreast of the doings of fellow elders. Among his kind, he was an outcast; his attitude to the better-known bloodlines was not untainted by envy.

'I know the vampire. The head of a blood-clan. Hasn't been the same since his dreadful daughter was destroyed.'

Almost surreptitiously, the Minister for Munitions pulled a large, insensible rabbit from a satchel. Churchill was overfond of his tipple. His particular quirk was to inject Madeira into the blood of animals. He fixed chubby lips on the rabbit's throat, sucking discreetly.

'Drink… good,' he mumbled. The rest of the room pointedly did not pass comment. Asquith, no mean imbiber himself, looked thirsty.

'General Karnstein has been arranging conferences and parties near the front,' Beauregard said. 'Besides expected names, like Anthony Fokker, we have heard the odd vampire elder has been included. And some unusual new-borns. Gertrud Zelle has been mentioned.'

'Your temptress, Beauregard,' Ruthven said. 'The mysterious and malign Mata Hari.'

'She is hardly mine.'

'You are responsible for catching her.'

Beauregard modestly showed open hands. Though she had featured in many newspaper articles, Gertrud Zelle was not the spy she was made out to be. After all, she had been caught and was awaiting execution. Her 'victims' were mainly high-ranking French officers, most notably the ill-favoured General Mireau. Pétain insisted on her ceremonial destruction, though Beauregard had asked the Prime Minister to plead for clemency. It was unlikely: as Ruthven reasoned, the Germans had burned Nurse Edith Cavell at the stake, so the Allies had to even things up and shoot Mata Hari.

'We are all men of the world here,' said the Prime Minister. 'I, for one, can think of a reason why the German High Command would see a need for the skills of a Mata Hari at Malinbois. The Graf always likes to reward his valiant warriors.'

Churchill, bloody rabbit back in the game bag, gurgled a laugh. With Madeira in his veins, his eyes pinked at the corners. His great face was otherwise powder-white except for the carmine of his flabby mouth.

'There is more to it than a debauch, Prime Minister,' Beauregard said, tactfully. 'The Germans would not be so secretive about simple hell-raising. Indeed, they take pains to inflate the amorous reputations of air aces, contriving romances with famous beauties which last only as long as a pose for the rotogravure.'

Ruthven looked at his advisers and tapped a foretooth with a fingernail. He made a great show of thinking.

'Smith-Cumming,' he said. 'What of our old friend, the Graf von Dracula?'

The spymaster consulted a notebook, where everything was kept in a cipher of his own devising.

'He has been seen in Berlin. He is to meet with the *Bolsheviki* at Brest-Litovsk next month. We assume the Russkies will confirm their withdrawal from the war.'

'A pity. I've always believed we should defend the British Empire to the last drop of Russian blood.'

The generals and ministers attempted laughter at Ruthven's joke. Even the dead-faced Mr Croft flashed a manufactured smile.

Smith-Cumming flipped a page. 'There is a suspicious consensus among our Berlin agents that the Graf has no intention of paying a visit next month to the Chateau de Malinbois. If true, it's curious such a fact should be so consistently available. After all, no one troubles to tell us when the Kaiser does not plan to visit his barber to have his moustache-tips waxed.'

'Next month?' Churchill growled.

'That is when the Graf will not be at Malinbois,' Smith-Cumming confirmed.

'Has Dracula ever visited this chateau before?'

'Not in this last century, Prime Minister.'

'Do we draw conclusions?'

Smith-Cumming shrugged. 'Some convoluted scheme is afoot, without doubt. We are matching wits with masters.'

'With the Russians out of the game, the Huns will launch an all-out attack on the Western Front,' said Churchill. 'It's the juggernaut strategy Count Dragulya has always practised.' Churchill favoured a curious pronunciation of 'Dracula'. It was not the least of his eccentricities.

'Ridiculous notion,' blustered General Sir Henry Wilson. 'The Kaiser doesn't have the men or the means or the guns or the guts. Haig will tell you Germany is an arrant paper tiger. The Huns are beaten badly, their heads are off. They can only flounder in dirt and bleed to death.'

'It would be pleasant to concur,' said Ruthven, 'but we do not just fight Wicked Willi. There are others in this business. Winston is quite right. A concerted attack will come. I know the Transylvanian brute of old. He is a veritable Piltdown Man, an unchecked Eoanthropus. He will not stop until stopped. Even then, he must be destroyed. We made the mistake once before of letting Dracula live.'

'I agree with the Prime Minister,' said Lloyd George. 'Dracula commands the Central Powers. It is his will that must be broken.'

Beauregard, wearily, had to concede he too believed a big push was in the offing. 'With the cessation of hostilities on the Eastern Front, a million men will be freed to fight in the west. Steel forged in the fire of battle, not green recruits.'

'And Malinbois?' Ruthven asked. 'Might this be his forwards post? He'll want to be in the field. He has a barbarian vanity about such things. He has not entered the lists, yet he must lust to do so.'

'The castle would make a suitable HQ,' Beauregard said. 'If a ground push is to succeed, he would wish to wrest from us our superiority in the air. Therefore, he would want JG1 with him.'

Ruthven slapped his desk, excited. His monotone became a grating whine.

'I have it! He wants to spread his black wings and fly. He'll be *up* in that dirigible of his, the *Attila*. He and I, we know this war comes down to the two of us. We face each other over the chessboard of Europe. To him, I am the Britain that humiliated and scorned him. To me, he is the past vampirekind must outlive. It is a philosophical and aesthetic battle…'

Churchill's belly rumbled and Lloyd George examined the cuffs of his striped trousers. Beauregard wondered if millions of truly dead thought it a war of philosophy and aesthetics.

'This is our duel. My brain and his. He has cunning, I'll give him that. And valour, for what it's worth. And he so loves his toys: his trains, his flying machines, his big guns. He's like a monstrous child. If he can't get his way, he will ravage the world.'

Ruthven stood and gestured dramatically, as if posing for a portrait: the Prime Minister in Full Flight.

'I see a way to trip the fiend, though. Beauregard, keep worrying at this Malinbois business. I want details, facts, figures. Mr Croft, this would seem a project suited to your skills. You will take Beauregard's reports and digest them.'

The hatchet man narrowed his dead eyes.

Ruthven continued, 'We can use Dracula's nursery enthusiasms against him, draw him into our trap and close our hands around his cursed throat.'

Ruthven strangled the air.

5

THE PROPHET OF PRAGUE

Knives of daylight glinted in cracks between the serrated tiles of the low, sloping roof. He grew weaker as the sun rose but his red thirst raged. He was starved for human blood. Edgar Poe, as usual, numbered himself among the most wretched of all his kind.

He sat on the cot, elbows on knees, head hung to avoid bumping. Books were stacked against the opposite wall in pillars two or three volumes deep. The bulkiest, least-consulted items of his travelling library were arranged into a literary ledge which served as a table. A jug half-filled with thick juice sat precisely on a circular dent in the cloth cover of his Schiller. His mouth and nose stung with the stench of days-old animal blood. His stomach revolted but soon he would be forced to drink.

Since turning, he had often suffered prolonged abstinence. Warm men felt hunger in their stomachs; the *nosferatu* ache was a pulsing fire in the heart, accompanied by a gnawing *need* in the throat and on the tongue. The sustenance of blood was as much in the taste as the substance, and in the spiritual mingling that came with the vampire communion.

Confining him to the ghetto, Prague's ancient repository for the alien and unloved, was ingeniously cruel. Under the Edict of Graz, proclaimed by Franz Joseph and Kaiser Wilhelm, it was forbidden for a Hebrew to be turned. Therefore Jews considered vampires predators and kept their women away from him. As with most edicts proclaimed at the dictate of Graf von Dracula, the specified penalty for transgression was impalement.

It was hard to nurture his inner vampire. He was reduced to procuring animal blood from a kosher butcher. The Israelite was a cursed gouger. In three years, the price of a few rancid drops of cow gore had risen tenfold. Sometimes the need for the sweet and scented blood of women took him to the brink of madness. Looking into a maelstrom, he was strong yet weak. With half dread and half delight, he foresaw a night when need would overcome him. He would claw ferociously into a nearby garret, forcing a fat wife or daughter to give herself up. Then, glutted, he would drift in poetic reverie, words flowing from his mind like water from a spring. Jews would come for him with a stake and his unhappy career would be at a sordid end.

In May 1917, Poe had risen from lassitude one evening to discover the myopic poltroon Wilson had committed the United States of America to the European conflict. With a pen-stroke, Wilson transformed Edgar Poe into an enemy of the Central Powers. He was then living in a moderately uncomfortable rooming house in the Sladkovský Platz, eking out an income as a lecturer. The brief prosperity of *The Battle of St Petersburg* had passed but his name retained some of its lustre. If all else failed, he could recite 'The Raven', the sole constant in his life and reputation. He no longer thought of the piece as something of his own creation, and had come heartily to detest its bleat of 'nevermore, nevermore'.

Eight months later, he was quartered in an attic little larger than a coffin. The ghetto was a slum labyrinth of narrow covered passageways, more like tunnels than streets. This hive of wood and plaster was infested with chattering, chanting Hebrews. Each room harboured unlikely numbers. Europe was choked with inferior peoples. If he ventured beyond the Salnitergasse, Poe was required to wear an arm-band signifying his status as a hostile alien.

Upon leaving the sullen and chaotic shores of his native Philistia for an old world of *kultur*, this was not the situation he had expected. He had sought freedom and found only his old enemies, the envy of lesser men and the temptations of despair. The few inclined to ponder his case treated him as a conundrum concealed within a nuisance, an occasionally diverting specimen but not one whose study offered much in the way of reward.

His gums receded and his sharp teeth hurt. An iron fist gripped and released his heart. He could bear no more. Despising his weakness, he took the jug and poured the sludgy remains into his burning mouth.

Indescribable foulness swarmed into his throat and a black ache split his skull. It was over quickly. Red thirst dissipated, for the moment. There was a nasty aftertaste, as if the blood were laced with machine oil.

Blood blurred his mind. He thought of pale women with active eyes, bright smiles and long, fine hair. Ligeia, Morella, Berenice, Lenore, Madeline. Many faces coalesced into one face. Virginia. His wife had died with blood in her mouth, child's voice choked in the midst of song. Later she returned from her grave, bestowing toothed kisses. She suckled him with her blood and turned him. Virginia was truly dead now, burned with Atlanta, but she was wife and daughter and sister and mother to him. He lived with her taste on his tongue and her blood in his undying body.

Something thumped mightily at the door. He jumped, alarmed, from his cot. His swimming head banged a beam and he groaned. He pulled open the door, scraping carpet away from bare boards. Outside, on the topmost landing, stood a uniformed vampire, glaring angrily from beneath an eagle-crested shako. He wore spiked and waxed moustaches. Poe recognised the Enemy Alien Commission's messenger.

'*Guten morgen*, Herr Unteroffizier Paulier,' Poe said. German was the official language of the Austro-Hungarian Empire. There were Czechs and Poles who did not know a word of their own tongues. 'What brings you to call on Prague's most dangerous belligerent alien?'

By way of an answer, Paulier stuck out an artificial arm. An envelope was fixed to his wood-filled glove by a pin. Like many functionaries, the messenger was a crippled by-blow of the war. His blood was not strong enough to regenerate a lost limb. Poe tore the letter loose and slit it with a sharp fingernail. Without speaking, Paulier turned and descended the many flights of stairs, false hand clattering against slats.

A door opposite opened a crack and, about three feet above the floor, large wet eyes glistened. The building was aswarm with rats and Semitic children. Degenerate races bred without restraint. Dracula was correct to bar them from turning vampire. Poe bared fangs and hissed. The door shut. He read the note from the Commission. He was summoned again to the tribunal chambers in the Hradschiner Platz.

Afternoon ground on. Poe sat alone in a cathedral of a waiting room, listening to the clock. He was sensitive to the passage of time. Since turning, his ears had grown so acute he could distinguish the workings of a clock. A plague of tiny creaks and clicks accompanied every second. Each tiny noise resounded in his head like raindrops on a drumskin. He thought of the offices of the Commission, to which he was frequently recalled, as the Palace of Vondervotteimittis. Its dusty corners and cold, hard benches were unaffected by the passing of history.

Four years ago, at the outbreak of war, the Empire had known what to do with enemy nationals trapped within its borders. There were internment camps and repatriation schemes. The bureaucrats and diplomats who dealt with those niceties were lost, gone into the armies and probably dead. The late entry of the United States into the war stranded a few citizens behind the lines. Poe, who had long ago ceased to consider himself American, was almost unique in his predicament. Few in the street understood precisely the significance of the ridiculous arm-band. He was more often harangued by gentlewomen who thought he should be doing his duty in uniform than by patriotic souls who recognised him as a deadly foe of the Habsburgs.

The face of the clock, wide as a wagon-wheel, was embedded in a classical orgy of grubby marble fixed above doors twice the height of a tall man. Its seconds were half as long again as those of Poe's watch.

When he checked his chronometer against the clock, the timepieces conspired to suggest they ran at the same speed. With his watch back in his vest, the clock slackened again. Excruciating pauses prolonged each tick.

A man without a country, his case was complicated by *The Battle of St Petersburg*. Though its reputation was entirely trodden into the mud, the book kept him out of a prisoner-of-war camp. If repatriated, Poe knew he would merit no kind reception in the land of his birth. An adherent of the Southern cause during the late war of Secession, he refused to recognise the United States as it was currently constituted. Wilson had preached hypocritical neutrality while surreptitiously succouring the Triple Entente; Poe openly and famously championed the inevitable and just triumph of the Central Powers.

At the beginning of the war, he had tried to secure a commission in the armies of Austria–Hungary. Kept out of the fight by envious fools, he whipped his long-silent muse to action. Written in a week-long white-hot burst, *The Battle of St Petersburg* foretold that the Kaiser and the King-Emperor would sweep through France within the month, then turn to the solemn duty of conquering the Russias. It was a story of gallant steam cavalry charges and aristocratic feats of daring, the fighting spirit of the great days allied to the marvels of modern science. All Europe was thrilled by his account of Zeppelin fleets laying siege to St Petersburg and the utter subjugation of the Cossacks by motorised Uhlans. Dracula himself was struck by the notion of locomotive juggernauts laying tracks before them as they thrust into the heart of the Tsar's dominions, and insisted the practicalities of such devices be gauged. Engineer Robur, the agitator for aerial warships, lent an endorsement. Pirate editions appeared in England and America as by 'the celebrated author of "The Raven"'. An unscrupulous Belgian calling himself J.H. Rosny *aîné* imitated the book chapter for chapter as *La Bataille de Vienne*, with German characters turned to Frenchmen and Russian place-names replaced by locations in Germany and Austria–Hungary. Poe recaptured the visionary reputation to which he had aspired in his warm days and was in great demand as a speaker. He visited gymnasia to share his vision with smart ranks of newly uniformed young men who would make it a reality. It seemed he would submerge forever the reputations of such infantile plagiarists as M. Verne and Mr Wells.

An old man scuttled through the waiting room, pushing a wheelbarrow piled with bulging string-tied bundles of yellow paper. He was warm but smelled bloodless and dry. The clerk ignored Poe and disappeared through a side door into a labyrinth of records. The tribunal hall of the Commission was a castle of forgotten fact, an Alexandrian Library of the irrelevant.

Even with the 'prophecies' of *The Battle of St Petersburg* scorned by those who had once hailed them as a model to be matched, Poe believed his vision truer than that of the front-line correspondents. His was the world that should have been; not the muddy, entrenched, life-devouring stalemate that existed across Europe. The British should have stayed neutral or ranged themselves against their hereditary enemy, the French. Truly, what did a Briton care for snivelling little Belgium? Zeppelins would now sail majestically over the enslaved hordes of the steppe. The great empires would purge themselves of impurities and govern the destiny of the planet.

Edgar Poe would be the prophet of the age. It was said no vampire could produce a work of lasting aesthetic or intellectual merit. He hungered to disprove the saw. But the world of glory that seemed about to be born was turned to a nightmare of boredom and starvation.

The cuffs of his trousers were frayed and he wore a celluloid collar that had to be cleaned with an india rubber. It was a mercy Virginia had not lived to see her Eddy reduced to this miserable condition.

An official entered. He wore a floor-length apron and an oversized cap with a green eyeshade. He held up a small bell, which he tinkled. The tintinnabulation assaulted Poe's ears.

'Herr Poe, if you will come,' the official said in formal German.

* * *

The meeting was held not in an office but in a high-ceilinged corridor. Thin windows allowed dusty light in. Attendants trundled trolleys by. Poe had to flatten himself against the wall to let them past.

Poe had dealt before with Kafka, a sharp Jew with queer batwing ears and a penetrating gaze. The clerk seemed to find the idea of an American in the ghetto disturbing and gave the impression of a genuine eagerness to help resolve the case. Thus far his efforts had yielded only a creeping plague of contradictory memoranda from higher-ups. Withal, he had almost taken to Franz Kafka. The only soul in Prague who had heard of Poe for anything other than *The Battle of St Petersburg* and 'The Raven', he had once asked him to inscribe a cheap edition of *Tales of Mystery and Imagination*. Kafka mentioned he was himself an occasional writer, but Poe had not wished to encourage further intimacy with the Jew and made a pointed display of indifference.

Poe was summoned to meet one Hanns Heinz Ewers. A vampire, of course, he was well-dressed and thought himself distinguished in several fields. Unusually for a German, he wore a suit rather than a uniform.

'It is ironic, Herr Poe,' Ewers said. 'We are truly doubles, mirror images, *doppelgängers*. When the war began, I was in your country, in New York City…'

'I have ceased to regard Federal America as *my* country, sir. I lost my nationality at Appomattox.'

'As you wish. I too was frustrated, as you must be now. I too was a poet, an essayist, a visionary, a novelist of sensation, a philosopher. I have conquered new fields of art, including the kinematograph. Employed by my Kaiser as a lobbyist, my efforts were insufficient to prevent the misunderstanding that exists between the New World and the Old. I was interned in and deported. I have long wanted to meet you, Herr Poe.'

Poe fixed Ewers's eye and found something lacking. He was a half-formed imitation, exaggerated to compensate for inner deficiencies.

'I once considered instituting a lawsuit against you, Herr Ewers,'

Poe said, plainly. '*The Student of Prague*, a photoplay which you signed, is an arrant plagiarism of my tale "William Wilson".'

Ewers was slapped by the accusation but recovered in an eyeblink. 'No more, surely, than your "William Wilson" is plagiarism of E.T.A. Hoffmann.'

'There is no comparison,' Poe said coldly.

Ewers smiled. Poe was struck by the man's detestability. His manner was as contrived, ungainly and fraudulent as his fictions. It was entirely fitting that he should work in motion pictures. There was a vulgarity about the stuttering, posturing, face-pulling foolery of the kinema that stuck to Ewers like mud.

'The case of Edgar Poe is under review,' Kafka reminded Ewers, holding up a thick folder of papers.

'No,' Ewers said, gripping the folder's edge with undead strength. 'As far as you are concerned, the case of Edgar Poe is concluded. Germany has need of him, and Prague will surrender him to me, as representative of Kaiser and court.'

Kafka's eyes wavered. Poe was unsure but it seemed the clerk was wavering out of concern for him.

A one-legged man, face hooded, stumped by, a basket slung upon his back like a peasant's pannier, half full of stopped watches.

'Herr Poe,' Ewers said. 'It has been decided you are just the man for a certain task of great national importance…'

'A tune has been changed, Herr Ewers. I've a distinguished military record in my former country, including study at West Point Academy, but my attempts to volunteer for the armies of the Empires were ungraciously rebuffed. Though I am an internationally recognised authority on the conduct of modern warfare, my many letters of suggestion to Generals von Moltke, von Falkenhayn, Ludendorff and von Hindenburg have gone unacknowledged…'

'In the name of the Kaiser and the Graf von Dracula, I extend the apologies of a nation,' Ewers announced, sticking out his hand as if offering a benediction.

Kafka's eyes darted between Poe and Ewers. Poe's impression was that the Jew shared his opinion of the German but had more empirical evidence to justify his dislike.

'What do you wait for?' Ewers snapped at Kafka. 'Herr Poe is an important man. Give him travel papers. We are expected in Berlin tomorrow.'

Kafka opened his folder and handed over a document.

'You won't need this any more,' Ewers said, clawing at Poe's sleeve, ripping away his armband. 'From now on, you are as safe in the Empires as if you were a pure-blood German.'

At a stroke, Poe felt himself transformed again.

6

MATA HARI

The prisoner had welcomed Beauregard's request that he be allowed to see her. Even were he not continuing the Malinbois investigation, he would have been inclined to pay a call. He had given evidence at her trial but they had never been introduced.

To step out of the staff car onto the parade ground was to set foot in a cemetery. The condemned woman was held in a barracks near Paris, long out of regular use, tenants gone to feed the war. The uncurtained windows of the long halls were dusty. Only one dormitory was inhabited. Eight men, pulled from the front to serve as a firing squad, slept in peace and comfort. To them, this must be a relief.

The night was black as ink. Like a warm convict, the prisoner was to be shot at dawn. Sunset would be a more appropriate execution hour for a vampire.

A lone light burned in an office. Beauregard rapped on a door. Lantier, a veteran with half a face, opened up and invited him in. Without a hint of insubordination, the turnkey made it clear he resented having his night disturbed by visitors pandering to the whims of an enemy of France.

Lantier looked over Beauregard's authorisation papers, clucking at each distinguished signature. At length, he decided in Beauregard's favour and ordered that the Englishman be allowed into the cell. A lecture was delivered in rapid French about the degree of intercourse allowed with the woman. There was to be no physical contact, no object was to be passed from one to the other.

The vampire's reputation was bound to outlive her. This fuss fed the greatly exaggerated stories they were telling. It was in the interest of the lady's 'victims' that she be considered irresistible, lest it be decided they had a degree of culpability in her feats of espionage. Surely, no ordinary woman could extract secrets from so many of the great and good. This was an extreme case of the brand of fascination vampires were popularly supposed to be able to exert over their helpless prey.

Of the officers whose names had come up in testimony at her closed trial, most who still lived remained on active service. Only a few insignificant lieutenants had been swept down with her. Even now, the odious General Mireau planned his next offensive.

It had been seriously suggested that the soldiers assigned to this detail be maimed veterans unmanned by the war. Following Lantier's slow progress to the cells, he wondered if the crackpot notion had been implemented. If so, it displayed an alarming ignorance of the physical act of vampirism.

Lantier opened a stout door and stood aside, allowing him into the cell. It was an unpainted room with barely the atmosphere of a cupboard.

The prisoner sat by a small window, looking at the last of the moon. With her hair roughly cropped and in a shapeless cotton dress, she did not resemble the jewelled seductress who had carried all Paris with her.

She turned to look at him and was indeed beautiful. She claimed to be half-Javanese, but Beauregard knew she was the daughter of a Dutch hatter and his provincial wife. After turning, her eyes had changed. She had slit pupils like a cat. The effect was enormously striking.

'Madame Zelle?' he enquired, politely but without need.

She stood graciously and acknowledged him. 'Mr Beauregard.'

He considered her extended, pale hand and shrugged.

'Regulations,' he explained, weakly.

The prisoner attempted a smile. 'Of course. Touch me and you would be my slave. You would overpower the guards and fight to the death to aid my escape.'

'Something like that.'

'How silly.'

A chair was brought for him by the turnkey. She resumed her own chair and he sat down.

'So you are the clever Englishman who caught me?'

'I am afraid so.'

'Why afraid? Did you not do your duty?'

Before the war, he had seen her famous Javanese Dance of Death. She was no Isadora and whoever schooled her was no Diaghilev, but the powerful effect she had on an audience, whether general or private, General or Private, could not be denied.

'You are an honourable English patriot and I am an unprincipled Dutch adventuress. Is that not true?'

'It is not for me to say, Madame.'

Her eyes were growing larger. There was cold, undirected anger in them. But also something else.

'You are a warm man?'

Had she expected him to be a vampire like her? Some *nosferatu* believed only their own kind could match them for brain-power.

'How old are you, Mr Beauregard?'

That was an unusual question. 'I am sixty-four.'

'I would have thought younger. By five or ten years. Some vampire taint has crept into you, retarding the processes of aging. It does not matter. It is not too late for you to turn. You might live forever, grow young again.'

'Is that such a pleasant prospect?'

She smiled genuinely, not for effect. A tiny, shining fang peeped between her red lips.

58

'Not, I confess, at this immediate moment. I am immortal and you are not, but you shall see tomorrow's sunset.'

He tried to look at his wrist-watch without being too obvious. The dawn was two hours away.

'There may yet be a reprieve.'

'Thank you for considering that possibility, Englishman. I am given to understand you personally pleaded for my life. You could only do that at risk to your own reputation.'

Unless she really could suck secrets from a mind with a single glance, she could not possibly know he had recommended lenience.

Her fang became more prominent as her smile broadened. 'I still have sources of information. Secrets are not hard to come by.'

'As you have proved.'

'And so have you. My poor secrets have been yours as many men's were mine. Simply by sitting in a room and thinking, you saw through my veils and schemes. I admire that.'

He tried not to feel flattered. It was one of her greatest weapons. Elderly officers had been her favoured prey.

'I have had fine tutors in the whole art of detection,' Beauregard admitted.

'You are a senior member of the Ruling Cabal of the Diogenes Club, the second or third most important man in the British Secret Service.'

She knew even more than was determined at her trial.

'Do not worry, Charles. I shall take to my poor grave those few of your secrets to which I am a party.'

Suddenly, she was using his Christian name.

'I am sincerely sorry, Gertrud,' he replied in kind.

'Gertrud?' she said, rolling the unfamiliar name around her pointed tongue. 'Gertrud,' she confessed, at last. Her slim shoulders slumped with disappointment. 'So ugly, so sad, so dumpy. Almost *German*. But it is the name I was born with, the name I shall die under.'

'But not the name of your immortality,' he said.

She dramatically framed her pretty face with long fingers, fluttering her nails in moonlight. 'No, I shall eternally be *Mata Hari.*'

She was parodying the American, Theda Bara. If they made a film about Mata Hari (certainly, they would make many) then Theda Bara, a professional vampire whose name was an anagram of 'Arab Death', was the only actress for the role. She was of a bloodline which took to photography. Many vampires showed up on film as a species of blurry smudge.

'They will remember me, won't they?' she asked, suddenly vulnerable. 'My reputation will not melt like snow in the sun, surpassed by some new temptress.'

It was possible this woman had acted all her life; underneath the veils, there was perhaps no reality. Or maybe there was a secret self she would take with her into true death.

'There will be no pardon, Charles. No mercy at the last moment. This is true? They will kill me?'

'I'm afraid a certain person has insisted,' he admitted, sadly.

'General Mireau,' she spat. 'His blood was thin, you know. Like English soup. I mean no offence. Do you know how many men died through his actions? He was more lethal to his troops on his own than under my influence.'

There had been a mutiny in the General's command. Mireau was one of the worst of the uniformed fools who thought the war a firepit that could be extinguished by pouring in living men. The General believed this woman's death would cleanse the blood from his record.

'The other side are no better,' she said. 'It was as easy to gull Germans.'

Early in the war, Gertrud Zelle had been in the employ of the French secret service. It had not been proved, but he knew she had worked for the Russians, the Hungarians, the Turks and the Italians. Even the British.

'At court, I was presented to the Kaiser. I was turned by the Graf von Dracula.'

In this cold new century, the Graf was careful with his bloodline. More than any other vampire elder, he was responsible for the spread of the condition through Europe. Now he controlled rigidly the selection of those he turned. Even warm, Gertrud Zelle had been a remarkable woman.

'I see I do not surprise you.'

She held up her hand. It was pale in the moonlight, blue veins distinct. In an instant, it was a webbed gargoyle's claw, thorny barbs tipping thumb and fingers. Then it was human again.

'Formidable,' he said. 'Only someone close to the bloodline could manage that trick.'

'Maybe not,' she said, mysterious but teasing. 'But in my case, it is so. As I have played the generals of Europe as puppets, so have I been played.'

It occurred to Beauregard that she could transform herself entirely. She could find the strength to tear through the walls. Something kept her here.

'At the last, I shall be free of him.'

So that was it. He felt a certain disappointment.

'I did not give myself up deliberately, Charles. Your victory stands as an achievement of note. It is just that I'm not necessarily despondent. It is a commonplace that many things are worse than death.'

From experience, Beauregard knew those of the Dracula bloodline often came to believe that.

'He is a monster. Dracula.'

Beauregard nodded. 'We have met.'

'You British,' she continued, 'you were right to throw him out.'

'It was not so simple.'

'Maybe not. Yet Britain would not long tolerate Dracula and Germany has become his paradise.'

'The Graf has the knack of gaining influence at courts. He's been at the business for five-hundred years.'

Gertrud Zelle leaned forwards and reached out. The turnkey

rumbled. The pistol in his belt was loaded with silver. The prisoner's hand halted, inches away from Beauregard's arm. She fixed his eye.

'He will make of this century a killing ground,' she said, seriously. 'In his warm days, he murdered one-third of his own subjects. Imagine what he would do to those he considers his enemies.'

'Germany is nearly broken,' he said, echoing the official position, wishing he did not know better.

'It's hard to deceive a deceiver, Charles.'

She sat back, straightening. A fringe of pre-dawn light haloed her cropped head. She looked more like Joan of Arc than a vampire spy.

'Your war is over,' he said, trying to be kind.

'You know much about us, Charles. Vampires. You must have had a remarkable teacher.'

He adjusted his collar, sure he was flushing.

'Who was she?'

'You would not know the lady's name.'

'She was old? An elder?'

Beauregard nodded. Geneviève Dieudonné was older even than the Graf. A fifteenth-century girl.

'She is still alive?'

'The last I heard, she was very well. In America, I believe.'

'Do not be vague, Charles. You know precisely where she is. You would make it your business to keep track of things.'

Gertrud Zelle had caught him out. Geneviève was in California, growing blood oranges.

'She was a fool to let you grow old and die, Charles. No, I take that back. That was your decision, not hers. If I had been her, I would have made you *want* to turn. I would have used my powers.'

'Your "powers"? Madame Zelle, it would seem you have been reading too many of your notices.'

'We do have powers, you know. It's not all conjuring.'

Dawn pinked the sky. Her face was paler than ever. They had been starving her in captivity. She must be in considerable discomfort.

Many new-borns would by now have been maddened by red thirst.

'I suppose it makes her better than me, that she would not change a man's mind through underhand means, even if it were for the best.'

'Believe me, Geneviève would not claim to be better than anyone.'

'Geneviève? A pretty name. I hate her already.'

Beauregard remembered pain. And more pleasant things. There was a fan of red in the sky.

'We don't have much time left,' Gertrud Zelle said, businesslike.

'It is regrettable,' he agreed.

'Very well. For the sake of your vampire lady, I shall pass on to you my surviving secret. You have been kind when you need not have been, and this is my gift to you. Use it as you will. Win the war, if it can be won.'

Was this some trick?

'No, Charles,' she said, either reading the surface of his mind or following his obvious thought process. 'I am not the Scheherazade of the age. I shall not delay my final appointment.'

He tried to think around this development.

'Convince me, Gertrud. Convince me I am not to be your last victim.'

'That is not unfair, Charles. I shall mention a place and a name. If you are interested, I shall continue.'

Beauregard nodded. Gertrud Zelle smiled again, as if laying down face cards.

'Chateau de Malinbois,' she said. 'Professor ten Brinken.'

This was what he had hoped for. Another strand of the spiderweb.

'I'm convinced,' he said, trying not to let his eagerness show.

'See,' she said, fang glistening, 'a vampire always *knows*. I'll make it brief and simple. You can take notes, if you wish. The world has made of me what it would, and I make no excuse for myself. I have followed the dictates of my heart, even when such courses were patently unwise…'

* * *

A small crowd of journalists and interested parties huddled around a brazier on the parade ground. The last snowfall was gone, though patches of gritty ice would have made an actual parade hazardous. Beauregard looked at the faces. None of Gertrud Zelle's 'admirers' thought it worth while attending this performance.

Was her story another farewell performance? It was possible she hoped in death to spread some misleading lie, distracting him from whatever the Germans were really about at Malinbois. He was inclined to believe her. The Graf von Dracula was a gothic thinker and her narrative was a gothic tale, with castles and crypts and blood and doomed noblemen. He had filled the remainder of his notebook with shorthand.

The soldiers of the firing squad stood as if for inspection. Boys with ancient eyes. After four years, not only the undead looked older than their faces. Beauregard wondered if these *poilus* would be happier if the prisoner at the stake were Mireau. In the ranks, the General was hated more than the Kaiser.

'Charles,' a woman's voice cut through his musings. 'We meet in the most odd places.'

The small vampire was dressed in jodhpurs and a Norfolk jacket, reddish hair done up under an oversized tweed cap, eyes shielded by thick blue-tinted glasses. Her clear voice retained a little Irish.

'Kate,' he said, surprised and pleased. 'Good morning.'

She slipped off her glasses and squinted at the fading blush in the dingy grey sky.

'It's morning, at least.'

Kate Reed was ten years his junior, turned at twenty-five. In thirty years of the vampire life, her eyes hadn't aged.

The journalist had been something of a heroine in the Terror, editing an underground periodical, two hops ahead of the Carpathian Guard. She was no less critical of authority in the age of Good King Victor. A Fabian Socialist and advocate of Home Rule, she wrote for the *New Statesman* and the *Cambridge Magazine*. Since hostilities had commenced, she had been twice expelled from France and once imprisoned in Ireland.

'I thought you were recalled to London,' he observed.

She gave a smart, sharp little smile, eyes twinkling. 'I retired from Grub Street, then volunteered as an ambulance driver. Our old friend Mina Harker is on the committee, still trying to make things right. I was shipped back on the next boat.'

'So you're not a reporter?'

'I'm an observer, always. It is a thing we vampires are good at. It comes from a long life and too much spare time.'

Dawnlight speared across the ground and she put her glasses back on.

He shared a history with Kate Reed. They were both creatures of another century. She was fitter by far to survive this new era.

'I have always admired you,' he said.

'You talk as if it were yourself they wanted to shoot.'

'Maybe they should. I'm tired, Kate.'

She took his hand and squeezed. He tried not to let her see she was hurting him. Like many vampires of comparatively recent vintage, she did not know her own strength.

'Charles, you are perhaps the last decent man in Europe. Do not be disheartened, no matter what. The "War to End War" talk may be rot, but we can make a truth of it. This is our world as much as it is Ruthven's or Dracula's.'

'And hers?'

He pointed with his head. As the sun cleared the barracks, Gertrud Zelle was led out by the turnkey and two guards. At her own request she was veiled to protect her sensitive face from the light. She refused the blindfold and insisted no priest be present.

'Madame Mata Hari has been silly,' Kate snapped. 'I've little enough sympathy for her. Good men died wholesale because of her wiles.'

'You are a Fabian patriot.'

'There's nothing wrong with Britain that impaling the Prime Minister wouldn't cure.'

'Now you sound like Vlad Tepes.'

'Another gentleman who would be much improved by the addition of a length of stout hawthorn.'

'I read your piece on the trial, Kate.'

She fluttered a little, trying to swallow vanity. 'And…?'

'You said what had to be said.'

'But the warm-blooded, cold-souled General Mireau still struts like a scarfaced peacock and rattles his medals at vampire fillies, kneeling at Mass with a conscience as clear as Vichy water.'

'You should know by now that commanders-in-chief make it a point of honour not to follow the advice of mere journalists. I am sure General Pétain read your articles with interest.'

'I have more to write. Mireau must be brought to book.'

'And Sir Douglas Haig?'

'Him too, and the bloody lot of them.'

Gertrud Zelle stood against a pole as a guard tied her hands. She held her veiled head high, unafraid.

'Queen of the May,' Kate commented.

The sergeant of the execution party read out the verdict of the court. His thin voice was lost in the bitter wind. At least ten counts merited death. With the sentence read, the sergeant rolled up the paper and stuck it in his belt. He drew and raised his sword; eight soldiers lifted rifles and took aim. Seven silver bullets and one plain lead. Any man could have the dud and tell himself he had not fired a killing shot.

The sword wavered and fell. Shots clustered in the prisoner's torso. A stray pocked the ground a dozen yards behind the pole. Gertrud Zelle's head hung and the veil slipped from her like a scarf, wisping away on the wind. Early-morning sun fell on her face, browning it quickly. Smoke seeped from her mouth and eyes.

'That's that, then,' Kate said. 'Beastly business.'

Beauregard knew it was not finished. The sergeant walked across the parade ground and stood by the truly dead woman, sword like a scythe.

'Good Lord,' Kate said.

With a stroke, the sergeant sank his sword into Gertrud Zelle's neck. The blade bit bone. He had to press gauntleted hands against hilt and point, forcing the silver-steel edge clear through into the post. The head fell to the ground and the sergeant picked it up by the hair, holding it for all to see. The face burned black, cat eyes shrunk like peas.

7

KATE

The whisper Kate had heard in Paris was true: Mata Hari had refused the offer of a priest to hear a last confession, but was willing to pass the night before her execution in conversation with Mr Charles Beauregard of the Diogenes Club.

Early in her career as a journalist, she had learned that following Charles at a discreet distance was an infallible way of hooking a story. Wherever found, he was the calm centre of a maelstrom of intrigue. If he told all he knew, history books would be rewritten. Probably, governments would fall, colonies revolt, duels be fought, marriages end. Charles was the linchpin of Britain; Kate was often sorely tempted to take hold of him and give a good pull.

What a vampire he would have made.

She was careful not to quiz Charles too much. He was too canny a customer to be duped like a subaltern by a girly simper and a casual question. Also, he knew her of old. The scatterbrained twit act, her primary tool in the trade of deceit, would not wash with him.

The sergeant in charge of the execution found a sack for the cinder that had been the spy's head. He made a solemn business of posing for photographs, holding the sack. The firing squad stood to order, presenting arms. At each explosive puff of flash-powder, young veterans cringed, remembering.

Kate watched Charles watching the photographers. His high

collar was not the sign of old-fashioned temperament but a cover for the unfading purple on his throat. A line of wine-coloured bruising fringed his collar. He was more handsome in age than youth, his hair was white but his chin was firm. He stood straight and years had smoothed rather than crinkled his face.

The elder Geneviève Dieudonné had been Charles's lover during the Terror. Some of her blood must have got into him. He had resisted the Dark Kiss, but it was impossible to be with a vampire for any time without tasting her blood, even if just a smidgen. Some warm men paid for tiny transfusions to keep their hair or tighten their tummies. It was a sounder rejuvenation treatment than monkey glands. Patent medicines hinted vampire blood was a secret ingredient.

The firing squad were dismissed. Reporters tried to interview them. Sydney Horler, a tub-thumper for the *Mail*, was in the mêlée.

'They love the war,' she said. 'Gives them something tastier to write up than provincial murderers and municipal adulterers.'

'You have a low opinion of your profession.'

'I like to think I'm not in the same line as the scratching vultures.'

'How does it feel?' shouted Horler. 'Shooting a woman?'

If any of the squad understood the question, none was inclined to answer.

'A *pretty*, wanton woman?' the Englishman emphasised. 'Would you say she was a fiend in human shape who deserved no more mercy than a deadly cobra?'

The sergeant shrugged. A singularly French gesture.

'You would say she was a fiend in human shape who deserved no more mercy than a deadly cobra, then?'

The soldiers started to walk away.

'I'll write that down then. Fiend in human shape. No more mercy. Deadly cobra.'

The excitable Horler began scribbling.

'I believe we have witnessed the birth of an evening edition headline,' she said.

Charles was too weary to respond. He consulted his wrist-watch and touched his hat, preparing to leave.

'Strange. A warm man who hustles to his bed at cock-crow. Are you sure you haven't turned?'

Charles summoned a smile. 'Kate, I've kept vampire hours for most of my life.'

His was a night-time profession, even in this topsy-turvy century where wars were fought and peace pursued after dark.

'With Mata Hari gone, you can rest now, surely. Your war is won.'

'Very amusing, Kate.'

She stood on tiptoe to kiss his cheek. His face was very cold. She held back in her hugging, so as not to crack his ribs.

'Goodbye, Charles.'

'Good day, Kate.'

He walked to a car and was driven away. She licked her lips and could taste him. His blood was strong. A mere brush of his skin was enough to give her an impression of his mood. She was excited, because she *knew* Charles was excited. Something had passed between him and Mata Hari that was important. She could read nothing more, nothing concrete. A shame. If she were an elder like Geneviève, she could suck his mind like an orange and know everything there was to be known.

If the trick were within her capabilities, the temptation would be too great to resist. As vampires lived through centuries, they gained strength and power. Many elders became monsters. They could do as they wished without fear of the consequences. The taste of Charles evaporated and her heart throbbed with red thirst.

In the early years of her afterlife, she had constantly tested her limits. Now she took them, along with her undead needs, as simply a part of night-to-night existence. Strangely, she still needed spectacles to correct the fearful myopia that had been the plague of her warm days. Most vampires overcame their infirmities upon turning, but she was a freak.

Her vision blurred as she tried to conquer her thirst. This was her own fault. If she had not tasted Charles, she would not now be suffering these pangs.

She did not care to consider herself dead but knew that was self-deception. Some, like Geneviève, turned without suffering true death. But Kate had certainly died. Mr Frank Harris, her father-in-darkness, liked to suck his get dry before dripping life-giving blood into them. She recalled the stopping of her heart, the queer silence inside her head. That had been death.

Her heart eased and she could see again. The day was overcast, so there was little direct sunlight to trouble her. She was not the species of vampire which shrivels and frizzles at dawn. She was of the bloodline of Marya Zaleska, an aristocratic parasite who claimed to be a by-blow of Count Dracula. In Kate, the fading Zaleska line was spiced by the powerful spirit of Frank Harris. In 1888, the famous editor had told her physical love was the gateway to womanhood and, on a divan in a private room at Kettner's restaurant, enthusiastically escorted her through the gateway. Having made a woman of her, he was obliged to make a vampire of her too.

Many young women succumbed to Harris's persuasion, but she was his only surviving get. Others had proved too fragile for such a strong line. Harris was gone too, murdered by Carpathians during the Terror. She was sorry; though a profligate who took little responsibility for his children-in-darkness, Harris was a good newspaperman. She was not ashamed to have him as her sponsor in the world of night.

Charles's car drove away, nestling secrets in a well-upholstered interior. The firing squad evaporated and the other journalists drifted off, filling in blanks in already-written stories. Jed Leland of the *New York Inquirer*, a rare competent American, touched a pencil to the brim of his straw hat. She returned the wave, worried he would delay her in unwanted conversation. Leland ambled along with the rest of the crowd, in search of an *estaminet* where they could scrawl out copy between *anis* and cat-blood.

Shortly after turning, her pierced ears had healed and, rather shockingly, she found herself a virgin again. The condition was swiftly, permanently, remedied. At the time, being 'ruined' was a bigger scandal than turning vampire.

She was still adapting, learning. It was hard to tell what she would become. She vowed not to be a monster.

Alone on the parade ground, she walked around to the guardhouse, keen senses alert. She did not want to share her lead. And she did not want to be involved with anyone above the rank of corporal. Her condemnation of General Mireau had won her many friends in the French army, but few in the officer class. Her articles about the Dreyfus case had predisposed them against her, and her recent writings had hardly regained their affections.

There was a French staff car parked in the road outside, just visible through a failing hedge. Its windows were dark. Had one of Mata Hari's conquests come to pay a secret farewell? Or to be sure she was truly dead?

Corporal Jacques Lantier was waiting for her in his pokey office. His face was an angry tangle of scar. After two days in which the enemy inflicted an eighty per cent casualty rate on exposed Frenchmen, the remnant of General Mireau's command had defied his 'to the last man' order and retreated across the hundred yards of dirt they had taken but been unable to hold. Lantier, alive and maimed, was one of the fortunate. In one piece, he might have been among the dozen men Mireau had had shot for cowardice. He was eligible for a place in the unofficial veterans' club of the disfigured, the *Union des Gueules Cassées*, the Brotherhood of Broken Mugs.

Lantier opened a hole in his lower face with the end of his little finger and stuck a cigarette into it. Kate accepted his offer of a cigarette and they both lit up off a single match-flame.

The corporal coughed and smoke clouded around him. He was, of course, grateful to one of the few journalists to condemn General Mireau but there were other considerations. Before the war, twenty francs might have purchased a horse. Now it might stretch to a slice of horse meat.

'They spoke softly, mademoiselle,' Lantier said, excusing himself, 'and my hearing is not so good…'

One of his ears was sheared off entirely, the other an inflamed lump.

'But you heard something.'

She added more notes to the sheaf in his fist.

'Scraps here and there… a few names… Chateau de Malinbois, Professor ten Brinken, Baron von Richthofen, General Karnstein…'

Each name unloosed another ten francs.

'Enough,' she said. 'Just tell me what you heard.'

Lantier shrugged and began…

It was nearly midday when Corporal Lantier finished. Kate had filled a notebook but was not sure what to make of it. There were gaps. Some she could fill in with her own intelligence but most were true blanks.

She had expected new light on the perfidy of General Mireau but this was entirely fresh. She would have to read up on the Richthofen Freak Show. If Charles was interested enough to hear Mata Hari out, there was certainly a story in it.

Lantier escorted her outside. Without its sole prisoner, the barracks were dead. The firing squad were on leave in Paris and would be back in the trenches by tomorrow's dawn.

They walked across the parade ground. She paused to examine the pole where Mata Hari had died.

'After the beheading,' Lantier said, 'young men pressed around and dipped handkerchiefs in the blood. For souvenirs.'

'Or to taste. It must be heady stuff. The blood of Mata Hari.'

Lantier spat and missed the pole.

'Vampire blood could help…' she began, indicating Lantier's face.

He shook his head and spat again. 'Curse you all, you bloodsuckers. What good have you ever done?'

She had no answer. Many Frenchmen, especially outside Paris, felt as he did. Vampirism had not taken hold quite as it had in Britain, Germany and Austria–Hungary. France had its elders — Geneviève, for one — and a growing swell of new-borns, often self-styled 'moderns' and 'decadents', but vampires were still not entirely welcome in the best circles. Alfred Dreyfus had been a scapegoat because he was at once a Jew and a vampire.

She bade Lantier goodbye and left the parade ground. Her trusty Hoopdriver bicycle was against an old cavalry hitching post by the main entrance. The staff car was still in the road outside.

Kate knew there was danger. During the Terror, she had developed the sense. Her nails slid out like cat's claws.

She stepped past the hedge into the road and looked at the car. There was a chauffeur in the front seat and the rear door was slightly open. Someone looked out at her with piggy eyes.

'*Ego te exorcisat*,' a voice shrieked. 'Suffer, foul harlot, suffer the torments of the damned!'

A black-robed man vaulted a low fence and rushed at her. A wild-eyed, white-haired priest had been crouching out of sight. She recognised him but had no time to summon a name from memory. Berating her in bad Latin and gutter French, the priest sloshed liquid in her face. Her glasses spattered with blurry blobs.

Her thought was that the lunatic had thrown oil of vitriol. Acid ate vampire flesh to the bone. She would recover, but look like Lantier for the next fifty years. There was no burning, no hissing.

The priest waved with his flask. Another splash struck her forehead and dribbled down. She tasted plain water. No, not plain water, she realised. Holy water.

She laughed in surprise. Some Catholic vampires were sensitive to such things, but she was an Anglican of long standing. Her family were Prod to the marrow; when told Kate had turned, her father commented, 'At least the fool girl hasn't embraced the foul antichrist of Rome.'

The priest stood back smugly, prepared to enjoy the dissolution of a corrupt creature of hell. He pressed a large, crudely detailed crucifix to his breast and held up a fistful of Communion wafers.

Her cap had come off and her hair flew loose. She picked her headgear up and patted her face with it.

'I'm all wet, you idjit,' she said.

The priest tossed the Communion wafer at her. He seemed to expect it to bite into her skull like a Japanese *shuriken*. The biscuit stuck to her damp forehead.

Annoyed, she crunched the wafer in her mouth and spat out the fragments.

'Where's the wine? I've the red thirst on me, now. Transubstantiate a bottle and I'll have blood to drink.'

This attack had spurred her bloodlust. She must feed soon.

The priest shook his cross and poured the curses of heaven on her. She saw a face dart back into the interior of the car. It had worn a French officer's kepi with a great deal of scrambled egg.

'You are Father Pitaval. You were at the trial of Mata Hari.'

Pitaval, some kind of renegade Jesuit, was Mireau's confessor. Also, it seemed, his tame vampire killer.

'You'll have to do better than this poor showing, Father.'

He shoved his crucifix at her face and she pushed it away.

'Look to your own conscience,' she shouted, at Mireau as much as the priest.

He raised his crucifix like a dagger and stabbed at her chest. The end was jagged enough to serve as the proverbial stake, but she deflected the blow. Her tinted glasses fell off and she was in a world of blur. She saw a black shape coming for her and stepped aside. She pushed hard, catching the priest and tossing him towards the car.

Scrambling in the grit, she found her glasses and replaced them. Pitaval crawled for the car. The door slammed shut before he could get there. The dark window rolled up, fast. Moving with vampire swiftness, she overleaped the priest and exerted an iron grip on the car door handle. She wrenched the lock open, enjoying the popping of the mechanism.

In the dark inside, General Mireau sat stiffly, staring hatred. He had a companion, a little new-born in a froth of white shroud. The minx had rouged her wrists where Mireau bound her with a rosary, misleading him about the effect of religious artefacts on vampire flesh. The General's taste for undead girls was predictable. Kate hoped this one was cunning enough to rob him blind and drain him dry.

She shook her head. Mireau shoved behind his companion.

'Sister,' Kate said, 'you have very poor taste in blood.'

The new-born wriggled. She was probably a dancer or an actress. Even more probably another spy.

Kate bent to get her head into the car. Mireau's cold eyes held flames of fear. He pushed the new-born forwards, encouraging a reluctant dog to fight. The vampire poodle opened its mouth to show tentative fangs. She attempted a hiss.

Kate considered hauling the foolish girl out and giving her posterior a sound spanking. It would be cruel: she might rot to nothing in the sun.

Father Pitaval was on his feet again, somewhat sheepish. The General was not getting value for his patronage.

'Mireau, have you no shame?' she asked.

Turning, she walked away from the lot of them. She heard shouting as the General abused his subordinates. A little spark of satisfaction warmed her heart. She had accomplished little, but at least Mireau was hurt enough to want to strike back. If she kept at it, she could have him.

Perhaps there were more worthwhile bones to worry. Especially the bone marked Chateau de Malinbois.

She got on her bicycle, and pushed off. On the road to the railway station, she whistled the 'Barcarolle' from *Tales of Hoffmann*, thinking of dancers and fliers.

8

CASTLE KEEP

Inside the Chateau de Malinbois, night was eternal. By day, the mediaeval slit windows were shuttered, the stone hallways lit only by infrequent candles. Deep in the damp guts of the castle, even a vampire felt the cold. Tiny drips of water were as constant as the granite-muffled pounding of the guns. Only the scientists' work quarters made use of electricity. In the examination room, dark corners were banished. Light shone without mercy. Merely to lie on the table was to expose one's interior workings.

Leutnant Erich von Stalhein wondered if General Karnstein had chosen Malinbois to give the fliers a feeling of being buried alive, to increase their desire to get into the air. Aloft, with the freedom of the currents and the strength of the moon, they were loosed from the shackles of Earth.

Stalhein lay prone as Professor ten Brinken checked another series of measurements. A brooding bear with shocks of grey hair on his beetle brows, the director was more dockyard bruiser than scientist. Perhaps his craze for the physical improvement of mankind sprang from awareness of his own ursine appearance.

An arrangement of directed lamps was fixed above the table. Stalhein's bloodline throve on moonbeams but glowing wires in glass bulbs were no use to him. Cold, artificial light was unsatisfying.

Dr Caligari, *Jagdgeschwader 1*'s alienist, was in the room. Stalhein heard his clumsy waddling, smelled his reeking clothes. He privately thought Caligari a quack. Like ten Brinken, he was fascinated by the vampire condition. In interviews, he always tried to draw Stalhein out, asking question after question about feeding.

'The muscles of the neck and chest are more developed,' ten Brinken told Caligari. 'It is pronounced enough to be calibrated. There would seem to be overall change. An evolution.'

The scientists discussed him as if he were a truly dead corpse, dissected for their edification. Stalhein was accustomed to this treatment. It was his duty to the Kaiser to endure such examinations. No flier of JG1 was exempt, not even the Baron.

Ten Brinken signalled the end of the examination by turning off the overhead lamps. With vampire quickness, Stalhein slid off the table and stood. Caligari, startled, cringed inside an ancient tailcoat. Stalhein dressed, pulling on breeches and boots, slipping into a good shirt. Ten Brinken, suddenly unctuous as a valet, held up his tunic. He backed into the sleeves, then fastened buttons from belly to collar.

'Fine, fine, Leutnant,' ten Brinken cooed. 'Most excellent.'

Naked, Stalhein was an object for study. In uniform, he was close to a demon prince.

Ten Brinken's lair was a fusion of ancient and modern. The walls were fourteenth-century stone, obscured by scientific charts of various vintages. The director scrawled hieroglyphics in a brassbound tome which seemed a thing of the monasteries, but the eye was caught by an array of shining surgical implements in a steel and glass stand. Ten Brinken and Caligari and the others — Dr Krueger, Engineer Rotwang, Dr Orlof, Professor Hansen — called themselves scientists, but alchemy was mixed in with their prattle of evolution and genetic heritage.

To men of Stalhein's father's generation, the vampire was a mythical beast. Within a lifetime, ancient magic had become a tolerated field of modern science. Understandably, the two scrambled. General Karnstein, the Graf von Dracula's overseer, was an elder; he had lived through centuries of persecution, perhaps believing himself a creature of darkness, only to emerge in the twentieth century and be restored to high estate.

Stalhein saluted and left the laboratory. His night eyes were better suited to the gloom of the narrow passageway, which ended in the staircase that led to the Great Hall. Music drifted down. A Strauss waltz.

Vaguely troubled, he climbed up to the Hall. Ten Brinken's endless examinations were rarely painful but always perturbed Stalhein. A secret purpose was kept from him. He told himself his duty was to do, not to understand. The fliers were not uninformed, but focused. Each victory was a building brick of the greater victory to come. He should pity the short-lived warmkind; they could never know what it was to master the skies, to taste the blood of a foe, to drink the light of the moon.

He wanted to be flying, bearing down on his prey. To feel the kick of discharging guns, to hear the whining of the air over his wings, to watch an aeroplane spiral in flames: this convinced him he was alive. His score was a respectable nineteen victories. In an ordinary *jasta*, such a record would be outstanding; but in this Circus, he was one of the lesser hunters. If he lasted long enough, he hoped to change that. The high-tide mark was the Baron von Richthofen's score, which stood currently at seventy-one.

The faded portraits and mouldy animal heads that had been on display in the Great Hall were consigned to cellars. The Circus had replaced them with twentieth-century trophies. Above a fireplace the size of a railway tunnel was crucified the top wing of an RE8, its forty-three-foot span of stiff linen dotted with bullet-holes. Hanging in the fireplace, anchored to the mantel by chains, was a rigged-up chandelier: the front of an engine, its cylinder heads stuck with lit candles. Spreading out from the centrepieces was an overlapping patchwork of serial numbers hacked from the fabric of Allied aeroplanes, many half-burned or badly holed. JG1 had collected specimens of Bristol Fighter, Dolphin, Spad, Vickers, Tabloid, Nieuport-Delage, Bantam, Kangaroo and Caproni. Also mounted in the display were scavenged guns, compasses and altimeters, human heads, leather helmets, single boots, broken cameras, bones, Constantinesco gears, propellors.

The magnificent horn of the new gramophone rang with an aria from *Die Fledermaus*. Hammer, smugly wearing the Pour le Mérite awarded him on his fortieth kill, played cards with Kretschmar-Schuldorff, the intelligence officer, and Ernst Udet, a promising flier neck and neck with Stalhein in victories. Grouped around an oil lamp, they were dwarfed by the vaulted space. Hammer was buried in a huge bearskin coat that made him look like a troll. Theo puffed on a cigarette whose smoke cloud was still rising but had not yet reached the distant ceiling. Udet, having succumbed to the latest vampire fashion, sported a fresh rack of antlers. Hung with ragged velvet, they sprouted through steadily trickling wounds in his forehead.

Night was hours away. Stalhein was down for the twilight patrol. He conquered impatience.

There were other fliers in the darks of the Great Hall, as eager as Stalhein for sunset and the chase. The sounds of tender feeding came from a curtained recess. The insatiable Bruno Stachel was lapping up the juice of another of his French girls. Stalhein thought a *nosferatu* should not feed by day; it made him duller when the time for real hunting came. A rare JG1 flier without a 'von' to his name, Stachel did not quite fit; in a cadre of hunters, he was merely a murderer. His score stood at thirty-one.

'Erich, hail,' shouted a young blond vampire, touching his fat hand to his cap-peak. 'General Karnstein sends his congratulations. Word is in. Your kill of two nights gone has been confirmed.'

Göring was the Circus's record-keeper. He maintained a chart of the individual victories.

Two nights ago, Stalhein had cruised low, hiding in pools of cloud, listening for engine drone. He rose sharply under an Avro 504J, firing into its underside. The aeroplane lurched off, fire spreading along its wings. He followed the descent, intending to land by the wreck and drain the pilot, but the Avro limped over the lines and came down in No Man's Land. Machine-gun bursts from the British trenches kept him in the air and he had no opportunity to finish the kill. Standing orders were that he was not to be sighted properly by the enemy; at least, not by an enemy who lived to give a report.

'The Britisher's name was Mosley. Of good family, apparently. A career has been ended before it was begun.'

Stalhein remembered bared fangs under an absurd fleck of British moustache, the rest of the face covered by goggles and helmet. It was a mediocre victory.

'Aren't you pleased, Erich?' Göring asked. 'You have twenty, now.'

'I did not drink blood,' Stalhein admitted.

'But you scored a victory. That is what counts.'

'Not to me.'

There was almost more frustration in a bloodless win than if Mosley had escaped altogether. At the end of the hunt, bloodlust must be slaked.

Göring clapped him on the back anyway. He had drawn ahead of the antlered Udet. At the beginning of the war, twenty kills would have earned the Pour Le Mérite; now, with so many competing, the number necessary for an automatic Blue Max was doubled.

'The Baron's kill, also, was confirmed,' Göring confided. 'A victory under the noses of the British. Captain James Albright, twenty-eight victories. A Yankee, one understands.'

Mosley was probably on a second or third patrol. An experienced pilot would not have been taken as easily. Yet his poor corpse counted as much as Richthofen's defeat of a gloried knight of the air. Göring, so boringly fascinated with statistics that he sometimes seemed close to ten Brinken, had an alternative chart, ranking fliers not by individual victories but by totting up the victories of those they bested. By this rating, the Baron's lead was even more unassailable. Early in the war, before the death of the great Boelcke, Richthofen had killed mainly sluggish spotters and stragglers; now his blood was up, he sought worthier prey.

Stalhein had been shot down once, by the modest British ace James Bigglesworth. That was long before he was skilled enough in the air to earn a place in JG1. The scars on his face and back took months to heal. He survived only through the good fortune of being thrown clear of his burning Fokker. There would be glory and honour in repaying that debt. Bigglesworth, twenty-two victories, was a prize worth the taking. According to Kretschmar-Schuldorff, the pilot was stationed at Maranique, in the same unit as the late Captain Albright.

A curtain was whipped from its rail by a living projectile and dragged across the flagstones. Something child-sized and barrel-shaped was wrapped in the cloth. It squealed, leaving puddles of blood in its wake. Lothar von Richthofen stepped out of the uncurtained passage mouth, holding a candelabrum. He grinned like a dog, blood smeared over his face and chest.

If Lothar was the dog, his brother was his master.

'Manfred falls back on the pursuits of his youth,' Göring commented.

The blood stench stung Stalhein's nostrils and eyes. Every vampire in the hall was alert. The squealing was like the scratch of claws on a blackboard. The bundle struggled with the weight of the curtain and shook free. Terrified animal eyes glittered.

Lothar stood aside for his brother. Rittmeister Freiherr Manfred von Richthofen was stripped to the waist, reddish fur wet and bristling. He was the best shape-shifter in JG1, main attraction of this Flying Freak Show. Usually reserved to the point of catatonia, Richthofen was in the grip of a passion. Killing Englishmen by night was not enough for him; he must hunt wild boar by day, as he had done as a child on his estates in Silesia.

The boar, imported God knows how and at what expense, wheeled and snarled at the hunter, froth dripping from its jaws. Richthofen stalked towards it. His feet were bare, but claw-spurs clicked on the stone. The boar, startled again, dashed off to one side.

Von Emmelman loomed enormously out of the shadow. He threw himself at the boar, intending to come down hard on its back. The slippery beast wriggled as the flier smacked against the floor, mossy hands closing around the animal's greasy tail. The heap-like Emmelman, permanently caught between *kobold* form and his former human shape, had the hog for an instant but its tail slipped through his fist. Richthofen skidded to avoid tripping over his comrade, then leaped over the fallen flier, yelling to his prey.

Lothar dashed after Richthofen, determined to be in at the kill. Stalhein and Göring were swept along in the brothers' wake. The pig's blood was foul, but stirred Stalhein's vampire spirit. Fangs grew and sharpened in his mouth. Under his shirt, fur swarmed up his back. The darkness lightened.

The boar rammed the stand of the gramophone and pitched it over. As the horn fell, a waltz was cruelly terminated. The boar shook its tusked head and scattered parts of the broken apparatus. That was an insult not to be brooked. The hog would pay for such trespass.

Fliers emerged from the shadows, devastated by the loss of the music, excited by the stench of blood. Angry red eyes followed the boar's tail as the animal sought egress. The vampires closed on the prey. Stalhein found himself in a perfect attacking formation. Richthofen was, as in the air, the point of the arrow. Stalhein was two fliers to his right, at the spur of the barb, a mirror of little Eduard Schleich on the left. Emmelman lumbered in the rear, wading as if through thick mud.

The boar was crowded towards an open doorway. The passage beyond led to the outside. Richthofen was a sportsman. By the rules, if the quarry could push through the main door of the castle, it was free and had earned the victory.

The formation advanced step by step. The boar backed away, trotters clipping stone. Richthofen had fixed the animal's eyes. He liked his kills to know him personally, to treat him with respect. As he moved forwards, his arms extended, the vestige of membrane-folds hanging beneath them. The fingers of his right hand bunched together, nails gathered into a thin pyramidal point.

The boar turned tail and ran. The fliers closed on it, bunching perfectly through the doorway with no crowding, easing out again to put on speed in the passage.

A side door opened. Caligari scuttled out, battered hat bobbing. He turned, the boar tangled in his legs, and looked aghast through his pince-nez as the hunters swooped at him. Richthofen swept the alienist aside, but it seemed the boar would have the victory. At the end of the passage, a shaft of daylight hung where the door was ajar. The light fell in a stripe on the boar's back. The animal must sniff the cold air of escape.

Manfred von Richthofen braced and launched himself. He leaped a full twenty feet, arms outstretched like wings. One hand latched on to the spiny bristles of the boar's neck and gripped firm. Richthofen fell on the pig with all his weight. Blood trickled down leathery hide. The hunter dragged his prey back into the darkness away from the door.

Stalhein was intoxicated by the blood. He fought to control base desires. There was purer hunting to be had. But a victory was a victory.

Göring clapped furiously at the Baron's feat. Fat Hermann was a born toady, a long-tongued second-in-command.

Richthofen wrestled the boar, then held it up overhead. For a moment, he was Hercules lifting Proteus. His face was that of a red lion, nose flaring, mane a-tangle from the chase, fanged jaws agape. He slammed the hog to the floor, stunning it. A flagstone cracked with a report like a gunshot. The beast squirmed, fight knocked out of it. Richthofen took his killing position like a practised matador, flexing his long right arm like a sabre, drawing back his barb-tipped hand. With a roar of triumph, he punched under the hog's tail, sticking the pig perfectly. He thrust his arm deep into his prey's insides. The boar's head, eyes empty of life, jerked upwards as a bloody fist exploded through the throat. The kill was spitted on Richthofen's extended arm.

He pulled himself free and admired the gleaming red sleeve coating his arm. Then he knelt by the fallen animal and, as was his right, lapped delicately at the gouting wound in its neck. He took little; this hunt was for sport, not lifeblood. When finished, the Baron stood and let his fellows fall upon the boar, tearing it to pieces. He stood over them, a master watching his dogs take their reward. Caligari, recovered from shock but still trembling, glanced at the feeding frenzy and waddled away, tutting to himself that the hunters were out of control.

In the mêlée, Stalhein fought for and won a ragged pig's ear. To gain such a mighty prize, he had to tear his arm open slamming against Udet's antlers and wrench his shoulder shoving Emmelman out of the way. He turned his back to the other vampires, protecting his morsel, and sucked the torn edge. Around him, fliers chewed and swallowed and retched and supped. The taste was vile but sparkling joys burst in his brain.

9

LA MORTE PARISIENNE

As the sun went down, he idled at a Montmartre pavement café. Even in the pit of this dreadful winter, *habitués*, not all undead, sat at street tables. They gossiped and flirted, read and drank. Doomed snowflakes melted on faces, hands and hats. Winthrop took a table inside, near the stove, and asked the patron for a pot of English tea. Experienced enough with British officers to know what was required, the Frenchman sadly turned from spices and coffees and liqueurs to fetch a shameful package of plain old Lipton's from a secret shelf.

In the minutes it took for the tea to cool to drinkability, he was propositioned by two *filles de joie* and a curly-haired youth; a fanged dwarf offered to sketch his portrait for the price of a loaf of bread; news swept through that the daring thief Fantômas had relieved a dowager of an emerald necklace in a nearby street; another struggling artist tried to sell caricatures of the Kaiser and Graf von Dracula; a naive Australian was asked to pay for a ten-centime *anis* with ten francs; and a knife-fight erupted between an *apache* vampire and a one-armed warm veteran who unexpectedly trounced the whole man. He supposed this was the famed *vie parisienne*; it struck him as mostly rather silly. Children pretending to be wicked.

When it was fully dark, he settled his bill and worked his way out of the *estaminet*, weaving between heavily populated tables. Americans, new to the war and Europe, were especially well-represented. Gawping and gazing at everything, they were most beloved by Parisian pickpockets. James Gatz, a 'lootenant' Winthrop knew slightly, hailed him with a reedy 'old sport'. Winthrop hurried off before he could be caught; now it was night, he was on duty. He wished Gatz well with a wave and hoped the young man would survive the evening with neck, wallet and heart whole.

In the Place Pigalle, children surrounded him, imploring *cadeaux*. On close examination, most of the creatures were vampires, probably his seniors. A golden boy made hooks of fingers and hung on to Winthrop's coat. The old-souled child cooed and hissed, attempting mesmerism.

Sergeant Dravot, Winthrop's inevitable shadow, appeared from a spot beyond the corner of his eye and detached the persistent parasite, tossing him back to his comrades. The savage children ran off, streaming about the legs of startled soldiers and their ladies of the moment.

Nodding thanks to Dravot, he checked that his buttons were all accounted for. He still felt the finger-points of the wild child on his chest. The sergeant slipped back into the crowd, prepared to see off Fantômas himself if the need arose. Though it was comforting to have a guardian angel, Winthrop was a little nettled that he was not entirely trusted out on his own. At times, Dravot was a nannyish presence.

He strolled with theatre crowds, studied in his air of aimlessness. The Grand Guignol offered André de Lorde's notorious *Maldurêve*, while the Théâtre des Vampires presented Offenbach's operetta *La Morte Amoureuse*, featuring the celebrated can-can 'Clarimonde'. At the Robert-Houdin, the warm illusionist Georges Méliès presented feats of prestidigitation which he defied any vampire to duplicate by supernatural means. Bernhardt was giving her blood-boltered *Macbeth* in one of many all-female productions currently gracing the Paris stage. With most actors gone to the war, the situation of Shakespeare's day was reversed and many masculine roles were taken by women *en travestie*. If the war ever ended, a second Revolution would be required to force the Divine Sarah back into frocks.

Squeezed into an unremarked side street away from the famous houses, the Théâtre Raoul Privache was neither magnificent nor celebrated. He had never heard of the place before receiving, in the note signed 'Diogenes', details of this appointment. A poster depicted a huge-eyed, gaunt woman in a leotard. The marquee announced, simply, *'Isolde — les frissons des vampires'*. A small press of devotees clamoured for entrance. Almost exclusively male and warm and mainly in uniform, they had a greedy, hollow-eyed look that matched that of the poster woman.

Joining the audience funnelling into the foyer, Winthrop looked about for Dravot. It was a game, sometimes, to locate the sergeant. Broad-shouldered and a head taller than most, the vampire did not exactly take pains to conceal himself but had the ability to fit in with any background.

An arrangement had been made at the kiosk. Winthrop was ushered down a narrow, unlit corridor to a private box. Dravot followed and took up a post at the door. He would not be able to see the performance. From the decayed state of the wallpaper and the faint smell of damp mould, Winthrop assumed the sergeant would not miss much.

Winthrop opened the door and stepped into the box. A man sat comfortably, puffing on a cigar.

'Edwin, you are remarkably punctual. Do sit down.'

Winthrop shook a firm hand and sat. Charles Beauregard had a full head of white hair and a clipped grey moustache. His face was unlined and he gave the impression of agility. Winthrop understood Beauregard had distinguished himself during the Terror, and once refused a knighthood.

Beyond the balcony, a muttering audience settled hastily into seats. A pianist tried to wring melodies from an ailing instrument.

Beauregard offered his cigar case but Winthrop preferred to smoke his own. He lit a cigarette and shook out the match-flame.

'I've read your report,' said Beauregard. 'A bad business, the other night. You mustn't blame yourself.'

'I picked Albright, the man who died.'

'And I picked you and someone picked me. No one of us is more responsible than any other. From Albright's record, I should say you couldn't have made a better choice for the show.'

A dark, winged shape flitted across Winthrop's mind.

'The Germans have awarded the victory to Manfred von Richthofen,' said Beauregard. 'If any of Condor Squadron had a chance against the Bloody Red Baron, it would have been Captain Albright.'

So the shape had been the Bloody Red Baron himself. Winthrop wondered what kind of kite Richthofen was piloting. Something new and deadly.

'German High Command are fond of building up their man-killers for the newspapers. We have no monopoly of jingo. If twenty Fokkers shoot at and down an Allied aeroplane, credit tends to be awarded where it will make the best propaganda.'

'There was only one thing in the sky with Albright.'

'I didn't say Richthofen wasn't a fearsome devil.'

An examination had shown Albright was completely dry, veins and arteries collapsed. Thorndyke, the specialist who performed the autopsy, reported the body was drained not only of blood but of every drop of liquid.

'Captain Albright was pulled out of his SE5a and killed in mid-air. I've never come across that before.'

'There's nothing new, Edwin. Even in this great modern murdering game.'

The house lights dimmed and the pianist tried harder. He wounded a theme from *Swan Lake* as the curtains parted. The stage was bare, except for a cane chair and an open steamer trunk.

A vampire woman walked out, a transparent moth-wing cape draped over her leotard. She was the Isolde of the posters. She had a hard face, not pretty. The shape of her skull showed at cheeks and temples. Fang-teeth stuck out of her mouth, wearing grooves in her underlip and chin.

The music continued and Isolde walked up and down the tiny stage, not even dancing. The audience was quiet.

'We are more and more interested in the Chateau de Malinbois,' said Beauregard, watching Isolde with half a glance. 'Strange stories are in circulation.'

Isolde spread out her long, lank hair with black-nailed hands. Her neck was painfully thin, prominently veined.

'The pilots all knew the place,' Winthrop said. 'Richthofen is an obsession with them. He's the man to beat.'

'Over seventy victories.'

'It would be a relief to see him downed.'

'Strange: the soldier who pulls a howitzer lanyard or works a machine-gun often kills as many in a few seconds as our Red Baron has during the entire war. Yet it is the flier who gets the press. Cavalry Captain Baron Manfred von Richthofen. He has the Pour le Mérite, of course, the Blue Max. That's the Hun Victoria Cross. And more lesser decorations than a man can list.'

Isolde undid the collar of her cape and let it float away. She was unusually skinny. Each rib showed like the slat of a fence.

'Watch this, Edwin. It's ugly but you'll learn something.'

The vampire solemnly took a knife out of the trunk and held it up. It seemed entirely ordinary. Isolde stuck the point into the hollow of her throat, dimpling the skin but not drawing blood, and ran it down the front of her leotard, slicing. Fabric peeled away from her chest. She had no noticeable breasts, but her nipples were large and dark.

Winthrop had no more than the normal experience of Paris frivolity, but the drab Isolde seemed to him underdeveloped to gain much following as an ecdysiast. The popular girls of the Folies Bergère were far more substantial than this poor creature, pigeons to her sparrow.

She shrugged and the upper half of her singlet slipped over her shoulders, falling to her waist. Her skin was unblemished but had a greenish undertone. Isolde put her knife to her throat again and repeated her cutting, this time slicing a red line down her sternum, to her stomach. There was very little bleeding.

'She's not a new-born,' Beauregard explained. 'Isolde has been a vampire for over a thousand years.'

Winthrop looked closer. He saw nothing that suggested the fabled strength and power of an elder. With her fixed fangs, Isolde looked forlorn, almost pathetic.

'She was guillotined once.'

Isolde clamped the blade between her thin lips and used both her hands. She worked the edge of her self-inflicted wound with her nails and peeled back the skin of the right side of her chest. As she moved, exposed muscles bunched and smoothed. With her whole hand under her skin, she loosened the covering of her shoulder and slipped it off like a chemise.

The audience were rapt. Winthrop was disgusted, as much at the spectators as at the performer.

Beauregard was not watching the stage but watching him.

'We do not understand our limits,' Beauregard said. 'To become a vampire is to have the potential to stretch the human body out of its natural shape.'

As Isolde turned, skin ripped down her back. Red-lined folds hung loose. With only her nails and a few slices of the knife, she methodically flayed herself.

A group of Americans, misled as to the nature of Isolde's exposure, stormed out, protesting loudly. 'You're all gooney birds,' one shouted.

Isolde watched them go, easing the skin off her right arm as if it were a shoulder-length glove.

'Some vampires, Edwin, have no more power to shift their shape than you or I. Notably those of the bloodlines of Ruthven or Chandagnac. Others, including those of the Dracula line, have capabilities that have never been tested to their limits.'

Isolde tore at herself, face impassive but gestures savage. Her skin hung in scarecrow tatters. Winthrop's stomach queased but he kept nausea down. The theatre stank of blood. It was a mercy there were few vampires in the audience; they might have been maddened. The performer detached scraps of her white skin and tossed them to her crowd.

'She has her disciples,' Beauregard said. 'The poet Des Esseintes has written sonnets to her.'

'It's a shame de Sade never turned. He'd have relished this.'

'Maybe he saw her in his day. Isolde has been performing for a long time.'

Her torso was a glistening dissection, bones visible in wet meat. She held up her skinned right arm and licked from elbow to wrist, reddening her tongue. Arteries stood out, transparent tubes filled with rushing blood.

Many of the audience were on their feet, pressing close to the stage. At the Folies, they would be cheering and whooping, making a display of gay goodfellow abandon. Here, they were intent and silent, holding breath, eyes on the stage, shutting out their comrades. How many of these men would want it known that they were patrons of the Raoul Privache?

'When she was guillotined, did someone stick her head back on to her body?'

She bit into her own wrist, gnawing through the artery, and began sucking. Blood rushed through the collapsing tube and she swallowed, gulping steadily.

'No, they buried her,' Beauregard explained. 'Her body rotted but her head *grew* another. It took ten years.'

She paused for breath and sneered at the audience, blood speckling her chin, then redoubled her attack. As she sucked, her extended fingers twisted into a useless fist.

'Of course, some say she hasn't been the same woman since.'

'How far can she go?'

'Can she consume herself entirely so that there's nothing left? She hasn't yet.'

Isolde's raw flesh changed colour as she sucked the blood out of it, but her face flushed, bloated.

'I think we've seen enough,' Beauregard said, standing.

Winthrop was relieved. He did not want to be a part of Isolde's audience.

They stepped into the corridor. Dravot stood by the door, reading *Comic Cuts*. Beauregard and the sergeant were old comrades.

'Danny, are you looking after our young lieutenant?'

'I do my best, sir.'

Beauregard laughed. 'Glad to hear it. The fate of the Empire may rest on him.'

Winthrop could not shake Isolde from his mind.

'Shall we take the air, Edwin?'

They left the theatre. It was a relief to get out into clean cold. The snow did not settle, leaving slushy residue on the pavement. Winthrop and Beauregard strolled, Dravot following about twenty paces behind.

'When I was your age,' Beauregard said, 'this was not the world in which I expected to grow old.'

Winthrop had been born in 1896, after the Terror. To him, vampires were as natural a part of the world as Dutchmen or deer. From his father, he understood what every Englishman of Beauregard's generation had lived through, the mental adjustments everyone was forced to make during the Terror.

'I remember a time when Lord Ruthven wasn't Prime Minister and Edward Albert Victor wasn't King. Since neither gentleman shows any intention of dying, it may be that they will hold their positions well beyond my lifetime. And yours, should you not take the opportunity to turn.'

'Turn? Become a thing like *that*!'

He nodded back at the Raoul Privache, thinking of Isolde's blood-veined eyes as she sucked herself stupid.

'Not all vampires are of her line. They are not a race apart, Edwin. Not all demons and monsters. They're simply ourselves expanded. From birth, we change in a million ways. Vampires are more changed than the warm.'

Winthrop had, of course, thought of turning. Shortly after his father's death, his mother tried to persuade him to seek the Dark Kiss, to preserve himself from mortality. At seventeen, he had not been ready. Now, he was no surer. Besides, he knew it was not a simple decision: there was the question of bloodline.

'The best woman I ever knew was a vampire,' Beauregard said, 'and the worst man.'

Miles away, there was an explosion. Tongues of flame licked the sky, outlining the whale-shape of a Zeppelin. There had been more air raids in the last month. Parisians had taken to calling the incendiary devices that fell 'Valentines from the Kaiser'. Zeppelins had to fly at such altitudes that it was impossible to drop bombs on precise targets, so anyone and anything could be destroyed. There was no real military purpose to the raids; Dracula had decreed a policy of *Schrecklichkeit*, 'frightfulness', to batter the morale of the Allies.

'Before we next talk, I want you to read this,' Beauregard said, handing over an envelope. 'You might call it a deathbed confession. A woman who was shot this morning told me her story and I've done my best to set it down in her own words. It's a trick worth cultivating, to remember exactly what people say. Often, you will find they have told you things they themselves are not aware of.'

Winthrop slipped the envelope into his pocket. Firebells clanged in the distance. There were bursts of Archie, too low to hurt the Zep. The dirigible drifted higher, pushing up into the clouds. There were usually five or six ships in a raiding party. If the Hun actually wanted to destroy something specific, they would send one of the big long-range Gotha bombers.

'I'd like to see one of those beasts brought down in flames,' Winthrop said.

Beauregard looked up to the skies, snowflakes brushing his eyelashes like tears.

'I'm tired now and I must go. Read Madame Zelle's confession carefully. Perhaps you will find something *I've* missed.'

The old man turned and walked smartly away, cane clipping the pavement. Drunken Americans courteously made way for him. In his day, Charles Beauregard must have been quite someone. Even now, he was the single most impressive individual Winthrop had come across in the service of the King.

Winthrop looked around for Dravot, and saw him after a few moments. The sergeant stood calmly in the shadows under an awning. Each time he played this game, he found Dravot more swiftly. He supposed he was learning something.

10

IN LOFTY CIRCLES

For all the magnificently painted ceilings and leather couches, this was another waiting room. He would pass the rest of his life in such places, hoping unconcerned dignitaries might conclude important business with time enough to spare for Edgar Poe. From terms in the army and at West Point, he was familiar with the ancient martial *dictum* 'hurry up and wait'. At the heart of the world's supreme military power, the rule was enshrined in national law. Prague was merely an outlying fiefdom of Berlin; this was the metropolis of waiting rooms, the central circle of prevarication. In Bohemia, Poe had fallen through cracks and been the last of the ignored. Here, he was merely the least of the hordes of the overlooked.

The hall was crowded with men whose finery suggested importance and worth. Within sight were enough feathered helms, gold tassels, sparkly epaulettes, polished buttons, medal clusters, white capes, shiny boots, brocaded waistcoats and striped trousers to outfit a comic opera company for a season. Yet supplicants paced with irritable energy or slumped in weary attitudes, revealing only powerlessness and irrelevance. Poe was a slumper, Hanns Heinz Ewers a pacer. He went back and forth like a sentry, hands clasped behind his back, neck stiff as a ramrod.

Their appointment was with Dr Mabuse, Director of the Intelligence and Press Department of the Imperial German Air

Service. At nearly midnight, the building was still busy. The most Poe had gathered was that he was to be asked to write a book. He did not mention that in the last three years, he had been unable to complete so much as a humorous couplet.

Junior officers clutched document bundles, desperate to be relieved of the bad news they brought. Colonels, generals, a field marshal were levelled in rank by an age of waiting.

A clerk, his hair a peculiarly shocked bird's nest, sometimes emerged, like a figure from a cuckoo clock, from a tiny door to call a name.

'Von Bayern,' he barked. 'Hauptmann Gregory von Bayern.'

An elder, neatly uniformed without the trimmings, stood at the sound of his name and was ushered out of the room. Ewers's envious eyes bored into von Bayern's uniformed back as it disappeared smartly through doors marked with a gilded bas-relief of the imperial German eagle.

'*They* always get preference,' Ewers stage-whispered bitterly, meaning elders. 'The centuried fools don't know what year it is, but are sure of a commission and the opportunity to eclipse the work of an able new-born.'

Obviously, Ewers was eaten inside by resentment. Poe was learning more of his *doppelgänger.*

In the first-class railway carriage, numbed by Ewers's reminiscences, Poe found his travelling companion tolerable only because his position guaranteed patronage, advancement or degradation. Ewers's stories of life in the service of the Kaiser were laced with the ironic, justified falls of those who had crossed or disappointed him. Each gem of truth in his autobiographical monologue was polished until it shone, then set in a tracery of arrant fiction.

It was an uncomfortable journey, with the etched faces of soldiers returning from leave always outside the compartment or in the darks between the carriages. The grey of their uniforms spread to their faces, showing colour only in the red around their eyes.

Apparitions haunted Poe still. On a nearby couch, squeezed

between a puffy diplomat and a mightily whiskered general, was a man from the front, a wild-eyed walking skeleton wrapped in a uniform. Jittery at every heel-click on marble, a muddied despatch clamped under his arm, he was one of the living dead, a warm man who seemed more dead than the vampires either side of him. His dented helmet was smeared with French dirt.

The stomach of his coat was pink-tinged with his own blood. Any rank insignia he might once have worn were obscured or ripped away. The man's stretched face was a mask of pain.

The General, fussily eating live mice from a brown paper bag, pretended not to notice the state of his comrade. He shrank to one side to avoid actual physical contact with such a disgusting remnant. The diplomat too, concentrated on a mid-air spot in a direction that did not require him to look at the soldier. The worthies, new-born vampires of the most distinguished station, conversed over and around the mud man, discussing the course of the war. Both were confident of imminent victory because the German fighting man was the best in the world. With the Russkies out of it, there was no excuse not to take Paris before the thaw.

The soldier held his stomach as if digesting a caltrop and looked at Poe with a terrible gaze. For a moment, he was certain he had been recognised as the author of *The Battle of St Petersburg*, and that he had been tricked into answering for his failure as a prophet of modern warfare. The thought passed but he seethed at the likes of the general and the diplomat. They were far more responsible than Edgar Poe for the divergence of the course of the war from his vision.

'Poelzig,' announced the clerk. 'Herr Oberst Hjalmar Poelzig.'

A sallow-faced officer arose and sauntered through the doors. Poe assumed he had shares in munitions. Only someone making money could look so arrogantly satisfied.

Ewers still paced, fuming. In the motor-car that conveyed them from the railway station to the Chancellery, Ewers had impressed the driver with the urgency of their mission. The name of Mabuse was well enough known to spur the man to an over-enthusiastic burst of speed. A ferocious honk on the horn startled a horse into rearing. Ewers chuckled while two soldiers tried to calm the beast and the car sped by, eagle pennants fluttering. Now, in this huge room, he was diminished. His true position emerged as each of his humble solicitations was pointedly ignored or waved away by hawk-eyed clerks. If he had not been so tired and thirsty, and conscious of his own bad clothes, Poe might have enjoyed the braggart's slow shrinkage.

A young veteran, a burned arm twisted into a batwing against his side, face snouted and angry with scars, entered with a trolley of newspapers which he hawked around the room. A colonel learned from the front page that secret information he was to hand over to his High Command was now common knowledge. Poe thought to buy a paper, but realised he had absolutely no money about him.

Ewers did his best to impress upon a clerk that his career would suffer dreadfully when it was found by Dr Mabuse that he, Hanns Heinz *Ewers*, had been kept waiting. He suggested darkly that a word from him ensured transfer to active service on the Western Front. The clerk humoured him but action was not forthcoming.

Strangely, Ewers was the only person in the room inclined to complain. The field marshal sat meekly, waiting. It was very German. Everyone knew their rank and place and stuck to it. All very reassuring, providing one had a seat on the pyramid. Anyone whose station could not immediately be determined from a glance at an epaulette was the equivalent of an Indian 'untouchable', excluded entirely from the caste system.

The soldier suppressed a groan and hugged his stomach as if a shrapnel fragment were working its way through. Poe thought a trickle of blood was seeping through the soldier's coat. His red thirst was excited but the battered and filthy soldier was revolting to his sensibilities. Poe would have to be starved indeed to feed on such poor meat.

The mood of the room suddenly changed, as if smoke had been

scented in the air. The supplicants were like a herd of grazing deer, alert to the tread of a hunter. A susurrus of whispering swept past like a wind and Poe heard a name, repeated.

'Dracula…'

The main doors were held open by attendants. A noisome party was coming into the room. Even Ewers stopped pacing to come to attention.

'Dracula…'

The Graf von Dracula was the Elder Vampire of Europe, Master Strategist and Great Visionary, Architect of Victory and Defender of the Kind. It was due solely to his colossal schemes that the vampire condition was spread throughout the world. Uncle-by-marriage to Kaiser Wilhelm II, he was rumoured to have a greater say in the conduct of the war than Hindenburg or Ludendorff.

'Dracula…'

Soldiers marched in, boots and breastplates clattering. Elders of the Graf's Carpathian Guard, they had fought at his side through the centuries. With them, they brought an icy stink of old spilled blood and discharged guns.

'Dracula…'

Poe had written to the Graf many times early in the war, encouraged by the elder's endorsement, never retracted but also not mentioned much these days, of *The Battle of St Petersburg*. He had never been granted a reply.

'Dracula…'

The repetition of the name was almost a cry, almost a prayer. An adjutant was dragged in behind a pair of wolves which snapped and snarled on leashes. Ewers jumped at the approach of the beasts. Poe had heard these were Dracula's lieutenants from his warm days, transformed by his powers into faithful familiars.

A tall vampire came through the doors at a striding pace. He wore a grey cloak over a simple uniform. Poe noted the leather holster at his belt, the shiny-peaked black cap, the pointed ends of his moustache.

While other elders clung to their own times, Dracula changed eternally with each war. While his generals advised the tactics of Waterloo and Borodino, the Graf deployed machine-guns against cavalry charges and ordered the digging of trenches across the whole of Europe. He was the great adapter, the supreme pragmatist.

A dowager knelt before the Graf and kissed his hand, pressing lips to spade-like nails. He tolerated her attentions but was eager to move on.

Though not given to fawning on the great, Poe stood to present himself. A word from Dracula would free him from the abominable Ewers and find him a suitable position. General David Poe, his grandfather, had been a warlord also, in the Revolutionary war. There were too many in the way. The Graf could not venture among the generality without being surrounded by the grateful, the solicitous, the opportunist.

Poe dashed forwards, running through his accomplishments in his mind. The conversation of Poe and Dracula. This was to be a moment in the history of imagination. As he neared the Graf's party, the air seemed richer, thick and liquid. Close to the warlord, Poe's step slowed as in a dream. Background noise was blotted out and Poe heard the beating of a huge heart, a drumbeat of life drowning all else.

The Graf's great head turned as he strode. His eyes passed over Poe without recognition. Poe skidded to a halt, gaping at the elder. Dracula hurried on. A pair of plumed Carpathians, one a warrior woman with a tattooed face, covered his back. Their hostile gaze drove Poe back. The elder swept through the room unquestioned, leaving supplicants in his wake. The weeping dowager had to be comforted by an aghast junior officer.

Poe felt the passing of the unusual conditions that obtained in the immediate vicinity of the Graf. Normal sounds and smells poured back in, setting his senses a-jangle.

The *presence* of the warlord was overpowering and did not fade fast. Ewers was electrified, unable to contain his nervous energies.

Newspapers riddled with bad news from the front were abandoned. Officers hung together to propose new paths to victory. Everyone knew a big push was in the offing, striking at Paris before the Americans arrived in force.

Poe could not forget Dracula's eyes.

The eagle doors were held open for the Graf's party. They moved into the hallway and mounted a wide set of stairs. The doors closed but Poe still heard boots on the marble steps. The heartbeat pulsed in his brain, setting a pace for the progress of empires.

Over three-quarters of the vampires in the room were of Dracula's bloodline. Poe felt excluded: Virginia never knew the name of her father-in-darkness, though she thought he might be a Spaniard. He called himself Sebastian Newcastle. The vampire had sought out the poet of the uncanny and found only Mrs Poe at home, then begun the process of her turning on a motiveless whim. That neither Poe nor Virginia demonstrated an aptitude for shape-shifting proved Newcastle was not of the Dracula line. At odd times, Poe was obsessed with tracking the vampire who had turned Virginia, but his enquiries always petered out.

The waiting hall settled again. Even the Graf's heartbeat, which had chimed with the throbbing of Poe's own blood, was gone.

He looked at the front-line soldier, alone on his couch. Unlike the general and the diplomat, he had not stood in the mighty presence. His lap was stained scarlet. Blood dribbled down his breeches and into his boots. A recent wound had opened. The man might die in this waiting hall.

His hollow eyes had followed the Carpathians and were fixed on the eagle doors. Sourly, the soldier turned away and spat on the floor. As he hunched forwards to hawk, his upper body shook badly. Having emptied his throat and nose, he sank back slowly into the couch.

'This is absurd,' Ewers said. 'Such foolishness will not go unrewarded, Herr Poe. Of that you can be…'

The clerk emerged again and looked at them.

'Ach,' Ewers was delighted, 'at last.'

'*Baumer*,' the clerk said, voice ringing. 'Feldwebel Paul Baumer.'

Ewers was enraged at being passed over again. He looked about for the unfortunate sergeant, ready to breathe fire in his face.

'Paul *Baumer*,' the clerk said again.

No one came forwards. Poe looked at the soldier and saw the last flutter of his closing eyes.

'I think this man is Baumer,' he said, looking.

The clerk tutted disapproval as his attention was called to the messenger from the front.

'Feldwebel Baumer,' he said, 'you may go in now.'

Baumer's shoulders moved but he could not lift himself. His despatch slipped from under his arm and plumped on to the marble floor.

'This is absurd,' Ewers said, as if Baumer were personally blocking his path to Dr Mabuse's office.

Poe could tell, from the change in the smell of Baumer's blood, that the man had died. His grip on his stomach relaxed and his arms eased away from his wet midriff. An insect landed on his hand and opened its wings, showing itself to be a butterfly. The clerk brushed the butterfly away as he checked the man's stilled pulse. He summoned attendants to remove the corpse. Blood pooled in the indentations Baumer left in the couch. The diplomat, indifferent to the death, caught the butterfly in his hand, considered its markings, then popped it into his mouth.

The desk seemed to cover the breadth of a tennis court. Dr Mabuse's chair was elevated so he could peer over his expanse of polished wood and gaze down on the heads of those seated on the other side. The Director of the Press and Intelligence Division displayed an obvious need for others to look up to him. Poe noted him to be a man of small stature.

Dr Mabuse had white, flyaway hair and the red eyes of a new-born who drinks too much. He wore a surgical white tunic, the Imperial

Order of the Iron Cross on a black ribbon around his neck. To the evident disgust of Ewers, the director exclaimed in delight at meeting Herr Edgar Allan Poe.

'I no longer use my stepfather's name, Doktor. Edgar Poe was I born, and am I again. The memory of John Allan need trouble us nevermore.'

Dr Mabuse's eyes gleamed. 'You were an inspiration to me, Herr Poe. Your tales, "The Facts in the Case of M. Valdemar" and "Mesmeric Revelations", excited my fascination with the hypnotic arts.'

Before the war, before turning, Mabuse had been an authority on the subject of mesmerism, lowering himself to public displays. Naturally, a man of his talents and influence was in charge of propaganda.

'All wars need heroes, Herr Poe. This war most of all. Since they tend by nature to be unforthcoming, all heroes need to be publicised.'

Dr Mabuse spoke as if delivering a speech. Lamps on his desk made a shadowed mask of his face, bringing out the glow in his eyes. Early in the war, Dr Mabuse had toured gymnasia, addressing students. It was not uncommon for an audience to enlist *en masse* following one of his lectures.

'You have heard, of course, of Manfred von Richthofen.'

'The flier?'

'*The* flier. Our premier warrior of the air. Seventy-two victories.'

Poe had always been interested in the possibilities of man-powered flight. When warm, he had written 'The Balloon Hoax', and in *The Battle of St Petersburg* he had predicted the use in battle of airships and fighter aeroplanes.

'It is the crowing claim of the Allies that they are our masters in the air over the Western Front,' said Dr Mabuse, lips curving in a one-sided smile. 'Before spring, that will change.'

'Germany has better aeroplanes,' Ewers muttered.

'Germany has better *men*. This is the secret of our victory. No matter what mechanical devices are ranged against us, we Germans will prevail through the strength of our spirit.'

Dr Mabuse took a document from his desk drawer and slid it across his desk. Poe caught it and looked.

It was the mock-up of a book cover. *Der Rote Kampfflieger*, by Manfred, Rittmeister Freiherr von Richthofen. *The Red Battle Flier.* The rough illustration showed a batwinged red shadow over a falling enemy aeroplane.

'Richthofen has written his autobiography?'

'The Freiherr is a fighter, not a man of letters. If his story is to be told, it will require a great spinner of tales. You, Herr Poe.'

He began to understand what was to be asked of him.

'You want me to ghost this book?'

'To "ghost"? Exactly. You shall be Richthofen's ghost.'

Ewers hovered in the shadows of the office. Poe wondered what his part in this was. If H.H. Ewers was so great a writer, why was he not clamouring for this honour?

'Herr Ewers will be on hand as a native German-speaker to serve as editor, should you need him.'

Ewers's brows contracted darkly. His pretended importance evaporated by the moment. It seemed he was less *doppelgänger* than messenger boy.

'Transport has been arranged to the Chateau de Malinbois, where Richthofen is stationed with his *Jagdgeschwader 1*. Our modest hero has consented to be interviewed at length. Use his words if you can, but work them up into something more than a set of dry war stories. To be frank, my experience is that true heroes tend to the tedious. Capture the truth but put your own shine on it, Herr Poe. Let us have some of the spirit of your tales. Thrilling battles, extreme characters, hairsbreadth escapes. The book will be useless if nobody wishes to read it.'

Anonymity did not bother Poe. Considering his current doubts, it might be best if this were not generally known to be his composition. He was unsure if he could even manage low hack-work. But he had always been as much a journalist as a poet. If anything remained of his ragged muse, it could be stirred to this purpose.

'You must to work fast. Events are moving swiftly, as you will find when you reach the front…'

The front! The Chateau de Malinbois was in the thick of the war. He would be in the glory of battle. Not as a soldier, but as a poet, he would take himself to war. This was a chance to right the wrong of *The Battle of St Petersburg*. If the world disappointed him, the world must be shaped to his liking.

'You must catch Richthofen's past but also tell of his present. As Germany retakes the air, you will be there to set the victories in stone for posterity.'

The director's voice was soothing and persuasive. Poe felt stirrings in his breast. A door opening in his mind: words would soon pour from him again. He stood to attention and saluted.

'Dr Mabuse, I shall endeavour to perform my duties, for the glory of the Kaiser and to the betterment of the cause of the Central Powers.'

'Herr Poe, that is all we can ask of you.'

11

WHAT KATE DID NEXT

She did not give the warmfellows cause to notice her, but her *nosferatu* senses were athrill. With the distraction of the air raid, Charles and his associate, Edwin Winthrop, should not catch her out. However, the tall, heavily moustached vampire watching over them was formidable. It was hard to stay on the track and not get mixed up with Dravot's boots. Of old, the sergeant was often found near Charles. Now his attentions were transferred to the younger officer. In itself, that was suggestive.

Kate had been Charles's shadow all evening. He was among the most perceptive of his ungentle profession but her night-skills grew more acute by the year. Paris offered crowds enough to be usefully lost in. Being titchy helped. Weaving between bigger people, she was a perfect mouse: scarf about her lower face, mittened hands muffed in her coat-sleeves, knitted cap over the tops of her ears.

Everyone else looked up but she regarded the pavement, hearing rather than seeing the way, fixing on Charles's voice. The racket of the air raid obscured most of what was said but Charles's timbre was easy to distinguish. Those of her bloodline had sharp ears, a useful trait in a reporter.

The Zeppelins were on the other side of the river. Hovering above the cloud, they could not be seen but the drone of engines was constant. Fairly distant bomb-bursts were overlaid by immediate

107

shouts of defiance and abuse. Useless shots were fired into the sky. The ground shook with each explosion. Fires spread.

Someone on the run bumped into her, dislodging her spectacles, and apologised in rapid French. Snake-quick, she caught her glasses and put them back on, blinking. The running man, scarlet-lined cape flapping, was lost in the crowd. For a moment, she thought her quarry lost but she caught Charles's voice, stray words drifting through din.

Panic spread as the Zeppelins drifted towards the quarter. Bombs still fell, whistling and bursting. Tonight, the Germans dropped only incendiaries, damaging buildings. At other times, Dracula's airships poured flaming liquid that adhered to living flesh. The stuff, which water would not douse, burned to the bone. Vampires might be hardy but fire and silver were lethal to them. With Europe overstocked by the undead, the war had prompted the development of infernal devices that would have given the late Van Helsing unpleasant delight. Manufacturers with stock in silver mines became munitions millionaires overnight. Lady Jennifer Buckingham of the Women's Volunteer Ambulance Brigade led a silver drive, persuading the wealthy to give up coffee pots and candlesticks for bullets and bayonets.

While Charles attended the Théâtre Raoul Privache, Kate had loitered outside, noting the comings and goings of patrons. Spotting Edwin at once, she was reminded of Charles in Whitechapel during the Terror, secretive yet puzzled. With Edwin came Dravot, a sure sign. Being familiar with the speciality of the Raoul Privache, she was unsurprised when the Englishmen left before the end of what might be termed the first act. Even after thirty years as a supposed creature of gothic dark, elders gave Kate the horrors. Isolde, among the oldest of the old, was hardly a healthy advertisement for eternal life.

A party of Americans blundered between her and the quarry. One was wounded, losing his footing through excess of champagne or in some incident related to the raid. Fresh blood poured profusely from a gash in his head, streaming down his young face, spotting his uniform. The blood was an endlessly fascinating mingle of gold and scarlet. She was twisted by desire. With sweet pain, her fangs slid from their sheaths. She had not fed in several nights. She would have to deal with the inconvenient business soon. Sharpened nails crowded inside her mittens.

The soldiers stared. She must look a fright. Her scarf fell away from her mouth. She could taste blood on the air. The wounded doughboy was terrified. There were plenty like him: farm lads who had never seen a real vampire, heads full of scary stories. With difficulty, she closed her lips over still-sharp fangs. She tried to smile but it hurt her face. Perhaps, after all, she was becoming a monster.

After a final huddled chat, Charles and Edwin parted. Charles, she realised, was returning to his suite at the Hôtel Transylvania. Dravot, on the other side of the street, ambled after Lieutenant Winthrop as if taking a nightly constitutional. Plainly, he was the latest catspaw of the Ruling Cabal. Kate was not sure the sergeant had not noticed her.

On impulse, she let Charles return to his deserved rest and took off after Dravot. As the sergeant shadowed Edwin, she shadowed him. It was another test of her abilities. With proverbial cat-like tread, she darted from dark to dark. Distinguishing the sergeant's heavy, distinctive bootfalls among the numberless sounds of the night, she fixed on them.

Emerging from the theatre, Edwin looked rattled by what he had seen. It was said Isolde had once regenerated her entire body like a lizard growing a fresh tail. There were similar stories about the resilience of the Dracula line. Considering the wretchedness of Isolde's situation, it seemed to Kate that absolute bodily indissolubility was not a path to perpetual happiness. Charles had shown him Isolde to make a point. What had the self-dissecting freak to do with Mata Hari? And, *pace* Corporal Lantier's account of Mata Hari's confession, the Chateau de Malinbois?

Having seen failed shape-shifters, Kate did not exert herself in that direction. Teeth and claws came when needed but she had no ambitions to extend her repertoire. When she was a warm child,

Mama warned her not to pull faces because 'if the wind changes, you'll get stuck that way'; now, there were too many would-be werewolves loping about, 'stuck that way'.

Edwin and Dravot walked towards an area damaged in the raid. A market building burned, surrounded by bucket-passing firemen and unhelpful crowds. The wrought-iron skeleton was black against harsh flames, buckling and screeching in the heat. The steam of overcooked vegetables stung her sensitive nostrils. Somewhere near, a horse whinnied in pained panic. Kate saw the animal struggling between the shafts of a fire engine. A shiny-caped man tried to pat out a persistent patch of flame on its flanks.

Dravot stopped and looked up. Kate did the same. Zeppelins were up there, arrogant crews calmly dropping fiery death. She heard engines buzz. French aeroplanes flew to defend the city. An airship could outclimb anything the Allies could put in the sky. Winged shapes passed overhead. The Allies prized their much-trumpeted 'air superiority' over the Central Powers, but Dracula and the Kaiser would not be content to let it lie. That madman Robur was still championing the cause of the aerial dreadnought.

The nails of her right hand became claws again, puncturing her wool mitten. Sometimes her body was alert to danger before her mind. Dravot was not where he had stopped. It was time to withdraw from the engagement. She had other ways of pursuing the story. Staunchly loyal to his masters, the sergeant was as much a killer as the men in the Zeppelins.

Frank Harris had taught her a journalist's first loyalty ought to be to the truth, not to patriotism or propaganda. The position did not find many supporters during the war.

A wall collapsed, scattering hot bricks across the street, pushing crowds back into side roads. A waft of hot air swept past.

Through a curtain of flame, Kate recognised Dravot. She was pleased there was a fire barrier between them and counted herself lucky.

'You, Miss Mouse, come here…'

The words were English, the tone commanding. It was Lieutenant Winthrop. She did as she was told.

A tumble of burning vegetable mush crept towards her shoes like molten lava. A warm grip took her arm and hauled her into an alley. If she fought, she could tear Edwin to pieces. Then she would have to face Dravot, who would doubtless render her the same service.

'Following in my footsteps, eh? It seems I've snared a little spy. A miniature Mata Hari.'

While she had fixed on Dravot, Edwin had hung back and waited to take her from behind. Her failing had been blithe overconfidence. There was no point in fighting it out. After all, they were on the same side.

'I have not the ssslightessst idea what you mean, ssssssir,' she tried to explain, hissing through a mouthful of jagged teeth.

This was no time to be aroused. She heard the tiny pulses of Edwin's neck and heart. As he smiled at her, the blue vein ticked in his temple.

Unexpectedly, Edwin laughed. 'I say, you sound fearfully silly.'

She willed her fangs to recede. Inside tight fists, nails dwindled.

'My name is Kate Reed, and I am a volunteer ambulance driver. You can ask Lady Buckingham or Mrs Harker for my references.'

He did not seem impressed.

'I assume you have followed me because of an intuition that I might come to some dire harm which would require your angelic ministrations?'

To pretend to be an even greater twit than she felt herself to be, she tried to project sheepish meekness. He let go and looked her up and down. She knew how odd she must seem in her disguise.

'I'm out for a stroll,' she claimed, loosening and rewinding her scarf with dignity.

'In an air raid?'

The fires were dying. Dravot had stalked around the blaze. He stood at the end of the road, a dozen yards away. She concentrated on drawing in her claws. It was important the sergeant did not think her a threat to his master.

'You've soot on your face,' Edwin told her, unkindly.

She rubbed her cheeks with mittens. He tapped his forehead and she concentrated on that area.

'You're just making it worse. With those specs, you look like a mole.'

As a child, Kate had been called 'Moley'. Penelope Churchward, the princess of their circle, thought the nickname remarkably amusing. No one heard much from Penny these days.

'You are gallant, Mr Staff Officer.'

'Lieutenant Winthrop, at your service.'

He presented his hand as if it were a calling card. She took his fingers and gave a gently painful squeeze. He set his teeth grimly but fixed a smile over the hurt.

'Pleased to meet you.' She curtseyed, letting him go.

He flexed his fingers to make sure they were all working.

'You're the Katharine Reed who writes so cleverly for the *Cambridge Magazine*, are you not? The intrepid lady journalist who called for Field Marshal Haig's prosecution on the grounds of criminal negligence?'

Kate's heart sank. If Edwin knew who she was, he would probably insist she get the Mata Hari treatment. She imagined Dravot wrestling her head off with quiet satisfaction.

'I have had the honour of writing for that periodical,' she replied, non-committally.

'I understand you're quite the heroine to those front-line troops who manage to have the *Cambridge* smuggled past the censors.'

He sounded as if that was meant as a compliment.

'And were you not imprisoned after the Easter Uprising? I seem to have your name lumped in with the Gore-Booths and Spring-Rices of this world. A Fabian and a Fenian.'

'I write what I see.'

'I'm surprised you can see anything through those goggles.'

He sounded as if *that* was meant as facetious.

'Has anyone ever suggested to you that alluding persistently to a person's infirmities might be considered impolite?'

Edwin smiled broadly but was not fooled. There was grit in him. He was not the usual silly-ass staff officer. Of course, she had known that. The lieutenant did not spend his time counting tins of bully beef. He was in with the Diogenes mob.

She decided to play the reporter.

'Do you have any views on the current state of the war? Is Allied command of the air under threat?'

He shrugged, unquotably.

'With the Russians out of it, do you fear a German spring offensive?'

His smile hardened slightly, but he said nothing.

'If you have nothing to say on the subject, would you mind if I bade you goodnight and went on my way? I, at least, have work to do.'

He stood back, spreading his hands.

'Not at all. Good night, Katharine.'

'That's only my name in print. Everybody calls me Kate.'

'Very well. Good night, Kate.'

She nodded, nicely. 'And a good night to you, Edwin.'

He was not caught. 'I didn't tell you my name.'

She tapped her nose. 'I have sources, Lieutenant.'

Before he could quiz her further, she withdrew. As she walked off, she heard Dravot move to confer with him. To her relief, the sergeant was not sent after her. The further away she was, the more comfortable she felt.

The Zeppelins seemed to have slunk back to Germany. Fire-fighters were getting the blazes under control. It was snowing again, slushing into the gutters. Within hours, all the water pumped at the fires would freeze, making a skating rink of the quarter.

She reviewed her sitiuation. Never again would she get within a hundred yards of Edwin Winthrop without being noticed. And he would talk with Charles, which would get her name added *again* to the list of those unwelcome in the vicinity of the war. She must come at this Malinbois business from a completely new angle. More than before, she was convinced something tasty was afoot.

12

BLOODLINES

'The world has made of me what it would, and I make no excuses for myself. I have followed the dictates of my heart, even when such a course was unwise. I am to be shot as a spy but, in truth, I have scant talent for espionage. You, above all, know that, Charles. I am a courtesan, simply. I am kindly called the last of the *grandes horizontales*. I suppose that in this cruel century I must be considered a prostitute, merely...'

The document was the holograph confession of Gertrud Zelle, known to the popular press by her stage name, Mata Hari. Winthrop had intended to defer studying the manuscript but found himself on the train to Amiens, confined in a compartment with a Captain Drummond whose win-the-war tirade was unutterably irksome. The red-faced, beefy vampire was a fine specimen of the bulldog breed, which is to say he was barking mad. An advocate of the 'one-big-push' strategy, Drummond insisted the blueprint for victory was that all the Allied armies should go over the top at the same time.

'The sausage-eaters will turn tail and scarper,' Drummond said, grin displaying interlocking fangs in his square jaw. 'Your dratted Germ-Hun doesn't have the stomach for a proper scrap.'

After four years of murderous, costly squabbling over a few muddy miles, Drummond struck him as insane. A pair of lieutenants, fresh from training, were converts to the captain's way of thinking.

Winthrop doubted they would survive a week in the lines. The Hun might not have the stomach of the Tommy, but he certainly had entrenched machine-gun positions.

'It's the only cursed way,' Drummond said, as passionately thick-headed as a campaigning politician. 'One big push to Victory.'

The lieutenants agreed, swearing to be in the first wave. Drummond had just killed them, and probably all the men under their command.

'If the fathead politicians would let us out of the trenches, we'd give the swine of Saxony and the poltroons of Prussia the sound biffing they so richly deserve. With the Kaiser hoisted on a sturdy stake, we should shove on into the Russias and sort out the blasted Bolshies.'

Winthrop imagined the tide of war surging around the world, sweeping through continents like a dreadful winter.

'Mark my words, the real enemy is the clique of homicidal, alien Jews that has done for the weak-blooded Romanovs.'

Drummond concluded his editorial and got down to gory stories of Germans killed with bare hands and teeth. Winthrop pleaded urgent business and read on.

I am Dracula's get. I was one of his mistresses. When the Graf settled at the Kaiser's court, he turned several of us. In life, he was an Eastern potentate. Always, he must have a harem. He would fiercely deny it, but his habits are Ottoman. Fortunately, I was a passing diversion. He is uncomfortable with women of this century. We are difficult to bend to his will. He prefers the pliable, superstitious fools of his own time. The favourites, the ones he calls wives, have been with him for centuries. They have child minds and beast appetites, all 'I want' and 'give me' and 'now'. I am not of that breed, but I fear degeneration is inevitable. Now I shall never learn whether my bloodline harbours the taint.

When he turned me, I was his property. His slave to use as was his whim. Even now, Dracula owns me. Dawn will set me free. After a few eternal months in the summer of 1910, the

Graf loosened the collar. First, he yielded exclusive rights. I was obliged to serve the pleasure of his Carpathian cronies. Many elders drink only the blood of new-borns. They regard the warm with disgust. I was the consort of Armand Tesla. Before his fall, Dr Tesla was chief of Dracula's secret police. A cruel elder, his amusement was to drip holy water on to the flesh of new-borns. It doesn't work on every line, but for some this is disfiguring. There is no explanation in science. The admission is unfashionable, but we are not creatures of nature. Vampires are *monsters*. When angered, Tesla would threaten my face. Even if I survived, my life as a courtesan would end. But the doctor came to value me, so I was spared.

Tesla schooled me as a spy and introduced me to diplomatic circles in Berlin, London and Paris. He became second only to the Graf in influence and power, which is why Dracula killed him. You knew that, too. I can tell by your face. A woman doesn't need to be able to read minds, though some vampires can. It is his weakness, Charles. Anyone about him who shows himself too able, he will become suspicious of. And he will destroy. He is a proud descendant of Attila but nations can no longer be ruled like barbarian tribes. Germany and Austria–Hungary *need* the capable men Dracula has assassinated. Only fools and the slyest of traitors survive. One man, even Dracula, cannot hold together such an empire. He failed in Britain and he will fail in Germany. Your responsibility is to ensure that enough of Europe survives his fall to start again.

Captain Drummond was still chuckling over his personal plans for 'Lenin, Trotsky and their unwashed shower'. Winthrop shivered. Dracula was hardly Europe's last monster.

When Tesla fell, I became an inconvenience and was sent to Paris. I was set up in apartments and resumed my life as a dancer.

Mabuse, Tesla's successor, ordered me to ensnare as many dignitaries as I could.

The woman was accused of prising the plans for a French offensive out of General Mireau, another advocate of the Drummond way to mass suicide. This was the charge upon which she had been executed.

The truth is I was delayed and passed on the information only minutes before the attack. If my report reached the German High Command, I would think them too busy gloating over dead Frenchmen to take notice. Mireau's colossal plan was to attack at dawn. That was it. He ordered twenty minutes' bombardment to clear the barbed wire and wake the German gunners, then breakfasted on cognac, snug in his field headquarters while a hundred-thousand brave *poilus* climbed from the trenches to be chopped up by concentrated mortar and machine-gun fire. I'm a whore with no more notion of military tactics than a goose, but even I saw the plan was astonishingly obvious. Attack at dawn, I ask you! Why not a token feint to draw fire, duping the enemy into signalling guns positions, then specific bombardments to eliminate defensive positions, *then* the big attack? Does it not seem strange *I* can come up with a sounder plan than the fabulous General Mireau? It is no wonder the ass is insistent I be executed (at dawn, of course), for fear Hindenburg might call upon my services as a strategist. Then again, I'm sure Germany has a surfeit of five-year-old schoolboys who could draw up battle plans that would baffle and overwhelm the good general.

Kate Reed had said as much in her articles on *l'affaire Mireau*.

'Hit 'em hard,' Drummond said, 'at dawn! Wake the blighters up with cold silver.'

This was a war fought by ferocious idiots.

* * *

Charles, you want to hear about the Chateau de Malinbois. Very well. It is the current headquarters of *Jagdgeschwader 1*, the group commanded by Baron von Richthofen. The press is full of their daring deeds. The expression 'Flying Circus' arose because of the unit's manoeuvrability. They have the knack of packing everything on to a train and moving to new positions. Early in the war, the Baron defied orders that his aircraft be painted *en camouflage* and insisted the machine be bright scarlet. Actually, as anyone who has tried to find a red ball in green grass will tell you, a red aeroplane blends surprisingly with the landscape. And by night, even to vampire eyes, red is black. It may be a surprise to you, but Germany's sky-high heroes are not universally beloved by their muddier comrades. The press blathers about the aerial feats of Richthofen's Flying Circus, but ground troops, and even fliers not assigned to JG1, call the squadron 'the Flying Freak Show'. The term is not inappropriate.

Malinbois is also a centre for research, under the directorship of Professor ten Brinken. From my nights as a bride of Dracula, I recall this scientist as a supplicant at the court. The palace was always full of crackpots of one stripe or another. The Graf is a fiend for modernity, as bedazzled by trains and flying machines as a small boy. The professor, one of a parade of geniuses, was granted a private audience with the Graf. I saw him then, a broad-shouldered warm brute, glowering as he paced outside Dracula's office. I understood he was not an inventor but a biological researcher. My instant judgement was that I did not like the man. His face was storm-clouded and about him was a creepy aura. At that time, there was a craze among some of the living for injecting themselves with extremely dilute doses of silver salts. Having thus polluted their blood, they felt safe from the thirsty undead. Even had ten Brinken not taken such precautions, I doubt I should have cared to taste his greasy blood.

When ordered to pay a visit to Malinbois, I assumed I was to be an ornament. Fliers are notorious for their parties. Germany indulges its heroes, and what greater indulgence could there be than Mata Hari?

I arrived late in the afternoon and was greeted by ten Brinken, who had me strip in his surgery. He subjected me to an intimate examination, as if I were a horse destined for the auctioneer's block. Yes, he graded my teeth. With all manner of callipers and probes, he noted even the minutest measurements. I have no qualms about being naked in public, but I was not comfortable with the professor's prying fingers. He took a sample of my blood for analysis and placed the phial in a cool cabinet with many other labelled specimens. He asked me to shape-shift, to become a wolf or a bat. I refused. I do not perform magic tricks. He again demanded. In the examination room also was a uniformed officer, General Karnstein. He kindly ordered me to accede to ten Brinken's request.

The Karnstein bloodline, which had its source in Styria, was one of the most distinguished in Europe. The General, one of Dracula's devoted allies in Austria–Hungary, was elder chieftain of his family-in-darkness. His involvement implied the Central Powers considered Malinbois a big show.

I changed, completely. I cannot *explain*. I simply *think* of one of my shapes and my body becomes malleable. I flow into another form. Like most of Dracula's get, I can take the shape of what I am told is a dire wolf, prehistoric terror of Europe. In Java, I learned the snake dance. I was the lover of a Malay elder, a *pontianak*. I have some of his blood in me. It sets me apart from the common *nosferatu*. For ten Brinken and the General, I assumed snake-shape then sloughed the new skin. Ten Brinken caressed the cast-off as if it gave him pleasure, holding it to the light and admiring rainbows in the scales. All men, Charles, are putty in my jewelled fingers, so they say.

Winthrop tried to envision Mata Hari's snake-shape. He had never seen her famous Javanese Snake Dance, but had heard accounts from besotted devotees.

Karnstein said I reminded him of some lost daughter-in-darkness who could become a large black cat. He likes new-born girls, that one. I knew if I turned my attention to the General, I could enslave him. Few elders are complicated. They may be powerful, but subtlety is beyond them. Ten Brinken filled out his charts and I was dismissed.

A wing of the chateau was set aside for those like me, courtesans. Rooms were stocked with unguents and face-paints. There were trunks of costumes. Much of the finery was rotted. I could tell this revel had been planned by men with little knowledge of or interest in debauchery.

I was not the only delight at this banquet. Other women and one youth, all vampires, were provided. In the dressing room, I found Lady Marikova, one of the wife-creatures who served Dracula in his Transylvanian exile. She had to be attended by Lola-Lola – a sharp, fat new-born minx – lest she get into a snit and murder an admirer. Old vampire bitches are terrible things, but pathetic. Also on the guest list were Sadie Thompson, an American adventuress with dead black eyes; the Baron Meinster, a golden-haired, girlish rake; Faustine, leading ornament of a Venetian brothel; and an elegant elder, Lemora. All whores of no little skill, we had another thing in common between us. We were all Dracula's get.

Dawn broke outside. Trees lined the railway track, many bent and broken. The fields were grey, thin snow layered over mud. The train neared Amiens. Winthrop heard the eternal muttering of the guns. Drummond flinched in the thin light and hauled down a blind.

Every schoolboy knew the spread of vampirism throughout the civilised world was almost entirely Dracula's responsibility. Before the 1880s, only a few superstitious souls *believed* in the undead. Dracula upset the board and set out the pieces in a new configuration. Vampirism spread from him, but his immediate get were fewer than some imagined. During his residence in England, he turned only three: Lucy Westenra, Wilhelmina Harker and Queen Victoria. Mrs Harker, now entirely forgiven and penitent, was his chosen conduit, extending the bloodline wholesale.

Many claimed to be Dracula's get but were usually merely of his line, many times removed from the source. So many of the breed gathered in one place was significant.

Baron Meinster and Lady Lemora, at least, were at the chateau against their wishes. Only one could have so much power over elders. As I said, our father-in-darkness never lets his get go free. We are all his slaves.

It seemed strange we should have been assembled. I was under the impression most, if not all, fliers were vampires themselves. Surely, a fitter reward for their valiant deeds would be a cattle-cart of strong-hearted, sweet-blooded warm wenches. They are not hard to find. I am sure the Allies feed their own heroes in the same manner...

So far as Winthrop knew, this was not true.

At the stroke of midnight – another predictable melodrama touch – we were escorted down to the Great Hall by liveried attendants. The men of JG1 stood to attention in full uniform before the vast fireplace. Lit from behind by pure flame, the fliers did seem the demigods the press would have them. Many a broad chest was insufficient to accommodate an accumulation of decorations. In this hall, Pour le Mérites were as common as brass buttons. The odd thing was that the Circus seemed turned out for a parade inspection, rather than, as I frankly expected, an orgy.

We were presented individually, announced to the company by General Karnstein. Then ten Brinken passed among us, one of his infernal lists clipped to a board. Like a dance director, he paired us off. Thompson was assigned to a predator named Bruno Stachel; Faustine with Erich von Stalhein; Meinster with a sad flier who preferred boys, Friedrich Murnau; Lemora with von Emmelman. Ten Brinken conducted business like a pig-farmer supervising a scientific breeding experiment.

When my turn came, I was offered to Manfred von Richthofen. I believe this suggests my status as Germany's première harlot. Strange as it seems, the Baron did not find the prospect of my attentions especially appealing. Other fliers passed comments or made enthusiastic noises when paired off. One or two couples – including Meinster and his flittery flyboy – were already embracing, drawing gentle blood. Ten Brinken was irritated by this immodest abandon but more tolerant of it than of the Baron's flat refusal. I confess I was somewhat surprised, even hurt. Any of these fliers could be dead within the night. In such a situation, a man is entitled to what pleasures may come within his grasp.

Winthrop thought of Cundall's Condors and 'mademoiselle'.

The Baron's brother, Lothar von Richthofen, was delighted to be given the Lady Marikova *and* her maid Lola-Lola, but distracted himself to try to jolly the Baron into going with me. As Lothar cajoled, I looked closely at Baron von Richthofen. I had imagined a giant but he is of moderate stature. His eyes are ice-blue and something is lacking in them. He is devoted, I understand, to hunting and has little interest in other pursuits. The hall is decorated with trophies of his kills but he is not as boastful as others with lesser scores. My impression is that he is not even a great patriot, merely a pure-bred hunting dog.

Winthrop remembered Albright's dry corpse and tried to envision the thing which had emptied him in mid-air.

Ten Brinken was agitated when one of his associates, a Dr Krueger, pointed out some were getting ahead of themselves. Stalhein's head was thrown back, eyes glazing as Faustine nibbled him. An attendant pulled the girl away and held her back. Her eyes were red and she had a full set of fangs. She panted like a cat, tiny blood dribbles on her chin.

'You must not drink from these men,' ten Brinken ordered, 'you must let them drink from you. This is of vital importance. Those who disobey will be punished.'

The stress ten Brinken laid on the word 'punished' was curiously sickening. I did not wish to discover what punishment he had conceived for us immortals.

Stalhein adjusted his collar and shook his head. Lothar was still trying to coax the Baron, who stood with arms resolutely crossed, Blue Max glinting on his breast.

As I said, many elders drink only the blood of other vampires. It is a way of taking on the strength of new lines. But the diet does not suit most new-borns. The Circus are, mainly, young in darkness, barely a year or two out of their graves. It is common in Germany and Austria–Hungary for the sons of the aristocracy to be turned in their eighteenth or nineteenth year. The blood of Dracula's immediate get is strong. The merest pinprick, squeezed onto your tongue, would be enough to turn you…

Winthrop had the impression Mata Hari was flirting with Beauregard.

He wished he had been present at the interview; so much meaning was lost without the inflection.

...and a taste would be enough to madden most new-borns. When *nosferatu* go mad, they lose control of their shape-shifting talents. It is not a pleasant way to die. Ten Brinken was playing a very dangerous game. Either he cared not for the survival of these heroes, or else he was confident of their qualities. I have no doubt the first condition is in some measure true: ten Brinken strikes me as a warm man fascinated and terrified by vampires. But I also think it a fair bet that any flier who had earned a place in JG1 would have the right stuff to taste the blood of Dracula's get and profit from the infusion.

'Drink their blood,' ten Brinken ordered, 'it is important.'

Lothar opened his mouth, transforming it into a snout bristling with teeth, and fastened himself to Marikova's swan-neck, chewing flesh, lapping spurting blood with a long tongue. The elder's wounds healed instantly, so Lothar tore again, smearing his face with precious gore.

'See, Manfred,' he said, voice surprisingly human through wolfish lips, 'it is not so difficult.'

Lothar's clawed hands rent Marikova's ball-gown, and his jaws tore her breasts and belly. He pushed the elder on to a divan and licked her open wounds. Lola-Lola held her mistress down, whispering soothing words into her ear, gripping her hand like a midwife helping a woman through childbirth. Marikova's face was frozen in indignation, but she was strong with the strength of centuries. I did not know if I could survive the rough treatment Lothar von Richthofen was meting out to Dracula's wife.

'Baron von Richthofen,' General Karnstein addressed the flier, 'it is necessary. For the war.'

The Baron looked at me without passion, without contempt, without interest. I cannot convey the emptiness of his eyes. Some *nosferatu* have a deadness in their heart that has nothing to do with true death. We vampires exaggerate the qualities of our warm days. You can imagine the traits I have carried over and amplified from life. In Richthofen, there must have been a coldness, a need to retreat from physical and emotional contact. For such a man to be a vampire, to be eternally dependent on such contact, must be very like perdition.

Winthrop could not bring himself to pity the Bloody Red Baron.

'Very well,' Manfred said, the good soldier obeying an order. He stepped forwards, close to me. I saw healed scars on his handsome, square face. Under his cropped hair was a fading red weal. He had recently been shot in the head.

'Madame,' he held out his hand. I took it. A queerly boyish look passed across his face, as if he did not know what to do next. I believe he had never before been with a woman.

Ten Brinken nodded to one of the attendants, who slipped my peignoir from my shoulders.

'You appear to be in excellent health,' he remarked.

Other fliers followed Lothar's example. Stalhein had Faustine pinned down, and drank from her slit wrist as from a public water fountain. Meinster opened his dressing gown like batwings and moaned in a species of pleasure as Murnau knelt before him, sucking intimate wounds.

Manfred dipped his head and touched a sharp tongue to my neck. When I say sharp, I mean it literally. Some vampires have barbed points in their tongues, to pierce their companions' skin. The Baron clamped his mouth to my wound and sucked, ferociously. I felt points of pain and an ocean of pleasure. I was near swooning. The experience had not been this intense since Dracula took me for the first time. I was warm again, alive.

'Not too much, Baron,' said ten Brinken, tapping Manfred's shoulder. 'It can be dangerous.'

I wanted to push him away but I had to hold him to me. I felt myself dwindling.

'Baron,' ten Brinken nearly shouted, fear lost in his devotion to science, 'enough!'

I shook. My vision clouded red. I was dying again. We can kill each other, Charles. I have seen Dracula do it, and contemptuously spit out in a great stream the blood he has taken. That was how he murdered Armand Tesla. This is true death, from which there is no returning. This is the death I shall meet at dawn.

Two attendants held Manfred's arms, wrenching him away from me. His mouth was still attached to my neck like the sucker of a carnivorous plant. With a wet snap, it came free. Manfred shook his head, my blood dripping from his lips. Unsupported, I crumpled. Ten Brinken stepped over me to examine the Baron. That told me where I was in his priorities.

The Professor clapped his hands and called for the fliers to leave off their drinking. For those who had lost control, attendants had wooden-handled devices like tongue-depressors. A touch of a silver spatula causes enough pain to shock a vampire free of red thirst.

I felt myself lifted into a sitting position. I was as pliable as a broken doll. General Karnstein had taken notice of me. With a pointed forefinger, he slit his wrist and raised blood to my lips like water to a wounded man. I had not the strength to swallow but Karnstein let blood dribble into me. His line is pure and strong, but it was hours before I was fully recovered.

From the floor, I looked up at Baron von Richthofen. He turned away from me, but I could see the flush of my blood in his shaved hackles. Then, I fainted.

That night, Meinster's flier died. Murnau's skull became that of a huge rat, but his flesh did not change. Bone burst through his skin. The next day, we were sent from the chateau, duty done. That is all I know. You must think of this, for I believe it to be the important kernel of my story: *he* has shaped them, *he* has given them his blood, *he* has made them into something new.

Beauregard must have asked her to be more specific.

I mean Dracula. He is the ringmaster of the Flying Circus, and the Red Baron is his star act.

13

DR MOREAU AND MR WEST

The duckboards were warped and ill-fitting, but it was best to walk on them rather than the mud. The top layer was frozen but boot-shaped holes showed where others had sunk to the knee in viscid filth.

'We don't see many civilians parading through here,' said Lieutenant Templar, a handsome new-born with a quizzical eyebrow. 'The breed prefer to fight their wars from armchairs in Boodle's.'

'Boodle's is not my club,' Beauregard said, treading carefully.

'No offence meant. It shows pluck to come this far when you don't have to.'

'You are right. Would it were that I was possessed of such spirit. Sadly, I *do* have to be here.'

'Worse luck, then.'

The slip-trench was ten feet deep. Its higgledy-piggledy sandbag walls were mortared with frozen mud.

A projectile overshot the line, sailed above at a decent altitude, and exploded a hundred yards off, where fields were patched with the last of the snow. Earth rained down. Templar shook like a dog, raising a halo of loose dirt. Beauregard brushed the shoulders of his astrakhan coat.

'A whizz-bang,' said the lieutenant. 'Nasty beasts. Fritz has been lobbing the little devils all week. We think they're trying to fill in this thoroughfare.'

The slip-trench fed men and *matériel* to the front line. If breached, the blockage would have to be cleared.

Another shell whizzed over and banged in the abused field.

'Fritz's calibrations are off. That's two they've laid back there.'

Beauregard looked up. The late-afternoon sky was grey, dotted with wind-whipped earth fragments, trailed across with smoke. Faint in the low cloud were the buzzing black shapes of flying machines.

'If those bats report back to Hunland, the gunners will make a few twiddles and drop whizz-bangs right where we stand. It won't be pretty.'

Early in the war, a reporter wrote up such a situation in *The Times*, boosting home front morale with a picture of cheery Tommies capering in the knowledge that the enemy's heavy guns consistently missed their positions. Devoted readers in Berlin passed on information to the German artillery, who made adjustments with devastating upshot. Journalism was now strictly regulated. Well-intentioned boobs did more harm with jingo puff than iconoclasts like Kate Reed with trenchant criticism. Beauregard would rather have the white cliffs of Dover defended by Kate than by a regiment of Northcliffe's flag-waving grubs.

'Hurray,' Templar exclaimed, 'the Camels are coming.'

A triangular formation of British aeroplanes closed on the German spotters. The gunfire was a tiny sound, like the chattering of insects. The aerial battle was fought in and above the clouds.

'There's one down,' Templar said.

A winged fireball burst through cloud, wind shrieking around it, and streamed towards No Man's Land. It ploughed noisily into the ground.

Air supremacy meant preventing the enemy from using his aeroplanes to gather strategic intelligence. The Germans, and to some extent the Allies, wasted column inches on daring deeds of the knights of the sky, but it was a nasty, bloody business. As things stood, a British observer, unless he ran into Richthofen, was more likely than his German opposite number to bring back details of troop dispositions and gunnery emplacements.

Another German came down, slowly as if approaching an airfield. The machine went into a spiral and crumpled in the air as if colliding with an invisible wall. The pilot must have been dead in his cockpit.

'The slip-trench stays open to fight another day.'

Looking about, it did not seem a particularly notable achievement.

It was a fairly quiet afternoon at the front. Both sides bombarded non-committally, but there were no big shows on. Rumours flew that enemy divisions from the Eastern Front were filtering through Europe, freed by the peace negotiated with the new Russia. Naturally, the rumours were true. Beauregard had reports from the Diogenes Club's associates in Berlin that Hindenburg and Dracula were preparing for *Kaiserschlacht*. In a last push to victory, the remaining resources of the Central Powers would be thrown into a costly stab at Paris. '*Schlacht*' could be translated as 'attack', but also meant 'slaughter'. Knowing what was to come might not be enough to put a stop to it, especially if carefully gathered intelligence was ignored by the likes of Mireau and Haig.

Now they were near the front itself. The impact of shells was a permanent low-level earthquake. Everything shivered or rattled: tin hats, duckboards, mess kits, equipment, cracking ice, teeth. Beauregard was interested not in forwards positions but in an odd, underground emplacement just to the rear of the line.

Some months ago, he had learned Dr Moreau was supervising a front-line hospital, presumably ministering to the sorely wounded. This was the same researcher whose vivisections had earned him repeated expulsions from learned bodies and exposure in the popular press. Beauregard had run across the scientist before, in the thick of another bloody business. By his estimate of Moreau's character, it seemed unlikely the man harboured a patriotic or philanthropic impulse in his breast. Yet here he was, in the worst place in the world, ostensibly risking his own skin to ease appalling suffering.

In consideration of Gertrud Zelle's narrative, he wished to consult

Dr Moreau. If anyone this side of the lines could shed light on the darkness of the Chateau de Malinbois, he was the man.

Towards the front, the trench narrowed. More sandbags were exploded. Major earthworks showed where breaches had been shored up. Templar whistled a little tune, a strange chirrup. Beauregard had heard the new-born was a good officer, concerned for the men under him.

Three Tommies sat at a wonky table, smoking and playing cards. A hand stuck out of the packed-earth wall, cards fanned in a frozen white grip. After a few visits to the front, Beauregard was not shocked by the grim humour. The unknown soldier was too well embedded to be dug free without causing a collapse. His release would have to wait till after the war.

Beauregard remembered a cartoon of two British soldiers chatting in a shell-hole. 'I'm enlisted for twenty-five more years,' one says. 'You're lucky,' replies his comrade, 'I'm duration.'

Two men threw in their cards and the third consulted the hand dealt the dead man. If able to bet, he would have won. Aces and eights.

'Moreau's show is down here, sir,' Templar said, lifting a stiff canvas flap.

It was like the entrance to a mine. A tunnel sloped down, shored up with bags, floored with boards, roofed with corrugated iron. An electric light was strung up about twenty feet in, but there was darkness beyond. Treacly mud ran slowly from the trench into the tunnel, but was diverted into sluices. Beauregard could not imagine where the liquid filth ended up.

A high-pitched scream came from the tunnel, followed by lesser yelps and groans. The cries sounded more animal than human.

'It's always like that,' said Templar, eyebrow raised. 'Dr Moreau says pain is healthy. A person in pain can still feel. It's when you can't feel anything that you have to worry.'

Another shriek was cut through by a rasp like the downstroke of a saw.

'It's unusual to have a clinic this close to the line, isn't it?'

Templar nodded. 'It's practical, I suppose. But not good for morale. The situation is fearful enough without all this. Some of the men are spooked by the confounded din. They're more scared of being taken into the hole than of being wounded in the first place. Silly stories go around about the doctor using the wounded as experimental subjects.'

Beauregard could imagine. Given Moreau's reputation, the stories might not be all silliness.

'As if there were anything to be learned from torturing wounded men. It's absurd.'

Templar was a decent sort, for a vampire; perhaps too decent. Such saintliness often overlooked man's capacity for pointless cruelty.

Beauregard stepped into the tunnel. A curious miasma filled the enclosed space, a strong sulphurous smell. Wavering electric light made the walls reddish.

The lieutenant stayed outside, like an old-world vampire at the edge of consecrated ground.

'You can go on without me, sir. You can't miss it.'

Beauregard wondered if Templar were as immune from superstition as he claimed. He shook the young man's firm hand and walked past the light into the dark.

The tunnel ended at a solid iron door. Getting it down here and set into stony earth must have been a herculean task. An extraordinary soldier stood guard. Stooped almost double, he barely came up to Beauregard's waist. His arms were six inches longer than his sleeves, most of his brown face was matted with hair, large teeth pushed lips out in an apish grin and red marks, like healed wounds, showed in loose folds of skin around neck and wrists. His uniform bagged in some places and stretched in others.

Beauregard took the guard for a savage, perhaps indigenous to a South Sea corner of the Empire. He might be a pygmy afflicted with gigantism. The war called upon all manner of King Victor's subjects.

At Beauregard's approach, the guard wrapped long fingers around a rifle and did his best to stand straight. He bared remarkable teeth, yellow bone-spurs in an acre of bright-pink gum.

'I'm here to see Dr Moreau,' Beauregard said.

The guard's tiny eyes glittered. He snorted, nose moving as if free of his skull. More screams sounded from behind the door. The guard, who might be expected to be used to the noise, shrank in terror, cowering into an alcove.

'Dr Moreau,' Beauregard said, again.

The guard's furry brows knit with extreme concentration. He unwound his fingers from the rifle and took hold of a ring set in the door. He hauled the iron portal open in a succession of creaking lurches.

A draught of bloody stink belched out. Beauregard stepped into a chamber hewn out of earth and rock. A row of cots took up fully half the space. On most were patients with terrible wounds, strapped to bloody mattresses. Some stared silently through bandage masks, others keened in idiot pain. A bin overflowed with cut-up uniforms and sawn-through boots. Electric lights pulsed in time with an unreliable generator grumbling in another room. The walls glistened with fresh blood. Everything was speckled. Even the light-bulbs were spotted, blood drops cooked to brown moles.

He saw Dr Moreau at once, a powerfully built old man in a vilely streaked tunic, with a leonine mane of white hair. The doctor bent over the living remains of a soldier, prising apart exposed ribs with a steel implement. The patient was a skeleton clad in wet scraps of muscle and meat. Hurt eyes shone in the red wreck of a face. Exposed fangs clashed in a devil's grin. Beside Moreau, holding down the patient's shoulders, was a smaller man. Moreau gave a cry of triumph as bones parted. A squirt of purple blood shot into the assistant's face, smearing his thick spectacles.

'There, West,' Moreau said. 'The heart still beats.'

West, the assistant, tried to find a clean stretch of sleeve to wipe off his glasses.

'I am right again and you owe me half-a-crown.'

'Certainly, doctor,' West said. He had a flat accent, American or Canadian. 'I'll add it to the tally.'

'You are a witness,' Moreau said to Beauregard, the first time he had acknowledged the intrusion. 'Mr West wagered it was impossible for the heart to continue to function under such conditions, yet the resilient organ beats still.'

Moreau lifted his arm to give Beauregard a view of the heart. It pumped like a squeezing fist, though most of its tubes were severed.

'This man could live,' Moreau declared.

'Surely not,' West countered.

'Your debt will mount, my man. Observe, how tenacious these little snakes prove…'

The cut tubes writhed swiftly. An artery probed like a blind worm and reattached itself, blood flowing through it, the break healing. Layers of tissue clustered, swarming over the heart, burying it. The pulled-back ribs closed like a trap, assuming their normal formation. A wash of musculature flowed over the bones.

'The resilience of the vampire *corpus* may well be infinite,' Moreau said. 'Only human despair permits death and a man whose brain has been halved can know no despair. Instinct takes over the animal.'

The patient's head was severely pulped at the back. Flesh swarmed strangely around the eyes. Every scrap of the soldier lived tenaciously. Beauregard remembered Isolde's sad performance. In thirty years' research, Moreau and his like had not set a limit on the vampire power of regeneration.

'But without the brain,' West said, tapping the area of activity, 'the creature has no purpose, no coherence…'

Muscle strands hungrily lapped West's fingertip. He pulled his hand away and watched smugly as a cheeklike slab of flesh formed *over* a startled eye.

'This is not a living man,' said West, 'just a collection of disparate, individually mobile, parts and functions. The template of human form is held in the brain. Without that template, this senseless creature can only flow in a random search for freakish shape.'

Skin formed over the patient's mouth, ripping on teeth and healing again.

Moreau's huge face reddened with anger. 'This man is guilty of a failure of will. He has surrendered his grip on human shape.'

Moreau stood away from the cot, disappointed and angry. The patient's jaw hinged open, fangs extending like poignards, rending the new skin. A croaking exhalation emerged from the bloody hole.

'The voice is entirely lost,' Moreau said. 'This is merely an animal. It cannot be saved.'

He took a scalpel from his tunic pocket. Its blade shone silver.

'Stand back, West. This could be messy.'

Moreau knelt on the patient's abdomen, thrusting his scalpel down, cutting warty skin that had already grown thick. He sliced between the knitting ribs and punctured the heart. The patient convulsed and died. Moreau's fist sank entirely into the chest cavity. He pulled his gory hand free and wiped it on the patient's bedding.

'It was a mercy,' he said, perfunctorily. 'Now, sir, who might you be and why have you ventured into my domain?'

Beauregard forced himself to look away from the ragged corpse. It putrefied fast, settling liquidly on the cot, dripping over the edges. The very old ones turned to dust. The patient had been a vampire for less than the lifespan of a normal man.

'Dr Moreau, you will probably not remember me. My name is Charles Beauregard. We met once, many years ago, in the laboratory of Dr Henry Jekyll.'

Moreau did not care to be reminded of his late colleague. Irritation boiled in his deep-set eyes.

'I'm attached to military intelligence,' Beauregard said.

'Only "attached"?'

'Quite so.'

'Congratulations.'

West was sorting through the detritus on the cot, picking out bullets and shrapnel. He wore black rubber gloves.

'I'm not yet ready to present my findings,' said Moreau, gesturing to direct attention to his array of strapped-down patients. 'I have not had enough vampires to work with.'

'You mistake my purpose, doctor. I'm not here in connection with your current work…'

(whatever that might be)

'…but to solicit information which may be of service. It is with regard to another researcher in your field, Professor ten Brinken.'

At the mention of the name, Moreau looked up, alert.

'A charlatan,' he spat. 'Practically an alchemist.'

According to Beauregard's sources, Moreau and ten Brinken had come to blows at a congress held at the University of Ingolstadt in 1906. That suggested the professor was not a man of insignificant stature.

'We believe ten Brinken is the director of a secret project given the highest priority by the enemy.'

'Too much mysticism in the German mind. The gothic imagination perverts their brains. I don't deny ten Brinken is a daring thinker. But none of his results are verifiable. He surrounds himself with Teuton blood ritual. No control group, no hygienic conditions, no proper records.'

Judging from this clinic, Moreau had a singular definition of 'hygienic conditions'.

'No,' Moreau said, definitely. 'Whatever ten Brinken works on will prove worthless.'

The assistant fluttered around, getting his nerve up to interrupt the great man.

'What direction was he taking in his researches?' Beauregard asked.

'Before the war? Crackpot studies of lycanthropy. Arrant nonsense. The old wives' tale that werewolves have reversible skin, hairy on the inside. Twaddle about animal spirits mingling with those of men. He seemed to suggest shape-shifters are subject to a form of demonic possession. It was all tied to bloodlines. Germans are obsessed with blood, with racial purity, with the strength of ancient vampire lines.'

'Like that of Count Dracula?'

Moreau snarled. 'There's an elder who has done his worst to sow confusion. In his superstition, he encourages fools to think of vampires as supernatural creatures. That's a sure way to stay in the dark.'

West finished his probings and peeled off wet gloves.

'I heard Professor ten Brinken lecture at Miskatonic University in '09,' he said. Behind his spectacles, he had watery, nervous eyes.

'This is Mr Herbert West of Massachusetts,' Moreau introduced his colleague. 'He has been of some minor help to me. In time, he might have the makings of a scientist.'

'What was the subject of the professor's lecture?'

'The effects of blending bloodlines. Like breeding cattle for more meat and less string. He claimed to be able to induce shape-shifting in vampires whose line does not entail the facility. Also, he suggested his methods could "cure" many common conditions and limitations of the undead.'

'Conditions and limitations?'

'The extreme sensitivity to sunlight. Fear of religious artefacts. Allergic reaction to garlic or wolfsbane. Even the universal vulnerability to silver.'

'Tchah,' spat Moreau. 'Blood, blood, blood. To the Germans, it's all in the blood. It's as if the *corpus* was constituted of nothing but blood.'

'Did the professor produce any of his improved specimens?' Beauregard asked. 'A vampire who could survive being pierced by a silver arrow, for instance?'

West shrugged and looked at the dead puddle on the cot. 'It was all theory.'

'To call it "theory", is to dignify muddle-headedness,' Moreau said, angry. 'Only I am doing anything like real work in the field. Ten Brinken is a dunderhead and a dullard.'

'Langstrom of Gotham University claimed results with ten Brinken's methods,' West put in, 'but his experiment ended badly. They still haven't caught him.'

'I remember you now,' Moreau said to Beauregard. 'You were with that elder girl.'

'Thank you for your co-operation,' Beauregard said. 'You have been most helpful.'

For a moment, he was afraid Moreau would ask him for news of Geneviève. Thirty years ago, he had seemed ready to exercise a scientific interest in her. And his scientific interests always appeared to run in the direction of taking a scalpel to the subject and peering into the works of life.

'If you come by them, I'd be grateful for a look at ten Brinken's experimental logs,' Moreau said, in an exaggeratedly offhand manner that told Beauregard how seriously he really took his rival's work. 'Drivel, I'm sure, but even fools can stumble over the odd truth. In Germany there are fewer legal checks to pure research.'

Beauregard turned to leave. The guard lurked beyond the open door, his shadow distorted on the floor.

'Don't mind Ouran,' Moreau said. 'He's been with me for many years. A good and faithful servant.'

Beauregard wondered if the red marks on Ouran's neck were surgical scars. Before the war, Dr Moreau had been forced to leave England and continue his work elsewhere. But this close to the killing ground 'legal checks' were not in operation. Humanity was suspended for the duration.

Half-way to the surface, the screaming resumed as Dr Moreau and Mr West turned their attentions to the next wounded vampire. After a few minutes in the clinic, Beauregard felt he should strip off every item of clothing and have it thoroughly cleaned. Better yet, burned.

When he emerged from the tunnel, Lieutenant Templar was waiting. Cigarette in hand, he watched a fresh-blown smoke ring drift upwards and apart. Evening crept near. Even the smell of the trench was better than the foulness of Moreau's dissecting chamber. The staccato chatter of machine-guns cut through the droning thuds of the usual mortar fire.

'Getting busy,' Templar remarked. 'How did you like the doc?'

Beauregard said nothing but the lieutenant got the idea.

'I tell you I credit no stories, but if any of my lads cop one, I'd rather have them dragged through the wire and driven in a bumpy lorry to Amiens than let them be taken down there.'

14

KATE AND EDWIN

Opposite Wing HQ in Amiens was a small café where Kate sat in wait for her prey. Fortuitously, there was a small café opposite every site of military significance in France. By now, Kate was on familiar terms with them all.

She sipped blood-laced *anis*, unable to tell from which animal the blood might have come, and kept an eye on comings and goings across the road. There was much activity; Wing was busier after dark than in the afternoon. The HQ was solidly built, a converted municipal building.

The trail had led her this far.

'Bone jaw, mamzel,' said an American. 'Je m'apple Eddie Bartlett. Private, First-Class.'

She looked at the doughboy over the tops of her blue glasses. The short, grinning, impossibly young warmfellow was confident of an eager reception. The gratitude of French girls was a major incentive to army recruitment in the United States.

'You've certainly learned to "parley-voo" mighty fine, Mr Yank.'

Private Bartlett was downcast. He must have been practising his line of chat ever since his troopship left New York. His comrades brayed with laughter. She smiled and her fangs peeped out. Bartlett apologised incoherently and returned to his friends' table. She hoped he found a willing mademoiselle before a bullet found him. He was a

141

nice-looking fellow and she regretted being cool towards him. It was not often she was mistaken for an alluring French siren. She liked the taste of Americans. Mr Frank Harris, of course, had been an American, a former cowboy. Unburdened by history, there was a lightness to their blood.

She was sorely thirsty. Blood-in-*anis* did little more than prick her appetites. Sometimes, she got so concentrated on one of her crusades that she misremembered necessities. She flicked her tongue over sharpening teeth. Amiens was near enough the lines for everything to shudder constantly. The surface of her drink wobbled slightly as she felt each bombardment in her gums.

Edwin Winthrop strolled out of Wing HQ, pausing on the steps to return the salute of a dusty sergeant. Kate pretended not to notice, but was so placed that Edwin could not help but spot her. The approach struck her as subtler than making a futile attempt to stay out of his sight. Pleased by his own perspicacity, he might in a burst of male confidence let something slip. For a moment, she thought he might add her presence to his report to Charles and pass by about his business. She tried to send out waves of vampire fascination by mental telepathy. It was all nonsense, at least in her bloodline, but it could not hurt.

Edwin made a decision. He crossed the street, dodging a motorcycle despatch rider, and bore down on her. She froze her face, suppressing a smile that might betoken a certain smugness and expectation of victory.

'Miss Mouse, is it not?'

She made casual play of noticing and recognising him.

'Edwin, good evening. You have not your guard dog about you?'

He looked about. Dravot was nowhere in sight. Even Edwin was not always aware of the presence of his protector.

'I dare say the sergeant might be concealed in a haystack somewhere nearby. In disguise, of course.'

'I should not be at all surprised.'

'He tells me you and he are old friends.'

Kate remembered the Terror. *Stories* circulated about Daniel

Dravot's role in affairs of great moment, stories she had never quite pinned down. The sergeant did his duty by the angels, but when an omelette was to be made he was the sort who willingly broke the eggs.

'He also tells me you are not as silly as you seem.'

She laughed to cover annoyance. 'No one could be as silly as I seem, surely?'

Edwin laughed too, genuinely. He was still puzzled by her. That was good. If he was puzzled, he was interested. As he tried to find out about her, she could learn from him.

'Are you chasing some poor general? Intent on wrecking yet another martial reputation?'

'On the contrary, I am composing an encomium to the steadfast qualities of our gallant staff officers.'

He sat opposite her. There was comment from Private Bartlett's table.

'Watch out, pal,' Bartlett shouted. 'She bites.'

'You have acquired a *claque*?'

Kate twitched her nose.

'You are blushing. It brings out your freckles.'

For a moment, she thought the bombardment was oddly regular, then she realised she was listening to Edwin's heartbeat, lulled by his strong pulse. Her glass was empty.

'Might I buy you a drink, Kate?'

'No thank you. I'm not thirsty.'

'I should have thought you were always thirsty.'

Her heart ached sharply. She would like a drink but not the sort Edwin might buy for her.

'My associate Charles Beauregard speaks highly of you, too. Though he made sure to remind me you were old enough to be my mother.'

'I am barely out of the cradle. I haven't been dead for thirty years yet.'

He was going to ask her what it was like. All young men did, eventually. It was a two-fold question: what was it like being a vampire, and what was it like to be bitten by a vampire?

The *patron* came over. Edwin ordered brandy giving her the chance to reconsider his offer.

'I'll take vanilla,' she said, like a silly girl in a Paris street café. Edwin hadn't heard the expression before. She moderated her request to another blood-in-*anis*.

When he had sipped his drink, he looked at her and began, 'Kate…'

'"What is it like?"'

He was astounded she had read his mind, convinced of her supernatural powers. She was amused and a little triumphant.

'It is hard to explain. It is one of those matters one has to experience for oneself. Like war and love.'

Edwin considered her answer and looked her square in the face. Her tinted spectacles were no shield against his gaze.

'You are after me, Kate Reed. I'm not sure to what end, but I'm certain you are after me.'

She shrugged. 'You have a sweetheart at home?'

He weighed the possibilities and nodded. 'Catriona Kaye. We're engaged. She's very modern.'

'Unlike myself, a cobwebbed relic of another age.'

'She is a century baby. I call her Cat.'

'And so might I.'

The tang of Edwin's brandy was in her nose. The *anis* taste on her tongue did not dull her sense of him.

'Does your fiancée want you to turn?'

'We haven't discussed the matter.'

'You'll have to.'

'I like being warm.'

'Not a foolish thought.'

'You are no propagandist for the undead state, then?'

Edwin's breath misted. There was a February evening chill. The warm wore scarves and gloves.

'I'll take vanilla.'

'Pardon?'

'I am the only one of my sisters-in-darkness to survive. It is a thorny thing, this condition, not predictable. After thirty years, the doctors don't fully understand it. To turn is to gamble on one's own strengths. Most new-borns die unpleasantly.'

She had no doubt Edwin would turn magnificently. Even as a warm man, he had a vampire sharpness about him.

'Catriona is my name in Scots. Katharine. Are we alike?'

He was surprised by the question.

'You must have something in common. She wants to be a journalist.'

'Will you let her follow a profession?'

'My inclination would be to insist on it. Her father takes a different view. He's a clergyman. She's an agnostic. They're always rowing.'

Annoyingly, she felt sympathy for Edwin's inconvenient attachment. Catriona Kaye sounded like an exact copy of her younger, warm self. Only prettier. Kate would not be able to win him away from the other woman and make of him a docile informant. Her career as a Mata Hari was ended before it could begin.

'Why the interest in my personal arrangements? I thought you ran more to politics and matters of great moment?'

'Journalism needs the human touch. Tiny insights to illuminate dry facts.'

Edwin finished his drink. His blood would be warmed by the brandy, flavoured strongly. An envelope edge peeped out of his jacket. He demurely pushed it out of sight.

'Sealed orders?'

He grinned. 'I couldn't possibly say.'

'I would be prepared to make a wager with you,' she said. 'That I know where you are to be sent.'

'If you could do that, you would indeed be a sorceress. I've no idea what is in these orders.'

She knew from his heartbeat that he was lying but let it pass.

'What would you be prepared to wager?'

She shrugged.

'A kiss?' he suggested.

Her eyeteeth lengthened minutely. She felt little pains, not unpleasant, in the nerves of her fangs.

'Very well,' she said. 'You are recalled to London.'

He took out his envelope and opened it. He read his orders, keeping them close to his chest, chuckling.

'You have lost your wager.'

'Am I to take your word for it?'

'As an officer and something reasonably approaching a gentleman?'

'Officers and gentlemen make the best liars. Especially intelligence officers. Lying is their profession, just as the truth is mine.'

'I could name the odd journalist not unaquainted with mendacity.'

'Touché.'

'You accept you have lost?'

'I suppose I shall have to.'

They stood, awkwardly, and looked at each other. He was not a tall man, within a few inches of her five-foot-one. He kissed her on the lips. His warmth shocked her, jolting fire through her veins. There was no blood but she had the contact she knew from feeding. It was not a long kiss. Bartlett's table cheered and jeered. She could not draw anything much from Edwin's mind. Just a drop of blood and she would know things. Edwin drew away. His hands opened and his orders drifted down past the table.

'That'd curl your hair,' he said, eyes wide.

With the swiftness of the undead, she bent down and picked up the paper, presenting it to Edwin. He was in a brief reverie, befuddled by the press of her lips. The paper passed only briefly through her glance but she knew Edwin was ordered to return to the airfield at Maranique and arrange another reconnaissance flight to the Chateau de Malinbois.

146

'Now that wasn't what you expected?' Kate said.

'I'll say not. You're electric, aren't you. Like an eel?'

PART TWO

NO MAN'S LAND

15

THE VILE, THE VIOLENT AND THE VEIN

'This is absolutely intolerable,' ranted Ewers. 'We were to be met at the station. A car was to be provided for us. This delay was not to happen.'

Poe dumped his carpet-bag on the platform as gloomy soldiers clumped around him. It was just past sunset. His red thirst was roused, an exquisite torture.

'Stakes will be hoist,' Ewers vowed. 'Guts will be spitted for this!'

Small irritations were disproportionately infuriating to Hanns Heinz Ewers. As his sense of self-importance was sorely exaggerated, so was his wrath when others refused to credit him with the inflated position to which he laid claim. Were he a subscriber to the theories of Sigmund Freud, Poe would be forced to conclude that Ewers's phallus was remarkably tiny.

Actually, he felt the Viennese Jew said much of interest. Also, he deserved his place in history. Franz Joseph had been on the point of acceding to a petition underwritten by the House of Rothschild and rescinding the Edict of Graz when Freud published *The Oral-Sadistic Impulse*. With its especial relevance to the undead, the book was evidence that the Hebrew race was so morally degraded, not to mention dangerously supportive of subversive notions, that the Edict should not only remain in force but be considerably strengthened.

151

'There should be no place for inefficiency in the German soul,' Ewers continued. 'It should be burned out with blood and iron.'

The station was Péronne, near Cappy. They were in France, only a few miles from the lines. This was the Somme. In Berlin, Poe had heard the bombardment as a tiny echo. The audibility grew as the train neared the war. Even Ewers heard it well before the French border. The noise wore on Poe's thin nerves; if he stayed too long near the front, he might go mad.

'Do they expect me to walk?'

In Ewers's tirade, 'us' had been replaced by 'me'. It was no feat of ratiocination to deduce that Ewers felt his was the important mission at Chateau de Malinbois, and Edgar Poe merely the hanger-on. If Ewers were such a magnificent wielder of the mighty pen, why had not he been engaged to create this marvellous book?

Ewers had two heavy trunks to Poe's one travelling bag and was unused to arriving at a station without exciting a swarm of gaudy-uniformed porters eager to serve his purpose to the death. Péronne was given over entirely to the military. Any Frenchmen normally employed as attendants were either dead or a few miles off, pointing rifles at the German lines.

Having borne its latest cargo of grey-clad bodies to the altar of war, the locomotive breathed angry dragon-steam. The huge, black engine had a smokestack to shame a paddle-steamer. The crest of Dracula was picked out in gilt on the boiler, somewhat obscured by mud and soot.

The Graf's first appointment in the Kaiser's service was as Director of Imperial Railways. Deviation from the timetable by more than five minutes was punishable by three strokes across the back with the flat of a heated sword. If a miscreant engineer committed a second offence, he was thrown alive into his own furnace. The Graf's foresight became evident in the first hours of the war: eleven-thousand individual trains were diverted from civilian service to convey several million reservists from their homes to regimental depots and then to the front. The Schlieffen Plan, devised under the Graf's patronage, was less a campaign strategy in the nineteenth-century sense than a colossal railway timetable.

'Hoy,' Ewers shouted, 'my luggage.'

Vast wheels ground as the train readied to move on. Ewers ran up and down, coat-tails flapping in scalding steam. Brass-bound trunks were tossed out of a carriage on to the platform. Good German workmanship showed as the sturdy cases buckled but did not break. Ewers shouted threats at the departing train, promising numbers and names had been noted down and that steps would be taken to ensure swift dismissal and punitive treatment.

There was a bad smell in the air. Poe recognised it from his last war. The war for Southern Independence. The one they had lost. He had never really purged the taste from his spittle. Mud, gunpowder, human waste, fire and blood. There were new ingredients, petrol and cordite, but the underlying stench was the same on the Somme as at Antietam. For a moment, he was overcome. Death crowded in on his brain, a black flag wrapped around his head, suffocating, blinding, choking.

'What are you standing there for?' Ewers snapped. 'You look like a scarecrow.'

Ewers did not feel anything. That said much about him.

'Pah,' Ewers spat, waving a dismissive arm.

Poe calmed. He must feed, soon. As always when at the lip of exhaustion and starvation, his senses were more acute. To feel too much is to be mad.

It was little wonder no car waited for them. Beyond the shuttered ticket office and a shelled-out waiting room was military chaos. Soldiers arriving at or returning to the front were sorted into divisions and found places on carts and lorries that took them to where the fighting was done. Sergeants shouted, with the universal bark of sergeants all through history. Men jumped, rifles and kit tangled.

Ewers reluctantly abandoned his trunks into the care of a starch-spined little corporal with a dash of moustache and a stiff-armed

153

salute. Poe saw in the man the makings of a martinet. They went out on to the station forecourt.

The wall of the ticket office was bullet-pocked at chest height. Rough wooden caskets were stacked to the height of a telegraph pole. An open coffin by the pile was filled to the depth of an inch with undisturbed snow, as if awaiting an Eskimo vampire who slept on a layer of his native ice. Péronne had been extensively bombarded several times and few buildings were undisturbed. Windows were blown out, roofs sundered, doors burned through, chimneys toppled.

'You there,' Ewers shouted at a sergeant, 'which way to the Chateau de Malinbois?'

The sergeant, a burly and moustachioed warmfellow, cringed at the sound of the name and shook his head, muttering darkly.

'You don't want to go to the castle, sir,' he said.

'Quite the contrary. We do the business of the Kaiser.'

Ewers was exasperated but Poe was struck by the sergeant's evident fear and disgust. Malinbois was obviously a house of unhappy and frightful repute.

'The castle is a bad place,' the sergeant explained. 'Dead things live there. Things that should be walled up and forgotten.'

Ewers snarled, showing fangs. The soldier was not troubled by the vampire display. So, worse things waited at the chateau. Poe's interest was almost excited. The sergeant tottered off, leaving Ewers exhaling steam like a train.

'Superstitious peasant,' Ewers spat.

Poe's fangs ached and his heart burned. He needed to drink. Ewers promised luxuries at Malinbois but this fabled castle seemed ever more remote. Official posters warned against fraternisation and disease. It was forbidden to drink the blood of French civilians. It might just as well be forbidden to breathe French air.

A child stood under a street-lamp watching the soldiers, a girl of eleven or twelve. Dressed in a clean pinafore, she had very white skin. In the fall of light, she shone. She was warm. Poe heard her heart beat, heard every rustle of her clothes. Through the fug of war, he tasted the sweetness of her breath.

She looked at him with old eyes. For an instant, she was Virginia. They all looked like Virginia, no matter the colour of their eyes or the style of their hair. There was always a touch of Virginia. He was drawn to the child, pulled across the cratered street. There was already an understanding between them.

'Herr Poe,' Ewers called, distant and irritated.

Reaching the light, he hesitated. The girl's face glowed with life. He was not sure he could touch her without being burned. Caution fought his impulses. She was not Virginia. This was a practised French flirt. She was here for someone like him. He saw scabs on her throat, healed bite-marks spreading like a rash from just under her tiny ear down to her collar. She smiled. Her teeth were not good.

Ewers, who had caught up with Poe, voiced exasperation, but did not get between them. He recognised Poe's need.

'If you must,' Ewers said. 'But be quick about it. We are expected at the chateau.'

Poe imagined Ewers was in another country. His voice was faint, the girl's heartbeat loud. With practised ease, she took his hand and tugged him past the light, towards an alley.

'This is what the posters warn against,' Ewers complained.

Ewers could not spoil the moment. There was already a perfect love. Poe could not close his mouth over his incisors. He cooed, trying to soothe the child. She was not disturbed by his fierce expression.

'Hurry up, Poe. Bite the whore and be done with it.'

Poe waved his hand to silence Ewers and was drawn into the dark, pulled down to his knees. He felt cobbles through his thin trousers. Rinds of hard ice lodged between the stones. The girl slipped into his arms and kissed him gently on the cheek and lips. Her taste was fire. Overpowered, he forced her head back and clamped his mouth to her pulsing neck. Old wounds opened as his teeth slid through her skin. Sweet blood seeped into his mouth, covering his tongue.

He drank, greedily, impassioned. The child writhed in his embrace. As he drank, he knew her. Her name was Gilberte, but her family called her Gigi. He saw her father shot, her mother run off. He saw her in other embraces, suckling other vampires. Her short life was beautiful tragedy. Her blood was poetry.

'Careful, you'll kill the little beast,' Ewers said, hands on Poe's shoulder, wrenching him away.

With a great effort, Poe left the flowing wound. The child's blood warmed and delighted him still, but he was overcome with regret and shame. His face was wet with tears.

'There'll be hell if she dies,' Ewers said.

Poe looked into the girl's face. It was a blank but he tasted her hate, her contempt. Gigi was cold in his arms, not dead but her mind flown for the moment, hidden deep inside as her body suffered this unpleasant transaction.

'Damn,' Ewers breathed. 'Poe, this is all your fault.'

Ewers was in the grip of sudden bloodlust. Poe had forgotten that the German was a vampire too. His eyes flushed red, his face roughened. Blunt fangs grew out of his unsmiling face.

'The least you can do is watch the alley,' Ewers ordered.

Gigi was not even afraid. It was only by force of will, compounded by Ewers's nagging, that Poe had resisted draining the child completely. He was not sure Ewers could exert as much self-control. His own past was not innocent of unwilled tragedies. With time, all vampires become killers. With more time, Poe feared, all vampires come to delight in killing.

Ewers fell on the shrinking child, ripping the collar from her bloody neck. He was a savage, brutally forcing her to yield what Poe had coaxed from her.

The German drank from the feebly struggling girl. His whole weight was on her. His back heaved. Two buttons above his coat-tails caught stray light, flashing like blind eyes. Poe imagined himself driving a length of sharpened wood into Ewers's back, piercing his dead heart.

This girl, tonight, would survive. Poe would see to that. But other girls, other nights, would not.

As he glutted himself, Ewers made noises like a pig. His face was bloodied. The red was black in the dark. Gigi was in a merciful swoon, great gashes in her neck and chest still leaking.

He took Ewers's arms and tried to lift him away. Ewers spasmed and was insensate in Poe's grip. He was easily rolled off Gigi. Poe ignored him and saw to the child. Her heartbeat was faint but strong. She would recover. He cradled the girl, not wanting to drink further. Their link faded, memories passing from his mind, but he wished to treasure her a few moments more. Only in these brief moments could he be calm in himself, at peace.

Cold doubts nibbled around the edges of his momentary contentment. Ewers, wiping his face, stood. He rearranged his clothes huffily, with pointed little gestures. He was angry, but smug.

'You are just like me, Poe. In us, desire runs strong. It is why we create.'

The child moaned, swimming from the pool of sleep towards the surface of consciousness.

'We are not alike at all,' Poe said, coldly.

Ewers brushed the thought aside and summoned concentration. He was unsteady. Gigi's blood was rich. Poe too felt added senses, a dangerous exhilaration coupled with awareness of the yawning abyss below. Scarlet sparks danced in the corners of his vision.

'We are expected at the chateau,' Ewers insisted. 'We must commandeer transport.'

Poe laid down the girl. She curled up like a cat. He rearranged her collar. Ewers had torn off too many buttons. Poe could not refasten her chemise and pinafore but made sure she was decently covered.

'Ewers, we have an obligation. To the child.'

Exasperated, Ewers fished in his waistcoat. He tossed a coin to the cobbles. Poe scooped it up and slipped it into the girl's hand. In half-sleep, she made a fist about the treasure.

They left Gigi and returned to the station. A car stood outside, driver at the wheel, officer standing by. When the officer saw Poe and Ewers, he snapped off a straight-backed salute.

'I am Oberst Theo von Kretschmar-Schuldorff. I have looked forward immensely to meeting the great writer, Mr Edgar Allan Poe.'

The officer spoke in clear English. He was a sharp new-born.

'Well, this is him,' Ewers said, in German.

Poe shook the officer's hand. Kretschmar-Schuldorff's eyes swivelled sideways tinily, taking in the condition of the new arrivals. Poe had wiped himself with a handkerchief but Ewers's clothes and face were spotted with drying blood. The officer had formed an opinion but would do his duty and keep it to himself.

Ewers stormed off to reclaim his trunks from the martinet-in-the-making. Poe was helped into the car by Kretschmar-Schuldorff. The Oberst treated him with the deference due a very old lady whose dreadful smell must never be mentioned.

What Poe had taken from Gigi was gone completely. His red thirst was abated but fearful realities returned. The noise of shelling and the stench of death were again paramount.

'I no longer use my stepfather's name,' Poe told the officer. 'I am simply Edgar Poe.'

Kretschmar-Schuldorff took mental note. Names and ranks were as important as uniforms and decorations to his class. He was a Uhlan, attached to the Air Service. Many gallant cavalrymen traded steeds for wings in this war.

Ewers returned with his serf, each dragging a trunk. The corporal's electric blue eyes were alive with resentment.

'We thought ourselves abandoned,' Ewers said, brusquely. 'What kept you?'

Oberst von Kretschmar-Schuldorff did not shrug, but his eyes narrowed minutely. Hanns Heinz Ewers was not making a comrade of this man.

'The war,' he said, explaining everything.

16

TWICE BITTEN

'The rule of "once bitten, twice shy" seems to have no currency with you,' said Major Cundall.

'Under the circumstances, you might say "once bitten" means we're on to something.'

Cundall sighed but his blood was up. Winthrop saw past the mask now. Behind the cynicism, the flight commander was a tiger. He had not won his DSO and Bar with wittily cutting remarks.

'So Diogenes insists we have another bash at Malinbois?'

'It's the general thought,' Winthrop explained.

Through an enchantment, Albright's cracked plates had been developed. Jagged white lines streaked across the photographs and areas were blank, but the castle could be seen. Winthrop laid out the photographs on the farmhouse table. The vampire pilots gathered round.

'This is the tower we're interested in,' he said.

Cundall considered the indicated area. 'Looks like a diving board. Do the air pirates of JG1 make prisoners walk the plank?'

The top of the tower was sheared off. A board affair jutted out of it. The area of interest corresponded with the most damage to the plate.

'What's that shadow?' Bigglesworth asked. 'Mostly under the blotch? Is that an observer? A gun position?'

Diogenes had also thought it a puzzle. Winthrop tapped the scale marks at the edge of the photograph.

'If it's an observer, he must be a giant,' he said. 'Fifteen feet tall.'

'It's a gargoyle, old thing,' put in Courtney. 'Devilish fond of gargoyles, the Hun.'

'Malinbois was French until JG1 moved in.'

'*Plus de* gargoyles *en France*, too,' said Courtney. 'You should have clocked the mademoiselle from Armentières I sported on my last leave.'

Some pilots laughed bitterly. Winthrop suffered less ragging on this visit. Nobody mentioned Spenser or Albright. He noticed the odd new face and tried not to think which old ones were absent. There was an army show on, readying for the enemy push everyone expected before spring. Cundall's Condors had spent the last few days knocking spotters out of the sky.

'Looks like we're in for a twilight patrol,' Lacey said, almost keen. 'If we flit over *en masse*, we'll ruffle the red fighting eagle's feathers.'

'Baron von Richthofen,' Roy Brown said, miserably. 'Someone has to kill him some time.'

'Someone has to kill everyone some time,' said Cundall, thinking it over. At bottom, he was a cautious sort. It was probably why he had survived this long.

'Diogenes suggests a full patrol this time,' Winthrop said, knowing the flight commander was entitled to be annoyed with the change of policy.

'Fair enough,' Cundall said, mildly. 'Courtney, pick an observer and take the Harry Tate.'

The pilot – a Tasmanian, Winthrop had learned – groaned. The RE8 was not a popular kite. They were called 'flapping ducks', close relatives of the sitting variety.

'I'll fly the tip of the formation. Don't fret so, Courtney. I'll baby you through.'

Courtney theatrically clutched his heart. For his part, Winthrop was pleased the flight commander was choosing the men for this patrol rather than delegating the task.

'Since we had such little fortune with the As last time,' Cundall said, cruelly, 'we'll put the Bs in the air this show. Bigglesworth, Ball, Brown, you're up. And, to add a little alphabetical variety, let us, by all means, have a Williamson to balance things out.'

The pilots began climbing into their Sidcots and hauling on fleece-lined boots. Albert Ball, bent the wrong way in several places, wriggled into flying kit by unorthodox but efficient means. Roy Brown, the sour little Canadian, drank from a pitcher of milk and cow's blood.

'Tummy trouble,' Ginger explained. 'Brown's soothing his ulcer.'

Brown looked pained but kept drinking. Winthrop understood how a man in this line of work could nurture an ulcer.

'I say,' Courtney said, 'my usual dance partner in the Harry Tate is Curtiss Stryker and he's off sick. Ate someone who disagreed with him, I fear.'

Allard looked grim, expecting to be volunteered. Instead, Cundall turned to Winthrop, smiling evilly.

'Winthrop, my precious prince, have you ever fired a Lewis gun in anger?'

'I know which end to hold.'

'That'll do you.' He thumbed towards the ceiling. 'Ever been up?'

'I've been given a lift across the Channel a couple of times. I've even held the stick and not plunged to Earth.'

'A veteran,' Courtney snorted.

'Topping,' Cundall said, 'you won't puke or anything. Care to come along on this jaunt? After all, it is Diogenes' show. Not mandatory, or anything. Just thought you might like the trip. The scenery is terribly picturesque at sunset.'

'I'd love to come,' Winthrop said, evenly. He was not entitled to be afraid.

'Good man,' said Cundall. 'Ginger, find our friend some kit, would you? He's a warm one, so we'd best keep him that way.'

Whatever the patrol was like, it could not be as bad as hanging around waiting for it to come back. If it came back. He had the impulse to jot a few lines. He pulled out his pocketbook and a stub of pencil.

'Last will and testament?' Courtney asked.

'No, just notes. Gathering intelligence is a matter of making notes.'

'Whatever you say, old son. I always cheer myself up thinking of people I owe money to. If I go west, plenty will be mightily browned off.'

Winthrop thought hard, and wrote 'Dear Cat, if you get this, I've run into serious bother. Don't let it knock you too much. Love you desperately. Edwin.'

It was feeble but it would have to do. He begged an envelope from Algy Lissie and gummed the letter in. It was a duty done.

Ginger returned with full flying kit. Winthrop did not ask who had last worn it. Like a discreet valet, the vampire helped him dress. First, he was required to empty his pockets of documents which might interest the Boche if he were captured. A couple of enigmatic despatches from the Diogenes Club went into a shoebox. He chose to keep his matches, cigarette case and a picture of Catriona.

'Pretty girl,' Ginger commented. 'Swanny neck.'

Winthrop shivered a little and signed a form pasted to the top of the box. 'I swear on my honour that I do not have on my person or on my machine any letters or papers of use to the enemy.'

Over his khaki shirt and trousers, Winthrop put on two ragged wool pullovers and a pair of arctic pyjama bottoms. Then he clambered into his Sidcot, a loose gaberdine one-piece lined with lamb's wool. Paying careful attention, Ginger practically mummified Winthrop's head: applying first a silk scarf to the neck, then a liberal smearing of cold whale oil to the cheeks and forehead, a thick balaclava helmet, a non-absorbent Nuchwang dogskin face mask and, finally, triplex goggles tinted for night-flying. The outfit was completed by thigh-high boots and muskrat gauntlets. With everything buckled together,

Winthrop was completely swaddled, a rotund snowman, his arms stuck out and he waddled rather than walked.

'It's getting hottish in here,' he said.

'It'll get cold sharpish up there,' Ginger said. 'Now put your cross on this.'

Ginger presented an FS20 for signature. Winthrop glanced at the form as he scribbled his name. After a list of the gear issued to him, it stated 'These are property of the public. Losses due to the exigencies of campaign must be certified by the officer commanding.'

'Grand,' Ginger said. 'Now, if you go down in flames, the RFC will dun your widow and orphans for the cost of your underwear.'

'I'm not married,' Winthrop said, thinking of Catriona.

'That's probably for the best.'

'Good old bloody old Harry Tate,' Courtney said, patting the side of the RE8. The two-seater spotter was supposed to be sheepish in the air, which was why Cundall was putting up five Sopwith Snipe fighters as guard dogs.

Winthrop gave Dravot his letter and told him to forwards it to the addressee if anything untoward happened. The sergeant nodded, understanding, and did not try to tell him he was certain everything would be all right.

Courtney helped Winthrop climb into the rear cockpit. It was not easy to slip his clothes-expanded bulk past the ring-mounted Lewis. Once he was in the wicker seat, the handles of the machine-gun stuck uncomfortably into his chest.

The pilot hauled himself up and hung on the machine's side, peering into Winthrop's cockpit. He showed him how to fasten the Sutton safety harness: four straps for shoulders and thighs, fixed together with a central pin held by a spring clip. If struck just right, the whole thing came apart allowing swift escape. Not that there was anywhere safe to go at 6,500 feet.

'A tip, old thing, if you see anything flitting past with a Maltese cross on its planes, fire about fifty yards in front of it. If you point at its side, it'll be gone by the time the bullets get there.'

'What if it's coming straight at me?' Winthrop asked.

'Then empty your drum into its nose and pray. Because there'll be a Hun behind a pair of Spandaus with exactly the same idea.'

'Where's the camera lever?'

Courtney tapped a toggle.

'I'll tell you when I'm taking pictures so you can steady the aeroplane.'

'You can tell me what you like but I doubt I'll hear a thing. It's noisy up there.'

He remembered his Channel flights. Even on a still day, the rush of wind was a roar. And even in mid-summer, the thermometer quickly fell below freezing. Recalling the stabs of colicky abdominal pain that had made a howling misery of his first flight, he summoned a mighty burp. At height, intestinal gases swelled to double their volume on the ground. Courtney did not pass comment on the big belch, but looked a fraction less worried about Winthrop.

'How's our new ace?' Cundall asked. The flight commander, helmet in hand, was looking over the RE8.

'He'll be the Hawker of 1918.'

The pilot was ragging him. In November 1916, Major Lanoe Hawker, VC, DSO, was Britain's highest-scoring pilot. Shot down and killed by Manfred von Richthofen, he was the Red Baron's eleventh victory.

'Just look after him, Courtney.'

'Not a hair on his head will be harmed. This I pledge on the honour of Cundall's Condors.'

'I'm a lost cause then.'

Winthrop no more truly felt brittle bravado than Courtney. It was how pilots were supposed to act, so they all did their best.

Courtney ducked under the wing and dropped into the forward cockpit, jostling the stick. The movable feast of Winthrop's Lewis was augmented by the pilot's fixed Vickers.

Winthrop found himself facing backwards, but twisted in the cockpit to follow Courtney's procedure. The pilot checked his Aldis sight and the engine gauges, humming 'Up in a Balloon, Boys' to himself. After tapping the compass to see if the needle moved freely, he confirmed that the height indicator was set to zero and the bubble was central in the spirit-level that showed if the machine was flying on an even keel. When Courtney slipped goggles over his eyes, Winthrop followed suit.

The Snipes taxied down the field in arrow formation, Cundall at the point. Courtney turned his engine a couple of times to check its air-worthiness, then let the petrol flood in. Most machine failure in the air was due to interruption of the flow of fuel. A ground man clunkily spun the RE8's propellor.

'Contact, sir?' the mechanic asked.

'Contact, Jiggs,' Courtney agreed, flicking switches as the groundman gave the propellor a whirl. The air-cooled Daimler engine caught at once, belching black smoke and raising a slipstream whirlwind that tore at Jiggs's hair and whipped everyone standing within fifty yards. The pilot advanced the throttle for two minutes, upping the revolutions, as mechanics got a hold on the strings attached to the wooden chocks jammed under the RE8's wheels.

Satisfied with the engine sound, Courtney waved his hand like a swimming fish. The mechanics pulled the chocks free and Jiggs gave the pilot a smart salute. Courtney replied with a wave and manoeuvred the ungainly aircraft into formation with the fighters, which were taking off at intervals of about a minute. All the Snipes were aloft by the time the RE8 got under way.

There was a lurch and Winthrop was forced to turn round by the rush of wind. A cold blast shot straight down the back of his neck, icy air ballooning inside his Sidcot. He looked down the field at Dravot and the ground crew, their long shadows stretched in front of them. He remembered to clamp his jaw shut to avoid biting his tongue. The RE8 bumped a couple of times on the iron-hard field, then lifted off.

The jogging shudder stopped and he was excited by the smoothness of the ride. There were no pot-holes in the air. He felt a thrill in his water as Courtney gunned the engine and the machine picked up speed and gained altitude.

The farmhouse and the people on the field receded. The sun was not yet down and stretches of unmelted snow shone grey. Flat, dreary ground sped by below them. Despite the wrapping, Winthrop was completely chilled. If he relaxed his jaw muscles a fraction, his teeth would chatter forever.

He moved steadily, swivelling his seat inside his cockpit, bringing the Lewis round with him. The gun was fixed to a scarf-ring, a rail rimming the hole in the fuselage. He wanted to see where they were going. Up ahead, Cundall's Snipe was a fixed point, streamers on his struts marking him as squadron leader. The other machines flew in perfect formation to either side. Ball and Bigglesworth were at the extremes of the arrowhead, flying only a little forwards of Courtney. It must be a trial to keep the nippy little fighters in pace with the lumbering Harry Tate.

He got more used to the cold. Flying was easier for vampires but a warm man could bear it. The exhilaration was undeniable. In this century, the skies would call to the adventurous as the sea had to their forefathers. It was a shame such romance was wasted in war.

Down below, in a wasteland where there had been a country lane, a sexless figure leaned on a bicycle and waved up. An unknown friend, though somehow familiar. Winthrop felt kindly towards the anonymous bundle and tried to get an arm out of the cockpit to wave back. The wind fell on his arm like a blow.

They passed a deep scar across the landscape. He realised it was the Allied lines. They were over No Man's Land. The ground below was pocked and ravaged as if a dozen earthquakes had struck at once, just as a hundred volcanoes were erupting and a thousand meteors pounding the landscape. Tons of shells had fallen on every square yard. After another scar, the German trenches, they were in enemy territory, Hunland.

17

A SOLITARY CYCLIST

She had to pedal at speed so her greatcoat's tails would not flap into the spokes. Given the state of the roads near the lines, she came off her bicycle at least once an hour. With vampire resilience, she felt hardly anything from her tumbles. Most bruises faded inside a minute. Kate would have enjoyed the rush if the air here had not tasted of ash and death. When life passes, blood spoils instantly like milk left in the sun. The stench of rancid blood hung miasma-like.

The lanes were narrow and shell-holed. She wove from side to side, skirting cavities. The old signposts were mainly blasted to splinters and replaced by sheets of painted tin wired to bushes. If further bombardment disturbed the bushes, the makeshift signs wound up pointing in wrong directions. Pre-war maps no longer resembled reality. Old routes were buried under rubble, new ones driven through fields. The courses of rivers were altered by the random landscaping of a million tons of shelling.

Still dogging Edwin, she looked for Maranique. Her reporter's sense, sometimes finer even than her vampire senses, twitched.

As the sun went down, a flight of aeroplanes passed over. She was on the right road: the machines came from the direction where she had guessed the airfield was.

The war in the air was changing. That was the story she had scented. Mata Hari had inclined her to look to the skies. Edwin had confirmed the insight.

She braked and touched one boot to the ground, then looked up through her thick glasses, afraid she would see black crosses on the undersides of wings. The blue, white and red roundels of the Royal Flying Corps (soon to be reconstituted as the Royal Air Force) told her she was at least not completely lost.

Pilots called their aeroplanes 'kites' or 'birds'. The wire and canvas contraptions were pitifully frail, ready to fly apart in a stiff crosswind let alone heavy fire. She was not convinced the things were safe even for peacetime use. At RFC flying schools, pupils were called 'Huns' because they wrecked more aeroplanes than the enemy. Half as many pilots were killed in training accidents as in combat. Wilbur and Orville Wright had much to answer for. Then again, her father had been certain bicycling would be the death of her.

She waved up but could not see any of the pilots return the greeting. It was possible this patrol was to do with the story. Once she lit on something, everything suddenly seemed connected, a dozen chance remarks and incidents forming a pattern.

The popular press in which Kate Reed was *not* published, typified by that fathead ass Horatio Bottomley's bloodthirstily patriotic witterings in *John Bull*, invariably called Allied pilots 'gallant' and 'dauntless'. Watching them soar away to probable death, it was hard to disagree. There was such a spirit in the fighting men. It was a crime the planners and the propagandists were so intent on wasting it with sheer carnage.

The patrol flew towards the lines in a neat arrow like a flight of ducks heading south for the winter.

Her position was not without risk. A reporter who seeks the truth is easily mistaken for a spy. GHQ concealed its blunders from press and public as keenly as it concealed its stratagems from the enemy. Like Mata Hari, Kate was forced to use her wiles, to cultivate friendly officers, to snoop where she was not wanted, to winnow out the germane from the gossip. General Mireau, for one, would be happy to see her go to the stake. She wondered if he still had his Jesuit after her. She would have to be wary: holy water and rattling rosaries were a joke, but silver bullets would be impossible to laugh off.

She wore the arm-band of an ambulance driver, which won her admittance to most military facilities. This close to the front, men were so pleased to see a female, even one whose attractions were as meagre as hers, that she could pass unquestioned in a mess-hall or a field hospital.

To the east, star-shells exploded, casting jagged shadows. Night-fighting had been fierce the last few weeks. The Germans did not want to give the Allies time to think. The patrol was over No Man's Land. She wished them well and pedalled on.

Maranique was home to Condor Squadron, which was an instrument of the Diogenes Club. Kate had gleaned that much from a canny interpretation of official releases before she even sneaked a look at Edwin's orders. She had spent an evening in the Paris HQ of the General Quartermasters' Staff, tracing requisitions and transfers, inferring a history of the squadron through the assembly of men and *matériel*. Charles Beauregard was often found in the paper trail. She was not surprised to learn how often he got what he wanted, even against the wishes of distinguished officers.

The road ahead was utterly devastated, hedgerows blasted, fields madly ploughed. Duckboards had been put down but most of them were smashed too. She got off her bicycle and hefted it easily on her shoulders. She hardly remembered being warm and weak, though she usually avoided ostentatious public displays of vampire strength. She stepped onto the impossible ground and waded on. Within a few steps, she was up to her puttees in grainy mud, extricating her feet with obscene sucking sounds.

All the aces joined Condor Squadron, but it was a sidestep in many a glamorous career. Considering their combined tallies before this assignment, Cundall's Condors logged comparatively few individual victories. For glory-hounds – it was naive to think no Allied pilot was as intent on racking up a score as Baron von Richthofen – it must be frustrating. The squadron must be engaged on work of such paramount military importance that the propaganda value of medal-laden valour had to be set aside.

She again found something resembling a road and got back on her old Hoopdriver. It was a man's bicycle, supposedly too big for her, but she was comfortable with it. Her first journalism had been published in the cycling press, back in the '80s. She was sometimes nostalgic for her warm days, when the right of women to wear bloomers on bicycle excursions was a fiercely contested issue. It was ridiculous to think of the period before the Terror as a sunlit idyll, but there had been something of comfort in trivialities now lost.

She came upon a sign ordering those without the relevant papers to turn back. The only paper in her voluminous pocket was wrapped around a package of blood sherbet. She kept notes in her head, where no one could get at them.

The road was marked with poles that reminded her of the stakes of which Count Dracula was so fond. They were mostly surmounted not with fleshless skulls but with battered German helmets. Another sign, in French and English (but not German), said, 'Unauthorised persons will be taken as spies and shot'. Kate was sure they meant it. Bottomley said journalists who criticised the conduct of the war should be executed as traitors.

One of Kate's sources, Colonel Nicholson, had been given the duty last September of escorting the great bloodsucking Bottomley on a tour of the front. He said the temptation to suggest the editor perch on the firing step and put his head in the way of a silver bullet was nigh irresistible. Having come as near as four thousand yards to the fight, Bottomley returned to the warmth of London and loudly trumpeted his own bravery at sharing the condition of 'our glorious lads' in the trenches. She remembered his article with a stomach-deep sickness: 'SOMEWHERE IN – HELL! What I have Seen – What I have Done – What I have Learned – The War is Won!' Most 'glorious lads' would cheerfully slip a bayonet into his belly rather than read another article full of sentiments like 'from Field Marshal Commander-in-Chief, right down to the rawest Tommy in the trenches, there is but one spirit – that of absolute optimism and confidence'. Nicholson told her, 'We put him into a gasmask for the purpose of a photograph and for a moment I had hopes that he would die of apoplexy.'

Laid over the war between the Allies and the Central Powers was a war between the old men and the young, between the politicians and tub-thumpers on both sides and the soldiers sent out to die. Kate had better cause than most to despise Dracula and recognised the need to check his ambitions, but many as bad held high office in Britain. That men like Charles Beauregard and Edwin Winthrop still served King Victor was fragile cause for hope.

She had thought a great deal of Edwin since their wager. They had made some contact she still did not quite understand. She wondered if he ever thought of her.

Coming upon a weary sentry, she meekly said 'Red Cross' to him as if it were the password of the day. He saluted and let her through without asking to see her fabled papers. Given the hell-raising disposition pilots were rumoured to have, women far more questionable than she must be coming on and off the field at all hours.

She found a shed and leaned her bicycle against it. Mud had spattered her entirely and was inches thick on the tops of her boots. Even her glasses were speckled with brown liquid. She was scarcely in a condition to beguile secrets from tight-lipped heroes.

The airfield still looked like a farm. Barns augmented by corrugated metal structures served as hangars. Just after nightfall, there were quite a few personnel milling about. In what had been a stableyard, two mechanics toiled on a Sopwith Pup which was leaking oil in a steady gush.

Kate walked past purposefully as if on important business, as indeed she was. One man whistled, testimony to the length of time he had spent away from home. She smiled back, hiding teeth.

She found the field itself. The patrol she had seen would have taken off from here. A knot of men stood near the farmhouse that must be their billet, watching the night skies.

It hit her that this must be dreadful, waiting and knowing the odds were bad. She had heard it was possible to become accustomed to the steady attrition as men you served with were killed off. It must take a fearful toll on anyone's sanity.

The group gradually broke up. First one man drifted off, then another, then all of them. They looked self-consciously at the ground, trying to fight the compulsion to gaze forever at the sky. Then they kicked a bit, muttered with mock cheer, and slipped back into the house. A gramophone croaked out 'Poor Butterfly'.

She felt, as she rarely did, that she was intruding, and wondered if she should get back to her ambulance unit. When she wasn't snooping, she helped with the wounded. The sobering duty reminded her why it was important to find and tell the truth.

'Miss,' said a deep voice. 'Should you be here?'

He had come up behind her without making a sound audible even to her bat-sharp ears. That marked him as a professional creeper. It was Sergeant Dravot, the hatchet man of the Diogenes Club.

She spread her hands in surrender and tried a mousy smile.

'I'm waiting for my soldier boy to come home,' she said, trying to sound like a tart.

Dravot looked up at the sky and, without a trace of expression, said, 'So am I.'

18

HELL'S ANGELS

Something exploded quite near. Winthrop felt a brief thrash of hot air. The RE8 whizzed past a blossoming black cloud. Archie. The spotter climbed sharply, faster than his stomach could manage. An unmeasurable distance below was a carpet of black bursts. The draught of explosions tossed the machine higher. Courtney rode the blast, keeping steady.

The RE8 was at its peak at 6,500 feet but its operational ceiling was 13,500 feet. Archie rarely got above 4,000. The weight of the shells dragged, thank God.

It suddenly occurred to him that they might not have the sky to themselves. In the circumstances, he was not best employed looking down. Most downed aeroplanes were shot from behind or above. He swivelled from side to side, turning through three-quarters of a circle. Nothing seemed to be creeping up on them.

They flew east, away from the sunset. The sky was red, darkness crowding around.

The RE8 tilted as Courtney executed a textbook aerial turn, following Cundall's lead. They were angling towards Malinbois.

The air whipped like a storm of fish-hooks. He tried to let go of the Lewis grips, but found his fingers wouldn't move. Biting on frustration, he forced his hands to work.

He fumbled for the camera toggle. He would have to sight the camera accurately, yet keep any spare eyes out for hostile fliers. Even by day, an enemy aircraft could seem the tiniest gnat in an unpeopled expanse of sky a couple of seconds before it was close enough to get in a killing shot. He needed a head like a multi-faceted sphere, with a compound eye on each facet. He wondered if there were vampires like that.

He turned round to his extreme right and saw the back of Courtney's helmet. The pilot held up his gloved hand, thumb up.

Beyond Courtney, the Snipes flew. Beyond them was shadow. The flight descended through thin cloud. A towered shape rose above the landscape. It was familiar from drawings and photographs as the Chateau de Malinbois.

Winthrop's arm tensed. He didn't know if he had the strength in his elbow to pull the camera toggle.

Something black and winged zoomed past. The RE8 banked, twisting away. The roaring in Winthrop's ears contained the tiny noise of gunfire. He adjusted to his new alignment. It was easier to think of whatever lay under his feet as down, even if the RE8 flew almost on its side. Sixty per cent of his field of vision was taken up by landscape. Against fields and roads, things were moving in the air.

He fixed on a field of virgin snow, a large-ish patch of white in the muddy grey. Something black darted across it and he angled his Lewis to aim in its path. He depressed the trigger and was shaken by the mule kick of the gun. He knew enough to fire only a short burst rather than waste limited ammunition in a futile spray. He could not tell if he hit anything.

The Harry Tate climbed and whirled. Amazingly, the formation was intact. Dark shapes flitted around the edges of the arrow, darting up. A line of painfully bright flashes ripped by. Tracer bullets.

The RE8 wheeled round above the castle. Winthrop pulled the camera toggle, waited a few seconds, and pulled again. Shadows passed over the spotter. Winthrop took his last two exposures and forgot the camera. He had both fists around the gun-handles.

They were in the middle of a dog-fight, an aerial mêlée. God knows how many fliers darted around, popped off guns, swore under their breaths, wrestled wings through wind resistance, prayed for victory or even another night of life.

His last letter was entirely inadequate. Catriona deserved better than a few lines of scribble.

Something knifed downwards in flames, screeching. He couldn't tell what markings were on its wings. It was impossible to count the shapes in the air.

Damn, he was going to die! Not in some remote white-haired future surrounded by grandchildren, but in the next few moments. He should have turned. But Courtney was a vampire and he was going to die too. Being undead was no use if you went down in flames.

They wove from side to side, up and down. Courtney must be some breed of genius to get so much out of a poor old bloody old Harry Tate. He dodged the best the Boche could put in the air. Clearly, Cundall's Condors were battling with *Jagdgeschwader 1*. Out there in the growing darkness was the Bloody Red Baron.

The Germans moved faster even than the Snipes, registering on the eye as an evil black blur. The darker it got, the more they blended with the night. Winthrop imagined the Snipes were luminous, attracting fire from all round.

The sky was beneath them and the castle was above his head. Courtney had flipped the spotter over. Winthrop's Lewis pointed down and backwards. Something climbed fast, a killer fish rising from the depths, eyes blazing red. Wings beat, displacing a great volume of air.

Tracer spurted up towards the RE8's tail. Winthrop returned fire, spitting bursts at the winged thing. Every tenth bullet was supposed to be silver. He realised he was firing not at an aircraft, but at a shape-shifted creature with multiple sets of batwings.

A creature with machine-guns.

He remembered the dark shape that had plucked Albright from his SE5a. And killed him.

A huge head, grinning bloodily, soared towards him, darting through gunfire. Terror reached out from the flying thing and clutched his heart. He was frozen, hung upside-down in his cockpit, unable to press with his thumbs.

Cat!

He did not know if he had shouted or prayed. There was a savage twist and the Harry Tate rolled right-side-up again. Winthrop saw two Snipes diving towards the Boche, spitting tracer.

Courtney climbed, trying to get above the fight. Winthrop looked down and saw dots of movement. There were bullet-holes in the underside of the spotter. His left foot stung; he wondered if he had been shot.

Before sunset, he had only fired guns in training. His whole war had been a staff officer's, fought in meetings and at desks. Dying and killing were not a part of it.

Courtney was clearing out. Though he could not know for sure, he must assume Winthrop had got his photographs. The primary objective achieved, it was now his duty to get home intact.

Red Albright had got his photographs too.

The problem was that, though the fighters offered more of a challenge and thus more opportunities for honourable victory, it would now be the duty of the German creatures to bring down the contemptible Harry Tate and prevent intelligence getting back to the Allies.

Winthrop still heard gunfire. His Lewis had been alarmingly loud and the echoes of his own fire-bursts tumbled around his skull. Forcing numbed fingers to unimaginable dexterity, he lifted the empty ammunition drum off the spike and replaced it with the fresh one stored under his seat. He fired a few shots to keep the barrel clear, hoping for a lucky hit on a darting batwing.

Little tears in the fabric of the upper fuselage flapped as they flew. The bat-thing had comprehensively shot them. Winthrop was sure the warm stickiness in his boot was blood. When would agony set in?

He looked down the tail at the Chateau de Malinbois. The famous tower was open to the skies, vast bats swarming around it. With a gasp, Winthrop realised what the diving-board arrangement was for. The shape-shifted fliers used it for take-off, leaping away from the tower to catch wind under their wings.

There were still at least three Snipes aloft, maybe more. The flaming thing that had rushed past had been one of Cundall's Condors. There was a bonfire on the ground near the castle, where the Snipe had crashed.

The creatures were as fast as Snipes and much more manoeuvrable. In the instant when the thing was bearing up at the RE8, Winthrop had taken it all in. Now, he remembered details. Slung round a thick neck was a harness with twin guns, hanging below a knife-edge breastbone. The large red eyes were those of a night-sighted beast. A human intelligence, a malevolence, made the vampire creature seem a refugee from Fuseli's nightmares. When he had called the shadow on Albright's photograph a gargoyle, Courtney had not been far wrong.

Winthrop shivered with fear, eyes forced open by the cold. He was not thinking clearly. It was important he lived to report this development. It was important to live.

Albright had been pursued back as far as Maranique before being killed. That showed a fine sporting instinct. The flier who claimed that victory was Baron von Richthofen. Could the bat-creature that had swooped up at the RE8 be the Red Baron? Winthrop doubted he would still be alive if that were so. Richthofen was not one to let a juicy victory escape him. He must have Harry Tates for breakfast.

Luck or providence was with them so far. He vowed not to die. He could not let Catriona read his silly letter. He had to describe this engagement to Beauregard. And he had unfinished business with Kate Reed.

There was an explosion over the castle. Another comet streaked to the ground. A Snipe had fallen. The formation was broken, though machines were fast catching up with the RE8. Snipes could manage a hundred and twenty miles per hour. Surely, nothing remotely human could match that over a distance.

Tracer caught his attention and he swung to the right, wrenching his gun round. He had little ammunition left. Machine-guns used bullets quickly. There wasn't space in the kite to store many extra drums.

A bat-shape plunged fast, wings rigid. The German vampire had three sets of wings, fixed together by some kind of twine. A human triplane. Winthrop got a fix and emptied his gun. Light darts shot at the vampire, who turned easily in the air to avoid the flow. His underside was lit up and Winthrop saw guns, dragging towards the ground, hanging below a coat of reddish fur. Was this the Red Baron? Arms reached like a diver's, claws extended in a point. He thought the vampire intended to shear through the canvas and wood of the RE8 like a living knife.

He kept his eyes open and thought of Catriona, of her taste, of her eyes. She said her hair was auburn, but he thought of it as red. There was nothing wrong with red hair. Damn, but this was silly. Dying.

The spotter was thumped and spun. Canvas tore and struts buckled. Wind slapped him in the face. The empty ammunition drum clipped his chin and fell upwards. He realised the RE8 was upside-down again. He *smelled* the animal scent of the flying thing and clutched convulsively at the gun-handles. His thumbs pressed and the empty gun clicked. Something long and leathery, like a whip, slithered across his cheek, tearing skin. The vampire had a tail. The blasted thing was a rat with wings. And the Pour le Mérite, no doubt. Then the vampire was gone.

He was suddenly calm. The RE8 was flying evenly and the wind slowed to a breeze. His stomach unclenched and he sucked in sweet air. He could still breathe. He felt nothing. Even his foot did not hurt. Was he dead? And if not, why not? Had the German spared the Harry Tate? If so, why?

He wrenched round to look at Courtney. His calm turned to ice. The horizon was up beyond the upper wing, a tiny wedge of sky at the top of an expanse of ground. Beyond the spinning propellor, darkness was dotted with fire. The forward cockpit was empty, straps and flaps of torn canvas streaming up.

The RE8 climbed, its balance shifted with the loss of the pilot. The flight was almost peaceful. Winthrop's skull rang with his own gunfire, but the rush of the wind seemed to quieten. There was still fire, a distant chatter. The fight was below the Harry Tate. He was out of it. Unless the engine died, the spotter would climb until there was no air to breathe. When it came down, he would be slumped lifeless in the rear cockpit and not even feel the inevitable fireball.

For a moment, he relaxed. His hands eased off the gun-handles and slipped into his lap. The fear and excitement that had turned every muscle and tendon to taut wire soothed away. Engine drone accompanied his drift into reverie.

He thought of the smell of Catriona's hair, damp after rain. It was goodbye to all that.

The RE8 flew in shadow. Between it and the moon was a bat-shape. The creature that had taken Courtney was still up there. The Boche's wings gave a leisurely flap. Was the monster entertained? Amused?

The RE8 angled, one wing raised slightly. Hundreds of feet below, tracer criss-crossed. A cloud of orange flame burst inside a Snipe. The fighter tore to burning fragments which fluttered downwards to the Chateau de Malinbois, fireflies around a fairy castle.

A tiny scream began inside his head. It grew, painfully shrill, popping his ears, forcing his eyes open wide. His lungs hurt, his throat caught. He realised he was shrieking at the top of his voice. His breath condensed with brief damp warmth in his mask and stinging droplets of ice formed in his moustache.

The Boche peeled away and flew off, leaving him to his fate. Given the choice of going down in flames or being sucked empty like Red Albright, Winthrop did not know which to pick.

The RE8 was not a dual-stick machine like the trainers he had
been ferried around in. If he was to take control, he would have
to be in the forward cockpit. The stick was all of a yard off. If the
now-useless Lewis were not in the way, it would have been perhaps
nine inches beyond his reach. The stick shuddered as wind streamed
over loose ailerons. Courtney's hands had been wrenched away but
the Harry Tate still flew on the vanished pilot's last course. It was a
miracle the machine had not instantly gone into a spin. The miracle
could not last much longer. Winthrop did not have minutes. He might
not have seconds.

He tried to get a grip on either side of the scarf-ring, but his gloved
hands were stubborn. Concentrating hard, he made fingers curl until
he had hold. Then he pushed with his upper arms, lifting his bottom
off its seat, shoving his feet against interior struts as he stood in the
fuselage. If he slipped, his boot would tear through fabric and he'd be
trapped like a fox in a snare.

As he stood, the RE8's balance changed. He leaned forwards and
the nose came down. His legs grew heavier, pulling him back into the
cockpit. Wind streamed hard against his chest as if he stood neck-
deep in a stormy sea. His goggle-rims pressed around his eyes like
biscuit-cutters.

Cruel, cold air tore at his agnosticism, ripping it off like a wrapping.
Dear God, if there is a Dear God, please preserve the life of this, thy
servant...

He was struck across the face by what felt like an iron bar. The barrel
of the Lewis gun. His nose and mouth filled with blood. One lens of
his goggles whitened into a spiderweb. If his head had not been triple-
wrapped, he could have been pitched, unconscious, out of the machine.

He prayed with his mind and swore with his tongue.

The Harry Tate was nose-heavy now. He saw the whirring blades
of the propellor. The engine was slowing. At any moment, it could
choke and die.

Clinging fast to the rim of the cockpit, he hauled his legs out of the body of the RE8. The wings were wavering. A triangular tear in the upper plane grew larger by the second. Snow and mud rushed by.

The nearer the spotter got to the earth, the more aware he was of the speed. In the heights, there was nothing to judge by except the instruments. As landmarks whizzed past below, it was possible to judge swiftness.

He rode the fuselage as if it were a horse, gripping with his knees. Catriona, a horsewoman from birth, said he had a good seat. The Lewis was in his way. Horrible silences broke up the drone of the engine.

Curse it, Edwin Winthrop did not intend to die.

He would reach the blessed stick, fly home to blasted Maranique, marry the sainted Catriona, become a damned vampire, return to filthy Hunland, slaughter the evil bat-thing that had taken Courtney, and drink the Kaiser's stinking blood from a bowl made of the fucking brainpan of the Graf von Dracula.

His left knee lost its grip. He wrenched round entirely at the waist. His legs flailed backwards. His fingers tore dope-stiffened linen. The propellor revolved as slowly as a windmill. Blood flew from his nose and mouth. He had lost his scarf. His Sidcot filled with cold air and he was a human balloon. If he let go, perhaps he would float to safety? No, if he let go, he'd be ripped into darkness and death. The air was infested with monsters. The Red Baron was still on his tail.

With his right hand, he let go of the cockpit rim and grasped for the back of the pilot's seat. His fingers slipped off greasy leather, then he found a purchase. He dragged himself eighteen inches forwards. It was like a mile. Hand over hand, he pulled himself over the cockpit. The stick was within his reach.

He must not touch it yet.

His back sang with pain. His eardrums must have burst. The blood on his chin was ice. He felt nothing from his legs.

Below the Harry Tate, the ground was near. He could see no sky.

One boot was hooked into the forward cockpit. He was crouched above Courtney's seat, wind rushing between his legs, looking down.

There were rips in the floor. To get into the seat, he had to do an impossible thing. He had to let go and trust to gravity. He knew he would be torn away from the Harry Tate and whisked off to death.

He thought of God, Cat, duty and revenge. And he opened his hands.

The seat slammed his spine as he fell. He bit his tongue. His elbows thumped the rim of the cockpit. His arms flapped in front of him like empty sleeves. He accidentally struck the stick. The Harry Tate, loyal for so long, betrayed him, banking sharply. With a terrible, slow rip, canvas detached itself from the upper plane.

He gripped the stick as if it were Excalibur's hilt and pulled it back. One of his feet found a stirrup under the rudder-bar and he pushed, flattening out the ailerons.

Once, he had kept a trainer up in mild skies for five minutes. That was not remotely preparation for this. For a start, he had never landed anything.

He pulled the stick back and pushed the rudder forwards, willing the nose up. Ignoring everything but the spirit-level, he tried to wrestle the bubble into position by force of will. The wind caught the dying propellor and whirled it. The coughing engine cleared and sounded healthier. A press of air below the Harry Tate tossed it upwards.

There was murderous ground below. Winthrop would have to deal with it. The upwards lurch was a temporary freak. Without a wing, the Harry Tate was liable to go tail-up and bury its pilot in the earth.

'Curse you, Bloody Red Baron von Richthofen, curse you and all your bloody batwing bastards.'

The thing was to get out of the sky without the petrol tank exploding. Fighting instinct, he let the stick out and relaxed his foot in the bar-stirrup. His air-speed gauge was broken, but he felt the slowing.

The important thing was to hit the ground slowly, with enough weight behind to stop the tail flipping up over the nose. The likelihood of a smooth and safe patch of earth this near the lines – if he wasn't yet over No Man's Land – was minimal.

For the moment, incredibly, he was not dying. How many of Cundall's Snipes were still aloft? Any survivors of the engagement should be making their way home. Somehow, he doubted Richthofen's Flying Freak Show – Mata Hari's apt expression – had let any prey escape. They were confident enough to leave him to this torture. Snatching the pilot from a two-seater must seem a fearfully good joke.

A stream of fire burst up from below but Winthrop laughed as the RE8 staggered past it. He was over the lines. Beyond his failing prop was home.

He flew low enough and slowly enough to be shot at from the ground. There were only a few seconds when the men in the trenches would be able to draw a bead. They passed and he was still alive, gulping down breaths that felt like draughts of iced water laced with splinters of broken glass.

His laughter tore at the air. He had to swallow it. He fixed his mind on home.

God Save the King... Britannia Rules the Waves... Dieu et mon Droit... Love you, Cat...

His wheels were only feet above the earth. Bursting shells and fire pillars revealed a landscape as pitted and cratered as the surface of the moon. Bad as it had looked from on high, it was worse from lower down. As soon as the RE8 touched a wheel to this surface, it'd be ripped off and the spotter would be strewn in pieces over a hundred yards of No Man's Land. There would not be enough left of him to bury.

He looked up. Dark shapes circled. Had the Red Baron kept pace, hoping to see the conclusion of his little jest? Another engine sounded. There was still at least one Snipe up there. The battle was not done.

He was sure the shape-shifter that had taken Courtney was Manfred von Richthofen. The fur had been reddish and the eyes had been ice-evil. No other Boche could be so complete a monster.

This was it. His last moments. If he could not be a vampire, he would have to settle for being a damned ghost. If nothing else, he would *haunt* his murderer.

Imagining a gap of inches between earth and wheel, he pulled back the stick, bringing up the nose. The wheels kissed ground but the tail ploughed into dirt, anchoring the machine. He was slammed against the seat as if by the slap of a giant's hand and bounced around the cockpit. He was sure the snapping he heard was his own bones. The Harry Tate screamed as it was ripped apart.

Earth was thrown up at his face. The RE8 dragged through No Man's Land. Broken wires twanged and whipped. A spar gashed the fuselage. The lower plane crumpled and was torn free. Winthrop threw his arms over his head and waited for the sudden thrust of death.

19

BIGGLES FLIES WEST

Below, the British Snipes were torn apart by the fliers of JG1. Stalhein and Stachel were the high men, observing the dog-fight.

After gaining the air from the tower of the Chateau de Malinbois, they flew straight up and hovered over the battle. If any of the Britishers made an escape, Stalhein and Stachel were to swoop down for a quick kill. It was an honourable and necessary position but frustrating for fliers whose immediate bloodlust was up.

At this altitude, Stalhein could glide, only occasionally flapping to remain in position. The span of his upper wings was thirty feet; excluding his whiplike tail, twice the length of his body. This span, the strong crossbar of his shifted shape, corresponded to the shoulders and arms of his human form. Membranes grew from his wrists to his sides, billowing like full sails. Bunches of muscle clustered around his rudder-like breastbone, giving him subtle control of his wings.

The lower wings were shape-shifted ribs, extruded from his body, augmented by canvas sheets. The stubby, functional arms that grew from his torso and worked the Parabellum machine-guns slung on the harness round his neck were made from whole cloth, flesh and bone grown by force of will. Learning to fly in this shape was trickier than mastering the use of one of Tony Fokker's fighters, but Stalhein was more manoeuvrable and as fast as any machine.

In his bat-shape, he was cocooned against the bitter cold by a stiff layer of natural fur over leathery skin. Seven-league boots the height of his human legs were hooked together at the ankles and knees. Otherwise, he wore only the apparatus that made him a flying weapon. The joints of his hips were locked and his vertebrae fused, turning the length of his body into an unbreakable spine.

The stink of discharged guns and burning fuel drifted up on the currents and caught in his huge open nostrils. His ears, thick-veined curls a foot across, picked up the chatter of discharged guns, the interrupted whines of failed engines, even the shouts of battling pilots.

One of the Snipes exploded. He saw a victorious Udet rise on the burst of hot air, swimming with his cloak-like wings. Stalhein heard the curtailed scream of a British pilot. Udet's score was level with Stalhein's again.

When word came in from observers that a full flight had left Maranique and was headed for Malinbois, Stalhein had assumed General Karnstein would again order a quiet night. Several times before, JG1 had been kept out of a fight because the time was not yet right to show their hand. Kretschmar-Schuldorff, whose job was to keep secrets, continually cautioned against premature deployment. Every man of the Baron's command devoutly wished to go into battle but they knew their duty. When the time came, they would serve the Kaiser as he saw fit.

The burning Snipe dwindled to a cinder as it plunged. Udet did a victory roll, easily slipping out of the path of a fusillade. There were still several Britishers aloft. JG1 was playing with them.

After consideration, Karnstein decided it was time to let slip the bats of war. He ordered Baron von Richthofen to take out eight fliers and destroy the patrol.

'Let us teach our enemy to fear us a little more,' the vampire elder explained.

Richthofen had been quiet as he accepted the order, but Stalhein and the others were unable to suppress their excitement. Stalhein began to shift even before he was picked for the flight, expanding inside his tunic until the buttons burst.

'Mark your man,' Richthofen told his fliers, 'and kill him.'

From his vantage, Stalhein saw how JG1 had carried out this simple order. Richthofen assigned his brother to the Snipe that flew the tip of the formation, taking for himself the spotter. An outsider might think this cowardice but Stalhein understood the Baron's decision. On its own, the RE8 was the easiest target, but it was also the most important. The Snipes were there to look out for the spotter and would protect it. By attacking the RE8, Richthofen made himself prime target. He would have to trust his men to make their kills and protect his back.

Lothar von Richthofen took his Snipe without even firing, soaring up from beneath the squadron leader and ripping off its upper plane, twisting the machine around in the air. The Snipe was hurled towards the ground in a fatal spin, discharging guns at random. Lothar followed the spiralling Britisher and wrested the pilot from his seat. Stalhein heard the screech as Lothar's jaws clamped around the flight commander's head.

Stachel, kept out of the killing, howled in frustration. Ropes of spittle flew from his shark-mouth. His mad eyes shone like flaming stars. Stalhein knew his comrade would not do. He thought only of Bruno Stachel, never of JG1 or the Kaiser or honour.

Huge and slow like a flying pancake, Emmelman flopped on his Snipe. He chewed into the aeroplane with great shaking motions of his neck, ripping canvas and metal with talons and teeth. To him, the machine was the hard shell of the nut and the pilot the meat inside. He didn't even fly with guns. His vast shape absorbed almost any punishment, spitting out spent bullets like drops of sweat.

The fight would be over before Stalhein got into it. A disappointment, but it was his duty to live with disappointment. This victory would be shared.

Manfred von Richthofen elegantly disabled the two-man RE8, snatching the pilot and leaving the observer to go down with the ship.

It was almost an artistic gesture, proof that aesthetic impulses did sometimes stir in the icy mind of the Red Battle Flier. Richthofen drifted lazily over the doomed spotter, looking down at the terrified observer. Waves of fear poured out of the man.

Schleich's Snipe was on the Baron's tail, trying to shatter him with gunfire. Whoever flew that machine was exceptional. No matter how far he shape-shifted from the human, Stalhein understood the mental adjustment that must be made by a man who expected to face a fighter aeroplane but was confronted by the fliers of JG1. Schleich's Snipe recovered from the shock and fought like a master. Schleich, left behind in the sky, fluttered awkwardly with a rip in one wing, trying desperately to get back on his man's tail.

It was not yet time to intervene, he judged. His orders were to stay out of it until it seemed a Britisher might be on the point of escaping. Schleich's Snipe dipped down and came up again, rattling off more fire. Richthofen danced in the air, not seriously endangered. The RE8 was still aloft, surprisingly. The observer had stopped screaming.

Stachel looked down, nodding ferociously. A fur ruff inflated around his head. His bat-shape had something of the howler monkey. Bold Bruno was eager to be in on the killing, keen enough to disobey the Baron's orders.

'Go down and you'll be dismissed,' Stalhein said. In this body, what seemed a normal speaking voice was loud enough to be audible over the wind. Stachel, desperate for blood and his Blue Max, shook his great head, but stayed in formation. Fear of loss of position was greater than the red thirst. No one had ever been asked to resign from JG1. Stalhein had the impression General Karnstein would insist on a permanent reassignment to Hades. Bound by fear and duty and bloodlust and honour, the fliers of JG1 were as much slaves as masters. They were not merely knights of the sky, but gladiators.

'This is a waste,' Stachel yelled.

Göring's Snipe began to go after the RE8, and Fat Hermann huffed through the air after it. Weighed down by the whale-like blubber which increased his shape-shifted bulk, Göring was the slowest of the flight. Still, he was a deadly marksman, setting his guns for short bursts and bringing his prey down with a big game hunter's precision.

The remaining fight drifted upwards, forcing Stalhein and Stachel higher through thin clouds. As moonlight fell on Stalhein's wings, his whole body tingled. New strength coursed like electricity through nerves and veins. He understood this was a characteristic of the line of the English vampire Ruthven, the Graf's former ally and now hated foe, but he did not understand how the strain had come to him. It had been a part of his *nosferatu* make-up well before Karnstein introduced him to the sweet Faustine, who passed on to him something of the Dracula line.

His body swelled with light and his strength grew. The cold he felt around his eyes and in his ears dissipated. The sustenance he took from moonlight was almost like blood. If he was deprived by clouds, he became listless. Like the proverbial werewolf's, his strength waxed and waned with the phases of the moon.

The RE8 was gone from sight, though Stalhein still distinguished the sound of its stuttering engine. In the observer's place, he thought he would go mad before hitting the ground. Göring's Snipe followed the spotter, Fat Hermann closing on his tail.

Only Schleich's Snipe was still in the battle. Schleich limped in flight, the rent in his wing expanding with each flap, too serious to heal instantly. The rest of the flight was in the Snipe's wake.

Schleich's Snipe climbed towards Stalhein and Stachel. Stalhein saw the tiny white face of the British pilot. It was Bigglesworth, the ace who tallied Erich von Stalhein among his victories. It was fitting that he should ascend to the heavens and find Stalhein waiting for him.

Stalhein waved Stachel back. This fight was his. Stachel was having none of it, so Stalhein shouldered his way in front of the other flier. He heard but ignored Stachel's scream of rage.

The whirring propellor of Schleich's Snipe rose. Bigglesworth fired bursts from his twin Vickers. Stalhein saw the flash of silver tracer and flew out of the path of the bullets. Stachel slipped to one side but caught the last of the fire with his wingtip. Enraged, Stachel lunged. Overcompensating for his wound, he disappeared into cloud, falling hundreds of feet.

Stalhein and Bigglesworth were alone. With calm excitement, he circled the Snipe, looking down into the cockpit. He saw the pilot's head swivel, the blessed moon reflected in his goggles. Before the kill, he paid homage to his valiant foe. This was a victory worth having.

The other fliers were climbing in a rough formation and would be here soon. There was no time to savour combat. He flew up on the Snipe's tailplane and took hold with his jaws, rows of teeth ripping through wood and fabric. With a toss of his neck, he wrenched the whole rear end off the fighter. He spat the dry stuff from his mouth and clawed his way forwards to the cockpit, thirsty for English vampire blood. With this kill, he would take on the valour of his enemy. With every kill, he grew stronger. That was the power Faustine had passed on with her Dracula-blessed blood.

With astonishing cool, Bigglesworth turned in his seat and levelled a thick-barrelled handgun, a Verey pistol. Stalhein laughed. Bigglesworth smiled. The other fliers were all around. Bigglesworth shot Stalhein in the mouth. Fire exploded on his tongue and burst around his snout, singeing the bristly fur of his face, searing his eyes. The smell was worse than the pain. He spat out the burning cartridge but had lost his grip on the wrecked Snipe. His body cried out for blood. His mouth still burned and his heart thumped like a war-drum with the vampire ache. He had vanquished, now he *must* feed. More than the victory, more than a medal, more than the mission, he needed *blood*!

The Snipe tumbled away, plunging through the fliers like a lead weight. The wings were torn off. The pilot was thrown out of the cockpit and fell independently, picking up speed. From this height, he would be smashed to useless fragments, sweet blood spread over a square mile.

Forgetting all else, Stalhein dived after his kill, clawing through the air. He folded his lower wings to decrease resistance and knifed down like a spear. Air screamed around his wings. His eyes, blobbed with fire-bursts, fixed on the falling pilot. It was hopeless. Bigglesworth had escaped him.

Unless he acted swiftly, he would plough into the hard earth on the very spot his victim fell. He, too, would be smashed to fragments. He struggled in the air, almost losing his mastery of the element. Extending his wings like sails, he halted his descent. It was as if his arms were wrenched out of their sockets. His tail lashed beneath him as he tried to attain an even keel. Finally, he pulled out of his dive. He drifted upwards on the current, scanning the black landscape for spots of burning light. He was somewhere this side of the lines, so there was no fire from the ground. His ears strained but he could not hear an impact. His foe was down somewhere, broken. The battle was over and Erich von Stalhein was unfulfilled. He began to growl.

20

FOREIGN FIELD

The stick was torn from his hands. Wind blast dashed his whole body. He realised the entire front of the RE8 had been wrenched off, ripped aside. His life was probably saved for a few seconds. The stove-hot engine was no longer three feet in front of his lap. Jolted out of its cowling, the contraption would have shot into the cockpit like a big bullet, punching through his soft body.

Winthrop was pushed back into his seat by the force of the crash, then thrown forwards into dark. Hard ground thumped him in the chest and face. He reflexively grabbed earth as if it were eiderdown.

His ears were still assaulted by the roar of the air and the grinding of the RE8 coming apart all around him. Something heavy fell on his back, forcing him further into the dirt.

The goggles prevented his eyes from being mashed into his head but his mask was ribboned. Dirt went up his nose and into his mouth. A sharp spar worked its way through his Sidcot into his side. Every part of him hurt, as if he had been beaten about the belly, kidneys and groin. Death was a single breath, a heartbeat, away.

Cat, he thought. Sorry for the silly letter…

He lifted his face from the ground, coughing and shaking loose matter from his mouth and nose. He breathed again. And again. His heart still beat. Maybe he would not die? Or maybe he was already dead?

This was something like the plain of hell he had imagined as a child, listening to the Reverend Mr Kaye, Catriona's father. There were distant screams and pillars of fire, and a deep darkness.

He shrugged violently, dislodging the broken wing-frame that had fallen on his back. His Sidcot tore as he extracted the spear-like end of a snapped strut.

On his knees, he froze, feeling only pain. His teeth rattled and were thickly smeared with blood and filth. He coughed and spat. His stomach rolled and emptied through his mouth. Being sick at least cleared his throat. He had no way of knowing which bones were broken and which just hurt. It might have been easier to determine which bones were *un*broken.

A burst of intense light flared nearby, searing his eyes. Flame seemed to brush his face and dissipate in an instant. The engine had blown up but there wasn't enough fuel left to make a proper fire. Dribbles of flame spread along a dark shape revealed as the nose of the good old bloody old Harry Tate. The machine had died but somehow cherished his life to the last, bringing him alive to the ground.

He should get away from the wreck before there was another explosion, but he couldn't move. He knelt, but it was as if his legs were anchored in the ground. His hammering heart slowed. Fumbling at his sooty face, he dislodged the remains of his goggles. It was as if the clouds parted. Moonlight flooded, spreading sickly. He pulled off his helmet and balaclava and wiped his face with the woolly rag.

No Man's Land was a mad landscape. Before the war, Winthrop had toured this country. It had been pleasantly wooded. Now there were no trees. The earth was pitted and cratered and denuded of all but the scrubbiest plant-life. Rolls of barbed wire were savagely strewn. The RE8 had gathered trails of the rusty stuff and dragged it, scratching deep ruts.

Mud-coloured corpses were beaten into the ground. A few feet away, a fanged skull in a *pickelhaube* lay on its side. It must have been there since the first push. The Boche didn't wear helmets like that any more. Winthrop tried not to make out disembodied limbs, tattered scraps of uniform, exposed bones. These former fields, fought over for four years, were seeded with millions of dead.

He checked his arms and legs and, though he found bruises and pain, thought his major bones intact. A bullet had creased his bootsole, burrowing like a worm. His sock was stiff with blood but the shot had done no more than tear his skin.

Standing, his right knee jolted pain. His Sidcot was torn and the pyjama trousers underneath were shredded, though his breeches were merely mashed into his leg. His footing wavered, as if on land after a month at sea. In the air, he had got used to the nothing under his feet. His balance was off but he struggled to recover it. His head swam and he blinked, yawning to open up his aching ears. He fought to regain his relationship with the solid ground, with gravity.

A star-shell burst overhead. The brightness hurt his eyes. White trails showered like jellyfish tendrils. Such infernal devices were to light targets for night-snipers. With what seemed agonising slowness, he crouched against the broken side of the RE8, shadow wrapping around him. His ears still roared, so he could not be sure no one was shooting. The star-burst trails fizzled to the ground and he was still alive.

He looked up at the skies for the bat-shapes. Would the Boche comb the wreckage for survivors? That was absurd. His survival was so unlikely and flopping down in No Man's Land so dangerous that even the Red Baron should leave him be. But he knew enough about vampires to guess the shape-shifted fliers would have their red thirst up.

He was not deaf. Besides roaring and ringing, he heard engine noise. There was definitely a machine still in the sky. One of the Snipes. He wrenched off his helmet and shook gathered sweat out of his hair.

There was gunfire. Specks of light in the air. In the direction from which the engine sound was coming.

He could see little, but imagined a fleeing Snipe, flying low, one of Richthofen's bat-*staffel* things on its tail.

More gunfire. Nearer. A machine passed over. He had the impression of swooping wings and wheels, a Snipe shimmering briefly in moonlight. He turned to follow the fighter's course.

A silent shadow passed, spreading a heart-deep chill. Like a bottom-dweller looking up at a manta ray, Winthrop cringed as the Boche flew over, intent on his prey. The Snipe streaked towards the British lines, wings wavering. It was gaining a lead, leaving the Boche behind. The shape-shifter rose in the sky like a hawk, pouring down fire.

Winthrop couldn't look away. Fire took the fighter in the tail. The Snipe went into a sudden spin. The fire-burst hurt his eyes before he heard the explosion.

The Boche hovered over the crash, underside reddened by firelight. A hugely distended white belly bobbed from the bat's midriff, blue and red veins swarming through the membranous canopies of the wings. He had never seen a vampire so completely shifted from human shape. Not even Isolde was so far gone. Richthofen's flying freaks had fed on Dracula's blood. He understood Mata Hari's confession. The Germans were scientifically cross-breeding to create these monsters.

The Boche rose from his kill on warm air and slipped into the dark of the sky. Slowly, with great straining flaps of his wings, the vampire circled away, returning to the German lines.

Winthrop cursed the murderer's tail. Something in him had died in the crash. Panic burned away, freeing a lizard-like cool from within his brain. This was what it was like to be reborn as a predator. His priorities changed. Immediately, it was important he survive the night and get back to the Allied lines. Beauregard must be told about JG1.

A painful step reminded him of his wounded knee. He needed a crutch. Stuck into the ground was the snapped-off blade of the Harry Tate's prop. It would do. At a pinch, it was sharp enough to pierce a vampire's heart. He wrapped his ruined helmet around the jagged end to pad it, and propped it under his arm.

The Snipe had been heading home. Now its fire was a beacon, signalling the direction he must take. He doubted the pilot would appreciate the use Winthrop was making of his flaming death but could afford no guilt.

There was no point in looking for the RE8's cameras. They must be smashed. If it came to it, Winthrop could draw pictures. Every detail was burned into his memory.

He set out, stumping towards the fire.

Alder, where he had grown up, was on the Somerset levels. In the wetlands, fields were divided by ditches rather than hedges. Outsiders often stood on the village green and assumed it a short walk across the moor to the church where Catriona's father was vicar. But if they took the 'short cut' rather than the winding lane, they would find themselves in a damp maze, forced to walk entirely around fields to find plank bridges laid over the ditches. It could take over an hour to cover the distance a crow could fly in a minute. No Man's Land by night was a similar matter of traps and blinds and dead ends.

Winthrop made his way methodically towards the Snipe's dwindling fire. After dawn he'd be a crawling target for any Boche sniper who cared to draw a bead. Actually, his baggy Sidcot was so muddy it might easily be taken for German grey and earn him a bullet from some enthusiastic but misguided Tommy.

He did not fret and swear when unbreachable tangles of wire or water-filled shell-holes barred his way. Patiently, he retraced his steps and found alternative routes.

His new-mended watch was broken again, stopped at quarter to nine. Possibly, it was not yet ten o'clock. Dog-fights rarely lasted more than a few minutes, though survivors often swore they had fought for upwards of an hour. There were hours before tomorrow's dawn.

Ground crunched and gave under his boots. He was walking on a horse that had been flattened like rolled-out dough. Birds had picked out the eye-sockets. The dead animal was alive with scavenging vermin. Squeaking rats writhed under their horsehide carpet and escaped in all directions. He didn't waste any effort on killing or hating rats. They were no worse than the human feeders-on-the-dead infesting this country.

His knee hurt more. The rest of his pains lessened, if only by comparison. The top of his jury-rigged crutch tore his armpit. His toes were numbed and he hoped the chill would set in around his knee soon.

Shells fell, but not too close. It was Allied policy to pour fire on No Man's Land by night, to discourage German excursions. As things stood, Winthrop considered the logic of the stratagem dubious, though he supposed it a mercy that he was unlikely to run into a lost scout out here in the mud. Even the most impoverished Boche would be equipped with a rifle and a bayonet and all he had to meet aggression was his trusty prop. This was such an impromptu jaunt he'd not even thought to bring a revolver.

The Snipe was directly ahead, its fabric completely burned away. Red-hot metal parts glowed in the last of the fire. It was impossible to tell which of Cundall's Condors this had been.

The daredevil Courtney was dead. Plucked and sucked by the Bloody Red Baron. Almost certainly, Cundall himself had gone west. Not to mention all the Bs: Ball, Bigglesworth, Brown. And, for alphabetical variety, Bill Williamson. Condor Squadron would be crippled.

A shell whistled and burst within a hundred yards. A scattering of dirt pelted his face. It was horribly possible an artilleryman was sighting on the Snipe's blaze, just to have a bright target in the dark.

When he returned, Winthrop would have suggestions to make which would, he felt, greatly improve the conduct of the war. After this picnic, he was entitled to bend Sir Douglas Haig's ear. He'd look up the journalist Kate Reed. As a matter of fact, he'd have looked her up anyway. An idea was forming, and Kate Reed was its budding heart.

With her red hair and sharp tongue, Kate was the vampire Catriona might become. Dainty little fangs in an appealing overbite. Behind her specs, she was smart and resilient. She was the nearest thing to a vampire elder in his circle of acquaintance. He would need an elder. There was no doubt of that. A new-born would not do. The strength was in the bloodline. The Red Baron and his murderous crew were proof of that.

A trap closed on his ankle, barbs sinking into his boot. He wheeled around, lifting his propellor-crutch. He aimed to strike at the thing which held him.

In the dark, there was a human croak. Winthrop saw large eyes in a black, charred face. And shining white teeth, extended vampire incisors exposed by the burning away of the lips.

It would be a mercy to stab with the prop.

The teeth parted with a hiss of breath. Another grip came, at his knee. The creature tried to climb up his leg, to haul itself upright.

It was the pilot. Winthrop couldn't tell which face this had been. The hiss died and the pilot let go of his leg, with an almost apologetic patting motion. The tatterdemalion stood, crookedly. From his twisted shape, he realised the vampire was Albert Ball. The pilot had survived another brush with Richthofen's Flying Freak Show, if barely. His Sidcot was fused with flesh, moulded black over his living bones.

'Good Lord,' Winthrop said.

The ruined leather of Ball's face made a smile. The pilot extended a contorted claw. Winthrop took the fragile hand and shook it, afraid fingers would snap off. He was grateful for the gauntlet that prevented him from touching the crackling greasiness of Ball's skin, but felt the cooked-through warmth of the pilot's grip.

'We'll have to get you home,' he said.

Ball nodded his bald skull. His flying helmet was burned on to him. Cloud drifted across the moon. The darkness deepened.

By himself, the chances had been slim enough. Now, Winthrop would have to get to the lines with the sorely wounded Ball.

These things were sent to try him.

'Come on, old son,' he said to Ball. 'It's this way, I believe.'

They walked towards the sound of the British guns.

21

THE CASTLE

With Prussian insouciance Oberst Kretschmar-Schuldorff dangled a Turkish cigarette from his lower lip. Smoke filled the car, wavering as they took the uphill road to the chateau. The officer sat opposite Poe and Ewers, sharp eyes glittering beneath his peaked cap, suggesting obscure amusement. None of the three cast a reflection in the dark windows. The driver knew his way by night, but the road was not of the best. Poe feared for Ewers's luggage, which was roped to the roof.

'We're not much used to visitors at Malinbois,' Kretschmar-Schuldorff admitted. 'So our facilities are primitive.'

Poe was prepared to be gracious. Any accommodation was likely to be an improvement on the ghetto. Ewers, irritability increasing by the hour, was less inclined to accept without complaint what life presented him.

'The chateau is ancient,' the officer said. 'There was a fortress on the site when Caesar divided Gaul. The current structure dates in part from the tenth century. It is of historical interest to vampirekind. It is named for the Sieur du Malinbois, an elder destroyed in the 1200s.'

'A sergeant at the station told us it was an evil place,' Poe said.

Kretschmar-Schuldorff shrugged without disturbing the smoke. A sardonic smile seemed always to underly his affectation of cool.

'Like your famous House of Usher, perhaps? Who is to say what is evil? In some, old feelings run deep.'

'He was not a true patriot,' Ewers said. 'He should be reported and demoted.'

'A man might be a patriot and not care for Malinbois,' Kretschmar-Schuldorff said. 'Who knows, Herr Ewers? You may not care yourself for our chateau.'

Through the windows, Poe saw the outlines of tall, broken trees pressing close on the road. The country here was dreary and uninviting. There was a centuried air of desolation, overlaid by the devastation of the last few years.

'There is a lake near the chateau,' said Kretschmar-Schuldorff, smiling more broadly, 'but it is not like the tarn of Usher. I think it unlikely that our quarters will crumble and pitch us all into stinking waters.'

'What an amusing thought,' Ewers said, trying to be cutting.

'It is the duty of all intelligence officers to have only amusing thoughts. Our primary responsibility is morale.'

Ewers looked as if, at this moment, his morale was at its lowest. Strangely, Poe took heart. He wondered if his own comparative lightness of feeling was sparked by the warm girl's blood seeping through his undead body.

'When we round the next corner, Herr Poe, you'll be able to see the chateau.'

The car strained and made the turn. Poe saw the castle with the moon behind it: a black shape with towers and battlements. In the silhouette, only one light burned, high up in the highest tower.

'Is that for us?' he asked.

The Oberst shook his head. 'It is for the fliers.'

They drove along the shore of a placid lake. Beside it was a cleared space Poe took for the airfield.

'Don't they tend to crash their aeroplanes into the tower?'

Kretschmar-Schuldorff laughed, musically. 'Herr Poe, you will be greatly surprised by many things.'

He had the idea a great mystery was being kept from him, and a thirst was excited. It was like his red thirst, but for knowledge rather than blood. He had always loved wrestling with puzzles and ciphers and conundra. He was a journalist and a detective, but it was as a poet he most desired to solve mysteries. He sensed a fresh challenge to his ratiocinative powers.

A castle, a mystery, blood and glory. All the elements were here for a romance of the grotesque and arabesque.

'Look,' Ewers said, pointing.

There were darker shapes in the dark sky, flapping things faintly outlined by the moon.

'Bats?'

'No, Herr Poe. Not bats.'

The shapes moved in formation. Poe judged them much bigger than bats.

'Vampires?'

Kretschmar-Schuldorff nodded and lit a fresh cigarette. Match-fire reflections sparked in his amused eyes.

In a flash, Poe penetrated the mystery. He knew what these creatures were.

'Shape-shifters,' he said, delighted with himself. 'These are the Baron von Richthofen's fliers. They don't fly aeroplanes. They grow wings.'

'Exactly.'

Ewers was astounded, annoyed not to be let in on the secret. Poe's heart and mind soared.

'It's a marvel,' he said. 'They have become angels.'

'Hell's angels, perhaps. Before the war is done, they might be fallen angels.'

The formation flew around the tower light. They must be huge, two or three times the height of a man. Their wings beat slowly, and they seemed to glide rather than fly. Poe would not have said it was possible, but here was the miracle itself.

'And all this is through the development of inherent vampire capabilities?'

Kretschmar-Schuldorff nodded. 'Tony Fokker has helped nature, designing contraptions they wear to increase airworthiness. And harnesses for the machine-guns. As yet, no vampire has been able to grow a set of Spandau teats and belch bullets at the enemy.'

'As yet?'

Kretschmar-Schuldorff shrugged. Obviously, that would come.

The first of the fliers turned in the air, wings spreading like sails as he slowed. He landed perfectly on the tower, wings cloaking around him. One by one, the fliers touched down. Smaller figures swarmed around them, confirming Poe's estimate of their height.

'Who would believe it? Even among those who have seen it, who would believe it?'

'Perhaps only a poet, Herr Poe. That is why a poet was required. You have seen it and you must convince the rest of the world.'

A straggling flier limped after the others. There was a great tear in the leather of one wing and he fought to stay aloft. Missing the landing site, this dark wounded angel slapped against the side of the tower and clung fast, barbs and claws gripping the ancient stonework. Tail dangling and wings folded, the injured flier climbed up to his fellows. Poe shared his pain, imagining what it must be like…

'I must see more,' Poe said. 'Take me up there at once.'

Kretschmar-Schuldorff waved away eager guards and startled sentries, clearing their way through the castle. Salutes were snapped off and papers were presented.

They ascended inside the tower, Poe taking the lead. He rushed eagerly up the stone spiral. The quietly intolerant Ewers followed, like a nanny who disapproves of the latitude allowed her charge by indulgent parents. Poe wanted to see the marvellous creatures. All other concerns flew.

The stairs widened and emerged in the flagstone floor of a large chamber. Moonlight sliced in through arrow-slit windows. Torches burned in sconces. A curtain billowed slightly, cold air wafting through. There was a powerful zoo-like animal smell.

He skidded to a halt in the bat-shaped shadow of a giant. The flier was taller even than he had thought. Poe's eyes were level with the tops of a pair of colossal, polished boots.

Lifting his gaze, he saw a lightly furred body still human in its underlying shape. The wings were folded, like a floor-length coat of living velvet. Hanging on the chest was a surplice affair of canvas and leather that supported a pair of machine-guns. There were other additions: straps to stiffen spines and wires to connect wings. Muscular arms grew from the wingpits, functional but inelegant, with three-fingered hands that reached the gun-handles.

A tight leather helmet became a loose cowl as the head dwindled, then was removed by orderlies who stood on elevated platforms. Fiery eyes shrank, flaring ears contracted, rows of teeth slid back into sheaths. The gaping red mouth closed, forming human lips. Fur faded like a dissolving mask.

'Herr Poe,' Kretschmar-Schuldorff said, 'this is Manfred, the Baron von Richthofen.'

Poe could say nothing.

The Red Baron was resuming human form. Orderlies swarmed around like valets, relieving him of guns, boots and straps. As he shrank, his flying gear threatened to crush him and had to be removed with care. There were racks for the equipment.

The baron's two personal orderlies worked swiftly and expertly. Surprisingly, they were warm men.

'These men have been with the Baron throughout the war,' Kretschmar-Schuldorff explained. 'Feldwebel Fritz Haarmann and Kaporal Peter Kurten. They are the squires of our knight of the sky.'

Haarmann and Kurten did not bicker as they carried out their duties. Poe assumed they must be in a state of perpetual awe. Richthofen's square, blue-eyed face emerged from the bat-mask. Poe recognised him from the Sanke card likenesses sold at railway stations throughout Germany.

The other fliers crowded into the chamber, pointed heads and hunched backs scraping the stone ceiling. There were dozens of ground staff to attend their transformations. There was so much activity that only Poe had the time to wonder.

'That is Professor ten Brinken, Director of Experimentation.'

Kretschmar-Schuldorff indicated a grey-faced, broad-shouldered man, hunched in a grubby white coat. The professor growled, checking measurements against a chart.

'And this is General Karnstein, commandant of the chateau.'

A distinguished elder, with grey hair and a jet-black beard, stood by with quiet pride. There was something of the eighteenth century in the cut of his uniform.

Richthofen's face was completely human now. He had shrunk to eight feet or so, half the size he had been. Muscles flowed into new configurations as the skeletal structure adjusted. Haarmann and Kurten produced large, soft-bristled brushes and swept away the hair shed as the Baron changed. In an instant redistribution of bone and tissue, the flier sucked his rudimentary arms back into his midriff. The shape-shifting was fluid and painless, apparently without effort.

It was wonderful magic. Wings stretched out and became arms, leather folding up like a Chinese fan, smoothing into fair skin. Richthofen's iron face betrayed no discomfort, though other fliers yelped and groaned as joints popped and bones reset. Ten Brinken, a stern but proud parent, observed with approval.

Medical men stepped in like the trainers of a pugilist, placing stethoscopes to chests, observing wounds as they healed, taking notes. Orderlies like Haarmann and Kurten provided robes for the fliers. They folded into themselves and grew down to their human heights, settling into their usual shapes.

They all looked human now. Vampires, obviously, but human. But these men, these fliers, were gods and demons and angels. Poe understood why he was needed here. Why the insignificant Hanns Heinz Ewers would not serve. Only Edgar Poe was genius enough to do justice to this subject.

In his own shape, Richthofen was a man of medium height, with a flat, handsome face and cold, inexpressive eyes. He settled into a fur-collared dressing gown. It was obvious he held within him great strength and a greater secret, but it would have been impossible to guess its extent.

'Manfred,' Kretschmar-Schuldorff said, 'this is Edgar Poe. He is to work with you on your book.'

Poe presented his hand. The Baron declined to shake it, less through arrogance than through awkwardness. There was a choirboyish prissiness to the hero. A man of action, he had Hotspur's distaste for the frills and comforts of life. He would have little use for poets.

'Herr Baron,' Poe stammered, 'I did not dream...'

'I do not dream either,' Richthofen said, turning away. 'If you will excuse me, I have a report to write. For some of us, words do not come easily.'

22

TROGLODYTES

In No Man's Land, it was impossible to accurately calculate the passage of time and distance. When fire-flashes lit up the burned-out Snipe, the sorry extent of their progress was revealed. It seemed hours had gone by, yet they had covered only a painful hundred yards.

He had assumed he would have to carry Ball on his back, but, despite fearful wounds, the pilot was the more fit to make headway. Ball surmounted obstacles that forced him to detours. The vampire was a miracle of the will to endure. It was as if the flaming crash had burned away all but the essential parts. He crawled crab-fashion, using his hands as adeptly as his feet, squirming over the terrain as if born to it. Through cracks in his black carapace of burned flesh and cloth, muscles and tendons glistened, working like oiled pistons.

Winthrop resolved to be like Albert Ball, to jettison excess mental cargo and concentrate solely on the needs of the moment. He was thinking too much of Catriona, of Beauregard, of Richthofen. He must think only of Edwin Winthrop.

Fingers of light waved in the sky behind them. If it was dawn, they were heading the wrong way, towards the German lines. It must be fire. After a pause, there were explosions, safely remote.

Winthrop found a French helmet for which the owner could have no further use. He detached it, without distaste, from an unrecognisable protruberance. Besides protection, the ridged Adrian helmet gave him an Allied silhouette. Now, he was less in danger from his own side. Of course, any good German they ran into would shoot him on sight.

He doubted the Boche regularly sent night patrols this far into No Man's Land, but if the big push everyone expected was in the offing there might be sneak parties out making maps and clearing paths. And there were probably Germans wandering around as lost as he was, in traditional blind, trigger-happy panic.

'And we are here as on a darkling plain swept with confused alarms of struggle and flight,' he remembered from 'Dover Beach', 'where ignorant armies clash by night.' Matthew Arnold was one of the prophets of the age.

While Winthrop outfitted himself through grave-robbery, Ball scrambled over the ridge of a shell-crater. Winthrop clambered over a shattered gun-carriage and, leaning heavily on his prop, looked down into the dark where Ball was crawling. In most circumstances, he would have found a vampire like Albert Ball disquieting.

His back, turned to Hunland, prickled. He anticipated bullets that would rip through him, ending this nightmare excursion. Suddenly alert, he jumped off the lip of the ridge and slid down in Ball's wake. His panic passed. He had no idea what had spooked him.

The jump jarred his bad knee and he almost lost hold of the propellor blade. He swore loudly and extensively. Not recommended conduct in a young officer eager to be advanced.

The crater was deeper than any they had yet passed. Under its rim darkness was complete, but the muddy bottom was gently moonlit. Another star-shell flared. At least from inside the hole they could not see the damned skeleton Snipe.

Ball made it to the bottom of the hole and waited for Winthrop. The pilot stood, limbs unkinking like the fake cripple faith-healed in *The Miracle Man*. His outstretched arms bent the wrong way.

Out of the firing lines of both trenches, the crater was an oasis of safety in a desert of peril. By the time Winthrop got to him, Ball had cracked open a pocket in his Sidcot, or possibly his skin, and slipped out a copper cigarette case.

'Care for a gasper?'

Ball stuck a cigarette into his mouth, nipping the end between exposed teeth, and patted his pockets for a box of matches. Winthrop took a cigarette and found his own matches.

'Ta, old son,' Ball said as Winthrop struck a light. 'Mine went off in the bad business back there.'

Without lips, Ball slurred his consonants badly. It was hard for him to suck flame to the tobacco, but a few strong draughts did the trick. His fused nostrils popped open as he exhaled.

Winthrop relished the tang of smoke. It was a living taste.

The crater was full of forgotten war dead, jumbled together, pounded into mud. Corpses of all nations were under them everywhere they trod. It was a mass grave waiting for earth to be shovelled in.

'This must be the proverbial pretty pass things come to.'

Ball looked around the hole. His eyelids were burned away. Winthrop saw the red tangle of muscle around his eyeballs. The crater was about thirty yards across.

'Been in worse. Last time, I was shot down in Hunland and had to slog through their trenches. That show was considerably bloodier than this jaunt.'

'But last time you were shot down by somebody in an aeroplane.'

'True enough, but wings are wings.'

Winthrop shook his head. It would not do to dwell on what had happened in the air. Not yet.

'Time to push on,' Ball said, stubbing out his cigarette on the steep incline of the crater's side.

They walked across the bottom of the hole. When he stood straight, Winthrop's back ached. He'd been crouching and cringing for hours, trying to present a smaller target.

Ball stopped and held his head like a dog cocking an ear, sensing danger. Before Winthrop could ask what was the matter, darkness swarmed up around them.

They were surrounded by a forest of living scarecrows. Suddenly electrified corpses rose from shallow graves or random piles. Guns were produced and pointed, and cold hands laid on them. Winthrop felt a clutch of pain at his throat and the prod of a bayonet-tip at his ribs. Again, he knew he was seconds from death. Foul breath wafted at his face. If the grip on his throat had relaxed, he would have choked on it.

He could not immediately identify the uniform of the soldier who held him. Tatters were applied to the body with mud, as if the man were an African savage. A cloak of camouflage netting was threaded with twigs and leaves. A necklace of cartridge cases and fingerbones hung on his chest.

A match struck and a thick-bearded face loomed close to his own. Red eyes shone from a mask of filth. Jagged vampire teeth gnashed, wet with bloody spittle.

'Who goes there? Friend or foe?'

The voice was British, but not officer-class. Winthrop would have put the soldier down as a Northcountryman. His terror eased.

'Lieutenant Winthrop,' he said, through a constricted throat, 'Intelligence.'

The creature laughed and Winthrop's terror returned. The throat-grip did not slacken. There were still malice and hunger in the red eyes.

'I know you,' the British corpse said. 'You're a poacher.'

Winthrop was slowly strangling.

'Hunting rights in this estate are exclusive,' the soldier said, indicating the death-strewn wilderness. 'I represent those who hold them.'

Another of the risen dead came to examine the catch. This one was well off his territory: the remnants of an Austrian uniform suggested he had deserted from the Eastern Front to get here. A gasmask, lenses gone from the eyeholes, made his head bulbous. Runic symbols were etched into the leather and a curly moustache was painted on the snoutlike filter.

'Ho, Švejk,' said Winthrop's captor, 'we've netted a representative of Intelligence.'

Švejk laughed too, a muffled malignance. Under the mask, his eyes were maddened.

'Good work, Mellors. Intelligence is a thing we've too little of.'

Švejk spoke thickly accented English.

Among the pack, Winthrop saw French, British, German, American and Austrian gear. Some combined equipment from different combatant countries. A golden-haired youth, face painted or dyed scarlet, wore a French tunic and a German helmet, and carried an American carbine.

Winthrop and Ball were manhandled to the other side of the shell-hole. Winthrop's propellor was torn away. He bit down on a scream as his knee exploded again. It would not do to show too much funk.

In the side of the crater was an opening disguised by netting and debris. A dirty curtain whisked aside. They were hustled into a tunnel.

'These used to be Froggie trenches,' Mellors, Winthrop's captor, explained. 'Then they were Fritzie trenches. Now, they're our bailiwick.'

'Who are you?' Winthrop asked.

'*Nous sommes les troglodytes,*' said a Frenchman.

'Correct, Jim,' barked an Austrian. 'We are the cave-dwellers, the primitives…'

'That's Jules for you,' said the Frenchman. 'Always explaining. I make the poetry, he adds footnotes.'

'We've gone to earth,' Mellors said. 'Down here, there is no war.'

After a few yards of downwards slope, the earth floor was boarded over and the roof was shored up by stout wooden pit-props.

'German workmanship,' Mellors said. 'More concern for the comfort of the fighting man.'

There was more laughter at this remark. Especially from Germans.

These were renegades, deserters from all sides. All seemed *nosferatu*. Winthrop had heard tales of such degraded creatures, maddened by continual combat, hiding in the thick of war, scavenging for survival. Up to now, he had classed the stories among the legends that had sprung up throughout the war, successors to the ghost bowmen of Mons, the crucified Canadian and the Russians with snow on their boots.

'We get few warm visitors,' said Mellors, with a tone of resentful mockery. 'This is indeed a privilege.'

Winthrop thought he heard Derbyshire in Mellors' voice. The soldier obviously had some education but spoke as if trying to forget what he'd learned. There was an ill-sewn set of lieutenant's pips on his shoulder. He might have won a field promotion from the ranks. It would not do to underestimate this unhappy rogue.

Held between Jules and Jim, Ball offered no resistance. He was gathering resources, trying to see a way through. Winthrop knew he could count on the pilot.

The passageway widened and they emerged into an underground dugout decorated like a neolithic cavern. Fires burned in oildrums, coating the ceiling with thick soot. Crude but striking images of violence and rapine were daubed on the walls with boot-black, dirt and blood. The collage incorporated newspaper portraits of Kaiser and King, images of generals and politicians, advertisements from the popular press of Paris and Berlin, and personal photographs of long-lost men. Sweethearts and wives and families were worked into a red and black inferno. All were swallowed by a many-eyed, many-mouthed monster that allegorised the war.

There was an overwhelming stench of decay, blood and faecal matter. Homemade coffins were laid out, each billet personalised with items that suggested its occupant's former life. Foraged weapons and clothes were piled in unsorted lots. There were also scatterings of human bones, some old, some disturbingly fresh. The troglodytes lived in this appalling bolt-hole, emerging by night to feed on the dead and dying.

'Welcome to our happy retreat,' Mellors said, gesturing freely. 'As you see, we have made for ourselves a utopia away from the idiocies above. We have settled our differences.'

'There are no German and French, British and Austrian here,' said Švejk. 'All allies, all comrades.'

Mellors let go of Winthrop's neck. As he bent over to choke and gulp in air, he was skilfully spun round. His wrists were bound with loops of barbed wire. Points stuck into his skin, discouraging struggle.

'And there's no rank,' Mellors said.

'You're still wearing your pips,' Winthrop pointed out.

Mellors smiled nastily.

'Don't make me an *officer* by your lights, *sir*. Not a scholarship boy.'

'I might have known,' the ghastly remnant of Ball said through shiny teeth. 'A grammar school oik.'

Mellors laughed deeply and bitterly. For a moment, Winthrop was almost embarrassed by Ball's sneering. He had been at Greyfriars himself but did not think that alone earned him a place in Heaven. Good schools produced as many swindlers and stranglers as missionaries and martyrs. After all, Harry Flashman was a Rugby man.

As a conclusion to the night's business, it seemed odd to listen to a debate between a pair of grotesque vampires on the merits of their old schools. The Nottingham-born Ball was not even that far removed from Mellors in background.

'The enemy of the soldier is not the soldier on the other side of the ditch,' Mellors said, 'but the high muckety-muck who sends him out to do and die. King or Kaiser, Ruthven or Dracula. They're all the same stamp of bastard.'

'We are good soldiers,' shouted Švejk. 'We are the troglodytes.'

Mellors took off his camouflage cloak and draped it over one of the coffins. The long box was fashioned from ammunition cases broken apart and nailed together.

'You are not our enemy, Winthrop,' Mellors said kindly.

'I'm glad to hear it. Now, if we could be on our way…'

'You are a living man and you can do us no harm. Only the dead hands of the old men hurt us. The century-befuddled fools with their titles and honours and bloodlines and lineage, they are the monsters who have reduced us to what you see.'

Ball's eyes swivelled. He was bound too, hoisted up by a couple of the troglodytes. There were iron hooks set into the concrete wall, high up and painted to fit in with the savage mural. Ball hung from the hook, shoulder-joints creaking, arms forced behind him. He hissed through lengthening teeth.

'This man has suffered,' Mellors said. 'That's obvious. Why should he suffer? What is it to him which weak-blooded parasite holds sway over the muddy stretch of countryside up above?'

Ball howled like a rage-maddened animal, showing the proper school spirit. He snarled abuse at his captors.

Winthrop's wrists were yanked upwards. Barbs tore flesh. Pain burned in his shoulders.

'No sir, you are not our enemy, but you might be our salvation. As you see, we are sadly short on provisions.'

Švejk's head expanded inside his mask. His eyes grew to fill the holes, wolfish hair swarming around them.

Winthrop was lifted by troglodytes. His wrists scraped as they were forced up over the hook. His heels scrabbled at the wall as his captors let him go. His weight dragged him down, but his feet did not reach the floor. A belt of agony fell across his shoulders and neck.

One of the troglodytes, a kilted Scot, sniffed his swollen knee. He pulled off the boot and rent apart Winthrop's layers of clothes, then ran a long, sandpapery tongue over the wound. Winthrop fought to keep his stomach down.

Mellors reached up and pinched his cheek.

'You might last for weeks,' he said.

23

SOME OF OUR AIRCRAFT ARE MISSING

Her best bet was to seem as small, harmless and mole-like as possible. She fluttered stupidly behind her glasses. She had survived childhood by such disguise. Somehow she didn't think the act would fool Dravot. At least she had not been thrown into a cell to await a formal arrest. Dravot favoured the use of the currently unoccupied pig-pens but, without an officer to back him up, had no real authority.

Kate was the latest novelty in the pilots' mess. At another time, she might have turned this to her advantage. Pilots were a nervy, chattery, show-offy crowd. If she kept her ears open, she could fill in blanks.

Dravot stood in shadows, head bowed by the low ceiling, eyes fixed on her. Even he did not suppose her liable to attempt an act of traitorous sabotage.

With Major Cundall, the flight commander, out on patrol, the ranking officer was a hawk-nosed American, Captain Allard. He peered into her soul with gimlet eyes, then allowed idle pilots to adopt her as a mascot while he decided whether she should be put to the stake now or at dawn.

Kate was in the custody of three absurdly young Englishmen: Bertie, Algy and Ginger. They offered her animal blood, which she kindly refused. She knew their type. They bantered continually and competed good-naturedly for attention, projecting boyish bravado by ever-so-casually mentioning feats of heroism and stupidity. When she asked what they thought of the war, they became embarrassed and clucked about 'duty, old thing' and the threat posed to cucumber sandwiches, country lanes and cricket matches if the Kaiser and Dracula were allowed to prevail.

Kate was not sure what use those things would be in the world she wanted to see after the war. If there was an 'after the war'.

'I say,' Algy began, 'are you one of these suffragette dollies?'

'Votes for women and all that rot?' chipped in Bertie.

'I'd like to see votes for everyone. When was the last time anyone in Britain got to vote?'

Lord Ruthven had suspended electoral process for the duration, calling a Government of National Unity. Lloyd George, notional Leader of the Opposition, was Minister of War. The Prime Minister still cited the twenty-year-old achievement of bringing the country through the Terror as qualification for continuance in office. His government might be inept, cruel and politely tyrannical, but it had emerged from the bloody nightmare of the Dracula years. By comparison, Ruthven was not so bad. At least he was a *British* bloodthirsty monster, and personally a modest, grey presence beside the fiery, imperious atrociousness that characterised the former Prince Consort. It was hard to think of a hard-and-fast decision made by the Prime Minister. His invariable policy was prevarication. Ruthven took blame for nothing.

'When the time is right, things will get back to normal, old girl,' Bertie said. 'We're on the side of decency, you know.'

The complacent smugness of these brave children was tragic. They were unlikely to survive the war, let alone the peace. Average life expectancy for a pilot on the Western Front was something like three weeks.

Ginger looked at his wrist-watch and tutted. All the pilots kept consulting time-pieces, even glancing at the stopped grandfather clock. It had been a good two and three-quarter hours since the patrol passed over her on the road.

'Never fear,' Bertie continued, 'it'll turn out for the best.'

A Sopwith Snipe fighter could stay in the air for only three hours. That nasty little fact concerned the men of Maranique rather more than one stray dotty lady journalist.

Kate knew it was rare for a whole patrol to be wiped out. Stragglers and survivors would always come through, limping home with smoking engines and singed wings.

She was received at the airfield with comparative kindness because she served as a distraction. If not for her capture and casual interrogation, the pilots would have listened over and over to 'Poor Butterfly', nerves tighter with each passing minute.

'I've an Aunt Augusta who was a suffragette,' Algy said. 'Chained herself to the railings outside Parliament. It rained like a drain and she caught a deathly chill. Had to turn vampire to come through it. Grew young again, ditched the old uncle, became a ballet dancer. Doesn't talk much about the vote and such these days. She wants to dance *The Rite of Spring* at Sadlers Wells. Slings around with that chap Nijinsky. You know, the bounder who shape-shifts in mid-*pas de deux*.'

'Three hours,' Allard announced, eyes cold. 'The patrol is lost.'

There was a long, wordless pause. The gramophone clicked, waiting to be rewound.

'Steady on,' said Bertie, finally. 'Give a couple of minutes' grace. Old Tom and the rest have come through many a scrape in extra time, on fumes and prayers. No need to spread despond at dear old Wing.'

'The three hours are up. No matter the quality of the men, the machines will fail.'

Allard was an American. He did not seem part of the club. Even for a vampire, there was something strange in his eyes. Kate was suddenly aware again that it was a long time since she had fed. Her heart felt like a concrete lump.

As the Captain picked up the telephone, Algy said, 'Come on, no need for that.'

Allard ignored Algy.

'Wing, Allard, Maranique,' he said, not wasting words. 'Cundall's patrol is missing. We have to assume they're lost.'

A voice at the other end crackled.

'Yes,' Allard said. 'All of them.'

Ginger, Algy and Bertie were disgusted. It was bad form to say such things, as if talking out loud made the loss more likely. If Allard were not so blunt, they'd blithely expect their friends to turn up, a little bruised, with exciting yarns of hairsbreadth escapes and daring wheezes.

Allard replaced the telephone. On a blackboard were listed the names of pilots, the serial numbers of aeroplanes, and a tally of individual victories. Several columns already ended with a chalked word, 'lost'. A column was not wiped out until a loss was confirmed. Allard wrote 'lost' against columns headed 'Ball', 'Bigglesworth', 'Brown', 'Courtney', 'Cundall' and 'Williamson'. His chalk scratched and skittered, setting Kate's sharpened teeth on edge.

'Don't forget Courtney's supercargo,' Ginger said, gloomily.

Allard nodded, acknowledging his omission but implying he had already throught of it. He chalked a new name on the board. 'Winthrop'.

'Some hero from Diogenes,' Bertie explained. 'Poor blighter. First time up and he gets shot down.'

Kate almost said something but thought better of it. Dravot's fixed expression did not change. She knew the sergeant must feel as keenly as it was possible for him to feel that he had not done his duty. He was supposed to protect Charles's protégé and had been unable to do so. If anything could hurt Dravot, that would be it.

When they had parted in Amiens, there had been something unfinished between Edwin and her. What was he doing in the air anyway? He was a staff officer, one of those stay-at-home souls never exposed to fire and blood.

'It'll be a devil of a job to replace that little lot,' Ginger said, contemplating the blackboard. There were more 'lost' columns than active pilots. 'Probably have to haul in a whole flight of Yanks. No offence, Allard. It just won't be the same.'

'Don't learn their names,' Allard said.

Ginger was devastated by the advice.

Kate had known too many truly dead, in the Terror and now in the war, to be entitled to feel any especial loss. But entitlement meant little. She had not earned the right to mourn, but she did. Her heart, starved of blood, ached.

24

HANGING ON THE OLD BARBED WIRE

Too exhausted to stay awake, too hurt to sleep, Winthrop hung on the wall like the Sunday joint. The pain in his shoulders, neck and knee was still sharp, but otherwise he was numb. His mind drifted, his senses slurred.

He and Ball were not immediately to be cut up and eaten. The troglodytes sat on their coffins and talked among themselves. Each retold his history as if blessing a class of children with a favourite fairy tale. Jules, an Austrian, recounted the story of his original separation from his unit. He had braved many perils before joining up with the tribe. Jim, the Frenchman, chipped in with his own variation on the theme, of desertion to escape the stake after ringleading a mutiny against General Mireau. Jim bitterly recalled the erosion of his patriotic fervour with each fresh injustice, inequity and corruption.

Winthrop shifted on his hook. Shards of pain speared through his shoulders. He bit back his impulse to yelp.

He could not pay attention to the deserters. Stories of privation, desolation and horror became scrambled and monotonous. Perhaps the narratives were embroidered with each retelling, incorporating favoured incidents from the stories of those who had passed on.

Though savage and socialist, there was order in this vampire community. Mellors said there were no ranks, but others deferred to him. He was called to arbitrate in disputes, to decide courses of

219

action, to pass judgement on the likeliness of a particular anecdote. Had it not been for his counsel, the troglodytes would have torn Winthrop to scraps on the spot rather than husbanded him against future need.

Mellors was chieftain and the snouted Švejk his Holy Fool. After the story-telling, Švejk got up and acted out a story his audience already knew, the saga of the capture of the burned men from the sky, eliciting harsh laughter by aping the crooked Ball and the upright Winthrop. The creature had Ball's mangled voice exactly, and provoked howls of humour with his imitation.

Ball's eyes were red and awake in the blackened mask of his face.

When Švejk had finished his performance, Mellors stood up and walked over to the prisoners. He looked at Winthrop's swollen knee.

'Nasty twist,' he said, not cruelly. 'But nothing broken.'

He unlaced Winthrop's remaining flying boot and wriggled it off, then stripped away the thick, stiff socks. After being hung, Winthrop could not feel his feet but he saw them as purple and bulging.

'The blood has rushed to your feet,' Mellors said, prodding an engorged toe. 'Perfect.'

Mellors sprouted a barb from his thumb and pricked Winthrop's foot. There was a tingling and a dribbling gout of blood.

'There's a taste for everyone, lads. Queue up for your char.'

Švejk was first, lifting his gas mask for a quick guzzle. Winthrop felt a warm wetness on his foot. And sharp little prickles. By turns, the troglodytes came forwards to lap his blood.

He had known vampires, of course. But he'd never before given blood. This was not what he had imagined. This was not pleasure or sharing. He had thought he might catch the eye of an elder and offer her his neck. Kate Reed seemed an interesting prospect. Or perhaps he and Catriona would turn simultaneously, tasting each other in a red communion. There would be fluttering curtains and moonlight, and tiny points of pain in a pool of pleasant submission.

Mouths battened on his feet, teeth tore, and his blood leaked. As he lost blood, there was less pain. His arms were ice-cold, his hands nerveless stone appendages.

Mellors looked up at him as the troglodytes fed.

'It's just nature,' the vampire explained. 'You can't complain of nature.'

If one of the creatures was in danger of supping too deeply, Mellors detached him and shoved him back to the pack.

'Hold steady, Raleigh. Not too greedy, now. Leave something for Voerman.'

A mad-eyed English subaltern made way for a young German with a long tongue. There was a doggy malleability to the tribe. They were probably a good fighting force. Winthrop felt as if his foot had been laid open to the bone by razors of ice. Finally, it was over.

Winthrop hung, drained and cold. One of the troglodytes produced a medical kit and expertly bandaged Winthrop's feet. As an afterthought, he took a poke at the knee, digging out fragments of grit, and bound it up tightly. When the medicine man had finished, he and Mellors were the only creatures out of their coffins. The others, fed if not satisfied, lay insensible under blankets or planks.

Mellors dismissed the doctor and checked Winthrop's wrists. With his full weight on the hook, he was not able to lift himself up and free. Ball hung like dried meat, twisted back and arms giving him a crucified appearance. His exposed eyes were unmoving. Satisfied, Mellors retreated to his coffin, hauling his camouflage cloak around him. In an instant, he was sleeping like a dead man. Winthrop fought exhaustion. His body weighed several tons. It dragged his mind down into the depths.

A stab of pain cut through his drowsiness. A barb gouged his wrist. The fires had burned to embers, lending the troglodytes' cavern a red-lit, infernal glow. The creatures lay unmoving in their coffins. Winthrop had no way of knowing what time, or what day, it was.

Something was moving. Unable to turn his neck, he swivelled his eyes, looking as far as possible to his left and right. Rats could not climb up to where he hung.

Ball was contorted on his hook. Winthrop realised the pilot's eyes were open and his mouth red. He had hauled himself up, further bending his already bent arms, turning on his side to press his hip to the wall. He had got his teeth to the twine around his wrists. No, he had got his teeth to his wrists.

Ball saw Winthrop was awake and gave a deliberate, silent nod. His mouth scraped at his left wrist, peeling back cooked skin to show red flesh. He chewed white tendons and exposed bone. As Ball bit deeper into himself, vampire blood dripped to the floor. Švejk snorted in his sleep. Ball was still for a moment, awaiting an attack, but renewed his efforts.

Winthrop felt useless. There was nothing he could do. The meat was gnawed away from Ball's wrist. His skeleton hand, gloved in flesh, flexed into a fist. The twine loop was loose but unbroken. Silver wire glinted inside the string. Only in this war would chandlers manufacture rope specifically for binding the *nosferatu*.

Ball hung on to the hook with his right hand. Setting his red teeth together in a jagged grin, cheek-muscles clenching with determination, the pilot pulled sharply, lodging twine between the bones of his left wrist, and swallowed a groan. The fist opened like a starfish, sticking out dead fingers. An artery gushed. Ball tugged again and the hand came off, falling with a wet smack to the ground. Blood welled from the stump. Ball, free, hung from the hook, twisting his legs in agony.

Even Winthrop smelled the rich vampire blood. Troglodytes stirred in their slumbers, nostrils twitching, mouths watering, claws scratching lids. When he let go of the hook, Ball did not so much fall as slide down the wall. For an instant, Winthrop was afraid his comrade had exerted himself so much that the shock of clumping against the earth had knocked him unconscious.

Ball held his stump with his unhurt hand. Blood oozed between his fingers. Shamefully, he dipped his head and licked his wound, sucking his own juice like Isolde at the Théâtre Raoul Privache. It was a perverse act among vampires, but clearly brought relief.

A troglodyte sat up stiff as a board, fencepost fangs sprouting from his mouth. It was Plumpick, a mad Scot with gentle eyes.

With a loose-limbed, liquid movement, Ball stabbed Plumpick's chest with his stump. The jagged edge of bone sank through the ribs and pierced the heart. Life died in the deserter's eyes and teeth crumbled like humbugs in his mouth. The weight of the dead vampire dragged Ball over and he was fixed in place over Plumpick's coffin.

With a quick fist-clench, Ball snapped his arm at the elbow and pulled free, leaving the spars of his forearm bones stuck through Plumpick's heart. He was coming apart fast.

Winthrop writhed on his hook, trying to edge up the wall with his shoulders and back. He knew he could not hope to duplicate Ball's stunt.

Ball silently and swiftly crossed the cavern, weaving between coffins, and stood before Winthrop. A man of his undead strength could easily take Winthrop by the hips and lift him bodily off the hook. A man of Ball's undead strength with two arms, that was.

It was awkward. Ball slipped his remaining arm between Winthrop's legs and made his hand into a seat which he jammed upwards. The slight, bent man stood up as straight as he could, making of his spine and arm a column which hoisted.

His bound wrists unhooked from their perch. His arms flopped down behind him and his whole weight fell on Ball, who staggered forwards and bent at the waist. In a tumble, Winthrop landed on dirt. His hands were on fire and his bandaged feet stung.

Other troglodytes stirred. Ball, with no regard for injury, scooped up a fistful of red embers from a fire drum and tossed it into Švejk's coffin. A nest of straw caught fire in an instant. The Bohemian hopped and yelped in the smoke.

Winthrop wriggled like a worm. He twisted his wrists round to free himself from the barbed wire. The damned stuff came off in a curl, leaving scabby stigmata on his wrists. He found his boots and hauled one on, ignoring the pain in his knee, then hopped upright and thrust his foot into the other.

Ball had a firebrand and was waving it from side to side, keeping the troglodytes back. Mellors was up, furious but amused.

Winthrop and Ball had their backs to the tunnel through which they had come. If they turned and ran, the troglodytes would bear down on them and rend them apart. But if they stayed where they were, Ball's torch would soon go out.

Mellors hissed curses in Derbyshire dialect. Surprisingly, Ball returned the favour in kind. Švejk rolled in the dust, stifling the flames that licked around his bulk. His coffin still burned.

Winthrop saw the opportunity. Shoving the surprised Ball from behind with his shoulder, he pushed vampire and torch into the faces of the troglodytes, who cringed backwards. Winthrop advanced and took hold of the casket of burning straw, which he pitched upwards, scattering fiery matter across the cavern.

Ball got the idea and touched the torch to the nearest troglodyte, Raleigh. A dirt-starched uniform caught light in an instant, fire swarming up to a bird's-nest beard and long straggle of hair. A high-pitched screech burst from the vampire. In torment, he ran back to his fellows, colliding with them, tripping over coffins, spreading fire.

The netting hanging from the cavern roof caught. Flames swarmed over the mural. The paper elements of the collage burned in flashes. A heated case in a corner exploded, stored bullets popping. Winthrop took to his heels, dragging Ball away from the cavern. They ran upwards.

25

DRESSING DOWN

'You are aware that under DORA, it would be quite in order for me to have you shot,' Beauregard told Kate, meaning it. Under the Defence of the Realm Act, practically any lawfully constituted minion of Lord Ruthven had the gift of life and death over any civilian. 'Really, what *were* you thinking? If you were thinking?'

There was too much other grief to be dealt with in this sideshow, but here he was, lecturing like a cross schoolmaster. Kate looked groundwards and twitched her tiny nose.

'And it's no use impersonating a Beatrix Potter rabbit on the brink of tears, Miss Reed. Remember, I've *known* you ever since you were as wet behind the ears as you like the warm to think. You're fifty-five this year, dead girl.'

She tried a feeble fanged smile.

'There's no excuse,' he concluded.

As he dressed the reporter down, he was aware of Dravot's cold, deep-buried fury. The sergeant would cheerfully cut Kate's head off and use it for a football.

The mess at Maranique was not crowded. Surplus pilots had beetled off to their coffins for the day. Only Allard, the acting CO, was left to face the inevitable enquiries. On the squadron roster, the word 'lost' was chalked by the names of the men who had gone out but not come back.

Furious as Beauregard was with Kate, he was angrier with Winthrop. He had no business going up and getting shot down. After Spenser, he was the Diogenes Club's second crack-up of the young year. Something in this duty sent men off their heads.

Allard sat, scarf over his face against the sunlight that flooded through windowpanes, wide-brimmed hat pulled down. He seemed all beaky nose and penetrating eyes.

'There is no hope?' Beauregard asked.

'I've telephoned every other field in the line,' said Allard. 'It was possible some of the patrol might have come down somewhere else. That did not happen. Major Cundall's flight is lost.'

Beauregard shook his head and damned himself for a fool. Every one of the dead men could blame him.

'Might they be prisoners?' Kate put in.

'The Germans have claimed the victories,' said Allard. 'They have the serial numbers. It is almost certain they will be confirmed. They claim kills, not captures.'

'That's remarkably swift.'

'It usually takes a day or so, but they were right off the mark. The RE8 is claimed by Manfred von Richthofen. A package of personal items was dropped on the field at dawn. Courtney's watch and cigarette case.'

Gloom spread.

'Anything of Winthrop's?'

Allard shook his head.

'There can't have been much left of the lad then?'

His born-dead boy might have grown to be a man like Edwin. Had he lived, his son might now have been a dead man like Edwin, lost to the war. He thought of Pamela, dead in childbirth, never knowing what would become of the world. And he thought of Geneviève, eternally between life and death, perhaps knowing too much.

Kate was upset. The snooping stopped being a game when lines were drawn through the names of the dead. It was odd: she had been indignant about useless death for so long that this could not be her first practical experience of it. She had come through the Terror. She was working as an ambulance woman. She must have seen dozens die.

· 'I'll talk to Mrs Harker. You'll be recalled to England. You'll be lucky to end up counting blankets in the Hebrides.'

'It's no worse than I deserve,' she admitted.

Beauregard was sorry. He had not expected her to give in. She could usually be depended on for an argument. As more and more lately, he was tired. At his age, this cruel game should be well behind him. But, as ever, England expected…

As far as could be gathered from scant reports and the German claims, Cundall's flight had made it to the Chateau de Malinbois and been surprised by the Flying Freak Show. It was a massacre. Six more victories for Richthofen's killers.

'Charles, aren't we supposed to have command of the air?'

Commander Hugh Trenchard of the Royal Flying Corps advocated a policy of offensive patrols. The skies over France were in theory so dangerous for the ordinary German flier that the German Imperial Air Service was useless as an instrument of observation.

'Yes, Kate. On the whole, we do. In this particular engagement, pitting Condor Squadron against JG1, we have come up short.'

'The enemy have done what you've tried to do, grouped together their best fliers, their worst killers, in one unit.'

'You're well up on all this,' he said.

'Condor Squadron was created to pick up intelligence about the spring offensive?'

'A spring offensive, now there's an idea. I don't suppose you can tell me the date Dracula and Hindenburg intend to launch the attack?'

'Don't be childish, Charles. Everybody knows there'll be an enemy offensive soon. Even Bottomley, and he thinks the war is won and the Union Jack flutters over Berlin.'

'My apologies. I am quite tired, you understand…'

Kate ignoring his sarcasm, continued. 'If Condor Squadron are to gather intelligence, then JG1 must be constituted to harbour it.'

Allard laughed bitterly. 'Not necessarily. Richthofen commands a Circus. It's a show, a glamour machine. No matter how many victories they log, fighters make little difference. An unarmed spotter which brings back a clear photograph of defensive trenches can turn a battle round. The air ace is too busy adding to his score to deign to look at the ground.'

Kate's little face scrunched in thought and she tutted. If she forgot to be self-conscious of her looks, she was appealing in a bespectacled way. When warm, she had been Pamela's friend. Kate sometimes used expressions the women shared, which perturbed him. It was as if his truly dead wife spoke through her undead friend.

'With respect, Captain, there must be more to it than headlines. It is all too elaborate. There is a secret purpose to JG1, just as there is a secret purpose to Condor Squadron.'

Allard said nothing.

'I think perhaps we should send you packing now,' Beauregard said.

Kate's cheeks reddened. 'Am I not under arrest? Due for the stake?'

'You'd like to be a martyr, wouldn't you?' Beauregard said. 'To what cause? The standard of the Graf von Dracula?'

That was unfair: Kate had imperilled herself enough through the years to demonstrate opposition to Dracula. But he was still annoyed with her.

'I certainly don't wish to die for Lord Ruthven and his kith and kind. The truth, perhaps. That might be worth spilling this vampire blood for.'

'Oh, go away, Kate. I've not the heart for this row.'

Suddenly, unexpectedly, Kate hugged him, face pressed to his chest. Her grip was fierce but not crushing. She measured exactly her strength.

'I'm sorry, Charles,' she said to his collar, so low Allard and Dravot could not hear.

His bites tingled. He held Kate to him. He remembered another vampire's arms: she reminded him of *her* sometimes, too. It was as if there were but one woman in the world, laughing at him from behind a dozen masks.

'I'm sorry too, Kate.'

Dravot had stood, ready to rip the reporter away from Beauregard and tear off her arms like a cooked chicken's wings. Beauregard motioned the sergeant to stay put.

'I'm still having Mina Harker pull you out of this.'

'I know,' she said, patting his chest, 'it's your duty. You have your duty and I have mine. It is the curse of our generation. Duty. Remember, we are the last Victorians.'

He was too empty to smile. Last night's losses were too terrible to shrug off.

'Captain Allard, can we find some means of transport to get Miss Reed back to her ambulance unit? Preferably something uncomfortable and undignified?'

Allard conceded that a cart could be made available.

'We'd better send a guard. In case she tries to make her escape.'

Allard nodded. He had a good man in mind.

'I'm doing you a great favour, Kate. Within the hour, we shall be answering to Mr Caleb Croft of the Prime Minister's office. You will remember the gentleman from the '80s, when he was given to placing prices on your head. Have *all* those insurgency charges been dropped?'

Kate's eyes, magnified by her spectacles, goggled. A dimple of wickedness crept into her cheek.

'I recall Mr Croft well. Does he still head the British *Okhrana*?'

'Britain has no secret police,' Beauregard explained. 'Officially.'

'Goodbye, Charles. Your loss is my loss.'

Kate left the mess. Dravot's eyes followed her.

'Keep her under observation,' Beauregard told Allard. 'She's cleverer than she looks.'

Allard nodded. He did not miss the implication.

'Make sure your guard isn't a warm man. If you have one about, send a homosexual or a monk. On second thoughts, I wouldn't trust Kate Reed with a monk.'

Weariness fell on Beauregard like a heavy mantle. He did not know what Croft would require of him but it was likely to be unpleasant. Old enmities lingered from the Terror. Croft's department would like to see the Diogenes Club wound up. A Whitehall school of thought held that the likes of Beauregard and Smith-Cumming were *Boys' Own Paper* anachronisms with no place in the harder, crueller secret wars of the twentieth century. That school did not appreciate how hard and cruel the secret wars of the nineteenth century had been.

He had not yet written to Spenser's people. Now, he would have to compose a letter of condolence to Winthrop's family too.

'Sir,' said Dravot.

The sergeant's face betrayed no feeling, but Beauregard understood what a blow this would be. Dravot was not in the habit of losing officers.

'There's no question of blame, Danny. If it rests anywhere, it must be with the dead. Major Cundall asked Winthrop if he wished to go on the flight. The mad, brave boy said yes.'

Dravot nodded once, accepting what was said. Then, awkwardly, he produced a letter.

'Lieutenant Winthrop gave me this.'

Beauregard took the letter. It was addressed to Catriona Kaye, The Old Vicarage, Alder, Somerset. With a dead heart, Beauregard could imagine Catriona Kaye. And he could imagine what was in the letter.

He hated: a directionless, all-encompassing hate. It was not enough to hate the war; he had to hate all the components of the engine that had ground up Winthrop and a million young men like him. He had to hate himself.

'I'll see the letter is delivered,' he told Dravot.

26

A WALK IN THE SUN

The tunnels were dark, but there was light ahead. The sun was up outside. He propelled himself towards the glimmering. Ball stumbled in his wake, determinedly covering ground. The troglodytes, occupied with their fire, did not give immediate chase.

As Winthrop ran, his knee hurt. The field dressing that had been applied was surprisingly sturdy. His booted feet were recovering sensation. He ignored pain.

There were shot sounds but he did not think they were being fired on. Another ammunition case had exploded. Something howled like an animal.

Only a few yards away now, the curtain hung over the tunnel mouth. White dots showed through the weave of camouflage netting. Once out in the sun, they should be safe. The troglodytes were newborns, not yet strong enough to stand daylight.

And so was Albert Ball. The thought hit Winthrop just as he pushed through the curtain. It was too late to change course. He staggered, sprawling, outside and tripped, falling flat onto the pitted bottom of the shell-hole. After the dark, his eyes hurt in the milk-mild light. Blinking, he recovered quickly.

It was a pleasant, quiet day. Not even much bombardment. The air was still sharp with February chill, but the clouds had drifted apart and the sun shone gently.

231

Ball shot out of the tunnel mouth and, smitten, fell. His limbs twisted as tendons shortened, giving him the look of an ossified Pompeiian. His chest and head began to emit tendril wisps of smoke. His face contorted further and stiffened in a scream that came out only as a gasp of escaping gas. He held his hand over his face.

Winthrop scrambled upright and ripped the curtain from the tunnel mouth. He draped it over Ball, wrapping the vampire in cool shadow. The ace's writhing stopped. Ball couldn't last long. Winthrop had seen men burst into flames on days more overcast than this. Vampires were frail immortals, he reminded himself. You had to get a good few years behind you before you could stroll in the sunshine.

The dark cave of the tunnel mouth was alive with eyes. A cruel laugh wafted across No Man's Land. Winthrop helped Ball stand, feeling growing heat in the vampire's body.

'Lovely day,' Mellors said. He stood in the darkness, watching his prey struggle. 'Just right for potting a few grouse.'

Winthrop choked on smoke. He had to get Ball into shadow.

In the tunnel mouth, Mellors raised a revolver. Winthrop pushed Ball to one side and shoved after him, getting out of the line of fire. Mellors fired a shot, which lifted a divot a dozen yards off. He could not draw a bead on them without stepping out into the killing sun.

The troglodytes would not come out until nightfall. But Ball wouldn't be able to make any distance in the daytime. He was shaking, containing an explosion by force of will. Winthrop had a vision of the vampire bursting. He was so close to Ball that his body would be riddled with shrapnel-like bone fragments. That would, at least, be mercifully swift.

Nearby was an isolated patch of wall, remnant of an unidentifiable building. In the lea of the wall was a deep, cool pool of dark. Winthrop gathered his strength and determination, then dragged Ball across the ground. Ball missed his footing but did not become a dead weight.

The wall would afford a shield against fire from the tunnel mouth, but they had to dash across the open to get there. Mellors fired again, with a countryman's accuracy. A red gobbet exploded in Ball's burned-black side. It was a plain lead bullet, for the wound did not slow the pilot.

Before the troglodyte chieftain could draw a bead on the living man, Winthrop was behind the wall, back slammed to shaking bricks. Darkness cloaked around and Ball collapsed. He tried to reach his wound with his remaining hand, but his elbow would not bend as required. Winthrop looked at the mawlike gape. Flesh and skin swarmed actively over shattered ribs. A tiny twig of new growth sprouted from the stump of Ball's lost arm, ending with a bud which might in time be a fresh hand. His healing faculties were exerted, but his wounds were too many and profound.

Having made it behind the wall, it was hard to feel the situation much improved. They had to wait for nightfall to move on. The troglodytes would then be able to bear down on them with despatch. It was unthinkable that Winthrop leave Ball here.

Shots thwacked against the wall, shaking the loose bricks. A few well-placed bullets and the wall would collapse on their heads. Winthrop dug out his cigarette case. He stuck two cigarettes in his mouth, lit them from his last-but-one match, and eased one between Ball's broken teeth. They sucked smoke and shook their heads.

'Really, this is foolish. You pop off home and send back for me.'

Winthrop coughed.

'Not likely help would arrive in time, I admit,' Ball said. Slabs of burned face had chipped away from his soot-blackened skull. One of his eyes was burst and congealed.

Slumped, Winthrop was overcome with weariness. He slid down the wall and hung his head. He wasn't sure he could even continue under his own steam. He had lost blood and been battered extensively. And, discounting his period of hung-up-to-dry unconsciousness, he'd not slept in nearly two days. It was also over a day since he had eaten anything.

'I always intended to have children-in-darkness. I wanted to pass on the gift.'

In his current state, Ball was not a good advertisement for the gift of vampirism. One of his legs was dead, broken in several places, slowly resolving itself to skin flakes, flesh dust and bone chips.

'If I hadn't accepted the Dark Kiss, I'd have been done for when Lothar von Richthofen shot me down. I've stayed on well past my time. Now it's over.'

Winthrop tried to contradict the pilot.

'No, old thing. I can tell I'm done for. There's less and less of me to save, and what's left is not much worth saving.'

'I can't go on either. I'm about done in.'

A shot ricocheted off bricks and spanged across the crater.

The pilot reached down to his leg and crumbled his thigh in his fingers. The skin came apart like burned paper, the muscle wafted to dust and the bone snapped into fragments like a length of chalk. A breeze scattered the dust.

'I'm finished, Winthrop.'

His jaw was loose at the hinges. Blood leaked from his mouth.

'Who turned you?'

Slug-like muscles over Ball's cheekbones twitched. Winthrop realised his lipless, fleshless face was trying to smile.

'A girl on Brighton pier.'

'Was she an elder?'

He was thinking of the centuried Isolde.

Ball shook his head. His scalp and helmet were fused into a loose, fragile covering. 'Just a new-born. An "artist's model". She said her name was Mildred.'

Winthrop could imagine a Mildred.

'Some vampires can regenerate entirely after decapitation.'

Ball's larynx clicked in an approximation of laughter.

'You're welcome to give it a bash, but I doubt you'd have much joy. I've an indifferent bloodline, I think.'

The dying vampire sat up, crinkling his stomach. Winthrop bent his ear to listen. Ball reached out and got a grip on Winthrop's shoulder. He still had strength in his wrist.

'There's only one way I can go on,' Ball whispered.

Thinking he understood, Winthrop loosened his collar. He would not mind Ball drinking his blood.

'It's too late for that.'

Ball's teeth were loose. One or two had slipped out of their holes. His purple tongue was swollen. He let go of Winthrop's shoulder and drew a sharp, thick nail across his throat, stabbing the jugular vein. Viscid blood oozed out. It was more like a jelly than a liquid.

'Take my strength, Winthrop. What's left of it.'

His throat rebelled at the thought. The vampire blood was strong-smelling. In shadow, it caught the sun and shone a pulsing mauve.

'You'll be stronger. You'll take a part of me with you.'

A cloud passed across the sun.

'Evening draws on, my boys,' shouted Mellors.

Ball's eye glowed. 'Winthrop, do it quickly.'

The decision was made for him. He held up the insubstantial Ball, feeling bones dissolving inside him, and touched his tongue to the snake trickle of blood. It was not the familiar, salt tang he knew. It was not human blood. A sherbet-prickle numbed his tongue, and he found himself lapping thirstily at the wound, swallowing ropy, sweet liquid.

Ball shivered in Winthrop's embrace but his slow blood continued to flow. Then, he came apart completely. A bad taste hit Winthrop's mouth at the instant of true death. Ashes fell away from his face.

He coughed, trying hard to keep the lumpy stuff in his stomach. His mind was cleared as if by a dose of salts. His eyes quickened, catching dozens of tiny movements. It was a sensation he associated with the early, pleasant stages of being drunk on champagne.

Ball looked as if he had been dead and forgotten for years. He decomposed drily. His head shrivelled to a thinly parchmented skull. It was detached from the body.

To turn vampire, you have to drink vampire blood at the same time as a vampire is drinking your blood. What he had done with Ball would not make a new-born of him. He was just like those old fools who dose themselves with vampire bloodsalts to retain their vigour. But he did feel changed. His knee ceased to trouble him, and the wire-gouges on his wrists healed over. His weariness was washed away and his hunger soothed.

'Come, civil night, thou sober-suited matron, all in black,' quoted Mellors.

'*Romeo and Juliet*, very good for a grammar school oik.'

'Which of you said that?'

It was strange: as if Albert Ball had spoken through Edwin Winthrop. In his mind, Winthrop remembered flying. Not his own memories, but those of the vampire.

'Both of us, Mellors, and a very good day to you.'

Winthrop stood up and stepped out of the shadow, keeping the wall still between him and the cave mouth. Sunlight did not hurt him, though his face tingled as if he had the beginnings of a tan.

'Ah, it's Winthrop, the observer. Do you plan to run off and leave your comrade. Surely, that's not cricket, not the school spirit.'

'Ball is dead,' he said, not sure.

There was no answer. Then, a shot dislodged some bricks.

Taking the camouflage netting, Winthrop wrapped Albert Ball's skull carefully. It made a bundle about the size of a football. He owed it to the vampire to carry his head as far as possible.

With his bundle under his arm, Winthrop launched himself at the side of the crater and scrambled upwards. Shots dug into the dirt yards either side of him. Then, a *push* at his side.

'A palpable hit,' Mellors shouted.

He gained the lip of the crater and threw himself over it, rolling downwards and lying flat in the blighted plain. Examining his side, he found that the troglodyte chieftain's shot had punched through his loose Sidcot without touching his body.

'You'll have to do better,' he shouted back in farewell.

* * *

Even more than in the crater, Winthrop kept his head down. Now he was exposed to snipers from both lines. Anything that moved in No Man's Land was in season. A bombardment had started. The British were hammering the Germans, which was fortunate. Shells whizzed across well above Winthrop's head and landed near the Boche trenches. That should keep German riflemen concentrated on other things.

He felt a stick in his hands, wind in his face, the thrill of a spin. For a moment, he saw the blue of a summer sky, tracer bullets flaring. He smelled burning castor oil, pouring out of the engine of a Sopwith Camel. Shaking Ball's memories from his mind, Winthrop got to his feet. After an experimental crouch, he stood gingerly.

Nobody shot at him. There was a strange peace. He was tiny and insignificant in this continental killing field. Nobody would notice him.

He walked away from the shell-crater and the troglodytes. By day, the paths between the barbed wire and the rubble-pits were easier. He darted from cover to cover, tacking towards the lines.

For the first time since the Richthofen creature had swooped at the Harry Tate, Winthrop felt it possible that he might survive the next few minutes. He might live a long life, if not a happy one. But he had business to take care of yet. First, he had to tell Beauregard about the bat-*staffel*. Then he had to get back in the air.

He was running, tasting the powdery breeze. It was easy to imagine leaving the ground, and being swept up into the clouds, there to joust with the dark knights of the sky.

He saw a wall of mottled sandbags, topped with swirls of barbed wire. He was moments away from the trenches.

He thought of the score that he must live to even.

Hurdling the wire with a new-found agility, he sailed over the lip of the trench and crashed down. He bent as he landed, coming down on his feet like a cat, and stood up straight.

'Blimey,' said a startled Tommy.

Winthrop handed over his bundle to the soldier, telling the warm man to take good care of it.

'Now, if you would be so good as to guide me to a field telephone, I have a report which must be made.'

The infantryman looked down at the bundle, which was trailing loose. A bony face was disclosed.

'Blimey,' the Tommy reiterated. 'Blimey.'

PART THREE

MEMOIRS OF A FOX-HUNTING MAN

27

THE RED BATTLE FLIER

Richthofen kept him waiting well into the afternoon. There was no reason for the delay. It was simply the habit of *junkers* to have vassals loiter. Poe supposed the flier had little interest in their collaboration. He must co-operate because he had been so ordered by General Karnstein. For Kaiser and *Vaterland*, Manfred von Richthofen would consent to be made immortal by Edgar Poe. To a physical immortal, perhaps the prospect was insignificant.

The Baron's private quarters were not quite spartan but hardly seemed the lair of a great warrior. There was an orderly desk where Richthofen sat to write terse, accurate, tedious reports of aerial exploits. In the last few days, Poe had examined numberless dreary documents. He understood why the Baron was not to be entrusted with the writing of his own memoirs.

Without permission to sit, he paced the room. On the mantel was a row of shining cups. Poe was drawn to the bright things. Each trophy bore a tiny plate, engraved with a formulaic notation: a number, the details of an Allied aeroplane, another number, a date. *11. VICKERS. 1. 23.11.16.* Each commemorated one of Richthofen's victories. The first number was the running total of the hunting bag, the second indicated how many had died in the downed aircraft. Every twentieth cup was double-sized.

There were about sixty of them. That was incorrect. Richthofen's score stood at nearly eighty.

'A silver shortage. The manufacturer made a special case for some months, but there was a tightening of regulations.'

Richthofen had come into the room without Poe hearing him, no mean achievement. He stood in completely human shape, calm and compact. Poe would never have discerned godlike potential in this ordinary soldier but could not forget what he had seen in the tower. Inside the Baron nestled the leather angel of the skies, the perfected vampire form.

'The tradesman offered pewter as a substitute but I took the opportunity to discontinue commemorating my kills with gaudy things. I know in myself my worth. Trophies have come to seem vulgar.'

Poe touched a cup. His fingers stung.

'Real silver?'

'I should give up these baubles for scrap. I'd rather have silver bullets in my guns than silver cups in my den.'

Few vampires cared to have silver around them. It showed daring. If Poe were to grip one of these trophies firmly, his hand would shrivel.

Richthofen stood beside him and regarded the cups. Each marked one or more dead. Göring, the recording officer, impressed upon Poe the arcana of the 'score'. Strictly, only victories over aircraft counted, not the number of dead or downed. A flier could claim a victory by sending a vanquished pilot to a prisoner-of-war camp. Few of Richthofen's cups bore a zero. His victories were kills. Oswald Boelcke, who formulated the tactics of aerial combat, liked to aim for the enemy's engine and let the pilot live. Richthofen always went for the throat. For him, a bloodless victory was no victory at all. Only a kill counted.

'They do not blur and become one. I remember each. I have made reports.'

Boelcke was truly dead, though not in combat: his aeroplane had crashed in mid-air into one of his fellows' machines.

The Baron sat at his desk, at attention even in repose, and indicated a chair. Poe folded himself into it. He was conscious of his shabbiness beside the correctness of the flier. Richthofen's uniform was pressed to perfection, knife-edge creases and drum-tight jacket ready for inspection. Poe's trousers were almost out at the knees. The buttons of his old waistcoat were mismatched.

'So, it begins, Herr Poe. Your book.'

'*Our* book, Baron.'

Richthofen waved an indifferent hand. He had the short nails and stub fingers of a cowboy, not the languid extremities of an aristocratic idler.

'I do not care much for writing. Or for writers. A cousin of mine has formed an unsuitable attachment with an English writer of repulsive reputation. A Mr Lawrence. Have you heard of him?'

Poe had not.

'By all accounts, he is a horrid fellow, dirty from coal mines and animal habits.'

Where to begin? Perhaps it was time to borrow from that queer Jew, Freud. 'Tell me of your childhood, Baron.'

Richthofen began a recitation, 'I was born on the second of May, 1892. My father was stationed in Breslau with his cavalry regiment. Our family seat is an estate at Schweidnitz. I was named Manfred Albrecht in honour of an uncle, an Imperial Guardsman. My father was Major Albrecht, Freiherr von Richthofen. My mother was the former Kunigunde von Schickfuss und Neudorff. I have brothers, Lothar and Karl Bolko, and a sister, Ilse…'

Poe interrupted, timidly. 'I have read your service records. Tell me *about* your childhood.'

Richthofen seemed to have nothing to say. In the depths of his eyes, there was (almost entirely veiled) drowning bewilderment.

'I do not understand what you want of me, Herr Poe.'

Poe did not expect to feel pity for the merciless hero. The Baron, though he would never let it show, was lost. Something was missing in him.

'What do you remember? A place, a pastime, a toy…?'

'My father told me I was different from the boys of the peasants who worked the land. They were Slavs. Orientals inferior to Prussians. Our family was Teuton, among the first to establish themselves in Silesia.'

'Did you feel different?'

Poe remembered his own childhood, estrangement from his fellows as an American in England.

Richthofen shook his head. 'No. I felt as I always have. I am myself. There has never been any need to question that.'

His backbone was as straight as a ramrod.

'What was your first passion?'

'That of any boy. Hunting in the woods.'

Richthofen was a hunter still. Was it too easy to deem him just a hunter, with no other light or dark to his soul?

'With my rifle, I shot three of my grandmother's tame ducks. I pulled a feather from each as a trophy. When I presented these to my mother, she scolded me. But my grandmother understood and rewarded me.'

'Like George Washington, you could not tell a lie?'

'I was admitting nothing. I was claiming my kills.'

'You saw no wrong in killing?'

'No. Do you?'

The drowning was gone from the Baron's eyes. There was a blue chill now. Poe thought of chips of ice in the streams of the Richthofen estate in Silesia.

'You were educated in Berlin, at a military school?'

Richthofen nodded curtly. 'Wahlstatt. Its motto was "learn to obey that you may learn to command".'

'Very German.'

Not a smile.

At West Point, Poe had been desperately unhappy, deprived by his stepfather of the funds he needed to keep up with comrades.

'You must have loved Wahlstatt?'

'On the contrary, I detested the school. It was built as a monastery and furnished like a jail. Not caring for the instruction I received, I did just enough work to pass. It would have been wrong to do more than just enough, so I worked as little as possible. Consequently, my teachers did not think a great deal of me.'

'But you learned to command?'

'I learned to obey.'

'You command this *jagdgeschwader*.'

'I pass on orders I am given. General Karnstein is commandant.'

It was like interrogating a prisoner of war. Richthofen would give away enough to pass, but no more. A lesson learned at Wahlstatt.

'When you were a boy, did you want to turn?'

'I was raised to know I would be turned in my eighteenth year. It is customary. Lothar, also, turned at that age. Karl Bolko, when he reaches manhood, will turn.'

'How was it done?'

'The usual way,' Richthofen said, brusquely.

'Forgive me, Baron, you must make allowances for my ignorance,' Poe wheedled, damping irritation by recalling the awesome winged creature that lurked within the cold fish. 'I turned in another age, when the change from living man to vampire was a rare, painful thing. I have known the grave and have been shunned as a beast of the night.'

'I did not die. My turning was hygienic. The results were satisfactory.'

New-born vampires usually described their transformations in the half-proud, half-ashamed, entirely excited manner in which the young men of Poe's warmth talked of their first visit to a brothel. To Richthofen, this miraculous metamorphosis was an uneventful appointment with a painless dentist.

'You turned in 1910. What is your bloodline?'

'It is of the highest. My family retains an elder, Perle von Mauren. Her line has become ours.'

This was a common arrangement. With Dracula established in

Germany, the spread of vampirism was regulated. In theory, every vampire within the domains of Kaiser and King-Emperor was under the patronage of Dracula. A new-born could not be made without the Graf's permission. Vampirism was a condition to which the nobility were entitled by birth. Many aristocratic families made connections with elders of whom Dracula approved. Women like this Perle von Mauren were advisers, mistresses and governesses.

'How do you feel about your mother-in-darkness?'

'Feel? Why should I feel?'

'Your line is important.'

'Strictly, I am not solely of her blood. Under the supervision of Professor ten Brinken, I have taken another as my father by proxy. I am of the Dracula line.'

He was not boasting but stating a fact.

'Are you greatly changed?'

'I am Manfred von Richthofen still. Most of those cups I won before I became a shape-shifter.'

'You flew in an aeroplane then?'

'An aeroplane is merely a gun with wings. Now I am my own weapon, my own instrument. Like the hunters of old.'

'Do you regret not living longer before turning?'

'I have never died.'

'But there are aspects of warm life lost to us. You set them aside before you could truly have known them.'

'War was coming. It was my duty to turn. Germany needed vampires of good lines.'

Maybe this empty man was the daytime shell and the giant Poe had seen was the *real* Red Battle Flier. This interview was like trying with thick gloves to pick up pins from a marble floor. Whenever a possibility was touched, it skittered away under a chest of drawers.

'After turning, you joined the lancers.'

'The First Regiment of Uhlans. I saw combat in '14, but the lancers were finished. This war has no place for cavalry.'

'So you exchanged your horse for an aeroplane?'

'I transferred to the Signal Corps and entered the Imperial Air Service as an observer. I made the decision to become a pilot. The position offers more opportunities for honourable service.'

'And sport?'

Richthofen considered a moment and gave a single nod. In a few minutes of unexpressive talk, he had disposed of an entire life up to the point when he found the vocation that made him famous. Poe had the bald facts of official record and tiny chinks of illumination that suggested a strange human story. It might be possible to frame the life of Baron von Richthofen as a tragedy. That was not what Dr Mabuse wished of the book.

'You spoke of dying, Herr Poe. As I said, I have never in truth been dead. But it seems to me now, looking back, that I was truly born not when I left my mother's womb, not when I drank Perle's vampire blood, but when I won my first victory. It was as an observer. I downed a Frenchman.'

Poe looked at the trophies.

'There is no cup. That aeroplane fell on the wrong side of the lines. The victory was not confirmed.'

'Does that bother you?'

Richthofen shrugged. 'One should receive credit that is one's due. An officer's word of honour should be accepted.'

'Why did you become a pilot?'

'So I could rely on myself. I lost kills because my pilot was not skilled enough to get me into position for a clean shot.'

Early in the war, observers – who were responsible for the guns – were the hunters. Pilots were in the same class as chauffeurs or beaters. Only after Boelcke laid down his famous *dicta* did the special skills of the flying warrior become generally appreciated.

'It is every man's dream to fly.'

Again, Richthofen was unaffected. 'As I believe I mentioned, I do not dream.'

'You are remarkably level-headed for a man on such intimate terms with the miraculous.'

The Baron had no answer.

'The world you were born into has changed beyond recognition. First, Dracula. Then, the war…'

'The world is beyond my control. I have only myself. I have not changed. I have only become more myself.'

THE MOON ALSO RISES

'You're an angel, Miss Reed,' said Dr Arrowsmith, gently squeezing the hand-pump. 'I wish we had a dozen of you.'

She was drowsy, as if slipping into vampire lassitude. The hollow needle in the crook of her elbow was an icy tick. Her already blurry vision dotted with smudges of grey fog. She could not feel her toes. Her fingers tingled. Her blood surged through rubber tubing, filled the valves of the pulsing pump, and disappeared into another tube, flowing into the patient's arm.

Vampire donors were prized at the military hospital in Amiens. The restorative power of their blood was remarkable.

Arrowsmith, a warm American whose face was prematurely scored with worry-lines, stroked her hair. He did not show he felt the chill in her but could not have failed to.

'We have taken enough from you,' he said, ceasing to coax the pump. 'We must be wary of going back too often to the well.'

Kate tried to tell him to go on. She wasn't even unconscious. Her body could regenerate its blood within an hour, especially if she fed.

On the other cot, the patient – an American captain, Jake Barnes – was mummified in bandages. The only inch of his skin exposed was stuck with the transfusion needle. Barnes was a new-born, his power of regeneration not yet developed enough to heal the wounds he had sustained. Hung on the wire during a bombardment, he had been pelted with a hailstorm of bullets, lead and silver. There was little left of him to save.

Her bloodstream connected with Barnes's, troubling her with flashes of his life. In her guts, she felt the stinging bites of silver bullets through a long night. It was hours before Barnes's comrades crept out to take him down. Despair had twisted his mind. She felt it like a poison.

Arrowsmith carefully took the needle out of her arm and pressed the open vein with his thumb. Her tiny wound healed over in an instant. The doctor examined the spot.

'Not a mark. A little miracle.'

Arrowsmith had scant experience with vampires. There were relatively few American undead. Barnes had been warm on the ship over, but turned in Paris. He thought the vampire state would better his chances of surviving the war. With distaste, Kate pictured the mindless can-can nymph who had turned him. Barnes might not be satisfied with the shape of his survival. His jaw was shattered, silver shrapnel embedded, spreading gangrene. He would not be capable of feeding himself in the near future. He'd be dependent on medical transfusions. He was, in many senses, no longer a man.

The doctor saw to his patient. Barnes could not talk, of course. His eyes shone angry and pained through slits in his crisp white mask. From their communion, Kate knew Barnes yearned to be allowed true death. Should she pass on his wishes to the doctors striving to keep him alive?

She tried to sit. Her head, a hundredweight of lead, dragged her to the pillow. She was weaker than she had thought. On the too-short canvas cot, feet stuck out beyond the sheet, she tried to summon her strength.

Arrowsmith was concerned. 'Be careful, Miss Reed. You're not right, yet. Don't try to talk. Rest. You've done enough today. Because of you this man will live.'

Her mouth opened and closed, but she had no words. Essentially, that was her problem. The war left her without words.

She knew she should not allow herself to feel so, but something had broken off with Edwin Winthrop's death. They had not been close but they might have been. It was not the truncation of a past that bothered her but the curtailment of a future.

Frustrated and exhausted, she had turned her body over to the Red Cross. As a bloodmilk cow, she was useful without having to take action, without having to think, without having to care.

When the war began, the first fought with significant numbers of vampires on both sides, it was assumed the undead would make unvanquishable, all-conquering soldiers. In magazine serials, *nosferatu* hordes swept across Europe, establishing tyrannies of centuried elders. As armies mobilised and diplomats manoeuvred in the summer of 1914, Saki's *When Vlad Came*, with its imaginary reoccupation of Britain by Dracula's vampire knights, was popular in railway station bookstalls. Hector Munro, 'Saki', was truly dead now, a Royal Fusilier shot by a German sniper.

She looked at the high ceiling. It was a grubby white, lightly spattered with blood no one could reach to scrub away. Fizzing electric lights hung from brass chandeliers, wires wound round wax-crusted candle-sconces. Before the war, the hospital had been a government building.

In the European stalemate, as the war of mobility turned to a face-off between entrenched positions, vampires did not prove all-conquering or invincible. But they survived injuries fatal to a warm soldier. It was an unappreciated curse of the undead. For a vampire, there were few 'Blighty' wounds, not mortal but dire enough to earn honourable discharge and a passage home. Aside from the odd Jake Barnes, a vampire who survived his wounds was liable to recover and be returned to active service. A good many preferred to stay warm and take their chances. The war was a plague of fire and silver. Its scythe swept away hundreds of thousands of new-borns along with their warm cousins.

In a hundred years, with Kate's blood in him, Jake Barnes might be ready to fight again.

* * *

Her bath chair was wheeled into the conservatory. Moonlight flooded down upon the row of convalescents. The illumination was a proven restorative for sorely wounded vampires. Kate did not feel it herself.

She was willing to give more blood but Arrowsmith ruled it out. She did not want to be left to herself, to think. She wanted to be useful.

Next to the swaddled mummy of Barnes sat Lieutenant Chatterley, who had received Kate's blood yestereve. Another rare Blighty case, his lower body had been blown to pieces. Though new bone-shoots sprouted from the stumps of his legs, they were dead. His body would become whole but he would not have the use of it. He contemplated his lack of reflection in the moonlit glass of the conservatory windows.

'Clifford, good evening,' she said to the Englishman.

He looked queerly at her. 'Do I know you? Were you one of the nurses?'

She shook her head.

A tic pulled at Chatterley's mouth. 'You're *her*. The elder?'

'An elder? Hardly. If I'd lived, I wouldn't even be dead yet. Probably.'

Chatterley would not thank her for his life and his dead legs. Like Barnes, he had a bitterness in his blood. He turned away, face to the moon. She had a touch of him also in her mind. From Barnes, she had only recent impressions, of Paris and his turning. From Chatterley, she had vivid pictures; a colliery wheel rising over a stretch of forest, a country house and grounds.

Kate was too tired even to feel any rejection. She could give nothing anyone wanted.

A pretty warm nurse fussed around Chatterley and Barnes. Neither showed interest.

'We've found you a cat, miss,' the nurse said to Kate.

Kate was too exhausted to fake a smile of gratitude. A cat would ease but not slake her red thirst. There would be little pain in a cat's life. She would drink without tasting agony.

'Thank you.'

'You're welcome, miss.'

The nurse did a tiny but perfect curtsey. She must have been a maid before the war. Kate noticed healed bites on her neck.

When warm, Kate had once been fed upon, by Mr Frank Harris, and she had died of it. Her memories were of turning, not of being food and drink for another. Now, she imagined she felt as the nurse must feel after letting her vampire lovers bleed her. She was empty.

'Someone to see you, miss...'

Kate had been in sleepless reverie. In the fogs of the '80s, dodging Carpathian Guards, scattering leaflets...

She stirred like a very old lady, bones creaking, limbs stiff. She could not turn in her chair, but she saw a shadowy reflection in the moonlit windows. A man in uniform stood with the nurse, leaning on a crutch.

The nurse wheeled her bath chair round. The visitor stepped into pale light. Kate felt a silver spasm in her heart.

'Miss Mouse,' Edwin said, 'you look like you've seen a ghost.'

WATCHING THE HAWK

'There is nothing here,' Ewers said, tapping the folder of notes. 'Nothing at all.'

At Malinbois, a tiny room had been found for him, a cubic bubble in stone. He was issued with a desk and chair, paper and pens. Each night, he was required to sign a requisition form and exhibit a burned-down stub before he could receive a fresh candle.

Poe sat, collar loose. Ewers stood, bowed by the low ceiling.

'I had hoped for an opening chapter,' Ewers said sniffily, 'and a plan of the entire work.'

Poe had hoped for a great deal more. By now, he should have half-completed the slim book Dr Mabuse required of him.

'Have you enjoyed much opportunity to converse with the Baron?'

Ewers was surprised by the question. Unnerved by fliers, he avoided them.

'He is not communicative,' Poe elaborated.

If it were allowed, Ewers would have been angry.

'The Baron has not co-operated? Have you been denied interviews?'

'No, it's that... as you say, there is nothing there.'

When he looked at a blank sheaf of paper, Poe saw the grey-blue eyes of Manfred von Richthofen.

'You are purportedly noted for imagination. Where there is nothing, you must make something.'

This commission was proving damnable. Wonders and marvels were eternally out of reach.

'The Baron is, I should say, a cold man,' Poe ventured. 'His reserve is an obstacle to progress.'

'I'll tell Karnstein. Richthofen will be ordered to be forthcoming.'

'I doubt if orders will help. It is not that the Baron is unwilling but that he is unable. He is not much in the habit of thinking. I sense he wishes not to ponder the darks of his life. Perhaps this is how he has been able to survive. On an unexpressed level, he fears that if he looks down, he will fall...'

'Alienist nonsense, Poe. The man's a hero. Heroes have stories. Find his story.'

Ewers stood straight to look down on Poe. As he left, he bumped his head on the lintel.

Poe was enough of a fixture at the castle to pass unnoticed in the hall where the fliers gathered to pass the hours of daylight. Perhaps he could find the Baron's life from his comrades. Each must have some story, some insight, which could colour the narrative.

'As recording officer, I must be strict with myself,' Hermann Göring declaimed. 'My victory is confirmed but I may not claim a kill. Ball did not die in the crash but at dawn. The British are sparing with details. It seems he was injured. The sunlight finished him off.'

'The kill should be mine,' claimed Lothar von Richthofen. 'If I had not crippled him in our earlier engagement, he'd have been safely home by sun-up.'

'Just be glad Ball is gone,' Erich von Stalhein said. 'He was a dangerous man. The skies are safer without him in them.'

Poe could not imagine the skies being dangerous for these creatures. In their shape-shifted forms, they were masters of the jungle of the air.

'I am afraid there is no confirmation of your kill yet either,' Göring told Stalhein. 'We have found the Snipe but the pilot's body escapes us.'

'Bigglesworth fell separately. I am satisfied our debt is cancelled.'

Pilots on both sides were ranked by their score. Some fliers affected indifference but Poe noted how attention revolved around Göring's chalked display of engagements, victories and kills. None of the fliers of JG1 could match Richthofen's line of cups, but all had impressive records.

'The Baron's bag is increased again,' Göring announced, not surprising anyone. 'Another useful victory. Captain Courtney.'

'What about the observer?' asked Theo von Kretschmar-Schuldorff.

'The British do not list him as lost.'

The intelligence officer was perturbed. The point of the dog-fight, from Theo's point of view, had been to keep intelligence from the Allies.

'He cannot have survived No Man's Land. Like Albert Ball, he must be dead.'

'You don't understand the British, Hermann. Too gentlemanly to lie, they omit information. Who was this observer?'

Göring shrugged. 'He is not listed as lost, therefore he is not listed.'

'If he made it home then they know all about you.'

'Nobody knows *all* about us,' Lothar commented.

Theo smoked furiously, thinking. 'Since they do not claim the observer as a survivor, the British may simply wish us to believe he passed on his intelligence, encouraging us to show our hand.'

'About time,' Stalhein said. 'We should be let loose.'

'Soon, soon…' Theo said. 'It's a clever game, and requires a cool hand.'

'I passed over the wreck of the Baron's RE8,' Göring said. 'There could be no survivor. The British wish to pretend they know our secrets. Typical of them.'

Poe saw shapes in the smoke-streams around Theo. The officer was disappearing in literal clouds of thought. Poe tried to follow his reasoning. Pleased his old knack for conundra had not deserted him, he penetrated the mystery just as Theo solidified his own conclusion.

'No,' Theo decided. 'The observer survived the crash and returned. It is the only possible interpretation of the facts.'

The fliers were mystified.

'You've lost me, Theo,' Lothar said.

'The observer must have perished,' Göring insisted.

Theo allowed a smoke ring to escape his mouth and smiled. 'Poe, would you care to explain our reasoning to these schoolchildren?'

Poe was surprised Theo realised he too had seen the answer. Fliers hauled their chairs around, very like children waiting for a story.

'The key is the fate of Ball,' Poe stated. 'The British claim he did not die in the crash of his aeroplane but later, some way from the wreck, at dawn. In No Man's Land, between the lines, during a bombardment.'

Göring snorted. 'This I have told you. It is in the record.'

'Who saw the crash?'

'Only myself. I would have finished Ball by drinking his blood, but there was fire. I judged it unwise to touch ground.'

'You have not recently been in communication with British Military Intelligence?'

Göring snarled, pig-like tusks sharp. 'You upstart cur, I'll have you whipped...'

'He's right, Hermann,' Theo said, calming the recording officer. 'Someone gave the British an accurate account of your victory over Albert Ball. It could only have been the observer of the Baron's RE8.'

Poe, vindicated, continued, 'If he gave his account to his superiors, he must ergo have survived and returned to his lines.'

The completed puzzle hung in the air. Theo waved his cigarette holder and his cloud drifted apart.

Lothar whistled. 'Manfred will *not* be pleased. It's rare that his little jokes backfire.'

The fliers seemed cheered that Baron von Richthofen had made a mistake. Maybe it proved the Red Battle Flier was made of the same stuff as they. Human stuff, after all.

'The Baron should have killed pilot *and* observer,' Theo agreed. 'It may be a great error on his part.'

'There is still no proof the observer survived, Theo,' Göring said. 'It is most unlikely.'

'There is no proof, but I am satisfied. And so is *Herr* Edgar Poe.'

The fliers regarded him with a mix of admiration and contempt.

'I understand you find my brother hard going? Can you imagine what it has been like having Manfred as an example for a whole lifetime?'

Lothar von Richthofen leaned against the battlements. The breeze riffled an aviator's scarf away from his casually worn Pour le Mérite. With white grin, shiny-peaked cap, black leather boots and breeches and loose crimson blouse in the Russian style, he looked far more the dashing hero than his brother.

'Even if the gods of battle will it and Manfred falls, I will never be the Red Baron. I will always be the Red Baron's brother. I have my medals. I have my score. But I fly in his shadow.'

The afternoon was overcast but Poe wore tinted spectacles with side-panels. He heard the minute sounds of distant birds more acutely than the nearby din of war. To his ears, the castle was a living thing of creaking stone and breathing wood.

'We are very different, he and I,' Lothar declared. 'Even when warm, Manfred was not "warm". Given that I have chosen a life of service which will, in all probability, not last long, I feel entitled to take my pleasures to excess. As a poet, you will understand what I mean. But I doubt Manfred has ever been with a woman except for feeding. Even then, he prefers his dogs. And his fallen foes.'

Lothar was his brother's opposite. He described exploits in embroidered detail, making an uneventful patrol one of Sinbad's voyages. In the Great Hall, he would give thrilling accounts of his battles, performing rather than reciting. Other fliers hung on every word, every turn of combat. It would be a simple matter to make of Lothar von Richthofen's reminiscences a heroic autobiography.

'He is a good soldier,' Poe suggested. 'He flies by the rules, fights by the rules...'

'The sacred *dicta* of Boelcke?' Lothar said, eyebrows arching. 'Manfred has made them his Bible, a manual for survival, for victory. As for the soldiering, it's hard to say. I fly close to the wind. I was always the boy who got in trouble while Manfred did his duty, or enough of it to get by. But it's open to debate whether he is really the better soldier.'

'I don't understand.'

Lothar watched a hawk wheel and circle over pigeons. Perhaps he was studying the tactics of aerial predators?

'Ask Theo if Manfred is a good soldier. That business with the RE8. You know what he did?'

'He took the pilot in mid-air and drained him.'

'And he left the observer. The man could not possibly have got control of the aircraft. Imagine his panic, his fear, as the RE8 went into a spin. Consider his frustration, his powerlessness.'

Poe thought it must be like being buried alive. Having written of the condition while warm, he had experienced it upon his turning. The stinking closeness still tormented his imaginings. No, that was a more protracted fate. To go down in an aeroplane must be like waking in a coffin as it is conveyed into the furnace of a crematorium.

'To Manfred, that man's fear was almost as rich as the pilot's blood. He *feeds* on that as he feeds on the fawning of his admirers. Secretly, he is delighted you are to write this book.'

'That is not my impression.'

Lothar's grin was wolfish. 'Make no mistake. He has heard of you, Poe. If only for *The Battle of St Petersburg*. You've been well chosen.'

One of the hawks took one of the pigeons. Poe heard the tiny neck snap. The sensations of the world crowded in on him. Little sounds from the countryside all around. The water lapping in the lake. Footsteps on frozen grass.

'It *was* impossible that the British observer could survive, but in war the impossible is commonplace. It is customary to kill one's foe as many times as possible, to be sure. It was *important* the observer be killed. It was the *primary objective* of the flight. Yet Manfred took delight in torturing him rather than going for a clean, certain kill. His pleasure, his feeding, his score… these were more important to him than executing his mission. In this case, that may have consequences we shall all regret.'

'This must be a constant complaint against heroes.'

'I am a hero too, Poe,' Lothar said, hands on hips, a deadly Adonis. 'I concede you are right. This is a part of all of us. Certainly, all of us in JG1. But it is *all* of Manfred. He is not a man, he is a weapon. I love him for he is my brother, but I would not trade hearts with him, not for his score, not for his fame.'

The hawk soared higher. Poe and Lothar both followed its path, turning to keep the bird in their sights.

'Manfred *kills*, Poe. That is what he does. That is what he *is*.'

30

RETURNED TO LIFE

Over the protests of the nurse, Kate walked with Edwin in the hospital grounds. Shortly after dawn, the moon was not yet down. Her glasses were sensibly tinted. Daylight hurt her only at the height of a cloudless summer day. The gauzy blue dawn light of French winter was as cool as a night of the crescent moon.

Edwin held her hand. His grip was firm, hers weak. He was changing. So, she supposed, was she.

He had not told her much of his mission to Malinbois, just that he had been in an aeroplane brought down by enemy action and had made his way back across the lines. Some of his reluctance to give detail was imposed by the Diogenes Club, who wished to keep their secrets. But there was in him some spark of strangeness. He now had his own secrets. This Edwin Winthrop who returned was not quite the man who had gone out.

'I'm in flying school. Diogenes is lending me to the new show. They'll need trained intelligence people.'

The Royal Flying Corps was being divorced from the army and reformed as a new service, the Royal Air Force. Edwin no longer wore his staff officer's pips.

'I'd have thought that after the last jaunt, you'd wish never to go near an aeroplane again.'

His face was set, his mind closed to her. 'Unfinished business in the air, Kate. I have to get back up there.'

The sun came out and Edwin flinched. His eyes closed to slits. She knew, at once, why.

'There's a demon in the sky and I must kill him.'

They stepped into the tangled shadow of a bare tree.

'You've vampire blood in you,' she said.

He nodded. 'A pilot I was shot down with. Albert Ball.'

She had heard of Ball, a decorated ace.

'Have you also given blood?'

He shook his head. 'Ball died before I could help him. It was his last wish I taste his blood. I think he believed he'd live on through me.'

'Now you're becoming a pilot?'

There was a strength in his eyes. Still warm, he had the beginnings of the power of fascination.

'In the air, I know what to do. I don't know if it's natural ability or something Ball passed on, but I'm jumping through the hoops faster than the instructors can credit. It must be Ball. Or maybe fear has been burned out of me.'

Kate was unsure about this new Edwin.

By mid-morning, they had taken refuge in Edwin's billet in a small hotel entirely occupied by the British. His small room was on the fourth floor, directly under the roof. Its ceiling sloped like a tent. Thick blackout curtains hung over a gabled window. Daylight seeped around the edges.

Kate sat on the narrow bed, pillows propped behind her. Edwin stood, head bowed by the ceiling.

She was weaker than she had thought. Walking in the sunrise had tired her. She could hardly move. By contrast, Edwin was accelerated, gestures and thoughts faster than hers. It was as if she were the sluggish, docile, warm fool, and he the predatory vampire, darting round her defences. Perhaps it was Albert Ball in him. And the despairing, ruined Blighty cases in her.

Edwin knelt and took her hand. A little of his vitality seeped into her.

An attribute of her line was a minor facility for psychic vampirism, the ability to drain energy without tasting blood. Those who knew Frank Harris, even before his turning, said he was an exhausting experience.

'Edwin, to state the obvious, you're alone in your room with a woman.'

He avoided her glance.

'Aren't you supposed to be engaged?'

Face down on the tiny bedside table was a photograph frame. A watch sat on it.

'I'm dead to Catriona. The war has made living dead of us all. Until it's done, there can be nothing else.'

He rose and sat beside her, still holding her hands. She heard his strong heartbeat. Her mind swam and she recalled falling under the spell of her father-in-darkness. Frank Harris's kisses were sour-sweet. Memory was blotted by a new taste.

Edwin kissed her deferentially and took her glasses off. She took them from him and placed them next to his watch, nails brushing the hardboard backing of the unseen photograph. His huge eye was up close, a blur of liquid gleam. His lips fixed to hers.

Without drawing blood, they drank from each other's mouth. His strength of purpose was a blast of wind against her face, streaming through her hair.

Something of her flowed back into him. She sensed his electric tingling. With a smear of guilt, she had an impression from his memory of a girl she took to be Catriona. A tall, delicate, grey-eyed willow in a white dress and a straw hat. The impression faded. Kate was overwhelmed by a heat in her heart. She hugged Edwin, vampire strength coming back to her arms, squeezing breath out of him.

They broke apart and went through the business of dispensing with clothes. Thirty years had brought merciful changes in fashion. In her warmth, undressing – even under circumstances which allowed full attention to be devoted to the chore – had been as complex a business as disassembling a rifle.

Under his clothes, Edwin's body was a map: seas of pale skin, continents of blue-black bruise, islands of red weal, archipelagoes of stitching, national boundaries of scar. An empire of injury. As she touched his wound-marks with fingers and tongue, he thrilled.

He stroked her shoulders and breasts and belly, covering her with moustache-tickle kisses. The tiny scars of her warmth, from childhood play or spills off her bicycle, had vanished shortly after turning, but she was still freckled like an egg.

With awkward shifting, they managed to get themselves side by side on the bed. Kate's back pressed up against the wall and Edwin's hip perched on the edge of the mattress. The space between them vanished. She felt his warmth against her from shins to neck. Her heart ached for his blood.

She touched him intimately, forcing herself against instinct to be gentle. Through her palm, she felt the heat of his gathering blood. He shifted her under him and entered her suddenly. She reached above her head and gripped the bedstead. Her eyes were shut, but she saw clearly. Images leaked from Edwin's mind. Faces and fears.

The heat built. Her fingernails were claws, hooked around the brass rails. Her fangs sprouted, forcing her mouth open. All her teeth were sharpened to points. She was dangerous to kiss.

'Careful,' she said.

His tongue flicked lightly against hers. Her arms seemed to become wings, cool air currents streaming over and under them. There was a great chasm of empty air beneath them, but they were sustained in flight. One drop of his blood now would explode in her mind. She would go down in flames. She tried to shut her mouth and swallow a scream.

Edwin took her right wrist and tugged, detaching her hand from the headstead. Her claws screeched against the brass.

'Be very careful.'

He kissed her fingers, touching his tongue to her barb-like claws. He took hold of her forefinger as gently as she had taken hold of his penis, and touched its tip to the hollow of her throat. She spent, violently. Her free hand made a fist, crushing flat a brass tube.

Edwin pricked her with her own fingernail. He punctured one of the tracery of blue veins in her chest. Scarlet blood welled and he pressed his mouth around the wound, suckling like a child.

Waves of warmth and pain washed about her. She was helpless, feeling him in every inch of her. She wanted to warn him about her blood. He drank without regard. There was a disturbing purposefulness in his tapping of her. She had been seduced. This was not what she would have willed.

Edwin gulped down swallows of her blood, then the urgency of his body overtook him. He held her close and spent inside her. The spreading warmth did not kill her red thirst.

As a dead thing, Kate could not conceive a child this way. She could only have progeny through passing on her bloodline. She might still become mother to her lover.

They lay together, one flesh, trickling into each other. A black dot of panic grew in Kate's mind. Edwin grew heavier on her. Sleep was overtaking him.

She struggled out from beneath his pressing weight. The hole in her chest closed, leaving only a smear of blood on her freckled bosom. There was no scar. Edwin's lips were red with her vampire juice.

She shook him.

'Edwin, if you mean to turn, I must drink from you to complete the communion.'

He moaned and his arms crossed over his throat, protective. Her blood matted his chest hair.

'It's dangerous unless we go through it completely.'

She had no children-in-darkness. She'd thought herself not old enough in undeath to be responsible. There were still too many things about her condition she didn't understand. Yet here she was, like a foolish warm girl overcome by passion, having to make a decision about motherhood in an inconvenient instant.

Edwin's eyes opened.

She *wanted* to drain him completely, to drink from him until his heart stilled, to watch over his corpse and coax him new-born into the moonlight.

'Edwin, I'm sorry, but you leave me no choice.'

The bones of her jaw unlocked as her mouth distended like a snake's. Extra fangs sprouted around the spurs of her incisors. She tasted her own blood-salted spittle.

Edwin put out a hand, pressing his palm against her chest, fingers splaying.

'No,' he said, weakly, 'no, Miss Mouse.'

She was torn by duty and desire, which told her she must feed, and Edwin's own gathering strength.

'You won't turn,' she said, words slurred by her fangs.

He shook his head. 'You mustn't make me. I must be my own father. Kate, please…'

He fell unconscious. His blood still raced, his heart beat strong and steady. She wanted to howl. He had unpenned the wolf in her, but would not let it feed. The room rippled, like a reflection in a disturbed pond. She was still troubled by sensations of flight and fire that spilled from his mind. She put on her spectacles and shut her eyes, trying to flush the wolf from her heart.

She got off the narrow bed. Edwin stretched out, smiling. She shook, as cold and weak as after giving her blood to one of the patients. But this was a more complex transaction.

If she were to ravish him as he slept, it would be understandable. Once turned, he would probably thank her. But there had been a force in his 'no', a determination.

Her knees were unsteady. She sank into a corner, bony legs to her chest, and pulled her clothes around. Making a nest, she willed herself into lassitude. Iron bands tightened about her craving heart.

31

A POET'S WARRIOR

There was whispering in the Chateau de Malinbois, rustling and cooing through passages and halls, slicing through cracks between great stone blocks. Poe's senses were ajangle with the murmurs of living and dead, the chattering of rats in the walls. He tried to shut out the eternal susurrus of words, words, words...

Theo Kretschmar-Schuldorff visited his room to give him a greatcoat.

'In this fastness, even the dead feel the cold,' the intelligence officer explained.

Poe accepted the gift with thanks. It was inches too long but of good quality, with a double row of shiny buttons. Rank insignia were unpicked from the shoulders.

'We'll have you fit for inspection, Eddy.'

'I was a good soldier, Theo. In wars fought before you were born. When alive, I served in the ranks and rose to sergeant by my own merits. As a new-born, I was an officer of the Confederacy.'

'I did not think poets made good soldiers. All the regulations and impositions...'

'When I first joined the army, I wished to take a holiday from poetic thought. And the war of Southern Independence was the poets' war, dreamers and idealists against factory-owners and puritans. Just as this is a poets' war.'

Theo was surprised by the statement.

'We fight for the future, Theo. The Graf von Dracula embodies the glories of the past but is not blinded by them. Under his standard, the world will change. To be a vampire is the essence of modernity.'

The officer shrugged. 'You are a rare patriot.'

'I see no other honourable choice.'

Theo ambled about the room, trying to sneak a look at the papers on the desk. Poe instinctively hunched over, a schoolboy trying to prevent fellows seeing his work in an examination. The officer laughed at the game. Poe straightened and relaxed.

'You've begun then? Ewers complains you drag your boots.'

Theo's opinion of Hanns Heinz Ewers had not improved.

'I have begun,' Poe admitted.

'And is it a fine tale of blood and glory?'

'It may be.'

'Our hero is a strange beast?'

'We are all strange beasts.'

'You would do well in my job, Eddy. You give so little away. Just like our Red Baron.'

Through a thousand fresh starts and strikings-out, Poe had assembled a patchwork of words and phrases into a chapter. Failing to find an avenue into Baron von Richthofen through the hero's own account, he had fallen back on his own impressions and sensibilities and constructed a narrative of his arrival at Malinbois, his first sight of the magnificent creatures of air and darkness.

'You'll have more glories to chronicle soon. I have been overruled.'

Theo argued in favour of deploying JG1 sparingly, believing the gradual spread of rumour would harry the Allies more effectively. He considered the shape-shifters a terror weapon, like gas. His belief was that JG1 were more useful for the enormous hurt they could do to enemy morale than for the limited, if impressive, damage they could inflict in the field.

'We are soon to show our hand.'

'A spring offensive?'

Theo shrugged. 'The worst-kept secret in military history. How does one conceal a million men? The British and French will throw up twenty-foot-thick walls all along their lines and pour Yankees into every emplacement.'

'Walls can be flown over.'

Whispering still pestered his ears. There were conspiracies in every corner. Each man was his own conspiracy, against all others. Alliances shifted and reversed, policies evaporated and reformed, loyalties strained and snapped. In this whispering was weakness. If the *Kaiserschlacht* was to succeed, the Central Powers must be forged into an iron hammer. In this castle, individuals were unstable atoms, whirling against each other.

'We shall have important visitors, I am told. You'll be close to the heart of things.'

Poe had a sense of the moment. It was dizzying, a maelstrom of history.

'Tonight, you should be in the tower. The Baron is going out. He will increase his score.'

'You are here,' barked ten Brinken as Poe stepped into the vaulted space. 'Good.'

The professor, once suspicious, had been persuaded Poe's book would serve his lasting reputation. He was given to addressing himself to the poet, phrasing statements as if they were suitable for publication.

Even wrapped in Theo's greatcoat (which, he realised, had come from the wardrobe of a dead officer), Poe was frozen. Exposed to homicidal winds, the tower was an arctic trap. Ice rinds mortared the walls. Every day, soldiers with mallets swarmed up scaffolding to knock off the night's icicles.

Baron von Richthofen stood in the centre of the chamber, to attention, in human shape. Poe gave Richthofen a salute which was not returned. The flier wore a long, quilted dressing gown. Scientists swarmed around. Ten Brinken brusquely directed operations, a corrupt priest hurrying through a devotion. The professor's colleagues were a half-mystical lot, caught between mediaevalism and modernity. Dr Caligari, the alienist, was a fount of peculiar practice and arcane theory. He lurked shabbily in the jagged shadows, scrawling his notes in runic scribble.

'If you would be so gracious,' ten Brinken addressed himself to Richthofen. 'Shift your shape.'

Richthofen nodded curtly and removed his robe. A naked Siegfried, he closed his eyes in concentration. His attendants stood close by, bearing the apparatus to be piled on the night warrior. Kurten was bent under the weight of the Baron's guns.

Something grew inside Richthofen. His shoulders broadened, his spine extended. He became wider and taller. Muscles swelled like wet sponges. Veins rose like firehoses under pressure. Fur swarmed over skin, coating now-leathery hide with a thick pelt. Bones distended, lengthened and reshaped. The face darkened. Horny skull-spurs prodded out around the eyes and the jaw. Bat-ears unfurled. The Baron's eyes opened, large as fists. The calm blue was unmistakable, a continuity between man and superman. Richthofen outstretched his changing arms. Joints grew spindly and sinewy as leather curtains fell, coalescing into wings.

Ten Brinken consulted his pocket-watch. His shock-haired associate Rotwang wrote down a figure on a form.

'Each time, Herr Poe, the process is more swift. Soon, it will be an eye-blink.'

Kurten and Haarmann helped the changed Richthofen into his boots and, scrambling up a climbing frame to reach, hung the guns round his neck. With arms turned to wings, the Baron grew fresh arms. Less rudimentary than the last time Poe had seen the transformed flier. Now, they looked like real human arms, skinned in leather. The hands, flexible and four-fingered, got a grip on the gun-handles. The barrels stuck up vertically.

'His shape improves with each shift,' ten Brinken explained. 'The ideal we have created becomes more perfectly attainable.'

Poe heard the beating of the Baron's enlarged heart, a strong pulse.

'Eventually this will be the true Baron von Richthofen. The mere human frame will be a disguise he may assume.'

'Might the change become permanent?'

Ten Brinken shook his head and grinned like a gorilla. 'Nothing will ever be permanent, Herr Poe. The forms of these creatures will forever be fluid. They will adapt to conditions wherever they are required to fight.'

The Baron folded his wings, still at attention, and looked through the aperture in the tower walls. Out there, stars glinted like razor-edges. The camouflage netting blew in. A strong wind swept the floor of the tower room. Scientists clutched rebellious notes. Poe shivered in his coat.

Ten Brinken and Rotwang circled the shape-shifted flier with prayerlike mutterings. Poe trailed after them, unable to resist the creature's pull. Manfred von Richthofen was no longer human. Animal smell seeped around him, raising tears in Poe's eyes and a sting in his nostrils. The musk was so strong it could be tasted like pepper.

Poe tried to conceive of comparisons: a gargantuan gargoyle, a beast warrior, a killer angel, a Teuton demigod. None would do. As the Baron said, he was himself and that was all there was.

The scientists backed away, leaving Poe at the giant's feet, looking up. The netting was removed from the aperture and Richthofen walked to the platform. His bootfalls shook the flagstones. Poe kept pace, striding in the shadow of the Baron's wings.

Drawing his shoulders in and bowing his head, Richthofen eased through the gap in the wall and stood on the platform. His chest expanded. His wings filled out, air pouring into them.

Poe followed, ignoring the windblast. The platform was suspended over empty space. Below was a sea of darkness. The stars mirrored in the lake were the only nearby indication of ground level. Fire-flashes marked out the trenches a few miles distant. Tiny screams persisted in the thunder of bombardment.

Richthofen stood on the lip of the platform, wings spread like black sails. Kurten, roped at the waist to Haarmann lest he be swept off the platform, fastened the hooks of the Baron's boots, binding his legs together up to the knee. Leather pouches slung round the flier's thighs were packed with extra drums of ammunition. An armoured helm fitted over his head, cut away from the flaring ears. Some of the Baron's comrades wore protective goggles in their shape-shifted form, but Richthofen scorned such comforts. His eye-sockets had risen into goggle-like ridged orbits.

Poe fought the wind and moved nearer the Baron. Theo called, telling him to be careful. Under his breath, Ewers prayed Poe be carried off into the air and dropped into the forest.

The Baron turned to look back and opened his mouth, baring foot-long fang-teeth. The inside of his mouth was a startling red, a wound in his black-furred face.

'I'm hungry, poet,' he said. 'How does their nursery rhyme go, "I smell the blood of an Englishman"?'

Poe was startled. He had not thought the shape-shifted Baron capable of ordinary speech. His voice was surprisingly little changed.

'If you have to, write my obituary.'

Richthofen's shoulder-joints revolved as his wings lifted. He tipped forwards, falling stiffly from the platform. His wings caught the air. A backwash forced Poe to his hands and knees.

The Baron dipped beneath the platform. Then he soared above it, spiralling towards stars. He did not flap his wings constantly, but glided on the currents, forcing himself through the air by will-power. An occasional beat was enough to keep him aloft.

Poe tried to stand, but was struck shivering. His boot slipped and he fell hard, sliding towards the edge. The Baron had been a wind-break. Now Poe was the only speck on the platform, winds threatened to dash him away. He stood again, carefully, and made a firm footing. Richthofen was nearly over the trenches, visible only because fires gave his underside a faint reddish glow. His flight was swift and elegant.

Returning to the tower, Poe was pulled inside by Theo.

'You should be more careful, Eddy. I'd have a thorny time explaining your loss to Mabuse.'

Poe was still shivering.

The scientists huddled, filling out forms, arguing minor points. The attendants put things away. General Karnstein stood where the Baron had changed, looking down at Richthofen's abandoned robe. Like a valet, Kurten whisked the garment away and brushed it off.

Theo clicked his heels and saluted. Karnstein returned the honour.

'Manfred is a brave lad,' the elder said. 'I pray he'll return safely.'

'If I chose to worry about anyone, I should save my fears for those who will be hunted down by Baron von Richthofen. He is, after all, invincible.'

Karnstein's face was grey, true age showing through apparent middle years.

'Kretschmar-Schuldorff,' he said wearily, 'no one is invincible.'

32

A RESTORATIVE

Kate awoke in the echoing dark of her skull, eyes sealed by the grit which formed if she slept through two or three days. The thread binding her to an unaging corpse was weaker than since her death. Her body was a hotel, suddenly emptied by a change of season or the outbreak of international crisis. No longer a home.

Fierce heartburn told her feeding was a matter of urgency. Extreme urgency. Her swollen and jagged fang-teeth were broken marbles in her mouth. She was drooling, losing needed fluid. With a gulp, she swallowed spit.

Her eye-gum cracked. It was night. She was still in Edwin's billet. In addition to her dress, a sheet had been tucked around her. The makeshift sleep-clothes smelled off. She wasn't wearing her specs.

A man sat on the bed. In the unlighted room, a cigar end burned like a distant sun. His silhouette was slumped.

'Edwin,' she croaked. Her dry throat hurt.

The silhouette turned up a lamp. It was Charles, his face shockingly aged by the lamp's deep-etched shadows.

'What have you done now, Kate?'

Stabbing pain pierced her burning heart, as if she had been roused from lassitude by a die-hard Van Helsingite with a stake of hot iron.

'Edwin…'

Charles shook his head.

'Winthrop is a changed man. A *much*-changed man, though not perhaps quite as you expected.'

It was not fair! Charles assumed too much, reached wrong conclusions. Blame was being unequally assigned. She could not make her voice work. She could not explain.

'I thought we agreed you were to leave France?'

Kate made fists and thumped her chest. She was embarrassed Charles should find her in this condition. Apart from wretched feebleness, she was unclothed.

'You are a sorry creature,' he said.

Charles stubbed his cigar out in a saucer and stood. He creaked a little like an old man, and hung his head so as not to bump the ceiling. He knelt by her, letting out a breath of exertion as his knees locked. There was an enamel basin under the bedside table. Charles found a damp flannel and applied it to her face, wiping dried trails from around her mouth and grit from her eyes. Satisfied, he took her glasses from the table, unfolded them, and eased them on to her face.

She saw the room in dizzying, sharp focus. Up close, the tiny lines around Charles's eyes were crevasses.

'Thirsty,' she said, deliberately. The word was unrecognisable, even to her own ears. She was furious with herself. She must be captain of her vessel. 'Thirsty,' she said again, clearly.

Charles half-understood and reached for a jug of water that had been beside the basin.

She shook her head. '*Thirsty.*'

'Kate, you presume a great deal on our friendship.'

She couldn't tell him what she meant. She could not explain why her red thirst was so urgent. She had lost too much blood, to Arrowsmith's Blighty cases, to Edwin...

He touched her throat. A spark passed between them. Charles understood. His time with Geneviève had taught him.

'You are close to starved. Bled white.'

He held the lamp close to her face. She blinked as he peered at her.

'There's grey in your hair, Katie,' he said, harmlessly gloating. 'You look as you would if you'd not turned. A shame you can never see the effect.'

Kate had no reflection. She did not show up in photographs. Sketches made of her could have been of a stranger. In warmth, she was hardly remembered for her looks.

'If you'd lived, you'd have been a fine woman,' Charles said kindly.

'I look like a mole, Charles. With untidy hair and freckles.'

He laughed, surprised she could manage a sentence.

'You underestimate yourself. Girls thought prettier than you grew fat and bad-tempered. You'd have become beautiful in your thirties. Character would have shown in your face.'

'Nonsense.'

'How would you know, Kate?'

'When we were all alive, you proposed to pretty Penelope and hardly noticed mole-face Kate.'

Old hurt wrinkled his brow. 'Young men make mistakes.'

'I'd such a crush on you, Charles. When you announced your engagement to Penny, I cried for days. I was driven to the arms of Frank Harris. And look what he made of me.'

She put fingers through her stringy hair, combing away settled dust.

'I wish I could stay angry with you for any length of time, Kate.'

He pushed his knees as he stood, and sat on the stool. She squirrelled back, hugging her sheet to her chest, propping herself against the wall.

'What happened here?' he asked.

'What has happened to Edwin?'

Ever the harbourer of secrets, he didn't want to give anything away.

'You first.'

'He took blood from me.'

He nodded.

'But I took none from him.'

He shook his head.

'He seemed to have some idea of assuming vampire strength without actually turning.'

'Is that possible?'

'I don't know. Ask an elder or a scientist. Or look in your heart.'

He did not pretend not to understand her. In his time with Geneviève, Charles had gained some of her strengths. Through love, Kate thought, or osmosis.

'What has… become of him?'

Charles was concerned for his protégé. That was why he sat in vigil, waiting for her to wake.

'He seems in good health. He has graduated from flying school. He will be the Diogenes Club's man in Condor Squadron. He has created a unique position and trained himself to fill it.'

'But you're worried?'

'As I said, he's changed. I do not say this lightly, but he frightens me. He reminds me of Caleb Croft.'

Another pain-burst racked her chest. Ribs constricted her heart like a bone fist. Hugging herself, she fought to control her twitching limbs.

Charles took out his right cuff-link, skinned his coat sleeve up to his elbow and rolled back his shirt sleeve. She shook her head, lips tight over jutting, aching fangs. Her heart yearned.

'Am I too old a vintage, Miss Connoisseur? Gone to vinegar, perhaps?'

Since Geneviève, Charles had not allowed himself to be bled. Kate knew this with certainty.

He sat on the floor and pulled her on to his lap. She was shocked by the warmth of him, realising how cold she was, how close to truly dead.

'You must, Kate.'

He presented his inner wrist to her. There were tiny, long-healed marks where Geneviève had suckled.

This came too late in their lives to be what she had once wished for, but it would mean survival. And with survival came unexpected second and third chances.

'I'll take vanilla,' she said. He smiled.

She took his hand and licked his wrist with her rough, long tongue. A healing agent in her saliva would smooth his wound within the hour. Charles smiled. He was familiar with this.

'Go ahead, pretty creature,' he said, gently. 'Drink.'

She sucked a fold of skin between her upper and lower incisors. Her fang-teeth gnashed. Blood filled her mouth.

The red taste exploded. Jolts ran throughout her body, more intense than a conventional act of love. Time concertinaed: Charles's blood sparkled on her tongue and against the roof of her mouth, trickled down her dry gullet and soothed her burning heart.

Suppressing shudders of pleasure, Kate was distanced enough to measure her feeding. If she drank from Charles's neck, there would be more to it. The wrist was far enough from heart and soul and head. Only sensations came through. His mind, with its secrets, was curtained.

She detached her mouth from his fresh wound and looked up at his face. His smile was tight. A pulse throbbed below his jaw, a blue finger beckoning. Her hands hooked into his coat. She might climb up him, drink from the source.

Her nose stung with the scent of blood. The trickle from his wrist called her. She drank, losing herself…

…she was in a reverie, blood warming her throat, stickily smeared around her mouth.

'Thank you, Charles,' she breathed, lapping again.

He stroked her hair gently. Her glasses skewed as she pressed her face to his wrist. He set them straight.

She did not take much from him. But he shared the strength of his spirit. She was no longer a stranger in her body. Her aches eased. She took command of her limbs. Her muscles were supple, comfortable.

She snuggled against Charles as he rolled down his shirt sleeve and retrieved a cuff-link from his waistcoat pocket.

He held up the lamp again and looked at her hair.

'The grey is gone. Red as rust.'

She stood, steady on her feet, holding up her dress to preserve some measure of modesty.

'A pity,' Charles said. 'I liked you older.'

She flicked him in the face with her sleeve.

'We'll have no more of your cheek, Mr Beauregard.'

'You're much more Irish when you're cross.'

She was blushing. After feeding, she was ruddy as a labourer.

Charles tried to stand, but could not. She had forgotten he'd be the weaker, temporarily, for their communion. She helped him up.

'There now, grandfather,' she teased. 'You should not tire yourself so. Not at your age.'

She kissed his cheek and, modesty abandoned, wriggled into her gamey dress, settling it on her hips. There were catches up the back.

'Could you do me up, Charles?'

'I doubt if anyone could, Kate.'

33

THE KILLER

'My father discriminates between a sportsman and a shooter. A shooter hunts for fun. My brother is, at heart, a shooter. Lothar loves to fly, to take risks. A sportsman hunts for the kill. I find my prey and I kill him, quickly. Each makes me stronger.'

Baron von Richthofen, going against instinct, made a genuine attempt to explain. Theo lagged behind them, saying nothing. Poe knew he remembered the instance when the Baron had chosen to play with his prey rather than kill, quickly. Albert Ball's observer still rankled with Theo.

'When I have killed an Englishman,' Richthofen continued, 'my hunting passion is satisfied for a quarter of an hour. Then, the urge returns…'

They walked by the lake shore. The day was overcast. All three vampires wore heavily peaked caps and dark glasses. Replete from a night's stalking, the Baron was more expansive than in earlier interviews. Theo had suggested Poe might find Richthofen more forthcoming outside the castle. To a huntsman, being within walls is like premature burial.

An animal was following. Poe heard its quiet rustle in the long grass. It was some sort of small dog. The Baron had also noticed their hanger-on and darted the occasional hungry glance at its position.

Last night, Richthofen had stalked and killed four times during a three-hour flight. His bag was an RE8 spotter, a French Spad, a Sopwith Camel and a British observation balloon. Six men were truly dead, four of them vampires. The Baron's score was increased by three victories. Balloons were reckoned separately. The Frenchman, Nungesser, had had a high score. This victory, which the Baron gave equal weight in his official report, would be remembered as one of his greatest.

'How would you rate your night's work?'

'It was good hunting. I drank from all but one of my kills.'

'Which is more important to you, the feeding or the killing?'

Poe regretted the question. It prompted Richthofen to throw up his guards. At first, Poe had thought the Baron genuinely baffled by such probing; now, he realised Richthofen merely measured his words, taking care to say nothing that might alert an Air Service censor.

The dog, a sad-eyed white beagle, emerged from the grass and padded over towards them. The cur must be surviving on dead men's scraps.

'The victory counts,' Richthofen said, at last.

'And what is a victory to you?'

Richthofen turned away and looked out over still water.

'And what is a lake to you, poet?'

It was an indifferent lake. Murky but not reeking, unbeautiful but not grotesque. A British fighter had come down in it the night Richthofen let Ball's observer away. Wreckage had been dredged out and fixed to the trophy wall in the castle. The body of the pilot had not been found.

'I can't tell you, but I can tell you what feeding is to me, what the blood of women means…'

'Women,' Richthofen snorted.

Theo looked up, killing a smile.

'I do not apologise for my nature,' Poe said. 'Though I have been, of necessity, a soldier, I am not a killer by inclination.'

'My brother claims he would prefer to be a lover than a fighter. But he lies to himself.'

'To me, the act of vampirism is a tender communion, an assuagement of solitude, a reaffirmation in death of life...'

'You lose me, poet. Do you not kill?'

Poe was ashamed. White, dead women haunted him. Teeth and eyes and long, long hair.

'I have killed,' he admitted. 'When I was a new-born, especially. I did not understand the nature of my condition.'

'I am a new-born. I have been a vampire for only eight years. Professor ten Brinken tells me I change constantly.'

'But you become more a killer?'

Richthofen nodded once. He drew a pistol from a leather holster and fired once, smartly. The beagle, surprised, was pierced through the head. It kicked, gouting blood from its ears, and lay dead.

'Absurd dog,' Richthofen said, suppressing a shudder. For some unknown reason, he found the harmless animal as repulsive as a plague rat.

Theo was alarmed by the casual kill. The shot resounded, assaulting Poe's sensitive eardrums. A flight of ducks burst from a clump of reeds. The dog-blood smell pricked Poe's red thirst. The animal was repulsive, but he remembered the sweetness of Gigi. At Malinbois, warm women were sometimes provided for the fliers. Poe hungered.

'My country requires I be a killer,' Richthofen said. 'I do my duty.'

'In centuries to come, you may change greatly. Your country's requirements may change, freeing you from duties. You may become a lover too.'

Richthofen, mild and cold and pale, looked directly at Poe. 'I have no centuries to come. I am a dead man.'

Poe looked at Theo, puzzled.

'I was given to understand that you turned without passing through death? You yourself told me so.'

The Baron looked disgusted. 'I do not mean that, poet. I am a truly dead man. All of us in JG1, we are dead men with temporary use of our corpses. It is likely that we will not survive the war.'

Theo's lips pressed in a serious line. He exhaled smoke and tossed the last of a cigarette into the lake.

'It's Nungesser. You drank his blood. You think his thoughts.'

The tiny coal of the cigarette hissed.

'I think my own thoughts, Kretschmar-Schuldorff. But you are right. The Frenchman was like me. He knew he was dead. Each victory for him was a reprieve. When I killed him, he was not surprised. He had known death would catch up with him eventually. I knew that as I tore his throat out and drank his hot blood.'

'Do you deem those you defeat your comrades?' Poe asked.

'The tragedy of war is the pitting of like against like. We fliers have more in common with those we fight than with those for whom we fight. I shall most likely die in the air. Oswald Boelcke, my teacher, died in the stupidest of accidents. All of us, us so-called heroes, die. We fall from the sky in flames. Only the plodding dogs will survive.'

Poe thought of Göring totting up everyone's score, of Ewers pestering officials for advancement, of ten Brinken taking measurements, of Kurten and Haarmann tending their master's guns. He thought of Edgar Poe stooping to the writing of propaganda.

'Professor ten Brinken claims he will make you invincible.'

'He follows us with callipers and a stop-watch, prattling of measurements and science. He has never been in the air. He cannot *know*. There is no science up there.'

'What is there?'

'You're the poet. You tell me.'

'I can't make poetry of what I don't know.'

Richthofen took off his dark glasses. His eyes did not shrink in the sunlight. His face was set like marble.

'Up there, in the night sky, is war. Eternal war. Not only with the British and French, but with the air. The sky does not wish us in it. Us, the presumptuous ones, it kills. It takes the Boelckes and the Immelmanns, the Balls and the Nungessers, and dashes them to the earth. We shall never be its creatures.'

He did not look up as he spoke.

'After the war, then what?'

For the first time in Poe's experience, Richthofen laughed. It was a brief bark, like a branch snapping.

'"After the war"? There is no "after the war".'

34

AN IMMELMANN TURN

There was an unspoken truce between them: no more talk of banishing Kate from the war.

Charles wanted her about because he wanted an outside view. Through their link, fading as his blood assimilated, Kate knew she comforted him. It was disappointing to be allowed into the counsels of the Diogenes Club not on her own merits but because she reminded this decent old man of other women, the women of his youth: his wife, Pamela, the sainted Geneviève.

As they were driven in an open car to Maranique, Charles dozed, exhausted, drained. She kept a blanket wrapped round his legs and held him upright. In sleep, he had his arm around her.

Who did he dream she was? Having survived Frank Harris, the Terror and thirty years as a vampire, she knew her character was firm. But Charles's ghost women were threatening. She risked becoming one of the phantom sisters who haunted him. Besides Pamela and Geneviève, there were Penelope, Mrs Harker, Mary Kelly, the old Queen, Mata Hari. Apart from Pamela, dead before the Coming of Dracula, vampires all.

Vampire personalities were unstable, shifting. Constantly taking sustenance from others, they became a patchwork of their victims' traits, shrinking in themselves, losing their original characters. Kate's sisters-in-darkness withered in their minds before their bodies gave out.

When she turned, Penelope, Charles's fiancée, became unrecognisable. A recluse now, she received warm young visitors in her dark house, clinging with tenacity to a life-in-death she despised.

Kate knew she was strong. She was still undead, still herself, still sane. Or as sane as she had ever been. If she'd lived, contrary to what the kindly Charles said, she'd have been a spinster freak, a dotty old aunt in trousers.

This was the road she had cycled the night Edwin was lost. Again the sky was muddy white. This time, it was near dawn not near dark. Again aircraft were aloft. Three Camel fighters returning to the field. They weren't flying from the lines, so they'd not been out on an offensive patrol. They were 'stunting', which was frowned on, turning wheels in the air, each trying to tie the circle tighter than his fellows. For every two pilots killed by enemy action, another died in training or recreational flight. Two Camels harried the third, hawks moving in on prey, trying to force him down.

A very few vampires could grow wings and fly. Kate was not one of those. Looking up, she felt the call of the sky. She'd like to fly one of these machines. As a child, she'd been teased mercilessly, by the same horrid Penelope whom Charles later failed to marry, when she admitted she wanted to dress as a boy and go to sea. This was the same impulse, something childish frozen in her by her turning.

The Camel which was leading its comrades in mock chase went into a spin, corkscrewing towards a line of shabby trees. She thought the fighter out of control. In her anxiety, she squeezed Charles awake, and pointed up.

'Damned fool,' he said.

The fighter brushed the tops of the trees (Kate heard branches snap, saw them fall) and, unbelievably, pulled out of the dive. Kate whistled. The Camel came up hard from beneath and behind, zooming up the tails of his fellows. If the pilot fired his guns, he could pot them both.

'That will be Edwin,' Charles said.

'Surely, that's an expert's flying. Edwin is a beginner.'

'An expert would know enough to be afraid.'

In aerial combat, the surest way to victory is to attack from below and behind, the position Edwin assumed against his mock enemies. Even a two-seater with a ring-mounted rear gun could rarely fire upon an attacker coming from below and behind. The tactics of the dog-fight, evolved in the last three years, boiled down to getting behind the target.

'Flies like a Hun, that fellow,' said the driver, not without contempt. 'A shooting star. VC in a fortnight, dead in a month.'

Edwin's quarry flew off in opposite directions: one tried to imitate his manoeuvre by throwing his Camel into a spin, the other made for the clouds.

'In a real dog-fight, they'd have escaped, despite his marvellous dive.'

Charles shook his head. 'In a real dog-fight, he'd have killed them before they could shake him off.'

There was a tiny chattering noise.

'Gordon Bennett,' the driver swore. 'That bloke just shot 'is mate.'

The Camel that was heading up was not hit, it seemed.

'It'll just be some sort of noise-maker,' Kate said.

'Don't think so, miss.'

The diving fighter pulled up, ragged and wobbly, but found Edwin still on his tail. There was another chattering.

Tiny flame-puffs burst in the Camel's tail-plane.

'He shot 'im that time,' the driver said.

They were at the main gate of Maranique. The guard passed Charles's car but did not salute. He might be a VIP but he was also a civilian. The guard was the same corporal who had let Kate in last time.

The car drew up at the farmhouse just as the Camels approached the field. Captain Allard, in a long black coat and a wide-brimmed hat, stood outside watching, along with a cadre of pilots, including old friends Bertie and Ginger. Allard was grimly silent, but the others argued heatedly. She guessed their point of controversy. Another staff car was parked by the farmhouse, chauffeur standing by. Kate caught the smell of Distinguished Personage, and wondered what else there was to worry about.

As the sun rose, the Camels landed. Edwin touched down first and taxied neatly towards the sheds. He was completely masked by helmet and goggles, but she knew at once it was the man who had drunk from her. A hot needle pierced her heart, reminding her of unfinished business.

The second fighter, tail-plane dotted with smoking holes, thumped down, one wheel slipping into a rut. It limped, turning awkwardly, to a halt. An incensed pilot jumped out and ran across the field, stripping off helmet and gauntlets. His big boots, designed for warmth not agility, made him as clumpily clumsy as a kinema comic.

As the third Camel made a careful landing, the angry pilot of the second tore up to Edwin, who was calmly lifting his goggles. Kate heard a blue streak of abuse.

She helped Charles across the field. Allard and the pilots also moved in on the argument.

'You shot me, you cold-hearted devil bastard! What the bloody hell are you trying to do? Win the war for the Hun?'

'Steady, Rutledge,' Ginger said. 'Give Winthrop time to explain.'

Rutledge, a vampire with tiny horns and a fierce moustache, was a new face.

'Well…?'

Rutledge looked up to Edwin. The pilot unwound his scarf, detached his mask and shifted his goggles. Black soot circles outlined cold eyes.

'He would have claimed victory,' Edwin said to Allard. 'I chose to mark my man.'

'Confounded dolt, you could have done for me!'

'I tagged you. I did not kill you.'

Allard, called upon to judge the issue, considered.

'Allard, if I'd meant to shoot Rutledge down, he'd be shot down.'

Allard, eyes burning, seemed to look into Edwin's heart.

'That is true,' he said.

Rutledge's mouth opened in protest. He thumped the side of Edwin's fighter. The canvas shook. The pilot was near hysteria.

'Captain, he shot me! An Englishman shot me!'

'He is telling the truth. He knew he would not kill you.'

'He damaged HM Government property.'

'Fined a day's flying pay.'

Edwin accepted Allard's verdict. There was cold understanding between the acting flight officer and the new pilot.

Rutledge stormed off. Edwin hauled himself out of the cockpit, hanging like a monkey from the cross-strut of the upper wing.

'Not a docile kite, the Camel, not like the Pups we trained on. This bird has to be broken in. Turns like a dream, though.'

Allard nodded.

The third pilot, a vampire American, had landed and ambled over. He was pale with excitement, but more exhilarated than angry.

'Lockwood, do you regret going for me like that, with such a comrade?' Edwin asked.

Lockwood shrugged. 'Seemed like a good idea at the time.'

The American walked off. Edwin took off his helmet.

'Hullo, Beauregard,' he said, acknowledging the visitors. 'Miss Reed.'

Miss Reed!

Kate, her Irish flaring, guessed a great many people would be in a permanent state of rage around this new, improved Edwin Winthrop.

'How did you enjoy the show?'

'You fly as if you were born to it.'

'I *am* reborn, Beauregard.'

Edwin dropped to the ground like a circus tumbler and stood straight. He was still warm, but there was a vampire sharpness to his smile, a thin coldness in his eyes.

She'd seen the look before: in the warm servants some elders impressed into their service, feeding them drops of blood and the promise of eventual turning. But Edwin was no vampire's slave. Certainly not hers.

'You fly like Ball,' Bertie said, stating a fact rather than giving a compliment. The new pilot accepted the judgement. There was something of Albert Ball in him, just as there was something of Kate Reed. But he ruled himself. There was an iron determination that all was down to Edwin Winthrop.

'Probably shouldn't have popped off at old Rutledge, though,' Ginger remarked. 'That sort of stunting's bad for morale. Never know when you'll have a Hun on your tail and Rutledge will be the only one who can shoot the blighter down.'

'I think that unlikely.'

Bertie and the others admired Edwin but did not accept him yet. They could not trust him not to value his own unfathomable cause over that of the squadron. Kate knew how they felt.

'I think it would be useful if we had a chat, Winthrop,' Charles said. 'You, myself and Kate. I wish to clarify a certain situation.'

'Is this a personal matter?'

'If you choose to make it so.'

Jiggs, the mechanic, opened up the cowling of Edwin's fighter. He tutted as a wave of oily heat wafted out.

'I have a patrol to fly in an hour. I'm the only warm man in the squadron. We're under strength for day-flying.'

Kate was not sure how warm Edwin was.

'This need not take long.'

'Very well.'

35

IMPORTANT VISITORS

A long black automobile was parked in the courtyard of the chateau. Six motorcycles, with uniformed outriders, formed a neatly serrated wall of defence around the car.

'Important visitors,' Theo said.

Poe, queasy from exposure to the risen sun, suppressed a cringe. In his experience, important visitors usually meant some new reversal. His dealings with publishers in America and Europe always involved violent argument, broken contracts and long-lasting bitterness. His current patrons might well be disposed to couch criticism of his work in terms of wooden stakes and silver bullets.

Imperial eagle pennants hung from the hood of the car. The outriders were sleek new-borns. Their undoubtedly military black leather uniforms were unfamiliar. Poe assumed this was a new outfit, an adjunct to the Air Service or Dr Mabuse's secret police.

In a German utopia, everyone would wear a magnificent uniform. Lavatory attendants would look like field marshals. Field marshals would stagger under the weight of braid and brass.

Poe was acutely aware of his status as the lone civilian at Malinbois. Even Ewers had taken to sporting a natty cavalry officer's outfit, earned by some obscure reserve status.

He had an impulse to conceal himself behind Richthofen.

A motorcycle rider, arm fixed in a salute, opened the car's rear door. An insectile elder unbent from the dark interior. A grave miasma emerged with him. Attendants held a black canopy aloft to keep the creature in shade. His rat face hung in the shadow, dirty white eyes shifting, as he stood up stiffly.

'It's the Graf von Orlok,' Theo explained. 'One of Dracula's closest advisers.'

Only the very very old looked this ghastly. Orlok wore an ancient greatcoat, fastened by dozens of buttons and hooks. He was hump-backed, spider-fingered, rodent-toothed and hollow-cheeked; his swollen head was bald under a fur cap and his hands were locked into arthritic claws. Poe had never seen a vampire so repulsive. This was one specimen ten Brinken would never be able to measure and categorise. Orlok was a fiend of hell, not a creature of science.

'I thought we had more time,' Theo muttered.

Poe would have pressed his friend for an explanation but Theo cut himself off. He had said more than he ought.

Orlok looked around, shaded against the sun. His eyes squirmed in their sockets. Poe tried to stand to attention. Richthofen was instinctively erect, ready for inspection.

General Karnstein marched out of the great doorway, ten Brinken and Dr Caligari flanking him. Sundry fliers lolled behind the General. They had done their best on short notice to get into dress uniform, the licence for individuality usually afforded heroes suspended for the moment.

The General saluted Orlok, who waved a claw and snarled. Poe realised the elder chose not to speak.

The little lakeside excursion party joined Karnstein's cadre. Baron von Richthofen took his place at the head of the fliers. Theo fell in behind the General and to his left. Poe stood by Theo and was eclipsed as someone – Hanns Heinz Ewers, of course – stepped in front of him.

The tallest outrider returned Karnstein's salute and removed his goggles. He was a handsome new-born Prussian with a clipped moustache, a fixed smile and a duelling scar.

'Hardt of the General Staff,' he introduced himself.

The new-born was Orlok's mouthpiece. He wore a black leather coat and helmet. Hardt looked around the courtyard and up at the skies.

'So this is the lair of our knights of the air. I'm a navy man myself. Submarines.'

Karnstein nodded.

'You've impressive quarters, General. And an impressive record. Which of your men is our Red Fighting Eagle?'

Karnstein gestured. Richthofen stepped forwards, saluting. Hardt returned the salute and shook the Baron's hand.

'It is a privilege,' Hardt said. 'You are a hero.'

'I do my duty.'

Poe could not look away from Orlok. The elder seemed almost frail, as if his long fingers would snap and crumble like old twigs. If a sunbeam fell on him, he'd burst into a puff of dust. But there was a strength in him that came with centuries. The spark in him that had clung to life must be hideously strong. The truly old were beyond comprehension.

'Sir,' Ewers addressed himself to Hardt, 'has Dr Mabuse had time to absorb the import of my report?'

'You are…?'

'Hanns Heinz Ewers.'

'The doctor will give due consideration to your complaint, Herr Ewers. As I'm sure you understand, more pressing matters demand his time.'

Ewers hung his head and chewed his lip angrily.

'And is this the cause of your trouble, Herr Edgar Allan Poe?'

Poe understood the brand of treacherous calumny Ewers had communicated to Mabuse. Ewers, no friend of his, must be working hard to undermine his position. Poe could only shrug. Hardt looked him up and down, grinning.

'Herr Ewers claims your reputation is inflated,' Hardt said, smiling.

Poe tried to return the new-born's steady gaze.

'On the contrary,' he said, hoping bravado would conceal unease, 'it might stand higher were I not plagued by arrant plagiarists. If my work is so overrated, one wonders why so many stoop to imitate it.'

Ewers glared evil at him. Poe had not realised the depths of the man's envy.

'We find Herr Poe's work satisfactory, sir,' put in Richthofen.

Hardt raised a sardonic eyebrow. Poe was himself surprised.

'You feel your collaborator is suited to his task?'

'Eminently so, sir.'

Hardt looked at Ewers with a sharp smile and a repressed, almost French shrug.

'It seems the matter is settled without further debate, Ewers. Our Fighting Eagle must be judged the expert. Thank you for calling attention to the matter, but it seems your worries are entirely unfounded.'

Ewers's face was red with swallowed fury. Veins in his temples expanded and pulsed. Poe gathered Baron von Richthofen had just saved his life. If not that, at least his position. And Ewers had tried to eliminate him.

'Shall we go inside?' Hardt suggested. 'The Graf von Orlok finds out-of-doors tiring after sun-up.'

Karnstein stepped aside. The fliers formed a guard, lining the entrance to the Great Hall. Flanked by his motorcycle guards, Orlok inched across the cobbles, taking care to remain inside shadow. Hardt took his pointed elbow and helped him on to the first of the three steps that led to the great door.

There was a pause. The silent vampire was a traditionalist. He would not step across a threshold unless invited.

'Graf von Orlok,' said General Karnstein, 'you are welcome to the Chateau de Malinbois. Please come and go of your own will.'

Orlok ground fingernails together like cicada legs. Hardt helped him up the steps. Once inside, surrounded by gloom, the elder wriggled away from his outriders. In the close confines of the passageway that fed into the Great Hall, Poe almost choked on the death stink of Orlok's old clothes.

Karnstein followed Hardt and Orlok up the steps, pointing out the way to the Hall. Poe stayed close behind, followed by Theo and Ewers. He felt a pricking in his spine as he imagined Ewers thinking of thrusting a dagger into his back.

Richthofen hung back, letting the elders go their way, and stood between Theo and Poe. He glared out through the door at Ewers, who remained on the bottom step, still digesting his fury.

'Ewers,' said Richthofen, 'I shall thank you not to concern yourself with the affairs of my biographer.'

'Baron, I…'

Poe, standing behind the Baron, saw only the neatly trimmed back of his head. Ewers was struck terrified. For an instant, Richthofen's ears were pointed and the set of his jaw changed. Turning round, he was as impassive and bland as ever. Poe was grateful he had not been staring the Baron in the face for the last few seconds. A blood tear trickled down Ewers's cheek. He was still gripped by terror.

They left Ewers in the courtyard and caught up with Orlok's party as General Karnstein showed them the wall of trophies, enumerating each flier's individual victories.

'This is most impressive,' Hardt exclaimed. 'The Graf von Orlok admires the achievements of JG1. As does his estimable cousin, the Graf von Dracula.'

'It will be a great privilege for these men,' Karnstein said. 'They are new-borns. Few of their kind are chosen for such exalted service.'

Poe had missed a vital point. What service was the General speaking of?

'To commemorate the significance of this position,' Hardt said, 'Berlin has decided its name should officially be changed. The Chateau de Malinbois is a little too *French* for our taste. From now on, in honour of the eagles of JG1, this will be the Schloss Adler.'

The Eagle's Castle.

Orlok prowled by the trophy wall, spindly claws tapping his chin as he looked at the relics of the dead. He seemed not to hear the talk, though his huge rat-ears must be sharp enough to catch the tiny sounds that plagued Poe. Hardt was merely the smiling mask, the dancing puppet. Orlok was the master.

'Now, if your intelligence officer can make himself available...'

Theo stepped forwards, smartly. His insouciant manner was gone. This was an Oberst Kretschmar-Schuldorff ready to stick at his post until the last trump.

'...we shall inspect the arrangements made to increase the castle's security when our commander-in-chief comes to be among his finest.'

General Karnstein cried clear stern tears of pride. Apart from the stoic Richthofen, the fliers were shocked, bewildered, ecstatic. Even these creatures could be impressed. The great commander was coming to Malinbois. No, to Schloss Adler. Sometimes, Poe hardly dared think the name.

Dracula.

36

DARK-ADAPTED

'It is as if I were about to be dressed down by my parents. You both look so earnest, so cross.'

'I am your mother in a way you don't yet understand,' Kate told Edwin, 'and Charles is your father. He brought you into this secret world. It is your duty to honour that.'

Edwin grinned, not understanding. His smile was easy but his eyes were hard. He was a wall to her mind; given their communion, he must work hard to be so impenetrable.

'Perhaps I shouldn't have peppered Rutledge's backside but I've likely saved his life. He was lax up there, careless. He'll be less so in future. The next fighter on his tail won't be a Camel. Lockwood got the point.'

They stood in the shed, between lines of aircraft. Charles leaned heavily on his stick. Jiggs worked nearby, patching the tail of the Camel Edwin had 'tagged'. The oily machine smell was strong.

Penned close between the aeroplanes, Kate saw the beginnings of the turn in Edwin. His movements were quicker. His face was colder. His sibilants hissed slightly, over sharpening teeth.

'You've taken from Kate,' Charles said.

Edwin, shame pricking minutely, looked down at the beaten earth of the shed. Then, flaring, he looked up and met their eyes.

'And I've taken from you, Beauregard. And Albert Ball. And

others. We all take. That is how we grow, adapt.'

He would be eating steak nearly raw, swimming in red juice. And he would have an appetite, burning fuel like a rotary engine. He would be always hungry.

'Don't you feel the danger, Edwin?'

'Miss Reed, without wishing to be offensive, you're a *vampire*. That hardly puts you in a position to lecture me about taking blood, taking *anything*, from another.'

The cut in her throat, made with her own claw, stung. Healed over entirely, the phantom wound throbbed, pregnant with blood.

'Edwin, you misunderstand the condition. You aren't a vampire.'

'I don't wish to turn, Kate. I don't wish to die. I have a duty and I can best do my bit with your blood in me. I apologise if I hurt or upset you, but there is a greater cause than us both.'

He looked up through the open shed doors to the sky.

'Up there lives a monster. I am pledged to destroy it. I owe it to Ball.'

'Either purge yourself or turn altogether. I've seen what happens to people caught half-way between warmth and undeath. You don't appreciate the risks to your mind and body.'

Edwin appealed to Charles. 'Beauregard, you understand the risks are secondary. We don't matter. Duty does.'

Kate squirmed inside. Her blood-links with Edwin and Charles were stirring. She sensed what was going on beneath their conversation.

'It's not duty, Edwin. It's revenge.'

Edwin's face closed shut.

'My blood in you. It's fogged your mind, twisted your intentions.'

'Richthofen must fall.'

'Richthofen will fall. Eventually. *Dracula* will fall. But it can't be just you. It has to be all of us. A consensus. You're becoming like the worst of them. This isn't a game for a few mighty knights and a million expendable pawns. This is about huge numbers of people, vampire and warm.'

'You're editorialising, Miss Mouse.'

She was angry. 'I'm trying to save you from a great misapprehension. Probably from madness and true death. You've been through something very like hell and have focused the blame on one young Hun, when you should blame the old men on both sides who have slaughtered millions because it was easier than living. The getting and keeping of power for a tiny minority in all countries has killed us all, is killing us all.'

'You sound like a Bolshevik.'

'If that's what it takes. I've been a Revolutionist, as has Charles.'

'I don't see what this has to do with me.'

'That's just it. It has to do with everyone. You see yourself apart from us all.'

There was a quiet, angry pause. Kate was flushed. Edwin, whom she had almost reached, retreated into the armour growing around his skull.

'Is this leading anywhere important, Beauregard? I have an offensive patrol to fly.'

After deliberation, Charles – older now than his years, slower and sadder – said, 'I believe you have returned to active duty too soon after your injuries.'

'I'm fit. I'm better than fit.'

Edwin did a deep knee-bend and sprang. He leaped twenty feet, grasping a cross-beam. His boots dangled above their heads. This was the sort of showing-off Kate expected from callous new-borns. The ones who wanted to distance themselves from the warm. The ones who wanted the living penned as cattle, who felt vampirism made them Darwinian aristocrats, princes of the Earth. The monsters. Edwin dropped like a cat and stood straight and cool, boyishly proud of his feat.

'In the first stages, it's like a drug,' Kate explained to Charles. 'There's a euphoria. Over-confidence.'

'She's wrong, Beauregard. I have been careful. I have made of myself a weapon.'

Charles was tempted to believe him, Kate knew. It would suit the purposes of the Diogenes Club to have this ruthless, agile creature on the books. But Charles was too good a man not to understand.

'I can't risk you, my boy. Kate has lived with her condition for thirty years. I have to listen to her.'

'But it's so *silly*,' Edwin said, turning away. His wide smile was almost hysterical. 'I can do so much. We have to destroy JG1. We have to persuade the Boche to stop making those creatures.'

Kate's ears pricked up. *Making* those creatures?

'You see my point. You are losing caution. You just told me something you shouldn't have.'

Edwin's eyes rolled, in irritation.

'Why are we having this argument? We want the same things, don't we?'

Charles was thinking. 'Kate, I want your word that you won't write anything about JG1 without clearing it with me first. Under DORA, you could be imperilled.'

She was on a hook now. 'Very well, but what is the story?'

'They're shape-shifters,' he said. 'Richthofen and his battle comrades. They don't fly aircraft. They grow wings.'

'Good lord!'

'They're Dracula's get. By proxy. His blood has made monsters of them.'

It was Kate's turn to keep secrets. She understood the import of Mata Hari's confession.

Edwin did not apologise for letting the wildcat out of the bag.

'I shall recommend you be relieved of your duties, Edwin. You need more doctoring,' Charles said.

Edwin did not protest.

'He is thinking of your interests, Edwin.'

He looked at her and kept his thoughts to himself.

'Very impressive,' she said. 'It took me years to master that trick.'

'Your face still gives you away. You blush like litmus paper.'

That was almost the old Edwin.

'I still have confidence in you,' Charles said. 'You'll be one of our best. When you've recovered from this taint.'

They left him in the shed. As Kate helped Charles out into the open, Edwin went to confer with Jiggs, casually poking about in a Camel's engine, debating mechanical arcana.

She worried that Edwin had not argued his corner as fiercely as she would expect. Vampire blood was stubborn stuff.

Especially hers. Perhaps the strain was growing weak?

In the sun, Charles cringed like a vampire. She hoped she had not made an invalid of him.

'Let me turn you, Charles. It's the least I can do.'

He shook his head. 'Not now, Kate.'

'You're not like Edwin. You have the character, the backbone. You could be one of us and not go mad. Unless people like us are vampires, the monsters will win.'

'This is dizzying, Kate. You argue your blood is poison, then you try to get me to drink.'

'You are like Edwin. Your mind is made up beyond reason and you'll stick by it until death.'

'Pot, kettle, black…'

Each word was an effort.

'Idjits, the lot of you.'

'The warm?'

'Men.'

Charles laughed.

They were outside the farmhouse. Charles pushed the door open with his stick and allowed Kate to step in. He followed.

Captain Allard, wearing a face-shading hat, sat at a desk, looking over papers. In an armchair nearby was a fish-eyed grey-suited civilian. With a razor chill, Kate recognised Mr Caleb Croft.

'You'll have to take Winthrop off the roster, Captain Allard,' Charles said. 'He's not right yet.'

Allard looked sideways, to Croft.

'Diogenes will find you another bright boy.'

Croft swivelled his eyes from side to side, an implicit headshake.

'We can't spare Winthrop, Mr Beauregard.'

Charles was startled by the refusal. He was on the point of blustering.

'It's too dangerous, Croft. The lad's a peril to himself and those who serve with him.'

Croft said nothing. His skin was lizardy. Brutality boiled off him like steam.

'This is too important to take the risk.'

A contest of wills took place. Croft exuded a damp, invisible cloud. He could sap the lives of others by breathing in. He was late eighteenth century. It was whispered he was once hanged. He wore high collars to hide the rope-burn. Now he was the iron instrument of Lord Ruthven's law.

'I fear I have sad news, Mr Beauregard,' said Croft, each syllable a hollow croak. 'Mycroft Holmes is dead. Your Ruling Cabal is inquorate.'

Charles was stricken. Mycroft had been his sponsor in the Diogenes Club.

'As a consequence, your operations here are suspended.'

Croft produced a document from his inside breast pocket.

'I have the Prime Minister's authority to take over. You have earned leave.'

Charles's face was as grey as Croft's coat. His heartbeat faltered. Kate had a stab of concern for his health.

'At least listen to me about Winthrop,' he pleaded.

'He is a valuable man. Captain Allard would find it difficult to run this show without him. Your concern is noted but the Lieutenant will remain on active service.'

'His promotion is coming through,' Allard said.

'On your recommendation, I understand,' Croft said.

Charles was shattered. Kate did not know whether to step in and hold him up lest he fall. No. He would not thank her.

'One further matter, Beauregard,' Croft said. 'It would reflect well on your unparalleled record if the last order you gave before you were relieved was to place Maranique airfield off-limits to journalists.'

Croft turned deep, dead eyes to her, and cracked open his lips in a scary smile, showing green-furred fangs. During the Terror, when the Prime Minister wavered between the Revolutionists and the standard of Dracula, Croft had issued orders that she be summarily executed on apprehension. Another woman, mistaken for her by the Carpathian Guard, was impaled in Great Portland Street.

'Why don't you personally escort – Miss Reed, isn't it? – to Amiens, Beauregard?'

Charles turned, hands useless fists about his stick. Kate picked up a strong impression: Charles saw himself drawing the silver-coated blade and sinking it into Caleb Croft's heart.

'Good day, Miss Reed,' Croft croaked. 'And good bye, Mr Beauregard.'

Together, they left. Outside the farmhouse, the morning air was chill. The clouds threatened. A flight of Camels rushed noisily past, rising into dangerous skies.

37

---◆---

MASTER OF THE WORLD

The Graf von Dracula, in consultation with Ludendorff and Hindenburg, under the direct patronage of Kaiser Wilhelm and King-Emperor Franz Joseph, had laid plans for the great victory of the Central Powers. Soon would begin the *Kaiserschlacht*, the all-or-nothing push of the German armies, backed by a million men freed from the Eastern Front, against the Allied lines and, once they were breached in a hundred spots, on to Paris. When Paris fell, France would be crushed, Great Britain cowed and America startled. The Allies would make what craven peace they could. Then Poe presumed the Graf would direct his attentions to the *arriviste* peasant masters of the new Russia and make ready for the next generation's war.

The newly named Schloss Adler would be Dracula's command post for this vital action. Flanked by his brood of flying demigods, the father of European vampirism would stand on the highest tower of the castle and watch his armies triumph.

Poe was possessed by the excitement of the moment. On the battlements as the sun set, he heard the din that rang throughout the castle as unused chambers were opened. A convoy of trucks had arrived, widening and flattening the road to the castle with their wheels. Efficient engineers were installing telephone and telegraph lines.

A group of men in uniform wrestled to erect a wireless aerial. A

304

new steel structure already arose from the ancient pile, topped with a huge inverted hook.

The uniforms reminded him of other soldiers in grey, of another just cause. Poe had felt as excited before, marching at the head of his troop into Gettysburg over fifty years earlier. That had been another all-or-nothing push, another turning point. Then, history had turned the wrong way. This time, that would not happen. Trains sped across Europe, packed with men and munitions. From his perch, he saw black segmented snakes winding across the sunset-bloodied land, heard the grinding of the wheels on the tracks. With every minute, Germany grew stronger.

In the last few days, he had been writing. *Der Rote Kampfflieger* was not the ghosted autobiography Mabuse had commissioned (Edgar Poe could not shackle his voice to another, not even that of Manfred von Richthofen) but a biographical sketch which spun out of control, scattering ideas and philosophies, mixing the politics of nations with the nature of the universe. Not since *Eureka* had he had a subject so vast.

It took all his concentration to hold the matter of his book in his mind. As he wrote, he realised this was his last chance to redeem a reputation compromised by the wide-eyed wrong-headedness of *The Battle of St Petersburg*. His hands were permanently stained, fingers black with ink. His cuffs were spotted. By writing, by envisioning in minute detail a world as it should be, mankind as it should be, he could make it so. His mind, stretched near madness, must prove strong enough for the task.

'Eddy,' Theo appeared, collar turned up against the wind Poe had not noticed, 'if you have a moment, there are a few matters we must discuss.'

Since Orlok's arrival, Theo was burdened with a thousand duties. Through the smiling Hardt, the elder insisted on supervising in detail all matters pertaining to intelligence and security. There could not be enough checks and examinations. Tiny flaws in the records of a dozen men, from an adjutant on Karnstein's staff down to one of the castle's troop of cleaners, had been exposed and the personnel removed.

Theo, like everyone, was newly formal. Fliers wore full dress uniform, breasts heavy with medals, at all times. Huge ledgers of military etiquette were learned by rote. Theo wore a fur-collared greatcoat over his immaculate uniform. On his tunic hung an Iron Cross earned on active service in Belgium. He had a large, flat box under his arm.

'Firstly, your problem with Ewers is at an end.'

Since his display before Orlok, Ewers had sulked, chattering out 'reports' on a typewriter, plotting his own advancement.

'The Baron has settled the matter personally.'

Poe tried not to think what that might mean.

'Now, as you understand, our little nest is to make accommodation for a very high-flying bird. Because of JG1's record, we have been able to adopt a certain casual attitude which will no longer be applicable.'

Theo was coming around to something awkward.

'I understand you held the rank of full colonel in the army of the Southern Confederacy?'

'I rose to that position. Under the name of Perry.'

Theo presented his box like a tray. He opened it, and thin paper was disturbed by the breeze.

'Matters are complicated, you understand, by the absorption of the Confederacy into our enemy, the United States of America, but it seems you are entitled to wear this.'

In the box, neatly folded, was the uniform of a *colone* in the Uhlans. Poe picked up the Ulanka jacket. The quality was of the highest. A double row of buttons glittered. Theo saluted.

'We have equal rank, Oberst Poe.'

He tried to get used to the continual saluting. His reaffirmed rank demanded salute of almost everyone in Schloss Adler, and he was obliged smartly to return the gesture.

'When they opened up the west tower, they disturbed the filth of ages,' Göring was saying. 'They had to send Emmelman in. He ate everything half-alive, and most of the dirt.'

Emmelman was the *kobold*-flier who never reassumed human shape. A shambling heap, he was a writhing mass of wormy appendages, lumbering alarmingly through corridors he filled entirely. Even this creature was crammed into uniform.

The Great Hall was being rearranged. The trophy wall was inviolate, but electric lights were strung everywhere, banishing shadow from the vaulted space. Centuried cobwebs were ruthlessly burned away. Cleaners grew fat on the spiders that were a perk of the position.

'Did you see the monster in the courtyard?' Göring asked Poe. 'Barrel wider than a factory chimney. Engineers claim it can hit Paris.'

Gun emplacements had sprung up all around the castle. Mainly anti-aircraft positions. JG1 expected to do a deal of air fighting close to home. The Allies knew what they were up against now, thanks to Albert Ball's lucky observer, and serious assaults were expected.

'You must set everything down. This is the sharp end of history.'

Poe outranked Rittmeister von Richthofen. He was worried this would prompt the flier to close up. Over the past weeks, he had just begun to tease thoughts and feelings out of the hero. This could bring down a steel shutter. He supposed that, if it came to it, he could *order* the Baron to be forthcoming.

Richthofen had been flying full-strength dusk-till-dawn missions for several nights, leading his hunting pack, bringing up his score until he was within sight of an unprecedented hundred victories. The general order was that no Allied aircraft be allowed to return to the lines with intelligence of the gathering forces of the *Kaiserschlacht*. In addition, JG1 were destroying balloons by the half-dozen, ensuring the Allies were running short of trained observers. The Baron was not tired by such exertions. Rather, with the glut of foes' blood, he swelled sleekly and seemed almost fat. He thought faster and was more expansive.

'I do not care for balloons,' he said.

'Because they don't add to your score?'

At the outset of the collaboration, Poe would not have dared make the suggestion. Now he knew his man, he could afford to be facetious.

'There's no sport in it. But it's dangerous. As you know.'

JG1 had suffered its first loss, to ground fire. Ernst Udet, swooping on a balloon, was transfixed by a lucky silver bullet and shape-shifted to human form, tumbling from the sky a broken wreck.

'Your father-in-darkness will be here soon.'

'I have met Dracula.'

A *Sanke* card, sold by the million, commemorated the event, the Baron and the Graf together. Though Richthofen could be photographed, Dracula had no reflection and so appeared in photographs as an empty uniform. The card showed the Baron posed stiffly, shaking the hand of a figure whose head was drawn in, a magnificent coin profile.

'On my twenty-fifth birthday, shortly after my fiftieth victory, I was summoned to Berlin. I met Hindenburg, Ludendorff, the Kaiser, the Empress and Graf von Dracula. I found the Empress to be a pleasant lady, very grandmotherly.'

'And the others?'

Richthofen hesitated, knowing praise of his superiors was his duty.

'Our Kaiser gave me a birthday present, a life-sized bronze and marble bust of himself. A characteristic gesture, I think.'

Poe smiled at the understatement. He was surprised the Baron should express even such mild criticism.

'What did you do with it?'

'I sent it to my mother in Schweidnitz, to be placed with my boyhood hunting trophies. In transport, one moustache was snapped off. I dare not exhibit an imperfect thing.'

'What of the others?'

'Hindenburg and Ludendorff lectured and asked technical questions, many beyond my poor knowledge. Hindenburg was struck by a nostalgic impulse when he learned we had occupied the same cadet room at Wahlstatt. I gather it changed very little between his time and mine, and that he had happier memories of the place than I.'

Hindenburg must have been at Wahlstatt only shortly after Poe was suffering at West Point.

'My own memories of military school have not become fonder with age.'

'That does not surprise me.'

'And Dracula?'

Poe remembered his own brief encounter with the Graf. And how overwhelming it had been.

'He is a huge person. He has his own gravity. There is a mental pull, an invisible fist. Those of his line, he has made his slaves.'

'New-borns who have been turned by elders are often bound to them.'

'It was not so with "Auntie" Perle. She is meek and knows her place. But with Dracula's blood in me, I am chained to him. To be in his presence is like being buffeted by strong winds which threaten to tear one's mind to fragments. This is not even his intention, it is what he is. I cannot best serve him by becoming like those creatures who have attended him down the centuries. His wives and his serfs.'

'Have any of the others…'

'…been in his actual presence? I hope we are strong enough to survive him long enough to do his will.'

A warm woman, Marianne, was presented to him in the evening. A train brought a company of such to the Schloss Adler, to feed those vampires not on active combat duty and reward those who were. The woman's neck was not too scabby, though she was rouged to conceal advancing years and so docile as to suggest she had been used by vampires for quite some time.

Her blood carried traces of the others who had tapped her. Poe sensed little of her own life. Her mind was almost drained, used up.

Still, she took the edge off his red thirst.

She was lulled into sleep and he drank again from the dribbling wounds on her neck and breast. Her blood cleared the fog from his mind, the jitteriness that he had, like the rest of the castle's inhabitants, been feeling since the changes began.

The door was rudely opened. Poe raised a sheet over Marianne's face.

'West tower,' Theo said. 'Full dress uniform. A quarter of an hour.'

Pre-dawn haze and thick cloud made the landscape seem like the bottom of the sea. Poe and Theo stood with General Karnstein. The fliers were out killing Englishmen, but the rest of the castle's staff were assembled in ranks as if for a parade. *Everyone* was in uniform: ten Brinken, Caligari, Rotwang and the other scientists had reactivated reserve ranks, even the Graf von Orlok wore a *pickelhaube* and braided tailcoat.

The fliers of JG1, a flock of giant bats, appeared from the west, in perfect formation. Richthofen was the arrowhead, wings spread wide. The sight of the creatures still awed Poe.

Through thin cloud which ripped as barbed wings sliced, the fliers approached Schloss Adler. The Baron landed on a stone platform, crouching slightly then standing erect. His men fell in smartly behind him.

Engineers fussed by the sky-hook set into the tower. A shadow fell on the castle and everyone looked up. A vast black whale-shape was descending through the clouds. A smartly assembled band struck up Wagner's 'Ride of the Valkyries' from *The Ring*.

Hardt gave orders as cables tumbled from the sky. Engineers scrambled to catch the whiplike things. A dirigible loomed lower. The cable was fixed to the hook and an electric winch whirred. It was rare to see a Zeppelin so close to the lines. This was a magnificent specimen, painted black as night. On the nose of the gasbag, just in front of the gondola, the crest of Dracula was picked out in scarlet.

All necks locked at an angle. All eyes fixed on the wondrous craft, the dreadnought of the clouds. It was the *Attila*, flagship of the German aerial fleet.

A trap opened in the underside. A batwing-cloaked figure stepped into empty air and floated down. He wore a face-covering helmet crowned with horns. His body was encased in burnished armour. As Dracula alighted on the tower, everyone saluted.

INTERLUDE

THE PRIVATE FILES OF MYCROFT HOLMES

Of the Cabinet, only Churchill attended the funeral. Lord Ruthven did not venture into Kingstead Cemetery under a lavender parasol to give the eulogy. That stripe of vampire known as 'murgatroyds' embraced the trappings of the grave, resting in catafalques, wearing shrouds and convening in crypts. Ruthven, however, deemed tombs and coffins common, the crutches of those pitiful warm who insisted on going through with the indignity of actual death.

Beauregard stood at the gravesite with Smith-Cumming. It was as wide and deep as the foundation of a good-sized cottage. Mycroft had been a Big Man in every sense.

This was an occasion for the Old Men, a dwindling circle of relics from a bygone age. They arrived in horse-drawn cabs, consulted pocket-watches and tutted about lost jewels of their youth: sweetmeats that couldn't be bought any longer, songs fallen out of the repertoire, famous beauties who faded rather than turn.

At the front, there was enormous resentment against this generation. The soldiers, the Young Men, believed hold-overs from the nineteenth century contrived the War solely for the purpose of scything the ripening corn. Considering the generals and diplomats who declined to come to the funeral, the Young Men had a point. There were fatheads in Britain to equal General Mireau, and knaves as black-hearted as Dracula.

The Reverend Mr Robert Elsmere, hardly a conventional churchman but an old friend, delivered a brief eulogy. Even now, it was impossible to give public specifics of the service Mycroft Holmes had done for his country. To the casual reader, his obituary in the *Times* was that of a minor civil servant who spent a great deal of time at his club in Pall Mall and very little in his supposed office in Whitehall.

Beauregard looked at the mourners. No mysterious veiled ladies. No vengeance-swearing gypsies. No long-lost sons back from Africa. Despite his profession, Mycroft had not lived a life of melodrama.

Smith-Cumming nudged Beauregard and pointed out a tall, thin old man with a prominent beak. Face seamed by suffering, he wore a deerstalker cap, peak pulled over dimming eyes.

'It's the Old Man's brother,' observed Smith-Cumming, 'the consulting detective.'

Another hold-over, another memory of bygone times. This place of the truly dead was full of them. Lucy Westenra was buried nearby. And Jack Seward. Names forgotten to history, but known to Charles Beauregard. The weight of his secrets bore down.

The coffin was lowered steadily into the grave. Dravot was chief pall-bearer. The coffin settled and Mycroft's brother dropped in the first handful of dirt. Then the small crowd broke up as a sexton, limping on a tin leg, began to shovel in the earth.

Beauregard offered conventional condolences to Mycroft's brother. They had never met, though they had aquaintances in common. The retired detective knew exactly who Charles Beauregard was.

'Tell me,' Holmes said, 'the Whitechapel business. It was Seward, wasn't it? Not the peer, not Holmwood?'

Beauregard was shocked to have old matters brought up. He had kept silent for so long he couldn't say anything out loud now. But he nodded, once.

'I knew as much,' Holmes said, relieved. 'The facts were there for all to see.'

Holmes was buttonholed by Churchill.

Smith-Cumming and Beauregard walked from the grave. Smith-Cumming's leg wasn't regenerated completely, but he got about with remarkable ease.

The path to the gate took them past the Westenra tomb, where once one of Dracula's get was destroyed. The door-stone was cracked across but the sexton kept the marble clean and changed the floral tributes. Beauregard detected the hand of his former fiancée. Penelope had known Lucy Westenra, the first new-born of the modern age, in life and followed her into living death, turned by one of her executioners.

It would be pleasant to lose track of the secret story. Let others follow the threads of incident and meaning which shaped the fates of nations and the lives of millions. Perhaps this was why he resisted turning; he knew that, in the end, he could not bear to keep up with the horrid course of history.

Tiny white flowers grew in the lea of the tomb.

'Snowdrops,' Smith-Cumming said. 'It must be spring.'

This year, spring did not mean joy and rebirth. This year, spring meant only the German Offensive.

The Diogenes Club was no longer open, even to members. The doors were under armed guard. An elder vampire and a new-born Tommy stood in the Mall, barring the way. The Prime Minister's dove grey Rolls was parked directly outside.

'Ruthven must be in the document room,' Beauregard commented. 'I'd hoped Mycroft would take the Club's secrets to the grave.'

'We should be there,' Smith-Cumming said. 'A last duty.'

'At least Caleb Croft is in France. I'd hate for those dead fingers to be flicking through the private files.'

'Soon enough, Beauregard.'

He wondered momentarily if the guard would have orders to bar them from the Club, but Dravot gave a salute to the vampires and they were admitted smartly. The Prime Minister occupied the foyer, leaning on a shooting stick, insouciance frayed by anticipation.

'Ah-ha, just the gentlemen required,' Lord Ruthven remarked. 'You will save us a tiresome chore.'

Lloyd George slumped in one of the chairs. An undersecretary, in shirtsleeves, eased a large Turner sunrise from the wall. Its frame was heavy gilt.

'Dreadful thing,' Ruthven commented, meaning the picture. 'All that fearful orange. It's a wonder you've put up with it for so long.'

Behind the picture was a strongroom door. Beyond were Mycroft's carefully-tended records. Fifty years of secrets. Beauregard knew of a hundredth part of the material.

'Maybe we shall at last know the true fate of the *Marie Céleste*?' mused the Prime Minister, as excited as a small boy on Christmas morning. 'The identity of the murderer of Edwin Drood? The whereabouts of the Borgia Pearl? The lost plans of the *Nautilus*? The formula for Griffin's invisibility drug? A treasure map marked with the locations of Lyonesse, Atlantis, Opar and Kôr?'

Ruthven was pricked by curiosity, but also by power. Knowledge, information, was power. Mycroft's files contained more secret knowledge than any other resource in the world. The solutions to petty mysteries were the least part of it. Having come to power late in life, the Prime Minister's first thought was always the perpetuation of his position. With Mycroft's secrets, Lord Ruthven might see in the New Millennium as absolute ruler of the British Empire.

'Now, to which of you gentlemen did the late lamented entrust the combination?'

Beauregard looked at Smith-Cumming.

Ruthven barked something that approximated a laugh. 'There is always dynamite.'

The undersecretary dropped the sunrise. The door was gleaming steel. Beauregard suspected dynamite would reduce the building to rubble but leave the strongroom unviolated.

The Prime Minister examined the door.

'It will be some tricky conundrum,' he said. 'A convoluted puzzle, a trap for clever minds. I know Mycroft of old. Too clever by four-fifths. Spent his life tying Gordian knots.'

Lord Ruthven was not the only elder vampire who fancied himself Alexander reborn.

Lloyd George snorted impatiently.

'So,' Ruthven snapped, 'what did he do? Give you each a piece of the puzzle?'

Smith-Cumming again looked at Beauregard.

Ruthven's smile grew fierce. 'He did just that, did he not?'

'We were entrusted,' Smith-Cumming said, 'but not with the full combination. I know a third, Beauregard knows a third...'

'And ... ?'

Beauregard, confident he knew to whom the last of the combination had been given, avoided Sergeant Dravot's eyeline. He said 'and Mycroft kept back the whole secret for himself.'

'This is silly. Children's games are being played with matters of national importance. David, go out and find the greatest cracksman in the world. That Froggie, Arsène Lupin?'

Lloyd George sat up sharply, shocked at being addressed as if he were a butcher's boy to be sent out for ten penn'orth of liver and lights.

The undersecretary laid hands on the cool steel of the safe.

'Sir,' he ventured, timidly.

'Maybe we require one of those Wild West Show brigands. Butch Cassidy? Buffalo Bill?'

'Sir,' repeated the undersecretary.

'What is it, Fink-Nottle?' said Ruthven, irritated.

The undersecretary pushed the door, which swung inwards.

'It's open, Prime Minister.'

A stale smell came out of the strongroom. Beauregard darted a look at Dravot, who was impassive.

'I ordered this place sealed,' Ruthven said. 'Heads will roll. That is not a metaphor.'

The strongroom was equipped with electric light. The under-secretary found the switch.

The room was lined with filing cabinets, but every drawer had been pulled out and piled up. Steel walls were streaked with soot.

'The door would have to have been left open a crack,' Smith-Cumming deduced. 'Or the fire would have gone out when the oxygen was exhausted.'

Mycroft Holmes' irreplaceable secret files were ash. The Prime Minister's grey face reddened with rage.

Ruthven rasped, 'Doesn't anybody but me appreciate there's a war on?'

PART FOUR

JOURNEY'S END

38

OFFENSIVE PATROL

Winthrop awoke before two in the morning. He hauled out the bucket stowed under his cot and was sick into it. With his changes, keeping down food and drink was difficult. His alarm clock was set to sound in five minutes. In the dark, outlines of objects were almost clear. Things seemed to glow with a deeper black. In the air, he was gifted with apprehensions and insights. Like a bat's, his inner ears sensed other creatures in the sky.

Sitting on the cot, he pulled on his Sidcot and boots. He didn't allow himself funk. This would be his first night patrol since... Since the first time.

Not quite a night bird, he needed a few hours' sleep. The vampires were downstairs, carousing. The *other* vampires? He was stricken with a shivering spasm. The queasiness in his stomach told him he was still warm. The sharpness in his mouth told him how close he was to living death. He couldn't afford to worry about such things. He must focus on duty and retribution.

Suiting up was automatic. He buttoned and strapped himself together, then stumped downstairs, joints thickened by protective gear. On the ground, he felt swaddled and stuffy. In the air, he was agile as his Camel. The cold cut through a dozen layers.

'Hullo,' said Bertie. War was a continuous rag to him. Those who went west had just popped out for a smoke and would be back in a minute. 'Wrapped up warm?'

'You've fixed up your Sidcot like Ball,' Ginger commented.

Winthrop had instinctively come into the mess through the low doorway and steadied himself by gripping Ball's hand-holds.

The boots made him clumsy. Suited-up pilots often fell over like clots. People were always saying he did things like Albert Ball: flying, shooting, crawling, fighting.

The pilots for tonight's jaunt were already in flying kit. Allard had a few veterans of the old Condor Squadron, but most, like Winthrop, were from the new intake. Mainly, they were American vampires, purposeful as blades, solitary as cats.

'Cheerio, old thing,' Bertie said as Winthrop left the mess. 'See you at dawn.'

Winthrop nodded ambiguous reply. He had no time to pretend each patrol didn't potentially end in true death. He made no arrangements beyond each flight.

Allard liked to have the patrol line up as if for inspection, and go over the particulars once more. Winthrop fell in by Dandridge, a Yank new to the war but skilled in predation. The elder had passed among the warm for centuries, stalking in the cities of the living. Others of the intake – the cowboy Severen, the insatiable Brandberg, the idealist Knight – were old, turned before the 1880s. Mr Croft reasoned that those who lived through ages of persecution must have the instinct to kill and survive. There was friction between these elder aces and Cundall's contemporaries. No arguments, just mutual distaste.

Winthrop, not a vampire, was apart from both factions. From Allard, he understood Croft approved of him. He had flown patrols with elders. They were better suited to daylight excursions than sensitive-skinned new-borns.

Allard appeared in front of his men, emerging swiftly from shadow.

'The objective of this patrol has been changed,' Allard said. Behind him stood Caleb Croft, greyness a gloomy gleam in velvet black. 'Tonight, we visit the Chateau de Malinbois.'

Icy calm radiated from Winthrop's heart. He must not let himself be excited or afraid. He had known this would come.

'Or, as it is now known to the German High Command, Schloss Adler.'

The intake had been briefed on Malinbois. Winthrop's report on his flight with Courtney was the only authoritative intelligence on the shape-shifters of JG1. While Winthrop was in hospital, Richthofen's bat-*staffel* had been glimpsed frequently from the ground, hunting spotters and scouts, killing balloonists, buzzing the lines. Only Winthrop had encountered the creatures in the air and lived to make a report.

Allard continued: 'Richthofen's brood have made it impossible to gather intelligence on the nocturnal movements of the German army. Vast numbers of men and much *matériel* are reinforcing their lines, to prepare for their push. This activity is being conducted by night. In this sector, no single aircraft has managed to return with information. We have no more balloons to put up or trained observers to put in them. It is vital the reign of JG1 be broken. To this end, we shall set out to engage the German fliers and prove they are not invincible.'

Suddenly, out of nowhere, observing the stricken expressions of even the oldest of the old, Allard laughed. It was not a reassuring laugh, but a sinister chuckle that grew to a maddened and maddening howl. Again, Winthrop noted that, for a comparative new-born, Allard was among the strangest of the strange.

The pilots dashed for their waiting aircraft. Winthrop was in his seat before the echoes of Allard's laughter died.

Condor Squadron had been equipped with new Camels. Tricky birds to tame, but on a par with any *machine* the Boche could put in the air.

Allard favoured a barbed arrow formation: taking the tip position himself, ranks falling back above and below and to both sides. Winthrop kept steady immediately above and behind the flight commander, with the high man, Dandridge, immediately above and behind him.

Without fuel, the shape-shifted Boche were not vulnerable to the most common killing shot of aerial combat. They could not go down in flames. But they were still vampires: silver in the head or the heart should do the trick. Every other bullet in the drums of the Camel's twin Vickers guns was silver. A twenty-second burst of fire cost a hundred guineas. Both sides were reduced to recovering silver from the amputated limbs or smashed corpses of casualties.

Winthrop carved crosses into the tips of all his bullets, silver or lead. Nothing to do with the supposed allergy of vampires to crucifixes, it ensured the bullets fragmented on impact, bursting inside a wound. In the course of a dozen daytime patrols over the last week, he had qualified as an ace, shooting down six of the enemy. He was happiest with the ones who had gone down in flames. He had a taste for the fray and Albert Ball's instinct for it. Now, he wanted to fight by night. He wanted to add a Richthofen to his bag. Then, perhaps, Ball would be assuaged.

His stomach spasmed again. He'd learned to live with the stitches of pain, not to let them show. Kate had tried to tell him his course was dangerous. He would make things right with Kate when it was all over. No, he would make things right with Kate *if* it was all over. No, he could not think of Kate, or Catriona, or Beauregard. Only the moment, only now.

He gripped the stick and kept level. The pain-burst faded. The night sky was alive. Without turning in his cockpit, he knew where the other Camels were. A picture of the arrowhead stayed in his mind.

Down below, a column of vehicles advanced along a road, feeding men and *matériel* to the Boche lines. He ignored it. This was not an observation flight. This was an offensive patrol, a hunting party.

A tiny noise. A lone Hun on the ground fired a futile shot upwards, at the Camels. Winthrop's thumbs almost depressed firing buttons. Albert Ball told him to be a cool hand. Ball sat on one shoulder, Kate on the other. Not a comfortable arrangement.

The patrol flew the course Winthrop had flown with Courtney.

Up ahead was the newly named Schloss Adler. This was where the Bloody Red Baron lived.

Reports were in from the lines. JG1 were out of their nest tonight, towards Amiens, attacking a row of patched-up balloons suitable only for hauling aloft Guy Fawkes dummies. They'd return frustrated to find a fight waiting for them. No one had ever *attacked* the shape-shifters before. That was a tiny advantage, a surprise.

Before he saw them, he *sensed* them. His ears thrilled. A silent formation returning to the castle. They flew like bats, gliding between wing-flaps, riding unmapped currents.

Allard saw the Boche too. He raised his hand. The arrowhead expanded. The Camels let distance grow between them, but kept in formation.

Remember, *short* bursts. Accurate fire, not hosepipe spray.

His mind stripped down, surplus thought and feeling done away with. He was a new person, unencumbered. A purpose behind Vickers guns.

They saw the Camels.

Allard was close to the flank of the enemy formation. He fired first. Silver flashes appeared in the wings of one of the creatures. The horribly human scream was louder than an elephant's bellowing. The injured monster fell out of formation. His wings were torn but bullets passed through. He'd have to be hit in the torso or head to be seriously damaged.

Winthrop watched the flier tumble, wings like an umbrella reversed by a sudden wind. He recovered and cruised downwards. Severen was on the wounded vampire's tail, whooping and firing like Broncho Billy. The elder had a killing thirst and was ignoring tactics. When his guns were empty, his enemy would recover and come for him.

The formations passed through each other. Winthrop smelled the shape-shifters' musk and felt the cold rush of their wings. Wheeling in the air, he tried to draw a bead on a black shape darting past. He nearly fired, but managed not to waste precious bullets.

The Boche weren't firing either. They would have used up most of their firepower on the dummy balloons. It was often the habit of fliers to get rid of the extra weight of ammunition by emptying guns into enemy trenches on the way home.

A wing filled his whole field of vision and he squeezed the firing-buttons. White flashes seared his eyes as his guns discharged. The wing was gone and he let up the pressure on the buttons.

The burst, only a few seconds' worth, jarred his ears. On instinct, he fired again, moments *before* another wing passed in front of his prop. This time, the shape-shifter flapped into his burst, and was twisted, screeching, in the air. A row of holes appeared in a curtain of wings. He was sure he had sunk a few into the furry barrel of the flier's body.

He tasted blood in his mouth. His own, mingled with Ball's and Kate's. His teeth were coral razors. This was as near to the vampire condition as he wished to come.

Another burst. Another miss. The bat-creature executed a perfect Immelmann and swooped towards the slice of moon. Dandridge was on his tail, firing scientific bursts. The Boche came out of his turn and spread wings wide. Dandridge had hit him. Red gobbets dripped in black fur.

With a sinking motion, the shape-shifter got beneath Dandridge's climb and latched like a lamprey on to the underside of the Camel, wings wrapping upwards, tail lashing. The Camel's frame buckled and its engine stalled. The prop sliced into the Boche's face but jammed.

Winthrop was appalled.

The Camel came apart. Dandridge's upper plane ripped off and disappeared like a kite in a storm. The shape-shifter detached from the aircraft. Dandridge's crushed wreck plunged, wind shrieking in the wires. As he went down, Dandridge emptied his guns.

The creature that had killed Dandridge struggled to stay aloft. He had taken many hits and the propellor slice was severe. His wings were ragged and torn. Ribbons of dark blood flew from wounds.

Was this the Red Baron?

Winthrop had the mutilated monster in his sights. He fired, pouring out silver and lead. He swooped down and over the creature, briefly worried that he might latch on to his Camel, repeating the manoeuvre that had defeated Dandridge.

His blood thrilled. There would be a reckoning. Turning for another pass, he saw Allard diving on the same prey. The monster struggled upwards to meet Allard. With what seemed a single shot, Allard put a lump of silver into the monster's skull. Instantly dead, the flier dwindled to human size, weighted by heavy guns, and fell towards black ground.

The creatures could be beaten.

His victory stolen, Winthrop wheeled, searching. He was at the heart of the dog-fight. Shape-shifters and Camels whirled around, firing guns, tearing wings. There was an explosion as a Camel (Rutledge's, Winthrop thought) burst into a fireball. An expanding ball of hot air hit his wings and forced him back.

Down below was the castle. And above was an immense dark shape that laid a shadow on the land.

Rutledge had not been killed by one of JG1. There was Archie all around. The Schloss Adler was defended by gun emplacements. Archie exploded below Winthrop, a carpet of fire in the night. Smoke smeared the lenses of his goggles and stung his eyes.

A bat came at him, and he turned the Camel's nose away. Detatching one hand from the stick, he wrenched off his blinded goggles, unmasking his face to the icy dash of open air.

Looking up, he realised a Zeppelin hung over the castle like a mammoth balloon, floating in thin atmosphere above the operational ceiling of any heavier-than-air machine. Only real monsters lived in those altitudes, where the cold froze blood in veins and made woolly flight suits into crackling ice chain-mail.

Allard signalled withdrawal. The shape-shifters were landing on their tower, retreating within stone walls.

Winthrop had been cheated of his kill. Perhaps the Red Baron was truly dead. Allard's kill. Angered beyond thought, Winthrop approached the Schloss Adler. A shape-shifter on the landing platform was shrugging his flying shape, bending to wriggle into the castle.

Winthrop fired a burst to get range. He heard his shots whine off stone. Half-way between human shape and bat form, the flier turned, attention caught by the fire, pointed ears swivelling. Winthrop's next burst caught him in the chest, bearing him backwards against the castle wall. Scarlet gouts blurted through thinning fur. A perfect heart-shot.

A seventh score. One that counted. One of the monsters.

No, it would not count officially. Winthrop, the killing urge briefly satisfied, realised he had gone against Allard's orders to withdraw. His victory would never be confirmed. Besides, what he had done was strafe a foe on the ground, not meet him in the air. The pitch was not level.

Still, the kill counted in his system. One of the monsters was gone.

It had been only seconds. He slid easily back into formation, behind and above Allard.

There were others. Brandberg, Lockwood, Knight, Lacey.

They sped away. There was still Archie but it was ineffectually distant. The shape-shifters were out of the air. The airship was too high to bring guns to bear.

Fourteen had approached the castle. Five were returning.

Winthrop had seen Dandridge and Rutledge killed and known Severen would lose his match. Now, he realised he had for a half-instant glimpsed one of the shape-shifters with a human rag in his mouth, shaking his head as blood-trails whipped. That had been another of the pilots.

The rest had been killed without his even noticing. Nine men exchanged for two monsters. The dog-fight couldn't have lasted more than two or three minutes.

The five Camels flew away from the rising sun. Spreading dawn fell heavily on Winthrop, like a blanket, sapping his energy, cooling his blood. They crossed the lines.

39

UP AT THE FRONT

'Your bus is wheezing a bit, miss,' said Colonel Wynne-Candy, 'I'll have my driver look it over.'

Kate, not attuned to the eccentricities of internal combustion, thanked the officer, whose staff car was mired at the side of the road. He had pulled over to let her ambulance past and suffered the consequences of gallantry.

There had been near-continuous bombardment all day. The enemy had brought up big guns and were hammering the Allied trenches. It would be heads down in the lines.

She looked up at a slate sky empty of all but cloud. To the east, the gloom was reddened by fire.

'A boy in the air?'

The round-faced colonel, cheerfully retained from the Boer war, was not the jolly fool he seemed. Kate shivered as she tried to shrug. She could usually put ideas into words, but was too involved in the business with Edwin to explain it easily.

'The lad'll be a lot safer with Richthofen down.'

'The Red Baron?'

'Word over the blower this morning. Not official yet. Boche won't admit a thing but our ears in Hunland have picked up a whisper. It seems Allied mastery of the air has been reasserted.'

Kate wondered if Edwin was disappointed. He had shaped himself into a weapon so he could go after the creature who had nearly killed him. Or maybe he had succeeded? No, he had not bested the Red Baron. In her blood, she would have *known*.

'Almost a pity, ain't it?' Wynne-Candy mused. 'The war will seem a spot less colourful. Richthofen gave our fellows something to shoot for.'

Something to shoot *at*, she thought.

A projectile whizzed into the mud a couple of hundred yards away and burst. Kate and Wynne-Candy cringed in a light patter of wet dirt.

'That's an overshot,' the Colonel said. 'No harm to anyone.'

A smoking crater marked the site of the shell-burst. There were more of them dotted about behind the lines than usual.

'Enough misses like that and our supply lines will be jiggered.'

'You have a point, miss.'

Wynne-Candy's driver, a muddy Cockney, reported on the ambulance, grumbling in the Colonel's ear.

'I say, that's not on.'

Wynne-Candy was shocked.

'I'm sorry to have to tell you, miss, but some unsportin' type seems to have taken a pot shot at you.'

The driver put his finger into a hole in the bonnet.

'Probably an accident. Any proper German officer who found one of his men sniping at an ambulance would have the bounder shot.'

The driver told her the engine was unharmed. With a good clean, the ambulance would run smooth as silk.

'Not easy, keeping things clean in this country,' Wynne-Candy said, looking about the plain of mud. 'Now, miss, be on your way. Boys are waiting at the front for a sight of you.'

With a khaki coat three sizes too big, a nest of hair plastered with mud spatters and a bad case of the distractions, she suspected she would not pass for an angel.

She bade the Colonel farewell and got back into the ambulance. When the army bought these vehicles, the assumption was that drivers would be six-foot-tall men. It had then been inconceivable that all those who fit the description would be required for the front and the position would have to be filled by a tiny vampire woman. She sat on three pillows and leaned forwards to reach the steering wheel, which seemed a yard across. Wooden blocks tied to the foot-pedals brought them within range of her short legs.

Every part of the ambulance rattled. Through the smeared windscreen, she looked at the sky. Even with the Red Baron gone, there were monsters up there. She sensed the tug of Edwin like a toothache. What he had taken from her would take months to recover. She felt she was half a person, fading into ghostliness.

Like a proper Victorian, she was throwing herself into duty. If it had been possible, she'd have picked up a rifle and fought the war. Geneviève, in her long life, had sometimes passed for a boy and served as a soldier: with Joan against the English, with Drake against the Spanish, with Bonaparte in Russia. Geneviève, of course, had done *everything*. Without meaning it, she went through life making other women feel inadequate. By 'other women', Kate meant herself.

In 1918, though she was stronger than most living men, the best Kate could do was drive an ambulance. The next war would be fought by men and women, vampire and warm. If she survived, Kate might be in that one. And the next. And the next.

Richthofen dead. She should follow the story. It would be news.

The road sank into the ground, banks rising to either side. She entered the maze of trenches. Corrugated iron grumbled under the weight of the ambulance. The main road was only just wide enough. Every time she made this trip, the route was different, as old avenues were blocked and new ones blasted.

Another shell exploded, out of her sight, but quite near. Clods pattered on the tin roof of the cabin. It was just earth, not shrapnel.

She was still a reporter, despite setbacks. She would try to learn more about the Bloody Red Baron. There were always the Musketeers of Maranique: Bertie, Algy and Ginger. They would talk to her. They were so good-natured they'd probably sent Christmas cards to the Kaiser during the truce of '14.

She could not go much further in the ambulance. There was a station where the wounded were gathered, laid out on stretchers. Casualties had been light recently. The Germans were preparing their offensive. That would be a military hurricane. Rear positions were deserted as every man and gun the Allies had in France was put into the front. It occurred to her today's heavy bombardment was to soften up the Allies. The offensive – *Kaiserschlacht*, they called it – was very close.

She wrestled with the brakes and the ambulance lurched to a halt. Hopping down, prepared for horrors, she sank up to her puttees in squelching mud. Under a canvas lean-to, the stretchers were all occupied. She had room for five patients, but there were at least fifteen men ready to be shipped back to Amiens.

The officer in charge of the post was Captain Tietjens, a decent man eroded by years in the mud. He recognised Kate under her layer of dirt and offered to get her a cup of tea. At the front, vampires took char with a squirt of rat's blood.

'No thank you,' she said, not wishing to use any of the meagre supplies. 'I've a parcel of scroungings under the seat. Some tea, a chunk of usable bread, a packet of humbugs. A few other things.'

She handed over the precious goods, which had cost almost the last of her money. She was a vampire, she could forage for herself. Tietjens made the parcel disappear: he would dole it out to the deserving cases.

Most of the wounded were Americans, a new development. The influx of Yanks was depended upon to block the offensive. Already, fresh troops were seeing action.

A doughboy, bent like an ancient crone, knelt by a stretcher, holding hands with a fearfully wounded comrade. The boy on the stretcher seemed to be only an upper body: below his hips, the blanket lay flat, soaked with sweet blood. Embarrassingly, her fangs popped.

The wounded man's friend looked at her, too numb to be afraid. It was Bartlett, the doughboy who had tried to pick her up in Amiens. He was changed. The cocky eagerness was blasted away: he seemed at once a lost child and a mad old man. From his mind, she took impressions. She wished she had been able to shut herself off.

'Bloody hell,' she said.

In weeks, Eddie Bartlett had lived through a million years of war. Apart from the half-man on the stretcher, Bartlett was the last of the group of friends who had been at the café in Amiens. He was practically the last of the boys who had come over together on the boat.

She wanted to offer herself to Bartlett. He could have her body, her blood, anything. She wanted to make things better.

Tietjens and she were the only personnel spare to lift stretchers into the ambulance. With extreme reluctance, Bartlett let go of his comrade's white hand to help.

'Hang on Apperson,' he said. 'Gotta *parlay-voo*, buddy.'

Carefully, the three of them got the first casualty – an American sergeant with rag bandages round his eyes – into the ambulance. When they came to Private Apperson, the boy was dead. Tietjens looked to Kate and shrugged.

The air was full of a whistling that hurt her ears. Tietjens, oddly, reached out and touched her hair.

She was about to apologise for having left her best bonnet at home when the whistling exploded. A wave of sound shocked Tietjens off his feet and threw him against her. They were both slammed against the ambulance. The sound was followed by heat. Then a great deal of earth. Something had hit very near. She saw a trench wall collapsing, slowly, on to the remaining stretchers, burying wounded men.

Tietjens was pulling something out from Apperson's bedding, robbing the dead.

Kate struggled towards the wounded. The next shell burst and she was knocked down again. Her back stung and she knew she was hurt. Tietjens was close behind her.

The officer jammed Apperson's tin helmet on her head. Seeing the sense in it, she fastened the strap under her chin. The rim rested on her spectacles, pressing them into her nose.

She dug with her hands, like an animal, trying to shovel the sliding loose earth off the face of a coughing warm doughboy. The more dirt she shifted, the more tumbled down. There was no room to pull the man out of the path of the earthslide.

As she dug, her claws came out. She scratched the earth. Her mouth was distorted by her fangs. She was reduced to the basest of monsters. The boy looked at her with panic and began to struggle, thinking she was attacking him. When he opened his mouth to scream, dirt fell into it, choking him. She thumped his chest, and he coughed up mud. She tried to tell him she was helping him, but could only snarl and hiss.

There was more whistling, louder and concentrated. Glancing up at the slice of sky visible from the trenchbed, she saw dozens of trails and sparkles.

Din, flame and force lifted her off the ground. The ambulance had taken a direct hit. Blood was in her mouth. The vehicle jolted into the air and came apart, screaming metal, spilling dead men. A hundred tons of mud flew up and fell down. Kate shut her eyes and her mouth as the grave-earth closed over her, pressing her down. There was sudden, shocking silence.

40

KILL THE DRAGON

Winthrop sat in Albert Ball's chair, staring at nothing. The mess was crowded but quiet. The new-born Cundall hands were playing cards. Some elders were toying with a plump French girl, exciting tiny squeals from her. She called herself Cigarette, and was shared like a smoke in the trenches, passed from mouth to mouth.

Since Ginger had passed on the rumour that Richthofen was truly dead, Winthrop felt like an exorcised ghost. There was no earthly reason for him to remain with Condor Squadron, but he was bound here. Ball and Kate were with him still, and his red thirst – worse, his red *hunger* – was rising, making him feel like a drunkard for raw meat.

His stomach was not improving. He could keep down only small amounts of very undercooked beef, swimming in blood. When sick, he disgorged alarming amounts of ground-up red meat.

The scabby necks of *filles de joie* like Cigarette had a fascination for him but he knew he could not drink warm human blood. He wished profoundly to be free of the dizzying taint that swarmed inside him, colouring his mind red.

If only he could kiss Kate again and set things right.

A shadow fell on him. Allard had appeared.

'Confirmation of our victory. The Germans have made an announcement.'

'Your victory,' Winthrop admitted. 'You finished the Boche.'

335

'It was a Richthofen but not the Richthofen.'

Winthrop's blood leaped.

'We killed Lothar, Manfred von Richthofen's brother. No insignificant ace. Forty victories.'

The Bloody Red Baron lived. The job for which he had transformed himself was not finished.

'I see what lurks in your heart, Winthrop. You are pleased. You want this prize for yourself.'

Winthrop did not try to blind the American with talk of all for one and one for all and winning the war and seeing it through.

'You may yet have your chance at the eagle,' said Allard. 'And maybe at greater prey.'

Winthrop was stricken with shivers.

Cigarette yelped through giggles. Allard glanced at the girl, not approving. She was in the lap of Alex Brandberg. His mouth was fixed to her breast.

Winthrop excused himself and got up, reaching for stirrups fixed to the timbers for Albert Ball.

'I need air,' he said.

It was March the 20th, official spring. In France, the weather was wintery. Winthrop stood outside the farmhouse, breathing cold air, concentrating. He still needed his vampire blood. The sense of purpose filled him again. But he was ailing. Every time he tried mentally to get above himself, to sort out Ball and Kate and the rest of it, he was paralysed. His mind was shrinking, intent merely on survival and murder. There was more, but a red mist hung over it. What separated him from the troglodytes? Or from old killers impressed into uniform?

Two orderlies struggled through the kitchen door, a long bundle between them. Winthrop smelled blood. The men carried Cigarette, drained unconscious. They left the girl in a lump against a fence by her bicycle.

Winthrop went over to see. The orderlies withdrew, wiping their hands as if they had disposed of something messy. The girl's shawl was wrapped about her. Banknotes rolled into a cigarette-like tube were tucked into her bosom. A spatter of rain, like tears, brushed Cigarette's face. Red-rimmed eyes sprang open. She reached for the money and pushed it deeper into her bodice.

He made no motion to help her. She would not thank him. With experienced fingers, Cigarette felt the bites on her throat and bosom, wincing as she probed ragged tears. She wrapped her shawl about her throat like a field dressing. The wool was spotted with old bleeding. She got deliberately to her feet, strangely dignified, like a drunkard doing his best to seem sober. She held the fence with one hand until she steadied. Her contemptuous gaze took in Winthrop, the farmhouse and the airfield. She was not squealing and giggling now. This girl could not hate the Boche more than she hated the Allied pilots who bled her for money.

He tasted blood in the rain.

Cigarette mounted her bicycle and pedalled off, leaning low over her handlebars, skirts tucked away out of the spokes. Did she have a family to feed? A husband? Children? Or was she a camp-follower, going wherever there were soldiers?

His sudden concern for the girl troubled him, then he realised it was the Kate in him. The rain washed it away. Only a fool stood outside in the rain when he didn't have to.

At sunset, Allard called a briefing. Winthrop knew at once that it was a serious matter. The board with details of the squadron's disposition was wiped clean. A large-scale map of the region hung from the wall. And Mr Croft sat by the captain, face unreadable.

Winthrop sat in Ball's chair, near Bertie and Ginger.

'Mr Croft would like to talk with you,' Allard said.

This was unusual. Winthrop could not recall the intelligence man actually saying a word.

Croft stood, bowing slightly to the room, and began, 'Gentlemen, conflicts of which you were not aware are taking place. A secret war, if you will. We have gulled the enemy. We have allowed him his knights of the air. We have helped build up the legends of men like Richthofen, have encouraged the enemy to trust in them, to prize them above their worth. It has been costly, but – as you will soon understand – a vital strategy.'

As Croft rasped, Winthrop burned. It was impossible to like this man. What he seemed to be suggesting was dreadful, that the Allies sacrificed good men like Albert Ball and Tom Cundall simply to lull the Boche into overvaluing their shape-shifting killers.

'You know that JG1 are stationed in Schloss Adler. On your last patrol, you brought back intelligence that a Zeppelin was moored above the castle.'

A great fuss had been made of that tid-bit.

'It is unusual for such machines to venture near the front. This is the flagship of the enemy's aerial fleet, the *Attila*. It is the position from which their commander-in-chief will observe their planned offensive.'

Winthrop remembered the black bulk of the thing.

'Are you saying Dracula's in that Zep?' Lacey asked.

Croft, annoyed to be questioned, continued. 'This is the end-game we have been manoeuvring. We have drawn Dracula out of his lair. We have brought him within our reach.'

Winthrop understood what Allard had meant by 'greater prey'. There were eagles in the sky, almost as common as sparrows. But there was also a dragon, the *dracul*.

'When the attack comes, it will be the purpose of this squadron to bring down the Zeppelin. Once the head has been cut off the beast, the body will wither. This single stroke will mean victory.'

'All very well, old thing,' said Algy, 'but we've nothing that can climb as high as a jolly Zep. One's eyes turn to iceballs in the upper climes.'

'He will come down to us. Lord Ruthven understands his arrogance. The Graf von Dracula loves this toy, this flying machine. He will want to be close enough to see his armies sweep across the lines. He feels secure in his guards, his shape-shifter aces. That childish overreaching will be the end of him. You men will assassinate Dracula.'

'I've always fancied a spot of Zep-busting,' Bertie said. 'Damned unsporting things, the Zeps. Bombing civilians and that sort of show.'

'This is not sport,' Croft said. 'This is war. In this instance, this is murder. Make no mistake.'

'What about dear old JG1?'

'Kill them if you must and if you can, but do not pursue any private campaign against them. The priority is the Zeppelin and Graf von Dracula.'

'Once Dracula's killed, will it be over?'

'This is his war. Without him, the Central Powers will collapse.'

'Without Dracula, who'll there be to surrender?'

Croft shrugged. 'There will still be the Kaiser. Without Dracula, he will be a lost child.'

Ruthven's man was convincing but his voice was hollow, his focus narrow. Croft said this was not sport but talked of end-games as if a continent of mud were a chess-board. From the air, in the air, Winthrop knew there was no order. Without its head, the beast might thrash until nothing was left alive in the jungle. All Europe might become a country of troglodytes. Winthrop could not think of that. He could think only of hunting hunters, of stalking eagles and dragons.

The telephone rang and was in Allard's hand. The captain listened, nodded, and hung up.

'It has begun,' he announced.

41

KAISERSCHLACHT

She could not breathe. Of course, breathing was a habit, not a necessity. Her chest was under something hard and heavy. All feeling was whipped out of her limbs. Jagged pain in her shoulder suggested silver.

Kate blinked in the dark. Her glasses, jammed to her face, kept dirt out of her eyes. Since turning, which had brought the vampire power of night sight, she had not known blackness so total. The silence of the grave was eaten by tiny, distant sounds. Screams, explosions, engines, single shots, machine-guns.

She had been dead for years. Her condition was not changed.

A pain rushed through her shoulder, down her right arm to her hand. She made a clawed fist, digging her nails into the meat of her palm. It was hard to punch earth. She had no leverage. Her whole arm strained. Her injured shoulder wrenched. She had to press her lips tightly together to swallow the shriek that wanted to escape.

There was a crack in her coffin of earth and her arm could move. Her fingers scrabbled filth as she reached upwards. She jammed her claws into a dead man and had to reach round him. Holding the corpse's arm, bearing the pain, she pulled hard, trying to shift her whole body upwards. The bar across her chest wouldn't budge.

If she fell into her lassitude now, she might live insensible through years, centuries. Perhaps she would awake into a utopia where mankind had outgrown war. Or perhaps she'd find Dracula absolute ruler of a desolate Earth. To sleep was to desert. Her responsibility was to the present.

Her fist burst through to the surface. She felt air on her hand and stretched out her fingers.

The thing on her chest was a beam, or maybe a heavy chunk of her ambulance. It was deeply embedded in the earth. She tried pressing herself down deeper, hoping to wriggle loose and burrow up like a worm.

If only her father could see her now.

Writhing her shoulders, she displaced soft earth beneath her. Everything was wet. Enough struggling turned packed-down dirt into moveable mud.

Someone took hold of her hand and gripped tight. She grasped a man's hand, trying to retract her nails so as not to pierce her rescuer. She tried to imagine the man. Hot pain came in her palm as a metal point – not silver – was forced through the skin into the flesh. Her saviour was shoving a bayonet into her. An eager mouth, tongue like a cat's, lapped blood from her hand, sucking greedily.

She grabbed a face, feeling a moustache, and tried to latch on to a skull with her nails. As the man who was stealing her blood stood, she was pulled through earth. The barrier scraped across her chest and hips. Then she was stuck again. Her shoulder burned. She thought her arm would be wrenched off. Then her face was out of the dirt and she was screaming.

Her glasses, miraculously unbroken, were smeared with earth, and the sun had set. But the light seemed intense. Her eyes stung. And she was assaulted by incredible din.

She stood up, still grasping the scavenger, and shook, trying to get the dirt-clumps off her clothes. Layers of earth between layers of clothes formed three or four skins of cold mud.

She let go of her captive. Her hand was enlarged and knobbly, meat stretched over a swollen skeleton. Her fingers had shot out, stretched to six-inch twigs with three-inch blades. As she thought about it, her hand dwindled. A deep-buried shape-shifting power had come with direst need.

If the new-born soldier staring at her had worn a German uniform, she would have killed him and eaten his heart. But he was a maddened Tommy, bleeding in a dozen places, her blood on his mouth. The soldier backed away and darted off, leaving Kate alone on a mound of mud. She was still enraged, fighting off the red thirst that came with this carnage.

As her eyes recovered, she distinguished pieces of her ambulance and the former trench-shorings. Dead men, smashed to pieces, lay all about. Mercifully, none was recognisable. She assumed Tietjens and Bartlett must be among them. There was no trench any more. Explosions had filled it in. She stood on the restored ground level, exposed. She saw the ditch-lines of nearby trenches. Most of the system was still intact. Men swarmed through, rushing to and away from the front.

A fragment worked its way out of her shoulder and she plucked it free. The pain was already fading.

There were explosions all around. Still ringing from the one that had nearly killed her, she was not further shocked. Turning, she looked to the front. Though her position was foolishly dangerous, she had a remarkable view. From her mound, she saw the busy line of the Allied trenches, the wire tangles of No Man's Land, and the puffs of the German guns. She even saw the distant fortifications of the enemy positions. Eerie music – Wagner? – was falling from the sky. In No Man's Land, steel monsters crawled. Above floated a leviathan of the air.

Again, Stalhein was high man. This time, he remained in his own shape and was detailed to the *Attila*.

The armoured gondola was a conclave of commanders, a nightmare of priorities eliciting a frenzy of salutes from the junior men of the airship service. The airship's captain was Peter Strasser, a fanatic for heavier-than-air flight who had carried out bombing raids on London early in the war. Outranking Strasser was Engineer Robur, director of the Imperial German Airship Service, the great designer of and propagandist for such devices. And outranking all was the Graf von Dracula, who stood alone, paces ahead of his black leather guards, looking at the mud-crawling battle through the observation ports. It was fortunate room had not been found for the Graf von Zeppelin, Field Marshal von Hindenburg and the Kaiser. The combined weight of their medals would have prevented the *Attila* from attaining operational altitude.

Everybody aboard the dirigible had precisely assigned duties, with the exceptions of Stalhein and the Graf von Dracula. Stalhein, feeling the cold of the height in his unshifted shape, had the sense he was being held back. JG1 would come into play soon.

From his chair, Strasser issued orders into a speaking-tube. His efficient crew scurried like uniformed monkeys through the fantastical arrangement of levers and struts.

A long shadow fell on the sunset-reddened land.

As befitted a craft of such magnificence, the *Attila* was equipped with a pipe organ. Robur sat at the keyboard, picking out themes from *Lohengrin*. The music was amplified through trumpets attached to the exterior of the ship.

Stalhein, with unaccustomed meekness, approached the observation port, a circular glass window three yards across set into the floor of the gondola. It was the eye of the *Attila*. The commander-in-chief of all the armies of the *Vaterland* stood, blunt hands resting on a brass rail, looking down on the battle. His face was grey in the artificial light, melancholy in aspect, slightly swollen. Stalhein had expected Dracula, the eternal warrior prince, to rejoice in the spilling of blood.

He had expected to feel more in the presence of the Graf. At one remove, Dracula was Stalhein's father-in-darkness. His bloodline, passed on through the elder Faustine, had given him shape-shifting aptitude. He was one of Dracula's creatures. Stalhein's blood did not sing. He did not feel compelled to kneel before his master. He joined Dracula at the port, and looked down.

There was light enough from the dying sun to see clearly. Formations of tanks crawled forwards, the first wave almost at the Entente trenches. Men advanced in their rutted wake. From this view, the troops were reduced to ants. The tanks seemed big beetles, ploughing through tiny obstacles. Bursts of flame flared throughout No Man's Land. This would be costly.

Spitting fire burst from the most advanced tanks, squirting liquid flame into the enemy trenches. Stalhein, though inured to fiery death, shuddered. This war prompted men of genius like Robur to develop weapons which could extinguish vampires as easily as gunfire and the sword killed warm men. Sections of the enemy trench system turned into rivers of fire, burning frontiers in the blackened map.

The *Attila* was over enemy territory, hovering above the range of anti-aircraft guns. Any heavy guns not yet overwhelmed would be occupied with the ground attack. There were no shells to spare for useless pot-shots.

A junior officer approached, terrified and awe-struck, and handed the Graf a note. He considered gravely and nodded. The officer waved an affirmation and Strasser gave orders into his tube.

Dark objects tumbled out of vents in the gondola, plunging to the ground. Mushrooming patterns of fire showed where the bombs burst. The Graf's eyes were balls of red, blood-blinded. His bloated face was lit by the fires below. He turned to Stalhein.

'God is with us,' Dracula said.

There were columns of fire all around. Kate realised how exposed she was on her mound. But, fascinated, she could not move. It was her job to be here, remember, to tell what she saw. She could not yet look away.

This was the German spring offensive, the *Kaiserschlacht*. Though everyone from Haig down to the dray-horses had known an attack was coming it had still taken the Allies by surprise.

As night fell, star-shells exploded above the trenches. The magnesium-flares of light stung her eyes. The land ironclads had advanced across the desert of wire and the dead, beating a path for the infantry.

'Who's that cretin up there?' someone shouted. Kate realised he meant her. 'Get his bloody head down before we have to pick it up in pieces.'

She was rugby-tackled by someone permeated with the smell of years of trench life, and dragged into a hole only half-filled with loose earth.

'It's a bint,' the soldier said.

His officer swore. Her Red Cross arm-band was slimed with mud. She wiped a swathe of grime away.

'She's a nurse, sir.'

'Bloody good for her, I say.'

'I think she's dead.'

Kate's fangs were poking out of her mouth. She felt her jaw distorting into a shark mouth.

'Bloody shame,' the officer commented.

'No, sir,' the soldier said. 'Not dead, *dead*, You know a vampire.'

This platoon was all warm. Some regiments insisted on living cannon fodder.

'You, Lady Bloodsucker,' the officer said, prodding her. He was elderly, about thirty. 'Are all your limbs working?'

'My name is Kate Reed. I'm whole.'

'Captain Penderel, at your service. You're conscripted.'

A spade was given to her. It had bloody handprints on it.

'See that earth there? Get stuck into it.'

Penderel's men shovelled away. The trench was blocked by an earthfall. Reinforcements, brought up from rear positions, were accumulating in the bottleneck. If the obstacle were breached, they could get into the fight. She saluted and started digging. Being a reporter was shame enough for her family; she would never tell them she'd worked as a navvy.

She hurled a spadeful of dirt over the top of the trench and stuck her shovel back into the packed, blasted earth. The blade struck something soft. A chunk fell from a face frozen into a dead scream. She flinched. Tommies pitched in, found the corpse's arms and pulled him out of the wall. The dead man came out in one piece. With a one and a two, the Tommies slung him into the air and out of the way, to fall where he might.

With the corpse gone, the barrier was greatly broken up. A man could scramble past it without sticking his tin hat over the top. Penderel approved the job and directed his men to advance. As he passed Kate, he saluted. She was left behind, still holding her shovel.

'The Hun has broken through, all along the lines,' said Ginger. He was the Squadron's telegraph expert. 'It's pretty much a wash-out.'

From the field, Winthrop could tell the battle was intense. The sky over the trenches was burning. The massed screaming of guns and dying men carried over the few miles.

Every man in Condor Squadron was in flying kit. Every machine was out of the hangars and fuelled.

Over the battle hung a dark shape, its underside crimsoned. It was the *Attila*.

'It's a big gasbag, remember,' said Bertie. 'It'll burst in flames with a few incendaries. Like a balloon.'

'It's a hundred times bigger than a balloon,' Allard reminded the pilot. 'It takes a big spark to set off such a firework.'

'Is he really up there?'

Winthrop had imagined Dracula would radiate an aura of evil and despair which would be unmistakable.

'Intelligence confirms the Graf von Dracula is aboard the *Attila*,' said Mr Croft. 'Your moment has come.'

The grey man had addressed himself to Captain Allard.

'Shouldn't we be strafing ground troops?' Algy suggested. 'Our lads must be taking a terrible pasting.'

Croft looked death at the young airman. 'Nothing matters but the *Attila*.'

Winthrop had the sense Allard was, for once, uncertain. In the end, he would obey orders.

If Dracula was up there, so was Baron von Richthofen. Every nerve in Winthrop's body thrilled. This must be what it was like to be a vampire. His blood sang, calling for victory. Tonight, he was sure, it would end one way or another.

The pilots clustered around Jiggs, handing over letters and keepsakes. Winthrop had nothing more to give. He hadn't told Catriona he was still alive. By tomorrow's dawn he might not have to. In the end, this was kinder.

The first Camels were aloft, circling the field, waiting for the formation to come together.

Equipment was piled on to trucks. There was not an idle man in Maranique. By the time this flight was through, the airfield might be in enemy hands. If there was fuel left, the squadron were to fall back to Amiens. There would be no fuel left. Condor Squadron would fight until it could fight no more.

He hauled himself into his machine, settling comfortably at the stick.

'Contact,' he shouted.

Jiggs spun the prop. The Camel moved forwards smoothly and into the air. The sun was down, but the land was burning.

Kate squirelled along, following Penderel's men. More reinforcements were on her tail. She knew her way, following the clattering troops as they rushed to the front. The trenches were partially covered, turning into tunnels. Candle-stubs stuck in tin dishes gave points of light.

She used the shovel as a scythe, getting things out of her way. She was stripped down to the animal, acting on instinct. No purpose but to be in the thick of it.

Popping out of a tunnel into the main trench, she found herself facing a fifteen-foot wall of collapsing sandbags. Men held ladders against them, but their upper reaches snapped.

A terrible grinding assaulted her ears. The treads of a tank churned at the top of the wall, shredding sandbags. The motorised juggernaut was jammed in mud and wire. Soldiers fired upwards at the plate-iron shell of the tank. Bullets spanged off metal, leaving dents. The tank lurched forwards a yard, great flat nose protruding over the trench, shadow cast down on the squirming men below.

Fumes leaked from inside the thing. Kate coughed, fearing gas. Gun turrets in the war-beast's side swivelled. She threw herself down into the liquid depths of the trench. A shell shot across the gap and burst against the mouth of the tunnel. Someone had drawn a bead on her former position.

The fire-flash lit the tank, showing every bolt on its side. It was a castle, with arrow slits and battlements. Shrapnel and fire spattered around. Men were pierced and fell, writhing bloodily.

Kate wanted to kill.

The tank's centre of gravity eased over the lip of the trench. The nose swung downwards, threatening to crush the men who crawled in the bed. The treads snagged on the rear wall and ground on, getting a purchase, pulling the machine level. It could roll over the trench as if it were a crack in the road. Men fired at the iron underbelly as it passed.

Kate bent low, like a frog, and leaped upwards, extending clawed hands, pushing against the ground with all her vampire strength. She shot level with the tank and grasped at the steadily moving tread. The grinding wheels caught a fold of her coat and pulled her into the side of the beast. She would be turned to paste as if thrown into the workings of a flour mill, but her broken body would stop this thing. A war cry began in her lungs and emerged as a death scream.

* * *

Poe had intended to present his manuscript to Theo this evening, but events had overtaken them. It started when the *Attila* detached itself from the castle, the signal for the offensive to begin. All along the lines, tanks trundled out of concealed positions, and men fixed bayonets to go over the top. The might of the Central Powers thrust forwards, trampling over the Entente. This would be victory.

On the tower, they watched fliers prepare to join the battle they could hear all around and see in the middle distance. It was still an awesome sight, the transformation of the fliers, but it had become almost familiar.

Poe and Theo watched Richthofen as he changed. Upon the death of his brother, he had shown no trace of anger or passion. But his armour, opening in cracks as Poe teased out material for his book, was entire again, locking inside whatever there was of him that had been alive.

Richthofen's calm face disappeared under fur. Poe thought the flier not even aware of their presence, but, as Kurten and Haarmann stood away, he bowed to his biographer, flourishing a wing-tip as if it were a courtier's cloak. Poe wished Richthofen farewell. The Baron leaped from the tower, followed by his fellows. The fliers swarmed around the *Attila*.

Theo watched his comrades slip into the night, eyes shaded by the peak of his cap.

'It is almost as if our duties here were over,' he said, at last. 'After tonight, what more use will we be?'

Ten Brinken's disciples had packed their records, preparing to withdraw. Karnstein was redeployed to the Italian front. Poe assumed the Schloss Adler was converted for use as the Graf's headquarters. As the castle became more significant militarily, its scientific purpose was wound down. Reports were written and despatched. The experiment was concluded.

'They will have won the war, Theo.'

Theo shrugged. 'That was what Dracula made them for, winning the war. But as Manfred said, there is no "after the war". They are the instruments of conquest, not rule.'

'There will always be conquests.'

'Eddy, my friend, sometimes for one with such foresight you are remarkably blind.'

Poe was shocked.

Though scientists were left behind along with ground crew, and Orlok scuttled about somewhere, the Schloss Adler seemed abandoned with the departure of JG1. The fliers could be seen converging on the *Attila*, tiny as flies. Poe's keen eyes distinguishing them from the morass of night.

In his last chapters, Poe had written of the Baron's reaction to the loss of his brother. It was as if both Richthofens had died, but he was cursed to walk the Earth a while.

'Poor Manfred,' Theo said, understanding Poe's mind. 'He is a loyal dog, for all else,'

'I'd give anything to be with them, Theo.'

Theo looked at him and tried to smile. 'It's too late for anyone to take any notice of what we do. There's a Junkers J1 fuelled, ready for an observation tour. Would you care to accompany me?'

'You can fly?'

'Only in an aeroplane.'

Pillars of fire rose from the battle. Poe thought of the skies over the decisive conflict.

'I've never been up in...'

'For a prophet of futurity, a sad omission.'

'Very well.'

Theo grinned, with some of his old sparkle. 'The raven has wings.'

In her last seconds, Kate would have liked to forgive everybody. But she couldn't.

Her coat tightened like a straight-jacket as more cloth pulled into the wheels of the tank-tread. She smelled heavy oil and grease as she was dragged into the killing gears. Then the engine inside the tank died and she was held, crucified against the machine's side. A mechanical failure or a chance bullet or the hand of God had saved her. Briefly.

One of her hands was free. She bunched her fingers and made a knife-point of her nails. She punched the taut sheet of her coat at the shoulder and tore. Stitching broke and she was free. She fell, but got her hand round the rim of one of the stalled wheels, gritting her teeth as her barbed nails scraped against greasy steel. Hand over hand, she climbed on top of the tank. The metal was heated, as fire had recently played across it.

There were enemies inside this moving cage. Warm or vampire, they throbbed with blood she needed to drink. A rifle barrel poked through a slit and angled round. She wheeled to stay out of range and took hold of the gun. With a wrench, she pulled the thing free – raising *hochdeutsch* oaths from inside – and hurled it off behind her.

Putting her face to the slit, she snarled like a beast. She smelled funk inside, heard tank-men scrabbling and panicking, trapped by the stalling of their wonderful war device. Fire would pour in and cook them.

Her face was close to a pair of boots. The only polished, ready-for-inspection boots in the whole of the armies of Europe. She looked up at the soldier who stood calmly atop the tank, uncringing as if the silver and lead bullets flying around were hailstones. He wore the uniform of the United States but this vampire was older than the country.

His boots grew insubstantial, whitening into a mist. She'd heard of the trick but never seen it done. The vampire gathered himself into a wraith-shape, glowing faintly. His clothes and kit dissolved with his body, as much a part of him as his hair. A bullet struck nearby, clanging against the tank. She cringed, but was mesmerised by the elder. A man-shaped cloud floated over the slit. It elongated and funnelled down, like a puff of smoke suddenly inhaled by a smoker.

Screams cut through layers of iron and steel, shaking her to the teeth. A pistol was discharged, shot rebounding in the confined space.

A red cloud burst from the firing slit, spattering her face with warm blood. She licked her face, impassioned by the blood, swallowing the terror that came with it.

Not waiting for the elder to emerge from the tank, she vaulted off the machine's back and felt earth under her. Looking back, No Man's Land was No Man's no more. Strung-out lines of grey uniforms advanced through the night in implacable ranks, stepping over their fallen, walking on in a human tide towards the Allied trenches.

A machine-gun, maybe thirty yards away, started up, and a fan of the advancing troops were scythed down. More men filled the gap. The gun ranged again, cutting more down. Then the gun was overwhelmed and silenced. The gunners were torn apart by the undead soldiers, blood splashing all around. The Germans' mouths were red.

The elder floated above the tank, reconstituting himself, pretty face reddened with fresh blood.

Someone shot Kate but only with a lead bullet. It slipped through her calf. The hole healed over immediately. She heard the shot long after the stab of pain passed.

Another tank spat a line of burning petrol towards the Allies, spreading fire on the ground. All about her, men retreated, falling back or just falling.

The elder drifted towards the second tank. He must be ancient to have such control of his form. Older than Dracula or Geneviève. Pre-mediaeval. Perhaps pre-Christian. An awesome thing to have hidden among mankind for so long.

He'd have numberless names.

The flame-thrower hitched upwards and belched another burst, catching the elder full in the chest. He burned like a butterfly. Centuries of unchronicled life were extinguished in an uncaring instant, blasted to sparking shreds by brute modernity.

Someone took her arm and saved her tiny life, pulling her backwards, along with the mass of men fleeing the front lines.

'Retreat, man,' someone told her.

42

NIGHT OF THE GENERALS

At HQ in Amiens, everyone was shouting at once. A double dozen telephone lines were manned, staff officers hopping to pass on grave news from points along the front. Lieutenants with brooms shifted markers on a map table the size of a tennis court. Bombardment shook solid walls. There were fires in the town. Shells were falling just short of the outskirts. Fall-back positions on the roads were being hurriedly manned. This was the big push everyone had expected.

Bone-tired after another stormy Channel crossing and dispirited in the aftermath of Mycroft's funeral, Beauregard was shunted into a corner by panicking strategists. It was coincidence he was so close to events. He was ordered to report to HQ to hand over to Mr Caleb Croft a list of the Diogenes Club's operatives behind enemy lines. It would be almost his last duty in the war. After that, he was free to go home to Cheyne Walk and think about writing his memoirs.

Croft was expected directly from Maranique. Condor Squadron were in the skies, represented on the table by a wooden arrowhead painted red. A broom pushed the arrowhead towards the black oval that was the *Attila*. The blocks representing Allied troops were mixed up, probably reflecting their actual dispositions. The Central Powers had thrown so many men into the onslaught that HQ had run out of the black blocks that symbolised them. To make up the shortage, a subaltern tore strips of paper and rubbed Maltese crosses on them with bootblack.

Beauregard rubbed his tired eyes. Battle smoke from a hundred cigarettes swirled over the map. The air in the command room tasted foul.

Field Marshal Sir Douglas Haig was on the telephone to Lord Ruthven, holding the receiver to his chest while he relayed orders to messengers, who passed them on to telephonists, who delivered them to officers in the field, who presumably told their men what to do. There was some sort of a plan. Haig was not at all discouraged by the attack. His red eyes glowed like electric lights. The pin-sharp points of his jagged teeth shredded his lower lip, spotting his chin with his own blood. As he commanded, he almost foamed.

Winston Churchill, despatched from London to be in on the bloodshed, was in the thick of the excitement in his shirt-sleeves, collar undone, silk hat on the back of his head. He shouted facts and figures around his burning cigar-stub. He must have fed within the hour, for he was blown up like a red balloon, fingers like sausages, veins throbbing in his temples.

General Jack 'Blackjack' Pershing, commander of the American Expeditionary Force, was eager to get into the game. He stood at one end of the map with clumps of American troop blocks in each fist, an eager gambler newly arrived at the table with chips to squander. By his side was 'Monk' Mayfair, a carnivorous apeman who might have been one of Moreau's surplus patients got up in a general's uniform and a cowboy hat.

The impression Beauregard got was that vampires like Haig, Churchill and Pershing welcomed this end to the boredom of entrenched squatting and bomb-ducking. They were fairly squiffy from the excitement of it all. According to reports, the lines were breached in a dozen places. German cavalry units were galloping into the fray in the wake of the tanks.

A grey presence made itself known. Croft surveyed the map

with a thin, smug smile. At the relay of another report, the Condor Squadron arrowhead was shoved against the *Attila* oval.

Croft ignored Beauregard. Since his advancement, the Diogenes Club had ceased to exist for him. Beauregard felt the list of names heavy in his inside jacket pocket. He could not help but feel that the agents he and Smith-Cumming had so carefully placed and nurtured would be literally wasted by a more ruthless spymaster.

Haig held the Prime Minister at bay and shouted 'Tell the bloody fool to retreat' into another telephone.

'This is absurd,' the Field Marshal announced to the room and Lord Ruthven. 'Damned Frog won't fall back. Mireau is shovelling his men under tank-treads when we've perfectly sound rear positions prepared. *Le* retreat *n'est ce pas français*. No wonder his men want him impaled.'

A blue block representing Mireau's French divisions was taken off the map and thrown away. A black block advanced over them.

'The Mireau problem seems solved, Prime Minister. *C'est la guerre.*'

Beauregard was chilled. From this room, it was too easy to believe the war a matter of maps and toys and blocks and brooms. Discarded blocks littered the floor, getting under officers' boots. Each meant a hundred or more casualties.

Enemy strategy was a three-pronged push, with Paris as the objective. With tanks and aerial assault and long-range bombardments, Dracula's forces were trying to stop the Allies falling back to prepared positions, spreading enough panic in the ranks to turn strategic retreat into a rout.

'It's a question of numbers,' said Haig. 'The enemy can't have enough troops to waste.'

Once the Allies had fallen back, unbelievable death would rain down upon the advancing Germans. On unfamiliar territory, after four years hiding in tunnels, they would be liable to be cut down by mortar, bomb, machine-gun, mine, flame-thrower and heavy gun. Both sides were abjuring subtlety to go at each other with sledgehammers, pounding directly at the most obvious spots.

'They may have a million men,' Churchill advised Haig. 'An iron steamroller ploughing across Europe.'

'We've more than a million,' the Field Marshal declared. 'We can pour in the Americans.'

Pershing bared fangs and whooped, 'The Yanks are coming.'

Mayfair capered off to take a telephone in one gloved foot and grunt orders to the American positions. Pershing, caught up in the moment, tossed American blocks on to the map, a desperate gambler trying to spend his way out of a losing streak by upping the stakes with each spin of the wheel. Mayfair kept up the stream of deployment orders.

The building shook from nearby shell-bursts. Dust sieved down from the ceiling on to the table. Beauregard brushed his shoulders. Winthrop must be with Condor Squadron, in the thick of it.

'We're digging in and fighting back,' Haig announced. 'We'll see some of those blasted black blocks off the map in no time.'

ATTILA FALLING

The observation port spread out the landscape like an embroidered quilt. There were no clear lines any more, just waves of ants and flame. It seemed the offensive was a complete success. Wireless messages came in from all along the front. Enemy defences were overwhelmed, targets taken, fortifications breached. The armies of the *Vaterland* rolled on.

'We shall be in Paris by tomorrow's sunset,' Strasser opined to his commander-in-chief.

Dracula said nothing.

The *Attila* descended gently. As enemy gun positions were taken or destroyed, it became safer for the aerial warship to approach the ground. With each confirmation, Strasser authorised a downward shift. The view through the port enlarged, showing more detail. The crawling ants became men, identifiable as things that fought and suffered and died.

The smell of battle seeped into the gondola. Stalhein was affected. His nose flattened into a snout. Vampire teeth thrust from his gums. The beginnings of a pelt pricked under his tunic. As his ears flared into bat-points, he heard more acutely.

Strasser, a new-born, was plainly alarmed by Stalhein's tentative shape-shift. Stalhein knew the type. Like all dirigible men, Strasser deemed aeroplanes trespassers in the sky. He was discomforted further by the idea of men who grew their own wings. His dream, inherited from the likes of the Graf von Zeppelin and Engineer Robur, was mastery of the world attained by floating serenely in an unassailable gasbag, making doughnut holes in clouds, occasionally deigning to drop a bomb or two. Creatures who buzzed and tussled at lower altitudes were insect nuisances.

All this, Stalhein knew from meeting the Kapitän's gaze for a moment. In his changed form, he acquired the ability to read the surface of a man's mind. He had to hold himself in, to prevent his spine swelling. If he were to transform completely, he would burst out of his uniform.

Through the side-ports, Stalhein saw his comrades of JG1. They fell into formation around the *Attila*, an honour guard of demon princes. Fear boiled up from the ground. To the Entente, the coming of the *Attila* and its attendants must be the Day of Judgement. Many would be converted to the cause of Dracula by the magnificence of the spectacle. And many more would become helplessly insane.

They were beyond the trenches now, sailing over territory that had been the enemy's less than an hour ago. The *Attila* kept level with the first wave of trundling tanks. Wherever the shadow of the dirigible fell was Germany's.

A young airman snapped a salute at his superiors and reported the sighting of hostile aircraft. Attention moved from the floor-port to the panoramic nose-window. A great bat-shape hung in front of the *Attila*. In his rightful place at the head of his formation, Baron von Richthofen held the air like a kite.

The night sky was warmed by ground fires. Stalhein saw the advancing specks that were enemy aircraft. Condor Squadron, the enemy's closest equivalent to JG1. Richthofen would appreciate the chance of a rematch with the men who had killed his brother.

'Now we shall see the invincibility of the airship,' said Engineer Robur, rubbing his hands. 'These English lords are fools to get into a fight with us. The pests will be swatted from the sky.'

Dracula nodded gravely.

'Take us down closer to the battle,' he ordered.

Winthrop's mouth was full of blood and pain. His teeth split his jaw. The vampire in him rose, reddening his field of vision. He tore off goggles and mask, eyes open against the wind. He drank smoky, icy air, swallowing the taste of war. His night vision was perfect. The Ball and Kate's voices whispered in his brain, urging him on to the arena.

The *Attila* was monstrously large. Its presence over France was an insult, but Winthrop didn't care about the Zeppelin or its passenger. His sights were on the creature that flew ahead of the airship, the Bloody Red Baron. Tonight, Richthofen would be destroyed.

The battle passed swiftly beneath the observation port. Stalhein saw fire dots as guns were fired at the *Attila*. The picture enlarged so that individual skirmishes could be seen. A tank rumbling through a farmhouse, rising to get over the hump of smashed brickwork. Infantry creeping up on a gun position, stick grenades falling closer to the target.

Dracula stood at the nose of the gondola, hands linked in the small of his back, surveying the scene, unsmiling as Camel fighters swarmed closer, spreading out to speckle the entire panorama of the sky.

The Kapitän spoke urgently with Robur, who leaned on his sticks and impatiently shook his head. There was a disagreement between the airship men. Strasser, reluctant and concerned, relayed more orders to his crew.

Stalhein's constricting sleeves split at the seams as his forearms swelled with sinew.

The first of the Camels fired. Tiny flashes popped around propellors. They were well out of range but the English liked to get a man's attention before engaging in combat. Stalhein respected that, though he thought it foolish.

Fliers came up from the sides of the Zeppelin and joined Richthofen in the forwards position.

There was a loud cracking rip. Airmen looked around. Stalhein's tunic had burst up the back. He shrugged out of the ruin and allowed himself a deep breath. His wings were forming, membranous folds blossoming in his armpits, running along the undersides of his arms.

The *Attila* was ahead of the German advance. The roads below were thronged with retreating British and American troops.

Strasser was briefly engaged in conversation with Reitberg, the master bombardier. Vital gun positions were to be destroyed. Such actions would transform the Entente's retreat into a rout. Reitberg tottered along a walkway to the bomb bay, muttering to himself.

A Camel, ahead of its pack as forlorn hope, swooped at the Zeppelin. Two fliers converged on it from above and below, firing Spandaus. The aeroplane's engine burst in a fireball that scorched Stalhein's eyes. Fliers flapped backwards away from the explosion and the burning machine spiralled towards the ground.

Strasser's men gave a hearty cheer which was frozen by Robur's glower. It did not do for an airshipman to hail the achievements of mere wing-jockeys. Strasser went to Robur again, grabbing his sleeve and insisting.

'We are too low,' Strasser said, 'too close to the ground.'

The engineer shook the Kapitän off but could not rid himself of dawning doubts. Robur, another Zeppelin fanatic, knew the limitations of the vessel he had designed.

Dracula half-turned, motioned with his hand. Lower still. Strasser almost protested but it was unthinkable that an order from the Graf be questioned. He stood back, unable to think, so Robur issued instructions, effectively usurping command. Airmen snapped to, pulling levers and wires that released pockets of gas, allowing the *Attila* to settle nearer the ground. Strasser threw up his hands.

Stalhein stepped forwards, round the observation port. Though only a little taller than in his man-shape, he was transformed into a flying beast, a man-bat. He spread his wings to steady himself.

He stood beside Dracula, watching his comrades engage the

Camels in a dog-fight. Several more fighters blew to pieces, raining fiery debris onto the countryside.

Robur settled into his chair by the organ, enjoying his authority. Airshipmen, awed by this legend of their calling, deferred to him. Strasser was cut entirely from the chain of command.

There was a rap at the window. A crack ran through the thick glass. A bullet-lump was lodged close to Dracula's head, tip sparkling silver. The Graf shrugged but Stalhein was close enough to notice the slight shiver of his shoulders. The commander-in-chief interlaced his fingers tighter behind him, quelling shaking hands.

Something was wrong. Dracula was not afraid. Dracula was fear.

Strasser was with them, awaiting the order to take the ship up. It was clearly time to withdraw to frozen heights and observe inevitable victory.

Dracula turned his face to the fire-blotched darkness.

'We go down more,' he said.

Winthrop had expected the *Attila* to begin ascent as soon as Condor Squadron hove into view. Allard had prepared them for an attack on the Zeppelin's belly, warning of the thinning air and gathering cold that would form a ceiling beyond which an airship was safe and an aeroplane was doomed.

Instead the *Attila* hugged close to the crowded ground, bombing retreating troops. It was insane. Something as dangerous as a million gallons of flammable gas should never be allowed this close to a firefight. Dracula, of course, was insane.

Winthrop's Camel climbed on the first pass, breaking formation. Allard's plan, to concentrate fire from below at the engine and fuel supplies, would have to be abandoned.

He passed over the gasbag, wheels almost brushing an acre of stiffened silk. One bomb could destroy the whole leviathan. But the Camel was not a bomber.

Knowing the terrible strain that would be put upon his upper plane, Winthrop angled the Camel nose down and pressed his thumbs on the firing buttons. His Lewis guns strafed the top of the *Attila*, ripping parallel lines of tiny holes in the gasbag. It was about as effective as sticking hatpins into Moby-Dick. Incendiary bullets must strike something solid to explode. The tiny charges spent uselessly in the empty bloat.

Winthrop overshot the *Attila* and ceased fire. He wheeled in the air for another assault. A batwinged thing had been on his tail. Now he faced it. Guns fired. He flew into a swarm of bullets.

Stalhein saw the faces of the Entente soldiers who fired up as bombs burst among them. The gondola rattled with direct hits.

Rifle fire would do little harm. The gondola was armoured and the gasbag big enough to sustain a million fleabite wounds before it was seriously ruptured.

But one explosive shell. One mortar bomb…

Reitberg, staggering back along the bucking walkway, tripped and fell, clinging to rigging. Blood burst from his collar. A stray bullet had sunk in his neck. The bombardier pitched off the walkway on to the observation port. The glass jarred in its frame but did not break. Trickles of blood ran across the circle, spreading over the scene below.

'We must climb,' Strasser shouted, looking urgently at Dracula, torn apart. The Kapitän could not question an order, only wait for it to be rescinded. Dracula watched the dog-fight, rigid as a statue. Strasser looked to Robur. The engineer was too delighted to have control of his creation to heed his subordinate's qualms.

Miraculously, Winthrop's engine was not hit. There were whistling holes in his fuselage, but he had come through. The shape-shifter he faced was not the Red Baron, but some smaller prey.

Winthrop turned the Camel on its side and fired. He sliced past the flier, ripping into his wings with an accurate burst. The creature tumbled in the air, shoulders dislocated as wind caught his wings wrong. Winthrop did not see him recover, so he assumed the German fell.

He flew fast, darting around the huge shape of the *Attila*, and kept losing sight of the battle. For a moment, as he replaced his ammunition drums, he thought he was alone in the air with the Zeppelin. Then he rounded the bulk of the gasbag, and saw Condor Squadron mixing with JG1 in a scramble of flame and wings. Aeroplanes exploded like comets.

A huge flapping fire-shape fell out of the path of a Camel. From the size, Stalhein knew it was Emmelman. Flames spread across the vast lump of his body and scattered across the canopies of his wings. Strasser gasped as Emmelman loomed close. If he were to plunge into the gasbag, the balloon would be burst.

A Camel zoomed down on Emmelman, who changed course, diving towards ground. The pilot pursuing the flier had unknowingly saved the *Attila*.

'Madness, madness,' Strasser screamed, tottering towards the wall of levers. 'We must climb.'

Dracula looked sideways, eyes flaming.

Hardt, the Graf's man, levelled a pistol and shot the Kapitän in the leg. Strasser screamed and stumbled, falling forwards, hands outreached.

'We shall keep to our course,' Hardt said. 'We are all brave men, are we not?'

Robur, mind gone, ordered his crew to hold the course. He turned to the keyboard and wrung chords from the pipes.

Strasser curled into a ball. Airmen closed around the Kapitän, and helped him up. He was fainting on his feet.

Emmelman hit the ground and exploded.

Something big burst in the trees below. Winthrop climbed, looking around. Just now, he was a monster. But it would take a monster to destroy the Bloody Red Baron.

Though outnumbered, the shape-shifters knocked down more Camels than they sustained casualties.

Brandberg passed. A bat-thing had claws sunk into the tail of his Camel and ripped towards the pilot with tin-opener jaws. The Camel went into a spin, taking the shape-shifter down. Another fire-burst on the ground. One for one.

There was no Archie. The offensive had swept past the lines. They were deep into what had been home ground. Winthrop could not think of the big picture. He had prey to find and kill.

'Gentlemen,' Hardt said, 'you have done your Kaiser a service which will never be forgotten.'

Dracula was turned away. Robur's mad music filled the gondola.

'Our lives will have brought victory.'

A scatter of bullets smashed across the windows. Glass burst inwards with a rush of wind. Stalhein's wings shrugged involuntarily. He was ready to take to the air. Hardt saluted the company.

Winthrop sought Richthofen, slipping through the dog-fight in the shadow of the *Attila*. He swooped upwards and looked down on the battle.

A tiny scrawl of flame clung to the Zeppelin's gondola. It was whipped to extinction by cold winds.

A Camel rose to join Winthrop. From the streamers, he knew it was Allard. A shape-shifter pursued the flight commander. Winthrop caught its chest with a burst of fire, and it sank, recovering balance. Wounded, the thing would be an easy target for another pilot. Only one victory counted. Confirmation didn't matter. Winthrop just had to know he had done it.

Allard flew away from the *Attila* and turned in a wide circle. Then he swooped back, closing upon the airship as if the length of its gasbag were a landing strip. He fired a Verey pistol over the side. The flare fell on to the skin of the gasbag, burning purple, lighting up

Allard's path. Seeing what the flight commander intended, Winthrop pulled up on the stick, gaining height. Allard's Camel scraped the silk with its wheels, ran into the spreading flame of the flare, then flipped up and over, prop shredding through the silk skin, wings buckling. A rent appeared in the top of the gasbag and Allard tumbled in. Gas belched out of the ruptured compartment.

Winthrop heard Allard's engine stall and buzz. There was gunfire inside the gasbag. Flashes showed through the silk as Allard emptied his Lewis guns. Then a spark of purple, as the flight commander, swamped by an atmosphere of flammable gas, fired another flare.

The *Attila* shuddered as something slammed down onto it. Robur screamed at the violation of his beautiful ship, jamming his hands against the keys. Tortured wind roared through the organ pipes, accompanied by the creaking and cracking of metal struts.

Hardt stood over the observation port, where Reitberg still lay, and kicked down with a heavy heel. The port fell out in pieces, dropping Reitberg like a loose-limbed tumbling bomb.

Stalhein was confined by the broken walls of the gondola. He should fly free.

Dracula was still turned away from the panic.

Hardt saluted, smiled and stepped out of the hole. He fell like a weight. Others of Dracula's guard followed. Some prayed, most were stone silent.

Strasser, conscious and intent despite the pain, pulled useless levers. Too many connections were broken. The organ pipes groaned.

The first of the big explosions came, discharging a foul smell through the gondola. Then the second.

A ball of fire burst out of the side of the *Attila*, ripping through the gasbag as if it were a paper lantern.

Winthrop felt the hot air rising.

He should look away but could not. The airship kinked in

the middle. One compartment turned inside-out in a gust of fire. Crumpling tail-planes angled up. The firelight showed a dozen flying shapes desperately trying to burst free of the gravity of the huge, doomed ship.

Another compartment, near the nose, exploded. Winthrop saw Camels and shape-shifters outlined black in the flames that consumed them entirely. He was calm. Richthofen would not be destroyed so easily, so stupidly. The Red Baron would be saved for him. Another compartment blew.

Through the hole in the gondola floor, the forests were as brightly lit as by day. The *Attila* was a burning red sun. Fires spread around, running along walkways, climbing ropes, chasing airmen.

Some of the crew had followed Hardt. Stalhein saw them break against treetops five hundred feet below. Some, by a miracle, might survive. He waited for his own last duty. Strasser, almost calm, stood away from the controls and smoothed his hair, then replaced his cap. He made no move to the hole. He would go down with his ship.

Robur turned away from his keyboard and looked at his disciple. He said, 'We should have won. If it were not for the insects.' He did not mean the war between the Entente and Germany, but the war between airships and aeroplanes.

Dracula stood. Knowing it was time, Stalhein rose from the floor, struggling with hot air under his wings, and took the Graf from behind, wrapping his legs around the commander. He surged forwards, dragging his burden, and burst through the last of the nose-port.

Something was ejected from the burning airship. A winged figure, something wrapped in its legs.

Winthrop let the thing pass through his sights without firing. He had more important prey.

He stalked the skies.

* * *

Above, as Dracula's weight pulled Stalhein down, the black canopy of the gasbag dissolved into a sky of fire. The organ, attacked in a final frenzy by the engineer, produced insane music.

His wingspan grew and Dracula was less heavy. They flew straight, descending towards the trees.

The *Attila* was lost, a string of burning balloons falling from the skies. The gondola crunched into treetops a hundred yards behind them.

Stalhein put on speed, outracing fingers of flame.

The dog-fight, scattered by the fall of the *Attila*, regrouped. The last of both sides forgot the possibility of surviving this battle and mixed in for death. He looked for a place to set down. Once duty was discharged, he should join his comrades in the sky.

An aeroplane was above him, closing. Though unarmed, he'd have a chance in a skirmish. He could drop Dracula and rip off the pilot's head. But he would not give up his commander.

At a glance, he realised he was spared. The aircraft was German, a two-man Junkers J1 spotter. It would give him cover.

They were past the burning forest. A straight road extended ahead. Glassy lakes reflected the fire. Stalhein spread his wings, letting wind slow him rather than speed him on, and settled towards the ground. They hit hard and he lost his grip on the Graf, sprawling in a mess of wings and limbs as he rolled across a field.

Thinking he was broken, he turned, trying to get the horizon level. After the even air, the ground was unsteady, rising and falling like the deck of a ship in a storm.

The Junkers, still aloft, circled like a protective spirit.

Stalhein saw Dracula rise from the field and brush off his uniform. He still did not understand why the *Attila* had been wasted, why an airship had committed suicide. The Graf walked over to Stalhein and looked down at him. His flat face was inexpressive, but Stalhein recognised the daze. In a lesser man, it might be called shell-shock. In Dracula, such weakness was unthinkable.

The field was not empty. Men shouted, in English. Shots were fired. Stalhein cringed.

Looking up, he saw Dracula was wounded. Blood soaked his chest.

'To die,' he announced, theatrically, 'to be really dead…'

Shadow-men gathered around in a circle. The Junkers uselessly strafed the field, hundreds of feet out of range. Silver caught light. Fixed bayonets neared.

The Graf still tried to speak.

'Poor Béla,' he said, incomprehensibly. 'The curtain falls.'

Blades moved, stabbed into the standing vampire, carving through his ribs and neck. Stalhein could not help his master. His wings were snapped. One of his legs was broken. Given minutes, he would heal and be well. He did not have minutes.

The enemy tore Dracula apart, spreading him across the field. Then they noticed the fallen flier. Gasping in revulsion at his changed shape, they closed in. Silver points pressed to his chest. Almost with pity, the British soldiers pierced his heart.

44

KAGEMUSHA MONOGATARI

Croft personally picked the black oval of the *Attila* off the map. His lips were a line of triumph.

'Gentlemen,' he announced, 'Dracula is dead. His head will be sent here.'

Beauregard remembered this had happened before. When Vlad Tepes was killed, his head was supposedly cut off and sent to the Sultan. Yet he had survived.

Events moved too swiftly for Croft's news to have much impact. Haig and Pershing were in dispute, competing for the honour of jamming breaches with their own dead. The telephone connected to the Prime Minister hung abandoned, twittering like a pathetic bird.

With Mireau gone, the French were rallying sensibly. American troops arrayed themselves against the German advance: raw recruits against combat-hardened veterans, or fresh spirited men against battle-weary remainders. And the British were dug in.

A shell burst on the roof of HQ. A patch of plaster fell from the ceiling, dusting Croft and Churchill like pantomime ghosts. Only their livery lips and fiery eyes were red in white faces. Subalterns with buckets were sent off to douse the fire.

'It is evident the Diogenes Club should have ceded responsibility for the secret war earlier,' gloated the phantom Croft. 'Great losses might have been prevented.'

The German advance came like a wave, spreading and breaking as it came up against the bulwarks of well-prepared positions.

Churchill did mental calculations.

'They cannot keep this up,' he said. 'With the *Attila* down, they will lose perspective. Confusion must set in.'

Comte Hubert de Sinestre, a sardonic general, reported a sighting of Dracula.

Croft paid attention. 'The *Attila*?'

'No,' said de Sinestre. 'Dracula leads his cavalry in full armour, mounted on a black horse, laying about him with a silver sword. Here, on the left flank. Where the gallant Mireau made his stand.'

The officer indicated a German charge.

Croft was perturbed. 'We have definite word the Graf was in his airship. He was killed by ground troops.'

The French vampire shrugged. 'English intelligence is notoriously suspect. I have the word of Colonel Dax, a most reliable officer.'

'He was in the air. It is his character.'

'The Graf proves remarkably mobile,' said Churchill. 'I've been handed a despatch from Captain George Sherston of the Royal Flintshire Fusiliers which tells me Dragulya has personally led a bayonet charge on the right flank and been peppered with silver bullets. Another cause for celebration, Mr Croft?'

Croft crushed the *Attila* oval in his hand.

'We have a plague of *doppelgängers*,' Beauregard offered. 'Next the Graf will be spotted strolling down Piccadilly with a straw hat on.'

'A mediaeval trick,' Churchill said, making a chubby fist. 'Impersonators to rally the troops, to draw fire.'

'The real Dracula was in his Zeppelin. I have affirmed it.'

Croft was green under his grey. His hands reached out involuntarily.

'The cavalry Dracula is down,' said de Sinestre. 'Cut in two by a machine-gun. His charge is broken. Mireau is avenged.'

'It will not do,' said Churchill. 'We must kill all of him.'

'He is dead. Truly dead,' insisted Croft.

'He'll be somewhere safe,' concluded Beauregard. 'In Berlin, probably. This has all been a distraction.'

'No,' said Croft, firmly. His fingers closed on Beauregard's throat. 'I am right and you are wrong.'

The face, rotten under the tight skin, came close, ghastly green powdered with plaster dust. Beauregard gripped the vampire's wrists, trying to break the choke-hold.

Officers tried to free him from Croft.

'I say,' snapped Haig, 'stop that, you two. I'll have no fighting in here. There's a war on, you know.'

Croft pushed him away, letting go. Beauregard coughed, breathing again, pulling his collar away from his bruised throat. The grey man calmed, deflated. Beauregard assumed the vampire's career was about to suffer a reversal.

Haig and Pershing came to an agreement and began piling American and British blocks on the road to Amiens. Black blocks, reinforced by cross-marked paper scraps, edged nearer.

Bombardment was constant and close. Blocks jumped on the table with each impact. Telephone lines were cut and reestablished.

Everyone looked at the table. The blocks were hopelessly mixed up.

Conceiving of the losses, Beauregard's heart ached.

'Oh the humanity, the humanity…'

45

TO END THAT SPREE

The wreck of the *Attila* burned so brightly Winthrop might have been flying by day. Beyond the forest, the landscape was covered with the straggling shadows of Allied troops falling back to Amiens. Lorries clogged roads and men waded through fields.

His face stung from the immense heat of the dirigible's death. He scanned the sky, above and below the Camel, for the enemy. Howling frustration gnawed his gut. He might be the sole survivor of the dog-fight, the last of both Condor Squadron and JG1. And he would never know what exactly had happened to Baron von Richthofen.

That would be worse than going down in flames. No. Nothing was worse than going down in flames. Nothing was worse than Allard's sacrifice, Brandberg's crack-up or the deaths of the dozens of men in the *Attila*. It occurred to him that he was, or had been, quite mad.

The Albert Ball in him urged him on to hunt out and destroy his enemy. But there were doubts. It wasn't so much the Kate Reed in him. She was not his conscience. He missed his old self, the boy he'd been before war made a man of him. The man he'd been before war made a monster of him. He owed explanations to Catriona. To Beauregard.

In concentrating on evening things with the Baron, he'd made of himself a freak. This strange Edwin Winthrop was as repulsive as Isolde, pulling out her veins on stage, or the bat-*staffel* of JG1, demon monsters for the Kaiser.

The rush of air on his face awakened him, purging him. He opened his mouth and let the wind blow in. Pulling back the stick, he made the Camel climb. The higher he went, the more distance he got from the brutish business. He could burst through the Earth's bubble of atmosphere and be free of the war and its eternities of killing and waste.

Then he saw the flying creature, hugging burned-out treetops, moving with purpose, as alone as a hunting shark. A flight commander's streamers flew from his ankle. It was Richthofen. In the firelight, the Baron was truly red.

Winthrop hoped this was the last of the shape-shifters. He'd seen enough of them destroyed. The charm was off. They were creatures who bled and died like any others.

His doubts drowned in a red tide. Icy calm, he took the Camel down, fast. The miracle was that he still had ammunition left. The shape-shifter couldn't fire backwards. From behind, the Baron was easy meat.

Richthofen was alerted. The bat-ears must be enormously sensitive. The German tried to climb and turn, bringing guns to bear on the Camel, but Winthrop harried him with a burst – short, for he must conserve his bullets for the kill – and forced him to dip down into the forest.

Winthrop pulled up and skimmed across the treetops, watching the Baron weave through the canopy of branches. He was unbelievably agile, but the forest slowed him. He seemed to be swimming through the dense trees. Fire spread from the *Attila*. Thick wood-smoke churned upwards, stinging Winthrop's eyes, swirling around his propellor.

If the Baron chose to land, he'd survive the night. He could wait for advancing German troops and be carried back to Schloss Adler a hero. But Manfred von Richthofen would not duck out of a fight.

The forested patch was small. Winthrop overshot the trees and flew over plain ground, rising towards low hills in the near distance. There were Allied positions in the hills. Men streamed back to them. This was where the German offensive would break. Or where the war would be lost.

Winthrop turned back towards the forest just as Richthofen flew out of the trees and soared upwards, a prehistoric monster with twentieth-century guns. The Baron fired and Winthrop returned fire. Bullets sparked all around. There was a hideous pranging noise. Winthrop thought he had taken a hit on the prop.

They rushed at each other, and missed colliding in the air. Winthrop felt the wind of the Baron's wings.

What must it be like to *be* such a monster?

He turned the Camel tightly. The Baron was far more manoeuvrable, so Winthrop had to push his machine to its limits.

Richthofen must have nothing. A warrior-monk, thoughtlessly dedicated to his country. That must be a weakness. He had nothing to fight for. Nothing but the empty achievement of an ever-increasing score.

Winthrop didn't want to be the Baron's victory. But he no longer needed to kill. He no longer wanted to kill. Nevertheless, he fired his Lewis guns at the bat-shape swooping at him.

The Baron evaded the stream of bullets. He passed by close enough for Winthrop to see his shape-shifted face. With blue human eyes and fixed bat-snarl, it was a tragic mask, leaking blood at the mouth.

There was another aeroplane in the sky, hugging the trees, moving slowly. A two-man spotter. At a glance, Winthrop took in the kite's colours. A Hun.

The Camel was above and behind the Baron. Winthrop fired single shots, conserving ammunition for the killing burst. He crowded and drove Richthofen onwards.

The bat-creature darted from side to side, but could not break free of the funnel in which Winthrop had him penned. His ammunition was nearly out. If the Baron stayed beyond range of accurate fire for a few more moments…

They were beyond the forest, half-way towards the hills, low enough to startle trudging troops. Men turned to whoop and cheer as Richthofen and Winthrop zoomed over them. Caps were whipped off by the windwash. Rifles were aimed at the sky and shots fired.

Bloody idiots. Both parties were moving so fast that a shot aimed at the leading flier could well strike the pursuer.

The spotter would be on the Camel's tail but Winthrop needn't worry about it yet. The fighter could outrace the pusher any night of the year and have juice left over to smash it into the ground.

A mortar barrage burst up into the sky ahead, startling Richthofen. The Baron soared up, flapping his wings. Winthrop gained on him fast, pulling back the stick.

The moon broke through the cloud like an eye opening.

Holding steady at speed, Winthrop realised the Baron was in his sights. If he depressed the firing buttons...

His thumbs were frozen iron.

There was Archie ahead. Gun positions in the hills laid a carpet of shellbursts. Richthofen winged towards heavy fire.

Late, startled by explosions all around, Winthrop pressed the buttons. A stream of silver squirted forth. Red wounds exploded in the Baron's hide. He had tagged Richthofen.

He was still pressing the buttons, but his ammunition was out.

Richthofen's wings seemed to spread like an enormous curtain, filling his sky. Winthrop knew he was caught without defence between the Baron and the Boche spotter. If they came at him together, he would be truly dead. Maybe that was for the best: to die, rather than live on and risk becoming even more of a monster.

In the creature's eyes, Winthrop saw killing frenzy. The Baron was about to add Edwin Winthrop to his score.

He reflexively thumbed the buttons. His Lewis guns clicked, empty...

But the Baron was struck again and again, as if Winthrop were hitting him with ghost bullets. Richthofen twisted in the air, wings struggling, riddled with bloody holes.

Winthrop was astonished.

It was ground fire, of course. Shocked out of his frenzy, he realised he was as likely as a Hun to be riddled by Archie and climbed above the dying flier. As he spiralled up, Winthrop saw Richthofen jittering in the air, as if kept up by the multiple impacts of shots fired from below.

The outspread wings were ripped ragged. The body dwindled, guns become anchors, limbs twisting. The dead thing fell towards the ground, disappearing into fire and darkness.

Shocked to his senses, Winthrop wondered what he was doing in alien air.

46

VALHALLA

When they touched ground again, Poe was changed. His first experience of flight had been unrelieved nightmare. Free of the Earth, he had been whirled into a sphere of chaos, a maelstrom of terror that destroyed the foundations of his vision.

The *Attila* was lost, a giant cloud of flame consuming the father of European vampirism. Baron von Richthofen was dead, a broken corpse transforming as he fell. *Der Rote Kampfflieger* was incomplete; it would have to be published with an afterword of obituary. The offensive had broken through, but at what cost?

Theo taxied the aeroplane along the little strip by the lake. The shadow of Schloss Adler stood against the sky. No light showed. The castle seemed deserted. The machine came to rest with a lurch, wheels sinking into grassy ground.

Poe was shocked by the calm that fell on him, the equilibrium he suddenly felt. His face was stiff with dried tears.

Theo crawled out of the fore cockpit and dropped to the ground. He tore off his helmet and gloves and threw them away.

What now?

The great gate hung open slightly. As he stepped inside, Poe knew the Schloss Adler was unpeopled. He had become used to the sounds of toil. Footsteps were hollow echoes, now. This position had been abandoned.

Theo was not surprised. 'Orlok will be on his way back to Berlin, to report to his masters. Dracula will want to know how successful his schemes have proved.'

'Dracula? He was aboard the *Attila*. He is lost, surely?'

Theo shook his head, weary and disgusted.

'That was an impostor, one of many poor fools dressed up to dupe the Entente. He was supposed to be a target. He did his duty. The enemy concentrated so hard on killing him in the air that they neglected to prepare themselves for the attack on the ground.'

'Who was he? The vampire in the *Attila*?'

'A Hungarian actor. A matinée idol from Lugos. One of Dracula's get. Moulded to serve as his *doppelgänger*. There were others. Maybe a dozen.'

'But… the men of the *Attila*, the airship itself?'

'Smoke and mirrors, scenery for the pageant…'

'Who could countenance such a thing?'

Theo thumbed towards a huge, indifferent martial portrait. Graf von Dracula standing beside the Kaiser, both in braid-heavy uniform, moustache points like needles.

'Them.'

Another had been left behind, Hanns Heinz Ewers. Someone had taken the trouble to shoot him but only with a lead bullet. He tried to hold his shattered skull together as it healed.

Poe's mind was whirling around. He had sought honour and glory, and found murderers and knaves.

Theo looked dispassionately at Ewers's wounds, and admitted the vampire might have a chance of recovery.

'Who was it?' Poe asked.

'Only one… flier came back,' Ewers said, eyes shut against the pain. 'He wanted your manuscript, Poe. It was Göring.'

'The recording officer,' Theo said. 'That makes sense. Eddy, this has all been about the writing of history. As long as records are kept, they'll have won. Germany has too many heroes. The book-keepers need to cull them. Göring, Mabuse, Dracula. Book-keepers, not soldiers. Think of the Graf and his beloved railway timetables. Deeds of glory reduced to numbers, like a stock exchange or a ministry for the collection of taxes.'

'My manuscript? Where is it?'

Ewers tried to smile. 'Göring was to take it to Berlin. To be published. It occurred to me to stop him.'

Ewers's eye rolled up towards his head-wound.

'I don't know why I chose to waste my brains on keeping your work from its publishers. I dislike you immensely but I would give anything to have your abilities, degraded and exhausted as they are. Call it jealousy, if you will. That is why I tried to suppress your book. Jealousy.'

The wounded man pawed at the top button of his tight tunic. Theo helped him, opening his clothes to give him air. Pages, covered in Poe's handwriting, spilled out.

'You are a great writer, Poe. I confess it. But you are hopelessly mad. I may have done you a service. Göring took the first three pages of your manuscript, bulked out with some of my own tales. Fine stuff, but wasted…'

Ewers lost consciousness. Theo stood up, his gloves bloodied. Poe had shrugged off his horror and was trying to catch up. The last pieces of the puzzle had been given him.

By the lake, Poe and Theo waited for dawn. The clamour of battle had passed, carried past the lines into enemy territory.

'Heroes make them uncomfortable, Eddy. Those little men with their little books. They need their glory, but they feed on it as we feed on blood. Your book was always supposed to be a memorial, a glorious tomb to inspire more heroes. They are to burn like comets and be snuffed out, while the book-keepers crawl on through centuries. Millions have died in this war. Anonymous statistics. That is what Dracula has made of us. Meaningless names in a book of the dead.'

Poe looked at his manuscript. There was a great spark in it. It was a dream, an inspiration. Reading of this knight of futurity, generation upon generation of boys would aspire to serve Germany as had Manfred von Richthofen.

'Dracula doesn't care for the Richthofens, Eddy. The excellent, the brave, the mad. He is happier with Görings about him, fathead bureaucrats of death.'

Poe let the first pages of the manuscript slip from the bundle, sliding towards the waters of the lake. As they rested on the calm surface, ink blurring, his heart ached. It might be those words were the last of his genius, the last he would ever write. Vampire dullness was settling around his mind.

Theo laid a hand on his shoulder, understanding. With a swift throw, Poe cast the pages into the air. They formed a cloud and settled into the lake, merging into sodden lumps, skittering across the surface for yards before being whisked under. Poe took off his greatcoat, ran his thumb over the newly earned epaulettes of rank, and tossed the thing into the water, disturbing the sargasso of pages.

'I consider my commission resigned,' he said.

The sleeves of Poe's coat tangled like the arms of a corpse. An unknown current, peculiar to the centre of the lake, sucked the morass of cloth and words into its heart. The deep and dank lake closed sullenly and silently over the fragments of *Der Rote Kampfflieger.*

'If you stay here, the French will come back, eventually,' Theo said. 'You can write another book. A clear-eyed book, conveying the truth.'

'The truth interests me little, Theo.'

The officer shrugged. 'That doesn't surprise me.'

'What will you do now?' Poe asked.

Before he turned and walked away from the shadow of the castle, Theo showed his old smile and said, 'Eddy, I shall fight for my country.'

47

AFTERMATH

Guns empty and petrol tank getting there, Winthrop had to land. Maranique, probably in German hands, was out of the picture so he looked for one of the fall-back positions towards Amiens. In the excitement, he had rather lost his bearings.

Sighting by the stars, he flew east. Below, convoys of reinforcements hurried towards the front. Streams of retreating troops passed them by or dug in to make a stand. At least Hunland hadn't crept out under him like a carpet. He didn't have to come down and surrender.

With Ball and Kate burned out of him, Winthrop was clearer in his mind, as if he had just awoken from an unpleasant but interesting dream. But he was exhausted, forgotten wounds troubled him again and he felt the loss. Without Ball's whisper in his mind, he found he was an indifferent pilot.

The stick wrestled in his grip. Previously, he had been a component part of his machine. Now he was mounted on a rebellious beast which would do its best to throw him if he showed any signs of weakness. The wires shrieked and the engine coughed.

There was a temptation to pull the stick back and let go, ascending towards nothingness. He was a ghost of a ghost now, no longer the man he was nor the creature he had become.

Some spark in him wished to continue with life. He fumbled the stick and evened the wings, keeping the bubble centred in the spirit-level. He was prepared to consider any stretch of uninterrupted road or grass as a landing site. But tonight the landscape was infested with men. Years of stalemate seemed over and the war of movement was restarted.

Familiar lights burned off to his left.

A field was marked out with fizzing Verey flares. He hoped whoever was running the show had the sense to keep the ground cleared. There wasn't enough fuel to circle and check out the terrain. He aimed the Camel between the purple lights and went down.

His wheels bumped in long grass. The Camel bounced off the ground, nose angling down. Winthrop knew the machine was going to turn tail and plough his head into the dirt.

Something snapped and twanged, whipping his face. The Camel was tumbling upwards and over. He hit the release mechanism of his straps and shot out of his seat. The stick jabbed his gut and groin. Wings crumpled around him. The ground came up and slammed against his head. A couple of hundredweight of debris came down on his back.

There were shouts. Liquid was trickling past him, smelling like petrol.

He was dragged boneless out of the wreck. He heard the crump of his remaining fuel going up, and felt the waft of warm, oily air. Flame darts rained down.

Death reached out a hand for him, closing on his heart and mind, but its fingers lost their grip and he screamed with life. He sucked down air, and was helped to sit up.

Opening his eyes, he saw the heaped bonfire that had been his Camel.

'You won't do that again in a hurry, I'll wager,' someone said.

She had been slung in the back of a lorry with the wounded. After a couple of miles of rutted roads, most of the wounded were dead. Kate had been hit a couple of times, but not with silver. The mud in her clothes had dried, mummifying her in stiff cloth. She had lost her scavenged tin helmet.

She was in a daze, curiously distanced from her body. It would be easy to flutter off into the dark and leave behind a living corpse. Would it continue without her? Perhaps this was how vampires became mindless thirsty things.

A boy in her arms called her Edith. She tried to comfort him anyway. Blood trickled through his field dressings but she would not drink from him. For the first time in her undeath, she'd had enough blood.

Geneviève had once told her, 'Vampires don't drink blood because we have to, we drink blood because we like it.' Kate was fed up with trying to be like Geneviève. It was time to become a twentieth-century girl. Rather than spend five weeks cleaning mud out of her hair, she'd have it cropped and bobbed. The earth mask on her face cracked and came off in sections.

The lorry kept pulling over to the roadside to let reinforcements pass. British tanks rumbled into the fray to counter the German machines. A platoon of Americans, new to the fighting, were driven past. They called out in sympathy to the lorry of mainly corpses, throwing across packs of cigarettes.

Kate stuck a gasper in her mouth but had no matches. The taste of tobacco was enough of a jolt just now.

Having been in the thick of it, she had no idea what had really happened. The German offensive had broken through. After the widespread breaching of the lines, the Allies had thrown hidden reserves into the fight. It might have gone either way. The war could be won or lost.

The lorry left the road and made its rough way over fields, creaking over newly laid boards.

A huge fire burned in a forested patch, where a Zeppelin had come down. Kate craned and saw the vast circles of the airship's ribs still linked in the forest of flame. The heat roused Edith's young man, who turned to gape.

* * *

'It's the plain of hell,' he said.

There were quite a few fellows mixing in the tent city at the edge of the field, pilots from forward outfits who had also fallen back. Winthrop found himself a dry-ish patch of grass and slumped there. Someone gave him a cigarette and a light. He asked if any other men from Condor Squadron had made it home safe. Everyone seemed to think so but no one could give him names.

Pilots stood about the field, sweaty in Sidcots, soot-rings about their eyes. Some were quietly wounded, most were exhausted. Acting Sergeant Chandler, an American in brand-new RAF fatigues, was responsible for compiling details of men and machines who had made it back.

'Are you a warm man?' he asked Winthrop.

Winthrop thought about it and said yes.

'Good for you,' said Chandler. He wasn't a vampire, but almost all the pilots he was herding were. 'Bloody good for you.'

'I'm with Condor Squadron. Have you logged any others from the outfit?'

He looked down his list.

'A white knight named Bigglesworth, shot down weeks ago, showed up tonight. Made it back through the lines on foot.'

'Good grief.'

'Otherwise, no one yet. But don't give up hope. It's a typical shambles, actually.'

Suddenly, a ragged cheer went up from the crowd. There was a field telephone in one of the tents and good news had come through.

'Have we beaten the bastards back?' Chandler asked a grinning young pilot.

'No, better than that. Richthofen's dead. Confirmed. Aussie ground fire got him. Heavy Archie.'

'It should have been one of our blokes,' a British flight lieutenant said. 'A pilot. Should've paid him back for Hawker and Albright and Ball.'

'Ball was the other Richthofen's. The brother.'

Already, the facts were blurring. Winthrop had shot Baron von Richthofen just before the German died. He could claim the victory. But he said nothing, just listened.

'They're talking about burying him with honours. Sporting spirit and all that.'

'They should cut off his rotten head and stuff the mouth with garlic, then bury him face-down at a crossroads with a silver spike through his black heart.'

'Taking it a bit personal?'

Winthrop didn't listen any more. It wasn't his war now.

Kate was recovered enough to feel she was using a space that would be more usefully occupied by a genuinely wounded soldier. She left Edith's young man to his own devices and slipped off the back of the lorry.

Her legs were still a bit rubbery.

As she walked, dry earth cascaded from her clothes. She'd have given a hundred years of her life for a hot bath. Wandering through crowds, as pre-dawn light filtered into the sky, she picked up snippets of gossip, rumour and news.

Most people agreed the German advance had halted. Some said the Allies had lured the Boche into a trap and cut them to pieces from entrenched rear positions. Some said German troops were so successful in the initial breakthrough that they were cut off from their orders and milled about with nothing to do, wondering at the supplies of food they found in the Allied messes. After years of starvation and blockade, the Hun was undone by the maddening smell of new-baked bread.

Kate did not know if she could write about the night.

She walked, not knowing where she was going. A rumour went around that Baron von Richthofen was dead. So that was that.

At dawn, the new-born pilots took refuge in the tents. Winthrop lay where he had fallen, Sidcot wadded into a pillow. The spring sun fell on his face. The noise of battle had receded.

Chandler told him word had come in from another of the temporary fields. A couple of Condor Squadron bods had turned up: Cary Lockwood, and Bertie and Ginger. So it had not been complete extermination.

Had any of JG1 survived? It didn't matter. The worst of them was gone. The terror was over.

Winthrop could no longer hate Richthofen. If the Allies buried the Baron with honours, he would stand as pall-bearer. He'd volunteer to fly over Hunland and drop whatever personal totems a shape-shifter took aloft with him. That, he hoped, would be his last flight.

The field and sunshine reminded him of a previous life. Cricket at Greyfriars. Spring walks with Catriona. He had a lot of things to mend. His knee burst with pain, reminding him of No Man's Land. Some things would never mend.

Kate found a fast-running stream. Not caring for modesty, she peeled off her mud-starched clothes, dislodging patches of encrusted dirt, and laid them on the stream-bed, weighting them with stones.

She looked down at herself and saw the body of a savage, marked with blood and different colours of dirt. Her wounds had healed over but were generously scabbed.

A passing line of troops whistled and cheered at her. Fresh from Paris, they must have seen better form at the Folies Bergère.

She sat down in the stream and let the sun-dappled water wash around her. Lying back like Ophelia, she allowed her hair to wave in the current. Trails of dirt rushed away from her. She closed her eyes and tried to wish it all away.

The warm men had a tea-urn set up. There were no mugs, so Winthrop drank out of a porridge-bowl. Someone from Condor Squadron finally came in. Jiggs, the mechanic, with tales of a hairsbreadth escape and a shiny pair of German-made boots.

The offensive was pretty much blocked, it seemed. A rumour buzzed briefly that Dracula had been killed, but it died almost as soon as it started.

'Our field has gained a water nymph,' Chandler said. 'There's a beauty in danger of drowning over by the temporary hangars. She's wearing a pair of earrings.'

A long whistle cut through her reverie. She opened her eyes and propped herself up on her elbows. A man stood on the bank of the stream, hands in his pockets.

'Why, Miss Mouse,' Edwin said. 'Doesn't the sun bring out your freckles nicely?'

She shut her eyes and let her head sink back under the water.

48

ENGLAND CALLS

He had not been accepting telephone calls. Beauregard sat in his house in Cheyne Walk. Unopened letters were neatly laid on his desk. Bairstow, his manservant, discreetly arranged them each morning.

There was a slim envelope from California, his address in faint violet ink. This, he was tempted by. But he feared that to open it would be to be pulled back into turmoil he had left. Geneviève attracted troubles, trailing them through centuries. He still loved her, he supposed. A dead weight of useless emotion. Official communications, stamped 'URGENT', had been brought by postman and personal messenger. They also lay unopened.

He did not read the newspapers, but Bairstow conveyed the barest outlines of the course of the war. It was little satisfaction to know Caleb Croft had been relieved of his duties. Ruthven had many other men of his stamp ready to step in.

Dracula had been seen in Berlin, storming out of the Imperial Palace in a black humour after an argument with the Kaiser. Hindenburg was promoted to the position of commander-in-chief of armies that were shattered and demoralised by their recent reverses. Dracula was shouldering the blame for the ultimate failure of the *Kaiserschlacht*. It seemed the sacrifice of his doubles created a great deal of confusion and loss of morale in the ranks. The mediaeval tactic should be retired in this century. Dracula's fall would be only temporary. The worst ones always came back.

He spent time looking at old, framed photographs. The camera made vampires of all, preserving the young for the alien future. In one group, Pamela was alive again, posed by the river with a flock of little girls in sailor suits. A blurred boat passed in the background. The girls were Penelope, Kate, Lucy and Mina, warm and untidy, ignorant of the things they would become.

Mrs Harker had also written to him. She was forever organising for other people. She wished to hustle him into a new programme of activities.

Bairstow entered, bearing a calling card on a tin plate. The silver had gone for the war effort years ago. Beauregard tried to wave him away, but the servant was swept aside by a long-legged spider in grey.

'Prime Minister,' he acknowledged, not getting out of his chair.

'Beauregard, this is absurd. Have you any idea how many pressing matters compete for my attention? Yet, here I am like a common tradesman, forced to hie myself to your doorstep to solicit an answer?'

Ruthven was plainly agitated. From Churchill, Beauregard knew the Cabinet were fractious. Lloyd George was proving more obstinate than anyone had supposed. The Prime Minister's position was entrenched, but hardly secure.

Lord Ruthven had not come alone. Smith-Cumming was with him, his leg grown anew.

'The Diogenes Club has reopened its doors to members,' Smith-Cumming declared.

'Croft's crew were worse than useless,' the Prime Minister ranted. 'His hare-brained assassination fantasies came close to losing us the war. The country needs living minds.'

'Mycroft's place on the Cabal is vacant,' said Smith-Cumming. 'Only one man can fill it, Beauregard.'

He looked at the two vampires, the shiftless elder and the solid new-born. Ruthven's hands were still on the tiller of state, embattled though he was. Smith-Cumming was a good man, blood-drinker or no. There were still good men.

Mycroft had preserved much of value from the past in this changed century. Without him, the Ruthvens and the Crofts crept on selfishly, wasting too many lives in a pursuit of power without purpose.

'Beauregard, please,' begged the Prime Minister.

In the absence of Croft and the Diogenes Club, the British Secret Service was run by a schoolmaster who concealed secret ciphers in sketches of butterfly markings. Results, obviously, had not been encouraging.

'England needs you, Beauregard,' insisted Ruthven. '*I* need you.'

But does England need Lord Ruthven, he wondered.

Pamela seemed to catch his eye from the photograph. She would have expected him not to yield.

'Very well,' Beauregard said. 'I accept the position.'

Smith-Cumming clapped him on the back. Ruthven allowed himself a smile of relief.

'But there are conditions.'

'Oh, anything, anything,' waved the Prime Minister.

'We shall see,' said Beauregard.

49

RESOLUTIONS

She would let him go, but first he owed her a debt which she insisted he settle. In a hotel room in Calais, after Kate and Edwin had made love, she bled him lightly. His taste was different now. The red thirst inside him was burned out. He warmed her, made her strong again.

Lulled by her, Edwin lay in a daze as she snuggled next to him. She was flushed, her freckles like pinpricks on her breast.

She was entitled to a little love. For almost all her life she had been too busy or timid. This time, even if she let her soldier go back to his rector's daughter, she'd have him for a while. If Catriona was the woman Kate thought she was, she wouldn't mind. This was France. This was the war. Different rules applied.

She ran her tongue over her teeth. Her fangs had receded with repletion.

Edwin held her close, murmuring the wrong name. She was used to that too. Everyone who got close mistook her for someone else.

Tomorrow they would both cross the Channel. But tomorrow was hours distant. Kate pulled herself on to Edwin's chest, pressing her face close to his neck. He stirred, responding. Her hair brushed across his face. His hands held her hips, settling her weight onto him. Her lips suckled his neck, but her teeth did not break his skin.

* * *

In England, things were different between them. Kate sensed an awkwardness in Edwin that gathered during the crossing. She was struck with a creeping melancholia. Knowing what would happen was not the same as being prepared for it.

In their nights together, she'd learned about his time with Condor Squadron. He had told her about his last flight. Officially, he made no claims, but she knew he had contributed to the shooting-down of Manfred von Richthofen. She had promised not to write him up as a hero.

This was a part of their lives they would always share. Others would never understand how they had allowed themselves to be changed so fearfully, to become bestial.

It was a fine moonlit spring night. In other circumstances, the voyage might have been romantic. Edwin was quiet, looking back at France from the railings. Europe would always be a cemetery for him, for all the survivors.

Sometimes, Edwin would go quiet and she could tell he was searching in himself for things irretrievably lost. She did not know if he was a broken man, or merely cracked. By the hour, he was cooling. There was still a speck of vampire in him, ice around his heart.

Neither of them had finished with the war.

At Victoria Station, Charles was waiting. For both of them. Kate was briefly worried he might have constables ready to place her under arrest and carry her off to Devil's Dyke. In the crowds, she spotted Sergeant Dravot.

Charles shook Edwin's hand and Edwin got out an apology which Charles waved away. He understood Edwin had not been himself.

'You have leave,' Charles told Edwin. 'I assume you will wish to spend it in the West Country.'

'I have to return from the dead.'

'That's not such a big thing as it's made up to be,' Kate said.

'Easy for you to say. You don't have to explain to Miss Catriona Kaye.'

'Neither do you, Edwin. Believe me, she'll need no explanation. Having you back will be enough.'

All this nobility was choking her. She shook his hand and darted a swift kiss at him. It was all very friendly. Tears stabbed the backs of her eyes, but she refused to have a weepy spell.

What would the rector's daughter make of the man who came back to her? Kate knew Catriona would get the worst of it, being with him through a convalescence that could never really put him together again.

'I shall follow your career with interest,' she told him, scolding. 'So be on your best behaviour.'

'I have taken out a subscription to the *Cambridge Magazine*, so I'll know what fevers your busy brain.'

Edwin let go of her hand, picked up his kitbag and walked away.

Charles laid a hand on her shoulder. She had forgotten he would know what she was feeling.

'He is too young for you,' Charles said.

'So is everybody.'

'As you well know, there are far older creatures than you strewn about the world.'

She turned to face Charles. He was calm again. Secret wars had been fought and he had his balance back. She was encouraged by that.

Edwin disappeared from sight, lost in the crowds of soldiers and their sweethearts. Their link was broken.

Dravot let Edwin go. He was staying with Charles now.

'So, will you depart for the Russias and become a heroine of the *bolsheviki*?' Charles asked.

She shook her head. 'Not yet a while, I think. This corner of the world interests me still. The old men are not exhausted. It would be a sin to let them be just now. There's the war, and then there's the matter of Ireland. Countess Markievicz and Erskine Childers have asked me to be on a committee for Home Rule.'

'Tell me no more. We may be enemies.'

She stroked his lapel. 'I hope not, Charles.'

'Ruthven still reigns, even as his Cabinet conspires against him. Dracula, though demoted, remains close to the counsels of the Kaiser.'

Kate considered the situation.

'All Europe is stark mad with red thirst. All America too, for that matter. All the world. But that's no reason to merge with the killing hordes, no reason not to struggle against the dead hands at the wheel.'

Charles was smiling. He looked younger. She knew he was on the ascendant. Edwin was dead to her, and maybe to himself. But Charles soldiered on.

Fresh troops, conscripts and volunteers as yet unblooded, broke from disorderly queues and shoved past to board the boat train. Their open faces, warm or vampire, bothered her. All they knew of war was fire and glory. Insanity would continue as long as lies were perpetuated.

'I should have you arrested,' Charles said, 'before you make more mischief.'

She thought of what she would write next. About the war, about the government, about the old men. She would write and shout and wheedle and nag until her voice was heard, drowning out the drumbeat of jingo and the blather of politicians. She could not be the last priestess of the truth. People would listen. Things would change.

'Mischief, my dear,' she said to Charles. 'You don't know the half of it.'

ANNO DRACULA 1923

VAMPIRE ROMANCE

1

GENEVIEVE BOBS HER HAIR

She was the last woman in London to go for the chop.

Unbound, Geneviève's hair was long enough to sit on. Before her monthly coma, she combed and arranged it like an eiderdown. She always woke up three days later to find it wound into a rope. Usually, around her neck – as if her unconscious needed to remind her she should have been dead for five-hundred years. From now on, her unconscious could keep its opinion to itself.

This evening, she would become 'modern'.

Her appointment at M. Eugene was for just after sunset. The salon was Cox and Box. Open round the clock: different staff, different clientele by day and by night. She didn't particularly need to shun the sun, especially in this dreary English autumn, but kept vampire hours anyway. Nearly fifty years after Dracula stepped into the moonlight, warm and undead shared the city in a reasonably civilised manner. The former Prince Consort had quit the country, leaving claw-marks on everything from the pre-broken 'Transylvanian' crenellations of Tower Bridge to the ugly bat frescoes of the Sir Francis Varney Memorial. Thanks to a *de facto* revolution, at least two *coups*, one world war and late-coming electoral reform, everything had changed again. Everything *kept* changing, to the accelerated, syncopated rhythm of the American music she heard in cafés and dance halls in Berlin, Paris and

London. In England for the first time since before the War, even Geneviève was changing.

The West End stirred into night-life. She loitered over a thimble of mouse-blood in the Maison Lyons on Shaftesbury Avenue during the Friday evening shift change. Warm people went home and vampires came out.

Leaving the restaurant, she had a *moment*.

In the 1890s, this district was a battlefield of fire and blood. Unconcerned people hurried along streets which had been fought for. Then, it was barricades in Leicester Square and impaled enemies of the State in Piccadilly Circus. Now, it was cocktails at the Criterion and a rag at the Troc.

She felt *something*. Her fangs sharpened, an instinctive response to danger or opportunity. She scanned the crowd as if the Carpathian Guard still had spies and informants out for her. Seeing only silly, happy people, she told herself not to be a fool. The Terror was over. New grief would come, but not immediately.

Dracula was no longer the most famous person in the world. The new holder of that dubious title was Charlie Chaplin. In films made in sunstruck California, the warm English comedian was 'the Little Vamp', a raggedy-fanged vagrant beloved by audiences who'd still cheerfully stake a real vampire. In the two-reeler *One P.M.*, Chaplin lampooned Dracula himself, playing a Lord of Vampires tipsy on booze-bolstered blood, tripping over his cloak while clambering into his coffin.

Graffiti was stencilled on a nearby hoarding, straggling across posters advertising Oxo concentrated blood cubes, 'Nutrax for Nerves' and NetherBeast gramophones. Kink-limbed and -backed stick-figure men followed a leader who carried a thin question mark. She'd been noticing similar scrawls around town. Sometimes just the question-mark man. A newspaper cipher competition? These nights, circulation-boosting stunts were a craze. But the crooked men seemed slightly too sinister for that.

In M. Eugene's salon, the shift change was not yet complete. Attendants hung black velvet – lesser *coiffeuristes* used crepe – over the wall mirrors. Some new-borns were sensitive about what they'd lost. She caught sight of the smoky smudge, which was all she could muster of a reflection, but was long past embarrassment.

For centuries, even scientific thinkers like Edmond Cordery – who tried to 'explain' the vampire condition as a 'benevolent mutation' caused by 'symbiotes in the blood' – couldn't account for the thing with mirrors. The world was forced to accept magic as part of nature. Max Planck's Black Blood Refractive Postulate of 1902 supposedly ended that. Geneviève had read summations of the physicist's paper and still couldn't follow his abstruse reasoning. She hoped she'd outgrown a mediaeval mindset, but was sometimes happy to fall back on magic rather than get a headache trying to understand science.

In the reception area, framed pictures – photographs or portraits indistinguishable from photographs – displayed varieties of bobbed hairstyle. The dancer Irene Castle, the elder Elizabeth Báthory, the *modiste* Coco Chanel, film stars Marian Marsh and Colleen Moore. Avant-garde adopters of the new look.

A warm girl in a trim white uniform like a nurse – actually, more like a chorus girl playing a nurse in a revue catering to (mostly male) sophisticates – replaced the day's roses with the night's lilies. She smartly modelled the style, a breathing advertisement. Her blond hair was cropped to show off her pretty neck. She had make-up over familiar nip-marks. The trend for dispensing with long, lovely locks was a convenience for (mostly male) vampires tired of trying to lift feminine falls out of their way yet still getting a mouthful of hair when they bit.

M. Eugene's other speciality was straightening curls with terrifying Heath Robinson contraptions of gleaming hooks and heated rollers. The devices were like something you'd find in a penal colony, but women willingly subjected themselves to being pulled, ironed, squirted and steamed to achieve a 'permanent wave'.

The salon was busy, every chair in use. The warm blond girl –

Miss Bunting, according to her nametag – consulted an appointment book. She said Geneviève would be seen to momentarily and took her coat and hat.

A new-born débutante with pearly fangs and bee-stung scarlet lips occupied the chair before her. From back numbers of *The Tatler* somewhat surprisingly piled in Charles Beauregard's Chelsea house, Geneviève recognised the daughter of the millionaire Percy Browne. Like many girls of good family, she had turned at twenty-one, commencing a season of midnight balls. According to gossip columns, she took to night-life like a proper flittermouse. The Polly Browne Set was notoriously flighty. She'd personally battened on half the young bloods in the Drones and begun to nibble through the officer corps of the Brigade of Guards.

Geneviève, while conceding she had no right to be waspish, wondered what use the future would find for a flock of immortal butterfly girls.

Waves of hair shrivelled on the drop cloth as one of the salon's nimble, slim young men snipped away with silver shears. Polly Browne's formerly pre-Raphaelite mane was trimmed into a shape like an aviatrix's helmet. All the while, the dresser gossiped: Ivor Novello was carrying on with the drag artiste Handel Fane, the organist Anton Phibes was squabbling with the management over billing at the Tivoli, Noel Coward was turning vampire. The cutter displayed skill. One slip with the blades and Pretty Polly would be marred for decades.

Geneviève didn't like silver near her face. Few vampires did, though Heidelberg fools still duelled with silvered rapiers to earn their distinctive scars.

Her turn came.

She sat in the chair, purple silk bib settled around her shoulders. Miss Bunting expertly took pins out of her hair and let it cascade. The chair was raised, so her fall did not quite reach to the floor.

Her hair brought out the proprietor himself. Eugene Suter was Swiss, with a curled moustache and long fingers. After Antoine de

Paris, the greatest hairdresser of the age.

'An elder,' he noted. 'How long has it been, Madame?'

'Mademoiselle,' she corrected. 'More than twenty years.'

Her last cut had been self-administered, a Joan of Arc crop needed after half of her hair – and most of her face – was burned off in a skirmish with Countess Verdel, one of Dracula's Carpathian she-wolves. She was assured her face had got better. She was also assured Verdel's head hadn't grown back on her shoulders.

Geneviève assumed the young man who had seen to Polly Browne would do the deed, but the *maître* waved him away.

'An elder, I cut myself,' M. Eugene declared.

No other customer commanded the personal attention of the proprietor this evening. Geneviève was not above enjoying the who-*is*-that-woman? puzzlement of haughty new-borns who expected special treatment.

M. Eugene's eyes flashed red and he opened his hands with a flourish, six-inch talons extruding from his fingertips, honed to an edge. Were he a mere barber, he could shave a man with those. She suspected that if he took to anatomy, he could slice through bone and tissue and extract a human heart, whole and without puncture, with one circular grasp.

He considered her head, finger-razors spider-walking through her hair. As he concentrated, bristles sprouted along his cheeks. His teeth enlarged, forcing his lips apart.

'Daisy,' he commanded.

Miss Bunting presented her neck. M. Eugene traced her jugular with his forefingernail, scratching through makeup. Blood welled and trickled along his talon. The *tang* made Geneviève's eyes water. M. Eugene poured the drop onto his long tongue and pondered. He announced, 'I am inspired.' The warm girl pressed a pad to her neck and stood back.

M. Eugene stepped behind Geneviève. She felt claws in her hair, lifting its weight. She had a qualm.

Apart from anything, it was going to be *expensive*.

It was over quickly. M. Eugene took off her hair with a precise frenzy, slicing rather than cutting. He hummed a *can-can* through fangs, accompanying himself with the clicks of his nails. She felt a chill in her now-exposed hackles.

'Hmmmn,' said M. Eugene, a sheaf of her blond hair pinched between talons. 'Curious. It rots not.'

'A peculiarity of my bloodline,' said Geneviève.

Should she be of a mind, she could furnish individual locks for an army of sweethearts. Then again, her soldier had other things to remember her by.

Charles. Another *tang*.

She was living in his house, though he was in India. She could taste him still. This was his city. The worst of the Terror reminded her of the best of Charles Beauregard. What she couldn't remember, now, was why she'd left England – and him – when the cause was won and Dracula flown. A Californian orange grove had been her whim…

Her bib was brushed and removed. She could not resist reaching for her new fringe. Her hair didn't cover her eyes any more. M. Eugene firmly pulled her hands away from his work. He gently slapped her wrists.

The hairdresser's nails were normal now, trimmed and manicured. He took a brush and made a few passes. He considered her head as a hedger might consider a topiary rabbit.

M. Eugene snapped his fingers.

A lad who'd been sitting on a stool, reading the latest number of *British Pluck*, scurried over and flipped open an artists' pad. M. Eugene stood over the mirror-boy as he made lightning sketches. Full on, profile, rear view. Here was a new profession for the *anni draculae*. The Old Count scorned mirrors as 'baubles of man's vanity'; now, fast-fingered draughtsmen served as looking glasses for the chic vampire. A good mirror-boy knew not to flatter the subject. The lad left her face indistinct and concentrated on her hair. She had bangs and cheek-guards. The back of her neck was shaved. She no longer looked Late Victorian.

'Satisfactory,' said M. Eugene. It was not a question.

She was gently hurried out of the chair. Others awaited the chop. Next up was a floppy-haired male dandy, an aesthetic remnant from before the War. Not a vampire, but a living man in aspic, with too-perfect, waxy skin. Monkey glands, perhaps. Or something worse. She had a shudder of insight: this was a character not to get entangled with. She got *impressions* from some people: usually people she was in sympathy with; in this case, not. The customer carefully held himself apart from contact, especially avoiding the mirror-boy. Perhaps he didn't like having his picture drawn. He looked enough like a living portrait as it was, the eyes not quite right.

The fellow who'd seen to Polly Browne popped up to look after the new customer. Instead of showbusiness gossip, the cutter chattered with horrified delight of recent criminal cases. Bywaters had gone to the gallows like a gent, swearing to his mistress's innocence (to little effect, Thompson was hanged too). The dreadful Dr Sheppard, guilty of the Ackroyd murder, would be executed in the manner reserved for condemned vampires: silver-bladed guillotine. The Crooked Men were marching through the East End, smashing newsagents and chapels. The sitter's cheek muscles tightened at the whisper of each act of violence.

Miss Bunting helped her into her coat and hat. The bonnet flopped over her eyes. She took it off again and stuffed it in her pocket.

'An excuse to buy a new one,' the girl said.

Geneviève had known she'd have to get a cloche or beret to go with the bob, but hadn't thought how immediate the need would be. There was a milliner's a few doors down. Caroline Reboux must do a roaring trade with newly shorn sheep from the salon. Ditto, The Bee's Knees – a fashion house, which sold Robe de Style, dresses, figure-flattening *Eulalie Soeurs* slips, ostrich feather boas and roll-top stockings. Several competing jewellers offered the ropes of pearls, which completed the flapper look. Garrard & Co. carried strings of all-black pearls, suitable for the thoroughly modern vampire.

'If I can *afford* a new hat after this,' she said.

'There's no charge,' said Miss Bunting. 'Your bill has been settled by the gentleman.'

The gentleman?

He stood near the door, waiting for her. A warm man: clipped moustache, maybe thirty-five or older, evening dress, sharp eyes. She shuddered. He didn't radiate wickedness like the dandy in the chair, but she perceived a flash of danger, a potential for practical cruelty, a scratch of attraction. He'd been *bitten*, at least once. Under his starched collar, he'd have marks like Miss Bunting's. Deeper scars too. The War. Even in this bright new age, it was always the War.

The gentleman raised his silk hat. And his eyebrows.

The face was new, but she knew where he was from.

The Diogenes Club.

2

MILDEW MANOR

Vampires were coming to Mildew Manor! Proper ones – young-old, Carpathian, *male*. Not just Bloody Aunt Agatha in the attic. This was the best night of Lydia Inchfawn's life!

Usually, nothing happened in the Lake District over the long vac, except rain. Whether chucking it down in sheets or drizzling semi-invisibly, rain was constant in these wild northern parts of England.

Even now, with the manor awaiting vampires (yes, *vampires*!), it was pouring steadily. The upstairs domain of B.A.A. was cursed with leaks and drips. Vampires preferred mist to rain, especially ones who could turn into fog and seep under doors or through keyholes. They liked full moonlit nights, for the pale glow it gave the skins of willing warm lovers. To vampire eyes, human veins throbbing red and blue in the moonlight. The moon was not full tonight – Lydia had checked the chart in the back of her diary – but cloud was so thick no one's neck would be lighting up like Piccadilly Circus anyway. Mouldy chiz. Trust the weather to spoil it!

Lydia's room did not have French windows to a balcony, suitable for a bat to alight on and gather wings into a cloak as she whispered an invitation. The stone sill *was* sturdy enough to stand on – even if Mother told her not to, for fear of falling and breaking her head – and that made it *almost* a balcony. In a pinch, it would do. The drumming at her window was driving rain, not the tapping of long, sharp nails. Any vampire who perched outside would get a thorough soaking for his pains. Bats didn't flap in muck like this.

She held her candle close to the window and tried to look out at the drive. The manor had electricity, but it came and went. Vampires would arrive in hearses drawn by black stallions, rat-faced minions to heft coffins, ancient Carpathian crests picked out in scarlet on polished wood. So far, nothing.

One good thing about rain: it stopped all that 'why don't you play outside instead of pressing your nose into a book all the time' rot. Playing outside could lead to catching a chill and dying. Once, when she was little, Lydia deliberately caught a chill because she thought Mother would summon a leech from Carlisle to turn her. Even then, she was potty for vampires.

Well before all the other girls at school took it up, she was a devotee of *The Dark Flame*. She resented the way her enthusiasm was now generally shared. Silly fillies who once blindly followed cricketers or tenors now put it about that they knew *everything* about vampires. One thing, though: a proper vampire could tell the difference between dilettante and devoted. A p.v. would hear the beating heart of a true devotee from a room away, could know with one look that a person's blood was sweet and pure. A p.v. would step callously over fair-weather fancies – like Imogen Ames, Kali Chattopadhyay or the rest of the witches of the Fifth – to batten on a t.d. Verity Oxenford, known to one and all as Smudge, her best (only) friend at school, agreed with her. Smudge had been *devoted* almost as long as Lydia.

That long-ago chill made her pale, which was good so far as it went. But that was it. She didn't make it to Death's Door. She didn't even get as far as Death's Garden Gate. Now, she was grateful. She wouldn't want to be a tubby child for all eternity. Ribbons and ringlets had made her look more like a pudding than a person. Even now, she wasn't sure this was the body she wanted forever. Despite a heroic abjuration of crumpets and jam, she hadn't become slim enough for the short-hemmed shrouds vamps wore in Paris. She cut out a pattern from the back of *The Dark Flame* and tried to sew her own shroud, but needlework was not her strong suit.

After turning, her *metabolism* would be different. She might be able to slough pounds by sheer concentration. A proper vampire could shape-shift into a panther or a she-wolf. Dropping dress sizes at will should be a doddle. Also, she could chuck her dratted specs. Mother said Lydia's eyes were worn out from reading and motion pictures.

Without reading and motion pictures, she wouldn't have known *anything* about vampires – except that the one in the attic was a fire-breathing dragon. She'd heard that from Cousin Bertie, who had no chin to speak of and was always getting into scrapes. Something was not right in Cousin Bertie's head. Mother said he would come to a sorry end unless someone took him firmly in hand.

Miss Carlotta Francis, *éditrice* of *The Dark Flame*, frequently addressed herself to the periodical's vampire readers – though the letters beseeching her advice, not to mention nine out of ten advertisements in the Heart's Blood section, seemed to come from warm girls. Insofar as personal columns went, living ladies – and a few funny gentlemen – seeking the attentions of vampires outnumbered the children of the night themselves. Another good thing about turning: a vampire would have her pick of the boys. Not that Lydia would be inclined to flightiness in anything but feeding (oh, and in flying). Fidelity would be her watchword, through the centuries to come.

She thought of *her vampire*.

He must be among the party convened at Mildew Manor. It would be too cruel otherwise. This weekend her true life, her *life in death*, would begin. The previous years – nearly fifteen of them – were a false start. Mostly school and governesses. Being told off and left behind on account of being a pudding.

She had no clear picture of *her vampire*...

...unless it was Rudolf Valentino as Magnus in *The Count*, the film of the famous novel by Elinor Glyn. Lydia and Smudge had seen *The Count* five times and came close to fainting at every visit to the picture house. Lydia could shut her eyes and replay the most swoon-worthy scene, the chapter entitled 'In the Count's Castle', inside her head – and did, frequently. Lady Diana, played by the kohl-eyed Norma Desmond – who was *all wrong for the part*, since Smudge said she pictured Madame Glyn's heroine as a slenderer, unbespectacled Lydia – meets a masked stranger at a Viennese ball, and faints in his arms as he waltzes her into the night. She awakens in an unfamiliar boudoir in a remote castle. A portrait over the fireplace shows a woman in Tudors-and-Stuarts costume who looks *exactly like Diana*. The room has French windows and a balcony. Diana is afraid, yet excited… her little fist at her breast, knotting and unknotting like a beating heart. A shape outside, wings spread. A scratching at the window. Fluttering curtains. Responding to a voice whispering directly to her soul, the Englishwoman opens the windows. And there *he* is.

The vampire, Count Magnus.

'What do you want of me?' she asks, in a trembling subtitle.

Valentino's eyes glow. Film magazines said he wasn't a real vampire and clever spotlights did the trick, but *The Dark Flame* hinted the Italian actor had turned in secret for the role. He smiles, showing sharp, yet even teeth. The other vampires in the film have rat-ears, wolf-fangs, enlarged and almost hairless skulls, talons and long, long faces. They dress in stinking, ancient rags and eat beetles. But the Count wears immaculate evening clothes. He has slick, thick, black hair and the face of a marble angel. An infinite sadness is in him, for he has not surrendered to the brutality of his clan. Later, it turns out he has a different bloodline and is English-born to boot. He has always known he was different from other *nosferatu*. The taste of Diana's blood makes him realise how *sensitive* he really is, for she is of a finer quality than the peasant wenches he has gorged himself on hitherto. She is the reincarnation of the princess Magnus loved and lost before he turned vampire. Only after all these years are their souls reunited.

But he doesn't know that yet, not in this scene.

'What do you w-want of me?' Lady Diana repeats.

'*Are you not woman enough to know?*' says the Count, licking his lips.

Only now does he have the daintiest, tiniest fangs.

Diana is overpowered, bodice torn away from her neck – and as much of her bosom as they could show in a cinema, whereas Madame Glyn writes that the Count impatiently tears off her nightie altogether. Diana swoons in terror and ecstasy as Magnus bites her. Afterwards, lips scarlet (well, in the book – shiny black in the film), the Count looks with infinite sadness at the girl in his arms, ashamed for the wrong he has done. English blood shows through Carpathian upbringing. Lady Diana, like every female in the audience, forgives him. She takes hold of his noble head and presses his mouth to her eager wound. Smudge had asked how a wound could be eager, prompting a two-day estrangement ended only with her begging to be forgiven and willing to take instruction from Lydia in the finer points of vampire romance.

There were other vampires. *The Dark Flame* couldn't fill every number with Magnus, though he did feature regularly. Smudge was an admirer of the (drippy, if appealingly floppy-haired) violin virtuoso Ralph Levé, who had extra-long fingers and was a pupil of Paganini. Lydia and Smudge had both been smitten, briefly, by George Valentin as Rupert of Hentzau in *The Vampyres of Zenda*. The Ruritanian baddie was much more appealing than stiff Lord Godalming (Lewis Stone), the hero who duelled him to a standstill at the end (but didn't shove silver through his heart). Lydia and Smudge both despised the Most Hideous Man in the World, Charlie Chaplin... his bowler-hatted, baggy-trousered, rat-tailed, *not funny* Little Vamp wasn't a *proper vampire*, but a reprehensible slur. Smudge got heated about what she'd like to do to Charlie Chaplin. Lydia had to calm her down by promising to write to Miss Carlotta Francis and get up a petition to have Chaplin's foul films refused a certificate by the Board of Trade.

Elinor Glyn was the greatest writer of the age. Lydia was impatient for *The Dark Flame* to begin serialising *Son of the Count* so Rudi could be in a film of it. But she conceded that Salome Otterbourne, Rosie M. Banks and Harriet Vane also wrote about *proper vampires*. Though all registered on the swoon scale, none were up to Madame Glyn's standards. Otterbourne's *Nitelite Saga* novels had *so much* swooning Lydia wondered if the authoress was prone to fits. Her hero glittered like a Christmas tree and her heroine was unconscious for at least seven chapters in each book, even though she was supposed to be telling the story. Banks's *Mal de Mer* mysteries were written in baby-talk and took about half an hour each to get through. She called warm characters silly things like Snookie, Lurline and Squits but stuck her vampires with peculiarly boring names as if they were someone's brother. Vane's *Vampyrrhic Chronicles* kept stopping for long lectures on ancient history and Roman Catholicism which Smudge said it was all right to skip. Miss Vane wrote from the vampire's point of view – she reputedly bit one of the Bloomsbury Group for research and nearly went to prison for it.

Even Bram Stoker's what-might-have-been novel made dull old Dracula out to be *almost* a proper vampire. *Dracula* wasn't banned any more but Lydia and Smudge had to read it in secret by candlelight lest it be confiscated. The real Dracula married the Queen. Siding with the Germans in the War showed Dracula up as a rotter and therefore not a p.v. at all.

Someone like Count Magnus was whom she saw in her future. It must be a *psychic bond*. She'd read about psychic bonds in articles by Dion Fortune or Luna Bartendale in *The Dark Flame*. If a person was predestined to become the lover – ultimately, the get – of a vampire, she would sense it for maybe years beforehand. She would see his face in dreams or have *flashes* of insight – sometimes, witnessing scenes from the violent, tragic history a vampire endures before finding his soul-mate – which could be taken by the unsympathetic and cynical for hysterical fits or mental disorder. Lydia had certainly suffered from that misunderstanding. She did see a face sometimes, though it was mixed up with illustrations of Count Magnus from the magazine, and Rudi V. and George Valentin in the photographs she had pinned up above her cot at school, and what she remembered of her brother Eric in his uniform when he went away to die in the War (she still had his watch, a parting present). She tried sometimes to get all that clutter out of her mind, to fix on the real face of *her vampire*, but only got an oval of fog with red eye-points. Perhaps that was what he would look like until he found her?

Lydia was a Greek name, from the Kingdom of Lydia, a satrapy of the Achaemenid Empire. Perhaps that was when and where she and *her vampire* first met and loved and were tragically parted? She as beautiful Niobe, proud daughter of King Tantalus... he as her lyre-playing husband Amphion, murdered along with his sons and daughters by Artemis and Apollo, only get of jealous goddess Leto. Niobe fasted for nine days while her husband and children lay unburied, and was then turned to stone, an outcrop of Mount Sipylus known as the Weeping Rock.

There was commotion outside. A horn honking.

She was at the window in a flash, looking out. Headlamps in the driveway. Not carriages, but motorcars – probably black, though it was hard to tell in the dark, struggling with the gravely mud.

Lydia Inchfawn's devoted heart raced. They were here! Vampires!

3

'TELL TOM TILDRUM THAT TIM TOLDRUM'S DEAD...'

At the kerb outside the salon was a green Bentley, black canopy up. Geneviève knew why she'd had her *moment* earlier. By the car, wearing chauffeur's uniform, stood a familiar vampire.

'Sergeant Dravot,' she acknowledged.

He gave the salute appropriate to a civilian.

Tusk-like permanent fangs curved below his grizzled moustache. Though big, he could hide in shadows and make no noise – but his presence had pricked her nerves. Danny Dravot was another holdover from the Terror. A good soldier: not necessarily a good man.

How long had the Diogenes Club been keeping this eye on her?

The gentleman steered her towards his car. Dravot held the door open.

'Let me take you for a drive, Miss Dieudonné,' the gentleman said.

'I've been in America recently,' she said. 'California and Chicago. Do you know what they mean when they say "take you for a ride"?'

The gentleman smiled easily. 'We don't misbehave like that.'

'You misbehave in completely different ways?'

'We might,' he conceded. 'At the mo, I'm only after a quiet chat. My motorcar is convenient. We can natter in confidence.'

'A proposition will be involved?'

'When a lady is invited into a Bentley, a proposition is often involved.'

412

She mulled it over. Unless she heard him out, she would be pestered.

'My name is Edwin Winthrop,' he said. She knew who he was. 'We have mutual connections.'

He didn't say 'friends'. He meant Charles, of course. But also Katharine Reed, who'd written to her during the War. Winthrop got his bite-marks from Kate.

'All right,' she said, slipping into the car.

Winthrop slid onto the seat beside her. Dravot sat up front and drove. The Bentley joined the flow of traffic, a jaguar among sheep. On the open road, it could break speed records. In the city, it was less nippy than a bicycle.

'Isn't this cosy?' said her host.

Winthrop took out a silver case and offered her a cigarette. She declined. He stuck one in his mouth and flicked a silver lighter. He drew in a breath and exhaled smoke.

'It's an honour to meet you, Miss Dieudonné. You're something of a legend in the Club. The first Lady Member.'

'And the last?'

'Not at all. We have women of distinction on our lists. Jennifer Chevalier... Grace Ki, the Ghost Lantern Girl... Lady Jane Ainsley. Admitted over the dead bodies of some senior members, certainly. But we're enlightened. No other way to be, of course. How did you like America? There are few of you there at present.'

'Few of me?'

'You plural. Vampires. You must have been a novelty.'

'For a month or so I was fussed over by reporters. Then, the press got a craze for human flies. Emphasis on *human*. If a vampire crawls up or down a building in America, no one cares. If Harold Lloyd does it, they give him the key to the city. Then there's Prohibition. Alcohol gets all the headlines, but the Volstead Act made selling blood illegal too. That's tantamount to hanging a "No Vampires" sign around the neck of the Statue of Liberty. Devil knows what's in the stuff you get from bootleggers. So I left. I was bored already. It's a young country. I felt like I was talking to children all the time.'

'That's terribly good. Do you mind if I write it down?'

He took out a little notebook and a silver extending pencil and scribbled. Three silver items about his person. That would be deliberate.

'I thought you were barred from writing your memoirs?'

'Not *barred*, my dear. It *is* frowned on, politely. We are a *secret* service. Not done to brag on one's achievements. I write things down for my friend Catriona Kaye. She keeps the records.'

'Another Lady Member?'

'Associate. She provides *outside perspective*. When you get to make up your own rules, you need someone to nag about niceties. Morality and responsibility and such. He who sets out to slay dragons risks becoming one. Nietzsche said that. Along with the even creepier saw about the abyss looking back. Cold, nasty German mind, Nietzsche. But you see his point. As constituted by Mycroft Holmes, the Diogenes Club is dedicated to the Greater Good. There's a tragic history of like institutions becoming tyrannies dedicated only to their own perpetuation. The Star Chamber, the Illuminati and so forth. We need the odd nay-sayer. The things we might have done, only for Cat to say nay. In a moment of crisis, you get this *clear vision* of the easiest solution and a terrible temptation to get on and do what has to be done. Only afterwards do you see what you've wrought and rue it. Then you wish someone had been around to say nay. Yes, I speak from bitter experience. Mycroft was a great one for *outside perspective*. The Old Man is even more of a stickler.'

The Old Man. It took a long moment for Geneviève to realise he meant Charles. If Charles Beauregard was old, what was she...?

'When the Old Man talks about checks and balances, he means you.'

That brought her up, sharply.

Since the second mutiny, when British troops and Indians alike rose against Dracula's Viceroy, Sir Francis Varney, the sub-continent had been fractious. The Cult of Saamri proposed a less gentle break with the British Empire than Mr Gandhi did. Charles, an old India hand, was needed. But the mission took him back to a part of his life she could never share. His wife was buried in the hill country. Pamela's photographs were displayed in his house, but Geneviève didn't show up. A vampire couldn't compete with a ghost. If Charles died out there – always a possibility in a war with the Cult of Saamri – he'd be buried with his wife. He'd been bitten since her death, not just by Geneviève, but Pamela's teeth had left his most lasting scars.

Charles had given her the use of his London house, but not been there when Geneviève arrived from the continent. She didn't think he'd fled the country to avoid her, but couldn't help wondering why the Diogenes Club had no one else to trust with India. With sharp new men like Edwin Winthrop and old vampires like Sergeant Dravot – not inexperienced on the North-West Frontier – at their command, why did it still have to be Charles Beauregard? He was nearly seventy. None of the staff in Cheyne Walk remained from the years she'd lived with him. The new servants were polite and efficient, but wary and impersonal. The place might as well have been a hotel, except for the memories.

'…so we hoped you'd be up for a little, well, let's call it intelligence gathering?'

'I beg your pardon.'

'Did I lose you there? Sorry. Should have known you were away with the fairies. Or did you *sense* something? I've heard you have *insights*. A gift of your bloodline.'

'Sorry.'

Winthrop smiled. 'It's a case of no one else will do, as usual. We have vampire members, of course. Sergeant Dravot was the first, but others have been admitted. Kate Reed, whom I know you know, is an Associate, though we've had a falling-out over Ireland and not heard much from her lately. A few useful chaps came out of the War and found peace on the dull side. Bigglesworth, Ultus, Hannay. Capital fellows, excellent sorts. When a bad hat needs a biffing, we send 'em in. Bad hats abound. There's been a curious crime wave lately. In America-Land, did you run into the Cat and the Bat?'

'The Kane papers are full of them. Masked criminals.'

'Yes, secret identity fellows. Cloaks and gloves, and murder at midnight…'

'Another reason I left. Whenever there was a "Bat" crime, the cops rounded up all the vampires. Being arrested in America gets tiresome after the third or fourth go-round. They really do use rubber hoses. The Cat was caught and turned out to be – *quelle surprise!* – a warm man. It didn't stop the harassment. If the Bat's a vampire, why doesn't he drink the blood of the people he murders?'

Winthrop raised an eyebrow. Geneviève had been hectoring him.

'Whatever the Bat is, he or she represents a pernicious fashion in villainy,' Winthrop continued. 'The trend started with Parisian perishers – Fantômas, le Rat, Belphégor. Thieves and anarchists, mostly. With a bit of *joie de mort*. Now, we've a plague of similarly got-up troublemakers in London. More organised than their Gallic cousins. They run their outfits like Yank gangsters. The Frog, the Ghoul, the Hooded Terror. Who thinks up these names? It's enough to make you think fondly of Professor Jim Moriarty or Arsehole Lupin, isn't it? Remember when crooks built reputations with daring exploits? Nowadays, your would-be diabolical mastermind hires a press agent and a costume designer before he coshes his first drunk.'

'You lot started it,' she said. 'Who made up "Jack the Ripper"?'

She knew Dravot could hear them.

Winthrop laid a finger by his nose and smiled. 'See what I mean about the unintended consequences of well-intentioned plans? When *whoever wrote those misleading letters* came up with a catchy moniker, how could he have foreseen it would inspire rotten johnnies yet unborn to come up with their own blood-curdling *noms de plume*?'

The driver grunted into a speaking tube: the nearest she'd get to an apology for an enormous quantity of grief. Necessary, perhaps? Forgivable, perhaps not.

'Any rate, we've red-blooded blokes – and a few lovely ladies – who can cope with your garden-variety Green Archer or Clutching Hand. Some Diogenes chappies can put on a mask with the best of 'em. Dr Shade, for one – though he's only an Affiliate. And Ghost Lantern Girl. Don't know why Gracie hides her face, but she does, the minx. She's the reason there isn't a Cult of Saamri Temple in Brixton Hill. Thanks to these sterling operators, the Diogenes Club stays in business.'

'I did wonder what you did when there wasn't a war on.'

'There's *always* a war on. Sometimes, you just don't notice it.'

A cheerful thought. Geneviève wanted to wriggle. Fine hairs went down the back of her dress when M. Eugene shaved her neck. She felt scratchy. Sitting straight, she tried to make the discomfort go away.

'Our thorniest problem just now is one of these masked murder-*wallahs*,' continued Winthrop. 'Hooded, from the descriptions we've had. He calls himself… dramatic drum-roll… *ta-daaa!*… the Crook!'

'That's a little obvious, isn't it?'

'He leans on a *shepherd's crook* when in his robes. Or perhaps it's an Episcopal crook, and he doesn't go by the Black Bishop because there's already a Black Abbot in the game. He sports a North Country accent, maybe assumed. Started in Leeds, but is getting a name in London. These criminals feud among themselves. The Crook is a coming man. His gang, the Crooked Men, cut Zenith the Albino out of a gemstone racket recently. That takes nerve. Rumour has it that the Crook was behind the dumping of the burglar Nighthawk in the Thames with his wings clipped. The Crook is – or claims to be – a vampire. We had a ringer inside the Crooked Men. Arthur Milton, a sharp operator. Haven't heard from him lately. *Not* a good sign. Before cessation of service, Milton passed on intelligence which connects with another matter we're following. That is where you come in, my dear.'

She had been waiting for this. It didn't escape her that Milton, the last man the Club had on the Crook, was certainly dead.

'As I mentioned, we have vampire members,' Winthrop said. 'But our bloods are – what is it you old sticks call them? – new-born. Not a one over a hundred. Dravot's only ninety-two. A merest babe in undeath. To get an invite to the weekend party we're interested in, you have to be an elder. The Diogenes Club has only one of those on the rolls. You, Miss Dieudonné.'

They had not crossed the river. Dravot was taking a circuitous route to Chelsea.

'Weekend party?' she prompted.

'In the Lake District,' Winthrop responded. 'A delightful spot, I'm told. Mildew Manor. The name doesn't mean it's a rotten hole. It's a contraction of "Mille Dieux". A Thousand Gods. A pre-Christian shrine existed on the site. Don't let that put you off. It's the least haunted house in England. All the modern comforts. A vampire named Agatha Gregson owns it. Strong-willed. She's drained two or three husbands – tends to pick on monied weeds who can give blood but not take it. They die of the bites but don't come back, or come back *twisted* and don't last long. Mrs Gregson – who is also Lady Worplesdon – has several absolute fortunes, no marital prospects and a tendency to meddle. She's taken it into her head that, with Dracula exiled from Britain and Germany – on that far Northern isle where it never gets dark – what vampirekind wants most is a new King of the Cats. You know the fairy tale?'

'"Tell Tom Tildrum that Tim Toldrum's dead... then I am King of the Cats", yes.'

'That's the one. I doubt anyone dared call the former Prince Consort "King of the Cats" to his face, but it's now deemed one of his titles... and up for grabs. Only elders need apply.'

'I did hear about this,' she admitted. 'I thought it was a joke.'

'It might be best if it were.'

'A lesson vampires should learn from the example of Dracula is that we don't need, can't use and shouldn't have a monarch. It's as stupid as someone declaring themselves leader of all the left-handed or red-headed people in the world. Vampires have no common cause.'

'You don't need to convince me. You need to convince Agatha.'

'Who's in the running? Ruthven?'

'Too clever. Kings get their heads chopped off. Ministers don't because the next king needs them. Which isn't to say Ruthven won't have a hand in it. He's been idle, which always sets him plotting.'

Lord Ruthven, Dracula's Prime Minister, was the Vampire Vicar of Bray… whatsoever king may reign, Ruthven would be at his side, picking up scraps. He remained securely in office from 1886 to 1918, but for a brief period after the Terror when he was replaced by Henry Campbell-Bannerman. He knew just when to break with the Prince Consort and side with the Restoration. Originally a Whig, Ruthven had called his administration Tory, Liberal, Tory again, and (during the War) a Government of National Unity. In 1918, professing to be weary of the struggle, he let David Lloyd George succeed him, probably because he expected the Coalition to collapse and take down whoever was at its head. Knowing he was popular with warm women – the fools! – His Lordship believed newly enfranchised widows would sweep him back into power with a proper mandate. He half-fancied he could mesmerise them in job lots at public speaking engagements. A crisis forced Lloyd-George's resignation in 1922, before Ruthven could position himself as leader of the Conservative Party. Andrew Bonar Law won an election while technically dead – in the throes of turning vampire. Like Agatha Gregson's husbands, he didn't survive. Britain's shortest-lasting Prime Minister, transformed into a giant dead bat with ragged velvet wings, was buried next to the Tomb of the Unknown Soldier. Now, the warm Stanley Baldwin was Prime Minister and would go to lengths to keep Ruthven out. He was widely quoted as having said he'd rather see Ramsay MacDonald, of the Labour Opposition, in Number Ten Downing Street than 'that murgatroyd atavism'.

Geneviève dreaded to think who else might fancy themselves King (or Queen) of the Cats.

'Elizabeth Báthory?' she ventured, shuddering.

'Too rich,' said Winthrop. 'She's on the Riviera, seducing millionaires on her black-sailed yacht.'

'Some Carpathian toady, then? Iorga or Mitterhouse or Vulkan. Bloated and fancying himself?'

'None of those are on the list, but the ones we have are pretty much interchangeable with them. Meinster, Zaleska, Karnstein.'

'Karnstein?'

'You knew the daughter, didn't you?'

'Carmilla. Mircalla. She kept changing her name round. Millarca, Marcilla. I don't think she really liked anything she could make from the letters.'

'General Karnstein was on Dracula's staff in Germany. Lucky to escape exile after Versailles. Might he consider himself the new Great Vampire?'

'He hates the living. After What Happened to Carmilla, you can see his point.'

What Happened to Carmilla was the prime example of how things were before Dracula insisted the world acknowledge vampires as a different kind of people rather than fiends from Hell. Her murderers kept her head as a souvenir. And stuck a stake through her. Then left the mangled corpse in the family crypt, for her father to find. To Geneviève's thinking, Carmilla was foolish, not wicked. She formed attachments to sickly warm girls who didn't survive her attempts to turn them. No one was more upset than Carmilla at the sad outcomes – except the families of the deceased, who put an end to her long, decorative existence.

'Will the General listen to you?' suggested Winthrop.

She caught his drift. 'Because he's looking to replace a daughter? If so, he won't pick me. He said I was a bad influence on the one he had. He's the most likely king of the three. Baron Meinster is a poltroon. Nice word, that: poltroon. If you're looking for a Dracula heir, Countess Zaleska says she's his daughter. She even might be, but I can't see her taking a throne. Too wet and world-weary.'

Geneviève, against her instincts, was interested. This game might be silly, but would have consequences.

'There are other players,' said Winthrop, consulting his notebook. 'Hodge, Kleopatra, Kah Pai Mei.'

She knew those names too.

'Richard Hodge, just back from Australia, is British originally, it seems. He's wealthy and has sponsorship. Croft's in his corner, which is to say he's Ruthven's man.'

Caleb Croft was Chief of Secret Police. At the end of the Terror, when deals were struck in Whitehall backrooms, he turned coat to keep his head and job. When Charles told her, Geneviève cried. Croft had murdered, probably personally, many of their friends. She'd damned Great Britain for a nation of lunatics. 'You'd have been better off keeping Dracula and getting rid of Croft!' The monster even managed to stay in office with Ruthven out of power. He knew where the bodies were buried and the mystic wards stopping them crawling out of graves to accuse or avenge.

'You know nothing about Hodge? That's not like the Diogenes Club.

'A "Dickon Hogge" was convicted of "assaulting cowes" at York Assizes and transported to Australia in 1786. A "Rich Hoggart" was suspected of double murder – two young children, throats cut in their beds – in Sydney in 1831. A "Richard Hogg" registered an opal mine claim at Lightning Ridge, New South Wales, in 1892. We believe they're all the same person, but would have a devil of a time proving it. "Hogg" is certainly Hodge. His fortune comes from black opals. It's anybody's guess what he was doing before the yokels caught him draining the livestock. It's likely he wasn't a new-born even then. He might or might not be the highwayman known as "Captain Hog", who plied his trade in the early 1700s, biting ladies whose carriages he stopped in Epping Forest.'

She threw back the other names. 'Kleopatra and Kah Pai Mei? What are their chances?'

'Not Europeans, not likely,' he said. 'Can you see your Carpathian Counts and Bulgar Barons taking orders from some dusky heathen?'

Dracula, sometime Hammer of the Turks, had set the fashion for European vampires to scorn cousins from other continents. That was a recent thing. Geneviève had spent time in China, South America and Africa – though not India, not yet – and at least respected their ancient bloodlines.

Kleopatra was, or said she was, a sometime Queen of the Nile, though not the one with Antony and the asp. She appeared on stage as 'Queen Katrina' and signed into hotels as 'Akasha Kemet'. Last season, she'd lucked into an opportunity to become the toast of Paris by performing a *danse du Nil* dressed only in strategically gummed crocodile scales. Hemingway called her 'the most sensational vampyre anybody ever saw'. Geneviève hadn't caught her act. She couldn't stand the frilly-shirted murgatroyds who managed and patronised the Théâtre des Vampires.

Kah Pai Mei was a martial arts *sifu*: Master of the Flying Guillotine, Practitioner of the Five Deadly Venom Disciplines, Adept of Mad Monkey Kung Fu, Calligrapher General to the Blood Blanket God and High Priest of the Temple of the Golden Vampires. Not exactly whom you expected to run into in Cumbria, but English weekend country house parties were cosmopolitan these days.

'If it were up to us as to who leads the armies of the night, I rather think we'd plump for None of the Above,' ventured Winthrop. She knew whom he meant by 'us'.

'I hope you don't want to nominate *me* as Queen of Air and Darkness? I've more important things on. Five new Charleston dance steps have arrived since last week and I've yet to master three of them.'

Winthrop blew smoke out of his nostrils. He was picturing her dancing.

'You couldn't keep up,' she told him.

He took her peeping into his mind in good humour. She'd not delved deep, where the real secrets were.

'All we ask is that you attend the conclave and keep your shell-like auricular orifice to the ground. This has blown up suddenly and we're on the back foot. It's Dracula's fault. He's been such a colossus for the last fifty years we didn't bother considering who we might have to put up with if he were scratched. We have lists of names, but don't really know the runners. You must have bumped into most of 'em.'

'Before Dracula came to Britain, vampires didn't have annual balls. Our best bet for keeping our heads was to lead quiet lives. We all knew What Happened to Carmilla. She wasn't the only one.'

Winthrop spread his hands. 'Before my time, remember?'

She let him off. 'Where does this Crook come in?'

'That's what set bells a-jingling. The Lake District isn't exactly his turf, but he has connections up there. Our late, lamented ringer suggested he – or she – might be at Mildew Manor this weekend.'

'So there's a hooded mastermind prowling the secret passageways?'

'How did you know there were secret passageways?'

'There are *always* secret passageways.'

'I suppose there are. In this case, a labyrinth of natural caves under the house. Not exactly secret, but deuced tricky. More than one potholer has disappeared. Those thousand or so pre-Christian idols are stashed there, in alcoves hewn from rock by ancient hands. No one has ever counted them twice and got the same number.'

'So, your Crook has a ready-made lair. What's he up to in it?'

'He has ambitions, obviously. We don't know if the Crook aspires to be King of the Cats. Only a maniac or an idiot would want that. Running a gang of criminals requires a practical mind. These fellows might *seem* lunatics, but they usually aren't. Be easier for us if they were cuckoo. We suspect that, like Lord Ruthven, the Crook is after *influence*... he could easily become a bigger nuisance if he had his hooks in one or more of the claimants. With, say, a High Priest of the Temple of the Golden Vampires in his corner, the Crook could challenge the Si Fan for the poppy trade. And a flow of fabulous opals imported without troubling Customs and Excise would make for a tidy war chest. Trivial as Mrs Gregson's party might sound, there are consequences on the streets of our cities we'd like to avert. You know the drill.'

Geneviève saw how she was being hemmed in.

'I don't know what use I'll be in this company. I may be an elder, but I'm not popular with the tribe. Especially with Dracula's hangers-on. Doesn't he still have "wives" in circulation? They'd like to kill me.'

'Agatha Gregson has promised a flag of truce over Mildew Manor. So you won't be beheaded in your bed.'

'I won't need a bed for a month. Not for sleeping.'

'Ah yes, you've just had your spell of "vampire lassitude" and can keep on the go night and day. Very useful.'

Someone in Charles's house had told Winthrop that.

'Have you fed? I know you need to after waking.'

'Yes, thank you very much.'

He couldn't keep his hands away from his collar when the subject came up. A warm man's tell. A warm man who's known a bite. Kate's letters had been explicit on the subject of Edwin Winthrop.

A man Not to Be Trusted. He might have the gentlemanly charm down pat, but he was not Charles Beauregard. In the Diogenes Club, Charles was the exception. Mycroft Holmes, the founder, was an unsentimental strategist. If not for Geneviève's unforeseen presence at the endgame, his master plan to unseat Dracula would have entailed loyal pawn Charles' death. Mycroft had needed someone like Charles, but the Club also retained back-alley knifemen like Dravot. Winthrop was what you'd get if you put Mycroft's brain and Dravot's heart into Charles' body. They could probably actually do that now, though the man had been grown conventionally – public school (Greyfriars), Oxford (Judas College), secret service (DMI6), with a detour into the Royal Flying Corps, courtesy of Kate Reed's blood.

'Did you really shoot down the Red Baron?' she asked.

'I was shooting *at* him,' he admitted. 'And he went down. Draw your own conclusions.'

'Australian ground fire?'

He grinned. 'Charles said you were a rose with thorns.'

He could take being needled.

She was irritated, but also at a loose end… and Agatha Gregson's notion of ordaining a new vampire monarch was one of those utterly stupid ideas that would take hold unless firmly squelched at the larval stage.

She didn't even have to accept.

'Welcome back to the Club, Geneviève,' said Winthrop.

Dravot had been driving north all the time. The Bentley was on the outskirts of London already. Winthrop had presumed. He would have to learn not to, but he was young. Even for a living man.

'Don't worry,' he said. 'We've packed for you. I had Catriona go shopping. You've an appropriate wardrobe to suit your new haircut. The least we could do.'

4

THE THRESHOLD

L ydia had been told to keep out of the way.

How did Roderick Spode get to be in a position to tell her what to do? It wasn't as if Mother approved of him. He was Bloody Aunt Agatha's minion and a very inferior specimen at that. He'd been bitten often and fed on live squirrels and bugs, but wasn't V at all. B.A.A. was an expert on who and what was and wasn't V. Her poor (well, rich, actually) husbands were all misleadingly promising but fell at the last fence. Non-V to the graves they didn't rise from.

Lydia would jump with ease, she was certain. If anyone in Mildew Manor was V, she was. She'd have her night-wings, soon…

Since Aunt Agatha seldom left her attic realm, her bidding was conveyed to the household via Spode. It was not done to accuse him of making it up, though Lydia suspected B.A.A. gave him a general outline of her bidding and he filled in the blanks with his own whims and pufferies. An odd egg indeed. He stalked the manor in a perpetual vile mood, bumping his head on low lintels even if he remembered to stoop.

Lydia had peeped into Spode's briefcase once and found sheafs of sketches. In his spare time, he designed uniforms (with black short trousers), insignia (upside-down crosses and skulls) and salutes (arrows indicating arm movement). He must be planning to start his own army. He took the trouble to design a girls' uniform, with black short skirt and beret, to go beside – or, more likely, twelve rungs below – the boys' version. Maybe it was more like Scouts and Guides than an army – though with pistols, since he put holsters on the belts.

Despite the orders of the Great Spode, she was not going to miss the arrival of the vampires!

She wore her best pale blue dress and lingered on the first-floor landing, in shadow but with a good view of the hallway.

If lightning flashed, she would be briefly lit up.

A vampire would notice her.

But it was just ordinary rain. No thunder and lightning.

She got tired of standing and sat on the top stair. No one noticed her.

The staff were assembled, for inspection. Spode marched down the line. He gave Matey, the butler, and the footmen only cursory nods, but fussed with the maids' uniforms, smoothing aprons and doing up top buttons. Lottie, the serving maid, was one for leaving her top button undone then bending over a little too far while pouring soup for gentlemen. B.A.A. would have dismissed her if she wasn't also a sneak who passed on what guests said when they assumed she wasn't listening. Lottie put it about that Spode once tried to bite her, though he was far from V. Lydia understood Lottie often let gentlemen guests bite her, or as good as bite her.

Spode marched up to Mother, who waved him away. She wasn't about to let herself be inspected. If Father were here, he'd be inclined to punch Spode on the nose again, but he was in Scotland, catching salmon, shooting grouse and drinking whisky. Harold Inchfawn had been a Prisoner of War and, Lydia thought, rather missed it. To hear him tell of wheezes PoWs got up to, captivity was like school. Father was one of those queer ducks who enjoyed his schooldays. His fishing, shooting and drinking party were muckers from Doberitz Camp, including a Russki who couldn't go home because of the Bolsheviks and two enemy officers who'd been guards. Father didn't hold it against the Germans that they'd killed Eric. Non-V to the kidneys, he muttered he'd take a warm Kraut over an undead Englishman.

427

Strictly, the front door should have been opened as the visitors' party entered the drive. But, with this rain, that would mean puddles in the hallway, soaked carpets and a bedraggled staff.

Lydia was excited, though. Vampires!

A hammering came. Mildew Manor had a mediaeval knocker, though the oak door was new. The old one had got woodworm. Father said the house was a vampire for money: it sucked and sucked and would never be satiated. Mother responded that, in that case, it was a good thing *her* Aunt Agatha had money. His major's pension wasn't replacing doors or getting drains seen to any time soon. Then Father would go for a long walk and come back squiffy.

The knocking resounded.

Matey opened the door, which needed a firm pull. Rain swept in and dashed the butler in his starched front.

They stood on the doorstep!

Lydia's heart stopped for a long moment.

There should have been lightning. So she could see their faces… so they could see *her*!

Mother was impatient. Spode was frustrated. Both tutted and fussed. Lydia saw what the hold-up was.

Vampires had to be invited in.

If not according to folklore, then according to manners. Who could extend the invitation? Debate might fill the letter column of *The Dark Flame* for several issues. The butler wouldn't do. Spode, a jumped-up minion, was scarcely entitled. Mother, a lady of the house, was a possible. Or could she only invite a vampire into her own room? Not that Mother would.

A chuckle behind Lydia scraped her bones. A hand fell on her shoulder. A grip pinched her nerves.

Bloody Aunt Agatha had her!

'Come, girl… help me downstairs.'

An order, not a request. B.A.A. wasn't half so feeble as she pretended, not with her iron grip. She just liked leaning on persons.

Vampires hundreds of years old looked young. Aunt Agatha, a vampire only since 1919, looked hundreds of years old. Bald, she wore a strange black wig with curls. Her only teeth were two long ones at the front.

Lydia stood and let herself be used as a cane.

Aunt Agatha paid for the doorstep, so she could invite the vampires over it.

Everyone turned to look. Even the red eyes of the shadowed folk on the threshold. Not at Lydia – though she liked the fact that she was almost included.

Aunt Agatha took her time lurching down the stairs.

'Come in, come in,' she said, at last.

Roderick Spode breathed again and the vampires arrived.

Lydia couldn't look at them properly, she was so excited. They were dark and fair, lords and ladies, elegant, pale, red-eyed, sharp-smiling. They were *old*, older than B.A.A., older than Mildew Manor's knocker. She was hot in the face.

'What a dump,' said a golden youth with powder in his hair.

'Hush, Herbert,' responded his grey-cloaked companion. 'It's only for a weekend.'

'A weekend can be forever.'

Yes, thought Lydia, thrilled – forever!

Aunt Agatha greeted her guests. Spode made himself useful for once by announcing their names.

Countess Marya Zaleska, a matron lady of haunted, nervous aspect, was with a lush-lipped vampire girl, her secretary Ilona Harczy. The Countess was solicitous of Ilona the way Sherringham, Drearcliff captain of hockey, was of Dimsie, her special pet in the Third. There were vampires 'like that'. Lydia had been warned against getting into black carriages with strange ladies who offered Turkish Delight.

Then came two sets of dressed-up natives… Kleopatra, black as coal and wearing too much gold, and Professor Bey, face like parchment and wearing a tarboosh… Kah Pai Mei, a wisp-moustached (and ridiculously long-eyebrowed) Chinaman in white robes, and a slant-eyed schoolgirl in a sailor suit with a sword strapped to her back. Lydia didn't care how old or important they were... natives! No possibility they'd turn out to be English all along, like Count Magnus. Lydia had standards. She would not be bitten by a darkie.

So far, so not promising...

The man in grey was David, Baron Meinster. His more colourful companion was Herbert, Viscount von Krolock. From *The Dark Flame*, Lydia knew Meinster was Dracula's get. In the 1880s, he'd been high up in the Carpathian Guard – not, as was apparent from his lack of scars, in the regiment's fighting arm, but a staff officer. His companion was the son of a Transylvanian big-wig. Since the Count von Krolock was likely to live forever, Herbert's chances of inheriting castles, estates and bank accounts were slim, which put him at a loose end. In a questionnaire, he listed his profession as 'party guest'. The Viscount wore buckle shoes, an electric blue blazer and matching plus-fours, a froth of lavender lace around his throat.

Rupert of Hentzau was a real person, not just made-up for a film. He'd been in the fighting part of the Carpathian Guard. He didn't make it to B.A.A.'s guest-list, worse luck. Baron Meinster was handsome in a spends-too-much-time-combing-his-hair sort of way. Viscount Herbert wore more make-up than a tart, including a star-shaped beauty spot gummed on his mascara-whitened cheek. The Transylvanian Twins wouldn't be interested in her, Lydia was sure. Like the Countess, they batted for the other side.

Mr Hodge, a tubby fellow dressed like an alderman who'd made money in trade, was the first vampire to pay attention to Lydia. He made her flesh creep. He had doughy cheeks and curly fangs. His head lolled this way and then that, as if he was considering her from different angles, trying to decide the best spot to bite. With Hodge was a Mr Croft, who could have been his manager, servant or jailer. The corpse-faced Croft was the most terrifying individual, not excluding Aunt Agatha in one of her towering bates, she had ever met. She didn't need psychic insight to know he was thinking of ripping into throats with his bare teeth – probably starting with Lottie's, but he'd get round to Lydia's soon enough.

Much as she hated to admit it, this was a wash-out!

'Prince Mamuwalde sends his apologies,' said Spode, reading a note handed on by Professor Bey.

Kleopatra laughed and hissed at the same time.

'He won't have anything to do with us,' explained Herbert. 'The African upstart says Europe isn't civilised enough yet. Whoever gets the Dark Crown will have to have that blood-monkey killed, you know.'

For some reason, everyone looked at the little girl.

Lydia hadn't expected a vampire her own age. Rather, a vampire turned – frozen! – at her own age. Spode didn't identify her so she couldn't be important.

There were more to come…

General Karnstein and family. A famous name, a Styrian bloodline. Harriet Vane – no less! – had written a biographical monograph about the Karnsteins, which *The Dark Flame* published in its Winter Special. The General wore dress uniform and medal ribbons. An Austrian, he sported white hair but a black beard. Austrians were almost as bad as Germans. The General's wife, Ethelind, was Irish. Though a lot of them were rebels, being Irish was like being English, only a bit more exciting.

The General and his wife stepped over the threshold…

…followed by *her vampire*.

Lydia knew him at first sight. There was no thunder and lightning, except when she remembered this moment – and she would, often – she'd *add* the thunder and lightning… the crash in her heart, the strike of a *psychic bond*. He was Amphion, she Niobe, their *love* the stuff of songs and stories.

Her vampire was beautiful. A pale young man, with sad red eyes. His hair stood up straight, like a brush… no, not like a *brush*, how could she think that! Like a proud coxcomb, like a lion's mane. His cheekbones were sharp. His teeth were even – no fangs! – and shining. His skin was unmarred, like soft marble. His ears were slightly pointed. He looked straight at her with green, green eyes. Her knees threatened to give out.

'Lady Worplesdon,' Karnstein addressed Aunt Agatha, 'this is our son, Liam…'

Liam. The name of an *angel*. The light under his skin was like diamonds in snow. An infinite loneliness in his mien.

He was perfect! *Her vampire*.

She couldn't wait to write to Smudge and tell her all about it. Her friend would be *livid*.

She would hide all her pictures of Rudi V. She didn't need them any more.

She tugged Aunt Agatha's sleeve.

'What is it, girl?'

Lydia was incapable of saying anything. She must be red as a fire engine. She would die.

'This is my sister's girl, Lydia,' said Bloody Aunt Agatha. 'Do not bite her.'

That was it. She really would die now.

Her life was *over*.

5

ON THE ROAD

They drove through the night and into the day. Winthrop, typically warm, fell asleep and made small, happy noises. Dravot wasn't Geneviève's idea of company on a long trip. She didn't attempt conversation.

Before dropping off, Winthrop gave her a sheaf of files. Background material the Diogenes Club had, or was willing to share, on the participants in Mrs Gregson's Vampire Weekend. About the guests, she found little she didn't already know except that General and Countess Karnstein had a son, Liam. Carmilla never mentioned a brother. So-called purebloods, Karnsteins married cousins and bore vampire children. Without ever having been warm, they grew slowly older over centuries. Was that why they all seemed to have something missing? The bloodline lacked the capability to turn others: Carmilla's efforts to give her special friends the Dark Kiss were futile.

Clippings in English and German detailed Karnstein's wartime command of the Schloss Adler. Home base of Winthrop's notable foe, Baron von Richthofen. A hive of sorcerous science and grotesque experimental medicine. The Adler Group – Caligari, ten Brinken, Krueger – made Jekyll and Moreau look like Alexander Fleming and Louis Pasteur. What had the mad scientists been up to since the War? Nothing healthy, she supposed.

A dossier on the Crook included transcribed interviews with

Arthur Milton, missing presumed slaughtered. The Crooked Men weren't just criminals but a political movement, recruiting from the ranks of the disillusioned, the disadvantaged and the dreadful. She'd seen the *Sturmabteilung*, the brown-shirted bullies of the Nazi Party, smashing vampire-owned businesses in Berlin, burning crosses outside the *nosferatu* ghetto. Crooked Men leaflets read like translated fascist propaganda, with added material invoking Arthur and Boadicea about resisting foreign monarchs. A mystery solved: the stick-figure graffiti were the marks of the Crooked Men. The thin question mark was their sign: both a shepherd's and a bishop's crook, suggesting a flock's need of strong leadership and the movement's semi-religious nature. She also thought of the music hall hook used to yank failing acts into the wings; the Crook often made people disappear as suddenly.

With the dawn, Winthrop woke up. They were in the North.

They stopped for breakfast in a depressing village, Royston Vasey. Mostly for Winthrop's sake. He had bacon and eggs and a gallon of tea. The café didn't offer vampire fare. Not much call for it in these parts. The moon-faced proprietor offered to send out to the local butcher for 'drippings'. Geneviève politely declined.

It was raining. Roads were in a ghastly state. The Bentley did not look its best. Winthrop claimed it had the same engine as the Sopwith Camel he'd flown in the War, inside a chassis that would do a motor-yacht proud. The canopy didn't leak, a mark of unostentatious British quality. It purred through mud and flood. Children braved the tempest to coo at the motorcar, though Dravot's scowl discouraged close inspection.

'Best push on to Mildew Manor before it's cut off,' Winthrop said.

'Cut off?'

'When the meres flood, the only road in and out is impassable. Except by boat.'

'So this weekend might last for weeks?'

'There's a cheerful thought,' he admitted. 'You can cross running water, can't you?'

'Yes. I don't know how that myth got about. It's ridiculous. What about water-mains?'

'There are cases,' Winthrop said. 'Our holding facilities for vampire Prisoners of War were hulks. Some had a, whatchumacallit, psychological block about running water. Never mind they'd been hauled across the English Channel. They read the restriction as not being able to cross running water *by their own volition*. A Dottyville report about it is buried somewhere.'

Before getting back to the car, they took advantage of the café's lavatories to change clothes. Winthrop transformed from a silk-hatted, tailcoated toff to a bowler-hatted, pinstripe-trousered functionary.

'Meet your new secretary. I have references.'

'They make you such good ones. Do you have a nice false name?'

'I'm sticking with mine own handle. I've met Croft before, with the Old Man. And Countess Zaleska, when she was petitioning mercy for her supposed father. She's pestered the Versailles Powers for visitation rights, which have been denied. That's as much mercy as Dracula will get from the vindictive so-and-sos. You'd think it would be us calling for his head on a spike, but the French are *much* more annoyed with him. And the Yanks.'

While in the lavatory, he had shaved. She scented spots of blood under his soft collar where he'd nicked old bites. Her eye-teeth extended a sharp fraction. Was Edwin Winthrop offering his neck? He smiled, raising an eyebrow which might express willing. He noticed her fangs. She wasn't in the grip of red thirst, but there was something... a temptation, an *interest*.

She had changed into new clothes from the several cases – monogrammed with her initials – Dravot brought from the car: an above-the-knee green dress with matching cloche and scarf, a wendigo-fur wrap worth more than this building.

'We need to represent you as a serious claimant,' Winthrop explained. 'And we've deep pockets.'

'You're not getting it back,' she said, hugging the white fur.

Now, she owed her lodging and her wardrobe to the Diogenes Club. They'd be feeding her schoolboy virgins plucked from Eton and Harrow next.

Obligations.

6

KEDGEREE

Lydia hadn't slept for thinking of *Liam*. Or maybe she had and dreamed of him. She began a long letter to Smudge, but abandoned the effort, deciding she'd telephone later. She wanted to hear the hissed intake of envious breath, rather than merely imagine it. Her news, her vampire, her triumph.

Of course, she was up hours before everyone except servants. Matey was in a fret. The butler, one for the gee-gees, had lost a packet on the races. Whenever he was out of funds, something small but valuable – a fag case, some earrings – would vanish from a guest's luggage. It was a reason few accepted invitations to Mildew Manor. That and the rain. Lydia trusted Matey knew better than to try to pinch anything from an elder vampire.

Mother wasn't down to breakfast.

Wet newspapers had been delivered by a lad more dedicated to getting his daily payment than the postman was to fulfilling his duty when the road was under water. Father took the *Telegraph*, Mother the *Mail*, Aunt Agatha the *Beast*. When the papers were dried out, Lydia would go through them and cut out articles about vampires for her scrapbook and unsolved crimes for Smudge's. Her friend took a keen interest in the criminal *demimonde* and had once had a passion for the decadent adventurer Anthony Zenith. That drug-addicted albino was last year's man. Now, Smudge fairly idolised the Crook, a masked gang boss whose reach, she said, was everywhere. He was always plotting a daring bank raid, lifting a Duchess's sparklers during a charity ball or arranging the mysterious strangulation of a witness before the case came to court. The Crooked Men stick figures were everywhere, including the walls at Drearcliff Grange. As it happened, those were down to Smudge scrawling them herself as she tried to work out the cipher. Upon leaving school, she'd either become a Scotland Yard detective and catch the Crook or a cat burglar and join the Crooked Men. There was debate about whether the hooded miscreant was a vampire or not. If so, he must be a hideous rat-faced one, or else why bother with the cowl?

As she ate her kedgeree, Lydia overheard the maids – Lottie, May, Janet and Ellen – gossiping about the guests. Janet said that Countess Zaleska had pinched her as if she were a side of beef laid out in a butcher shop. May didn't think it right that English girls should have to wait on coloureds and chinks. Lottie said Meinster and von Krolock, 'the pretty ones', insisted the beds in their room be pushed together. She made a gesture with fist and forefinger which excited a fit of giggles. Most of the elders' servants were roomed with Mildew Manor staff, but Kah Pai Mei's *geisha* and Countess Zaleska's secretary stayed with or near their masters. No one knew whether Professor Bey was Kleopatra's servant or consort.

'Bet he's her *lunch*,' said Lottie.

Lydia set down her spoon loudly, to announce her presence.

'You shouldn't disrespect the vampires,' she said, conscious of squeakiness in her voice. 'They are guests. And masters.'

The loose talking maids were shocked silent. They hadn't noticed Lydia the way many didn't notice sharp-eared servants.

For a moment, she thought they'd laugh at her.

Most were her age or only a bit older. She realised she'd always been a little afraid of them.

'Sorry, mum,' said Lottie, stricken.

'So you should be,' said Lydia, awakening to power.

In Mother's absence and with Aunt Agatha snoozing the daylight hours away, she was mistress of Mildew Manor. She could tell servants what to do, what not to say, what to think…

They didn't know *anything* about vampires.

They *should* be afraid. At the slightest hint of insolence, there'd be consequences.

At least they hadn't talked about *him*.

'I'm sure you've work to do.'

Dismissed, the maids curtseyed – not satirically, she saw – and scattered.

She was alone in the room, thrilled.

Already, things were changing. She tucked into her kedgeree with renewed appetite, and cleaned her bowl.

7

ARRIVAL

The rain drummed on the Bentley's canopy and washed across the windscreen. The odd drowned cow stuck in runnels between the roads and the low stone walls which bordered fields. New ponds formed in depressions. The Lake District's lakes were enlarging.

'Ark-building weather,' Winthrop commented.

'A little late for that,' Geneviève responded. 'I'd suggest evolving gills.'

'Can you do that?' He puffed out and sucked in his cheeks like a goldfish. 'Turn mermaid?'

'I can't. Some can.'

'You learn something every day.'

'At my age, you have to forget something too.'

'Wish I could do that. I've a long list.'

Dravot coughed into the speaking tube. An announcement.

The Bentley eased through open gates into a drive lined with megaliths. When the ancient temple was demolished to make way for the house, ringstones were shifted to serve as markers for the approach road. Mildew Manor lay ahead – a patchwork English country pile, partially knocked down and rebuilt over centuries, none of the pieces fitting together. She supposed the window shutters were against the rain, not to shield sensitive vampire guests from daylight. It was hard to believe the sun was up.

The drive was a fast-flowing stream. The Bentley glided

amphibiously to a forecourt where other cars were parked. If any careless chauffeur left a window open a crack, he'd be driving a fish tank when the time came to go home. Rain lashed the gravel, washing reddish grit into the lawns.

Dravot, playing his part, had to get out to knock at the front door. His peaked cap got blown off and he had to chase it out of a bush. Geneviève quite enjoyed that.

Eventually the door opened. Winthrop and Geneviève made a dash.

In the hallway, servants waited along with a big, warm man. His frown might have been permanent. Bites on his wrists and under his cuffs marked him as some vampire's bleeding boy.

Geneviève handed her new wrap to a maid who was less dumbstruck than she might have been but promised to 'keep it safe and dry, with the others'. Geneviève supposed lady elders already present had deposited even more expensive fripperies.

The frowning man was about to ask who the hell they were.

'This is Geneviève Sandrine de l'Isle Dieudonné,' said Winthrop, with confidence. 'An elder of the House of d'Acques. She is expected.'

The frowning man was the fretting man for a moment.

Then, he asked the maid if rooms were prepared for the late arrivals. Eyeing them up, she said Geneviève and Winthrop could go in the Blue Suite. A berth for Dravot would be found in the servants' quarters.

'I'm Roderick Spode,' said the frowning man, as if they were supposed to recognise the name. 'I advise Lady Worplesdon.'

If that was the extent of his duties, Geneviève had drunk a lot of advice in her time, straight from the vein.

'The first session begins in an hour,' Spode continued. 'You are a claimant?'

He was addressing her, but Winthrop responded. 'Lady Geneviève will chuck a *chapeau* in the ring.'

Trust the Diogenes Club to give her a title.

Spode scowled.

'Don't you think she's Queen of the Cats material?' said Winthrop, blandly. 'She has a distinguished history.'

'I've heard of the lady.' Spode tried to conceal distaste.

'Good-oh. Half way there already, then.'

'At the session, a claimant is permitted to have one representative present.'

'That'll be me. I'm Winthrop, Her Ladyship's secretary.'

Spode did not take the offered hand. Winthrop withdrew it as if he hadn't noticed the sleight.

The advisor snorted as if there were a pong in the air, and rattled saliva with his tongue. Was he smelling out interlopers?

No. Geneviève caught it too. Blood. She kept her mouth firmly shut, so as not to startle the servants.

Winthrop was bleeding from the neck, where he nipped himself shaving. Had he deliberately opened little wounds to give an impression? Lady Worplesdon's minion now thought Winthrop was her own Renfield.

'Are we last to arrive?' he asked.

'Barring more surprises,' responded Spode.

'Top hole, Spode.'

8

NEZUMI

The new one was boring. French, blonde and too thin. One of those anaemic-looking vampires forever on the point of fading away. Her warm chap was tolerable. Bite-worthy rather than swoon-worthy.

Lydia was getting ahead of herself. Before she could think of outside dalliances, there was *Liam*.

Impatient for the vampires to rise – late afternoon, she supposed – she went back to her room and did prep.

She found *The Dark Flame* Special with Harriet Vane's monograph about the Karnstein family and re-read it. Disappointingly, there was no mention of Liam... unless he was the same person as Karl Carnstein (or Carl Karnstein), listed (albeit with a question mark) as a son of Ludwig (or Leopold) and Ethelind (Fionguala) Karnstein. Ludwig-Leopold was General Karnstein, though the authoress called him Count Karnstein. Over the years, elders picked up a string of aliases and alternate titles. Miss Vane expressed scholarly impatience, devoting an angry footnote to the number of anagrammatical names used by the late Mircalla Karnstein, most famous of the clan. The writer was piqued at her celebrity, earned by being silly and getting killed. She deemed many Karnsteins of more interest. If Liam and Karl were one and the same person, Miss Vane knew next to nothing about him. She went into depth about the family's unusual Austrian-

Irish commingling, which went back centuries and involved bog creatures called Durward and a dislike of the English. *Her vampire* wouldn't have inherited *that*.

She turned to the latest issue and tried to read an instalment of a new serial, 'To Love a Vampire' by Richard Lestrange. Words swam before her eyes and illustrations blurred as if seen through rain-washed windows. With *her vampire* in the house, the attractions of made-up ones dimmed.

As the afternoon dragged on, Lydia put aside *The Dark Flame* to make a Plan. She *must* see Liam again and make a better second impression.

For that, it was vital B.A.A. not be there. She would always say something dreadful. For preference, Lydia would come across Liam alone. Better still, he would chance upon her! Might he wander the estate, contemplating those weathered stones strewn about the place, trying to make sense of nearly-worn-away runic carvings? Perhaps he would search the library for a book of romantic poetry he wrote centuries ago to a lost love and happened not to have his own copy of? At present, the former wasn't likely. Even vampires didn't go for contemplative walks in mucky weather like this. And any long-lost books of romantic poetry in the Mildew Manor library had been bunged out by Father in favour of bound volumes of *Punch*. So, no go. There was the music room, where Liam might pick out an old air on the pianoforte – only it hadn't been tuned lately and tended to ker-plunk every few bars.

In the end, she gave up imagining meetings and crept out to contrive one.

The vampires were risen – if not from coffins, from beds in the guest rooms.

On the landing, Lydia found one. Not Liam, but the oriental girl with the sword. She sat where Lydia had been last night, cross-legged at the top of the stairs, satchel for a cushion, keeping an eye on the hallway.

The new vampire and her chap were downstairs, waiting by the door of the music room, where Aunt Agatha's boring meetings were to be held. Only B.A.A. could host a gathering of vampire elders and make it tedious. If it were up to Lydia, the vampires would duel for the top spot, with the losers getting their heads chopped off and (of course) Liam winning the last fight by hacking up that Frog twit. Instead, they were going to talk it out, like a meeting of the school fete committee.

She was about to creep back to her room, when the girl turned and reached for her sword. Lydia was sure she was about to lose *her* head, but the girl didn't draw her blade. She looked at Lydia and nodded, some sort of acknowledgment.

Talking with this creature would be good practice for talking with Liam. There wasn't the risk of making a complete clot of herself or blushing red as a fire engine. Getting used to vampires who weren't Aunt Agatha was essential.

'Hello, I'm Lydia Inchfawn,' she announced.

'I know,' said the girl. 'I am S.'

'S? The letter S?'

S nodded. Funny sort of name.

'I'm sixteen,' Lydia lied. 'How old are you?'

S thought a moment and said 'I don't know. A thousand, perhaps.'

Lydia was impressed.

'Or thirteen,' S said. 'I have been thirteen since I turned. I will be thirteen until I die.'

Lydia sat on the step next to the vampire.

The French vamp – Geneviève – was dressed like a Sixth Form girl sneaking out to do the Charleston or the Black Bottom at a bash in town. Yank dances were silly and too much like something a native might do. Lydia hadn't spent painful hours learning the waltz, the quickstep and the mazurka in Miss Downs' dance class to give in and hop like an epileptic kangaroo. Under Miss Downs, girls took turns being the man. Smudge said she wouldn't mind taking the lead all the time if it helped.

'Are you the oldest here?' she asked S.

'No. Kah Pai Mei, to whom I owe fealty, is older. Kleopatra, the Egyptian, is much older.'

'You owe fealty? Are you a servant?'

'I am *yojimbo*, bodyguard. I follow Kah Pai Mei to discharge a debt. You are unmarried?'

Lydia was shocked at that. 'Yes, of course. I'm, ah, only...'

'Sixteen.'

Lydia supposed that where S came from an unmarried sixteen-year-old might be written off as an old maid. Plenty married at not much older in England. Several girls in the Upper Sixth were informally engaged.

'I was married,' S said. 'When I was alive.'

'Did your husband turn too?'

'We never met. We were married by our families, as babies. To seal an alliance. Like this meeting. Someone will be Mikado of Vampires... then, alliances, marriages.'

Some of those Upper Sixths were similarly pledged. The English ones had at least met the cousins or family connections to whom they were to be shackled. Olivia Gibberne, the Head Girl, was set to become Countess of Chelm through marriage to a hideously aged forty-one-year-old earl. Jungle drums said Gibberne borrowed books on poisons from the school library. Smudge said if she wanted to get away with it, she should hire the Crook.

'Gosh,' said Lydia. 'Do you miss him? Your husband?'

S paused. Her face went blank rather than showed concentration, but Lydia could tell she was thinking.

'Yes. I have always missed him. More than I miss many people I've met. If I had met him, I would have forgotten him by now.'

'I'm sorry.'

'It's not your fault.'

'I know, but, well... it's sad.'

'Yes.'

'I'm fourteen, really,' Lydia owned up.

'Are you in a school?' the vampire asked.

'Yes, worse luck. Drearcliff Grange. In Somerset. Mangle-wurzel country. Fouler weather than here. It's why I'm not there now. So much rain that the roof fell in on my dorm. The teachers are nitwits. And there are harpies all over the show.'

S touched the hilt of her sword. 'Flying demons?'

'No, harpies. Prefects. Hostile to all living things. Oh, I'm sorry. I didn't mean to say that. Is it offensive?'

S shook her head. Her hair was very black and cut sharply, fringe over her eyes, square at her chest. She looked so *solemn*.

'I know what prefects are,' S said. 'Also, hockey and cricket. And "midnight feasts". You are in a house?'

'Desdemona. Drearcliff houses are named after Shakespeare women. Goneril, Tamora, Viola, Ariel and Desdemona.'

'You are loyal to your house?'

S seemed fiercely interested. Lydia didn't want to disappoint her. 'Yes, of course.'

She'd been randomly dumped into Desdemona, which was where girls who weren't anything in particular fetched up. She liked her housemates no more than she liked the rest of the school; she only saw them more often, which on the whole made her dislike them more than girls she seldom met. Frankly, Lydia didn't see the point of houses.

'It is as it should be,' S responded. 'Loyalty is important. And "school spirit". "Playing the game".'

This was not what Lydia expected of a samurai vampire.

'I say, S… how do you know all this?'

Shyly, the vampire shifted herself off her satchel and took out a book. It was in Japanese characters. Columns of splotches. Remembering they read from back to front, Lydia looked at what would normally be the back cover. A big-eyed, yellow-haired girl in school uniform – skirt shorter than acceptable at Drearcliff Grange

– was chasing a burglar, waving a cricket bat. At least, she supposed the bald fellow with striped jersey, domino mask, fangs and a bag of candlesticks was a burglar.

'*The Head Girl at the Gables* by Brazil Angela. I have read other books by Brazil Angela. *The Jolliest Term on Record*, *The Leader of the Lower School* and *The New Girl at St. Chad's*. My favourite is *Monitress Merle*. I think Merle is "spiffing". That is correct, no?'

'Spiffing, yes. But it's Angela Brazil.'

S nodded, with a touch of shame. 'Of course. In English, the family name succeeds the given. Have you read Braz... Angela Brazil?'

'One or two.'

Before her V passion was properly enflamed, Lydia had been potty for books about schools. Actually going to a school somewhat spoiled them. Real monitresses weren't forthright and decent like Merle, but pernicious rats. Books never conveyed the bum-numbing tedium of Double Geog on Wednesday afternoon with Frightening Fritton scratching diagrams of terminal moraines on the blackboard and flinging chalk shards with deadly accuracy at girls who nodded off. Angela Brazil schools weren't heated by radiators which failed in winter so that windows frosted from the inside or mysteriously came on during heat-waves to turn classrooms into tropical greenhouses.

'Have you fought for the honour of your house?'

Lydia was a duffer at games. Always picked last, even after Smudge. When it was Lydia's turn to bowl, Witch Walmergrave drawled 'another six wides' before she'd thrown her first. She held a house record for windows broken, which ought to count for something.

'I won a prize for knowing all the Kings and Queens of England in order.'

That was true. Crawford of Viola, up against Lydia, forgot Edward V, one of the princes in the Tower. Edward reigned for less than three months before Richard III locked him away with his little brother and – according to Shakespeare – had him stifled. The prize was a pen, which she had since lost.

S was impressed.

'Honour was satisfied. I salute you, Lydia Inchfawn.'

'Call me Niobe. Everyone does.'

Only Smudge did. At Drearcliff, everyone else called her 'Inchworm'. Or 'Four-Eyes'.

'Niobe,' repeated S.

'Do you have any other names? Besides just the letter.'

The vampire girl looked downcast, fringe over her eyes. 'I lost them. When the clan debt was incurred.'

This was the opposite of the problem Miss Vane noted.

'I would like an English nickname,' S said, shyly. 'A girl should have a special name, for her house friends.'

'Do you remember what your family called you? It can't have been S.'

After a long time, S said, '"Nezumi". Parents might call a girl "Nezumi". I do not know if I am remembering or dreaming or thinking of another girl.'

'"Nezumi",' Lydia repeated.

Despite the sword, S looked younger than thirteen. And very, very far from home.

'What does "Nezumi" mean?' Lydia asked.

'Mouse.'

'I'll call you that, then. Mouse.'

'Thank you, Niobe. I would like that.'

For some reason, Lydia felt tears coming.

This conversation with a vampire was not what she expected. It was ordinary, and – because of that – strange. Aunt Agatha, the only vampire she knew, didn't have conversations. She issued pronouncements, talked over Lydia's head, or tossed off cutting remarks. S wasn't what Lydia expected. B.A.A. would have called the Japanese girl non-V, which went to show how peculiar her thinking was. Only now did it strike Lydia that this sharp-toothed Mouse's idea of a midnight feast might wriggle and bleed more than the hampers girls shared in Angela Brazil books.

She had an impulse to put her arm around this thousand-year-old child and tell her things would be all right.

Other vampires came down from their rooms. Mr Hodge and Mr Croft and the Transylvanian pretty boys. Spode was with them, explaining about Geneviève, the late vampire. None of them were happy. Meinster, in particular, was incensed. The French woman had done something disgraceful, but, annoyingly, the Baron didn't come out and say exactly what it was. With vampires, what counted as disgraceful behaviour? Saying your prayers properly, burning down someone's castle, biting off a goat's willy?

S stood.

'What are you looking at, China Doll?' Mr Hodge said to her, rudely. 'Caught yourself a snack? Nice fat lass, eh?'

Fat! Lydia's face burned.

Mr Hodge licked his lips. Most of his teeth were yellow and rotten, but his fangs were white and perfect. He tried to look jolly, but something was wrong with him. More than being the wrong sort of vampire, the bloated leech greedyguts sort.

Lydia backed away, behind S.

'I am from Japan,' said the girl. 'Not a china doll.'

Mr Hodge's breath was foul. His neck kinked the wrong way for a moment as if he had been hanged and not completely recovered. Mr Croft, biting distaste, pulled him away from the girls and escorted him downstairs.

'All right, Caleb, I'm coming,' said Mr Hodge. 'I'll stick to your bloody schedule.'

Mr Hodge didn't *like* Mr Croft, though they were supposed to be in cahoots. Mr Croft was so used to not being liked he didn't think anything of it, but was wrong. When Mr Hodge took a dislike to someone, he didn't do anything about it straight off but would in the long run. For the moment, he was going along with what Mr Croft, Spode and Aunt Agatha wanted – but he had ideas of his own. And he thought about killing people, all the time.

An insight – Lydia had just had an *insight*. About vampires.

Later, she would tell S.

'Don't mind him, loves,' said Herbert von Krolock, 'he's from Australia, where they stand upside-down. Blood goes to their heads and makes them doolally. He's fed off aborigines and sheep-shearers.'

S watched the other vampires go downstairs.

Kah Pai Mei, her master, appeared on the landing. She bowed to him. He said something to her in Chinese, Japanese or Double Dutch.

S's face *was* like a doll's, now. A mask.

Kah Pai Mei proceeded downstairs. Not looking at Lydia, S followed.

Lydia felt strange. Vampires were here, all around – and they weren't what she'd imagined. Not at all. A tiny worm of doubt curled. What if Madame Glyn and the other authoresses were as misinformed, blinkered or downright *wrong* about vampires as Angela Brazil was about girls' boarding schools?

At the bottom of the stairs, S turned and looked up at Lydia. She made a funny little gesture with her hand – bunching up her fingers like the head of a mouse, nibbling a piece of cheese. A smile flashed on her doll face but was gone when Kah Pai Mei turned to her.

Lydia hoped her new friend wasn't stuck with the High Priest much longer. He was a millstone.

Despite what they said about her behind her back, the pretty boys descended on Geneviève and told her how lovely she looked, clucking over her dress and hair. They complimented her on being thoroughly modern. The Viscount was especially fulsome, as if trying to make the Baron jealous.

Lydia heard a breath behind her and turned.

Her heart leaped with shock. *His* face was close to hers, almost translucent. Like a mask hung over a light bulb. Liam, *her vampire*. How could she have forgotten him? Yet, when talking with S, he had faded in her mind... though she had vowed to think of no one else all day, to strengthen their *psychic bond*.

He might have said something. She couldn't be sure. A *rushing* in her head blotted everything out.

Lydia was standing in his way, at the top of the stairs. General Karnstein was with him in a fancier uniform than before. Liam wore a cadet's tunic. He was close enough for her to taste…

…but she couldn't.

He was there, yet faint. She thought she could see through him, as if he had coalesced out of fog but not yet set. Points of light glittered on his sculpted cheeks.

She blushed – yes, like a fire engine, but it didn't matter somehow – and stood aside. He was beside her now.

His lips parted. He must be asking her name? As if he didn't know, on sight, everything… perhaps he just knew her face, and some other, long-ago name?

'Lydia,' she said, in a raspy whisper that came out wrong.

'Lydia,' Liam repeated.

He had said her name! Like no one else did… not Liddy-*ahh*, like Mother and B.A.A. when they were nagging about her being a useless lump sitting about dreaming over a book… but Li'*di*-ah, as she thought of herself, like the call of bird on Mount Sipylus, a name for taking flight.

When he said her name, his eyes flashed.

Her knees gave out – a *swoon* was upon her – but, cat-quick, he caught her. His arm was solid, not at all made of mist.

'You must be careful,' he said.

There was an Irish lilt to his voice, but also clipped precision. From foreign girls at school, she recognised the stilted perfection of English learned as a second language.

His face was *enormous* now, so close to hers.

He escorted her down. She thought they floated, for she couldn't feel her heels on the stairs.

Her vampire!

9

CAT'S EYES

Given that this weekend promised to seesaw between bore and nightmare, Geneviève was prepared to snatch small pleasures.

In the hallway of Mildew Manor, she enjoyed Meinster's discomfort in a situation where he was obliged to be polite to her. The Baron ground his fangs as Herbert von Krolock gushed about her new look. Meinster had been a golden-haired youth when turned, but the clock hadn't stopped properly. He looked embalmed rather than forever young. She was taller than him by inches, though he wore shoes with lifts. Like many Carpathians, he claimed to be Dracula's get. Geneviève was sure the Count – who had a bat in his belfry about 'relations' between men – only ever bestowed the Dark Kiss on 'brides'. If the Baron *was* of Dracula's bloodline, he must have swallowed distaste and cadged a nip off one of those she-cats. The more Meinster fumed, the more his boyfriend fussed over her. The Viscount – whose rust-coloured quilted floor-length smoking jacket could pass as a ball-gown – posed as a harmless ornament with poor taste in patrons, but perfumed swishery covered a mind as sharp as his eye-teeth. He hadn't put himself forward as King of the Cats.

'You *must* meet Mr Hodge, Gené,' said Herbert. 'He's from Australia. A very *manly* country.'

Hodge wasn't much to look at, though he had powerful arms as well as a flabby stomach. He had Caleb Croft – who knew *exactly* who she and Winthrop were – two paces behind him. Hodge grunted and she smiled in response. Winthrop and Croft exchanged cutting looks.

'Have we met before?' she asked the claimant.

''Appen not.'

There was *something* about him, though. Then, she saw it.

'When did you turn?' she asked, trying to seem curious rather than rude.

'Fifteenth century,' he said, too surprised by the question to lie. 'You?'

'Snap! 1432.'

'1485. You're older than me, lass.'

She could always tell a vampire who had turned in what she still thought of as her day. It was seldom a delight to run into a fellow survivor of her warmth. Dracula, another fifteenth-century vampire, was typical of their age in a way Geneviève strived not to be.

Vlad Tepes turned in 1476. Was there a connection? Hodge's bearing had something of Dracula. Blunt, unconcerned with duplicity. His world was simpler than, say, Lord Ruthven's or Mycroft Holmes'. Just appetite, ambition and brute force. She hoped Hodge wouldn't turn out to be a long-lost, British-born son of the Wallachian *voivode*. Though that might explain why someone so obscure would be claimant to the throne.

'Mr Hodge was recounting delightful exploits in Van Diemen's Land,' said Herbert. 'Hunting cannibal convicts in the wilds.'

Hodge grunted again. Geneviève remembered he'd once been called 'Hogg'. After a razorback, presumably.

The Chinese priest joined their party. Kah Pai Mei was a considerable personage. His moustaches and beard reached to his waist. He had long, straight black hair. An unbidden thought: how would he look with a M. Eugene bob?

Stifling a smile, Geneviève bowed and addressed him in Mandarin.

'It has been many years since I studied at the Temple of the Golden Vampires, but I think often of lessons learned there at the feet of the venerable masters.'

'It is regrettable you were let through the gates,' Kah responded in contemptuous English, affronted a barbarian should sully his own tongue. 'A former High Priest was unforgivably lax. Your "venerable masters" were destroyed by Portuguese ruffians. Westerners are now forbidden. We no longer countenance the pollution of our techniques by lack of discipline.'

'That puts me in *my* place,' she said.

She understood the High Priest had three ways to kill her with his eyebrows.

Why did so formidable a person need a bodyguard? To keep face. Other candidates had retainers, so Kah brought one too. Geneviève didn't recognise the Japanese child. The silver-plated *katana* slung on her back wasn't for flower-arranging or pouring tea.

Meinster, Kah and Hodge glared at each other.

It was dawning on Geneviève that there was a reason she'd spent so little time in the company of her fellow elders these last few centuries.

Something made her turn to look at the stairs.

She could have sworn she saw a ghost. Carmilla Karnstein, dressed as a young man, with a dazed warm girl on her arm. No, it must be the brother. Liam. The resemblance was exact. They couldn't be twins. She'd have known if Carmilla had a *twin* brother.

Liam Karnstein looked at her. Even his eyes were his sister's. In a certain light, Carmilla's eyes had slit pupils like a cat's. In the dark, they flashed green fire. Liam's were the same. Except they weren't, exactly. In her right eye, Carmilla had a slight imperfection, a reddish squiggle. Liam had the same thing, but in his left eye. He was his sister's reflection. The one she didn't have.

Geneviève was fascinated by the vampire youth. And suddenly weak in his presence. It was like being in a stuffy, overheated room, or noticing too late that you'd slipped into a bath without tending to

455

a slashed femoral artery. She felt what the warm felt – herself, slowly bubbling away.

Meinster and Herbert were struck too. A gaggle of warm maids peeped out of a door to catch sight of Liam Karnstein. He had 'it', the famous vampire power of fascination. Like a cobra, he could mesmerise the most unwilling prey. Geneviève didn't have 'it'. Life might be easier with an ability to bend others' wills, but she didn't regret the lack. Most who mastered the trick became self-cantered monsters given to whims, tantrums and random cruelty. Big bloodthirsty babies. Exhibit One: Count Dracula.

Carmilla had 'it' and it hadn't made her happy. Whenever she charmed a companion, she fretted that she wound up talking to herself. Also, 'it' was only good until a brighter bulb happened along. Baron Meinster had low-wattage glamour, but was a candle next to the searchlight of the Karnstein boy. Geneviève, who'd thought herself immune, couldn't look away.

Liam Karnstein gently deposited the girl who had floated at his side on a divan. She looked like she might need to be fanned. Who was she? Geneviève hadn't asked Winthrop about the warm people who lived at Mildew Manor. Servants were all about and Mrs Gregson presumably had living relations.

'Geraldine, you look ridiculous,' said General Karnstein. He had the habit of giving everyone he met English names and sticking by them no matter how often he was corrected. 'What have you done to your hair?'

'What all the girls in this century are doing, General.'

'Tchah – this century!'

He'd been like that with his daughter when she refused to be sewn into constricting mediaeval bodices and started wearing loose dresses cinched under the bust. Then, when he said 'Tchah – this century!' he meant the *eighteenth* century. It was all downhill since the Holy Roman Empire so far as he was concerned.

'I like it,' said Liam, eyes flashing green. 'I can see your ears. You have pretty ears.'

His voice had an Irish lilt, but the timbre was his sister's.

Geneviève had forgotten how overwhelming Carmilla had been when she put her mind to it. For someone so doomed, she'd had a powerful glamour.

'Thank you,' she said. 'I'm Gené. I was a friend of your sister's.'

For a moment, she saw puzzlement in those strange eyes. That red squiggle seemed to contract and expand.

'Of course,' said Liam, regaining composure, kissing her hand. 'I know you. I've always known you.'

His touch was electric. The minute stubble on her neck prickled.

For some reason, the lumpy warm girl on the divan was snarling.

'I don't think we've met,' said Geneviève. 'I would remember.'

Liam smiled, enigmatically. With a hint of fang.

If his brand of 'it' could be bottled and sold at Boots the Chemist, a fortune could be made. So far as Geneviève was concerned, they could call off the election now. If anyone was fit King of the Cats, it was Liam Karnstein.

She bit her tongue.

'Miss Dieudonné,' said Winthrop, who'd been watching. 'Is there something?'

She concentrated. She made the fog go away.

'There was,' she said, 'but there isn't now.'

Winthrop stood down.

Right. She knew something. Liam was dangerous. If he was like his sister, he was as dangerous to himself as to others.

Damn! She'd nearly been *bitten*. She'd certainly been befuddled.

She should have known better. After all these years…

10

FLASHING GREEN

The *witch* was ensnaring him. Lydia saw it happening, but was helpless.

She was so *old*. Not just old – Liam was probably old in years – but old-*looking*. Who was she fooling with her indecent dress and bobbed hair? She was a remnant, a relic, a fossil.

Her vampire would see through the charade.

She trusted him. His heart beat with hers. He had touched her, let her touch *him*. The seconds it had taken to come down the stairs had lasted for an age, the most perfect moments of her life.

They had been in a bubble together, on a cloud.

Love. She dared think it. This was love!

The General sternly spoke with the creature who had the bloody cheek to look at Liam with lizardy eyes. Geneviève's fangs were practically three inches long, the shameless hussy! Lydia knew what that meant. Red thirst was on her and no one was safe!

Liam took Geneviève's withered claw and pressed his full lips to her bony knuckles.

Uck! Foul.

There were ways to kill a vampire. Interfering witches should be burned.

S – Mouse – was her friend, now. If Lydia asked her, would she lop off the frog princess's head? She'd like to see the wretched tick bite persons then! Her eyes wouldn't be so bewitching as dead red marbles in a rotten mask of human hide.

Lydia bet Geneviève dyed her hair that colour. Really, it must be greasy grey. No, green! Looked at in the proper light, she'd have warts! And wattles. Her knees knocked, from gripping a broomstick. The jasmine she wore was only to cover the whiff of grave-mould.

Then, Lydia's heart soared.

The woman backed away from Liam. It was over between them.

He was on to her now. Lydia had never had any doubt. Not really. Liam saw through the mist. There was only one soul for him.

He was, now and forever, *her vampire*!

11

THE CROOK STRIKES!

A partially shrouded piano and a harp in the shape of a lumpen angel with strings for wings marked this as the music room. Portraits of stern composers hung on the walls. Geneviève imagined the infinite evenings stretching out here. The piano stool was probably stuffed with sheet music for 'The Okefenokee Swamp Stomp', 'The Vampyres' High Noon' and 'Alexander's Ragtime Bat'.

The electric light burned unsteadily. Lamps and candles were set all around the house, with matches handy, in case the power gave out. Judging from the way every bulb in the place pulsed and fizzed, the generator was ailing. On arrival in the servants' quarters, Sergeant Dravot was asked if he knew about fixing electrical works; when he said he didn't – though Geneviève would have laid a sovereign to a thimble that he did – the butler just said 'pity'.

Herbert von Krolock idly plucked a harp-string. It twanged, loudly. Baron Meinster glared. The Baron was often irritated. Not a desirable quality in a would-be monarch of the undead. Dracula got angry and killed people. Lord Ruthven was unflappable and got round them. A sulky, tutting king would be hot-collared before the week was out.

Undiscouraged, Herbert arranged his skirted jacket over the stool and sat at the piano. He pushed back frilly cuffs from delicate hands and tinkled a sombre snatch of *Swan Lake* before segueing into a rinky-dink 'Tiger Rag', played from the shoulders *à la* Chico Marx or Jimmy Durante. He winced exaggeratedly whenever a wrong note sounded, but cheerfully bellowed '*a reţine tigru… a reţine tigru*' over the tune.

'*Der* Mildew Manor joanna *ist kaput*,' commented Winthrop.

Meinster shut the piano as if he wanted to chop off Herbert's fingers, but the Viscount snatched his hands away in time.

'Just trying to brighten up your drab, dreary lives, dollies,' he explained. 'I shall now retire from the performing arts and devote myself to good works among fallen seamen.'

Herbert pulled his chin and lengthened his face. A little bat-shape was stuck to his cheek and a crescent moon rose above his eyebrow.

The warm-up act curtailed, Agatha Gregson took her place in a throne-like armchair on a raised dais. Fed recently, she had spots on her collar and chin. No one liked to mention it. Geneviève looked at the hostess and indicated to her own chin. Mrs Gregson frowned, then dabbed herself clean with a handkerchief.

Seven seats were arranged in a half-circle. Comfortable leather chairs, suitable for dozing away an afternoon like an ordinary member of the Diogenes Club. With no obvious order of precedence, Geneviève claimed the second chair from the left. Winthrop made do with a stool placed to one side and a little back – perfect for conspiratorial whispering. Except he wouldn't risk it. Too many sharp ears about.

In her new profession of spy, she supposed she should watch out for clues. Try to overhear stray, telling thoughts.

'Why don't we plump down here,' Herbert told Meinster, seating him on the far left, 'next to the scrumptious Gené.'

She smiled sweetly at the Baron, who stuck out his lower lip like a little boy told to stand in the corner.

Hodge sat at her right. He sank rather further into his chair than he was expecting. Croft stood, rather than squat on the stool.

Then, beyond Hodge: Countess Zaleska, Kah Pai Mei, Kleopatra and Liam Karnstein.

461

Liam was in the chair. The General on the stool.

Karnstein wanted the position of King of the Cats for his son. Liam could certainly pull off regal charisma, but otherwise seemed a nebulous choice. Did his father expect him to breeze onto the throne on cheekbones, a sad smile and sparkling eyes? Judging from their little encounter in the hall, he might pull it off. Then what? Dracula recruited his court by making fresh minions, turning women – his so-called brides – who passed on the Dark Kiss to useful men. The thinner, more refined Karnstein bloodline couldn't match that trick. It would take too long to raise a new generation of Liams and Carmillas to fill out a junta.

The General's perch was further back than the other representatives' stools. He didn't like to be close to others. Why was he so fastidious about keeping himself apart from his own son?

Countess Zaleska was as Geneviève remembered: thick-hipped in a heavy velvet evening gown and matching turban, projecting elaborate, jaded melancholy. Her secretary – a prize baggage if she ever saw one – curled at her feet like a cat. The Countess stroked Ilona's short thick dark hair. Geneviève suspected Miss Harczy went to M. Eugene too. She caught Winthrop ogling the lushly upholstered vamp the way everyone else sneaked looks at Liam. Mercifully, modern fashion favoured the ephebic figure. Nineteenth century formal wear had made Geneviève look like a schoolboy forced into a dress for an end-of-term play. The bustle, which she'd seldom worn, was no use when you couldn't put up a matching front. If you asked most men, and many women of la Zaleska's persuasion, Ilona's deep *décolletage* was unlikely ever to go out of style. Even a Symington Side-Lace brassière, essential underpinning of the flapper look, couldn't flatten *that* silhouette. Geneviève trusted the Diogenes Club put stuff in Winthrop's tea to render him immune to such temptations. The last thing this conclave needed was a Feydeau farce of after-hours bedroom-creeping.

Ilona was modestly dressed beside Kleopatra, whose gold chains and pearl ropes were held together by flimsy wisps of silk. Her exposed skin – ie: most of her – was flawless and dark brown. Her face was a tribal carving, commandingly beautiful if ferocious. Geneviève wasn't entirely convinced the Ancient Egyptian toast of Paris wasn't a new-born kooch dancer from Spanish Town, Jamaica. Her pharaonic shimmy might be an extravagant imposture. She never spoke, so an accent didn't give her away. She couldn't be quizzed on history she'd lived through to catch her out. She communicated via snarls which her associate, attuned to lip-curls and nostril-flares, translated into sentences. Where had Kleopatra dug up Professor Bey? He wasn't even a vampire, though Geneviève would hesitate to call him warm. He was safe among bloodsuckers; anyone who bit the desiccated scholar would draw only a mouthful of dust.

Hodge snacked on blobs of coagulated, crusted gore from a brown paper bag. Pig-blood, dripped from a fresh-cut throat into a pan of sizzling batter. Kenyon Produce marketed these gruesome remains as 'scratchings', but only in the North. Not suited to London vampire tastes, apparently. Noticing her disgusted interest, Hodge mockingly offered her the bag. She wrinkled her nose.

'Please yourself, lass,' he said.

Everyone else was trying to seem refined, but the opal millionaire liked to show an earthier side. Hodge's deliberate vulgarity made him stand out amid these prissy, delicate monsters. He was hardest to read of the claimants. He reminded Geneviève of Al Capone, with whom she'd had an uncomfortable meeting, but also of the thug nobles she'd come across in her warm days, assisting her physician father in the aftermaths of battles which settled nothing. Had Hodge been like that in 1485? Selfish by right of birth and banditry, contemptuous of compassion, impatient with subtleties – but sly with it, not above doing his own butchery. He must have lived through the Wars of the Roses and died at the end of them. Also: Croft's man. Never forget that. With Ruthven behind Croft.

So, the claimants and their advisors? A mixed bunch. Throw in Agatha Gregson and Roderick Spode and this was a desperate crowd.

Winthrop sat, notebook ready like a devoted minion, working on a funny drawing of Agatha and Spode. He was a talented caricaturist. A humorous spy.

Was someone in this room the Crook?

Everyone had something to hide. Including herself. It was up to the outside observer to suspect *everyone*.

That logic would nominate Winthrop as the Crook.

Or the butler. She could tell Matey was a wrong 'un and wouldn't leave valuables on her dressing table. Not that she had any. The butler must have keys to every door and desk in the manor. It didn't make him a mastermind, just a light-fingered chancer. Out here, it must be impossible to get quality servants. Or did Mrs Gregson have uses for someone she could have jailed if he failed to follow orders?

If it was just a matter of putting on a hood and waving a shepherd's stick, the Crooked Men could take turns. If they were anarchists, she'd suspect they put up a straw man to mislead the authorities, but their lunacy hared off the other way. Fascists were big on *führers*. So, there was a real Crook.

How did she get to be a detective anyway? She'd trained as a doctor – several times. She usually thought crime as much a social as a moral issue. She'd been chased by too many policemen, inquisitors and fearless vampire killers to put faith in the law of any land. This monied shower weren't driven to crime by economic circumstance. Except General Karnstein, who'd maintained a show of aristocratic pomp to cover genteel lack of funds for centuries… his motive wasn't slum-born, twelve-in-a-room, fighting-with-rats-for-stale-bread, father's-wages-gone-on-gin poverty, but lost-the-castle-to-the-bailiffs, pawned-the-family-jewels, can't-find-a-rich-merchant-to-marry-the-spare-daughter poverty.

Spode rapped on an occasional table with a gavel.

'Elders, welcome,' he said. 'Lady Worplesdon would like to say a few words before this session goes into, ah, session.'

Cold eyes swivelled.

Agatha Gregson sucked in air around her fang-teeth and met every chill gaze with a freezing stare. Herbert von Krolock whimpered satirically.

'Vampires have gone to the bloody dogs,' their hostess announced. 'I know it, you know it, every fool knows it. The generation of the '80s has turned out feebly. No backbone. No fibre. Thin blood. Scarcely V. Say what you like about the Prince Consort, but he had standards and held to them. No laxity. No fuss. A firm, iron hand. And no nonsense about a velvet glove, either. We all miss Dracula.'

So far as Geneviève was concerned, Mrs Gregson was speaking for herself.

'I intend to do something about it,' she continued. 'Someone here, someone in this room, must step up. We are a rudderless ship, a leaderless tribe. One of you will become King of the Cats.'

The title still sounded like a ragtime ditty.

'Ma'am, if I might athk a quethtion,' began Professor Bey. 'How do you have the power to confirm any claim which might be made?'

'The late Lord Worplesdon owned controlling interests in three national newspapers and the *Leeds Mercury*,' said Mrs Gregson. 'Those interests are now mine. If headlines run declaring so-and-so King of the Vampires, it will be accepted.'

'In England, only,' ventured the Egyptian.

'In the Empire,' insisted Mrs Gregson. 'A situation that obtains in the Empire will become universal. Even in the heathen states of America. Beyond the press, we have a movement ready... a movement which will support whosoever we choose.'

Geneviève looked at Winthrop. Had Agatha just owned up to alliance with the Crooked Men?

'How will the choice be made?' said Herbert. 'Shall we draw straws? Or cut cards?'

'We shall hear each other out and come to a decision.'

Very British and hopelessly optimistic. Everyone would vote for themselves. Except Geneviève, which gave her surprising sway. If she backed someone else, that claimant would have twice the number of votes of his or her nearest rival.

She was sorely tempted to do some mischief.

'No,' said Kah Pai Mei.

Mrs Gregson was astonished.

The High Priest stood, and repeated himself 'No.'

'No, sir?' responded Mrs Gregson.

'No, woman,' said Kah. 'I say no. It will not be. This will not happen.'

The Chinese vampire had the floor. His minion had a hand casually on her *katana*.

'I have come far. I have walked across continents and sailed across oceans. This has not been pleasant. These are barbarian lands. Your European Lord Dracula was a braggart and a dunce. We should curse his name. For centuries, *jiang shi* – what you call vampires – were feared. Now motion picture actors make joke of us. Merchants sell us bags of fried blood-clots. Legend says we shrivel in sunlight. The meaning of this is that we lose power in the open. To remain strong, *jiang shi* must be invisible. The Temple of the Golden Vampires rules in secret. An Empire larger than that of your British Crown, lasting thousands of years. The lords of warm men paid homage in gold, slaves and their daughters' blood. Any who spoke against *jiang shi* were smashed, their names scratched from the parchment of history. Only we had the secret of taking an enemy's past as well as his future. This is as it has always been in the civilised world. When Dracula – an impatient, thoughtless individual – sat on your British throne and shouted, "Look at me, here I am!", it was inevitable he would fall. He must not be replaced. It is time for us to be feared once more. I offer you a choice so simple even a Westerner can understand it… pledge allegiance to the Temple, let every Western vampire become subject to the Golden Masters… or else be cut down as reed before the scythe.'

At that point, the lights went out. There were a few groans.

'If you'll all remain seated,' said Spode. 'The electricity will come on again in a moment... and we can address the *very interesting* points Mr Kah has raised...'

Geneviève saw green Karnstein eyes flash in the dark.

There was a strange, sweet yet sickening smell.

The lights came on again for an instant, then went out. Geneviève retained an image of the face of Kah Pai Mei, eyebrows dangling several feet, eyes bulging, long tongue unrolled.

'Winthrop,' she said. 'Light.'

Winthrop gave her his lighter, which made her hand tingle. Silver. 'Sorry,' he said.

She flicked on a flame. Then the electric light came back.

'Swipe me,' exclaimed Hodge.

'Whatever that means, I second it,' said Herbert.

Countess Zaleska screeched and fell into a faint. If she was Dracula's daughter, Geneviève was Charley's aunt.

Kah still stood, but his arms hung slack. A pole driven through his ribs rested on the floor, propping him up like a scarecrow. Blood rotted through his robes like acid. Corruption hissed inside him. His face was melting, gobbets dribbling down his remarkable eyebrows. One of his fangs fell onto the carpet.

At moments like this, Geneviève regretted her vampirish acute sense of smell. Meinster and Herbert had scented handkerchiefs over their noses.

'Should we take him off that pole?' asked Ilona.

The girl did not look as if she wanted to soil her hands on the task. Maggots writhed in Kah's shredded cheeks. His hair was dirty white and stringy.

'This chappie is properly skewered,' said Winthrop, getting close and peering at the wound. 'Truly dead. He came a long way for such shabby treatment.'

Winthrop was about to touch the corpse. The bodyguard drew her sword and put its edge to his throat.

'A bit late for that, old thing,' he said.

The Japanese vampire's eyes burned with shame.

'Put the pig-sticker away, would you? I call this a black mark in your exercise book, Miss *Kyûketsu Shôjo*.'

She followed orders. Winthrop had promoted himself from secretary.

Geneviève glanced around. As before, *everyone* looked guilty. Matey was in the room, which she hadn't noticed before the lights went out. If this homicide were investigated by an American police department, the butler could expect a couple of nights' assault and battery before – guilty or not – they got a confession from him and shut the book.

'Nasty,' she commented. 'It would take a lot of strength…'

…which every vampire here had, not excluding the sissy boys and the old woman who acted like an invalid.

'…to do this. Plus, stealth.'

That was rarer.

Some of the company could see in the dark better than she could. No one piped up with an accusation.

'I… did not hear, did not sense…' said the bodyguard.

The samurai looked like a lost little girl. A tear of blood on her cheek. No, it had fallen from her master's wound.

'Gené, consider the weapon,' said Winthrop. 'The proverbial sharpened object.'

A length of wood like a quarterstaff had been shoved into Kah from behind and below, thrust up through his heart and out of his chest.

'He should not have spoken of Prince Dracula so,' declared Baron Meinster. 'He has earned his impalement.'

Kah *did* resemble Vlad Tepes' hoist-on-stakes victims. She was not about to try to pin the crime on Dracula's ghost.

'Interesting,' said Winthrop, 'but that association is not what I meant when I said you should consider the weapon.'

Winthrop pointed down, at the carpet.

The end of the staff had rucked the rug around it. Winthrop knelt, avoiding trickles of ichor. Nasty, acidic stuff, it would eat through floorboards.

Winthrop flattened out the carpet. The staff ended with a curve like a question mark.

'It's a crook,' she said.

12

BRITISH BUSHIDO

'Hello, police,' Spode shouted into the telephone, 'there's been a murder... yes, someone's been *murdered*... by person or persons unknown!'

Lydia's heart knotted.

Liam!

No, it was all right. Liam came out of the music room with the others. The tightness in her chest eased.

Who was missing?

She hoped it was the French cow, but – no – she was still lolling about, worse luck.

'A Chinese gentleman,' Spode shouted, as if the telephone only worked if yelled into.

It must be Mouse's employer, the High Priest.

Crivens! Where was Mouse?

Lydia had arranged herself on the settee in the hallway so as to look her best for Liam. She'd expected him to come out on his own, to search for *her*, rather than in a clump of perplexed, horrified vampires. She might even have dropped off once she got comfortable, but was wide awake now.

There'd been screaming. It seemed a bit Non-V. The twittering and the bother. V ought to mean unruffled, icily undemonstrative, always composed. Not like this mob at all. Yet, these were elders, *proper vampires*. She felt a spark of superiority, an impulse – usually spurred by soppy or senseless girls – to snap 'Oh, *grow up*!'

'Yes, Inspector, ah, Hound,' said Spode, who got the cord knotted about his waist while trying to talk into the telephone and keep up with what was going on inside the manor at the same time. '…right away… I'll take charge until you get here.'

Spode untangled himself and replaced the receiver. He coughed loudly. The chatter continued. Aunt Agatha stamped. Everyone shut up and looked at her.

'The police have asked me to keep you all here,' Spode announced.

'As if we could go anywhere in this filthy English weather,' sniped Viscount von Krolock. 'The motorcars are underwater.'

Mildew Manor was always being cut off. Once, Lydia missed three weeks of school because of a flood – so wretched roads and an easily washed-away bridge weren't entirely bad things. Mother had worried Aunt Agatha would go mad from blood deprivation and attack the servants.

'This will be got to the bottom of, mark my words,' said Spode. 'A claimant has been killed…'

'I don't think Kah was a claimant,' said Mr Winthrop, Geneviève's chap. 'He made a speech about it, remember? Seemed to disapprove king-anointing.'

'He's not a claimant now,' said the Viscount. 'He's a puddle. You'll never get that stain out, Lady Worplesdon. The only thing for it is to burn the carpet.'

Aunt Agatha did not look best pleased.

'Are we to be eliminated, one by one?' demanded Liam's father. 'Is this English treachery?'

'If you would all calm down,' boomed Spode.

Matey sidled up to Spode and discreetly said something.

'I've just been informed that… ah, the road to the estate *is* impassable…'

…which meant someone had tried to scarper and got stuck. Matey had muddy shoes.

'…this may delay the arrival of the police.'

Commotion. Only Matey looked relieved. He probably had a swag bag which needed hiding.

Spode raised his voice, again, 'So we shall just have to make the best of it!'

'There's an assassin among us!' exclaimed the Viscount. 'Make the best of that!'

The darkie woman – who wore practically nothing, so you could see she really *was* that colour all over – made a disgusted sound. Her fingernails were six inches long. Did she do special bottom-flexing exercises to get her bum looking like two cushions of muscle?

'Kleopatra is not thatisfied,' said her pet mummy. 'Athurantheth were given. We were to be under a flag of truth. Protection was promithed.'

Flag of truth? Lydia worked it out: truce.

Spode pulled out a revolver and waved it.

'You're all protected *now*,' he insisted. 'Except the one of you that's a bally murderer! He's not protected, at all. He's hunted!'

More commotion. Lydia was afraid Spode would shoot at the ceiling. The electric chandelier, unstable at the best of times, might crash down on someone's bonce.

'I didn't come here to be accused of murder,' exclaimed Hodge.

'Really, old chap?' said Winthrop. 'Where do you go to be accused of murder, as a rule?'

For a warm man, Winthrop was droll. And dishy. But nothing next to *her vampire*.

Liam kept quiet. Alone of the household, he wasn't in a tizzy over the Celestial's death. Calm, smooth, clever.

He would have a plan. When white wolves besieged the castle, Count Magnus had a plan. He didn't let the pack fetch Lady Diana away to make her their captive queen and bear litters of cubs.

Lydia knew something she must tell Liam. Something important. A clue!

Might she and Liam catch the murderer together? An adventure!

In books and motion pictures, persons grew close to each other while having adventures. It could happen.

Countess Zaleska was helped out of the music room by her secretary. The Countess was whiter even than usual, but Lydia saw she was not as overcome as she pretended. Her head was on Ilona's shoulder and she was hugging the girl, which made it awkward for both of them to walk. But she looked out, carefully, through slit eyes. She licked her lips, then sneaked a kiss – a bite – of Ilona's neck. Used to it, Ilona carried her mistress along and helped her onto the settee. The Countess fanned herself.

Lydia was drawn to the music room. The door was open.

'Where do you think you're going, child?' said Spode. 'Come away, girl. There's nothing to see.'

Through the doorway, Lydia saw that wasn't true.

Mouse sat, cross-legged, head bowed, by what looked like a melted wax statue. With a thrill, Lydia realised she saw her first dead body. Well, her first dead body which wasn't a vampire and still walking about.

The High Priest was so old he was rotting to nothing. They'd have to scrape him up to bury him or send him home to be burned or whatever the heathen did with their truly dead in China.

Ugh!

He was stuck on a pole.

'Is that a crook?' she asked.

'Well spotted, young Lydia,' said Winthrop. 'It is indeed.'

The Crooked Men had committed an atrocity in Lydia's home! Smudge would go purple! Perhaps the Crook himself was nearby?

'Let's all go into the drawing room,' said Spode. 'Matey, if you could have, ah, refreshment sent up from the kitchens. A hot drink will calm everyone's nerves. Hot, with something in it, eh? Do the world of good. A nice pot of tea.'

'I never drink… tea,' said Baron Meinster.

Aunt Agatha was addicted to a tea Lipton's sold for vampires.

Darjeeling with blood-clots. Rosie M. Banks must have shares in Lipton's, because the vamps in her mysteries drank Tea-Blood all the time and kept breaking off the story to say how lovely it was. When the vampire romance craze bit, Lydia had tried drinking it and upset her tummy. Mother forbade her from touching the stuff again.

Despite complaints, the company did what Spode suggested. Most grumbled, but all marched into the drawing room. Mother was there, rattling her necklace like a rosary. She would start one of her headaches soon. She always got them when Spode took charge.

Lydia hoped Liam would stay in the hall, but his father hustled him along.

Spode ordered Matey to have a footman guard the music room. The body – what was left of it – was not to be fiddled with. He was particular on the point.

'You,' said Spode, pointing at her, 'go to bed.'

Lydia curtseyed but stuck her tongue out when Spode turned his back.

She had no intention of going to bed. Not when it was getting exciting.

Besides, it was *ages* till her bed-time. She looked at Eric's watch and saw it wasn't yet eight o'clock. It was hard to tell day from night at Mildew Manor, and evening just got lost. Thick cloud cover and unending rain effectively brought sunset forwards to just after lunch.

Matey scurried off. Spode went into the drawing room and slammed the doors. Lydia walked towards the stairs, to fool him. Alone in the hall, she stopped and listened.

There was shouting in the drawing room. Perhaps the vampires would kill Spode? Or the murderer might get him with poison smeared in his teacup. Maybe God – the proper God, or one of the thousand old ones from the caves – would finally pay attention to Lydia's prayers and strike the Odious Spode with lightning.

Someone was dead already. Chances are there'd be more corpses before morning. So, it wasn't unreasonable to suppose – to *hope* –

Roderick Spode would be one. The Crooked Men *must* have him marked for death. Split from gullet to giblet with an ornamental dagger. Shot in the eye with a stone scarab fired from a catapult. Or defenestrated, from one of the high windows. Geneviève Flirty-Bat could get it, come to that. Maybe a quarrel from a trick crossbow rigged up behind the books in the library straight through her heart? While she was wishing, Lydia wondered if Aunt Agatha might finally die peacefully in her sleep at some point – which didn't happen to vampires that she knew of, but there was always a first time. With B.A.A. gone, Mother and Father could sell Mildew Manor to an American and move somewhere decent – with proper drains, electricity that worked and a picture-house within a bus-ride's distance.

Cheered by contemplation of the probable happy outcome of a Mildew Manor massacre, Lydia skipped into the music room and stopped short as if slapped. She'd read about what happened when vampires were killed, but hadn't expected the stink. Kah Pai Mei was a skull on a stick, face flaked away. His eyebrows still clung to the bone.

Mouse looked up at the High Priest.

A spot of blood marred her perfect cheek. Lydia wiped it away with her thumb, but a stain – a scar – remained.

Mouse had a short knife in her hand. Too dull for cutting. Her scarf was wrapped around a part of the blade.

'Niobe,' she said. 'I am glad it is you.'

'What a turn-up for the books,' Lydia said. 'Spode is going spare!'

'I have a favour to ask.'

'Fire away,' Lydia said. 'Anything I can do.'

'I must cut out my insides, but that will not end my shame. Another must help. Please…'

Mouse put down her knife and drew her *katana*, which she passed to Lydia.

'This Yasutsuna blade is older than me,' said Mouse.

Lydia had hefted a sword when she played Tybalt and had to

perform duels. She'd enjoyed killing Carstairs' Mercutio more than being killed by Trevlyn's Romeo. Mouse's *katana* was heavier, more beautiful than the button-ended foils from the school prop-store. Lydia caught sight of herself in polished silver. The sharp edge caught the light and she saw a black, red-eyed, writhing horror. Mouse's reflection. Lydia turned the sword so she wouldn't see that again. She tried to scrub the glimpse from her mind.

'When I have disembowelled myself, you must strike off my head.'

Lydia was appalled. She nearly dropped the sword.

'Why would I want to do that?'

'Honour. I am *yojimbo*. I have failed my master…'

It was hard to argue the point. Kah Pai Mei's arm fell off. It clattered on the floor, bony forefinger pointing.

'Your Mr Winthrop says I have a black mark in my exercise book.'

He wasn't *her* Mr Winthrop (worse luck).

'But it's not as if *you* killed him, Mouse.'

'I was pledged to protect the High Priest.'

Mouse untucked her sailor-collared tunic from her skirt, showing her flat tummy. She picked up her knife again and pricked herself in the side, not breaking the skin.

'I must atone for my shame…'

The vampire tensed, ready to press the knife into her bowels. Mullane, a girl with a freakish passion for things Japanese, had delighted the dorm with a detailed, gruesome explanation of *hara-kiri* or *seppuku* (the same thing, in spoken and written language). When a noble Jap let the side down, he (or she) was obliged to commit ritual suicide in messy, yet elegant fashion. Mouse was supposed to saw through her belly with the *tantō* (a blunt knife) and tumble her innards into her lap. A *kaishakunin* (loyal retainer) should be on hand with a *katana* to sweep off the disgraced samurai's head if they hesitated during the gut-gouging part of the evening's entertainment. Strictly, the retainer was supposed to use a *dakikubi* cut, so the head remained attached to the torso by a flesh-hinge, but flopped forwards onto the chest.

Lydia did not hold up the sword.

'Dash it all, Mouse, you can't do this.'

Mouse looked solemnly through her fringe.

'Really, you can't,' Lydia said, het up. 'It's not playing the game. It's giving in.'

'It is the way of *bushidō*.'

'It's not the way of Desdemona House,' Lydia said. 'We don't cut out our stomachs when we're down a man. We get up and… well, do something about it.'

Mouse was listening.

'School spirit, you know – British *bushidō*.' Lydia tried to remember her Angela Brazil. 'You can't just be out for a duck and toddle back to the pavilion. The game's not over. There's another innings and all to play for. If you kill yourself, Mr Kah will go unavenged. You should at least take a chuck at it. Someone did for him and nobody knows who. It's a mystery. A *murder* mystery. The rest – the grown-ups – are nattering uselessly about it. They're nowhere near finding out who the murderer is. Surely, the best thing you can do is catch the killer. Then you can stick your knife somewhere useful…'

Mouse relaxed and let her knife-point hover – away from the dimple she'd made in her side.

'That *would* be honourable,' she agreed.

'Of course, Mouse,' said Lydia. 'There's a madman on the prowl. It's up to us to stop him before he kills again. Or after he's killed a few more, but before the sun rises on a house full of corpses.'

'Us.'

'You, me… and Liam…'

'Liam Karnstein?'

Mouse frowned slightly. Lydia hadn't told her vampire friend about her and Liam, she realised. An incredible oversight.

'He's our age,' Lydia explained. 'Not a grown-up.'

Lydia realised something, or thought she did. Vampires were the age they turned, not the number of years since they were born. Aunt Agatha could boss about vampires who'd been around for centuries.

Mouse seemed unsure. 'He will help?'

'Yes, of course. We're… we're very well-suited, if you ask me. I *know* something, Mouse. Something important no one else does. Except one person who's trying to keep it quiet. Something *relevant to the case.*'

Mouse returned her *tantō* to its wooden sheath. She stood up, brushed carpet-fluff from her knees, tucked in her tunic, retied her scarf and took back her *katana*. She considered the shining blade for a moment – some ritual, looking at the horrid face reflected back at her? – and sheathed it too, with a *snick*!

Now, Lydia shared what only she knew.

'Spode talked to the police on the telephone.'

'Yes?'

'He says they say they can't come straight away because the Manor is cut off by the floods. Spode is telling everyone someone called Inspector Hound put him in charge. He's striding about like a sergeant-major, giving orders.'

Mouse nodded.

'But, not twenty minutes ago, I tried to use the telephone…'

…to call Smudge, to tell her about Liam.

'…and the line's down. Spode only pretended to talk with the police!'

Lydia took the receiver and toggled the cradle. Not a sausage.

'Crumpets,' exclaimed Mouse.

'Double crumpets,' agreed Lydia. 'With strawberry jam!'

'…and cream!'

'Now, we've got to tell Liam,' said Lydia. 'He's a boy. He'll know what to do.'

Mouse said nothing, but gave a sharp nod.

'That's the spirit,' said Lydia. 'Chin up and soldier through.'

'Lydia,' said Mouse, 'you are a prick.'

'You mean "brick", Mouse. A prick's a tiny little wound or… well, or the thing a boy has…'

They both giggled, like schoolgirls.

13

IN THE DRAWING ROOM

'Any one of us could have killed the High Priest,' said Spode.
Except you, thought Geneviève.

Whoever had done it was fast, strong and quiet. A vampire.

That probably put Winthrop out of it too. But not Dravot, who must be about somewhere, up to something.

The Diogenes Club weren't above 'bold strokes'. If the Ruling Cabal – in Charles' absence, she had no idea who they were – decided it was for the greater good that an elder vampire be stricken from the lists, they wouldn't take her into their confidence. She remembered why she'd quarrelled with them in the first place.

'When the police get here, they'll want to speak with us all,' Spode continued. 'It might be best if we settled on what to tell them. We don't want to go contradicting each other accidentally.'

'A Chinaman is dead,' said Meinster. 'Is that even a crime?'

'Are you volunteering a confession, Baron?' asked Winthrop.

Meinster shut up. Herbert fondly patted the Baron's hair, experimentally stroking it the wrong way so it stuck up like Liam Karnstein's. The Viscount would dress Meinster up in Oxford bags and a straw boater next, and pack him off for banjo and Charleston lessons.

'We are all *doomed*,' lamented Countess Zaleska. 'It is for the best.'

Geneviève wasn't ready to surrender just yet. Elders like the Countess often complained – frankly, *whined* – about the *ennui* of eternal existence. Always, elders with enough money not to be troubled by worries other than those they invented for themselves. Recently, a breed of Viennese quackery had sprung up to prey on them. Geneviève respected Freud and his circle: Ernest Jones's monograph on 'Dracula and the Oral-Sadistic Impulse' pertinently suggested trouble might have been avoided had the Old Count talked about his dreams before making them come true. However, Freud inspired bearded, bespectacled confidence men to set up as psychoanalysts. For ridiculous fees, they would pretend to be awake while vampire clients lay on couches and retold convoluted, trivial life histories. You couldn't pay Geneviève to listen to Marya Zaleska for five minutes. As a qualified physician, she'd prescribe a spending spree, some nice new turbans and a fling with a warm chorus girl to pull the Countess back from the abyss.

Geneviève found the world, on the whole, more annoying than boring – and hadn't grown out of wanting to see what happened next.

Hodge got up and walked to the door.

'Fook this for a game of soldiers,' he said. 'I'm off.'

'It would be best if we stayed together,' said Spode.

'Where's Yum Yum, then? She were next to Chu Chin Chow when he got spiked. Best placed to do it.'

Much as she disliked agreeing with Hodge, that made sense. Who better to kill someone than their own bodyguard? Precedents went back to Caligula. Whisper was Vlad Tepes originally died at the swords of his own guards. Having dressed up as a Turk for a laugh, he was surprised when his fellows took it seriously enough to kill him. Later, they said they didn't recognise him and it was all a mistake… but Dracula was never that good an actor.

Geneviève hadn't got an impression of treachery from the girl, but her instinct wasn't infallible. She'd worked with Jack Seward for months, not suspecting he was the Silver Knife.

'Mr Hodge, would you be happy to stay if we brought the girl – what's her name? – here?'

'What do you think? No. I'd not be bloody happy to stay. And what about Mrs Karnstein? She's loose too.'

Hodge hadn't noticed Dravot – servants were invisible to these people, even formidable vampire servants – or else he'd lump him in with the other suspects.

'My wife rests,' said General Karnstein. 'She is not to be disturbed.'

That might bear investigation. Geneviève exchanged a look with Winthrop, who'd also noted Karnstein's oddly uxorious spasm. There was *something* about Ethelind. Like her son, she gave the impression of not being all there. Yet, she was a practiced deceiver.

When Carmilla was alive, the family m.o. was to palm the girl off on *nouveau riche* boobs as cuckoo in the nest. After a convenient carriage accident or fainting spell in the vicinity of a nice villa, the Countess dropped hints until the near-invalid girl was put up in the spare room, where she could batten on the spare daughter. Meanwhile, the General (who went by 'Count' then) persuaded a wealthy fathead or said fathead's social-climbing wife to invest in a military riding academy or subscribe to a fund to erect an equestrian statue of his heroic cousin Lord Durward. Without promising, he would off-handedly mention that when next the matter of ennobling bourgeois clods came up he might have the ear of the Emperor. What Happened to Carmilla put paid to the scam.

'Rests? Hah!' said Hodge. 'Pickled more like. The micks are all soaks.'

He was still determined to leave.

'I say, old man, it's probably best if you didn't toddle off just yet,' Winthrop said to Hodge. 'Might look suspicious, don't you know?'

Hodge stopped short and really looked at Winthrop.

'Who're you, lad?'

'Lady Geneviève's secretary. Edwin Winthrop, at your service. I'm here in an advisory capacity.'

'Take your bloody advice and stuff it up your bloody arse. Do I make mesself clear?'

'Pellucid, Mr Hodge. Still, if you leave, you'll be sought to "help the police with their enquiries" by dawn.'

'Why would I want to kill the chink?'

'Why *wouldn't* you? I daresay most of us would want to kill Kah Pai Mei. He was a horrible, horrible person. If I thought about it, I'd *want* to kill him. But I'm not one of you vampire bods. It's highly unlikely I *could* kill him. Everyone else here could, though. The elders, that is. Not you, Spode. You're a bark-not-bite cove. Must be funny for you lot. *Nosferatu, upiór, jiang shi, kyûketsu.* Vampires. You had centuries in the dark. Oh, I know, you were persecuted... my condolences, General, I heard what happened to your daughter. But you had a *power* then. Kah said as much. When you weren't in the open, most folk didn't even believe you existed... well, you could get away with practically anything. With powers of fascination, strength of ten mortal men, speed of a rattlesnake, claws of a panther, ability to take other shapes. Must have been a temptation. Getting away with murder, I mean. For all those years, if you wanted to kill someone... well, then, you bally well did. The plods could do little about it. If they even had plods in the dim and distant. No, if someone ticked you off by – oh, let's say, making a speech about how you're all lower than vermin and should pay obeisance to some Yellow Peril Temple in Far Cathay, you could just top him and be done with it. Even before you were vamps, most of you were barons and earls and princes... back in your day, 1066 and all that, you could flap a languid hand or throw a hissy fit and have villages who refused to pay tribute burned to the ground or the wench who spilled the stew on your doublet and hose drawn and quartered. When Dracula left his castle and changed the world, you were kings again, openly... then the rest of us got used to you, and suddenly you're just people. Extraordinary people, no mistake. But rules now apply. The tax-man comes round. The boot-black must be paid. And, as the Book doth say "thou shalt do no murder". So, my question – my *theoretical* question – is: after all those years of being able to kill without consequence, is it a habit you, any of you, can easily give up?'

'*Who* are you again?' asked General Karnstein.

'Winthrop, General,' he said, smiling and holding out a hand he knew damn well no one would shake. 'Just making an observation, not an accusation.'

Hodge hadn't left. Winthrop's little lecture had sunk home.

'I've never murdered anybody and I wouldn't lower myself to it now,' said Herbert. 'I am blameless as new-fallen snow…'

'New-fallen snow has killed a lot of people,' Geneviève said.

'Good point. The warm, if they get cold enough, they die, don't they? I should have thought of that.'

Geneviève rather liked Herbert von Krolock. He made no pretence of being useful. If he were a claimant, she'd vote for him.

Baron Meinster, however, was a malign little slug. A Woolworth's Vlad the Impaler.

'If I might be permitted to athk, why were you tho contherned with the hook?'

Professor Bey – someone else who wasn't an idiot – addressed Winthrop.

'What hook?' blustered Hodge. 'What are you talking about, cloth-head?'

'It's a *crook*, Professor. Like a shepherd's. You know, the ones who washed their socks by night.'

'But what ith the *thignificanth* of the crook?'

'I just thought it interesting,' Winthrop said, weakly.

'You were thure to tell thith lady,' said Bey. 'Motht inthithtently.'

'Tell them, Winthrop,' said Caleb Croft.

Everyone perked up to hear from the man who spoke so seldom. Some must know who he was, but even those who didn't would know to be afraid of him. Croft didn't have the knack of seeming harmless. Even if Winthrop were right, and almost everyone in this room was a murderer many times over, there were degrees. Barring truly extraordinary revelations, Caleb Croft was the worst man here by an attenuated stick of sedimentary calcite.

'What does this mean?' demanded Agatha Gregson.

Winthrop had the floor again. Something about him made people listen. If he were a vampire – rather, if he were more of a vampire – he could be King of the Cats by snapping his fingers.

'Do you hold some sort of official position?' demanded Spode – who was only now white with terror.

'Not *official*,' Winthrop admitted. 'Not like our secret policeman, here. But I am a concerned citizen.'

'*What about the hook?*' repeated Bey.

'Have you seen those stick-figures on walls? The Crooked Men?'

Most looked puzzled at that, or pretended to.

'I have,' said Ilona Harczy, putting up her hand. 'Like gypsy marks, but in the city.'

'There are scratches like that on the stones outside,' said General Karnstein. 'By the drive.'

Geneviève hadn't noticed that.

'I too have theen the thingth,' admitted Bey.

'The scribbles are all different, but the leader of the procession, the bent-over figure, always carries a crook. The leader of the Crooked Men is called the Crook. He – or she – will be your vampire killer, unless I miss my mark. Mr Croft can fill you in with the *curriculum vitae* of this dangerous bounder.'

Heads swivelled.

'The Crook is a criminal,' said the secret policeman. 'If he exists. The Crooked Men are real. Enemies of the State. The Crook is a phantom. A story to frighten children.'

'Interesting that you should think so, old bean,' said Winthrop. 'Didn't you once knock about with Jonathan Wild? Back when you called yourself "Charles Croydon"? In the jolly days of highwaymen and rogues like Dick Turpin and Captain Hog and Jack Shepherd. I've heard it said that you learned your trade from Wild...'

Croft admitted nothing.

'Fascinating fellah, J. Wild, Esquire,' Winthrop carried on. 'Rose from humble origins to become Thief-Taker General, the most powerful, ferocious policeman in London. But he had another job. As the biggest thief – the biggest *crook* – in the city. A clever game, playing both sides. The more Wild thieved, the more he was needed to catch thieves. One job fed the other. You wouldn't happen to have a second career, would you?'

He was taking a chance.

Croft's fists knotted and unknotted. His nails grew. He might rip out Edwin Winthrop's heart. Or, worse, mark him down as 'future business' and take his time to think of a fitting punishment for insolence.

'Stand down, Croftie,' said Hodge. 'Winfield, or whatever your name is, I don't like you. Or your doxy. You talk round a thing rather than come out and say it. But you're not a fool. I've a job for you, if you'll have it. In me court. One thing's plain now. There's only me. Nancies and darkies and fainting biddies. They won't do, will they? It's me. I'm King of the Cats.'

Mrs Gregson started applauding.

Geneviève looked at the others. Karnstein would still argue for his son and Meinster for himself. They cancelled each other out. Zaleska was too feeble and Kleopatra not interested.

'Any other nominees? Good, let's get to the bloody coronation.'

'There's…' Winthrop looked at her.

Damn, she thought. Not me.

'I nominate… Liam Karnstein,' she said.

Even the General was surprised. His black eyebrows shot up towards his white fringe.

She'd had to pick one of them. And Liam had… those eyes. Carmilla's eyes. She couldn't believe that had been it. Meinster was a petulant, spiteful weakling and the others had no chance. So it was Liam. Beautiful, blank Liam.

'I second the nomination,' said Herbert. 'I think Liam would make a perfectly delicious King of the Cats.'

Herbert would need a new boyfriend. Meinster's face looked like a hot iron mask.

The General held back. If he could get what he wanted without personal effort, why waste words?

If Hodge was angry, he didn't show it.

'I've a nomination, too,' he said.

Croft gave him the nod. And, in pique, so did Meinster.

'Want to back down, lad?' Hodge said to Liam.

The Karnstein boy hadn't shown interest in his possible elevation.

'I would prefer not to,' he said.

'Then it's on. Between us. You and me. For the crown.'

Winthrop nudged Geneviève, but she stood with her arms folded. She'd told him she would not be a claimant.

'Mrs Gregson declares this session closed,' said Spode, who'd been clawed by the hostess. 'We shall take a break and reconvene at midnight.'

14

THE INTREPID THREE

Lydia thought getting Liam away from his father might be a problem, but *her vampire* was left alone.

The grown-ups were preoccupied. General Karnstein, Baron Meinster and Countess Zaleska were in an aristocratic foreign huddle in one corner of the hall. Mr Hodge, Mr Croft and Mr Spode had an untitled British conspiracy in another. Plotting was about, she could tell. The Chinaman's murder was only one item on the agenda, a late addition to the weekend's subjects for discussion. In novels and moving pictures, proper vampires spent less time on boring politics. If they had to establish who was clan chieftain, they'd turn into big bats and have at each other with fangs and talons until there was no doubt who ruled the roost. The fight was over with quickly, the better to get on with swoonworthy matters. These elders would rather pass a procedural motion or make a point of order than alight on a person's balcony or climb up the outside of a gothic tower to suckle from a soul-mate. Unthinkably, they were rather dull.

Liam was on the settee, unmoving: a dummy abandoned by a busy ventriloquist. Was he in that dead-to-the-world state vampires assumed while passing daylight hours encoffined on beds of their native soil? That aspect of the condition sounded a) uncomfortable and b) filthy. She hoped after she turned she wouldn't have to drag about a carpet-bag full of Cumbrian sod. Still, as Smudge said, a layer of dirt could hardly be *worse* to sleep on than the lumpy cots of Drearcliff Grange. Liam was not asleep, just still, observant. He might have been thinking of her − in fact, she was sure of it. He could *only* think of her. Their *psychic bond* was an invisible elastic string between their souls.

Peril arose. The ghastly Geneviève looked set to swoop down like a vulture in roll-top stockings. If Liam was lyrical Amphion reborn, the French creature was cruel Leto. Providentially, Viscount von Krolock and Miss Harczy got in the witch's way. They fussed over her for reasons beyond the understanding of mortal woman.

'Come on, Mouse,' Lydia said, dragging her friend to the settee.

When the two girls stood over him, Liam stirred to life. He was elegant, but quick. He looked up − with those *eyes*, ye gods! − and Lydia was rapt by flashing green. He didn't smile − his unlined face wasn't shaped for silly grins − but his lips parted slightly. His red tongue slipped across his white teeth. He was *tasting* the air, tasting *her*.

'Liam,' she said, concentrating. It was the first time she said his name out loud in his presence − she would remember that, and so would he. 'You must come with us, with me and Mouse. It's *important*.'

A moment passed. Liam seemed uncomprehending, but Mouse tugged his sleeve and he came to life. He stood − taller than her, of course, so she had to look up at him − and let them lead him into the library. He was dreamily biddable, open to suggestion. He instinctively knew to take her seriously. Another sign of their *psychic bond*. They'd barely spoken, barely *touched*, as Liam-and-Lydia, but their Niobe-and-Amphion souls were entwined.

The library was the least-used room in the house, and no wonder. A patch of ceiling was rotted. Rain seeped in somewhere and flowed through holes in the plaster, dripping into an array of china − old chamber pots, mostly − with a chorus of plinks and splashes.

Mouse was one of those persons who can't enter a room full of books and not look at the spines. Within three or four seconds, she determined that Mildew Manor offered nothing worth reading.

Lydia kept *her* books in her room, where they didn't get damp and mouldy. *The Count* had pride of place, propped up so the eyes of Count Magnus – a portrait photograph of Rudi V, with a bat-wing collar – could transfix her as she fell asleep. She rearranged the books of Salome Otterbourne, Rosie M. Banks and Harriet Vane weekly, unsure whether to shelve them in order of publication or internal chronology. Vane created the problem by writing her story out of order. No matter how boring the *Vampyrrhic Chronicles* got, Lydia had to buy each novel to keep the set complete.

She must remember to turn her copy of *The Count* spine-out. Rudi V had oodles less 'it' than Liam.

'Spode's in on the murder,' she said. 'He fibbed about talking with the police.'

Liam nodded, encouraging.

'It's up to us, to you, me and Mouse,' she continued. 'None of the grown-ups will help. They're either in it too or too thick to notice.'

'Us,' he said, hissing the S slightly.

'We three,' said Mouse. 'We must be intrepid. We must catch this Spode out and bring him to justice.'

'Justice,' said Liam.

Mouse was resolute. A staunch friend and a tireless fighter. With the samurai filly on their side, Lydia and Liam were sure to prevail.

Though Mouse looked as if she was coming down with something. Lydia hadn't known vampires got tired or unwell. Count Magnus never had to go to bed with a head-cold for three weeks.

'Where should we start?' Lydia asked.

Liam said nothing. His face was still. He was thinking.

'Spode's room,' chipped in Mouse.

Liam nodded. He must have been about to say the same thing…

…did he have a psychic bond with, with… *Mouse*? No, they were only thinking along the same lines. Lydia didn't have to worry about her friend, any more than she'd have to worry about Smudge. Of course, the Japanese girl *must* be in love with Liam. Smudge would be too, if she were here. It was *her vampire*'s special curse that all who saw his face were smitten. He would be practiced in kindly letting down girls who weren't Lydia. Mouse, poor butterfly, must love with a selfless, foreign devotion, knowing Liam was destined to be Lydia's soul-mate. She would have to content herself with sighing and pining under cherry-blossoms. Lydia took a moment to feel sorry for her tragic friend, forever just too young – though, not, she remembered, unmarried – to be a part of the world of *vampire romance*. With a rush of pity for the excluded girl, she resolved that Mouse would come visit for tea, or Tea-Blood, every Monday and Thursday.

Mouse was a vampire – which, according to *The Dark Flame*, ruled her out of the running when it came to undying true love. Did vampires love other vampires? Some leading men in books had vamp former girlfriends, the she-fiends who bit them in the first place. The meddling tarts provided plot complications, but were no real threat to the heroes' devotion to the heroines. Smudge heretically said these vixens of the night seemed a tad more *exciting* than the milk-and-water warm girls who narrated the novels. That was the point, though. The former girlfriends were like the vamp women at Mildew Manor, the French flirt and Miss Harczy and the Mostly Naked Egyptian: too flashy, too fleshy, too *obvious*. Black underthings and red, red lipstick. The love that mattered was the *psychic bond*, a predestined once-and-forever love truer than any temporary entanglements. With Liam, she expected harmony beyond even the sharing of blood and ascendance to immortality. Niobe reunited with her Amphion!

For the moment, though, there was an adventure to be had. To think on their future gave her tingles, but things had to be done first. She and Liam would have eternity for their love. Here and now, they were with Mouse and after a murderer.

'We shall be the Intrepid Three,' said Mouse. She held up three fingers, pressing her little finger against her palm with her thumb. 'This is our salute.'

Lydia matched it.

The girls looked at Liam. He mimicked the sign.

Mouse reached out and scratched three parallel lines on the wallpaper.

'This is our mark,' she said.

Properly, you needed vampire fingernails to make the Mark of the Intrepid Three. Had Mouse forgotten normal persons didn't have them? Lydia supposed three scratches with a nail-file would have the same effect.

'Now, where's Spode's room?'

'On the third floor, just by the spiral staircase to Aunt Agatha's attic.'

'What are we waiting for?' asked Mouse.

Lydia looked to Liam. He was their leader.

Eventually, he nodded.

'Let evil-doers beware the Intrepid Three,' Lydia said.

She and Mouse made the sign. After a moment, so did Liam.

15

THE NAME GAME

'Why Liam *Karnstein*?' Winthrop asked, annoyed.

'Least worst choice?'

Geneviève still wasn't entirely sure why she'd nominated the Karnstein boy. His eyes? Carmilla's face?

'You'd really prefer Hodge?' she asked. 'Croft's man? Ruthven's man?'

That brought him up.

'*Is* he Croft's?' He was asking himself as much as her. 'Croft nominated him, but they aren't singing from the same hymn sheet. Our Mr Hodge or Hogg or Hog isn't anyone's man but his own. We should know more about him. And about your pale wonderful boy.'

'Isn't it supposed to be your job to know about everyone?'

'I am not Mycroft Holmes.'

'No one is. Not entirely a bad thing, in my opinion.'

'You didn't altogether care for our sainted founder, did you?'

'Do we have to go into *that* again?'

Winthrop smiled, irritation expended. He was more curious than angry.

They were in her room, theoretically preparing for the next session, called for the ominous hour of midnight. If anything, the rain was worse. A real storm was rising. Winthrop paced, all nervous energy and quick movement. She could tell he still had some of Kate's blood

493

in him. Had he topped up his vampire infusion lately? He had little concern for any danger he – or she! – might be in. She knew the type: intellectual sleuth. To him, murders were puzzles. This murder, of the unlamented High Priest, was just a piece in a larger puzzle.

Should she put on a fresh dress? Would Countess Zaleska or Kleopatra? Or Meinster? Herbert von Krolock would change. He'd worn three different ensembles since mid-afternoon. Between the session where Kah was killed and the after-murder meeting in the drawing room, he'd quick-changed as if fearful of specks of dead Chinaman clinging to his cravat. At that, she couldn't be sure her dress was free of decomposing spatter. Which decided her.

Off with the green silk. On with the light mauve.

She undressed behind a screen. Winthrop threw himself on her bed and lay back, pondering aloud. It was an irritating habit. He was the most infuriating man. And yet…

'I do not like thee, Mr Hodge,' he said. 'All that blunt plain-speaking. The worst mendacity announces itself as unvarnished honesty. There's a cloud over the fellow. I wonder if Croft isn't having second thoughts. Ruthven wants a marionette King. Dick Hodge shows signs of wanting to reign. And your choice, young Liam Carl Karnstein… well, he's not a vampire who has no reflection. He's a reflection who has no vampire.'

Lightning struck. Then, beats later, thunder rumbled.

'Say that again,' she said, leaning out from behind the screen.

'Pardon my blushes, but… you're not clothed properly.'

He latticed fingers over his eyes, though he was peeping out. She wriggled her dress down so it settled.

'What you said about Liam…'

'It was droll, I suppose. He's not like a vampire who…'

'No, not that.'

'Not that? Then what?'

'His name.'

'Liam Karnstein. Liam Carl Karnstein. Or Carl Liam. No one is sure.'

'Carl Liam?'

'Yes.' He saw it. 'Oh. Oh dear. Oh dearie me.'

Those dratted anagrams, again. Liam Carl. Carl Liam. Mircalla. Marcilla. Carmilla.

'No,' he said. 'Surely not.'

'Everyone knows General Karnstein has – had – a daughter. What Happened to Carmilla is the most famous thing about the family. No one mentioned until this weekend that he had a son. It's her. Carmilla. She's back. Somehow, head on her shoulders. Dressed as a boy.'

Winthrop sat up.

'I saw a vampire dancer in Paris during the War,' he said. 'Isolde. The Old Man took me to her show. Bit of a gruesome spectacle. She's supposed to have been guillotined and grown a new body.'

'This isn't like that. Liam is the wrong way round. A reflection, as you said. It's in the eyes. Carmilla had a red blotch in one: Liam Carl has it in the other.'

'What is he? Or should it be she?'

'Not a girl, not a boy, not anything. Edwin, I'm not even sure Liam is a vampire.'

'Mercy me.'

'Mercy all of us.'

16

THE SECRET LIFE OF RODERICK SPODE

The higher up the house, the less reliable the electricity. The ground floor was well-lit, except when the generator conked out. Above that, lights burned dimmer and bulbs often popped. Unguarded candles were useless because of draughts.

Lydia could get about Mildew Manor without a light. She'd been going up and down these stairs in pitch black so long she knew every creaky board, loose carpet-rail and wobbly banister. Mouse could get by in the dark. Liam, peculiarly, couldn't; his eyes were meant for better things. Between them, the girls managed to get Liam to the third floor. Servants' quarters. No matter how he barked orders, Aunt Agatha's minion was just a jumped-up servant.

Spode's door was locked.

Neither vampire was of the turn-into-mist variety, so flowing under the door wasn't an option. Mouse offered to smash the door down but Lydia had a hairpin and practice at picking locks. Getting into the desk drawer where Frightening Fritton kept confiscated items was one of her party pieces. When that talent was needed, she had more friends than otherwise.

Spode's room wasn't even as tricky to break into as the teacher's desk. The first time she cracked that, Smudge had raised the possibility it might be booby-trapped – but it wasn't. Lydia didn't seriously think Spode left open mantraps lying about either. A few moments operation and – *click!* – the door was open.

'Well played, that girl,' said Mouse.

Liam might have nodded approval.

Her concern that, as a warm person, she was feeblest of the Intrepid Three evaporated.

They slipped into the unlit room. Lydia shut the door behind them. She felt Liam's overwhelming *presence*. It was exciting that he was here in the dark, sharp ears attuned to her racing heart. His red thirst must quicken with her pulse, to the point of nearly overwhelming his finer instincts. He kept his beast on a leash. An awful effort. She respected his self-sacrifice at not pouncing on her veins when she was powerless to resist. She thrilled to contemplate the eventual slipping of the leash.

Mouse found an oil lamp, lit it and turned up the flame. Spode's room was the size of Lydia's. The single bed was made military-fashion, folded and pressed striped pyjamas displayed on the pillow. The edges looked sharp enough to cut yourself on.

Pinned above the bed were pictures from magazines. Lanky, pale vampire women in their underthings and warm men in uniforms. Lydia thought for a moment that a signed, framed photograph on the bedside table was the Most Hideous Man in the World, but it was only that Austrian politician with the Chaplin moustache. Spode had several pictures of Mr Hitler and was also a fan of the fat Italian who looked like a weight-lifter in a tunic two sizes too small and wore more medals than he could possibly have won.

'We should look for clues,' she announced. 'Murderers always leave clues.'

Mouse nodded and glanced, swiftly, around the room.

The obvious place was a roll-top desk. Locked, but pregnable. Lydia took her hairpin to it.

'Can you show me how to do that?' Mouse asked.

Lydia gave a demonstration. Mouse followed intently.

The trick was in the last wiggle. *Click!*

Liam drifted off to look at Spode's pictures. Did he see clues they'd missed? It was possible he recognised more people than she did. Maybe he knew some of the underdressed vampire hussies.

The desk-top rolled up to disclose a mess of papers.

'The man's *obsessed*,' said Lydia.

There were sketches – not bad, actually, though she didn't like to credit the artist with anything like talent – of women with no faces and limbs that trailed off without feet and hands. The women were faint pencil lines, but their lingerie was inked in detail. Slips, pantalettes, brassieres, hose… not the navy blue knickers and chest-restraining vests which were the only admissible underwear at Drearcliff Grange. Spode spent a lot of time drawing frills.

She looked through the papers until she found one which didn't match: a chart of kings and queens of England, a subject she knew well from her prize-winning triumph. The recent succession was a fudge, with an interregnum between Victoria (1837-88) and Victor (1897-1919) to account for the Terror. Several of Victoria's children and grandchildren, warm and vampire, were put forward as kings but the country was too busy rising against Dracula to determine which should have the crown. Drearcliff Grange history textbooks, published in 1893, listed Vlad I (1886-) as reigning monarch. Upon Victoria's suicide, he tried to claim succession. There was heated debate, with Crawford of Viola taking the opposing position to Lydia, that Dracula merited a listing (1886-1888) the way Philip of Spain earns his (1554-1558) because the terms of his marriage to Bloody Mary made him co-ruler of England while she was alive. Upon King Victor's death from silver poisoning while trying to turn vampire – still not exactly explained – his (warm) nephew became George V (1919-).

Oddly, the chart was folded so the uppermost section showed the Houses of Lancaster and York. Her special period, thanks to murdered little Edward V. Spode or someone had drawn crooked men (a cipher!) between Richard III (1483-1485), wicked smotherer of the Princes in the Tower, and Henry VII (1485-1509), first of the Tudors. Lydia couldn't immediately see what this had to do with anything. B.A.A. and Spode were trying to settle on who was King of Vampires. Were they looking for historical tips on how to drag in some prince and puff him up to plop on a throne?

By right of nobility, the title should be Liam's. Of course.

He hadn't said anything about it, though. Too modest. He'd have to be persuaded it was his duty, for he'd not seek the crown. Like Amphion, he'd rather pluck his lyre and tend his love. Would Lydia sacrifice a portion of her happiness if Liam became King of the Cats? Could she share *her vampire* with the world? Only if, say, another Great War or similar crisis required him – and him only – to step into the breach. Painful joy stuck in her heart at the thought. He was hers as she was his, but he was too pure to turn away if needed by his kind, by all mankind!

Mouse knuckled the walls, oak over stone, listening for hollows. A *thunk* sounded.

'A secret panel,' said Mouse.

'More of a wardrobe,' said Lydia.

'A *secret* wardrobe?'

Now Mouse came to mention it, the wardrobe in Spode's room was slightly secret. The one in her own room could be mistaken for a door since it was built into the panelling. It had a handle and a latch, but no lock. Spode's wardrobe had a lock but no handle. You could see where a knob had been removed, despite a splotch of new varnish which hid the spot. The keyhole was easy to miss, too.

Mouse asked for the hairpin and fiddled with the lock.

A fast learner, she was rewarded with a *click!* She used her suicide knife to pry open the wardrobe door.

Perfumey smell wafted out.

Spode didn't just draw expensive ladies' underthings. He collected them! Smudge said she'd read about men like that in Krafft-Ebing. Possessed by paraesthetic fetishism. One should pity such persons, not laugh at them – according to Dr Krafft-Ebing. Smudge and Lydia had still barked like seals at the very idea. Imagining broad-shouldered, brutish Roderick Spode prancing in a *Eulalie Soeurs* slip made Lydia titter.

Really! Uck!

Did this tie in with the murder? Had Kah Pai Mei threatened to show candid photographs of Spode dressed like a tart to B.A.A. unless he… what? Supported the High Priest in a claim to be the ruler of all vampires? Embezzled from Aunt Agatha's bank accounts? Locked himself in the library with a loaded revolver?

The idea of Spode's brains splattering over volumes of *Punch* distracted her pleasantly while Mouse delved into the wardrobe. It was unlikely Spode had anything in the tiny girl's size.

Mouse lifted aside an armful of lingerie, like a curtain. A draught came out of the wardrobe.

'The mystery deepens,' announced Mouse. 'It's not just a wardrobe. There are stairs, going down…'

Secret stairs!

17

WHAT HAPPENED TO CARMILLA

'We can't just ask the lad to open his shirt to show if he's a she,' said Edwin. 'There are *some* proprieties, you know. Guests under the same roof and all that.'

'One of our fellow *guests* thinks it's *proper* to skewer Chinamen.'

He inclined his head, thinking it over. Edwin wasn't averse to skewering so long as the right people – which is to say, the right people as determined by the Diogenes Club – got the sharp end.

The midnight session wasn't for an hour or so. Watches and clocks didn't agree with each other in Mildew Manor, so no one could be sure. The meeting would convene on Mrs Gregson's time.

Geneviève was determined to find out about Carl Liam before then. If he became King of the Cats, it'd be her fault. She'd *nominated* the phantom Karnstein. What had she been thinking? *Had* she been thinking? That damn glamour again!

Carmilla Karnstein had been – was? – her *friend*.

When you came back from the dead, you told your friends pronto. Observing Edwin's *proprieties*, you posted engraved announcement cards. When you came back from being *destroyed* – decapitated *and* dismembered! – you sent up balloons. If there was a fresh chapter to the sorry saga of What Happened to Carmilla, Geneviève should have known.

The guest rooms were all on this floor. Oil-lamps on the landing burned smokily. Lightning briefly made Edwin's face skull-like.

'Which room are the Karnsteins in?'

She knew he'd know. It was his job to keep track of things.

He pointed at a door. She rapped smartly and let herself in before being invited or turned away.

Yes, she could cross a threshold unbidden.

At first, she thought no one was home. A candle had burned low in a dish on a table beside the canopy bed. Framed pictures were propped on the table. Liam and/or Carmilla's portrait was illuminated. Travelling trunks were open.

'Steady on, old girl,' said Edwin, hand on her shoulder. 'There's…'

In the bed, someone stirred. Edwin's grip grew tighter. He pushed the door silently shut behind them.

'Who's there?' came a weak voice. The canopy curtains opened.

It was the General's wife. Ethelind's eyes were milky white. She was blind. When had that happened?

'It's Gené Dieudonné, Countess. Carmilla's friend. Do you remember me?'

'Yes,' she said. 'The *clever* one. Has that made you happy? Being *clever*.'

The Countess said 'clever' as if she were biting a lemon.

'Not really what I want to talk about,' said Geneviève.

'The Count says a clever woman is a contradiction in terms. He has all the brains in the family. All the brains the family needs.'

Geneviève sat at the end of the bed.

In the candlelight, she saw Countess Karnstein was withered. Her bare arms were skin-sleeved bones.

'The Count knows best,' she said.

'It's about your son,' Geneviève began…

'I have no sons,' said the Countess, definitely, bitterly. 'Just an idiot daughter. I'm useless, you see.'

Edwin was interested enough to approach.

'There's a man in the room,' said the Countess, looking around with blind eyes.

Ethelind Fionguala had been a famous stunner in her youth, which extended over centuries. Geneviève remembered her as a statuesque, mature beauty – an older, dignified version of her daughter. Now, she was close to being a hag.

'I'm Edwin Winthrop, ma'am,' he said.

'My secretary,' Geneviève explained.

'Secretary!' the Countess snorted. 'Is that what they're calling it these days? You're her bleeding boy and no mistake.'

Her Irish came out.

Geneviève wouldn't be distracted. 'Who is Liam?'

The Countess was distracted, irritated.

'The young fellow travelling with you,' said Edwin. 'The lad your husband represents as your son?'

Now, the Countess concentrated, maliciously.

'A *thing*,' she said. 'Grown from seed, like a pot-plant. No child of mine. No child of anyone's. An *homunculus*. A *monstrum*.'

'That is not true,' said someone.

One thing about the Karnsteins. They could sneak into a room without Geneviève noticing. Carmilla had been quiet too. Sly and crafty. A bloodline trait.

General Karnstein held a revolver. She didn't need her meagre psychic abilities to know it was loaded with silver.

'You're troubling my poor wife,' he said. 'She is not well.'

'Not well, not well,' she shrieked. 'He says I'm not well. Ask him *why* the Countess isn't well! Ask him what he's done!'

There was evidently disharmony in the family.

'I don't think you want to shoot us, General,' said Edwin. 'Mrs Gregson wouldn't approve of more of her guests getting killed. Word will get round that her soirées are unsafe. Invitations will be refused. A touch humiliating, what?'

Karnstein smiled, which he only did to be cruel. 'A murder has already been committed. If there are intruders in my room, I am justified in defending my family. For all I know, you two did kill Kah Pai Mei.'

'There is that, of course. On the other hand, if you eliminate Miss Dieudonné here, you'll need another nomination for your candidate. Might not be such a doddle. We can't be the only folk who've twigged he's not what you say he is.'

'A monster,' said the Countess.

'In this company, a serious accusation,' commented Edwin. 'Think of it: *more* of a monster than Dickon Hodge, Queen Kleo or Davey Meinster. One might almost admire the achievement.'

'How did you do it?' Geneviève asked. 'Is Liam Carmilla?'

'He is what Carmilla should have been,' said the General, stiffly. 'A son to the House of Karnstein.'

'I bore no sons,' said the Countess, close to wailing.

'Quiet, Ethel.'

'General, you're just bursting to tell all,' said Edwin. 'It's the curse of doing something amazing no one knows about. You can't brag. Now, to be friendly, I'll help you along. I *have* a clue. If I'm thinking on the right lines, just nod.'

General Karnstein pointed his gun at Edwin.

'Schloss Adler,' Edwin said, airily. 'Professor ten Brinken. The Alraune Experiment. As your lady wife says, "grown from seed, like a pot-plant".'

Karnstein nearly shot Edwin in his surprise.

'You had to have a seed. Not the head. What was it?'

'It was her heart,' said the Countess. 'Her broken heart!'

Now, the General smiled. Edwin was right. He did want to brag.

'This ten Brinken johnnie,' Edwin told her, 'was one of Dracula's pet alchemists during the late unpleasantness. I ran across the products of his beakers in the skies over France. He is a monster-maker. Young Liam is more presentable than von Richthofen's Bat-staffel, but even further from human. That's ten Brinken's special trick. Scrambling up vampire, vegetable and mineral. You were right when you said Liam wasn't even a vampire, Gené. Not a proper one. He's as much mandrake as man. A touch of the turnip, eh? What does a veg vamp suck? Sap? Karnstein, d'you really think you can put a heap of compost on the throne of Dracula?'

'I don't see why not.'

Now it was all on the table, General Karnstein would kill them. She saw it coming. He'd shoot her first – because he'd been looking for an excuse for centuries (he really did have extreme views on cleverness in women). Also, if he shot Edwin first, she was quick enough to take him down before he could level the gun at her.

'Open that wardrobe,' the General ordered, indicating which one he meant with a flick of his gun.

He was one of those officers who couldn't be bothered hauling corpses. In war, he was the kind of bastard who'd have a prisoner to dig his own grave before summary execution.

'This one?' asked Edwin, cheerily. Karnstein nodded.

The door behind the General opened slowly. The Countess, of course, couldn't see it. If her other senses were sharp enough to determine something was happening, she kept quiet. Of all people, she must have had enough of her husband. Geneviève always rather admired Ethelind for putting up with her family. She didn't like to see what had become of the woman.

Edwin took the wardrobe handle and made a show of pulling.

'Seems to be stuck. Warped. No wonder with all this rain. You can see why they call this place Mildew Manor, eh?'

Karnstein was impatient. His fangs stuck out. After shooting her in the heart, he might feed off Edwin.

Sergeant Dravot stood behind the General. She reconsidered her position on Danny Dravot. Good old Sergeant Dravot. He had his uses.

Edwin yanked open the wardrobe and everyone was surprised at what fell out. Except the Countess, who only heard the thump and said 'what what?'

Dravot took away the General's gun and got an arm round his neck.

Karnstein was furious, but too astounded to complain. His face went red, as well it might.

On the carpet lay Countess Marya Zaleska. Shot through the heart with an arrow.

A rumpus on the landing. People crowded into the room.

'This looks awfully bad for you, General Karnstein,' said Edwin mildly. 'Would you happen to have an explanation?'

Wide-eyed and desolate, Karnstein shook his head.

'Thought not,' said Edwin. 'Slap the darbies on him, sergeant.'

18

IN THE MAZE OF A THOUSAND GODS

Lydia led the way, holding the lamp. Liam followed, stooping so as not to bump his lovely hair. Then came Mouse, *katana* drawn. The lamp got hot. Were the Intrepid Three to stick with solving mysteries, it'd make sense to invest in a battery torch.

A secret spiral staircase wound down through Mildew Manor.

No cobwebs, so obviously in regular use. Were there doors in other wardrobes? Did Aunt Agatha know the home she'd bought came complete with hidden passages? She couldn't see B.A.A. squeezing in and tottering down these steep steps, though she only pretended to be feeble. It would be like Spode to discover the passages and take advantage. But for what?

They descended for *ages*. The air grew damper and cold.

The stairs went below the ground floor, kitchen and basements. Brickwork gave way to hewn stone. Rings were set in the rock at intervals, as handholds.

Eventually, the steps led out into the caves. Stalagmites grew up, stalactites grew down: both sharpened like stakes. Sconces held burning torches. Who lit the things? How did they stay alight with all the dripping, seeping and pouring? The uneven rock floor was criss-crossed by runnels. Liam seemed not to want to get his shoes wet, but Mouse nudged him.

There was human noise. Vaguely churchy, like an incantation.

These caves were once used for heathen worship. Obscene idols stood, sat or squatted in alcoves. Some of the more obscene had been sold off to private collectors. Baphomet and Baal. Mythwrhn and Pazuzu. Shuma-Gorath and Shub-Niggurath. Azal, Azazel and Azathoth. Abracadabra, Abanazer and How's-yer-father. Their parsons didn't deliver sermons about continence and charity but pulled out parishioners' lights and livers to drape on the altar. Viler tribes conducted themselves indecently without clothes in honour of high holidays and beat out ragtime rhythms on tom-toms made from skin flayed from the bottoms of Christians. Lottie said looneys from London were always trying to get into the catacombs to revive olden days religions. A previous owner put up iron gates at the hillside cave entrance to keep out cranks. Providing a suitable bribe crossed his palm, Matey let one or two through. Some never resurfaced, so degenerate devil-worshippers might wander here still.

Lydia turned down the lamp. No sense giving away their presence.

Cautiously, the Intrepid Three crept towards the noise.

She should have worn Wellingtons. Her shoes were soaked through. She was shivering. Vampires didn't much notice cold and wet. She had to put up with small discomforts for the sake of adventure.

She felt Liam's presence in her heart. A constant thing, now.

It was curious how happiness changed her. It almost hurt.

They followed a path between shallow pools, smoothed by generations of pagan sandals. The murmuring grew louder. Spode wasn't in this wickedness alone.

Firelight flickered from a chamber up ahead. Mouse pointed at the cave wall with her sword. At knee height were scrawled broken-backed stick figures, a procession of mediaeval cripples struck with dancing sickness. The Crook was definitely behind this! Lydia had a pang for Smudge, stranded with her parents in Prestatyn, left out of the adventure. She would seethe to learn Lydia had found vampire romance *and* confronted the Crook in one weekend! Were the signs a warning against trespass or directions for the heathen faithful? The

Crooked Men all headed in the same direction. Towards the fire.

Mouse and Lydia pressed close to the wall. Liam hesitated, as if deception were beneath him, then followed suit. Lydia took advantage to wriggle a little closer to him. An electric thrill passed between them.

Now, she could pick out the odd word in the hub-bub.

Peeping ever so slightly into the fire chamber, which was the size of a small cathedral, she saw an unholy gathering. Galleries of rock formations rose forming a high ceiling. Hordes of bats could hang in the natural, glistening vaults.

Spode was among a crowd, in a monkish waterproof robe, hood doffed. These were the Crooked Men! The waterproof was sensible wear for a conspiracy meeting in these conditions. Some she recognised: May, the tweeny who disapproved of coloureds and chinks... Ilona, Countess Zaleska's secretary... the local curate, Hartley... and one of the footmen, George. Two or three more, new to her, looked collectively like a right shower. All wore waterproofs, each with a different Crooked Man design on the chest.

The fire burned steadily. Enough smoke poured back over the congregation to make robed plotters stifle coughs and rub their eyes. In a throne-like chair on a raised rock sat a hooded, robed, hunched-over person. On his chest was a unique design, a picture of a pig. He held a pole with a hook at the end and wore a white mask as well as the hood. The Crook!

Frankly, it could have been anyone.

But she knew at once who it was. From the way he held his head. From the shape of his shoulders.

The Crook was Mr Hodge!

Smudge would be disappointed her criminal idol wasn't someone more... well... *glamorous* than the grunting, fat-faced guest. No wonder Hodge thought the hood and mask a good idea.

The thing was – and now Lydia felt like the bee's roller-skates, for no one else would guess it – she knew also who Mr Hodge was really. It had just come to her.

Crumpets! A cat was among the pigeons. Rather, a *hog*.

She had to tell Liam. And Mouse.

Turning, she saw robed figures – late-comers – in the tunnel behind them. Mouse scythed with her *katana*, but the Crooked Man who snatched at her wore armour under his waterproof. The sword sliced through cloth but struck sparks from metal. Large already, armour bulked him out to giant size. The Crooked Champion rammed a mailed fist into Mouse's face, making it a bloody mess.

Lydia knew Liam would save them now.

She waited for him to become a hummingbird whir, besting the thug who had hurt Mouse. Count Magnus, in similar situation, would duel five or six men at once, and take on a dozen more once they were down.

But Liam simply stood there, impassive. He had another plan.

Mouse, undaunted, thrust her sword at the Crooked Champion's throat. He knocked her blade aside with an armoured wrist and grabbed her by the shoulder and hip. He raised Mouse over his head, armour-plates creaking. Mouse slashed at his helmeted head, which clanged like a broken bell. The Crooked Champion shoved the vampire girl upwards, impaling her on a field of stalactites. Mouse bled and writhed, but was fixed, pierced several times – if not fatally since nothing stuck through her ribs. Blood rained on the now-tattered robes of the Crooked Champion, splashing his revealed armour. A white rose was enamelled on the helm.

Hands seized Lydia.

19

A CROWDED ROOM, WITH ABSENCES

Kleopatra took one look at the corpse of Countess Zaleska and shrieked, setting Geneviève's teeth on edge. Funny how elders who'd – by their own account – relished centuries of bloodletting turned squeamish when one of their own kind was murdered.

'Someone took the old bat at her word,' said Herbert von Krolock. 'Marya droned incessantly about how weary she was of the burden of eternal life. Finally, it's been lifted off her.'

'You can't think I have anything to do with this,' said General Karnstein.

The confidence man's fall-back: if things look bad, bluster pompously.

'Of course not,' said Edwin. 'You wouldn't lower yourself to mere homicide… except, now I come to think of it, you were just threatening to shoot Gené and me in cold blood. *And* you indicated this wardrobe was your favourite place for stashing *corpi delicti*. Under any circumstances, a corpse in the cupboard would be a mite suspicious. Since you admit you'd happily commit the odd double murder if you had an earthly chance of getting away with it, twelve good men and true will have few qualms about fixing you up an appointment with the silver guillotine.'

Geneviève knelt and checked the Countess.

Lacking pulse, heartbeat or mirror-misting breath were not

511

infallible indices of true death – though they were seldom signs of rude health. Without instantaneous putrefaction, Geneviève relied on what student wags at Barts called the rule of thumb: gentle pressure to the eyeball. Even comatose vampires didn't lie doggo for that. She put a thumb-print on Marya Zaleska's open eye and elicited no response. She tried to shut the woman's eyes, but the lids resisted.

The Countess was dead, but not rotten. Some stayed fresh.

The arrow transfixing her was the sort used by mediaeval English archers. Another fifteenth-century killing. A pattern emerging? The shaft was finely etched with bent stick-figures. A calling card. She was minded to let Karnstein stew, but this was the work of the Crook.

She didn't think the General *was* the Crook. Unless he was framing himself to throw off suspicion. Karnstein wasn't subtle enough for that.

'This is an outrage,' said the General. 'Someone does not want a Karnstein to be King of the Cats.'

'You don't have to be a murderer to think that a bad idea,' said Geneviève.

'You nominated Lovely Liam, dearie,' Herbert said.

The Viscount had a point. 'I withdraw my support,' she said.

'That'll have to wait till the midnight session,' said Baron Meinster, huffily. 'It's a point of procedure.'

As far as Meinster was concerned, another claimant was out of the ring. He was pretending not to be delighted. Wasn't the freshly deceased Countess a cousin-by-bloodline of his?

'Must follow protocol,' said Herbert, larkish. 'Especially when elders are being felled like trees.'

'Some vampires are more like trees than others,' said Edwin, dryly.

'I can't think *what* you mean,' said Herbert.

'Haven't you heard the latest?' said Edwin. 'The General grew his son from a cutting. In mulch.'

'Oh, *that one!* Too beautiful to be true.'

Herbert clapped daintily manicured claws to his cheeks in an exaggerated show of surprise. Von Krolock was beyond shocking, but not beyond playing to the gallery to increase Karnstein's discomfort.

'I will not hear this calumny,' said the General.

'You'd better invest in ear-plugs then, old thing,' said Edwin. 'Because a lot more calumny is due to be slung your way before sun-up.'

'I insist this oaf lets go of me,' said the General, meaning Dravot.

The Sergeant held the General by the arms. A full foot taller than his captive, Dravot looked as if he could bite off Karnstein's head like a gingerbread man's.

Edwin gave Dravot the nod and the General was released. He made a fuss of brushing off his tunic. Medals clattered.

'I shall lodge a complaint with our hostess.'

Though Ethelind Karnstein was scowling, Geneviève had an idea that her husband being pushed about delighted her.

The bedroom was crowded. Lots of witnesses. Accusations bubbling over. Kleopatra leant on her professor. Herbert sardonically observed Meinster's clenched-jawed cool. Croft kept quiet and looked deader than the woman on the floor.

Mrs Gregson sailed in, accompanied by the shifty butler and a put-upon warm woman. The hostess had changed into a black formal gown with fur trim. Her black wig was wound through with little green silk snakes.

Everyone looked at the Countess. And the General.

'One fewer setting for late supper, Matey,' said Herbert.

Croft was on his own here. Cut loose by his claimant? Not a happy association, even if Hodge now had a clear run at the crown. Ilona Harczy was scarce, too. She'd not be grief-stricken at the loss of her employer. Ilona would swiftly secure another position as a companion. She was *very* companionable.

Another face was absent.

'General, where *is* Liam?'

All the bluster seeped out. Karnstein's green eyes flashed panic.

20

LIAM BITES

The Intrepid Three were hustled into a smaller chamber. Lydia thought the Crook's underground lair should be packed with barrels of gunpowder, cases of rifles and armoured tunnelling machines. This was more like a big stationery cupboard. Tea chests stood about; one with its lid off was half full of reams of blank paper. Nearby stood a hand-cranked printing press. Leaflets written in the cipher of the Crooked Men were piled up neatly in a dry spot.

Mouse's sailor suit was ripped and bloody. She was unconscious, but her injuries were healing. Her face was already fixed, blood-crusts flaking away from porcelain skin. She was curled up in a corner, like a real mouse. Her sword and knives – several more than Lydia had known about – were gone. She was in no state to help.

What was Liam thinking? Lydia didn't like to ask.

He sat on a tea chest, smiling absent-mindedly. Calm in the face of danger, unconcerned for himself.

But unconcerned for Mouse too.

He could have helped her friend, Lydia felt. He must know something.

The Crook – Mr Hodge – took time off from addressing his followers to look in on the prisoners. He didn't give Lydia more than a second glance and plainly thought Mouse done for, but was intrigued by Liam.

'Bright lad, not to fight,' he said. 'There's something about you, Karnstein. Something *unusual*. Crooked, even. We can use a good Crooked Man. I'm going to keep you for a bit if you don't mind. 'Appen, I'm going to keep you for a bit if you *do* mind. Don't want you going to waste. If you get thirsty, that bit'll do for snap.'

The Crook pointed at Lydia with the straight end of his crook.

Liam didn't seem interested in anything. If he heard Hodge, he paid him little attention. He was deep inside himself, thinking.

Lydia still had not shared her *deduction*. The right time would come. Once they escaped. She had no doubt they would escape. Liam wouldn't have let them be captured otherwise. He'd know a way out of this prison.

The Crook left two followers – no one Lydia recognised – to keep an eye on the prisoners, and hurried off to whatever business he had. The trailing edge of his robe was filthy from dragging about these caves. He leaned on his crook, trying to conceal some infirmity of the spine. She remembered Hodge's oddly lolling head.

Lydia looked at Liam, and thought he was thinner – not in the way a person gets thin, but in the way paint thins with water. If he could turn invisible or – better yet! – insubstantial, he could easily get them out of this pickle. It wasn't that, though. He was weaker, somehow – less *there*.

Then she realised. Hodge was right. Liam hadn't *fed*. Since meeting her, he had held back, out of consideration for her feelings…

A wave of love swept over her. And an ache.

He shouldn't have deprived himself. She should have sensed what he was doing and not let him. If he'd been at full strength, Mouse wouldn't have got hurt. They wouldn't have got caught.

Their *psychic bond* had missed a signal.

She knew what she must do now. The sacrifice she must make.

The Crook had made a mistake by contemptuously leaving Liam with her. '*That bit'll do for snap,*' he'd said. *Snap!* He'd not thought Lydia might willingly surrender blood, to give *her vampire* the grit to soldier on. Later, Mr Richard Hodge would regret that. Dick the Hog!

She undid her collar and the top buttons of her shirt. Her heart beat fast, and she felt flushed. Her jugular pulsed.

'Liam,' she said. 'Take me…'

He did not respond. He was sinking.

She looked for something to scratch herself with, to pique his interest. She rejected the rusty nails of the tea chests. She didn't want tetanus, thank you very much. A splinter, maybe? No.

Sitting next to Liam, she took his hand – it wasn't cold, but it was odd to the touch, pliant – and held it to her heart, then guided his fingernails to her throat. They were long and sharp and should do the trick.

She looked into his liquid green eyes.

This was the moment she had been waiting her whole life for. A moment of perfect communion.

She made herself ignore the Crooked Men, who watched the scene without comprehension.

Liam's beautiful lips parted. His teeth showed, sharp and ready.

'It's all right, Liam,' she told him. 'You can't hurt me.'

Lydia's whole body was eager for his razor-kiss. She was woman enough to know what the vampire wanted… but woman enough also to know what she wanted, what she *needed*…

'Bite me, my Amphion,' she said.

Liam's eyes – his whole being! – fixed on her. She had goosebumps all over. Then his gaze swivelled, shifted away from her, towards the dark corner, towards Mouse.

Mouse!

He was at Lydia's throat, whole face pressed into her neck. She felt a tongue on her skin. The wet touch thrilled her.

He pulled away. The wetness went cold.

'Too young,' said Liam. 'Not enough years.'

Now he moved fast, as vampires could. The tea chest toppled without his weight. Lydia bumped her behind on the floor. Liam leaped across the room like an insect and battened onto Mouse, sniffing her as she slept. She stirred a little.

'Years,' said Liam. 'Many years.'

Mouths opened in his hands. Mouths ringed with green teeth. He thrust his hands through the rips in Mouse's clothes and pressed them to her skin. Vampire blood flowed. His stiff hair stood up like porcupine quills. Electricity crackled.

A snow-white streak grew in Mouse's raven-black hair.

Her face shrivelled like an apple left too long in the bowl. Her arms and legs shrank and bent.

And Liam filled out. He became more *there*.

One of the guards said a dreadful swear, several times. The other ran off with 'The Crook'll want to know about *this*!'

Hot tears burst from Lydia at this... this betrayal, this vileness, this cruelty!

The Intrepid Three were broken. How had she ever thought she could be friends with them... with vampires!

Mouse's eyes − her *old* eyes − opened. She mewled, in childish panic. The tiny elder tried to struggle, but was weak and senile now. Liam had swallowed her strength. Her little fists thumped uselessly against his chest.

He did not leave her dead. He was crueller than that.

When he took his hands off her, his palm-mouths detaching like suckers, he left her just enough substance to cling to life. Where he had touched, Mouse's body was ravaged.

Liam stood.

His green eyes took in the room. He was alert, now. Quick. He saw Lydia, but took no more note of her than of the tea chests, the printing press, the boxes of paper. To him, all were just *things*.

Liam walked up to the guard, who backed off, afraid. Liam held up his hands. The mouths were closed now, invisible. There was a crackle around his hands, like electricity. It was *vitality*, stolen from Mouse, spilling out.

The guard broke, and ran. Liam strolled after him, unconcerned.

Liam passed Lydia, ignoring her. She thought to follow him, if only to get out of this place.

Her heart was dead. She would never be a vampire. She was just one of the walking dead. She'd trail along in Liam's wake, out of habit. But she didn't mean it. She didn't mean anything.

A voice croaked from the corner.

'Ni,' said Mouse, trying to get a name out from a throat dry from a thousand years' use. 'Niobe.'

Liam was leaving.

Lydia stepped out of the store room.

'Niobe, help me.'

The hook in her heart tugged. And she turned back. To Mouse. To her true friend.

21

REVELATIONS

The company left Countess Zaleska under a sheet and reconvened in the drawing room. Mrs Gregson had a maid serve bloody apéritifs. Wet logs tried to burn in a fireplace the size of most flats Geneviève had lived in. An ugly ormolu clock set in the stomach of a reclining psammead dominated the mantel, ticking eccentrically towards midnight. Another session of the (dwindling) elder vampire conclave was still supposed to commence at the witching hour.

Geneviève did a head count. No Liam Karnstein. Also, no Mr Hodge, no Roderick Spode, no Ilona, no *Kyûketsu Shôjo*… and hadn't there been a doughy, angry warm girl loitering earlier? She never had found out how that one fit in.

Everyone sat or stood around. Mildew Manor was full of mismatched furniture from various periods, mostly in poor repair.

'The *monstrum* is below,' said Ethelind Karnstein, from a settee. She had insisted on a cold compress for her forehead.

'What? Where?' asked her husband.

'Under the house. I can *feel* it, moving. I can always feel it. It has *so much* of me.'

Geneviève had thought Ethelind disowned whatever Carmilla had grown into. Then, she understood. Liam literally had 'so much' of his mother.

'He feeds on you,' she said. 'It's why you're…'

'*Old?* Yes.'

The others understood at once. Meinster, Kleopatra, Herbert, Croft. Few things could discomfort such creatures, but the concept was an affront – a threat they had to take seriously. Used to being predators, they were outraged to be treated as prey.

Liam couldn't survive off the blood of the warm. He sustained youth by stealing from those who'd lived beyond their natural lifespans.

He was a vampire of vampires.

Edwin caught up quickly. Had he a notion beforehand?

'That's… that's disgusting,' said Meinster.

'Come off it,' said Herbert. 'You'd bleed your own mother. In point of fact, you did…'

'That was different. She was warm.'

According to Carpathian Guard gossip, Meinster had turned his mama. He couldn't bear to be without her in undeath, though they had never got on. She'd kept him on a chain, apparently. The Baroness Meinster didn't last long after receiving the Dark Kiss from her blessed boy.

So, Liam was a danger to elder vampires. How did the process work? Not by conventional bleeding? Geneviève had felt weak in his presence, but put it down to a draining glamour. Now, she understood. Carmilla wasn't just a walking carnivorous orchid. She was reborn as a sponge.

'A *monthter*,' diagnosed Professor Bey. 'Horror of horrorth.'

Geneviève sensed a lynch mob forming. She was honour bound not to let the company get carried away with a futile witch hunt.

'Whatever he is,' she said, 'Liam didn't kill the Countess or Kah.'

Dead, Marya Zaleska showed the same face she had for a hundred years. The High Priest putrefied normally. If Liam leeched off them, they'd methuselate like his mother, winding up enfeebled but not truly dead. So far as she knew, Liam's youth-stealing wasn't even fatal. After repeated sucklings, Ethelind only *looked her age*.

'We still have a murderer among us,' said Edwin. 'Fancy that.'

Everyone took the time to look at everyone else, with suspicion. Except Mrs Gregson, who just looked like she owned the house and wished everyone would keep to her schedule.

'It was Hodge,' said Caleb Croft.

Now, everyone looked to him. Including Mrs Gregson.

'He's quick,' Croft elaborated. 'When the lights are out, he's quicker than you think. He killed the High Priest when we were all there. I knew he was doing it and I couldn't see it.'

'You didn't try to stop him?' accused General Karnstein.

'Did you try to stop your son feeding off your wife?'

The General and Mr Croft had both brought monsters to the party and lost hold of the leashes.

'How'd he get the crook into the room?' asked Edwin.

'No idea,' said Croft. 'You'd have to ask him.'

'Hodge is the Crook?' Geneviève asked.

Croft shrugged. 'So it seems.'

'And you are sharing this information with us only now?'

Croft shrugged. 'Mr Hodge has not been… entirely forthcoming… in his dealings with… ah…'

'You and Lord Ruthven,' Winthrop prompted.

The *eminences grises* of elder vampiredom seemed to have been duped by the Crook. That was almost funny.

'What about the marks on the arrow?' asked Edwin. 'Are the little crooked men some sort of message? Or just for show?'

Croft looked blank.

Edwin took out his notebook and flipped the pages to show copies he had made of the cipher. Croft shrugged.

'You're not really her secretary, are you?' observed Herbert.

Edwin smiled.

'He's from the Diogenes Club,' said Croft.

'And you're a secret policeman,' responded Edwin.

Croft looked, as usual, as if he'd like to kill someone. In this instance, Edwin Winthrop seemed likeliest candidate. Sergeant Dravot shifted slightly, just to remind the grey man he was there. Croft backed down, closing dead lips over thrusting fangs.

'Anyone else want to own up to a hidden identity?' asked Herbert. 'I myself am exactly who I've always said I was. I am not a policeman, secret or public. I am not, indeed, anything.'

'*So* glad that's cleared up,' said Croft.

'Croft,' demanded Meinster, 'do you withdraw your support for Hodge's candidacy?'

The Baron was still playing that game.

'It's not about being King of the Cats,' said Croft. 'Absurd title, of course…'

Meinster huffed at the dismissal. He and Mrs Gregson might be the only ones, but they took the title seriously.

'It's about being King of…'

Then the lights failed, again.

When they came back on, Croft was gone. Scratched into the carpet where he had been standing was a crooked stick figure.

'Merciful Mithras,' swore Herbert, 'here we go again…'

22

A MIDNIGHT FEAST

Only one medicine could help Mouse and Lydia didn't have enough in her veins. Liam had taken too much. It would take a river of blood to restore her.

A practical solution must be found.

She shouted 'fire'. In the caves, her shout echoed off the altars of a thousand forgotten gods. Smudge said the *Police Gazette* advised those being attacked to shout 'fire', not 'help'. People usually run to a fire. People often ignore a cry for help.

She kept shouting.

Crooked Men came, nearly tripping over their robes. The guard who'd fled was back, with Mouse's *katana* held all wrong. His fellows had mediaeval vampire-killing weapons. Lydia ducked back into the storage chamber and pressed against the cave wall.

Four monk-robed characters crammed in.

Crooked Men bumped into each other. The cowardly guard fell over and lost his grip on the stolen sword. Heart hammering at the risk, Lydia got her shoe under the blade – quivering as if it were a venomous cobra – and kicked it away, out of the Crooked Man's reach.

Then Mouse was on the guard, rummaging through his robe. She was a small, white-haired monkey with long nails and teeth. She bit and chewed. The Crooked Man screeched. The scream cut off. Lydia heard sucking. She saw mess. Her friend's feeding wasn't dainty.

One of the other Crooked Men – George, the footman – pulled a knife from a sheath hung on the rope around his middle. Hissing, Mouse took it from him and sliced him open. His blood poured on her.

She was red and sticky now, a wild thing – worse than the reflection Lydia had glimpsed.

Lydia looked at the wall.

The screams didn't last long. The feeding did.

She didn't know how she felt any more. These were bad men. They wouldn't hesitate to kill her or Mouse if the Crook told them to. Her friend *needed* a river of blood. This was for the best.

Madame Glynn never wrote about the *sounds* of vampires feeding. Or the smell. She mentioned Lady Diana's 'sweet-scented trickle of blood' and how it 'excited Count Magnus's dark passions'. Blood wasn't sweet scented, it stank of hot copper and foulness. It didn't only trickle. It spurted. It gushed. Vampire teeth and claws didn't just bring blood welling to the surface to be lapped at like cream off a saucer of milk. Mouse pulled stringy, pulpy, gruesome stuff out of the Crooked Men.

When Lydia turned, Mouse was covered in red muck.

Her friend stood over four Crooked Men. George the Footman and Hartley the curate and two she didn't know. They really were crooked now, backs bent the wrong way, necks dislocated to stretch open throats. Mouse had her sword and knives back, but they were clean. She had done all the damage with her hands and mouth.

Mouse's face and arms were normal again. Normal for her. A child's. But her hair was still a shock of white. Liam had taken something Mouse would never get back.

'It's not safe here,' she said, sheathing her sword.

Lydia agreed.

Mouse took hold of Lydia's arm and squeezed. She ponged something horrid.

'Thanks, Niobe,' she said. 'I owe you my life.'

'Don't be a drip,' Lydia said, kindly. 'House honour and all. You'd have done the same for me.'

Mouse kissed her, quickly, stickily on the cheek.

'Silly sausage,' said Lydia.

Mouse saw the muck she'd left on Lydia's face.

'What do I look like?' she asked. 'A sight?'

'A perfect sight.'

'Rats.'

They ran through the caves. Lydia let Mouse pull her ahead. They didn't smack into too many walls. There was surprisingly no clamour. Were the Crooked Men Mouse fed off the only ones left down here? Where were the rest? What was Liam – the *monster* Liam – doing now? He was out there somewhere.

Lydia's feeling for *her vampire* had turned cold. Liam was no more capable of love than a cactus. He was not the kind of vampire she had taken him for. What he had done to Mouse wasn't a communion, but mere selfish slaking – an unforgivable affront, an assault on friendship. If she lived until Monday, she'd cancel her subscription to *The Dark Flame* and pen Miss Carlotta Francis a considered letter about her periodical's irresponsible fostering of misconceptions about vampires in general and handsome male vampires in particular.

They came to a large cavern, with a deep pool and a running stream.

'Help me get cleaned up,' said Mouse. 'I can't go about looking like a hullabaloo in a butcher shop.'

23

UNDER THE HOGGE

'There must be a secret door,' said Edwin, knocking on wood panels. *Everywhere* sounded hollow. 'The Crook was listening.'

'What crook?' asked several people.

'*The* Crook,' said Edwin. 'Do pay attention.'

Geneviève was more interested in what Caleb Croft had been saying than in where he'd got to and what had happened to him. If the Crook throttled Croft, that was a sole tick in his Good Deeds column.

'It's about being King of…'

Not… the Cats. So, King of the Khyber Rifles? Jazz? Spades? Carpathia?

There was only one obvious answer.

…a penny, suspended in the back of her mind all evening, dropped.

Hodge turned vampire in 1485.

So, what else happened that year?

Working as a battlefield nurse, she was traipsing around a particularly fruitless Franco-Breton conflict known to history as 'the Mad War' (she wasn't the only person to say 'aren't they all?'). Under the regency of Anne de Beaujeu, 'least foolish woman in France' (incidentally, populariser of the handkerchief), the country fell to plots, uprisings and power-grabs fomented by would-be monarchs in the outlying duchies. Hence, the Mad War.

In World News... Matthias of Hungary took Vienna from Frederick III, and made it his capital city... Spanish Inquisitor Peter Arbués was assassinated, allegedly by Jews – justifying centuries of disproportionate persecution...

In England, Richard III fell at the Battle of Bosworth Field.

'I know who Hodge is,' she said.

'The Crook,' said Edwin. 'It's obvious.'

'Not just the Crook. He's the Crook-Back!'

Edwin stopped tapping and looked at her. So did everyone else.

'It's in his name. The Hog, remember? The Duke of Gloucester's crest: the white boar. As Richard III, his cronies were men called Catesby and Ratcliffe and Francis Lovell, whose emblem was a wolf. "The Catte, the Ratte and Lovell the Dogge... Ruleth all England under the Hogge."'

'What *is* she on about?' demanded Mrs Gregson.

'Shakespeare, *mes braves*,' said Herbert, posing against the mantelpiece. 'I've always longed to strut the boards. I've the legs for tights, don't you think?'

'Richard III is an elder vampire?' said Edwin.

'Now you mention it, I believe he came to a ball my father held once,' said Herbert. 'It's been nagging me all weekend where I met him before. Talk about tripping the light fantastic. Tripping over the carpet, more like.'

'Pish-tush,' said Mrs Gregson. 'What are you wittering on about, woman?'

'It's about being King of... England,' she said, completing Croft's sentence. 'The United Kingdom of Great Britain and... what's the status of Ireland since that treaty? Any rate, Richard III wants his throne back.'

With a ghastly grinding sound, a stone door opened behind the grate in the fireplace. Hodge stood, dramatically lit by flames, in red robes with a white pig on the tabard, leaning on his crook. He had Crooked Men with him, including Spode and – no big surprise

– Ilona Harczy. Dragged by a giant in armour, bleeding from the throat, was Caleb Croft.

'And why not, lass?' said Hodge. 'I were the last English King of England. Since me, it's been a dog's breakfast of foreign bastards, pooftahs, whelps, harridans, lunatics and whoreson knaves. Taff Tudors, jock Stewarts, double Dutch, fat Krauts, and Count Fookin' Dracula. Me country needs me!'

Hodge stepped around the fire and limped into the room. Turned vampire, he'd had his back broken and set, crudely dispensing with his warm infirmities. It hadn't broken his habits. He stood straight, but – unless he concentrated – walked like a cripple.

One of the maids was with his retinue, face painted with white roses. The King had four followers: two (Spode and the maid) definitely warm, one definitely a vampire (Ilona). The man in armour could have been anything; Geneviève pegged him as muscle.

'Why bother with this charade?' she asked. 'King of the Cats?'

'Don't make me laugh,' he sneered. 'It were never about King of the Bloody Kittens. Let one of these foreign pillocks call hisself that… you, Meinster, you're as good or bad as any. I'll let you have that crown. Only I'll want sommat back. I want you lot – foreign bloody vampires – to leave England be while I conquer me own country. Oh, and bloody Wales! I'm going to ravage the fookin' place! I'll stuff the coal mines with the drained corpses of male-voice choirs and rugby forwardss.'

'Doesn't England already have a king?' said Herbert. 'An Edward or a George or somesuch?'

'A sausage-eater at bottom, lad. Nowt to me. Nowt to England.'

The Crooked Men were a more ambitious conspiracy than even the Diogenes Club knew, a political movement calling for Plantagenet Restoration and a return to feudal values. In propaganda, the Crooked Men harped on the society-sapping menace of 'alien rulers'. She'd read that as lingering resentment against Dracula, but Hodge deemed Victoria and her heirs as foreign as Vlad the Impaler.

'Who turned you?' she asked.

'What is this, Twenty Questions? If the name means anything to you, it were Gregory von Bayern. Fought wi' me at Bosworth. Kraut vampire mercenary. Got to me as I lay bleeding. You know that story. "A horse, a fookin' horse, me kingdom for a blah de blah…" I *hate* that play, you know. All lies. Well, most of it. Von Bayern didn't bring me a horse, but he bled for me, bled *into* me. He's still about, I reckon.'

'I know him,' said General Karnstein. 'Hauptmann von Bayern was on Dracula's staff in the War.'

'You can thank him from me for nowt. Fooked off after he turned me and left me to fend for mesself. Back then, you couldn't return from the dead and hang on to your lands and titles wi'out some prawn in holy orders coming for you wi' scythe and stake. I've had hundreds o' years o' beetlin' about while jessies and whoreson knaves run me rightful kingdom into the muck. Couldn't say owt. That's all over.'

'I say, we did manage an Empire without you,' pointed out Edwin.

'It'll be a bloody sight more imperial wi' me,' announced Richard.

'*Vivat, vivat… Ricardus*,' declaimed Mrs Gregson, lowering herself creakily on one knee and kissing Richard's crook.

Was the hostess in on it? No, she was just a sudden convert to Yorkism.

Few others in the room were potential subjects. Geneviève would bet Richard remembered Anne de Beaujeu sent troops to support Henry Tudor at Bosworth, and still planned on paying France back with interest. So that was her out. Croft was English, but gurgling his own blood. Edwin was too appalled to take Hodge's claim seriously – which might, she judged, be a mistake. It didn't do to underestimate the kings of the middle ages. Men like Richard and Dracula fought their own battles, for a start. With swords and bows. Without the patience for politicking, they took an Alexandrine approach to the knotty problems that troubled subtle minds like Croft or Ruthven or, come to that, the Ruling Cabal of the Diogenes Club.

'You, big lad,' Richard said to Dravot. 'What sort o' King do you want? Beardy Georgie? One o' his stammering sons?'

She might not like Dravot, but he was loyal, wasn't he?

Loyal to what?

The Diogenes Club always said 'the Crown' or 'the Throne'. That meant more than a jewelled hat and a fancy, uncomfortable chair. More than a vampire bloodline.

Why did she even care? What was it to her who was King of England?

She'd not liked Kah Pai Mei. She loathed Caleb Croft. Killing or cutting them weren't serious crimes in her book.

She couldn't see the harm in Marya Zaleska, though.

And she didn't like what she knew of the Crooked Men. Any more than she liked what she'd seen of Hitler or Mussolini or, in France, the noisy, nasty, hateful patriots in *les Camelots du Roi*.

Once before, she'd been unwittingly instrumental in deciding who sat on the Throne of Britain.

'You'll all support me,' he said. 'The vampires, any rate. You warm ones, you'll do what's good for you.'

Edwin looked at Mrs Gregson's female relation, who might have been slapped with a wet haddock. Technically, Professor Bey was also a non-vampire.

Richard directed his attention to her.

'I can make you kneel, lass,' he said.

'How, pray?'

She saw the ghost of Shakespeare's Gloucester in his one-sided smirk. Determinèd to prove a villain.

'You're an elder. Like me. Like a lot in this room. Us elders, we don't fear death. The Countess begged for it, you know. Most of you've already been dead and it didn't take. You've got spine and pride. Even you, nancy boy Herbert. Fight like a caged rat, you would. Wi' ten like you, I could take a city. Birmingham, say. No, death is nowt to us. Makes us cocky. But I've someone in me pocket who can put the fear into an elder vampire. And I've got you to thank, General Karnstein. Your fairy princess is now my hunting dog.'

Liam Karnstein – elegant, beautiful, remote – strolled out of the fireplace.

'What this lad can do to you, you're all afraid of!'

24

DE PROFUNDIS

Lydia explained to Mouse who Mr Hodge was.

Richard of York. A very bad king.

But she didn't know how he'd become the Crook, or why he was pretending to be friends with Mr Croft. Grown-up stuff. Politics.

It was easiest to think of him as a murderer. A gangster, like in America. The robes and armour and crooked figure writing were just fancy dress.

'You're so clever, Niobe,' said Mouse. 'To see through him.'

Lydia *was* proud of that. She knew her kings and queens.

But knowing didn't seem to help.

They cautiously made their way through the caverns, back to the stairs up to Mildew Manor. No Crooked Men were left down here besides the four Mouse had fed off.

Her friend had put one of the Crooked Men's robes over the tatters of her sailor suit. She had to gather it in at the waist and tie the rope over the folds to avoid tripping.

Lydia could not think of *her vampire*.

After what had happened in the store room, something was missing in her.

What would she tell Smudge?

Was vampire romance dead?

25

THE MIDNIGHT HOUR

All the elders in the drawing room backed, stepped or squirmed away from Liam Karnstein, as if he exuded an invisible cloud of plague bacilli. Geneviève found herself nearly colliding with a waxy potted aspidistra. Now she knew what this pretty youth could do, she struggled with instinctive terror.

Richard smirked and dragged his foot, but kept his distance too.

How secure was his hold over the creature?

'Carmilla,' she said. 'Is there anything of you left?'

Richard laughed. 'Go on, lass. Try owt.'

She approached Liam.

'Carmilla?'

The green eyes were empty of expression, recognition, intellect.

She felt the pricking of tears. This creature offered worse than death, but was tragic too. Poor Carmilla, so fearfully treated... so poorly used... now, even as a vegetable homunculus, so wasted and exploited. Useful to Richard, as she had been to her limpet parents, she was no use to herself, and never had been.

Geneviève reached out, towards the carved beauty of Liam's face.

Kleopatra made a noise of disgust, fearful for her own looks. No one else said or did anything.

Geneviève felt the flow of her life pulled out of her into the pulsing orchid heart of the Karnstein creature. She was tired, and *ached*.

She couldn't bring herself to touch it.

She stepped away. The eyes followed her.

Was Liam *hungry*?

'Kill it,' said Ethelind, the thing's mother.

'Family ties, eh?' said Richard. 'Even the lad's mam's afraid. So cruel, Mrs Karnstein. You made something beautiful and threw him away.'

Geneviève remembered the Princes in the Tower. Killed on the orders of their wicked uncle.

'The play's wrong there,' said Richard, picking up her thoughts. 'I didn't send murderers to stifle the tykes. I always say: if you want sommat done, do it yourself.'

His big hands opened and closed and twisted as if little necks were gripped in them.

'The thing about killing kids: it's habit-forming,' he said, smiling. 'Little lives, so easy to snuff. When I were alive, I'd got so I could do it wi' me thumbs or a pillow. Or that grip, hand over mouth and nose. They call it "Burking", as if the Edinburgh beef-snatcher invented it. Pah, it should be called "Dicking", after me. I've "Dicked" my share, all right.'

'Nobody ever denied that you were a Dick,' said Edwin.

Richard chuckled mirthlessly, and – she could tell – made a mental note to do something mediaeval to Edwin's bottom. His hands were bigger now, thick-fingered, extra-knuckled, stubby-clawed.

He touched Liam's shoulder and wheeled the creature around, directing its bright green gaze at everyone in turn.

'General, you want to take a go?' he asked, mock-genially. 'Your hound is on my lead. Think you can call him back to heel?'

Karnstein concentrated. He must have had some control over the creature made from his daughter's heart and God knows what animal and vegetable matter. Liam, she understood, was essentially mindless and needed direction from a strong-willed master. Like Rossum in the play, Professor ten Brinken had grown a robot. The General could make no connection to Liam. Karnstein's ambition was stronger than his willpower. Richard III was, as Shakespeare said, *determinéd*.

Edwin casually reached into his dinner jacket, as if for a cigarette case. He got a silver-plated automatic halfway out before the armoured giant smote with a mace-like fist. The gun skittered across the flagstones. Edwin crumpled.

'Wondered who'd have the balls to try sommat,' said Richard. 'Might have known it'd be the Man from the Diogenes Club. Yes, I know all about you lot. From Croftie here.'

He kicked Croft, who fell over, leaking blood. His throat was cut deeply.

Dravot stepped to help Edwin and the giant got his chest in the way. The Sergeant looked ready to head-butt the Crooked Man's helmet. Neither stood down.

Edwin, dazed, got upright. Geneviève helped him balance, though the blood on his face made her fangs start. She had her arm round his waist.

Richard scooped up the gun, balanced it on his fingertips so as not to grip the silver barrel, and tossed it into the fire. It lay on burning logs, heating up.

'Why did you kill them?' she asked.

'Who? The little princes?'

She shook her head.

'Oh, *them*. Tonight's crop? Well, Chinky-Chinky-Chinaman were bloody rude. I didn't take to his notion we should all bow to the East. In my line, I get enough aggravation from Limehouse tongs, ta very much. The Countess, like I say, were begging for it. She and me go back a way. I had her vote at midnight. But she wanted something I was not prepared to give. A dynastic marriage. The House of York wi' the House of Dracula. I'll not be wed to a bloody foreign tart, especially a bloody foreign tart what goes wi' lasses. So that partnership needed dissolving. But a foreign tart who knows her place is welcome, missy. Like little Ilona, here. She got the Countess in me sights.'

Richard mimed twanging a bowstring. Ilona purred like a kitten.

Shakespeare had caught one of Richard's habits, the need for an audience to take into his confidence, to confess and boast to. This, she realised, was why he was even here. He wanted his peers to know what he had done, to express grudging admiration, to acknowledge heroic villainy. He hadn't changed. He was a big little boy with a toy theatre. All these years after Bosworth, he was addicted to melodrama – dressing up as a hooded fiend, passing notes in cipher, killing when the lights went out.

The gun in the fire started popping off.

Professor Bey got shot in the knee and loosed a fluent, lisping string of oaths in a language she didn't recognise. Others flinched and hopped, while Richard laughed heartily. He'd made sure to stand out of the way. The aspidistra pot burst, exploding dirt all over the carpet.

The clock chimed elaborately, then began sounding the twelve long strokes of midnight.

'Now,' said Richard. 'Who wants to try and stop me being king of whatever I fookin' claim?'

A small person leaped through the fire, clothes catching light, and bounded across the room, sword-point steady.

The *katana* pierced Richard's adam's apple and slid out the back of his neck.

'Bloody 'eck!' he croaked.

The Japanese vampire, fire springing up from the remnants of a robe, bore Richard down. Grip firm on her sword-hilt, she pinned him to the floor.

The armoured giant, slow to react, made a move, but Dravot got him in a wrestler's grip, wrenching off his helmet. Inside he was a pockmarked bald vampire Geneviève didn't recognise.

Still a weight on Richard's chest, Kah Pai Mei's bodyguard produced a silver throwing star and flung it with casual accuracy. It embedded itself in the bald vampire's forehead. He was suddenly a dead weight in armour in Dravot's hands.

Spode and Ilona were in check. Meinster and Herbert hissed at them through mouthfuls of sharp teeth. Kleopatra took hold of their necks, lifting them off their feet. She had a dancer's strength. Cords of muscle showed in her arms.

The Yorkist maid fainted in a corner.

Liam didn't move.

That stray warm child gingerly stepped out of the fireplace. Geneviève still didn't know who she was.

Richard tried to speak around the silvered steel transfixing his voice box.

'My kingdom,' he said, 'my kingdom for…'

The Japanese girl – her hair was white, now! – twisted the sword and chopped down with it, one way and then the other.

Fast, she stood up, wiped her blade, and sheathed it.

The final stroke of midnight sounded.

The head of the last English king of England rolled into the fireplace.

26

---◆---

WHO MOURNS FOR ADONAIS?

'He was Richard Crookback,' said Lydia. 'I could tell from the pig on his chest.'

'Lydi-*ah*,' said Mother, in exasperation.

No one else even noticed her.

Mouse had, she supposed, restored her honour by killing the man who had murdered her master.

Right now, her friend needed patting down. Her robe was still on fire.

None of the vampires in the room made the effort, so she did. She burned her palms and, in the end, found it easier to pull off the robe completely and throw it away.

She'd have to lend Mouse some clothes, though they'd be too big for the tiny girl.

The darkie woman had hold of Spode and the Countess's secretary. Her teeth were huge. She looked angry enough to eat them both.

The Crooked Champion was ashes in armour. And Richard of Gloucester was truly dead.

The Crooked Men were smashed, at least at Mildew Manor.

But it wasn't over. All the vampires in the room – except Mouse – were still, holding their breath if breath they had, as if any movement would attract the darting bite of a black mamba.

They were terrified of Liam. Even his parents – *most of all*, his parents.

For a moment, Lydia wondered whether she could set him off. If he was pushed, would he serve these vampires the way Mouse served the Crooked Men? Tearing from one to the next, sucking elders empty and tossing aside the husks, glutting himself on stolen lives.

They wouldn't be so beautiful then. Geneviève and Kleopatra... Meinster and von Krolock... They'd be shrunken scarecrows.

Even Bloody Aunt Agatha and the big chauffeur with the moustache.

She *could* do it.

Liam had followed her, for a while, until the hunger took over. It wasn't a *psychic bond*, she knew now. Liam would follow *anyone*.

He had been following Hodge, but that was off. Obviously.

Lydia looked at *her vampire* and saw only carved ice. He was not different. She was.

'What's to be done with... ?'

Geneviève said it, not finishing the sentence.

'My son will do his duty as a Karnstein,' said the General.

'But this is not your son,' said Geneviève, 'this is your daughter. What's left of your daughter.'

Liam was a *girl*! Lydia had a spasm of horror.

She looked at his face and saw it, a softness she had mistaken for masculine beauty. Yuck!

No. Liam wasn't *even* a girl. Liam, in the end, was nothing. Under his clothes, he – she? it? – was a mannequin, a dressmaker's dummy who was whatever the tailor wanted. An idol no longer worshipped, like the gods in the caves.

Because no one else would, she took Liam's hand and pulled him into the fireplace, back into the dark passages and secret stairways.

He did not resist.

He could not feed off her. She was safe with him.

27

CARMILLA'S LAST REPOSE

'What *is* that girl doing?' said Mrs Gregson's warm relation, Mrs Inchfawn, who was – Geneviève gathered – the mother of 'that girl'. She came with the house.

So far as Geneviève was concerned, 'that girl' – Lydia – was saving all their lives.

Carmilla was far gone. Liam had never existed. The creature Karnstein called his son was a danger to other vampires.

She had felt his spell, but mistaken it for 'it'. A draining. They'd all been off their game when Liam was in the room. Even the General kept away from his son, for fear of going the way of his wife.

The Japanese girl had suffered worst.

Because Mrs Gregson didn't seem inclined to do anything but look pop-eyed with apoplexy, Geneviève took it on herself to send a maid to fetch a dressing gown for the white-haired, singed child.

Edwin was still dazed from being thumped with an iron fist. He complained less than Professor Bey did about being shot in the knee. First aid was applied. Mostly hot towels and whisky.

Ethelind Karnstein sat up and kept asking what was going on.

Dravot could hold the fort up here.

Geneviève took the Japanese girl, who said her name was Mouse, and also volunteered Herbert von Krolock.

Together, they went through the fireplace and followed the trail.

It wasn't difficult. No one ever swept secret passages. Scuffmarks in the dust and broken curtains of cobweb showed which routes were travelled.

Mouse, a quiet little thing, led the way.

'Are you going to kill it?' Herbert asked. '*Can* you kill it?'

Geneviève wasn't sure. But she wanted to see.

Under the house were caves, the home of the thousand gods. Lately, the Crooked Men had been using the place.

They found the girl and Liam in a huge cavern. Lydia had manoeuvred the creature into an alcove. She stood back, admiring a thing which was now more statue than creature. Liam was turning into one idol among many.

Lydia held up her hand, warning the vampires to stay back.

'Without you, he's nothing,' she said. 'Keep away.'

Geneviève saw what the girl meant. So long as the thing with Carmilla's heart was removed from the society of vampires, it was inert. A mandrake, like Professor ten Brinken's other experiments, it would sprout roots. Tubers and leaf-buds already wormed out of its flesh, bursting through clothes. The skin was greenish in this light. The eyes still burned green.

Lydia began piling up stones to seal the alcove. There weren't enough to make a sill, let alone a wall.

'Come away,' said Geneviève. 'The butler can do that. With bricks and mortar. You've done enough.'

Mouse bravely walked on and laid a hand on Lydia's shoulder, then brought the girl back. They were a safe distance from Liam Karnstein.

'Niobe,' said the Japanese girl.

'Call me Inchworm,' said Lydia. 'Everybody does.'

Geneviève took a last look at the face of her friend, and said a last goodbye to Carmilla's heart.

28

DEPARTURES

The next morning, the rain stopped. Matey reported the road out was passable again.

The vampires made excuses and left early. The question of who might or might not be King or Queen of the Cats wasn't settled to anyone's satisfaction.

Aunt Agatha was in her attic, sulking. She had been an enthusiast for Richard III. Matey, following Mr Winthrop's orders, was supervising the bricking-up of the Person She Would Never Again Think of by Name.

So Mother had to handle the departures, though she was still mostly terrified of creatures of the night even in the cold light of day. For her part, Lydia had learned much about vampires, though she didn't know how she'd tell it to Smudge. Some were frightening – she still thought Mr Croft, who'd survived near decapitation, the worst of the lot – and some were useless. Most were ordinary.

Kleopatra and Professor Bey left first. Lottie reported that all the bed-linens and towels from their rooms were missing. In the last day and a half, she had acquired little bite-marks about her throat, so someone had been nipping her.

In the hall, with the great doors open, Lydia heard gushing gutters and saw the green, waterlogged lawn. The cars were all in working order and not washed away.

'Mrs Inchfawn, thank you for a delightful weekend,' said Herbert

542

von Krolock, dryly. 'Please pass on our gratitude to Lady Worplesdon. So much entertainment. I look forward to doing it again soon.'

The Viscount's teeth got longer when he lied, Lydia noticed.

Baron Meinster was still annoyed at not being elevated to the vampire monarchy. She saw he hadn't given up his ambition. Herbert just thought it a fearful bore and wanted to get back to civilisation quickly. By civilisation, he meant a suite at the Savoy with reliable electricity and hot and cold running chorus boys.

'Come on, Molly,' he said, dragging the Baron to a sporty roadster. 'Toodle-oo, new chums.'

Meinster and von Krolock had a vampire chauffeur Lydia hadn't even noticed before, an Italian-looking fellow with a tight uniform, nice eyes and an easy, ready smile. He gave her a thrilling wink, which – she realised – nearly set her off again…

After she'd gone to bed last night, the grown-ups had a meeting about what was to be done with the Crook's surviving followers. This morning, over breakfast, Mr Winthrop and Mr Croft were tidying up. The telephone was restored and Mr Winthrop made lengthy calls to people she gathered were above the police when it came to sorting things out. Mr Croft could only communicate via written notes. Mr Winthrop – who had to make calls for the vampire – pretended he couldn't make out his handwriting. This annoyed Mr Croft a great deal, which amused Mr Winthrop all the more.

Ilona, it seemed, had slipped off at dead of night. Lydia bet she had planted one on that vampire bruiser with the moustache, Dravot, to get him to look the other way. Apparently high-tailing it across the fields, she would be in dire peril of ruining her stockings. If Miss Harczy had problems with running water, she'd be bogged down and easy enough to net.

Spode was under something like house arrest. For a change, he was not booming orders. Lydia doubted he'd learned a lesson, but it would be a long time before anyone dressed up in silly uniforms and followed him.

No one but Lydia had noticed May was one of the Crooked Men. That meant she had a slave for life. Which could be useful.

If the Karnsteins were reluctant to leave the PSWNATobN behind, they didn't show it. This morning, Countess Karnstein looked fresher, cheeks filling out. Lydia saw where the Person etc got his/her/its looks from, which had literally been the case lately. The Countess could see, now: if she looked directly at a thing or a person. She swivelled her head with a snakelike motion that drew attention to her unnaturally long neck. The General carried the bags. In daylight, his uniform now made him look more like a hotel commissionaire than a power behind the throne.

Mr Winthrop popped out to see the Karnsteins off.

'Are your passports in order?' he asked. 'I've heard there's likely to be a swoop on visitors to our shores with dodgy papers soon. You might consider a sojourn on the continent.'

'We're going to the Irish Free State,' said the Countess.

'Very nice at this time of year.'

'It's horrible any time of year, Mr Winthrop, but it's my native soil. I think we won't meet again.'

'A shame. Might I say how well you're looking this morning, Countess.'

She gave him a cold dead stare. Her husband dragged her away.

Mr Winthrop looked at Mother and her, smiling. He had a bandaged head, but was enjoying himself. Just being alive with the sun out made things better. His vampire bit wasn't about this morning.

Lydia supposed Geneviève wasn't *completely* hideous. But, still…

Mouse came down, dressed in Lydia's outgrown third-form Drearcliff Grange skirt, blazer and straw boater. Her hair was permanently white.

'*Yuki Onna*,' said Mr Winthrop.

Mouse nodded, solemnly.

'It means "woman of the snow",' she explained. 'A famous Japanese vampire.'

The only cars left in the drive were Mr Winthrop's Bentley and Mr Croft's Sunbeam.

'How did you get here, Mouse?' he asked.

'We walked.'

'From China?'

Mouse shrugged. 'Mostly. Kleopatra gave us a lift from Preston.'

'You are *ronin* now?'

Mouse nodded. Thanks to Mullane of the Fifth, Lydia knew *ronin* meant 'masterless samurai'.

Mr Winthrop gave Mouse a card. 'If you need employment, present this at the Diogenes Club in Pall Mall. England owes you, Miss Mouse. Is there anything England can do for you?'

Shyly, Mouse said 'I should like to go to school.'

Mr Winthrop looked rather surprised.

'That can be arranged. Have you a school in mind?'

'Oh yes,' said Mouse, holding Lydia's arm.

'You've made a friend,' Mr Winthrop observed. 'Good, I approve. Lydia, isn't it? Well-played, by the way.'

Lydia felt her face going red again. Mr Winthrop's eyes glinted when he smiled. His face wasn't smooth like a vampire's. He was crinkly round the eyes, and he'd missed a bit while shaving. But he was more than just alive.

'Cheerio,' he said, and walked away.

Lydia sighed and Mouse thumped her in a friendly way which hurt more than she wanted to admit.

'Come on, Inchworm. I want you to teach me cricket.'

Lydia had a notion this coming term at Drearcliff Grange would be different.

29

CHELSEA MORNING

After a long day's drive, they were back in London. Well past midnight. It was Monday morning.

Edwin was satisfied at the weekend's outcome, if not their performance.

'We didn't emerge from this little contretemps covered in glory,' he admitted. 'Two vampire elders got murdered, two more got justifiably homicided, I got bonked on the head and our collective bacon was saved by jolly hockeysticks schoolgirls.'

Geneviève thought that a fair, if limited account.

'At least the King of the Cats thing is done with.'

'Kicked into long grass, more like,' he said. 'Molly Meinster is still rooting about for it.'

'*Molly*?'

'It's what Herbert calls him. The Viscount let it slip.'

'Deliberately?'

'What do you think?'

Geneviève laughed. 'I think… Herbert von Krolock is a wicked boy and will bear watching.'

'Oh, we'll watch them all from now on.'

The Bentley cruised down the King's Road, past St Botolph's. Geneviève saw a line of Crooked Men graffiti on the kerb.

'What about that lot? The organisation's still there.'

'Headless chickens, I hope. Ordinary criminals and crackpots with useless monk togs in their wardrobes. We'll round up the dangerous ones and find something to charge them with. Spode will name names. Croft won't even have to drag the blighter to the Tower. Our Mr Spode has had a fright.'

Not half the fright he'd have when Croft got his voice back. She was almost sorry for him. If Croft got his way, the purge of the Crooked Men would be enacted without legal niceties. Admittedly, it would have been the same or worse for the enemies of York if Richard had won. The business of the secret state depressed and enraged her.

'Mrs Gregson wants shot of Spode for messing up her weekend,' Edwin said. 'So he's lost his patron there.'

'She was all fired for a Plantagenet Restoration.'

'A woman of enthusiasms, Mrs Gregson. They wax and wane, like the moon. With Dickon decapitated, the craze passes. I hope she latches on something harmless next. Like country dancing.'

'There've been some dangerous country dances.'

'I suppose there have. This is your stop, old girl.'

Cheyne Walk, Chelsea. A comforting row of lamp-posts. Dravot parked outside the house. The curtains were drawn but the lights were on.

She kissed Edwin on the cheek, slightly enjoying his wince. That bonk on the head was a near-concussion, she'd judged while bandaging him. She deflected any attempt to palm one of those sign-up-for-eternity-in-the-secret-service cards on her.

'Be seeing you,' he said, giving a secret salute.

'Not if I see you first,' she said, fondly.

Getting out of the Bentley, she realised she was stiff from so many hours in the car. And thirsty.

The Bentley drove off. She wasn't alone. People were always about in Chelsea, vampire and warm. An open-top Alberford full of bright undead things roared past. In the back, Polly Browne sat on the shoulders of a titled twit with a monocle, dress hiked up above her stocking-tops, fringes shimmering, tiara of black ostrich feathers askew on her bob, red mess smeared about her pretty lips and tiny chin. She had a bottle of champagne in one hand and a blood-leaking weasel in the other. Whoever thought that made a happy drinks mix? Half her party gave voice to 'The Darktown Strutters' Ball'. The other half roared 'The Roast Beef of Old England'. Neither faction were in tune. A girl in an oversize check cap who was wrestling with the driver's wheel accompanied the choir with car-horn poots. Polly waved a yoo-hoo to Geneviève, perhaps half-remembering her from M. Eugene's, perhaps just hoping to snare a new catch for her fast set. The tourer turned a corner, jumping the kerb, scraping a lamp-post, making a policeman jump. The bobby tooted his whistle but the Polly Browne Express was gone, leaving empties, items of clothing and an insensible warm Boy Scout in the gutter.

'Evenin' miss,' said the constable, passing her by.

'Good evening,' she responded, through closed lips, not wanting to show fangs.

She had her key out of her purse as she walked up to the front door, but it was open before she got there.

It wasn't the butler who's name she couldn't remember.

'Hullo, Gené,' said Charles. 'Was that Winthrop's bus? Have you had an adventure?'

He was sun-browned and the lobe of one ear was missing. He wore a crimson smoking jacket and held a balloon of brandy.

'I certainly have,' she said, kissing him on the lips, tasting the brandy. 'Dire peril to the realm averted. Virtue triumphant and the wicked laid low. True hearts broken but on the mend. What about you?'

'Oh, the usual,' he said. 'The Empire is marginally less doomed than it was last month. The sun's still going to set, though. Chilly out here on the steps, old girl.'

They went indoors and she kissed him again, taking more time.

She thought of Carmilla, the sponge. She thought of Lydia

Inchfawn, leading Liam into the caves under Mildew Manor. What had been going on between them?

She broke the kiss. Her fangteeth were sharp enough to cut her lips – and his if she wasn't careful.

'Charles, I'm a vampire,' she said. 'What do you see in me? We're a sorry lot, really. What's the appeal?'

'You're a vampire? Can't say I'd noticed. Apart from the bites. I noticed the bites. Still, quinine seems to do the trick. And beef tea. Good as new after quinine and beef tea.'

He tweaked her nose. Her mood changed.

'More of that and you'll be bitten again,' she said. 'Soon, and badly.'

His eyes – young eyes for a man of his years – glinted with mischief. 'Promise?'

'Promise.'

ANNOTATIONS

A s with the new edition of *Anno Dracula*, I'm not going to tag every borrowed, misappropriated or historical character, setting or bit of business. However, I am happy to acknowledge my major sources, and highlight a few elements that might otherwise escape the reader. It has been sobering to re-read the book and realise how much of my research I've completely forgotten. In some cases, others will have more luck tracking down what or who I meant than I have. Again, I want some mysteries to remain. Obviously, this is a fantasy novel – but much of the most unbelievable material in it is true; I have refrained from too many 'yes, this really happened' and 'my god, they actually said that' notes.

EPIGRAPHS

It is a testimony to Manfred von Richthofen's fame – and perhaps the different mores of 1918 – that his autobiography should have been translated into English and published successfully in Britain while the Great War was still being fought and the author was on active service as an enemy ace. Richthofen, incidentally, dictated his memoirs to a stenographer; they were almost certainly touched up by professional editors and propagandists before publication – but, as Grey notes in his preface, are surprisingly frank and forthright. All Richthofen biographers treat the book as a primary, mostly trustworthy source – though some members of his family disparaged it as a complete fabrication. On balance, it seems likely *Der Rote Kampfflieger* was an 'as told to' celebrity autobiography rather than 'ghosted'. I wonder who, if anyone, saw royalties from the British publication.

PART ONE: ALL QUIET ON THE WESTERN FRONT

The section title, of course, comes from Erich Maria Remarque's novel of the trenches, *Im Westen nichts Neues* (1929). An approximation of the German ('Nothing New in the West'), the title was coined by Remarque's English translator, Arthur Wesley Wheen. Lewis Milestone's Hollywood film, *All Quiet on the Western Front* (1930) was the *Platoon* or *Hurt Locker* of its day, a Best Picture Oscar winner combining a realist, yet exciting view of a particular war with general anti-war sentiment.

CHAPTER 1: CONDOR SQUADRON

Edwin Winthrop. I salted this character throughout my earlier works, and have revisited him outside the *Anno Dracula* continuum. He appears in my one-act play *My One Little Murder Can't Do Any Harm* – I took the part in its only production to date (1981) – and a flashback section of my novel *Jago*, and is mentioned in the Jack Yeovil novel *Demon Download*. Subsequent to *The Bloody Red Baron*, Edwin has shown up in 'Angel Down, Sussex', 'Clubland Heroes', 'Seven Stars' and 'Sorcerer Conjurer Wizard Witch', which can be found in *Secret Files of the Diogenes Club* and *Mysteries of the Diogenes Club* (MonkeyBrain).

Sergeant Dravot. He returns from *Anno Dracula*, though the non-vampire Dravot perished at the end of Rudyard Kipling's 'The Man Who Would Be King'. Being undead has straightened out his character somewhat.

Elliott Spenser. Thanks to Clive Barker, Pete Atkins and Doug Bradley for him and his 'Moldavian headache remedy'. Yes, I know the IMDb, Wikipedia and other sources say 'Spencer', but I double-checked the spelling with Pete, who actually named the character.

The habitués of Condor Squadron are a mix of real people, like Albert Ball and Arthur Rhys-Davids, and air aces from pulp and literary fiction. Most are too well known to need tags, but especial credit to V.M. Yeates for Tom Cundall, who comes from Yeates' outstanding autobiographical novel *Winged Victory* (1934). Written partially as a response to W.E. Johns' 'boys' adventure' collection *The Camels Are Coming* (1932), it's still the best of many books about WWI air combat. List-makers who distinguish on Wikipedia between my 'real' and 'fictional' characters have a problem with Henry Williamson, who is both – a character in *Winged Victory* and its editor/dedicatee. Nods also to Johns, Walter Gibson and John Monk Saunders, of course.

Boche. The derogatory term derives from the French slang term '*alboche*', which literally means 'German cabbage head'. I first came across the insult in a commando comic in the 1960s, where a French hero was forever fuming about terrible things done by *les boches*. I assumed there was an especially evil Nazi General called Leslie Botches.

CHAPTER 3: PAST MIDNIGHT

The gramophone record of 'Poor Butterfly' is from John Monk Saunders' screenplay *The Dawn Patrol* (1930).

Sidcot. A flying suit, named after its inventor, the Australian flier Frederick Sidney Cotton. Before the introduction of the Sidcot in 1917, pilots found it impossible to keep warm in the air – shaking hands and chattering teeth added greatly to the other perils of combat flying. Cotton also devised various photographic equipment used in early air reconnaissance.

CHAPTER 4: GREY EMINENCES

General Karnstein. His 'dreadful daughter' features in J.S. Le Fanu's 'Carmilla'. In *Anno Dracula*, Geneviève thinks more kindly of her.

'He's like a monstrous child.' In *Dracula*, Van Helsing holds similar views, referring to the Count's 'child-brain'.

CHAPTER 5: THE PROPHET OF PRAGUE

Edgar Allan Poe. Turning him into a vampire means that the alternate world of *Anno Dracula* differs from ours even before Dracula defeated Van Helsing's group c. 1885. I did this to set up a story which I now can't write (see the note on Billy the Kid in *Anno Dracula*). I wasn't the first to rank Edgar among the undead: in Shimako Sato's film *Tale of a Vampire* (1992), Kenneth Cranham plays a vampire Poe. I featured Poe in my Jack Yeovil novel *Route 666*, and return to him in the short stories 'Just Like Eddy' and 'Illimitable Dominion'.

CHAPTER 6: MATA HARI

Theda Bara. In 1917, if you asked anyone to name a vampire, they would first think not of Dracula but Theda Bara, and wouldn't mean an undead bloodsucker but a predatory seductress. This meaning of the term goes back to Rudyard Kipling's poem 'The Vampire', source for the 1915 film *A Fool There Was* which made a star of Bara (real name: Theodosia Goodman). It wasn't until the success of the play and then the film of *Dracula* that the older meaning of 'vampire' eclipsed the Bara-type 'vamp'. Bara never did play Mata Hari, but in an era when only bad girls could be sexy in films, she was Carmen, Cigarette, Camille, Salome and Madame Mysterieux (she played Esmeralda and Juliet too, but always more popular as a vixen than a heroine). An iconic poster of her clad only in jewels as Cleopatra was popular in the 1960s; I grew up in a house where it was wallpaper along with the classic images of Bogart, Bardot, Gable and W.C. Fields.

General Mireau. He's the worst villain (played by George Macready) in Stanley Kubrick's film *Paths of Glory*. In Humphrey Cobb's novel, he's called General Assolant. The character is based on General Gérard Réveilhac, who once ordered the shelling of his own men to encourage an advance against an impregnable enemy position (the artillery officer refused to carry out the order unless it was put in writing, and Réveilhac backed down). Mireau/Assolant is ostracised (if validated) by high command; Réveilhac was made a grand officer of the Légion d'Honneur.

Poilu. Nickname for the French infantry soldier from Napoleonic times to the Great War. Literally, it means 'hairy one'.

CHAPTER 7: KATE

Sydney Horler. 'Exciteable Sydney Horler', as he's called in Colin Watson's indispensable study of British pulp, *Snobbery with Violence*. He worked for the *Mail* during the war. He was also attached to the propaganda section of air intelligence – which would give him another reason for loitering about the plot of *The Bloody Red Baron*, though I probably didn't know that when I wrote the book or I'd have made more of it. In the 1920s, he became a prolific writer of thrillers in imitation of Sapper and Edgar Wallace. His not-well-remembered work combines bluff hearty British masculinity with an almost neurotic dislike of sexual activity and foreigners. Horler's *The Vampire* (1935), an arrant imitation of *Dracula*, features the evil Sovranian nobleman Baron Ziska.

In earlier editions, Charles consulted a wrist watch in the previous chapter and a pocket-watch in this one. Tut tut. I've 'invisibly' fixed a few other glitches from earlier editions – the spellings of some names, Kate's inconsistent height, Hitler's eye-colour, etc. Thanks to all who've pointed these out.

CHAPTER 8: CASTLE KEEP

Professor ten Brinken. He comes from H.H. Ewers' best-known novel *Alraune* (1911), which was filmed several times. Like Dr Caligari, he was played in a German silent movie by Paul Wegener.

Doktor Krueger. Most of the scientific staff at the Chateau de Malinbois are too well-known to need a note, but some have assumed the Professor to be related to the child murderer Fred Krueger (which, who knows, is possible) so I thought I'd clear up the ambiguity and acknowledge a key influence. Krueger is a recurring villain in Robert J. Hogan's pulp *G-8 and His Battle Aces* stories, appearing many times (devising many demented schemes) from *The Bat Staffel* (1933) to *Scourge of the Sky Monster* (1943). The Chateau de Malinbois project is exactly the sort of thing one could expect from someone whose bright ideas included bat-shaped planes, zombie aces, defrosted Viking warriors and giant fists/skeletons/arms in the sky. In *The Blood Bat Staffel* (1936), Krueger deployed 'weird-looking bat men'. It's a good thing our side had G-8 – unless you're reading the German edition, of course – and similar flying heroes, or we'd have been overrun by Krueger's Kreatures.

'A rare JG1 flier without a "von" to his name.' In assembling fictional enemy aces from various sources, I had a slight problem in that almost all of them – Bruno Stachel is an exception – are versions of Manfred von Richthofen, so I had to leave out some (like 'Baron von Richter' from *The Dawn Patrol* and 'the Red Max' from *Wacky Races*) or wind up with a squadron of clones. Thanks to W.E. Johns, Harry Stein and Mort Leib, Robert Kanigher and Joe Kubert, and Jack D. Hunter.

CHAPTER 9: LA MORTE PARISIENNE

Ecdysiast. A correspondent kindly pointed out that this term was coined well after 1918 by H.L. Mencken, at the request of Gypsy Rose Lee – who wanted to call herself something more dignified than a stripper. I noted in the afterword to *Anno Dracula* that Bram Stoker's *Dracula* is already set in a parallel universe where expressions come into use before they did in our relatively vampire-free history. So, here's another instance of that phenomenon.

CHAPTER 10: IN LOFTY CIRCLES

Gregory von Bayern. He appears in John M. Ford's *The Dragon Waiting*. A mediaeval alternate history, with magic, vampires and British Royals, the book was – along with Brian Stableford's *The Empire of Fear* – responsible for convincing me that readers would understand an alternate world vampire novel. Everything Mike Ford wrote is worth reading.

Sebastian Newcastle. Don Sebastian de Villanueva appears in Les Daniels's excellent historical vampire novels, *The Black Castle*, *The Silver Skull*, *Citizen Vampire*, *Yellow Fog* and *No Blood Spilled*.

CHAPTER 11: WHAT KATE DID NEXT

The Hôtel Transylvania. See: Chelsea Quinn Yarbro's *Hôtel Transylvania*, first in another fine historical vampire series.

CHAPTER 12: BLOODLINES

Lady Marikova. Stoker does not give names to Dracula's three wives. Others have remedied the omission. Marikova was named by R. Chetwynd-Hayes in *The House of Dracula*.

CHAPTER 13: DR MOREAU AND MR WEST

The University of Ingolstadt. Victor Frankenstein's alma mater.

CHAPTER 14: KATE AND EDWIN

Eddie Bartlett. The James Cagney character in Raoul Walsh's *The Roaring 20s* (1939), another of my templates for the *Anno Dracula* series. The three characters found in a foxhole just before the Armistice in the opening take different courses in life Stateside, enabling multiple viewpoints on a turbulent society in a lively decade. With songs, montages and that particularly exhilarating Warner Brothers wisecrack dialogue.

'I'll take vanilla.' Like the expression 'it seemed like a good idea at the time', the catchphrase 'I'll take vanilla' was popularised by the movie *The Last Flight* (1931), scripted by John Monk Saunders from his novel *Single Lady*. The line is associated with the character of Nikki, played in the film by Helen Chandler, who was Mina in the Bela Lugosi version of *Dracula* that same year.

Catriona Kaye. Though barely present in *The Bloody Red Baron*, Catriona Kaye was Edwin Winthrop's partner in the play *My One Little Murder Can't Do Any Harm* – she's named after the actress who played her, Catriona O'Callaghan – and has turned up in my novel *Jago* and several stories in *Secret Files of the Diogenes Club* and *Mysteries of the Diogenes Club*. She'll be back.

PART TWO: NO MAN'S LAND

I intended to take all the section titles of *The Bloody Red Baron* from famous WWI stories. Though the German film *Niemandsland* (1931) means I just about fulfilled this remit, it's generally known in English as *Hell on Earth*. *Niemandsland*, which I've never seen and had barely heard of when I wrote the book, deals with soldiers of warring nations living together in a refuge between the fronts.

CHAPTER 15: THE VILE, THE VIOLENT AND THE VEIN

Poe also fights for the Confederacy in Walter Jon Williams' 'No Spot of Ground'. Another fictional use of Poe that resonates with me is Manly Wade Wellman's 'When It Was Moonlight', in which the poet meets a vampire.

CHAPTER 16: TWICE BITTEN

Harry Tate. Rhyming slang for the R.E.8 aeroplane, taken from a popular comedian whose pop culture legacy includes owning the first recorded personalised license plate (T8) and the phrase 'Goodbye-eee' (taken up by a song used in *Oh! What a Lovely War!*). The plane was disliked by pilots and the term 'Harry Tate' came to mean outmoded or useless in the services.

CHAPTER 17: A SOLITARY CYCLIST

Colonel Nicholson and Horatio Bottomley. Some have assumed Nicholson is the character created by Pierre Boulle, played by Alec Guinness in *The Bridge Over the River Kwai*. Not so. Colonel W.N. Nicholson, CMG, DSO, 15th Highland Division, was the author of the memoir *Behind the Lines: An Account of Administrative Staffwork in the British Army 1914-1918* (1939). I took his remarks on Bottomley's visit to the front from *1914-1918: Voices and Images of the Great War*, edited by Lyn Macdonald. Bottomley, massively influential in his day, was convicted of fraud in 1922. Though the most obnoxiously jingoist of all British publications, Bottomley's *John Bull* rather surprisingly lobbied (unsuccessfully) for mercy in the case of sub-lieutenant Edwin Dyett, who was shot for desertion in 1918.

CHAPTER 18: HELL'S ANGELS

The chapter title comes from the 1930 talkie, directed by Howard Hughes and James Whale, which was – along with William Wellman's silent *Wings* (1928) – important in post-war myth-making about the fighter pilots of 1914-18. The title was adopted by a unit of the Flying Tigers in World War Two, and then – without the possessive apostrophe – by the motorcycle gang. Thanks to Hughes' obsessiveness, the making of the film has its own legend, as reflected in a series of films about the perils of making air ace movies: *The Last Flight*, *The Great Waldo Pepper*, *The Stunt Man* and *The Aviator*.

CHAPTER 19: BIGGLES FLIES WEST

The chapter title comes from a 1937 novel by W.E. Johns. Obviously, the Biggles books – which I read assiduously as a pre-teen – are a pervasive influence on *The Bloody Red Baron*. It's possible that their pre-eminent position in British popular culture was shot down by devastating parodies on *Monty Python's Flying Circus* ('I don't understand your banter'), which Michael Palin at least must have come to regret. The joke title *Biggles*

Flies Undone was playground currency long before Python cited it, though. The early Johns stories, which have a World War One setting, are a little grittier and more personal, though they don't aspire to the qualities of Cecil Lewis (*Sagittarius Rising*) or V.M. Yeates. As a child, I especially liked the later, more fantastical books. John Pearson's *Biggles: The Authorised Biography* (1978) was useful.

CHAPTER 21: THE CASTLE

Sanke card. The publisher Willy Sanke issued a series of postcards between 1909 and 1918, commemorating German aviators. A collection can be found online http://www.sanke-cards.com.

CHAPTER 22: TROGLODYTES

The Miracle Man. Winthrop must have seen a production of the George M. Cohan play or read the Frank L. Packard novel it's based on. The Hollywood film version, in which Lon Chaney made his first great impression unkinking his limbs in the healing scene, came out in 1919.

For our troglodytes, thanks to Jaroslav Hašek, D.H. Lawrence, Henri-Pierre Roché (and François Truffaut), R.C. Sherriff, F. Paul Wilson, Daniel Boulanger and Maurice Bessy.

'To the ghost bowmen of Mons, the crucified Canadians and the Russians with snow on their boots.' These are folk-tales of World War One: the legend of the ghost bowmen (or angels) of Mons seems to have got started with Arthur Machen's story 'The Bowmen', but became prevalent and controversial; the crucified Canadian, reputedly fixed to a barn door by German bayonets, was a widely-circulated atrocity story and depicted in Allied propaganda posters ('your liberty bond will help stop this'); Russian forces sent incognito to the Western Front (or even to Scotland) were supposedly recognised by the snow on their boots.

PART THREE: MEMOIRS OF A FOX-HUNTING MAN

The section title comes from Siegfried Sassoon's autobiographical novel.

CHAPTER 27: THE RED BATTLE FLIER

'A cousin of mine has formed an unsuitable attachment with an English writer of repulsive reputation.' In 1912, Frieda von Richthofen – then married to an academic named Ernest Weekley – eloped with the author D.H. Lawrence. When her divorce was secured, they married. While visiting his wife's family in Metz before the War, Lawrence was accused of spying for the British. Later, he was accused of spying for the Germans, and signalling to submarines, and hounded under the Defence of the Realm Act.

Perle von Mauren appears in 'Revelations in Black' (1933), a story by Carl Jacobi published in *Weird Tales*.

CHAPTER 28: THE MOON ALSO RISES

For the staff and patients at the hospital in Amiens, thanks are due to Sinclair Lewis, Ernest Hemingway and D.H. Lawrence.

When Vlad Came. Saki's novel *When William Came*, which I first read in Michael Moorcock's anthology *England Invaded*, was one of the templates for *Anno Dracula*. Written in 1914, and set in a near-future Britain occupied by the Kaiser Wilhelm's armies, it's the best of the many future war stories published after the success of George Tomkyn Chesney's *The Battle of Dorking* (1871). Noel Coward's 1947 play *Peace in Our Time*, an alternate history drama (one of the first in the field) set in a Nazi-occupied Britain, is a conscious revisiting of Saki's themes.

CHAPTER 33: THE KILLER

The absurd dog. I admit this is the second time I've used this bit of business. The first is in *Back in the USSA*, which I co-wrote with Eugene

Byrne. If ever Manfred von Richthofen appears in anything else I write, I'll have him shoot the beagle again. Take that, Great Pumpkin!

CHAPTER 37: MASTER OF THE WORLD
INTERLUDE: THE PRIVATE FILES OF MYCROFT HOLMES

This short chapter was deleted from earlier editions, but appeared (in a slightly different form) in a convention booklet (FantasyCon 1996) and an issue of *Crime Time*. The original reasoning for taking it out was to stay in France where the action was, rather than nip home for a single scene. In putting it back, I've placed it between the third and fourth parts of the book, so it can be easily skipped if you prefer to read the novel as originally published. With these new editions, I think Mycroft's funeral is a useful – even crucial – part of the attenuated overall story running from *Anno Dracula* through to *Johnny Alucard*. It's the only onstage appearance by Mycroft Holmes' more famous brother in the series.

PART FOUR: JOURNEY'S END

The section title comes from the 1928 play by R.C. Sherriff about life in the trenches. James Whale directed the original production, and a 1930 film version. A 1931 German movie adaptation, a forgotten mirror image of Hollywood's *All Quiet on the Western Front*, is called *Die andere Seite* (*The Other Side*). The 1976 film *Aces High* switches services, making Sherriff's infantrymen into pilots.

CHAPTER 38: OFFENSIVE PATROL

For the new intake, thanks to Tom Holland, Eric Red, Cash Markman and James D. Parriott and Barney Cohen. Alex Brandberg may be the most obscure pre-existing vampire character in the whole *Anno Dracula* series.

Broncho Billy. Broncho Billy Anderson was a cowboy star in early motion pictures. Born Max Aronson, he became known – at a time when film stars weren't generally billed onscreen – by the name of a continuing character he played in a string of Westerns. In Howard Waldrop's 'Der Untergang des Abendlandesmenschen', Broncho Billy and William S. Hart pursue Graf von Orlok from *Nosferatu*.

CHAPTER 39: UP AT THE FRONT

The chapter title is from an unused alternate title of the 1972 Frankie Howerd vehicle *Up the Front*. In that, Zsa Zsa Gabor – who has a role in the *Anno Dracula* universe as one of Dracula's later wives – plays Mata Hari.

CHAPTER 43: ATTILA FALLING

Man-Bat. Just as Herbert West acknowledges 'Langstrom of Gotham University' as a pioneer in the field of man-to-bat shape-shifting, my idea of what the transformed Stalhein and his comrades look like owes a great deal to Frank Robbins and Neal Adams' creation Man-Bat. He's not yet shown up in any of the live-action Batman spin-offs, but features in 'On Leather Wings', the pilot episode of *Batman: The Animated Series*.

CHAPTER 44: KAGEMUSHA MONOGATARI

The chapter title is Japanese for Tales of the Double; it compounds the titles of Akira Kurosawa's *Kagemusha* and Kenji Mizoguchi's *Ugetsu Monogatari*.

AUTHOR'S NOTE AND ACKNOWLEDGEMENTS

This should be considered an addendum to the already lengthy enough roster of credits and mentions appended to *Anno Dracula*. Works that have proved useful for *The Bloody Red Baron* are: *The Imperial War Museum Book of the First World War*, Malcolm Brown; *Vampire: The Encyclopaedia*, Matthew Bunson; *Richthofen: A True History of the Red Baron*, William E. Burrows; *Reel America and World War I*, Craig W. Campbell; *Voices Prophesying War: Future Wars 1763–3749*, I. F. Clarke; *The Encyclopedia of Science Fiction*, John Clute and Peter Nicholls; *The Transylvanian Library: A Consumer's Guide to Vampire Fiction*, Greg Cox; *Lugosi: The Man Behind the Cape*, Robert Cremer; *The Haunted Screen*, Lotte H. Eisner; *Rites of Spring: The Great War and the Birth of the Modern Age*, Modris Eksteins; *A Nation of Fliers: German Aviation and the Popular Imagination*, Peter Fritzsche; *The Great War and Modern Memory*, Paul Fussell; *The Blue Max*, Jack D. Hunter; *A War Imagined: The First World War and English Culture*, Samuel Hynes; *The Camels Are Coming, Biggles in France, Biggles Learns to Fly, Biggles Flies East*, Captain W. E. Johns; *Richthofen: Beyond the Legend of the Red Baron*, Peter Kilduff; *From Caligari to Hitler: A Psychological History of the German Film*, Siegfried Kracauer; *Sagittarius Rising*, Cecil Lewis; *1914–1918: Voices and Images of the Great War*, Lyn Macdonald; *The Golem*, Gustav Meyrink (Introduction by Robert Irwin); *The Extraordinary Mr Poe*, Wolf Mankowitz; *The Pocket Encyclopaedia of World Aircraft in Colour: Fighters, Attack and Training Aircraft*

1914–1919, *The Pocket Encyclopaedia of World Aircraft in Colour: Bombers, Patrol and Reconnaissance Aircraft 1914–1919,* Kenneth Munson; *Winged Warfare: The Literature and Theory of Aerial Warfare in Britain 1859–1917,* Michael Paris; *The Life and Death of Colonel Blimp,* Michael Powell and Emeric Pressburger; *Imaginary People: A Who's Who of Modern Fictional Characters,* David Pringle; *The Red Air Fighter,* Manfred von Richthofen (Preface by Norman Franks), *Edgar A. Poe: Mournful and Never-ending Remembrance,* Kenneth Silverman; *The Monster Show,* David J. Skal; *Dracula,* Bram Stoker; *Snobbery with Violence: English Crime Stories and their Audience,* Colin Watson; *The Fossil Monarchies: The Collapse of the Old Order 1905–1922,* Edmond Taylor; *Queen Victoria's Children,* John Van Der Kiste; *The First of the Few: Fighter Pilots of the First World War,* Denis Winter; *The Annotated Dracula, A Dream of Dracula: In Search of the Living Dead,* Leonard Wolf; and *Winged Victory,* V. M. Yeates (with a tribute and preface by Henry Williamson). For historical, aviation and cultural input, I'd like to thank Eugene Byrne, Mark Burman and Tom Tunney. For other kindnesses, thanks are due to Gail Nina Andersen, Susan Byrne, Cliff Burns, Jacquie Clare, Julia Davis, John Douglas, the Dracula Society, Martin Fletcher, Christopher Frayling, Gabriela Galceran, Kathryn Greene, Antony Harwood, André Jacquemetton, Peter James, John Jarrold, Stephen Jones, John Phillip Law, Paul McAuley, Thomas Mohr, Bryan and Julia Newman, Sky Nonhoff, Jenny Olivier, Quelou Parente, Marcelle Perks, Stuart Pollak, Mandy Slater, Adam Simon, Helen Simpson, Richard Stanley, Jean-Marc Toussaint, Caroline Vié, Nick Webb, Linda Ruth Williams and the Lord Ruthven Assembly.

Kim Newman, Islington, 1995

RED SKIES

In the Titan edition of Anno Dracula, *I included extracts from a screenplay adaptation written shortly after the book's publication. I've not done a* Bloody Red Baron *script, so I can't provide similar material this time round.*

However, here's an odd footnote. I had enquiries about the film rights to The Bloody Red Baron *from legendary producer Roger Corman, whose 1971 movie* Von Richthofen and Brown *(aka* The Red Baron*) was an influence on the book. When I did an onstage interview with the lively, always entertaining Roger at the Edinburgh Film Festival, I talked with him about the book… as I suspected, he was mostly interested in finding a project which would make use of leftover flying scenes from his earlier movie. He hadn't realised my novel was part of a series (which complicates the rights situation) and that my von Richthofen didn't actually fly a plane, so wouldn't cut together easily with footage of John Phillip Law in his scarlet Fokker. Roger's idea was to come up with a monster movie to pitch to the SyFy Channel, which would mix biplanes and flying monsters. He thought it would be neat if the Baron's victories were sacrifices to Valkyrie.*

Naturally, I rushed off and wrote up an outline for a Red Baron/Valkyrie movie. Annoyingly, Bryan Singer had just used Valkyrie *as the title of his plot-to-kill-Hitler movie, so this couldn't follow the SyFy pattern of just naming the film after the mythical CGI beastie of the week (cf:* Hydra, Cerberus, Ogre, Goblin, *etc). I looked again at* Von Richthofen and Brown *and took notes on footage which could be used again, and how it might be assimilated into new material. I dug out my* Bloody Red Baron *reference books and notes, so I could re-use some historical or borrowed characters to increase the cross-over quotient.*

Here's what I came up with….

RED SKIES

AN OUTLINE BY KIM NEWMAN, BASED ON AN IDEA BY ROGER CORMAN

'...once upon a time, in the dark heart of Europe...'

Prussia. The Middle Ages. An ancient forest. Nightfall. Fires. Blood on the earth. A battle is lost. Asian INVADERS are sacking the district, murdering the wounded. MANFRED – a bloodied, exhausted young man – has survived the battle. His father/commander has been killed. He flees from the enemy, hampered by armour. Seeking sanctuary in a Christian shrine, he finds the NUN who tended the altar dead. Shocked by the enemy's sacrilege, he runs deeper into the forest. Three especially persistant INVADERS are on his tracks, hunting him like an animal. MANFRED sheds his armour to make better speed, and drops his sword while crossing a stream. Inhuman eyes watch from the trees. MANFRED has entered a more primordial, magical region of the forest.

MANFRED comes to a waterfall – there is no way forwards. The INVADERS are close after him, so there is no escape. MANFRED falls to his knees and prays, not to the Christian God but to the old Norse Gods of Germany – Odin, Freya, Thor. His prayers are answered by eerie, wordless singing voices. Three beautiful women – LORELEI, BRUNHILDE and KARNILA (two blonde, one dark) – appear through the curtain of water. These are the VALKYRIE, handmaidens of the Norse Gods.

Back at the stream, the INVADERS find a trickle of blood washed from the sword, and get back on MANFRED's trail.

***

The VALKYRIE, who cherish warriors, are contemptuous of MANFRED, as much for losing his sword as losing the battle. Their faces shift, becoming vampirish, hawklike, glamorously scary. MANFRED, all hope gone, conquers his fear and stands up to them, calmly awaiting death. LORELEI, lead Valkyrie, sees a warrior spark in him, and offers a bargain. If MANFRED offers up blood sacrifices in battle, the VALKYRIE will make him invincible and immortal. He will become the eternal German hero.

The INVADERS are near the clearing. From the waters, LORELEI produces red armour marked with a black double-headed eagle. BRUNHILDE and KARNILA help MANFRED into the armour, which gives him strength. LORELEI cuts open her chest with sharp nails, and draws a bloodied sword from her own body. She washes the blade clean in the waterfall – bloody bone turning to polished steel – and presents to MANFRED. The INVADERS come into the clearing. MANFRED defeats two of them quickly, slicing them to pieces. The THIRD INVADER surrenders and offers his scimitar, which MANFRED throws away. Drawing his side-dagger, MANFRED slices off the THIRD INVADER's ear and holds it up. Blood scent excites the VALKYRIE, who begin to transform into harpie-like winged monsters. We don't see them clearly at this stage, but aerial shots from their POV show them harrying the THIRD INVADER and eventually tearing him to shreds with talons and fangs. The pool at the foot of the waterfall is scarlet with blood. The VALKYRIE, transformed back into womanshape, bathe in it.

MANFRED kneels by the bodies of his slain enemies. LORELEI now has a falcon on her arm, a hunter's bird. She tells MANFRED that Germany is proud of him, and that he is called to battle again. A pigeon passes by, and MANFRED looks up at the sky. LORELEI throws the falcon into the air, opening her mouth and giving voice to an inhumanly beautiful sound – the song of a siren…

* * *

We follow the falcon's path towards the pigeon, cutting through the clear skies. Then, with a match cut, the birds are replaced by World War One biplanes in the middle of a dogfight. The credits play over an aerial battle, seen through the distorting ripples of the waterfall pool. The theme music incorporates the siren song, perhaps sampling Wagner's 'Ride of the Valkyrie'.

Here's a paragraph Roger − living up to his reputation for frugality − suggested would be too expensive, and requested be dropped from the outline:

[Blood swirls in the waters of the waterfall pool, and ripples over the montage that makes a credits sequence. Stock footage of Germany's wars down through the ages − the Thirty Years' War, the Napoleonic Wars, the Franco-Prussian War, the First World War. (Basically, the wars seen in *Alexander Nevsky*, *Barry Lyndon* and *Waterloo*). Knights in armour with elaborate Teutonic headpieces. 18th Century cavalrymen. Cannons. Sieges. Muskets. Rifles. Chattering machine guns. Throughout all this carnage, we see MANFRED − reincarnated each generation − in different war uniforms, always with red metal and the double-headed eagle about him. The beating of huge wings, an ululating siren song and the shadows of the VALKYRIE over all the explosions, battles, charges and victories. The overlay of bloody ripples finishes as history reaches a German airfield in France in 1917.]

MANFRED strides out, in flying suit and helmet, and approaches a plane made of scarlet metal. It bears the sign of the double-headed eagle. MANFRED's armour is now an aeroplane; his sword and dagger are the plane's twin Spandau machine guns.

An ATTENDANT salutes 'Rittmeister Baron von Richthofen'. MANFRED looks back at the base hospital − where the VALKYRIE stand in nurses' uniform − and nods to them. He gets into his plane and takes to the skies with the battle squadron (Jagdstaffel) commanded by BOELCKE. The VALKYRIE watch hungrily, and walk out onto the runway, capes spreading like wings. Over the countryside, the German Squadron seems to own the air – but a British formation appears and an aerial mêlée ensues. Several planes are shot down on both sides. As MANFRED machine-guns the enemy, he hears the VALKYRIE song. We get glimpses of winged monsters in flight.

MANFRED engages in a fight with HAWKER, a British ace. This does not go completely his way. Separated from the rest of the battle, MANFRED pursues HAWKER into clouds, and finally puts bullets into his plane, wounding him in the side. LORELEI tears HAWKER from his cockpit and rips him to shreds. On the ground, a motorcyclist (BROWN) wonders if it's beginning to rain, and raises a hand – which is spattered with blood. In the air, MANFRED sees LORELEI in her monster form: she's a combination harpie, vampire, gorgon, witch and siren.

The Germans return to their airfield. The other fliers congratulate MANFRED on his tenth victory, which makes him a double ace, and plainly hero-worship him. They also envy him the nurses, who they believe are his personal harem. BOELCKE, however, is angry. By pursuing his own score, MANFRED neglected formation. Their supposed missions involve aerial reconnaissance of allied positions, but MANFRED takes scalps not spy photographs. BOELCKE knows MANFRED's victories are good for propaganda – but feels something is wrong with the flier and suspects the nurses are involved. MANFRED is toasted in the field's officers' club, and adds a silver cup to his row of trophies. BOELCKE goes to his office to write letters to the families of the pilots who were killed today, and finds his way blocked by the VALKYRIE, who taunt him ambiguously. BOELCKE resolves to get rid of MANFRED somehow.

***

BROWN, the motorcyclist, arrives at the British field. Taking the loss of HAWKER hard, the fliers are holding a raucous funeral. BROWN, a new pilot, enters the pub-like officers' club and is swept into a dance by JIMMY BIGGS, a young flier, and shoved into a table. COMMANDER CUNDALL, the senior officer, insists the drunken BIGGS apologises – which he does. CUNDALL checks BROWN's orders, and assigns a billet in BIGGS' hut. It's HAWKER's old space, which sets the other officers against the 'jonah' newcomer. BROWN, hefting the near-insensible BIGGS, gets to the hut. CATRIONA – HAWKER's girlfriend, a nurse – is clearing away his things in a box. She breaks down at the sight of the new flier, whom she thinks is doomed. She says there's an unbeatable red devil in the sky. CATRIONA leaves and BROWN gets BIGGS onto his cot. BROWN finally takes off the leather helmet, goggles and big leather jacket. BIGGS, vision still blurry, looks at BROWN. From his POV, it is obvious that the new pilot is a young woman. Assuming he is drunk or dreaming, he flops back on his bed.

The site of HAWKER's crash. MANFRED comes to cut away the roundel from his plane as a trophy and look into the dead eyes of his bested enemy. LORELEI watches him. Centuries of easy victory have turned MANFRED into a hollow man, but the VALKYRIE are still bloodthirsty. MANFRED laments that the British offer no challenge. LORELEI cautions him to be wary. Britain, like Germany, is an old land, and is defended by great powers. They leave. Seen only by us, mystic forces swirl around the crashed plane. HAWKER's corpse transforms into an old, long-bearded, robed, living man with fiery eyes.

The next day, BROWN – passing for a young man, exciting comments about how they're sending 'em to war before they can shave – reports for duty. BIGGS, hung over, suggests an easy patrol, well away from the Red Baron's hunting ground. This goes awry as the Jagdstaffel show up and give the Brits a hard time. MANFRED gets BIGGS in his sights, but BROWN roars in with an unexpected display of virtuoso aerobatics and drives MANFRED off. MANFRED is annoyed but excited by a challenge. He is eager to take out the new British flier, but his plane is shot up and he reluctantly leaves his prey free. This annoys LORELEI, who is cheated of blood, and the skies darken. BROWN inelegantly lands her plane, which falls apart. Reddish rain starts to fall. Everyone congratulates her. BIGGS admits he's in her debt. He remembers thinking she was a woman.

CUNDALL introduces the fliers to MALLEN, a newly-arrived civilian advisor (the transformed HAWKER) sent to help with the squadron's Red Baron problem. The young men are sceptical but MALLEN impresses BROWN. She gets psychic glimpses of his wizardly look when she is introduced to a man in tweeds with a clipped moustache and wise old eyes. She helps him set up his teaching area, in a corner of a hangar – and notices that he has spasms of pain. He admits he won't be here long, and they have much to do.

MANFRED is joshed by comrades about letting one get away, and is coldly furious. He goes to his rooms and the VALKYRIE, angry and semi-transformed, demand a replacement sacrifice. He has to fill one of his silver cups with his own blood, which they drink. Making his evening worse, BOELCKE summons him with good news – he's been awarded yet more honours by the Emperor, and Berlin wants him to go on a propaganda tour of Germany inspiring youth to join up and fly for the Fatherland. MANFRED realises this is a ploy to get him out of the front line, but has no choice. After MANFRED leaves, BOELCKE is afraid but relieved the confrontation is over and his problem is solved. He is startled by a face at the window – the monster LORELEI's – illuminated in a flash of lightning.

MALLEN takes an especial interest in BROWN – Jane Charlotte 'Charlie' Brown – because he knows about her potential destiny. He is

Merlin, recalled in England's hour of need, and she is the latest avatar of the ancient British warrior queen Boudicca and the Arthurian female knight Bradamante, reborn to counter the mystic forces arrayed against the Allies. MANFRED is eternal, because Germany is always at war; BROWN is newly-incarnate because Britain fights only when she must. BROWN's comparative inexperience is a disadvantage to be overcome. MANFRED is the red dragon, who can be slain only by the purest knight. MALLEN knows BROWN is a woman. She and her brother were pre-war aviators, though he got all the headlines and she was a better pilot. Her brother fell off his motorbike and broke his back on his way to join up, so she took his place. She resists MALLEN's mystical talk, and insists the war can only be won with modern science and tactics – but is surprised he doesn't give her away for serving in the Royal Army Air Corps under false pretences.

MANFRED reports for what BOELCKE intends will be his last day's duty – and, in the confusion of an aerial battle, fires on his commanding officer, whose plane nose-dives and crashes. BOELCKE crawls out of the wreckage alive – with the battle still going on overhead – and is relieved to see an ambulance trundling towards him. The VALKYRIE emerge from the vehicle and get him inside, where they take on monster-form and tear him apart.

At BOELCKE's funeral, command of the squadron is passed to MANFRED. Some cheer, but others – who knew of the hostility between MANFRED and BOELCKE – are worried. MANFRED orders the planes be painted in garish colours, creating the Flying Circus. He privately paints his own plane with blood the VALKYRIE have taken from the murdered BOELCKE. However, he finds it difficult to reconcile murdering his commanding officer with his sense of honour, and feels the beginnings of resentment against his supernatural patrons.

* * *

In the air, the Germans have more and more success, and MANFRED offers more and more victims to be shredded by the VALKYRIE and blood rains down on the soil of Europe. More silver cups appear on the Red Baron's mantel, representing each victory. We also see trench warfare, gas attacks, bombardments, exploding Zeppelins and other WWI stock footage stained with blood to give a sense of the enormous blood-feast the war is for the VALKYRIE.

BROWN becomes more skilled as a battle pilot, and survives hairy situations on a daily basis; she has to go through tests and ordeals on a magical level to become a fit incarnation of the warrior queen. She is romantically drawn to BIGGS, who finds himself helping with her training – and conceals the fact that she's a woman from his comrades. MALLEN has only a short time to teach his pupil – he has a streaming wound in his side, carried over from HAWKER's death, that dressings won't staunch. BIGGS is torn between desire to protect BROWN and a growing understanding of how important she is. BROWN still resists a mystic interpretation of the conflict, but BIGGS – who has glimpsed the VALKYRIE – is already a believer. MALLEN tells BROWN that training is important, but not enough – she will need a weapon, the right material forged in blood, to slay the red dragon.

Christmas, 1917. Guns still. An armistice. At an inn halfway between the German and British fields, the two squadrons have an uneasy shared meal – toasting each other, bristling with resentments about who shot down who, and who's committed more atrocities (strafing downed pilots, etc). A fight nearly breaks out between BIGGS and MURNAU, a German flier, but CUNDALL separates them. MANFRED makes an entrance late, attended by the VALKYRIE – the British are impressed and envious of his entourage. BROWN has psychic glimpses of them as they really are, nudging her towards a fuller realisation of her own mystic status. MALLEN says grace before the meal, which makes the VALKYRIE hiss – and CUNDALL weakly toasts fliers of all nations who have fallen (the idea is that this occasion was more convivial in earlier years before the war got really nasty).

After the meal, musicians play. MANFRED asks BROWN to dance. By now, all the British know she's a woman and go along with it – it seems no more insane than anything else in the war. MANFRED and BROWN dance faster, exchanging barbed words about who'll kill who. MANFRED sees in BROWN something he has missed in his centuries of bloody service. BIGGS, in love with BROWN, tries to cut in, but gets flung across the room with inhuman strength. At midnight, the armistice is over. A brawl erupts between the two squadrons. Blood on the floor, with spilled beer and wine – and a French hostelier laments it would have been better if England and Germany had settled their differences in one of their own countries.

Outside, MALLEN is ringed by the VALKYRIE, who probe his magical defences with siren song. They all show their true natures and have a mystic battle – with MALLEN exhausting himself as he sees off the VALKYRIE. Dying, he gives the last of his strength to stop the VALKYRIE simply killing BROWN on the ground and removing England's champion from the field. BROWN – who has seen enough of this to realise all the mystical business she has scoffed at is true – cradles MALLEN, half turned back into HAWKER. He finally expires, willing her to go on and bring down the Red Baron – which ought to mean the beginning of the end of the war. BIGGS, witness to this, serves as BROWN's squire, and receives a portion of MALLEN's knowledge. As BROWN stands, she shimmers – and BIGGS sees her as Boudicca or Britannia, in armour and robes.

MURNAU, who has seen the real nature of the VALKYRIE, spreads rumours around the Jagstaffel. Any rebellion is quashed when the VALKYRIE 'come out' as magic creatures and exert their will over the squadron. They know things are urgent, and decree that a raid be made against the English on Boxing Day, while they are opening presents and tucking into figgy pudding. This is a Pagan feast of sacrifice. MALLEN is slain, but they want BROWN killed too. MANFRED, long-dead emotions stirred by BROWN (who reminds him of the murdered NUN in the prologue), bridles against his bloodthirsty mistresses but centuries of habit compel him to follow their orders.

The Germans make a devastating raid on the British field, and many – including CUNDALL – are killed. The VALKYRIE ride the skies, openly, along with German planes, and attack the British from the air, slaughtering pilots, civilians, nurses, dogs, whoever is around. Blood soaks the ground. BROWN fails to get in the air, held back by BIGGS. She is furious, because she now believes she's the only one who can end this. He tells her she doesn't yet have the sword that can slay the dragon.

Back at the German base, the blood-crazed fliers hold a celebration – chasing a boar through the mess hall and sticking it with swords. The VALKYRIE exult, at the creation of a dozen new bloodthirsty champions, including proto-Nazis and serial killers. BRUNHILDE and KARNILA take lovers from among the company, and the party turns into a pagan orgy of sorts. MANFRED is struggling with the waking of conscience. He has a moment with LORELEI, who offers herself to him – he asks about the price of victory, and she tells him it's never been about victory. It's about blood. Valkyrie bear the valiant dead to Valhalla, and so they need an endless supply. To fulfil their purpose, they need spilled blood, and victory would mean an end to that. They are stronger now than they have ever been because this war has spilled more blood than any other in history. MANFRED sweeps the silver cups from his mantel.

BIGGS and BROWN walk in the forest. She's still angry with him, but he tries to explain how she's more important than him. Only she can prevail. They are deeper in the woods than they intended, away from the war. They kiss, finally. Then become aware of eyes on them. Red eyes. BIGGS draws a pistol and fires. MANFRED emerges from the dark, uniform smoking but unharmed. He says that ordinary bullets can't hurt him, and throws down a sack which bursts, spilling silver cups. 'Silver, stained with blood.' He takes the gun from BIGGS and knocks him out. BROWN hits MANFRED with a length of wood, like a quarterstaff and he parries the blow. They have a flirty dance/fight, which ends with MANFRED stealing a kiss – leaving blood on BROWN's lips. She says he could just quit the war, defy his mistresses. With his honours, no one would complain. He considers it, but regrets that his sense of duty makes it impossible. He is Germany's dragon – and dragons don't retire. They must be slain. He disappears back into the dark. BROWN has a vision of MALLEN, who tells her she has been given the weapon she needs. BIGGS comes round, surrounded by silver cups.

The British scrape together a determined squadron, and BIGGS – the new commander – orders a 'vengeance raid' against the German field. BROWN, now fully aware of her destiny and shining like a knight, is above all that, but gets into her plane anyway. The British attack the German HQ – bombing the hospital where the VALKYRIE have been feeding off wounded and dying men. MANFRED and BROWN are in the air, duelling. BIGGS intervenes and BROWN sees the VALKYRIE coming for the man she loves. She dogfights the monsters. MANFRED has a chance to kill her but doesn't – which prompts LORELEI to tear at him in his plane, peeling him like an apple. BROWN, the champion of Britain incarnate, fires at the VALKYRIE.

Flashbacks show that – following MALLEN's teaching – BROWN and BIGGS have had the silver cups melted down into bullets, though it's the blood on them not the metal which gives them magic power.

***

BROWN pots BRUNHILDE and KARNILA, who transform into crones as they fall into a forest and a lake, where they become pools of blood. BROWN shoots her last blessed bullets at LORELEI, who is wounded and leaves MANFRED – horribly mauled – in his plane. Accepting his lot, MANFRED lets BROWN shoot him – and his plane lands, intact, in a field. MANFRED, dead, is finally at peace.

BROWN, emotionally wrung out, returns to the British base, where her famous victory is already celebrated and disputed. BIGGS, whom she embraces, tells her others are already claiming the kill and that there are insane stories – like the rumour of the ghost bowmen or angels seen at Mons earlier in the war – spreading about winged monsters mixing in with the battle.

In the forest, wounded, LORELEI turns back into a beautiful woman, and is on the point of bleeding out. She begins a death-song, eerily beautiful – which carries through the trees. A soldier, carrying a despatch from the front line, finds her and their eyes meet, electrically. He sees her as a monster, and smiles. She touches his face, finding her next catspaw. A comrade calls out, 'Who have you found there, Adolf?' and young Hitler responds 'An angel, a German angel.'

NOTES ON RED SKIES

OUR VALKYRIE

Though our Valkyrie are based on pre-existing legends and traditions, they are a new monster so we can make up our own rules for them. The implication is that these creatures have inspired myths of sirens, gorgons, lorelei, harpies, vampires, Rhine maidens, lamias, Norns, witches, etc, which is why they have attributes found in each of these archetypes. They can look like beautiful women, but can turn into winged monsters. They feed off blood, symbolically as well as literally. They are seductive, but terrifying. They are pitiless, but sensual. They are tied to the soil of their native land, and have always been the feared yet loved protectors of the Germanic peoples. They are fliers – but more like hawks or eagles or falcons than vampire bats, so their monster forms should have a birdy look rather than the traditional reptile-rodent demon features (though fangs work better than beaks).

OUR CHAMPIONS

Manfred and Brown are champions of their respective countries – Germany (by extension, the whole Nordic peoples) and England (by extension, Great Britain and the WWI Allies). Manfred serves our version of the Norse Gods, while Brown comes from the Arthurian tradition whereby celtic or wiccan religion is channelled into a form of Christianity. Manfred is long-lived, fighting from generation to generation, because Germany is always a warrior nation. Brown is a youth who has to come into knowledge of her position, because England fights only when challenged – this is why King Arthur sleeps until 'the hour of greatest need'. Yes, I know this is a hideous simplification of history, but it's strong on a symbolic level and means that our mystic antagonists aren't just mirror images of each other. I'd like to hint that the other combatants in WWI have their own warrior goddesses in play – an Ice Queen for Russia, Joan of Arc for France, someone like Annie Oakley or Calamity Jane for the vital young Americans.

OUR CHARACTERS

Manfred, Baron von Richthofen. Historically, von Richthofen was 26 when he died. Our Manfred should look that age, but have an immortal's world-weariness in the Dorian Gray/Wandering Jew/ soul-in-torment-vampire tradition. Initially, he turns from the failure of morality to darker Gods – but he has a vein of honour which makes him not completely happy with being a villain. That said, he's a ferocious, savage warrior and should be a formidable antagonist.

Roy Arthur Brown. A nineteen-year-old, born in England, raised in Canada – obsessed with flight. He's the type who built his own aeroplane, and learned to fly by himself. He comes to the war as an idealist with illusions of knightly combat in the air, and ironically becomes an incarnation of an actual knight. He is impulsive, open-hearted and thinks fast, but hasn't yet learned caution or the cost of heroism in human lives. He is an avatar of King Arthur ('Roi Arthur'), who is supposed to return to defend his homeland in 'England's hour of greatest need'. Only – thanks to the intervention of the Valkyrie – the hour of need has come early, and Brown isn't ready to counter the mystic forces arrayed against the Allies. Manfred is eternal, because Germany is always at war; Brown is newly-incarnate because Britain fights only when she must.

[This characterisation was added when SyFy didn't buy the 'disguised as a boy' bit. I'd originally gone with that because Roger has a history of doing pictures in which women take the sort of active protagonist roles usually reserved for men, cf: Beverly Garland in Gunslinger, *the lead cast of* Viking Women and Their Voyage to the Waters of the Great Sea Serpent, *Shelley Winters in* Bloody Mama, *Claudia Jennings and Jocelyn Jones in* The Great Texas Dynamite Chase.*]*

Mallen/Merlin/Hawker. The reason for reincarnating Hawker as Mallen is the possibility of recasting Corin Redgrave to match the old footage – if this can't be done, maybe the roles could be rejigged. He has a Fisher King side-wound for further Arthurian associations, and of course fulfils the Obi Wan/Gandalf role (then again, they're both rip-offs of Merlin in the first place) as hero's tutor.

[Sadly, Corin Redgrave – at that time, a survivor of the earlier film – has subsequently died, which probably mothballs Red Skies *for good. Unless Vanessa wants to play it in drag.]*

Catriona Kay. A nurse, engaged to Hawker – she doesn't realise that she has been drawn to this part of the war by her own destiny, in that she's the embodiment of Britain's presiding goddess, a nurturer rather than a nurse. She is the Lady in the Lake, but also Guinevere and Britannia. She stands as a positive example of mystic female energy – a living reminder of why our side is better than theirs.

[This role grew to provide a strong woman on the Allied side when Brown changed sex in the revision. I prefer the earlier version, where there's sexual tension between the antagonists, but came to see that doing the picture with Brown as a man and Catriona as the semi-mystic woman could still be interesting.]

[Here's how the armistice dance scene would have played in that version: MANFRED *asks* CATRIONA *to dance, which prickles* BROWN's *jealousy.* MALLEN *advises caution, knowing that jealousy was the original Arthur's fatal flaw.* MANFRED *and* CATRIONA *dance faster, and she is semi-transformed into the Lady in the Lake/Guinevere/ Britannia, the British equivalent of the Valkyrie.* MANFRED *is struck by the difference between this nurturing goddess and the vampire harpies he serves.* BROWN *finally snaps and tries to cut in, but gets flung across the room with inhuman strength.* BROWN *and* MANFRED *face off, personal hatred sprung up between them – though* CATRIONA *tries to keep them apart.]*

Biggs. A Boys' Own adventure hero stuck in the middle of a war which isn't an adventure and isn't for boys. Probably drinks too much and drawls in public school slang to cover perpetual terror. He was Brown's idol at school, a hero on the cricket pitch – but now seems decades older than his friend, and isn't exactly happy to be reminded of who he used to be.

Boelcke. Our token sensitive German, who worries about the monsters on his own side.

584

Cundall. The British squadron's C.O. In war movies, crusty old character actors tend to get these roles – but in WWI, someone in his job would probably not even be thirty.

Brunhilde and Karnila. Lorelei is the dominant Valkyrie, so she gets most of the screen time and carries their end of the story. However, her sisters should have their own distinct personalities. Brunhilde is the stern, dark, melodramatic one. Karnila is crazier, sexier and the most sadistic one.

My assumption is that this sort of project tends to get filmed in Eastern Europe, where they have handy forests, disused military facilities, etc. This makes it convenient to cast out of Europe: I'm assuming you can bring in an American leading man (the real Roy Brown was Canadian), then cast British actors as the Allies and Germans as the Germans, with maybe Russian or Hungarian women as the Valkyrie.

I noted earlier the considerations of blending stock footage into the new material without showing obvious joins (the flying scenes in *Von Richthofen and Brown* all take place in bright daylight, but monster scenes would work better at night or in dramatic cloud). I emphasise that the presence of the Valkyrie affects the weather – hence the tentative title *Red Skies* – and we can digitally tinker with the skies to cover the matches. One of the commentators tactfully raises the issue of the quality of effects work. I've looked at a bunch of comparable SyFy Channel films, including *War Birds* (WWII pilots vs pterodactyls) and *Aztec Rex* (conquistadors vs dinosaur) and they often stumble over the iffy CGI monsters. I assume it's easy enough to handle the Valkyrie in gorgon/vampire shape on the ground with prosthetic effects, but care will have to be taken with the aerial scenes. Having the monsters move very swiftly in flight and shown at first only in glimpses will help. In my earlier draft, I put in a little more sex: I'm not sure if this is entirely within the SyFy brief, but it fitted in with the Corman horror filmography back to *The Burial of the Rats* or *The Velvet Vampire*. With female monsters, it's obvious we can stretch to some risqué scenes – though beware the casting of silicon-enhanced pole-dancers which often renders such characters more ridiculous than scary or sexy. Such scenes could be cut back in the broadcast version but included for DVD release.

SO, WHAT HAPPENED?

SyFy didn't bite. They wanted more Sharktopus, *and who can blame them?*

ABOUT THE AUTHOR

Kim Newman is a novelist, critic and broadcaster. His fiction includes *The Night Mayor*, *Bad Dreams*, *Jago*, the *Anno Dracula* novels and stories, *The Quorum*, *The Original Dr Shade and Other Stories*, *Life's Lottery*, *Back in the USSA* (with Eugene Byrne) and *The Man From the Diogenes Club* under his own name and *The Vampire Genevieve* and *Orgy of the Blood Parasites* as Jack Yeovil. His non-fiction books include *Nightmare Movies* (reissued in 2011 by Bloomsbury in an updated edition), *Ghastly Beyond Belief* (with Neil Gaiman), *Horror: 100 Best Books* (with Stephen Jones), *Wild West Movies*, *The BFI Companion to Horror*, *Millennium Movies* and BFI Classics studies of *Cat People* and *Doctor Who*.

He is a contributing editor to *Sight & Sound* and *Empire* magazines (writing *Empire*'s popular Video Dungeon column), has written and broadcast widely on a range of topics, and scripted radio and television documentaries. His stories 'Week Woman' and 'Ubermensch' have been adapted into an episode of the TV series *The Hunger* and an Australian short film; he has directed and written a tiny film *Missing Girl*. Following his Radio 4 play 'Cry Babies', he wrote an episode ('Phish Phood') for Radio 7's series *The Man in Black*.

His official website, 'Dr Shade's Laboratory', can be found at www.johnnyalucard.com